THE TRANSCENDENCE

The – Foundry – Book 2

J Fitzpatrick Mauldin

For all the children who stared at the sky wondering what was out there.
For those who grew up and found the world wasn't what they thought it was,
and so, they dreamed of a better future.
For those who did not give up on hope.
For those who did not give up on wonder.
For those with which an ember of life still burns in their soul,
driving them to make a difference in the world.
Never give up.
Always protect life.
You are the Universe.

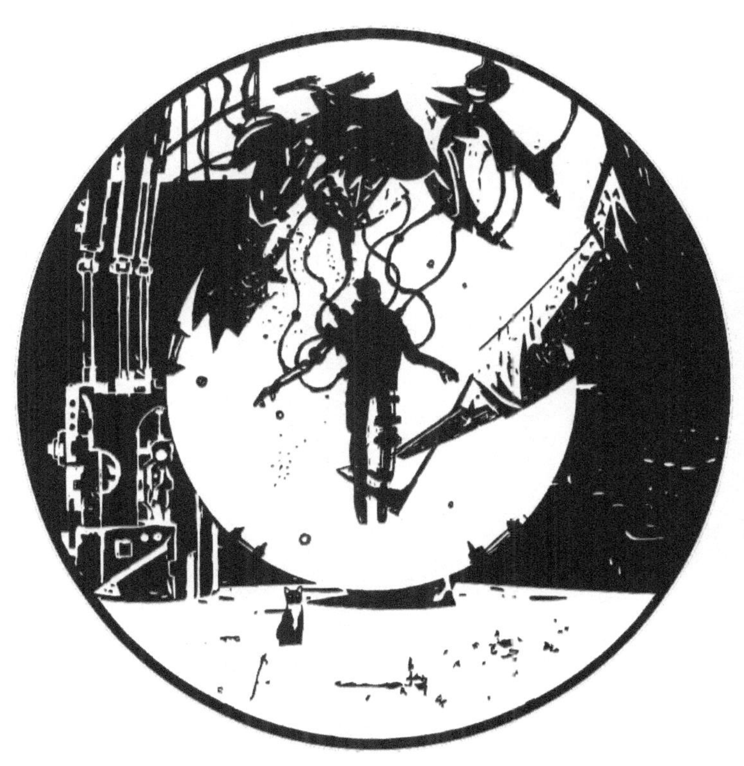

PART I

CHAPTER 1

The fate of humanity was undecided, and I wasn't sure if I could change that. We were here. We were alive. We'd seen progress. And yet, I couldn't shake the feeling deep down in my gut that the rug was about to be pulled out from under us.

Someone was going to screw it all up.

On the hillside beside Perry's bar, I stood watching as twilight on Novae was pushed back by fire, thinking to myself the entire time: *How much longer can we keep this up? When is the other shoe going to drop?*

A wingless shuttle in the shape of an aeronautical lifting body descended from orbit, the brightness of its drive flame lengthening the shadows cast by nearby trees, their large, fan-like leaves dancing along the dappled slopes northeast of the fledgling human colony of Novae. I could only hope this expedition brought us good news and not more disappointment. We'd find out soon enough.

Orange and white fusion exhaust reflected back in the eyes of many a creature, who all took flight in response to the unexpected light and noise, hiding themselves someplace safe, someplace finding prey might be easier. Among them were flocks of the bird-like analogs native to this temperate world, wings spread wide, as well as an assortment of scavenging mammals no larger than wildcats who preferred keeping out of sight.

From the shuttle's belly, landing struts extended, their edges glimmering, making contact with the landing platform. Once firmly on solid ground, the shuttle's engines died, and I was left with only artifacts in my vision, purple spots like upside-down teardrops preventing any chance of stargazing. I tried to rub these blots away with the heels of my palms out of instinct, but that never worked. Not really.

The rumble of the shuttle's engines translated across the landscape to me and was gone, the thump of music from the patio over my shoulder rushing back in to fill the void. Patrons whooped and hollered at its arrival, before returning to their drinking, their talking, their dancing. There were no shortage of momentary distractions tonight at Invictus.

I wondered, who'd gone out? Where did they go? It was likely a set of scientists from the Security and Exploration Arm. Maybe even Mom or Dad. I could use my neural implants to ping the local network and check, but with all the outages eating up our meager bandwidth, too many frivolous queries, I decided not to overburden our systems. I only hoped they'd found something good out there. The better we understood our new world, where the dangers were, what resources lay in wait, the better our chances for survival.

The year was 03 NCE, the third year of the Novae Common Era. We lived in a frontier colony in every sense of the word, hanging off the edge of anything humanity ever thought possible, and yet, here we were. We were surviving. The Isoptera had not killed us at the first Foundry facility, or on our own ship, nor had they the crew of the *Brilliance*—another United Exploration Initiative FICSE Mission ship, whose people lived here with us. The Gene Brokers had not irrevocably altered our DNA, beyond the small modifications on Creatus that had kept us from dying from the silica dust we were breathing in. With a few unlikely friends and the Foundry's unusual brand of assistance, humanity had persisted. We'd traveled to an unknown place, made contact with a fathomless alien intelligence, been hurled across the Milky Way through the Wandering Gate, and found ourselves on a world untouched by the unforgiveable sins of sentient life. A world without war, without crime, without so much of what we left behind on Earth. We could start over in this place. Stay forever. A society of the best and brightest, built on abundance and logic, not scarcity and emotion.

We just had to figure out the abundance part.

Novae had not been our intended destination. The UEI had borne a world-wide project that all of Earth bought into, not just with their minds, but with their pocketbooks. Taxes had been levied in almost every industrialized country to build five massive, fusion-powered starships set to discover the nature of the signal the Foundry sent to us. When we'd left

Earth, everything was in shambles. Climate change had created a vast disparity between the haves and have-nots. Population growth was off the charts, unsustainable. The air was becoming unfit to breathe. Economies were pushed well beyond the breaking point. Our species was desperate. Then a voice from the dark said, *'Hello, humanity. We are the Foundry, come see us soon'.* Something in that signal, a feeling, an impression, told us everything would be okay. That the Foundry would help us survive. This became our mission, the only mission: FICSE, Foundry Intent, Contact and Save Earth.

Five ships set off for five different stars: the *Brilliance*, *Galileo*, *Star Stream*, *Revelation*, and of course, my childhood home, the *Vasco Da Gama*. Three went into the dark and were never heard from again. Two ships, ours and the *Brilliance*, made contact with the Foundry at different facilities. Through this process, we learned that the Foundry itself was dedicated to "Protecting Life." It sought to awaken the Universe's collective consciousness by helping fledgling species like our own survive and thrive. Yet there were rules. We still didn't fully understand what those were. All we knew was that it disabled our ships and after a series of tests, it gave us new ships, better ships. It was never hostile, like the Isoptera or Gene Brokers, but it was not always a friend. We did not know who was in control of it, if anything, or what all its motivations might be, but it helped us survive. We were grateful.

We had kept good on our original mission. We made contact and were still doing what we could to determine the Foundry's intent. As for saving Earth… Novae kind of put that on hold.

"They're back," my wife, Shelly Williams Hughes remarked, sneaking up beside me and giving me a start. I hadn't heard her approach, with all the commotion. "Hope the survey went well."

My lips compressed into a hard line. "Same here. As much as the Foundry has helped us, you'd think…well…"

"You'd think it would have given us a little more than this?" Shelly supplied. "We've been given just enough to get by. Just enough to get started. Access to a few 3D nano printers, a dwindling supply of staple foods, and orbital defense provided by your and Karianna's ships. All things we need, sure, but it still looks like they want us to stand on our own two feet."

"You've been going over Johan's estimates again, haven't you?"

She frowned. "I have. Every month the Foundry is giving us a little less charity. Within five or six months we'll have to be self-sufficient, or people will begin to starve. Think we can retreat back into the Foundry vessels? Is that even an option?"

"I don't think so." I shook my head, considering the idea. "Not unless we're leaving for good. We put down roots. I suppose it wants to see us make use of them."

"Unwritten rules…"

"Certainly not posted ones. Typical Foundry. Hold us accountable to a set of laws and procedures without telling us what they are."

I turned to face her, and saw her body silhouetted by the light of white glow ropes and globes within the open-air bar. It was strange, but despite not being able to see her face in the dark, I knew her expression. Hopeful with a touch of cheer, a half-smile, encouraging. Ever optimistic, just like her father. I reached out and took her hands in mine, placing a kiss on the knuckles of her right hand.

This was my wife. My wife. The love of my life. The woman I had wanted to be with since the first time we doodled pictures in school aboard the *Vasco Da Gama*. No matter where the universe took me, I needed her at my side. She'd been saved from the ills of the Gene Brokers by the likes of the Melcorin, no thanks to me, and I could have kissed the leathery, blue-skinned bastards for it—if they had allowed me.

After getting settled on this world, I had popped the question, using a ring made of junk metal and a piezo electric crystal I'd found in a broken transmitter. Our friend Mary had officiated the quiet ceremony on a hillside to the east of the colony, my parents and a few friends present, and it was done, Shelly in white, her long dress flowing in the wind, me dressed in black, a leather jacket with a crimson, razor-sharp edge blossom pinned dangerously to its right lapel. We'd given our vows, kissed, and tripped over one another's feet as we spun to face our audience, the two of us tumbling onto the dirt in a heap. The blossom had cut me on the arm in the fall, drawing blood, but I'd hardly felt the pain as the purest form of laugher escaped us.

Shelly squeezed my fingers.

"We'll be fine," I sighed, and let go. My attention fell on my right hand, the end of the ivory-and-gold prosthetic arm given to me after the *donation* of my arm to the Foundry. My fingers flexed like flesh but were anything but. Four years of subjective time I'd had this thing, and the matching leg. I wasn't sure if I'd ever get used to it, but at least I wasn't the only freak who'd made a donation. The donation was a part of me now, a reminder of how I'd changed since leaving Earth, of what I'd given up.

The Foundry protects life.

I raised my eyes once more. "FICSE mission folk are tough. We've been through worse. We'll get through this too."

"Funny thing," she started, her tone wistful, hair falling into her eyes, "you dreamed of touching stars, but in the end found yourself digging in the dirt."

"Such is life." I brushed her curls back behind her ear, allowing her eyes to glimmer in the dark. "We all have to do our part. Maybe I can help with the food crisis and cut back a bit."

"You?" She patted my belly. "No. You're already skin and bones. You eat any less and they'll think you're some *moleque* from the *favelas* who snuck onto Novae."

I chuckled. "You've been hanging around Mom, haven't you?"

"Portuguese is a wonderful language."

"You guys want a drink?" an older middle-aged man with bug-like optics asked us, appearing just outside the open-air bar, a pair of glass mason jars in one hand, a jug of sloshing amber liquid in the other. Perry was always an excellent host, but now wasn't the time.

"I'd rather not wake up feeling like my head is in a vice tomorrow morning," Shelly replied before I had the chance.

"Did you say headache?" he asked, shocked. The goggles over his eyes, meant to replace his vision after a failed experiment had taken it, made a whirring noise as they adjusted focus. "A headache? No. No. No. I've got it all worked out now. That Santi-berry business stuff I made last. I'll admit, it was bad. There's a protein in the fruit that caused all that mess. It's fine now. We're using Yellow Rondure. My sweetgums says it's safe, by the way. Tastes just like an apple. I promise, one sip of this, and you'll be transported to the shady groves of red deliciouses back on Earth. No shoddy products at Invictus, not anymore."

"What if I have no idea what an apple tastes like?" I asked, being honest. I was pretty sure I'd eaten an apple aboard the *Vasco Da Gama* at least once, but I had to have been no older than six. Trees didn't travel well through deep space. They needed room to grow and thrive, a place like this, not a garden in a steel box.

Perry's brows crinkled at the edges of his visor. Pretty sure he was narrowing his eyes at me. "Well, I suppose it doesn't matter. Tastes good either way. Come on, let me pour you some."

I raised my hands in objection. "Not today, barkeep. A part of me knows trying this today is a bad idea."

"Bad idea? No, no. A bad idea is being a fish who thinks a hook is a great way to get a lip piercing."

Shelly gave me a withering look, clearly unamused. Perry's jokes hadn't gotten any better with time. "Look, Perry, when the Cultural Center is complete, please don't start up a comedy night. I'd hate to have to boycott you."

"I will have you know that everyone at Invictus loves my jokes!"

"But after how many drinks?" She pointed at the amber jug he carried.

He scowled. "So mean."

What Perry lacked in comedy, he made up for a hundred-fold in other ways. I had known him almost my entire life, and we had become close friends in the past five to six years of subjective time. Acting as a kind of therapist, he had helped me work through much of my mixed feelings over my parents, and been an important part of my crew aboard the *Fidelis*, the ship the Foundry had gifted me.

"Here's a good one," Perry went on, ignoring Shelly's annoyance. "If April showers bring May flowers, what do May flowers bring?"

I rolled my eyes. "What, Perry? What do they bring?"

"Pilgrims!" he said, raising the sloshing jug above his head in exclamation. "Ah! Ah? Come on. It was great! Didn't you get it?"

"No. I don't get it."

Shelly grinned and patted me on the back. "Seasons, love. He's talking about seasons and the start of America."

"Oh. Wait. Like, the *Mayflower*? The ship? Columbus?"

"Yes, like the ship."

"Still don't see how that's supposed to be funny."

"Come on," Perry said, then laughed. "It's great. Pilgrims…"

Across the colony came a thundering boom, and the lights and music of the bar went dead, leaving my ears buzzing in their absence, my vision filled with spots. The fragile network my implants connected with was no longer present, leaving me feeling empty, exposed. I reached for a weapon on my hip that wasn't there.

The crowd of Invictus began to murmur in alarm.

"Shelly?" I whispered, hand searching in her direction. She took hold of my fingers, and I felt my heart calm if only a little. I blinked several times, trying to adjust to the darkness like I had with the bright lights of the shuttle's engines.

"Christ on a cracker," Perry cursed, and something shattered at his feet, the smell of alcohol in the air strong, burning the hairs of my nose. "Damn it. That's a wasted batch. Nothing to do about it now. Did another one of the generators go down? Or did we run out of feculent coal?"

"Hard to say," Shelly replied, her voice calm as ever. "But the cause doesn't matter right now, we need to get everyone inside. Sawtooths like to hang around in the dark. Pretty sure they might like the taste of humans."

A cool wind whipped over the hillside, pulling at my jacket, reminding me that bundles of quills and rows of teeth were hiding in the dark. Were my mechanical augmentations enough to fight back against this apex fauna? I hadn't put them to the test.

Hand lights began to switch on around us, shooting out at every angle, their sharp lights casting heavy shadows, making it somehow both easier and more difficult to see. Some held theirs in their palms, while others clipped them to their chests. Thank the Universe we had these. It was a moonless night, despite Novae having two, and even with a brilliant view of distant galaxies wheeling overhead, our little settlement seemed swallowed by the void.

Perry edged towards his patrons, careful not to trip over broken glass, and began gathering them up. "Come on everyone, come on. Invictus is closed for the night. Let's get you safely back home. No worries, here, we'll get the power situation worked out."

"What about the backups?" someone asked.

"I don't know if I can walk."

A woman sighed. "I've got you."

"This place needs walls," another grumbled. "A hard day's work behind you and can't even get a drink in peace."

"Calm down," Perry assured them. "We'll sort it all out in the morning."

There came a cry in the dark, a shriek like a large bird with an edge like an idling chainsaw. Commanding shouts came from the other side of the bar towards the center of the colony. Security was sweeping the area, which was good, but people could easily be dragged out into the night with little or no way to stop it.

The hairs on the back of my neck stood on end. That sound meant feline forms stalking the dark around us looking for morsels. A pack of nocturnal hunters with iron-hard quills and mouths jointed too many times to ever be mistaken for terrestrial. They were the stuff of nightmares, which didn't answer to sharp words, screams, or the wild waving of the arms like the other animals might, but only to that of a fully jacketed round. Hunters who embraced the dark and loathed any form of light, for which we now had little. Every ecosystem had apex predators, a creature at the top of the food chain, and sawtooths, well, they sat at the top and called Novae home just like us. The trouble was, they were here first, and they knew this place better than we did.

"Everyone calm down, stay together," Shelly said, helping herd the departing crowd. "Let's get indoors. Storage Warehouse 3 is not far away, just down the hill. We'll be safe in there till they get the lights back on. Afterwards everyone can walk home."

"Perry!" a man called from off in the dark, appearing before us a moment later with a wispy, older woman dressed in dirt-covered overalls at his side. He was broad shouldered, dressed in well-worn work clothes, and bore a shoulder-length crop of golden hair as well as a thick, golden beard.

"Lance," Perry said, relieved. "Good to see you."

"Alyssa and I are headed over to work on the generator."

"Okay," he replied, and went to the woman, giving her a tight hug. "Glad you're okay, sweet cheeks."

"I'm fine," she said, kissing him on the lips, having cocked her head to avoid her nose colliding with his goggles. "Though a touch tired of putting out fires. I signed up to save the world, not be a stinkin' pioneer."

The kiss put a bit of steel in Perry's back, standing him upright. It did wonders for your confidence, having someone in your life who loves and believes in you.

"Hey, Lance," I said, reaching out my prosthetic hand in greeting, for which he accepted. "We're going to get these drunken idiots to safety. After that, need any help? I'm at your disposal."

Lance Brittan shook his head. "Nah, we got this. Not sure what the issue is yet, but it's likely we ran out of feculent coal. Great biofuel, sure, easy to get and all, but a pain in the ass to burn right. This will be the last time we make that mistake."

"You're doing great," Shelly assured him. "I've gone over the numbers a hundred times. At a specific temperature, that fuel burns three times as fast. Unfortunately, that temperature can change based on far too many factors. Humidity mostly. Compression too. Our Arm will keep at it. You have my word."

"Abundant fuel. Couldn't be simple."

"Never. And we're working on it. Okay?"

"I know. I know." Lance spun around and raised his voice, shouting at someone I couldn't see in the dark, "Hey! Donaldson! Anyone out there sweeping for those things? It's too dark out there. You tell Chevelle she needs to get your asses organized."

It had taken years for Lance and me to reach a good place. He had been Shelly's other half several times growing up, especially during the period of years she and I hadn't been talking. The son of one of our former pilots, he had lived a life of additional privileges, much like her, and as a result he had turned out to be a bit of a self-centered adult. Time and circumstance had softened his edges. Sure, he could still be an asshole, but he was a good kind of asshole. Most of the time.

We urged the crowd towards the center of the colony, down the main road. I could see armed personnel weaving through rows of buildings made of smooth stone, flashlights mounted at the end of their weapons. Chevelle and Donaldson had roused the minutemen and were hunting sawtooths. If there was one thing we'd gotten good at over the past few years, it was getting our asses in motion during a crisis. You just couldn't live in a crisis all the time.

A few warning shots were fired near the edge of Eighth Street. Colonists shouted in response and redoubled their efforts to keep everyone moving.

"Milo," a voice rang out inside my head. *"Milo."*

I skidded to a halt and closed my eyes.

"Everything okay?" Shelly asked, taking hold of my arm.

I shook my head in response. "Proxy," I whispered, and pointed up to the sky.

Her face blanched. "Oh."

I took a deep breath and opened the connection. My little, all-knowing, orange-striped tuxedo cat needed to talk, and at a time like this, I couldn't imagine it was anything good. Rarely did the Foundry's AI have something positive to say.

"Milo," Proxy reported, images without context appearing in my mind as it spoke, *"I have detected five unknown vessels on course to hit high orbit. I recommend we investigate."*

"A little busy down here," I replied, using thoughts, not words. The trajectories of the arrivals appeared within my mind's eye in wireframe above Novae, a pentagonal formation screaming towards the surface. If this squadron of alien ships did not change course, they would hit the outer atmosphere of Novae in less than an hour.

"I have been keeping track of your situation," Proxy went on. *"And while it might be a bit chaotic on the surface, my assessment is that these contacts are potentially more dangerous than your local wildlife troubles."*

"Who are they? Jevox? Melcorin? One of the others?"

"As I said…" The AI sounded somewhat annoyed for a moment. *"They are unknown. They are of a design with which we are not familiar."*

"Hah. So, the almighty Foundry has no idea what they are?"

"We do not know everything, Milo. And sometimes, even when we do, we do not have ready access to that information."

"Okay. Okay. Fine. Tactical analysis?"

"I have already given it to you. Get into orbit and we will intercept them."

I closed the connection.

"Shit," I growled. "I have to go. Something's headed our way, but I can't leave you down here in the middle of a crisis."

Shelly shook her head. "We'll be fine. On the other hand, if something destroys us from orbit…"

"You could go with me," I offered. "There's no safer place than on my ship. They've got this covered down here."

She leaned in and placed a kiss on my cheek. "Be careful, love."

With a sense of resignation, I let out a long sigh. "You're right. You're right."

I turned to leave, the lights from the crowded group fading over my shoulder, leaving me in the dark. Though I knew my way to the platform by memory, I found myself tripping over rocks and catching my feet.

A growl came from the shadows off to my right, that idling machine shriek, and I took off running. I could see the outline of my shuttle over the trees ahead, its shape blocking out a series of flashing lights. Though I had the mechanical augmentations of my arm and leg, it did not make me much faster.

Something hard slammed against me in the dark, knocking me off balance yet not onto the ground. I twisted around, arms raised, my hand light shining in the direction that it had gone. Gravel shifted on my left, tiny stones crunching, then on my right. An ominous, guttural purr rose a series of needles across my back. I was not prepared to fight a sawtooth. I was unarmed and alone.

From the dark came three bursts of light and crackling booms. A bleeding alien form slid to a halt at my feet, its multi-jointed face and jaw twitching.

"God, I freakin' hate nature," Karianna growled, walking into the glow of my hand light. "You okay?" I raised my shaking hand, pointing the light at her face. The blade of a woman raised her prosthetic hand, metal bracelets jingling, and squinted her eyes. "The hell, dude."

"Sorry," I breathed out, lowering my light. "Thanks."

She shook her head at me. "Whatever." And reached for a pistol tucked in the back of her jeans, tossing it to me.

I caught the weapon and clutched it tight.

"Milo, what did you plan on doing? Karate chopping the damn things?"

"Forgot my gun at home," I replied.

"Good thing I carry a spare."

"Look, I'm a lover, not a fighter."

She barked a laugh, the serious features of her hawkish face exaggerating. "Says the man who has one of the most powerful war machines in existence waiting for him overhead."

"It's a responsibility, not something I was looking for."

"Mmmhmm."

A moment later the two of us were hopping into our respective Swift Shuttles, stripping out of our clothes and submerging ourselves into orbs of clear liquid eight feet across. After the near miss, I was more than grateful for my ship's protection.

As we sank to the bottom of the Star Spheres, a series of tentacle-like umbilicals interfaced with our bodies, providing us with air, with nutrients, with a constant feed of information. Connections sprang to life, and in an instant, we were one with our ships, and the ships were one with us.

Our triangular shuttles ignited their engines and screamed off into the night at a breakneck twenty-five Gs of acceleration, a delta in velocity so great it would turn an unprotected human into a pile of mush. They sliced through the atmosphere like a pair of curved and jagged blades, but Karianna and I felt no discomfort. Our Star Spheres, the machines the Foundry built for us to pilot our ships, were specially designed to protect us from intense G forces, their fluid distributing the pressure such that no one part of our body was overtaxed. This made flying any Foundry-made craft from within a Star Sphere feel as if it were an extension of your own body, not just a machine at your command. The Swift Shuttle was no exception.

"Two minutes for coupling to the Fidelis," I heard Proxy say before the cat appeared beside me.

My body was floating in a field of endless stars, both outside of the shuttle, and not yet within the *Fidelis,* a virtual environment to help me control and contextualize the information given to me. I had three-dimensional, free movement in local space, complete with prismatic visual feedback and streams of data, granted through a mental projection the ship gave me from within the sphere.

I reached down and gave Proxy a scratch behind the ear and the cat began to purr. While it might not be a true feline, and just some weird AI facsimile, this warmed my heart nonetheless.

As the Swift Shuttle broke free of Novae's atmosphere, Prima, the equatorial continent our colony was founded upon, became a shrinking expanse of a few scattered lights, this side of the planet shrouded by night. The *Fidelis* was up ahead, beckoning me, a skyscraper-sized hunk of white and gold the shape of a crystal shard, flat at one end, jagged at the other. North of it, towards the planet's pole ten thousand one hundred and fifteen kilometers away, was Karianna's ship. It was made of the same material as mine, but instead mostly gold and black, and was shaped like a three-dimensional diamond printed on a deck of playing cards.

"You ready to kick some ass?" Karianna asked, her voice echoing into my virtual environment.

"Only if we need to," I replied. "Not every answer comes at the end of a gun barrel."

"You're no fun."

"Let me ask first. Have we gotten executive approval?"

"Who's going to stop us?"

"We live in a democracy, not a dictatorship."

"Fine, fine." She paused for a moment. *"Novae control, this is Karianna Torlen of the Reverie. Requesting orders of engagement for unknown spacecraft headed towards the colony."*

A moment passed. No response came from the surface.

"Don't be a smart ass," I replied.

"Power is out, Mr. Hughes. Looks like we're going to have to use our best judgement."

"Fine. Let's do everything in our power to keep from firing. If they get too close, we'll do what needs doing."

"Much better."

"We don't need to make enemies unless we have to."

Karianna let out an exasperated sigh. *"Ugh. I guess you're right. Not as fun, though."*

"You want to blow things up? We'll go bust some rocks in the asteroid belt later."

"Now you got yourself a date, fly boy."

"Sorry, miss. If you haven't noticed, I'm taken."

"Alright, alright. Stick with your wife, or whatever. Bring her along."

"She doesn't care much for flying."

"Really? Well, that's too bad. Flying is life."

My Swift Shuttle slipped into a port on the belly of the *Fidelis* and locked into place. There was no time to move into my primary Star Sphere near the bow of the ship, nor was there any need. I was aboard my battleship, and I could control it from anywhere within.

The targets were less than two hundred thousand kilometers from our position and screaming towards the surface. I ramped up the main drive and brought the *Fidelis* around, activating the Mercurial Integumentum as I did so, the protective shield of nanobots swarming around me like a second skin.

"Proxy," I said, peering down at the cat that weaved itself between my floating legs, rubbing them with its face. "Have you attempted to make contact with the targets?"

"Yes. No response." It purred against me.

"Do we not understand their language, or are they just being difficult?"

"Hard to say."

"Let's try and scare them off. Power up the Para Lux array. I'm going to get between them and the planet. Karianna, why don't we take a wide formation. You head them off so they can't cut around and go for the colony."

"Alright. Going to get all my weapons up and bright. Time to look like a big, terrifying animal."

The unidentified ships drew closer, their shapes resolving into something substantial. I got my first glimpse at them and frowned. Each were about as large as an acre of land and were shaped like starfish, their orange and black hulls covered in fractal patterns that reminded me of the inside of sunflower blooms or the outside of pinecones. While they appeared organic at a distance, nothing about the scans that returned supported this idea. Far as I knew, there was nothing truly organic living in the void.

"Any weapons?" I asked Proxy.

"There are high-energy signatures near the center of mass in excess of ten terawatts, but that is all I can see. They are fusion-powered. Not of Foundry make."

"That's reassuring."

"Hardly. If they were of Foundry make, we would know what we are up against. Tactical analysis is much simpler that way. This is an unknown."

A valid point. This was one of the reasons the Foundry recycled all arriving ships when a species visited its facilities, regardless of their technological level. It gave every species who took their assistance an even playing field.

"Almost in position," Karianna said, *"they're still coming."*

"Proxy, keep trying to make contact. Karianna, let's give them a light show."

"Hell yeah."

The Para Lux arrays on both the *Fidelis* and *Reverie* blossomed as we began to cast beams of high-intensity light all around the unknown ships, careful not to cross their paths and slice them in two. The rainbow beams of pure light flashed within our virtual spaces but were hardly visible on the visual spectrum without any atmospheric gases to reflect against.

We got the desired effect. The starfish-like craft broke formation and began to scatter, fusion drives flashing bright. Two turned the opposite direction, slowing themselves to head away from us at a dangerous, fifty G shift, while two angled themselves to miss Novae and head off into the void. The last of them, however, deviated only a little.

"That one's headed for the surface," Karianna said.

I threw the *Fidelis* into a hard burn and moved to intercept. While this ship could travel faster than fifty percent of light speed, it was massive and required considerable effort to turn. The starfish ship shot past us.

"We have to scare it off."

"Fighters?"

"No ancillary pilots on board, just us. I can't control more than about four at a time by myself."

"This isn't a dog fight, Hughes. Throw a damn swarm at them, they won't know the difference."

She had a point. "Okay. Proxy, launch a wing of drone fighters."

As I pivoted the *Fidelis* around to pursue, a half-dozen diamond shaped fighters shot from my belly and rushed towards the unknown ship. I did my best to plot courses that might make them appear as if they had physical pilots.

A few thousand kilometers separated the invader and the surface of Novae. My heart thundered in my chest.

"Get ready to shoot it down," Karianna said.

"No. We wait."

"Do you see how close it is to Novae? I'm serious. We have to kill it. Now—while we can."

"We don't know what it is or what it wants."

"I'm taking it down."

"Wait! Please wait. We can't make more enemies."

Karianna screamed into the open channel, *"Pacifist!"*

"I've been called worse," I mumbled.

Just as the starfish was about to hit the upper atmosphere, the first of our fighters reached it. Without preamble, the unknown ship took a hard turn in response and banked upward, heading off into open space, a trail of blue, ionized gas at its tail.

"They are retreating," Proxy reported. "I would keep an eye on the closest of them, but the rest are accelerating away."

"That was an unnecessary risk," Karianna told me.

I swallowed. She was right, but did attacking someone who showed us no direct threat make any sense either? In the end, no weapons had been used. No overtly aggressive actions taken. They had merely entered our airspace as explorers while keeping their lips sealed.

"They'll come back, ya know?" Karianna ventured when I had not responded.

I shook my head. "Not this time."

"We'll see about that. We'll see."

CHAPTER 2

To ensure the Starfish did not return, Karianna and I spent the rest of the night within the Star Spheres of our respective ships parked in orbit around Novae. My Proxy, as well as hers, monitored our instruments and tracked the ships as they moved across the system. There was no need to remain at high alert as far away as they were, so bedtime was in order.

Resting on the surface of any world was never quite as good as it was aboard the *Fidelis*, the only exception being when my wife snuggled close at my side. Sleeping within a Star Sphere was quite the experience. While my body was fully relaxed in a tank of water to restore itself, my mind could be transported anywhere, real or imaginary. If I wanted a lavish bed laid out beneath a sea of stars in a forest, I could have that. If I wanted a bed deep within the caves of an alien world, I could have that too. Most often, though, I found myself a place far more ordinary: the bed in my quarters aboard the *Vasco Da Gama*, my home until a few subjective years ago. Nothing fancy, just a ten-by-ten box with white and cream walls edged with lines of LED lights, a square-edged, queen-size bed with a semi-firm mattress at the center, and two white, unadorned side tables with drawers. I had lamps on either side of the bed, a cerulean tablet within arm's reach, and a body pillow to wrap myself around. It was familiar, comfortable.

I was used to sleeping with Shelly next to me, so I stacked a pile of pillows at my back simulating her presence before burying my head in the body pillow. Once I was comfortable the lights of my room dimmed, and I was plunged into total darkness.

Hours flashed by. Dreams of impossible sights flowing in one side of my head and out the other like water, impossible to retain but for a few drops of silty memories left behind. While I often dreamt no matter where I slept, something was different here within my sphere. I felt connected to that same presence I had felt when the ship had been nearly destroyed during the battle with the Kabosai. The presence I felt when I touched stars. There was an understanding just outside my base-line perception. Some sort of truth that, like a leaf on the surface of a pond, the more I reached for it, the more I pushed it away.

I was someplace else.

I was someplace new.

A black hole resolved into existence before me, hungry and dying, with little else to feed upon throughout all creation. Its singularity was trapped by an unfathomable structure of metal and glass, geodesic panels reflecting its emissions back upon itself, amplifying them, scattering, containing energy.

It was an end.

A beginning.

A moment of both death and life.

From above my position hovering at the edge of the accretion disc, something bright glimmered, its light somehow escaping the pull of this monster. I turned to peer toward it, catching sight of a square room mounted to the inside of the expansive, glass structure.

Was it a habitat? Could that even be possible? Was someone observing this cosmic beast with naked eyes as it went about its work, turning the final cycles of this machine of reality?

"Milo," a voice said. "Milo. Time to get up."

I cracked open my eyes. The lights of my quarters brightened.

That other place… it was…

"Is it that time already?" I asked Proxy as I sat up, bedsheets and pillows piled around me like a soft fortress.

"Yes," the cat said, leaping up off the floor onto the bed, seeking a crook among my tangle of sheets that it could sit down. "Power on the surface has been restored. The executive Arm has called a meeting, and the Council is gathering."

"Should have expected it." I rubbed my face and found both my hands made of flesh. In this virtual place, I was fully human. No machines made up parts of my body, just normal flesh. I was not a freak. "I was having the weirdest dream."

Proxy cocked its head at me. "Oh? What was it about?"

"It was about." I scratched my chin and peered at the wall, trying to recall what I had seen. "Funny, I can't remember."

"This is not uncommon for humans, is it not? Forgetting your dreams?"

"No... I mean yes... This is normal. Frustrating as hell, and normal. I swear, some of our best ideas happen when we sleep, then we wake up and forget all about them."

"Perhaps the Universe is protecting you from dangerous ideas."

My heart skipped a beat. Something about that statement struck home. I wasn't sure how to respond. "Maybe," I yawned.

"Are you ready to return to the surface?"

"Almost. Do me a favor before I head back down?"

Proxy lowered its head. "I am here to serve."

"Pack a breakfast for Shelly and I."

The cat twisted its head. "Are you sure? You have been receiving nutrients through the Star Sphere's umbilicals and I have been monitoring your vital signs. You do not require sustenance at this time."

"Yeah, well, maybe not, but I enjoy it. Besides, Shelly will appreciate a hot, fresh meal, not just another pile of meadroots and stone bison sausage."

"As you will."

Less than an hour later my Swift Shuttle landed back on the surface of Novae, Karianna seconds behind me. As soon as I was secure, I climbed out of my Star Sphere, toweled off, and slipped on fresh clothes. A wicker basket with food wrapped in cloth sat by the exit. The savory scents of sausage fat, cheese, butter, and fresh biscuits crawled through the cracks of the wooden lid, elevating my state of mind. Proxy had done as I asked, and I was always grateful for it.

"Hope you got some for me," Karianna said as I stepped out onto the landing pad. She too had changed into different clothes from the last time I saw her, a pair of dark-wash jeans, fitted t-shirt and an asymmetric black leather jacket complete with a pair of matching knee-high boots. Her raven hair was still damp from the Star Sphere, pulled back into a ponytail with a pink, rubber hair tie.

I gripped the handle on the basket and smiled at her. "You can get your own. You have a Proxy, too."

"Maybe I forgot to ask."

"Not my problem."

She ran her mechanical fingers down the length of her ponytail, squeezing out water before shaking it dry. "You're an ass, you know that?"

"Think that if you like," I replied, then reached into the basket and removed a warm biscuit wrapped in cloth. "Here. Just so you won't bitch and complain the whole time."

She snatched the biscuit from my fingers and narrowed her eyes at me. "You really know how to charm the ladies, don't you? Ooo, it's got cheese."

By the time we walked to the north end of Novae, though the winding streets of squat, yurt-like homes made of smooth, white stone, the Council Chambers were nearly full. The colony was made up of only about seven hundred humans, but we could not seat them all. People were lined up outside, begging to be let in to the recessed, cylindrical building we used as our seat of government, security insisting that some of them stay outside or go home.

The local network was back up and running, my neural implants able to interface with it, but every port was so clogged with traffic I gave up trying to query for any valuable information. It was wasted effort. Intuition was enough to know what was going on.

As Karianna and I descended the steps inside, colonists parted to let us in. As pilots of the Foundry ships, we were special, important. That afforded us some privileges, as well as a heap of responsibility.

Shelly raised a hand at me from across the curve of the Council Chambers. Karianna followed me through the press of colonists as we made our way to her. A few people said their hellos as we passed, patting us on the back or reaching out to bump fists.

It was all so overwhelming. The room was abuzz with a thousand conversations, so many it was near impossible to focus even on one. I waved to my parents who were sitting several rows up with Ada Mitchell, Gino Cassini, and Johan Van Niekerk, all of which, along with Shelly and many others, made up the Technology and Development Arm of the colony— which my mother naturally led. They smiled and waved back.

All five Arms of the colony, our organizational branches of service, were represented. Emilio Sanchez, as well as Perry and Alyssa, were off to my left representing the Agriculture and Labor Arm. To my right, Charlotte Patterson, Leo Nelson, Marissa Martin, and Dante Vasquez, sat together, representing the Culture and Xenology Arm. Folks from the Security and Exploration Arm were scattered throughout the chambers. Chevelle Young, their head, was near the front of the room. Rowan Donaldson, the hero of the *Reverie*, an imposing man who had saved the *Brilliance's* crew from several Isopteran boardings was near the back, his protégée, Jaxson Zager, beside him. The energy today was tense after the events of last night, of which they only knew half. This would prove interesting.

"It's just about to start," Shelly said as I took a seat on the stone bench beside her. "So happy to see you. Everything go okay up there?"

I gave a shrug. "Almost didn't make it."

"What? What do you mean?"

"Well, I was jumped by a sawtooth near the platform. Karianna saved me. Again."

"Forget your pistol?"

"Yeah."

She tsked at me. "What about the rest? What happened in orbit?"

"The rest was fine, I'm fine."

"Fine? That isn't a good response. Are you frustrated, insecure, neurotic and exhausted?"

"More like feelings inside, not expressed."

"I see." She patted me on the thigh and grinned. "Talk later?"

"Sure. They'll have me fill everyone in soon. I'm just glad you're okay."

"Me too, babe." Her head cocked, nostrils flashing as she sniffed the air. "What's in the basket?"

"Breakfast," I offered, opening the lid.

Shelly gave me a broad smile and squeezed me around the shoulders before kissing me on the lips. Her kisses were the best, soft and sweet.

"Get a room," Karianna groaned and rolled her eyes.

"You are a saint, love," Shelly whispered and reached for a slice of spinach and ham quiche. "I miss eggs. Too bad all the chickens died in the attack."

"The Foundry makes a good substitute," I said, and caught the look of several others eyeing our breakfast with more than a curious look.

"Maybe, but how much longer will it do this?" Shelly took a bite of her food and let out a subaudible sigh.

"For me? For us, me and you? Forever, far as I know."

She took her time chewing as if this might be the last quiche she ever ate. After a moment she went on, "Doesn't seem fair to everyone else. Not that

I don't appreciate it, and trust me, I do. But everyone else has to eat whatever we can grow or find, and here you are bringing back gourmet food from the *Fidelis* any time you wish."

I let out a long breath. She had a point. We were eating a specially designed meal created by the Foundry from human memories. A luxury we could not extend to everyone in the colony, not so long as we lived on the surface. While in transit between worlds, the Foundry would feed us however we liked, but here… Here it wanted us to find our own way.

Five or six months. Was that all the time we had? Were Johan's estimations correct? Was the Foundry tapering its caloric assistance?

"You're right," I said. "I shouldn't have brought this."

Shelly licked her fingers clean and shook her head. "Now, now—don't say that. Maybe we should just share it with those sitting around us."

I gave a nod and reached into the basket, removing and omelet wrap, as well as a handful of sonhos—a sort of Portuguese donut ball *minha avó*, my grandmother, used to cook at holidays. After I was satisfied that this was all I wanted, I turned to those sitting nearby and offered up the rest. There was far more food than Shelly and I could think to eat, and this painless act of charity seemed to alleviate my guilt, if only a little.

A bang came from the front of the Council Chamber and the room went silent. From hidden alcoves next to the dais at the front of the chambers, six people appeared, each well-dressed in dark suits with either pants or skirts, a pin on each of their left chests with the image of a FICSE Mission vessel curving into space. This insignia was fast becoming the seal of Novae, a reminder of what we were and where we came from.

The councilors of the Executive Arm took their places behind a series of podiums arrayed at equal distances. On the right wing of the dais, our left, was Ricardo Perez, a squat man in his fifties born of Cuban immigrants in South Florida. A brilliant student, he'd gone to graduate school on scholarship for both political science and law, earning him a place on the fleet. Beside him was a petite woman with shoulder length waves of blonde hair and bright eyes, Sydney Clark. I had seen her from time to time growing up on the *Vasco Da Gama*, a doctor in agricultural studies, but she had never been well liked. That had all changed on Novae. Next in line came Sofia L'Agnese, a sturdy woman from Rome, Italy, taking her spot beside Sydney. She gave the room a curious look, and her soft, olive toned face pinched.

At the right end of the dais, Rebecca Crawford found her place, her tangle of red curls pulled back into a bun. She had a stack of papers in her hands I did not see the rest carrying. Beyond her, Alexander Halifax came next. Alexander was the youngest on the Council, and one of the most brilliant minds I had ever known, even including my parents. A child like me at the onset of the mission, he had lived his younger years aboard the *Brilliance* and studied mathematics, earning remote PhDs in both applied and theoretical disciplines from MIT. He was a good-looking man, handsome with a close-cropped beard and close-cropped hair, of African descent, skinny but not without definition, always cheerful and smiling. It was a wonder he hadn't remarried after his divorce with Ada, well-loved as he was.

Last but not least, Mary Stablecamp, the head of the Executive Arm settled into place. Sister of Perry Stablecamp, former lover of Esteban Lopez, my brother by circumstance who had been lost in battle to the Kabosai, and my friend. Novae had voted for her to lead our colony. Out of everyone here she was the oldest, having remained free from hyper suspension during our journey to Ph0nx so that she could live a life with Esteban. She'd never gotten over his death, and likely never would. And so, in remembrance, her once luscious, colorful hair, dyed something new with each time she had a fresh romantic entanglement, from pink to blue to green to purple, was now lifeless and grey.

In this sorrow, she and I would always have something in common. Anytime I thought of Esteban, my heart ached. He'd been a good man, a best friend, my adopted family. He'd helped me through the darkest days after the fall of the *Vasco Da Gama* and shown me how to grow up and take responsibility. A brother not by blood, but by circumstance and fire.

He would be so proud of Mary. She had become the figurehead of our Colony. Our unofficial leader. She was the Speaker.

Our six duly elected leaders stood before us, none of them career politicians, all scientists in their own right, a legacy no other human colony has had the opportunity to leave until now.

"Order in the Council Chambers," Mary said, her voice amplified by the slender microphone on the podium before her. "I call to order this special meeting of the Executive Arm to discuss our recent, persistent crisis. Miss Clark, report if you please."

"Yes, Madam speaker." Councilwoman Clark lifted a sheet of paper and began to read. "Last evening at 23:32 Central Novae time, Generators M-

114, and M-116 went inoperable. This plunged the colony into near-total darkness, other than a few backup systems in the medical buildings and Council Chambers. Sawtooths were immediately heard prowling through the streets. Captain Young of Security and Exploration deployed armed guards to sweep the streets for anyone in danger. Four human-sized specimens were found and put down. Eight people were injured, mostly quills, a few bites. Germane Daw lost two fingers. We're working on prosthetics to replace them."

She paused for a moment, sighing as she pinched the bridge of her nose. "You know, it sure would be nice if we knew where those ugly things hid during the day, maybe thin out their ranks. Anyways, Gino attended the injured. With the hard work of labor team, Lance Brittan, Austin Dardar, and Alyssa Robinson, restored power to the colony. This was not before a report of something dangerous in orbit was communicated to both Foundry pilots."

"Milo, Karianna," Mary said—no, the Speaker said—raising a hand in our direction. "Would you mind debriefing us on the events of last night? Being that we have not heard a word from you since."

Karianna and I gave one another a look, then stood. We remained silent for a moment, waiting to see which of us would speak first. When she said nothing, and the awkward silence of several hundred eyes rested upon us too long, I started.

I waved to the gathering with my prosthetic hand. "Good morning, everyone. Council members. Moments after the power outage, our respective Proxies informed us of a potential threat headed for orbit. They were something the Foundry had never seen before, ships the shape of starfish with massive fusion reactors at their cores, possibly for some kind of weapons, maybe just for space travel. There were five in all, moving in formation towards Novae, with no open lines of communication. We made the decision to wait to see if they were hostile before engaging."

"*You* made the decision," Karianna said, finally speaking up. "Not me."

Heat gathered around the collar of my shirt, sweat breaking out on my back. Was she seriously going to throw me under the shuttle with the engines on?

"*We* made the decision," I hardened my voice. "We don't need to make more enemies than we already have. When we gave them a light show, all broke off but one. The final ship was scared off with drone fighters. At this moment, they are burning away from us towards the edge of the system."

"Where did they come from?" Councilwoman L'Agnese asked.

"We don't know," Karianna replied. "The Foundry was pretty tight lipped. Besides, I don't think it knows."

"You made the right choice," Councilman Perez said, his tone thoughtful. "We cannot bloody the nose of every species who comes within a reasonable distance to us without cause, no? How do we build bridges? Make allies?"

Councilwoman Clark set her papers down and frowned. "If we kill them, a few ships are dead, but if they kill us, humanity may be at its end. Extinction. We hope the mission is still alive, that we can get help from the Foundry and go back to Earth, but with time dilation, there's no telling how much time will pass. How much time has passed on Earth? We could be it. All the more reason we should protect ourselves. We may have others counting on us."

"Heavy handed nonsense," Councilwoman Crawford interjected. "The Foundry ships are remarkable, yes, but there are only two of them. Two. We already rely on the kindness of others too much. What of their interconnected alliances? Hurting one without cause may initiate a chain reaction where others are no longer willing to do trade. While Chevelle and her team are devoted to our ongoing surveys of this world, it will take some time to create the infrastructure to exploit any of the resources we discover, least of all the feculent coal."

The room fell into a reflective silence.

"Alexander?" Speaker Stablecamp asked after a few moments. "Your thoughts?"

The councilman rubbed at his jaw, thinking. "I mean, I get it. We're not in the strongest position at this point. Shoot first and ask questions later is what we're doing with the sawtooths, but far as we know they're just animals. Not sentient. We have to keep ourselves safe, but making everyone mad usually doesn't help either."

"Is this a policy we want to adopt in the future?" the Speaker proposed. "Prudence in first contact?"

"You should have reached out for guidance," Councilwoman Clark declared while leaning forward on her forearms, an edge of anger in her voice. "We are a democracy."

"And just how was I supposed to do that, huh?" My reply might have sounded a bit petulant. "Power was down, and what shoddy communication network we have was not available."

"In fairness," Karianna raised her prosthetic hand, fingers wiggling in a kind of wave, "he did try. As annoying as it is, he insisted that we do that first."

Councilwoman Clark crossed her arms and turned her attention back to the papers on the dais.

"Thank you, pilots." The Speaker gestured for us to sit.

Shelly grabbed my hand after I sat back down, then laid her head on my shoulder. "You did good," she whispered. "You did good."

Damn. I did not like being in the hotseat.

"Now to the matter of the generators," the Speaker resumed. "Mr. Brittan, report."

Lance stood and gave them a nod. "An honor, madam Speaker. We have uncovered the cause of the outage. A three-way gas exchange had a leak, and as a result it altered the chemical properties of our supply of feculent coal. As we all know, it's an easy to find fuel, pretty much anywhere you look, stone bison crap it out all over the place, but its finicky. Maintenance seems to have been the cause this time. A failure in the exchange allowed moisture into the system, which altered the autoignition temperature, which in turn altered the burn rate. When fuel ran out, the excess heat buildup ruined several of the finer components, turning them into literal slag. We've got it up and running again, but this sort of system is prone to failure. It is my opinion that we need to get the photovoltaics up and running as soon as possible, or we'll keep dealing with this. And to do this, well… I need help."

"What are we short of?" Perez asked.

"Mostly pure silicon, gallium arsenide. A few other trace elements. We just don't have a good supply of our own right now."

"I see. And what else?"

Without being called on by the Council members, a man named Johan Van Niekerk stood up, a scowl on his face. While no objections came forth from the crowd, he did receive a few sour looks. Johan was a fit, broad shouldered South African man in his middle sixties with narrow eyes and thinning hair that was slicked back. He kept his grey and white beard full, but not long, and wore fitted clothes in the fashion of those twenty years his junior. Like many of the colonists, he was intelligent and driven. His personal expertise was in the fields of computer science, economics, and data analytics, giving him insights few besides Councilor Halifax might have. But however brilliant he was, there were times he lacked social graces or any willingness to follow protocol. Times like now.

"Silicon? Gallium?" Johan asked, his harsh, South African accent thick with the occasional Afrikaans word mixed in. "*Asseblief,* no major issue to me. We can trade for those items. We have seeds in stock. So long as we are careful to allocate them over the next few months."

"Yes," Lance said, turning to face Johan. "But do we have enough? Pretty sure everyone here still likes to eat. Are we forgetting about the food taper? Hmm?"

"No one has forgotten about the food taper. It was my find. I have revised the numbers once more. Everyone needs to listen to me and listen good. If the Foundry keeps reducing its food drops from the *Fidelis* and *Reverie* as it has, in five months there will be no more. We have five months to be self-sustained before *baba* puts us out."

There were murmurs around the room, hushed conversations and uneasy looks. This was not truly anything new, but there were still naysayers.

"Has this been peer-reviewed?" someone shouted from across the room. I couldn't see who it was. Others grumbled in agreement with this question.

Halifax raised his hand. "I have. Pretty sure Johan is right. Might look like a lot of food is coming on each pod, as in the same quantities, but the Foundry is packing them different to look this way. There's less material in there. His conclusion—accurate. Five months are all we have, unless something changes."

Johan turned to Karianna and me, giving us a pinched expression. "Anything we can do to encourage the Foundry's help?"

The Foundry had been supplying supplemental foodstuffs to keep everyone fed over the past three years as we built our shelters and infrastructure. These foodstuffs had been simple, base proteins, grains, those sorts of things, airdropped by pod every two weeks to a spot at the edge of the colony. Nearly a year back, Johan had begun carefully weighing the supplies given to us under the suspicion that something wasn't right. What he discovered was that the Foundry was sending down less and less, the quantities decreasing on an exponential curve. One day, it was going to seem fine, and the next, the pod would be empty.

Karianna and I shook our heads. We had both asked our Proxies to help, and they had given us no answer other than, "This is how things must be", in response.

"Very well," Johan said, then looked to the stone ceiling, scowling.

"Materials are all well and good," Lance started again, clearly annoyed at Johan, "but we need labor for the PV project too. We need workers. We need muscle. We're building acres and acres of solar arrays in not the best conditions."

"And where do you see this labor coming from?" Johan pressed.

Lance cocked his head to the side at a condescending angle. "Thank you for asking, sir. As you just mentioned, our seed stocks are rapidly piling up. If I could borrow five or ten people from the agricultural projects—"

To my surprise, Johan raised a hand to hush Lance. "What I hear from you are not rational reasons, they are excuses. Listen, I come from a time in history when we hustled to make the most meager livings." He shook his fist in the air. "This made us strong. It made us hard. It made us resilient in the face of unspeakable odds. Look where we are now. Hm? If not for hard work and grit, the FICSE fleet would never have been built. Without hard work and grit, we never would have crossed the gulf between stars." He slowly spun, regarding the many faces in the room who had focused on him. "This spirit is still alive in each and every one of you. We carry the pride of humanity and their plight on our shoulders. We cannot be absolved of that. You say you need help? Why not just work harder?"

"Pretty words," Lance said, his eyebrows raised, "but why do you even care? Agriculture isn't your concern. That's my Arm, not yours. My dance space."

"Our survival is my concern. Earth is my concern. The mission, son. It's all that really matters. Trade and self-reliance get us home quicker."

"The mission," Lance muttered, shaking his head. "What a load of stupid shit."

"We cannot abandon all hope of the mission," Johan replied, his voice becoming hard. "FICSE. Foundry Initiative, Contact and Save Earth."

"Look where we are, papaw." Lance raised his arms wide, palms up. "We're on a damned alien planet lord knows how far from our birthplace. The mission to save Earth is nothing more than a goddamned pipe dream at this point. We aren't going back. This is it. This is our reality."

"I don't accept that."

"Accept whatever the hell you want, old man. Novae is our reality. And I don't know about you, but I want to keep living. I'm happy here."

Once upon a time, I had had passionate feelings about the mission. I can recall arguing vehemently with Captain Williams over this exact topic, but at that time I was naïve. I did not understand the bigger picture. I did not understand how things change. How objectives change. We are scientists, not animals. We made changes when the data supported it. And right now, the data did not support our original mission, it supported our personal survival.

Just as Johan was about to interject, he was interrupted. For once he shut his mouth and did not argue.

"We no can take five or ten people from agri-work," Emilio Sanchez, head of Agriculture and Labor declared, finger pointed at Lance. "Impossible. Forget trade with Jevox, how we feed everyone?"

"PVs mean safety and security for all the ends," Chevelle Young, head of Exploration and Security, spoke next. "Soon as they up, soakin' in starlight, those can run back to crops. Power means we get on with it, proper cordon around the village. Fixup. Everyone haps."

"Unacceptable!"

"Hear me. Physical security comes before trade. The Foundry will provide for now. Let's lean on that. Lighten the load."

"But we need materials coming from our trade agreements to finish PVs. You no been listening to Lance?"

"Move from me, we 'ave enough, I know. We can make work if we go with three-phase plan. Could take longer than we like to meet goals, ya, but we be safer this way."

"That heap of *basura*? It no' been peer reviewed. Es outside of your arm, Chevelle. This is Agriculture and Labor work, not Security and Exploration, *hermana*."

"Ay ay, pattymout, I have two PhDs, I know good science. This good science."

Emilio threw up his hands and began to shout. "*Uno* PhD, *dos* PhD. We all have them. You think that makes you special, no? Did you rescue dozen varieties of grape seeds from Earth and make them grow in soils of different composition, on other worlds? Tell me you do that. No? You not? Didn't think so. Good science…"

"Look to me, my job is to provide safety to the colony. My job is to procure resources, material. We might have less trade if labor is put on PV project, but my team can snag the rest. We've had many promising surveys lately. Peng spots. Good places."

"Only thing you've been good at procuring lately is piles of *caca* for the compost hut. So, thanks. We do need help to fertilize our future wine crop."

"Pussy hole."

"Order! Order!" Speaker Stablecamp banged her metal gavel upon the dais and the room began to quiet, though not all at once. It took several moments for the angry murmurs to die down. "We are a civil society built on intellect and reason. We will not be overcome by emotion and fear. Emotion and fear are what drove the decline of the nations of Earth. These are all valid arguments. That said, I will not allow us to become fragmented. This talk of 'not my Arm', 'not my job' has to stop. We are one colony, one people. Your Arm's specializations do not exclude or prevent you from helping others. Do you understand?"

The room was silent. Those who had been speaking took their seats without a word, even Johan, despite the furious look on his face. Madam speaker had put them in their place for the moment.

"Hear me clearly," she boomed. "I believe in what we are doing here. We will survive. We will create a viable place for humans to live beyond SOL."

A chirp echoed through the Council chambers. A soft ping came to the back of my mind. Arrivals were incoming, and this time, they were not Starfish.

"Speaking of trade," Clark said. "It seems that the Jevox will be here soon. Speaker, do we wish to take a vote on this matter and adjourn to tend our guests?"

Speaker Stablecamp paused for a moment, taking a slow breath. She scribbled a few notes on a sheet of paper at the dais, thought about what she had written, then nodded. "Call for a vote?"

The other Council members nodded.

"The vote is as follows. We will transfer eight workers from the agriculture projects to the PV project at Lance Brittan's recommendation. Is that sufficient, Mr. Brittan?"

"Yes madam," he said, keeping his head down where he sat.

"All in favor?"

"Aye," Clark voted.

Councilman Perez came next with, "Nay."

"Aye," L'Agnese said.

"Nay," Crawford said.

Councilman Halifax scribbled on his tablet, working through some sort of math problem. He would be the tie breaking vote. While Mary could cast her own, it was general practice for her to lead the discussion, not determine the outcome. If she felt the need to deadlock the vote for more discussion, she could, but rarely did so.

"Alexander?" the Speaker said.

He set down his pen and frowned. "No good answer. No good solution. I vote nay."

Madam speaker nodded. "Thank you, councilors. That is two in favor, three against. Motion to transfer workers has not passed. Mr. Brittan, you will have to find another way for now."

Even through the crowd of people, I could see the slight sag in Lance's shoulders. He was disappointed, and understandably so. But what was the right answer? I wasn't sure. I wasn't even sure I should have an opinion. Having access to the *Fidelis* meant I lived above these concerns, good or bad.

"This meeting of the Council has come to a close," the Speaker said, banging her gavel.

The room swelled once more with conversation as everyone shuffled and made their way for the exit. Karianna gave a wave and darted off to catch up with someone. Shelly and I remained seated where we were as people cleared out.

"Well, that went okay," Shelly said over the noise while letting out a sigh.

"What do you think?" I asked.

"About what part? Our priorities? What you did?"

"Any of it."

Her eyes went wide, and she reached for her hair, twisting the curls at the ends with her fingertips. "We're in a tough spot, but I believe we'll get it figured out. We just need solutions. Logic may make people think, but emotion is what makes them act. Emotion isn't always a bad thing, and we should not forget that."

I frowned at her. "You're right. We're still human."

"For now, at least. And because of that, we act irrational at times. Such is life." She took me by the arm and smiled. "Come on, let's go. I think both of us could use a little time away from the crowds."

"Mom! Dad!" I waved at my parents who were walking back across the aisle in front of us towards the exit.

Mom opened her arms wide and wrapped them around both Shelly and I, squeezing us so tight I could smell the soap she used. "Look at the two of you, *doce doce*."

"Stop it," Shelly said, waving a dismissive hand and chuckling.

My parents, like most who had been adults at the onset of the mission, were getting older, but were not old. They were both in their late fifties, but took good care of themselves for the most part, working full-time. There was no opportunity for retirement in this society. Mom's tight curls had only a few sprigs of grey, her dark skin smooth but for thought lines upon her forehead and around her eyebrows. She was strong and fit, her eyes kinder than in those years aboard the *Vasco Da Gama*. Dad on the other hand, had gone nearly bald, his pate a brilliant beacon of white under any source of light, and he carried a few too many pounds around the middle. It was clear we needed to do some more hiking, and soon. Might not be as thrilling as when we rode motorbikes in our Virtual Environments back on the *Vasco*, but it was far more kind to the midsection.

I was so very grateful to still have them both. Things had been rough when I was a kid, they had snuck us onto the launch craft illegally, determined to be part of FICSE no matter what, then became so obsessed with their work I felt like little more than a footnote in their great scientific careers. We had had some time to work through this since arriving on Novae, but it had not been easy. It was like getting to know them all over again.

Shelly's parents, on the other hand… this mission had claimed them both. Maybe that's why Mom pretty much adopted her.

Dad sighed and put a hand on my shoulder. "They've lost it, son. They've lost their damn minds."

"Lost it how, Dad?"

"We've got to do everything we can to protect the people of this colony, and that isn't just about guns." He pointed a finger at the dais. "I keep hearing this argument pop up again and again. The Mission. The Mission. What mission? Those days are gone and done for. We left Earth, became part of this strange galactic system. We lost our ships and still don't have any way to help out those back home, if we can even find it again. And now? We're on the ass-end of nowhere. You know what I say? I say we survive here and forget the rest. What other options do we have?"

"Should we not care about it?" I asked, then raised my open palms to forestall his irritation. "The Mission, that is. Not that I'm arguing for it. Just want to understand."

"If there was a way to go back, then yes, we should care," Mom supplied, lowering her voice. "Is there a way, Milo?"

I gave a shrug. "The Foundry ships are capable, no question. Just don't know if they are willing. I have no idea where Earth is in relation to us. I mean, we've discussed the pulsar maps from Voyager to get back, but those were cleared from all our devices. Far as I know, at this point the Foundry won't help us anyways. Maybe we have some tests to pass, or something, I can't say. The Foundry exists to protect life, and let's be honest, humans don't always do the best job with that. I think we're on our own for now."

"Doing just what it wants us to do…" Dad mused, fingers rubbing his chin. "What do you think, Shelly? What's the best course of action?"

"What do I think?" she asked, looking surprised. "Well, I think we should make the best of our situation, live our days to the fullest. It's our best trait as humans. Adapting. If we can't go back to Earth, then there's no sense in getting upset about it. We're here, many of us are still alive, and life is to be enjoyed."

"Life is to be enjoyed." Dad smiled at her. "You got yourself a good one, son. You got yourself a good one."

CHAPTER 3

As we exited the Council chambers, we came upon Johan and several others from the Technology and Development Arm. They had gathered in a circle and engaged in a heated discussion. As head of their Arm, Mom hurried over, Dad, Shelly and I following.

"This is getting old," Johan was saying. "No one is listening to what I've told them. Time is running out. We've got to tighten the belt and get ready. Being on UEI ships for so long in homeostasis we got spoiled. The world was handed to us. Everything we ever needed, at our grasp. Now, look at us, the Foundry has become our benefactors. That didn't go so well for you from the *Vasco Da Gama* with the Gene Brokers, now did it?"

"How are we to tighten?" Gino Cassini asked. "My husband Emilio does not tell lies. It is hard work for agriculture. We don't have many modern conveniences of farming. A few ploughs and other equipment, not much else. Nothing is efficient. They need help there, too."

"We all need help sometimes," Ada said, shifting her weight to poke out one hip. She narrowed her eyes in thought while rubbing her right thumb and forefinger together. "I'd love to get the resource allocation system up and running. Pretty sure buff Santa here agrees with me on this. One sure-fire way to tighten this up is to keep a running tab of everything in a central place, accessible to everyone. You know, it'll make sure that people are responsible when a resource is used. Right now, about all we have are a few clipboards and an old set of tablets. Getting people to log every little thing is next to impossible. Only good thing I can say about this crazy situation, is it keeps my ass busy. Just the kind of challenge I enjoy."

Johan gave her a withering look. "Did you call me Santa Claus?"

"It's a compliment, sir. He can like, you know, deliver presents all over the world in a night. Who else can do that? It's high praise."

He groaned and went on. "But to get that system up and running we need more network bandwidth. Too many people sending worthless queries and eating up what little we have. The heavy lifting of our implants is not done in the head, it's done on the network." He tapped his temple with a finger. "This hardware is for interface, not much more."

Ada made a finger gun with her right hand and pulled the trigger, clicking her tongue against her teeth. "So that's the ticket. Bolster up the network. Get it running more efficiently. Open the way for us to all work better."

"That will help, Lovelace," Shelly added as we arrived, taking a spot next to her before giving her a bump with an elbow. "If we can push the firmware updates we're working on to the implants, they'll use less data. No sense running two-way protocols for integrity. If a few packets get lost when we query, it's not the end of the world."

"So proud." Ada patted Shelly on the shoulder and smiled. "Miss Perfect is starting to accept that things don't always have to be… perfect."

Shelly rolled her eyes and put a hand to her chest, feigning embarrassment. "Stop it."

"Come on, come on." Ada crossed her arms and tossed back her head, chewing on the ring at her bottom lip. "Look… If you had it your way, there would not just be two-way protocols here, but four. Send a packet, make sure it was received, send it back to know it was received, then send the packet back to say that what was received was received, only to send it back to see if it was received."

Shelly narrowed her eyes at her, the look on her face a kind of forced smirk. What a dichotomy as friends. Ada was all ripped jeans and tattoos, with a constellation of piercings, her ears, nose, and lip threaded with silver. She had half her hair shaved across one side, its cut length asymmetric, a rainbow of pastels hidden beneath shoulder length sections of dark brown. She was the very picture of a punk, a rocker, whereas Shelly was all strait-laced and starched like an Ivy League legacy, not a wrinkle in sight. God forbid.

"Stop exaggerating," Shelly chuffed. "I'm not that bad."

Ada raised her eyebrows at me, not at Shelly, saying something without saying something. She wasn't wrong.

"Okay, okay, lots to untangle there," Mom said, raising her hands and settling in beside Johan. "Is everything okay, Van Niekerk? I sense a whole lot of frustration here."

At the right side of our circle stood a couple, a petite woman my age with long, red hair, and her stocky, baby-faced husband, both dressed in dirty overalls patched several times.

I gave them a polite nod. "Harper. George."

"Hey, Milo," George said, reaching out a hand. "How've you been, man?"

Harper did nothing but sigh. Years had passed, but my one-time girlfriend still hadn't gotten over Shelly slamming her in the face with a lunch tray.

"So, it's true," I ventured to the group. "Most of our network bandwidth is being eaten up by people screwing around on their implants. I've done a little frivolous file sharing myself, sure, books, VEs, but nothing else. I saw where Perry and Alyssa had put up the message board to name plants and places. Think that's what's doing it? People chatting it up on boards?"

"No," Shelly answered.

"It's nothing like it used to be," Gino said. "The internet. Social media. Back on Earth it was a legitimate addiction, digital candy, tiny bursts of dopamine on demand."

"What do you mean?" I asked. "People used it to share files and ideas, right?"

"No," Dad cut in, a single finger raised. "And umm, sort of. It was created to be a library, a place where the world could share research, expression, and make connections in a decentralized manner. Mostly, though, it was used as a means to waste time sending videos back and forth of people who couldn't dance to save their lives."

Gino nodded. "Then there were recipes on how to make bread from foods like acorns. Tried it once, forage diet. Terrible."

Dad leaned in. "Animals doing cute things."

"Of course, of course. And let us no' forget dank, seventh tier meme dumps."

"Dank meme dumps?" I asked, looking to those my age for guidance. From the blank looks on their faces, all were equally as confused as I. "That's weird. Why would people waste such a resource?"

Dad sighed, his hands clasped together, fingers squeezing. He wasn't the only one who seemed a bit uncomfortable around this topic. "If I don't ever see another person's legs stretched out on a beach with a drink in hand in a feed, it'll be too soon."

"Social media was the downfall of society," Johan said under his breath. "We began to curate images of who we wanted others to believe we were, true or not. No depth. No reality. Ideals no one could live up to. Thankfully, we do not have the same economic pressures to keep us engaged with a platform like those, or the same population. Seven hundred colonists can't make anything go viral. If we can just cut down on trading useless pings on the network for a while, it should be enough."

"For once we have something we can agree on," Dad told Johan. "That aside, Parallax is still the superior band."

"Billie Rayne and the Quad."

Dad raised open his hands and repeated, "Parallax."

"Billie Rayne…"

Mom shook her head and brought everyone back to the subject at hand. "Look, fine, the internet was terrible. What's really wrong, Johan? Tell me what's really wrong."

"What's wrong?" He scowled at Mom. "They don't listen. No one listens, and this is getting old. We're all scientists, and yet, it seems that that doesn't prevent people from acting irrational."

"That's humans," Mom said, crossing her arms. "We can either lead through it or go around it. No other options. *Que coisa.* For now, I intend to lead our Arm through others. What do you want from everyone? You essentially called us all out for being fat and lazy."

"*Asseblief,* don't you see?" Johan pointed towards the cylindrical shape of the Cultural Center under construction, its main structure in place, most of the working now moved to the interior. "Earth got so bad because people didn't listen. People tried to kick the can down the road. It's not my problem, it's someone else's, living in their stupid, insulated little universes, VEs, social media, escapism. Earth has problems, sure, but that's for another generation. Nothing went down how the masses expected. But when the food stopped coming or became so expensive that even Americans were forced into austerity, it all heated up. We coordinated a world of nations to take a risk, build the ships, and send them off in hope of something better. And yet, what did they do while we were gone? Nothing. Nothing at all. Their hope fell on us, is still on us, a prayer that some great machine god would save them.

"We delved into the void. We faced fire and demons both alien and human. The *Brilliance* had a mutiny aboard the Foundry facility, people died, and those interlopers, those assholes Justin led, were cast out because they wanted to lay waste to all we had fought to save. Our crew endured three attacks from the Isoptera. Three. And we survived. Then there's your people from the *Vasco Da Gama*; the attack, the Kabosai, the battle of Ph0nx. These events brought us to an apex, a moment where we could make a choice to be better, to do good. And all I keep seeing are a bunch of spoiled humans looking to turn a blind eye to the truth and settle back into complacency."

No one said a word for a moment, not even Ada. Personally, I felt we all needed a bit of time to heal from what we had been through. My physical wounds might be gone, but the mental ones were fresh enough. The level of change we'd been forced to endure, the terrifying things we saw. We looked into the black and the black looked back at us. We saw madness, and it said hello. We had people to mourn, ya?

Shelly gave me a look and knew what I was thinking. I missed my surrogate brother. Esteban wasn't here, and it hurt terribly, and Johan, he just wanted us to move on. He wanted us to let all that go. Wanted us to forget that it ever hurt.

"I get it," Mom said, putting a hand on Johan's thick shoulder, her expression softening. "Trust me, I get it. The question is, what do you want? What do you really want? How do we change it? Only way I see, is to work together as one."

"Times were better when we had a unified purpose," he said, lowering his voice. "We have too many people wanting too many different things."

"We knew this might happen."

"Would happen. We knew this would happen. We've got to change that."

"Is survival not enough of a unified purpose?"

"For a while, maybe, but I think people need something else to believe in. Something bigger. A cause."

Gino nodded. "We are building a future without war, my friend. A future without hate. Is that not enough of a cause?"

"Wait till the lights go out," Johan replied. "See how long that aspirational hope of yours holds up. We've got a window to make it right. We have to make it right."

"What do you suggest?" Harper asked.

"I keep looking at this like a business. We're not making enough, and we're spending far too much. It puts us in the red. We've got to increase our revenue or reduce expenses. We're just not doing enough. We need to do more."

"So, we work harder? Put in a few more hours? Cut back on off-time?"

"Not sustainable," Mom said, waving her hands in front of her. "I've been there before, and Perry's blindness was the result."

"But he was a result!" Johan declared, becoming visibly angry. "He was a result, and if not for him, none of us would be here. The protein treatment saved us all."

Mom's expression went dark, her hands at her side balling into fists. This was dangerous ground for Johan to tread on. Santa might find himself without a head. Dad took a step closer to her.

"Besides," Johan went on, heedless of the social cues, "there are other Arms stealing resources from us, just not sure how."

This comment drained all the anger from her. "What do you mean?"

"I had planned on starting the next batch of network nodes, and when I went to look for the necessary goods from the warehouse, they were not there."

"Just to be clear," Mom raised her hands, "you're saying someone has been stealing electronics materials from us?"

"Finished chips and processors, yes. There is nowhere near enough. Funny, I want to say that those missing materials are also used in PV construction. Curious."

It was hard to tell if he was being honest, or just stirring the pot. Johan did enjoy getting others riled up.

"Let me guess," Mom went on, "the raw materials to make more aren't available right now?"

Johan smiled. "You're starting to get it, Hughes. Unless I'm wrong, most of Chevelle's people will be pretty much tied up for the next week with defense work after that outage last night. Might be some others were encouraged to take the initiative."

"And that's why you butted heads with Lance."

He shrugged. "Not the only reason."

Whatever the solution for the sawtooths was, we needed one. I didn't want a repeat of last night. Those things scared the shit out of me.

"Ok, Johan," Mom said, fingers rubbing at her temples. A headache was on its way. "Let me talk to her and see what I can work out. We're due to put in some time on surveys anyway. If she can pilot the shuttle, we can be her team. Would that be fair? I'll talk to her as well about the possible theft."

"Adding bandwidth to the network would help in the short-term," Harper said. "Ada and I can get the resource management system up and running, I think. Maybe we can tag some of the components to catch the thieves."

Ada let out a sigh, making it clear that she was not enthused to work with Harper on any of this. "Alright, fine, dude. I suppose I could use the help with data tables."

"It's a start," Johan said. "They'll still have to cut back."

"One step at a time," Mom replied. "Look everyone, last night was rough. Work to be done or not, I want all of you to get some rest. The Jevox will be here in a few hours, and I get the feeling we aren't ready for them."

Harper rolled her eyes at the comment, disgust twisting her lips. "Isn't this just typical for them? Agriculture didn't keep up, did they? Too busy dicking around with other projects. Emilio spends too much time working on his vines than hard crops. Wine tastes like shit anyways."

"That's not fair," Shelly said, her back bowing up. Ada put a hand on her shoulder to calm her.

"We could have helped them with the water purifiers," Mom chided Harper. "I bet having better access to potable water would have helped the plants grow quicker, considering we're in the dry season.

"Listen to me everyone, and listen to me good. I want to get one thing clear. To echo the Speaker, we are one colony, one people. I won't have any of that back-talk within my Arm, you hear me?" She paused, then annunciated each word, "Do—you—hear—me?"

The redhead eyed Mom and Johan, then crossed her arms. George reached for her, then thought better of it. He reminded me of a kid who'd been told "no" too many times questioning their place in this world.

"So, you saying we can't have opinions?" Johan asked, his hands raised in a what's the big deal kind of gesture. This made Harper smile.

"Each of you elected me to serve in this role," Mom replied, "if you don't like how I am running our Arm, take it up with the Speaker."

"*Asseblief,* no need to be like that. Only trying to help."

"Enough," she said, waving a hand. "You are all dismissed. Get to work."

The circle broke and everyone but Mom, Dad, Shelly and I departed, a sullen mood hanging over us. Mom kept her face hard until the rest were far enough away, then began to massage her temples to release the tension. Dad put an arm around her.

"Too many projects," she lamented. "Too many threats. Too little time."

And she was right. Five months was all we had to get our act together, and that was creating a squeeze on every possible resource. Was this the Foundry's plan all along? Did it want to see how we would act under pressure? Would it make our people starve if we couldn't see it through? I sure hoped not.

CHAPTER 4

Shelly and I didn't need much encouragement to rest after last night's events, just permission. We scurried home to our single bedroom habitat dome on the southwestern end of the colony to recollect ourselves. Shelly hadn't slept well without me there, and I had had too much on my mind. What were these Starfish? Would they come back? What did the Foundry want out of us? Would they ever help save Earth?

All valid questions for which I had no answers.

Emotions were running high, and those who passed us were both relieved and annoyed at the Council's ruling and direction. As Shelly had said, we were in a tough spot. Economically, we weren't of much value to any of those sentient species who had settled the 75-DFX system, and yet, there were a few niches we did fulfill. We did not quite have the ability to stand on our own, but that was coming. It was so close I could almost taste it. If only we could make it till then.

Nevertheless, people weren't happy. People always found reasons not to be happy.

I extended my hand for the door handle of our tiny stone house, and as I did, something dark leapt into my field of vision, its shape all teeth and quills. I stumbled back out of reflex, tumbling full speed into Shelly, nearly crashing us both on the dirt, my heart racing. I reached for the pistol gifted to me, but to my dismay found that it wasn't there. I had forgotten it again, left it universe who knows where.

What was I going to do to…

Laughter came from the other side of the floating, bloodied head. I paused, taking in a shuttering breath.

Once able to take a second to assess the situation, and not just react, it appeared that Karianna had leapt from behind our house holding the rotting head of a dead sawtooth. She hurled it to the ground with a thud, then rested her sticky palms on her stomach, body bent over, trembling.

"That wasn't funny," I barked back at her, while trying to swallow down my fear response. Adrenaline was pulsing through me so hard my hands shook. "The hell was that for!"

"Oh, my god!" Karianna shouted, shaking her ichor covered hands, bits of blood and unidentifiable fluid dripping to the dirt. "You should have seen the two of your faces. Classic."

"Not cool," Shelly said, eying the dismembered sawtooth's head, then glaring at Karianna. "Not cool."

"Rawr! Chirp. Chirp. Chirp," Karianna went on. "Come on, now. You have to admit. That was great. Right? So great."

"I could have shot you," I replied, my fear replaced by white-hot anger. "You think about that?"

She shook her head. "No, you wouldn't. Because you misplaced your gun again. I bet it's in your Swift Shuttle, packed right beside your sphere."

I shook my head at her and shooed her away, heading back to the door. "Take that *thing* with you. I don't want it stinking up our entryway. We'll get bugs, or worse."

Karianna rolled her eyes at us and kicked at the head with the toe of her boot as we stepped inside and closed the door.

"Bitch," Shelly mumbled.

And I let out a small chuckle, hand on my heart trying to calm my nerves. "Language."

We needed a minute to calm down.

It would be some hours before our guests arrived, and there was no way we would miss the opportunity to see them again. So we spent that time reading on our hand terminals, kicked back on our primitive couch made of metal storage crates and stuffed stone bison skins, trying to distract ourselves for a moment from the challenges facing the colony.

For my part, I enjoyed the third book in a series of steam punk pirate novels Karianna had brought with her from the *Brilliance* called *The Children of Black Flag and Steam*. The story had lots of swashbuckling, betrayals, black powder, and naval battles, all sprinkled between pages of witty banter and some explicit sexual content. It was entertaining stuff, sure, if zero in substance.

Shelly, on the other hand, was pouring over an alien scientific codex, titled *Applied Neurotech-Five*, which she had traded for years back on Cynosure with a Liowin merchant. Books one through four were not part of the collection, and the few times I had tried reading it with her it had made my head hurt. The Foundry had given us some translation improvements along with the universal inoculant. However, it seemed to miss most colloquialisms, figures of speech, and metaphors. Trying to untangle the meaning of seemingly nonsensical expressions was maddening. This did not perturb her in the least. She knew there was something valuable in those pages and was determined to mine that information for all it was worth. Her intensity and devotion were admirable. If anyone could figure it out, I was confident it was her.

I found it interesting that despite losing both our ships to the Foundry's reprocessors, the crews of the *Vasco Da Gama* and the *Brilliance* had retained massive collections of books, movies, music, and art. Most admitted to keeping backups of their personal caches on hand terminals like ours, but I had come to believe the Foundry itself might have made its own backups before destroying our ships, then distributed those copies into our portable terminals without us knowing. Curious, though, there were some pieces of data that were missing. Data like star maps, or probe information from early unmanned spaceflight. It was as if our history had been intentionally edited to omit important details.

About the time I had started the third to last chapter of *Gold Beard's Fall*, a sonic boom rocked the colony, my collection of tiny figures I'd made of nano-fluid rattling on the shelf above my head. They were here.

Shelly sat up and reached for her boots.

"Do we have to?" I asked, tapping my hand terminal against my forehead. "I was just getting comfortable."

Truth be told, I really wanted to know if Metal Beard was going to use the Artifact of Fate, even if it meant forfeiting his immoral soul. Why wouldn't he? Bastard captain.

She gave a shrug. "You're comfortable on the couch? That's too bad."

"Why too bad?"

"Thought you might be interested in getting more comfortable elsewhere."

I shot up onto my feet. "I'm game if you are."

She goosed me in the ribs in response, eliciting a laugh.

"But, in the interest of peace," she said, "I think it would be a good idea for us to go."

"Alright, alright." I rubbed my side. "Think there will be trouble?"

"Not sure. Best to be vigilant."

"Vigilance is exhausting."

"Don't I know it."

We made our way across the colony, joining a procession of curious people. Despite how crowded the alien travel schedule had seemed lately, arrivals like this were not so common, with one every half cycle or so, no more. We'd seen the Melcorin visit, as well as a semi-aquatic race called the Vancor, the plant-like Bruche, and of course, Jevox.

It made my heart swell to see that many of the women joining our procession moved a little slower than the rest, their bellies full and round. It seemed that the birth control measures aboard the UEI fleet had begun to wane in their effectiveness. Several colonists had found themselves delightfully pregnant. Alice Jones, Lena Grace, Georgia Stanton, and Charlotte Patterson, the head of Culture and Xenology, were among them.

Life was moving on. People were having families and putting down roots. And why wouldn't they? This would become the only home some would ever know, a thought that was both wonderful and saddening.

It was a clear day out, with a smattering of clouds in the blue skies overhead, the sound of work all around us. Stone habitation domes like mine and Shelly's were being erected on the southeast of the colony, and storage warehouses on the west. Farm equipment was prepping soil for new seeds in the northeast, and at the center of it all, dozens worked on an ornate cylinder of concrete and steel twice the size of the Council Chambers inlaid with images of humans going about everyday life. This would be the Cultural Center, and it was near complete, a place to help us all remember, to help us all reach further. A place for music and paintings and human expression. A dream of many made form.

The Cultural Center was the vision of a child from the *Brilliance*, Marissa Martin. Though not introverted, she was not outspoken like some others in the colony, such as Johan, or any of the Councilors, and hardly ever seen in the middle of a crowd at Invictus. She spoke only on matters of great importance. She had grown up en route, taken on scientific education and a role in biotech, but found her passion elsewhere. Oil on canvas had been her forte, painting hundreds of them while in transit. When the *Brilliance* was disabled at first contact, she had lost it all. The Foundry might have a desire to protect life, but it did not understand protecting expression, history, or culture. She had lobbied the colony for a repository of our unique culture. We were not like other humans. Our fate had diverged, and we needed a place to celebrate that divergence.

Then there was the matter of Marissa's musical talents. As of late, she had teased us on many occasions that when the Cultural Center was complete, she had a symphony to share with the colony about our journey to this place. To this point, there was no real music which was uniquely ours, born of the FICSE fleet. While I couldn't speak for everyone, Shelly and I feverishly awaited that day.

As we passed the construction site, we turned to the empty plinth by its main entrance.

Shelly gave the white marble block a long look as we passed. "I wonder what it will look like?"

"The statue?"

"Yeah."

"I've heard Leo is already working on it. Who knows what it will be?"

She nodded at this and said no more.

The Jevox craft had settled into place on the northwest landing platform fifty feet away from our survey shuttle. Water vapor poured from their cooling engines, a plume of white towering over the colony.

A crowd of two dozen colonists were gathered here, waiting for the aliens to disembark from their shuttle. As a cool breeze rushed over the hillside, the vapor cleared, revealing a craft of smooth, aerodynamic edges, with five circular engines strapped to a central core and fins of equal number that swept between them. Its construction made me think of a sea creature who'd mated with a rocket, its skin metallic red with lines of black and silver shot through with stylized geometric symbols and foreign mathematical scripts. Just like with Shelly's book, even with the Foundry's translation enhancements, I was left wondering what it all meant.

A door appeared out of the solid hull, nano-machines peeling away to reveal an interior like an abstract artist's fever dream. There were bright lights within its halls, and colors, more colors than could be perceived by the human eye, garish and upsetting in their intensity. We had not evolved to even comprehend, much less appreciate this level of beauty.

At the front of our welcome party stood the Speaker, ready to greet them. Charlotte Patterson, head of Culture and Xenology, whispered in her ear while making several small gestures with her fingers. Mary nodded fervently, then took a deep breath.

"You got this," Charlotte mouthed.

The Jevox appeared in the opening, five abreast. They were bipedal like humans, and mammalian, but this was where our similarities ended. Standing at about four feet tall, their arms and legs had several more joints than ours, allowing them greater dexterity in movement. While it was my understanding that they were oxygen breathers, they wore partial masks over their faces, which in themself seemed half again too large for their bodies. The front of their masks was a clear pane of curved glass which allowed them to see with all five of their eyes arrayed in a star pattern. Their reddish-brown skin could be seen around the necks of their clothing, a set of loose-fitting cerulean blue robes with deep sleeves and wide cuffs, with capes that hung near to the ground.

They stepped foot onto the landing platform, their straight backs drooping as if a sudden weight were put upon their shoulders. I got the impression that gravity on Novae was a bit more than they were used to. It was clear that their muscle tone wasn't as defined as humans either, which seemed to track, but what they lacked in physical strength they more than made up for in a single purpose. Something we didn't seem to be doing so well with lately.

Arms wide, the Speaker began a dance of sorts, bringing both hands into the middle, palm to palm, then reaching out with the right, then with the left. She twisted her arms in a circle counterclockwise, right hand drawing the top, left drawing the bottom, before reversing directions and bending her knees in a bow, head tipping forward, eyes closed. She repeated this five times with slight variations in her movement, each time the lights within the Jevox's ship becoming brighter, abstract patterns shifting, turning wild.

The Jevox blinked, then returned her fluid gestures, movement for movement, yet mirrored, the platform going silent. I wasn't sure what I was watching, what it all meant, but we were somehow showing them great respect, and they were showing it in turn.

"We say, hello," the Jevox on the far right said.

"We are well met," the one on the far left said.

The one in the center went next, "How fare our Novae humans?"

Speaker Stablecamp raised her right hand, showing all five fingers.

Despite the gravity, the Jevox straightened their backs. Something about the number five pleased them. Five engines. Five fins. Five fingers. Five Jevox.

"We are well," the Speaker said. "All our best to the hive."

"The hive endures."

I felt a hand rest on my shoulder and found that Dad had snuck up behind me. He smiled at the Jevox like a kid high on candy and let out a long sigh.

"Never ceases to amaze me," he whispered. "We aren't alone, not at all."

"Want to know something interesting?" I asked, leaning in.

"Always."

"I once asked the Foundry how safe hyper suspension was."

"That so? What did it say?"

I cleared my throat and put on my best imitation of the Foundry's monotone voice, *"Of the more than six thousand species who have undergone hyper suspension, only three have suffered negative consequences."*

"Six thousand…" he hissed. "We were never alone."

"The Foundry protects life," was all I could think to say, and Dad nodded in response. It was an immutable fact.

"We have come to trade," the Jevox at the center of their group said. "Do you wish to trade?"

"We do," the Speaker replied.

"Have our requirements been met?" one of the Jevox near the middle asked, though I wasn't sure which. While they were not identical, their voices were similar to one another, as was their appearance. "We are eager. Seeds of Earth plants in exchange for the refined materials you require."

"That is a matter I wish to discuss."

"Did you know they're expert terraformers," Shelly said, drawing my attention away, her tone conspiratorial. "They like helping other species prepare new worlds to survive."

"Terraforming?" Dad's eyebrows raised. "Doesn't that take hundreds, if not thousands of years? Imagine the engineering involved. They can't be as powerful as the Foundry, can they?"

"Maybe not as powerful as the Foundry, but they have something not many intelligent species other than the Isoptera have. They have a hive mind.

While each Jevox is an individual, they are also not. As I understand it, the logical portion of their brain is dominated by a single mind which interacts over a local bio-electric network. This breaks them into individualistic enclaves unless they are together in a large colony or on their home world. Inside that hive-mind there's a hierarchy, multiple personalities that fit together like puzzle pieces, but I don't know all the details. Nevertheless, one mind, no queen, one team."

Dad raised his finger and began to nod. "Which allows them to work as one entity. Damn, what an advantage. We want to bicker over where the network relays and latrines go, and they just get to work digging."

I blinked at Shelly, feeling quite dubious. "Where did you learn all this?" She always knew something I didn't. It would not have surprised me if she had pulled this out of thin air. "The Council has been pretty tight lipped on what they have learned about the Jevox, and all Proxy has told me is that they are friendly, and do not wage war. Ever."

She gave me a sheepish grin. "Remember, love, I have traded for many books. Some are more comprehensible than others."

"I really need to read more," I told myself, "having Proxy in the corner of my head is making me lazy."

"Yes." She goosed me in the ribs once again. "Yes, it is."

"Remarkable." Dad beamed with child-like wonder. "One mind. No war. A single objective. I wonder, does that leave no place for individual expression?"

"The art on the walls inside their craft seems to disagree with that idea, Mr. Hughes."

"Hmm. You said they like helping others terraform. Wonder why that is?"

Shelly pursed her lips. "Now that is a good question."

A mumble went through the crowd, drawing my attention back to the conversation at the front.

"Is something amiss?" one of the Jevox said, cocking its head at the Speaker.

Mary took a moment to collect herself, a smile forming on her calm, practiced face. "Nothing is amiss. We are waiting for the current crop to seed. While we have gathered four fifths—" She paused, correcting herself. "Most of what was agreed upon, the balance is not yet ready. We are learning to best make use of this world."

"It does not fit your needs fully, does it?" another asked. "The world."

The Speaker considered her answer. "Not entirely; nor did Earth, our home world."

The Jevox paused for a moment, looking at one another. It was now clear a conversation was happening between them.

"It is inconvenient," they said, their voices synced. "But we will wait. If this takes too long, however, we will be forced to leave. One quarter yuniea, and we must go without any trade. The hive needs us."

"We understand," the Speaker said, and gave a bow. I noted how much she had changed in those years between Creatus, Ph0nx, and here. There were moments that felt weird, and this was one of them. Not that Mary wasn't capable of this position, far from it. I just never expected to see her leading our people, building bridges with alien species. Then again, who the hell else was better?

She raised her hand once more, splaying her five fingers. "Come, let us gather someplace more comfortable. I do not wish for this world to cause you too much discomfort."

The Speaker led them away with a small retinue, Councilman Perez, Councilwoman Clark, and Councilman Halifax at her side. Alexander walked close beside one of the Jevox, the two of them chatting in hushed tones. The crowd dispersed as we watched them leave.

Among the mix one person hung back, talking to a group of three ladies— one blonde, one brunette, one with red-hair, all pretty. As he spoke, they laughed and covered their mouths to hide embarrassment. He was my age, fit in a lean way with tight fitting clothes, his arms all muscle, inked in esoteric tattoos, hair dyed platinum with a perfect fade, eyes the kind of blue that made women's legs weak.

He raised his hands and framed those leaving between his L-shaped index fingers and thumbs, as if viewing the departing procession through the lens of a camera.

"A moment of history," he said with a flourish of his hand. "This will be my next piece."

The ladies giggled again, and one of them put a hand on his right arm. He looked at it, then into her eyes. She looked away from him, cheeks blood-red.

"This was the day we fell short of our commitments," he went on, his tone a touch pretentious. "All because of poor planning and a lack of action. How will humanity be a great shining beacon to others if we cannot meet simple promises? Thus is the struggle. The pain, and the failures. Is this what makes us human? Are we measured by our success, or our failure? When will we learn as these noble people have? To keep to a single mind that we might achieve greatness as one? We infight, we bicker, and we get nothing done. Why? Because so many have not overcome the attachment to antiquated concepts of possession, have not overcome dangerous emotions of greed and pride, have not transcended to higher ways of thinking and being. We can ill afford to offend our guests. We must be open, willing to share with one another. For when we share, it is when we reach the highest heights of pleasure and fulfillment."

He leaned close to the dark headed girl on his right who was about a foot shorter than him, took a deep breath and placed his lips beside her ear. He whispered. She shuddered.

Shelly groaned.

Leo Nelson was one of my least favorite people in the world. I did my best to love everyone, accept everyone, but his self-possessed ego rubbed against me like a metal file on an open wound. He had been raised aboard the *Brilliance* and was an accomplished mixed-media artist. There wasn't much he could not do to express the human experience with the right tools in hand; putty, mud, camera, he even dabbled a bit in fashion. Yet what did he do most of the time? He squandered his talent getting as many pretty things into his bed as he could. The guy might know art, but he didn't understand basic math. Some point in the near future, he was going to piss off enough jealous ladies in our little colony to find himself sleeping alone for good.

Dad started his way over to Leo, making me nervous. What in the hell was he about to say? Opinions were something Dad had a hard time keeping to himself at times. Even more so the older he got.

"Where are you going?" I asked, reaching for him.

"Don't worry about it, son, head home." He waved a hand in the air. "Meet you lovebirds for dinner later."

Shelly eyed me. "Oh, shit."

"Oh, shit is right." I took off after him.

At Dad's approach, Leo narrowed his eyes and kindly dismissed the gaggle of ladies. They gave him smiles and headed off, taking a few quick glances over their shoulders at what they could only see in this moment as an Adonis.

"Poor planning and a lack of action?" Dad said, repeating what had already been stated, a finger raised.

Leo just stood there, expression slipping into a superior scowl. "It's pretty clear what happened today. We had an opportunity to build bridges and show a powerful species we were capable of living in our corner of the galaxy. What did we do instead?"

"Have you ever studied botany, agriculture? Have you ever attempted to grow plants on a world that the seeds weren't evolved to live on in more than a greenhouse?" Dad poked him in the chest, forcing Leo to take a step back. "No, that's right. You played with finger paint and panties while everyone else was busting their asses. So, before you go talking down to hard working colonists, take a look in the mirror."

"Hard working? A fallacy of success to the proletariat."

"Proletariat! What in the hell do you take this place for? Some kind of Marxist society? We are an egalitarian democracy."

Leo raked a hand through his platinum hair, pushing it back. He gave Dad a hungry smile. "People like you will be forgotten in time. Your names will be nothing but dust on the wind. Maybe a single line of code lost in a sea of data. It is those who express history, who craft the lens by which all future humans look through who will be remembered. Da Vinci, Van Gogh, Jackson Pollock, they were not remembered for how hard they worked, but how they touched on the very spirit of what it was to be human."

"Comparing yourself to them is like me comparing myself to Einstein."

"Genius knows genius." Leo gritted his teeth and narrowed his eyes. "Johan was right."

"Wait, what? Van Niekerk was right about what? He been talking trash about Parallax again?"

"Trash music."

Though it was nice to see Dad give Leo what he deserved, this argument would not help matters. Leo was heavily involved in the construction of the Cultural Center and for the most part, everyone in the colony loved him, not just the pretty ones. To many he was a symbol of progress and evolution. Having him as a social enemy wasn't a good idea.

"Hey, Dad," I said as I eased up beside them. "Leo, so nice to see you."

"Hughes," he replied, unamused.

"Dad, weren't we about to go check on the nano-vats? The next batch is nearly at phase four."

"The nano-vats?" He scratched at the back of his head, confused. "They're not due to be flashed for at least another week."

"Still, I think it's a good time."

"But I'm not done talking to Nelson here. We were just starting a spirited discussion."

"No," Leo said, offering us a cold smile. "I think we're done. It has been a pleasure, sir." He turned to walk away.

Another crisis averted.

Though Dad had calmed down over the years, from time to time he could get riled up over something and there was hardly any stopping him. He had a good heart, with good intentions in mind. He just didn't care who got pissed off or why. When he thought he was right, damn it, he was right, and there was no dissuading him. Might need to check with Mom and be sure he was still taking his bipolar meds. I'd not seen him in a bad spell for years, but when he was on his highs, he was manic, and when he fell, he crashed and burned. This was likely just his normal bravado, but it didn't hurt to check.

"We're gonna go for a walk," I told Shelly, and she nodded.

"I think it's great you're spending time together. See you at home."

"See you at home."

"Wait, what?" Dad spluttered. "This isn't…"

"You boys go have fun!"

I led Dad away with a gentle hand on his arm.

"But I didn't…" He looked between Shelly and I, then stamped his right foot on the ground. "I don't have to be handled."

"I'm not handling you." I let go. "Look, is everything okay?"

He started walking, heading away from the platform along the hillside through knee-high red grass and scattered scrub. I followed him into a colorful field of edge blossoms several acres across, doing my best to walk with the grain of their leaves as not to get cut. These particular flowers, while dangerous at times, were just as beautiful. They liked to mimic rainbows, their petals transitioning from one side to the other like light through a prism, each blossom a different solid color, pixels in a giant matrix, but their sharp ends ran a single direction. Walk against that, and you are in for some cut up legs.

"I'm fine," Dad replied, carefully plucking one of the violet, razor sharp flowers from its stalk between patches of red grass. "Why wouldn't it be fine?" He twisted the blossom in his fingers, inspecting its vascular, paper-thin leaves.

"You were about to make a scene with Leo. He may not be my favorite person, but he pulls a lot of influence around here." I put a hand on his shoulder and squeezed, then realized it had been my mechanical one and I might have gripped a little too hard. He didn't seem to notice. "Talk to me. Please."

"I understand what everyone is feeling," he said after a moment. "I get it. I feel it too. Old habits. Old situations past their expiration." He sighed. "When we were aboard the *Vasco Da Gama* things were easy. They were simple. Prepare for our arrival at the Foundry facility and stay alive. This made our priorities easy. Maybe Johan was right in that, over time we've taken our unified purpose for granted. I don't know. I just want to be sure we're focusing on the right things. It's not so simple to know what that is anymore."

The edge blossom fell from Dad's fingers, and he moved ahead, pressing through the transitioning colors of blossoms. Purple to blue. Blue to green. Green to yellow and orange and red. I kept a careful eye on the wind to be sure we did not find ourselves stuck out in the middle.

"I know it's not easy," I told him. "And I hate that."

Dad stopped and frowned at me, a look of remorse on his face. "Sorry I came unglued, but when he started spouting about people being lazy… There isn't a soul on either ship who has ever known what that word means. We all got here because we busted our asses, or at the very least, their parents busted their asses. And we will survive because of it. Just seems there's a lot of this talk going around. Leo isn't the only one. Alyssa too. I even overheard that old girlfriend of yours going on about it the other day at the commissary. What's her face?"

"You mean Harper?"

"Yeah, that's her. Can't ever remember that girl's name, and she's on our damn development team. This whole idea Johan is pushing about us being lazy, it's going around. It's infectious, working its way through the colony like a virus. He's on my team, part of my Arm, and it makes me want to stop playing nice. What a slave driver. Not even Tobias pushed us that hard. And yet, I know we still need to go hard. Pure grit."

"You know, Dad," I said, smiling at him. "There's more to life than just hard work."

"I know. I know." He paused and raised his hands, looking back towards the Colony. It was late afternoon, and our star, 75-DFX, was dipping down to the horizon, casting long shadows between shafts of golden light on half constructed buildings, fields of crops, human ants hurrying from one task to the next as night came. "Hard to slow down though, and I don't think I want to either."

"Well then, what do you think we should do?" I asked and focused my attention on the scaffolds around the Cultural Center. "Do you have a plan?"

For once, Dad did not respond. We needed more reliable power. We needed food, and trade. We needed the labor to get things done. We needed to create infrastructure to help us communicate better, to travel. We needed safety and security. We needed a lot of things. Not all could come at the same time, or at the same rate, but this fact did not preclude those needs.

Five months…

"Can we keep walking?" he asked after some time. "The flowers are beautiful, and it's not so late. I could use the moment to stretch my legs."

"Sure, Dad. Whatever you like."

And that's just what we did.

"Did I tell you I've been studying our system?" He smiled. "Had them make me a print of a 356mm telescope."

And in truth, he had, but I didn't see any reason to bring that up. The Foundry had given me all the data on this system I needed, but what did that matter in this moment? Astronomy was Dad's passion, his life. Let him discover the universe his way.

"You didn't," I lied. "What did you find?"

"I must tell you about the reddish gas giant I've been studying. Thirty AU away from 75-DFX, one hundred and twenty thousand kilometers in diameter, with six rings, one of them forty-one degrees to the elliptical, with dozens of satellites."

"Really? That sounds amazing."

CHAPTER 5

I woke up the following morning to a network ping from the Council. As tired as I was, the tiny message ping felt like a metal pin being poked into the side of my head. It tapped me once and waited. Then twice… Three times… I rolled over, unable to ignore the sensation, kicked off the sheets, and let out a groan. A curious mixture of thoughts swirled around in my mind as I sat up. I could almost remember something, but the memory's edges were too slippery to hold on to, and so it fell back into the depths of oblivion, dissolving into nothingness.

Just another stupid dream. Another stupid dream.

Shelly was already awake, having fixed breakfast, two plates of stone bison sausage, a loaf of black bread, and a handful of grapes, with a steaming cup of rog on the side—a hot beverage that was like coffee.

"Sleep okay?" she asked, taking a seat at our improvised dinner table, no more than a set of storage crates with a sheet of scrap metal laid on top.

I shook my head, gave her a peck on the lips, then sat down. "Not really. I keep having these crazy dreams."

"What about?" She grabbed one of the sausage links and took a bite.

"I don't know. Lots of darkness, and then I wake up. By the time I start putting it all together, I forget what it was about."

"Sounds like everyday existential dread to me."

"You're probably right." I dug into my food, cutting the sausage into pieces before placing it between thin slices of bread. "You know what's funny?"

"What?"

"I talked to Proxy about this the other day. Had dreams when I was in orbit. You know what it told me?"

She leaned forward, urging me to go on.

"That maybe, well, I forgot what the dream was about because the Universe doesn't want me remembering."

Her upper lip curled. "That's not creepy or anything."

"No. Not creepy at all."

The ping went off again, nearly making my vision go blurry. I rolled my eyes at it, and Shelly shook her head.

"Haven't read it yet?" she asked.

"Can't I just wake up first? Is that too much to ask?"

I took my time eating before I read the message, grateful for breakfast, and even more so that Shelly made it for me. Though as I ate, I was reminded of something. Food on Novae here never tasted quite right, but for Emilio's grapes. Everything had an odd sourness to it, an overly fibrous texture. And yet, food was food.

Breakfast finished, I could no longer avoid the ping. I took my cup of quasi-coffee in hand and pulled it up, sipping as I read the message.

In the wake of the Council meeting, the various project crises, and the arrival of the Jevox, all Arms of the Novae government were being asked to re-evaluate their resource allocation and systems of use. Another vote would be taken later in the week to determine what the top three priorities of the colony would be for the near future. Each Arm was charged with either reducing consumption of key resources by ten percent without a loss of throughput, or to increase throughput by twenty five percent given the same resources.

Thinking through what this would mean for several Arms, several projects underway, I had to figure out where I could be best utilized. While I did have experience in nanoscience, my current batches of nano-machines were nowhere near ready. Once complete we could use them to fabricate all sorts of small components, including the network and PV electronics, given we had the proper resources. And so, this stream of thought gave us only one real choice.

"What a squeeze," I said, then took a sip of my rog. "Did you talk to Mom by any chance? Did she convince Chevelle to pilot a survey?"

Shelly tipped her head. "We spoke. Metallurgical survey happening in the mountains up north."

"Well then, I guess I better go along and help. Want to come with me? Could be fun."

"Wish I could, love." She gave me a wink. "But I have work to do. Us humans got far too used to having access to easy information. Network is still acting up. Another few fixes to add into the patch Ada and I are working on. Just a band-aid till we get upgraded, and that can't happen until…"

"Until we find more copper and silica and Universe knows what else."

"Pretty much."

"Be so much easier if the Foundry would just give us what we need. The nano-vats aboard the *Fidelis* can make damn near anything we want, they just won't."

"You've asked Proxy nicely, right? Scratched it behind the ear and given it a little cat nip?"

"Yes, yes. Even petted its belly and rubbed its tail."

"That's too bad."

I double checked the survey schedule then slipped on a fresh set of clothes, not that I'd be wearing them for long, before giving Shelly a hug and a kiss and heading out. The day was overcast, dark but with no more than a mist for weather. While there was a storm off in the east, it was far enough away that it wasn't worrying.

I gathered up my jacket and pinged Karianna to see if she wanted to help. *"I got nothing else better to do,"* she replied, her tone chipper. *"Meet you at the platform."*

As I crossed the footbridge of a freshwater stream heading towards my shuttle, I was intercepted.

"Good morning, Milo!" Xuan Nguyen, a member of the Security and Exploration Arm, shouted. The broad-shouldered, thickly built woman ran over to me, a smile cracking her ever-cheerful face. An attitude like hers could make an Eipren shudder.

"Morning. Nice day out."

"You good, dude?" She pulled a few lose strands of black hair out of her face, those sticking where the mist had left her skin wet. "Looks like you woke up on the wrong side of the bed. Get some coffee. Do a dance. Say a few kind words to yourself."

"I'm good," I told her, then rubbed my eyes and yawned, my foot catching for a moment on small rocks I hadn't seen hidden in the red, knee-high grass. "Slept funny is all. Maybe I got spoiled sleeping in a Star Sphere."

"You and me both. So much better than a regular bed. If I were you, and was sleeping up there, I'd get a huge ass feather bed, silky sheets, pillows as long as my body. Maybe a canopy too? Listen, you ever need a drone pilot on one of those missions, hit me up, alright? I'll take a few nights in orbit as a vacation from this place. You know, a chance to fly through space in my head."

I gave her a shrug and continued towards the platform. "That's the complete opposite of what Shelly likes to do. She prefers ground under her feet. Hates being in space."

"Serious?" Xuan's expression twisted into something peculiar. "None the less. Consider me?"

I paused for a moment, thinking the idea over. It was a shame to have these fighters in orbit without any pilots. Having Lance and the whole wing had been invaluable in taking on the gene brokers. "Alright. I will consider you."

She beamed, palms on her cheeks. "You would? No kidding?"

"No kidding." I gestured ahead with my right hand. "You going on the survey today?"

"Not today." She patted the rifle slung over her shoulder. "Someone has to stick back just in case those stone bison decide to roam into town. We've had several close calls in the past week. They're big as hell, and even though they aren't aggressive, they can be crazy dangerous."

"Always the one who's busting ass while Hy lounges around at home, huh?"

She let out a barking laugh, then covered her mouth. "That husband of mine has his uses. Not everyone in the house can be a badass like me." Her right arm flexed.

I smiled. "True that."

"Go find us some lithium today, would you?"

"Add to shopping list," I replied and drew a checkmark in the air with a finger.

"Tell Shelly hi for me! We should meet up at Invictus sometime soon."

"So long as you two don't make me dance."

"Hah."

"Don't let Rowan work you too hard!" I shouted as she went on her way.

At my arrival on the platform, Karianna waved, and we stepped inside our respective Swift Shuttles.

"Survey team," I called as I descended into my Star Sphere. "This is Milo Hughes. Miss Torlen and I would like to join you on today's expedition to lend some help."

Chevelle's voice came back over the comm channel, her tone delighted. *"Ey, Mr. Hughes. Safe to 'ave you and Miss Torlen on this mission, fam. Let's hope we come back with more than just crumbs, yeah? Hold tight for the preflight check."*

Data came back through the connection with Chevelle and the survey shuttle. The team had a full crew today. Johan was with them, no doubt trying to prove to others he wasn't lazily spending time in a lab, even though he could have been helping Shelly and Ada with the local network issues. Mom was aboard as well. Harper and George were here, and also James. Pretty sure this was the first time in years the three of us troublemakers, as they used to call us, were occupying the same basic space at the same time.

"Hey bro, what's up?" James called on the open channel. *"Ready for some fun?"*

"So long as it doesn't land us in too much trouble," I told him. "Haven't you heard? I'm reformed."

"Reformed? I doubt that."

"Don't drag me into your drama."

"Me?" he ventured, a hint of a chuckle in his voice. *"Drama? Perish the thought. I never encouraged anyone in our group to make poor decisions."*

"I've had enough trouble for a lifetime," George added out of nowhere. *"Thing is, it keeps finding me."*

"Don't be a baby," Harper told him, and from the tone of her voice it was not playful.

"Wasn't George the creator of the super saturation of troublesome events theory?" I asked.

Karianna popped in on the channel. *"What the hell is this idea? You've got my attention. I'm curious."*

"Maybe later," George told us. *"You can read my thesis. It's quite extensive."*

Karianna and my Swift Shuttles rose on jets of air and hovered towards the survey platform. Chevelle worked through the checklist, and a few moments later, the survey shuttle began to ascend, its thick, snub-nosed form rising several thousand feet along beside us, a set of airfoils unfolding into wings, their tips pointed out rather than at the sky as they had been during reentry. Along its side was a row of windows through which I could see the faces of our fellow colonists.

Chevelle pinged the channel and began giving instructions, *"Aight then, mandem, here's the plan. We head north and keep two kilometers between us. We'll spread out wide, eyes open. Bare caves I wanna check out, ok? Without the heavy kit to use, these holes our best shot."*

"What are we after?" Karianna asked. *"I'll go on and have Proxy calibrate the equipment."*

"Lithium, gold, and iron."

"Copy that."

"You hear that Proxy?" I asked, words projected by my mind, not my mouth.

The tuxedo cat appeared beside me in my virtual environment, tail snapping around in the open air. "I have made the necessary adjustments to our instruments."

"Thanks. Do you think this is a good plan? How we're going about this?"

"It is reasonable. The caves of this planet should contain many of the substances the Novae colony needs for survival."

"Okay."

"Here we go," Chevelle called, and the survey shuttle roared off into the north.

I floated high above the surface of Novae, arms wide, marveling as the world rolled out before me, forests of green and red, hills with grazing stone bison and striders, my mind no longer confined to the walls of the Swift Shuttle. The sensors and cameras and science instruments of this Foundry vessel called back to me as extensions of my perception just like the *Fidelis*. They were my eyes, my ears, my fingers and toes, reaching out, hungrily seeking information. Air flowed over my body, making the hairs of my arms stand on end, a rush of excitement coursing through me at the acceleration. It was exhilarating, freedom in its purest form. I could go anywhere with this vessel, do anything, see anyone. The temptation to burn away and disappear forever was palpable. I couldn't be the only one who felt this way.

On my left several kilometers away, Karianna did the same as I had, though all I could see was her shuttle, not her. Had she ever thought of running away? Had anyone who had given their donation just taken the gift and traveled for all time?

Out of nowhere, Karianna's shuttle shot up several thousand feet, cutting a line through the cloud ceiling. She banked right, then left, made several barrel rolls, then shot down towards the surface. I took a deep breath as she thundered towards a lake nestled in the valley of two tall hills. But just before she hit the water, she broke off and shot skyward, leaving a trail of ripples across its once placid surface.

I chuckled to myself as I discovered I was rocking my own shuttle. This was pure, distilled freedom.

Never wanting to be left out, I drifted from formation. I leaned forward and urged my Swift Shuttle faster, its engines whining. The valley swelled around me, mountains shooting up on either side. I navigated the narrow passage at several hundred kilometers per hour, skimming over the tops of trees, the backwash of my fusion engines blowing scores of fans off of their tops, forcing herds of stone bison and striders to scatter.

A strange urge overcame my sensibilities, but I did not fight it. I acted like a kid, flipping myself upside down so that blood could rush into my head. I watched a world of green and brown flash overhead, my feet planted in the deep, blue sky. The valley I thundered through began to narrow. I fell into the vast and open airspace, my feet tickled by clouds, before looping back around to my original location, feeling the slightest bit dizzy as I leveled off.

Proxy looked up at me from where it stood at my feet, a curious expression on its face. I smiled back. Smiled until my face hurt.

My moment of pure bliss came to a close as an audio ping hit the communications channel like a pebble tossed at a glass window. Someone wanted to chat. It wasn't Chevelle.

"*Milo,*" Johan said, his tone flat. "*What do you believe we need to do for the Foundry to help us go back and fix Earth?*"

It was at that moment I knew this was going to be a long survey. That running away idea felt even more appealing.

"I don't know," I replied. "It hasn't exactly been clear about that. I have a feeling we're in the middle of a test."

"Asseblief, *a test? So, it's toying with us. Playing with us to see what we'll do. We're rats in a cage.*"

"That's not really how it works," I replied, carefully choosing my words. "It doesn't get pleasure out of this. It just is."

"*What do you mean?*"

My attention drifted as the mountains rolled beneath us, turning ever rockier the further north we went. It would not be easy to get a ground car through such terrain without any roads. Although I hoped we found what we were after, getting it back to actually use it would be a challenge.

Johan called again, *"Hughes?"*

"Let me think of a good way to explain this," I said, a bit more irritated than I had intended. "When it storms outside, rain can fall. Think of the rain as a test. If you have a raincoat, you'll stay dry, mostly. But if you have no raincoat, you get soaked. The storm has no cares over if you get wet or not. It just is."

"You're saying the Foundry is a force of nature, not an intelligence?"

"Yes, and no. I think it's both. But I don't think it has emotion. It acts in certain ways because of what it was made to do. It has a directive."

"To protect life," Mom added. *"Always to protect life."*

"Protect life," Johan considered. *"Whatever motivations it has, it should support us getting aid. Saving Earth is protecting life."*

"The Foundry is very big picture," I told him.

"Which are worthless to our needs."

"Maybe yes, maybe no. It's big picture, like beyond our comprehension big. Maybe letting us suffer helps other species thrive, I just don't know. Proxy won't tell me."

Johan let out a low rumble over the channel. *"Sounds to me like you're saying it will never help."*

Anger welled up from the pit of my stomach. "We're still here, aren't we? We're still alive. In my opinion, the Foundry has been pretty damn gracious."

"Easy to say when you've got wings," Johan replied, his voice low.

Karianna reeled back from her aerial acrobatics and fell into formation.

"It comes at a cost," Mom said in my defense. *"Milo's wings were not free, and they carry a terrible responsibility."* Though I could not see her face over the channel, I imagined her expression soft and caring. I was surprised she didn't interject some Portuguese. Embarrass me by saying something like *meu lindinho filho*, my beautiful son, as part of her reply.

"Of course, Mrs. Hughes," Johan back peddled. *"Ek is jammer. I'm sorry. There's a cost to all things."*

"Well, I think you're right, Johan," Harper said, her tone far more interested than I had expected. *"The Foundry has done little more than bring us trouble. We*

should demand it takes us home. Maybe the Jevox would help us clean things up. They're terraformers, right?"

"The Jevox?" Johan mused. *"Maybe. If the Foundry won't give us the help their signal promised, that leaves us back at square one. We've got to do it ourselves."*

"Can we even demand anything from the Foundry?" George asked. *"Again, to Milo's example, it's like a storm cloud. You can't reason with weather."*

Harper groaned. *"Better to try than to let it just walk all over us."*

"How has it walked all over us?"

"Milo's right," Karianna spoke up, and the chatter died down. *"You don't really understand till you've been part of its network. In my heart I know it wants to help, or at least Proxy does, but it can't. There's a wall of some kind. Things that need doing first, ya know? Like—"*

"Like a test?" Johan ventured, his tone more than a little sarcastic.

Karianna sighed. *"Yeah. Like a test."*

"Listen up," Chevelle cut in. *"We can chat about 'what ifs' all day and end up looking like wastemen. As mum always say, look after the pennies and the pounds will sort themselves out. We got survey work ahead. Grab what we need out here, and we be blessed. Won't have to trade for every kilo of materials. Safe? Let's not get rinsed out."*

"Bob's your uncle," James added.

"Ain' funny," Chevelle told him.

"Who's Bob?" I asked and got a few chuckles in reply. I hated it when I didn't get something. Besides, Chevelle was damn hard to follow anyways.

"We're coming up on the mountains," Chevelle said. *"Milo, Karianna, spread out, see what you can find. Off to stick our head in a few crannies. We'll keep close. No going on foot without backup."*

"Copy that," I replied, then veered off towards a steep, snowcapped mountain with a network of valleys and streams at its base. Karianna broke, heading off in the opposite direction.

"Let's find something good," James called over the comm channel.

"Big money," I said, mumbling. *"Come on, big money."*

CHAPTER 6

As I neared the face of the mountain, I slowed, my readings drawing me towards an opening on the western slope. My Swift Shuttle hovered just over the treetops as I reached out my senses, attempting to feel what was inside the tunnel. At first all I could see was dirt and biomatter. I drew the shuttle closer, bringing me a few dozen meters from a dark opening, a cloud of dust kicking up around me.

The communications channel buzzed, static kicking back. *"We've—got—a good—"*

"What was that again?" Karianna asked. *"Didn't catch that."*

"A good cave—checking—"

"You getting the same thing, Milo?"

"Yeah," I said. "Chevelle's signal is bad. These hills are wreaking hell on their communications."

"But not ours?"

"Neutrino beams. Goes right through most matter, little interference. Since we made so much of the survey shuttle ourselves, they're still using radio."

The cave before me lit up as I sent several small drones into it. I gave a start as their visual feed came back to me, walls covered in moisture, great stalactites hanging from thirty-meter ceilings almost touching the floor. And then there was something moving, hundreds of somethings, a writhing, roiling mass of leathery dark skins, quills, and teeth. I'd once seen photos of a rat king, something that occurs when too many rats live in tight spaces, their tails interlocked until they were a singular, massive, suffering organism. This was not so different, only that these were not rats. Rats did not grow to the size of mountain lions.

"Holy shit," I said, throwing up my hands. For an instant I forgot that I was safe within my Star Sphere aboard the Swift Shuttle and not on the ground.

"What's wrong?"

"The inside of this cave is full of sawtooths, hundreds of them. This must be where they go during the day." I made a gesture to share the feed with Karianna. "Take a look."

There was a pause before she spoke. *"You know, Milo. Next time you want to show me something disturbing, think twice. I'm going to have nightmares again, and I just got over the freakin' Isoptera. I really don't care for wildlife, Novae born or not. Why do you think I carry a side-arm?"*

"How does that help with zipzaps?" I asked, thinking of the biting insects that wandered through the colony in swarms from time to time. They were like mosquitos, so I was told as I'd never seen that brand of nuisance, but worse. A thousand biting heads in a ball of fury.

"It doesn't help with zipzaps, but it makes me feel better. I keep a blowtorch ready for those."

"Sorry." I knew all about bad dreams. For me it was first the Isoptera and the attack on the *Vasco Da Gama*. Later, it had been the Frendol when they kidnapped me on Cynosure and planned to vivisect me. Then there was the Kabosai when they took our people on Creatus. My nightmares had plenty of fuel. "You're right."

"Are you seeing anything valuable in there other than those things?"

I reviewed the sensor data. "Proxy, what are you seeing?"

"There are bands in the walls comprised of sedimentary rock," the cat replied, its head twisting in a curious fashion, tail flicking at the non-existent floor. "These caves are comprised of hematite and magnetite, as well as limestone. Their iron composition is high. Considering the presence of a weak magnetic field, there are likely deep deposits before and beneath us."

"Well, it's on the shopping list, though we've got some unwanted tenants. Nevertheless, pretty lucky I'd say."

"Indeed."

"Let's tag it." I placed a pin on a virtual map and uploaded the data gathered. It would be a challenge to use this space with its current residents but might prove useful in the future. "Survey team, call back."

The drones returned, and I stowed them in their hidden ports. I backed away from the cave's mouth and scanned the slopes, looking for another opening.

"Survey team, call back," I repeated, anxiety building. This wasn't like them. "Survey team?"

A moment passed. Nothing. Not even static.

"Karianna, are you seeing anything? Do you know where they went?"

"No. Let me climb to a higher altitude and get a better view."

"Where did you guys go?" I turned my ship towards the north, where a single summit reached high enough it almost touched clouds.

"I'm not sure," Karianna said. *"I'm not seeing any sign of them from here."*

I did my best to swallow my fears. Nothing worked perfectly in the field. "Okay. Just communication challenges, that's all. There's line of sight issues and magnetic interference. I'll head off in the direction they went. You check out that side of the mountains."

"Can do. Already found several promising sights."

"Glad to hear it."

Karianna and I split up and continued the search. While I was supposed to be looking for caves that might contain what we needed, I couldn't stop wondering where our people had gone. We could get back to surveying when I knew they were safe.

Something metal gleamed in a copse of trees along a shallow slope two kilometers ahead. I leaned in and hovered in that direction, attempting to get a better look.

"Proxy, what is that?"

"A metallic rod of some kind. Maybe an antenna."

I nodded slowly, then noticed an opening up ahead. Another cave, sure, yet this one was massive, wide enough that perhaps an egotistical pilot might believe they could fly right into it. As I scanned the outside of the cave, I found signs of lithium, something we needed by the truckload for goods from heat-resistant glass to batteries.

"I think I found where they went," I called out.

"Oh?" Karianna said. *"Where are they?"*

"Found a big cave. A real big cave. I think they flew inside."

"Flew inside a cave?"

"Yeah."

"Why not hang out there a few minutes, maybe they'll come out."

I shook my head as if she could see what I was doing. Habits. "No. I don't think so. Something isn't right. They lost one of their antennae, it's how I located their path. My guess is that there is a substantial lithium deposit down here. They already made a commitment not to get out and walk."

"And so, flying inside made sense?"

"Says the daredevil pilot."

"I might be a daredevil, sure, but I'm no dumbass."

If they were inside and trapped, they could be in trouble. I trusted Chevelle to pilot well, even in tough conditions, but if she damaged the survey shuttle and had been forced to land… And what's to say this cave wasn't filled with sawtooths? They'd have no easy way out.

"I'm going in after them," I said, and began lowering myself to line up with the opening.

"Have you lost your goddamned mind? What happened to prudence?"

"Prudence goes out the door when my friends could be in trouble."

"Oh, lord. You're one of those."

"One of what?"

"A lawful good. A freaking paladin. Always doing the right thing. Always rushing into a burning building."

"You can either support me and watch my back or keep making fun of me."

"I prefer making fun of you."

"This is serious!"

"Duh, I know it is. That's how I deal with stress." And from what I knew of her, this made a lot of sense. *"Don't get killed, alright? This being a freak gig is a little easier when you're not alone in it. Feel me?"*

And I did. Donations had changed us in so many ways. "I won't get killed."

My Swift Shuttle hovered just a couple of meters off the ground, kicking up dust, leaf fans, and straw. Now that I was closer to the surface, I could see where the survey craft had done the same. They were in here.

"Survey, call back," I tried again. No response.

"I do not advise this action," Proxy objected while rubbing up against my leg. "It is putting us both at unnecessary risk."

"What are you worried about? You aren't even here, you're up in orbit on the *Fidelis*."

"But *you* are here, Milo."

"We're going in, and that's that."

A long breath eased out of me as I brought the jagged edges of the craft into the embrace of the cavern. Lights blossomed around the hull of the Swift Shuttle where the vertical thrusters burned, and I felt for an instant like a blazing star. Where the other cave had been full of rock formations that might have blocked any hope of something this wide traveling within it, this one was open, a tunnel leading deep into the mountain like the mouth of a beast.

"There is little margin for error," Proxy said, and I knew it was right.

As the stone of the mountain enfolded me, the path narrowed, from four or five wingspans, to two or three, to just over one. Proximity alarms shouted.

"I got this," I said. "So long as I go slow, it will be fine."

"What if you clip an airfoil on a wall, and that wall is weak?" Proxy asked. "We do not know how strong the ceiling above us is. You cannot take on the weight of a mountain."

I tried not to let that thought overtake my outlook, millions of tons of dirt and rock collapsing on top of me. This was like playing that game from history class, Operation. All I needed to do was not touch the walls. No buzzer.

As I navigated to the back of the main chamber, around collections of stalactites and pillars, a single path appeared that was not much wider than my wingspan.

"Don't touch the sides," I told myself and eased into the gap. My right airfoil scraped the top of a pile of rocks, and I felt a stab of pain shoot down my arm. That was how it worked with anything Foundry-related. This ship was like a part of my body. All damage to the ship fed back to me as physical pain.

The air foil slid free of the wall, and I glanced over my shoulder, checking to be sure the ceiling wasn't coming down on us. It held, and I moved ahead.

Tunnels began to branch off, and I swore my external lights dimmed. There was a haze in the cave system, a mist. Yet even still, I could detect that a lithium concentration was here, if not a significant one. It seemed that even on Novae lithium did not occur in a pure form but was part of igneous rock formations. I was no geologist, but what this told me was there was a good chance this channel was, or at least used to be, a magma flow.

The walls and ceiling began to close in, tapering down and branching off into two options, the brightness of my external lights waning against dark stones. If anything went wrong down here, there was no easy way out.

"Where do we go?" I mused.

Proxy's body twitched as if having been doused with water. "There is a scuff on the right tunnel."

"I see it." And squeezed us through, wishing for once that the Swift Shuttle could become a pancake.

The air displaced from my engines began to vibrate the chamber, creating a feedback loop of rushing noise. I attenuated its volume within my perception and threaded through the hole, taking a single look back at what I had passed through. It was too small. Too tight.

The tunnels branched again, and I followed the path of the survey shuttle, seeing small signs of their passage, displaced water, broken rock formations. The noise from my engines was growing louder as the space widened, then grew ever smaller. The weight of the world was pressing down on my mind, the freedom and ecstasy I had felt over the skies of Novae having long fled at the arrival of claustrophobic terror.

I found myself in a broad cavern, cathedral in shape, and felt some relief. As I took the opportunity to breathe, giving myself a little positive self-talk, I remarked on this chamber's towering ceiling and arches, crystal formations of gypsum and quartz hemming the edges of the floor, jagged stalactites hanging overhead like inverted spires. The roar of my engines redoubled.

To my right came the crash of a stalactite, its rocky form slamming into a pool of fetid, green water. I jerked away from the impact out of reflex and found myself drifting to the left.

"Watch out for—" Proxy began but was cut off when the left airfoil of the Swift Shuttle slammed into the chamber's wall.

Chunks of stone tumbled down from its weakened surface, pieces large as trucks slamming onto me and forcing me to the ground. The engines sputtered for a moment, and I lost altitude control. I looked up to see the stalactite above me wavering side to side. The entire room was trembling, hundreds of spikes dangling in rhythm overhead.

Then it hit me. I knew why. I knew what was happening.

"The vibrations of the engine noise," I said. The roar of the Swift Shuttle had reached the exact pitch of the stalactites' resonant frequency. Bridges had been ripped apart by this principle of physics. Glass could shatter with noise. Car tires had gone flying off their axles from lug nuts vibrated off their pegs. If the room continued to resonate like this, the noise could bring the whole damn ceiling down.

Proxy did not respond in affirmation, only nodded. Ever see a cat nod in resignation? Neither had I.

There were two options before me. I could stay and try to figure this out, avoid the falling spikes of deadly stone, or press on before more fell. The tunnel before me and to the right appeared to be the clear winner, damage to the nearby walls indicating this was the most likely direction they had gone.

Stalactites crashed around me. I sucked in a breath and punched it, but before I could, a section of the wall behind me weighing several tons collapsed, pinning me to the ground.

The Swift Shuttle went down, my body screaming, a dozen alarms letting out their cries. I willed the nano-repair bots into action.

"It is coming down on the east side of the chamber," Proxy reported.

Everything went black for a moment, my perceptions blocked with a wave of overwhelming pain.

I struggled against the pile of rocks pinning my shoulders. Every time I twisted, attempting to break free of their crushing weight, all I managed to do was grind up bits and pieces, filling the space beneath my belly with rubble. I managed to wiggle far enough ahead I could again see two things. The vibrating stalactites overhead, and the exit.

"More power, Milo," Proxy said. "It is the only way."

"Damn it. This was so stupid."

"Yes," it groaned. "Yes, it was."

Closing my eyes, I focused my mind on the passage ahead, imagining our path as we shot through the narrow gap. I only hoped it went somewhere that wasn't a dead end.

"Stupid, stupid, stupid," I grumbled as I ramped up the engines.

When the fusion core had reached one hundred percent, I gave it a quick boost. The Swift Shuttle burst from the pile of rocks like a missile, and off we went, casting shattered pieces of limestone and chert everywhere. Newtonian physics took over, and it was all I could do to steer.

We shot through the narrow gap ahead. My airfoils screeched as they were dragged against the volcanic walls. My heart thundered in my chest as I twisted and turned down a serpentine path with no models or maps of what was ahead, avoiding pillars of rock, ceiling scuffing against the top of my head, the tips of my elbows, leaving the skin raw. Everything was aching.

I tried with all my might, but I couldn't slow fast enough. I had too much velocity.

"I sense seismic instability," Proxy reported. "This is not the result of your engines."

"What? What do you mean?"

"The ground, the walls. They are vibrating. An earthquake, perhaps?"

"You've got to be fucking joking me."

Proxy seemed confused. "Is fucking a joke?"

"I eh—Depends on the context?"

"You seem to take it seriously with Shelly."

"Not now, Proxy. Please, not now."

The tunnel corkscrewed, and I flowed along with it, traveling way too fast for such a tight space, walls rushing past in lines of black and silver. Several tense moments passed in which I did not take a breath. Thank the Universe, I did not die.

I emerged on the other side of the tunnel without critical damage and reversed my engines, bringing the Swift Shuttle to a rapid halt. My stomach was flipping end over end. I wanted to puke. This had been reckless and stupid.

"Mi—Milo, do you copy?" my communications channel crackled.

My heart leapt at the sound. Could it be? Was that…

"Chevelle?" I asked, hopeful.

"Milo! Thank the big man you here."

I eased my banged-up body forward and could see the survey shuttle stuck sideways between a set of narrow walls.

"Are you okay?" I asked.

"We're alive. Caught up. Got wedged. This is where the tunnel ends, innit."

"We'll get you out. Is anyone hurt?"

"No, just stuck."

"Alright. Any luck with what you came for?"

"No. I'm sure you saw that spread of lithium. Some down here, eh, just not anything like we'd hoped. I've gone dizzy and broke the shuttle."

"It will be fine," Mom said next over the open channel, an edge to her voice. *"If we can just get it out. You shouldn't have come in after us, Milo."*

I groaned. "Glad you're okay too, Mom."

"What a royal waste of time," Johan put in. *"This is why we're at the mercy of alien charity."*

"No one makes it alone," James said. *"We made the decision as a group to check this out."*

"I did not vote for it. This was Chevelle's impulsiveness"

"Neither did I," Harper agreed. *"It was dumb. We should have gone on foot."*

"No griping. No backtalk," Chevelle told them. *"Long as you ride on this shuttle, I'm the captain. We chose together."*

"Not that I am agreeing with your little errand," I said, drawing myself close enough I could deploy the shuttle's grapples and start to pull them out. "But it's a good thing you didn't go on foot. I stumbled onto a haunt where sawtooths go during the day. Trust me, you wouldn't want to pop in unannounced."

"Well then, it's a good thing we didn't," James said, relief in his voice. *"I think I've had quite enough gunplay for a lifetime."*

The cave gave a shudder, and I knew we needed to hurry. If an earthquake was coming this would be the worst place to be.

"Karianna," I called over the open channel. "I'm sending you a 3D map. We need to get these people out before the mountain comes down on us all."

CHAPTER 7

"What in the hell did you do to this thing?" Lance said, his eyes wide as moons as he stared at the smoking survey shuttle resting on the landing platform. He raked a hand through his blonde hair, and I could see the mental calculations burning up his brain. "Perry?"

Perry walked around the shuttle, ducking under the wing, running his hand over surfaces, peeking into engine slots. "Has to be an interesting story here."

"Oh, I promise, there is," Karianna said before I could speak up.

"Geez, Chevelle, did you get into the hooch first? Don't drink and fly, sister."

It had taken Karianna and I the rest of the day to get the survey shuttle free. After I had tugged it from the narrow crevasse inside the cavern, Karianna helped me walk it out. We deployed every drone we had available to lift the survey shuttle inches off the ground and moved it one foot at a time. Other than the largest of the chambers where the ground was covered in debris, our exit had been far less eventful than my entrance, if tedious. Once we were back outside sometime mid-afternoon, Karianna and I transferred the crew to our Swift Shuttles and carried the survey shuttle between us on grapples back to the landing platform.

Lance and Perry inspected the damage, each with a tablet in hand, tapping on pipes and panels. Chevelle had managed to cause a lot of damage in a short time. Thank the Universe I had not done the same.

"Stupid," Mom whispered under her breath, standing close beside me.

"I thought you voted to go in."

"Well, maybe, but she was in charge. Guess I should have been enough of a leader to stand up to her."

I gave Mom a pinched expression. "You're not one to shift blame."

"You're right, son." She rubbed her face and groaned. "Ignore me. I'm just tired, and we need a lot of things. Time to own the good and the bad."

"I'll help where I can, if you want," George offered.

Mom whirled on him. "We need you on networks!"

He took a step back in response and blinked at her. In that instant, George appeared legitimately scared.

A moment passed, and she took a deep breath, then shook her head, hands coming to rest at her sides. "I'm sorry, Ramirez, that was uncalled for. Please, go in and see if you can help Shelly and Ada with anything."

George gave a shrug. "Alright, fine." He motioned for his wife, Harper, to follow, but she remained behind, talking in hushed tones with Johan. George made one more failed attempt to get her to join him, telling a joke and smiling, but when she shot him an annoyed look, he headed off towards the tech lab alone.

"How bad are we?" Chevelle asked. "Don't mess around."

"How bad are we?" Lance rounded on her, hands shaking. "How about you get back with me in a little while. It's a hell of a project just to figure out how bad you fucked up. How's that?"

"It's an answer," Johan said.

"What compelled you guys to fly into a cave?" He raised his hands and pointed at the twisted airfoil on the starboard side. "I mean. What the hell?"

"Lithium deposits," Chevelle suggested.

"Lithium?" Lance pinched the bridge of his nose. His pale face was turning red. "I don't care if you discovered Cortés' gold, don't do it again."

Sensing the only way that this might go, Mom gave a wave and gestured with her head back towards the colony. "Let's leave the experts to their work. We can regroup and figure out where we go from here. Survey shuttle is down for now. We're not going back out today."

"It's just like the broken perfume machine," Perry declared, his visor reflecting the light of high afternoon onto the exterior of the scratched passenger cabin.

"How's that?" I asked, knowing full well that this was a dad joke trap.

"It's out of odor."

And on that note, our group turned and headed back, not a single person laughing under their breath. I swear. Not a single one. Certainly not me.

Mom led us back to the tech labs where we unloaded our gear, found places to sit and relax, and get something to drink. On our walk over, James and Karianna broke off with some vague excuse about business to attend to.

Shelly greeted me with a hug and a confused expression. "Not a good day?"

I shook my head. "Survey shuttle got wrecked. Flew it into a cave."

"Like, into the side of one? Or like, into, into a cave system?"

"Into, into."

"Oh damn."

"Yeah. Damn."

She narrowed her eyes at me. "Whose brilliant idea was that?"

"All of theirs, apparently." I gestured in the survey team's direction. "We just pulled their asses out. My Swift Shuttle took a good bit of damage, but the Foundry nano-machines will have it fixed in a few hours. Too bad our technology doesn't work like that. I got pinned under rocks for a minute, and it was pretty scary. Flying underground—not advisable."

"Milo, a cave," she said, leaning in and lowering her voice, tone hardening into iron. She took hold of my upper arm and squeezed. "You could have been killed. What were you thinking following in after them? You can't be reckless like that."

I closed my eyes and let out a sigh. "Mom was down there. Stupid or not, I couldn't just leave them."

"There are better ways."

And with that I resigned, raising my hands in apology. She was right. I could have sent some drones in first. I could have called for help, and we could have taken a ground party. As open as the cave was, one of the trucks would have done just fine getting around most of the space. Instead, I decided to be all action hero.

"I can't lose you too," she said, her expression turning soft. "Mom's gone. Dad's gone. You're my family."

"I'm sorry," I mouthed, and she nodded the slightest bit, accepting my sentiment.

Our little excursion had worn me out. I searched for a place to sit and rest for a while, and as I did, I noticed that at the far end of the lab we had visitors. The Jevox were here with Shelly, Dad, and Ada, inspecting our tools and the various technological components that were scattered across workbenches. Twenty-five eyes hidden behind breathing masks. Arms with too many joints, fingers too much like ours. Robes the same cerulean color, though with differing abstract patterns of red, gold, and white. Getting used to how other species presented or conducted themselves was a challenge at times, my mind working overtime to fit them into a box that they just didn't fit. But for all their strangeness, all their unusual synchronicity, I'd prefer to look at them any day of the week over those horse-sized Kabosai slugs.

I gave Dad a wave, and he waved back. George was helping him with something electronic, a network relay, remaining silent.

"The Jevox have been hanging out with Ada and I all morning," Shelly offered in a low voice. "Must say, though, they are courteous guests. I've learned a lot about them."

"Oh yeah?"

"Yup. We know they have two colonies here in the system, small ones at that, stations basically. One is in the asteroid belt between planets four and five, they call it Preste. The other, somewhere deep on that unnamed, lifeless rock, planet four. But their home world, Rix, really isn't too far away in the grand scheme of it all. It's only ten light years."

"They say what it's like?"

"They did." She smiled at me, the curious learner in her brain lighting up. "According to them, it's a union of nature and engineering. The entire world nearly covered in buildings where the hive lives. You know how we wondered if they have any individuality?"

I nodded.

"They do. It just isn't expressed in logic. They tried to explain it to me, and I don't totally get it, but the emotional part of their brain is the individual. They still choose mates. The enclave that has joined us, that's what they call their groups, three of them are male, two are female. Two sets are paired. One is unpaired."

"Wait, I don't understand. How can logic and emotion exist separately?"

Shelly shrugged. "Well, they've figured out how. That's where their artistic expression comes from. Just look at their robes, they are the same, but different."

The enclave of Jevox stood in the corner of the lab, passing a series of silicon chips between one another, then to Ada, who returned them to the storage containers at the end of the work bench. Each of them were inspecting the components, and not just with their eyes, but their fingers, their noses. While they might speak with one mind, one will, there were subtle differences to their actions. The one on the far right seemed to favor visual inspection. The one to its left, testing to see if it could guess the weight of the object with its hand. While the next in line compared the chips to one another, counting sub-components on their green surfaces. Were these strengths? Weaknesses? Or was this how individuality showed up in their hive group? A propensity towards certain interests?

Shelly turned towards the group of Jevox. "May I ask something of you?"

One of the Jevox turned its head while the rest continued with their tasks of inspecting human technology. "What would you ask?"

"Would you happen to know anything about the Starfish? We were recently visited by some unknown ships."

My eyebrows raised. Why hadn't I thought to ask them? The Jevox were far more well-traveled than we were. Of course they might know.

"Starfish?" they asked as one. "What are Starfish?"

"Five sides, like your ships, but flattened." She gestured with her hands, drawing shapes in the air.

"Oh," they said, looking to one another. "The Pentaray."

"Pentaray?" I whispered, rolling the word around on my lips.

Shelly gave me a glance, then turned back to our guests. "Is that what they're called?"

"It is what *we* call them," one of them replied. "What they call themselves, we cannot say. You call yourself Human. We call ourselves Jevox. What do they call us?"

A curious thought. In the absence of proper names, we come up with whatever comparison makes sense, good or bad. As humans, we had called these unknown ships Starfish. The Jevox, Pentarays. It made me wonder if Pentarays were animals from their home world that they used purely for comparison.

"Are they dangerous?" I asked. "They came here a few days ago, and we scared them off with the Foundry vessels when they would not communicate. No shots fired."

"We know little of the Pentaray," another Jevox said. "They are benign for the most part. Stay to themselves. Are scared away by energy weapons."

"What do they want?" Shelly asked.

The Jevox spoke among themselves again for a moment. This went on longer than normal. Were they arguing? Could Jevox even argue?

"Crystallized oxygen," one said after a while.

"Crystallized oxygen?" I mused, fingers rubbing my chin.

Both Chevelle and Johan raised an eyebrow at one another, then proceeded to fix themselves a kettle of hot water on the stove in the corner of the lab. Chevelle found a stool beside the station and sat down, letting out a bone-tired sigh as she did.

"Why would crystallized oxygen be on Novae?" Shelly mused. "I didn't think it was anything but theoretical, and even so, it could only exist in conditions close to absolute zero. Those do not exist here."

"They search all places for it," the Jevox on the far right said while raising a compact formfactor motherboard, inspecting its many card slots. "Once they are aware of it, they can be aggressive."

"But why?" I asked. "Materials science isn't my field, but wouldn't it theoretically be a superconductor? There has to be better options, right?"

"Other properties exist," the one at the front of their group replied. "We believe their technology to be part organic. Could be used for cellular respiration, not just super conductivity."

"*Asseblief*, organics in space?" Johan asked while dipping a tea bag in his steaming mug. "Is that even possible?"

The Jevox did not reply.

"Hey, Milo," Shelly asked, dragging a stool over and setting it beside me. "Since you're already here, do you mind helping us test something?"

I sat down and gave a nod. "Sure, what's up?"

"I've got a patch ready for the neural implants. I'd like to run it through both of us, make sure it's stable. Thought maybe Proxy could help us out, roll back the firmware if something goes wrong."

"Should be safe," Ada said, nose scrunching up as she smiled. "I mean, even if it's not, it won't kill you or anything."

"How reassuring," I replied.

"Lovelace is right," Shelly said, eyeing her friend. "We've run plenty of models to be sure it won't scramble your brain, and with Proxy's help, we can make this test safe. Won't take long."

"Proxy?" I spoke aloud.

"*I have been listening,*" it replied, but only in my head.

"Does the Foundry restrict you from helping with this?"

"No. We would be happy to assist. Please, ask that your wife grant me network access."

I gave Shelly a hand gesture. "Proxy's all in, just grant him access."

"Dunno if I'd let machines creep 'round in my skull," Chevelle commented. "Might mess with my head. Might make me lose it."

"Am I mental?" I glanced at her over my shoulder.

Chevelle gave a shrug. "Hard to say, bruv. Real talk here. You came screamin' in after me, not the other way. We just lay there."

Shelly gestured at the air before her and took a seat again.

"Alright," she said after a moment, then took a deep breath and forced a smile. "If we're right about this update, and we're stable, it should let us use less bandwidth for common inquiries over the network. It will be error prone in some circumstances but takes off much of the pressure. It's as we discussed, Johan, UDP protocols for queries level four and below."

Johan raised his mug of steaming tea and nodded. "Did you check the ports and transmission frequencies?"

"Three times."

"Test the time rules for buffer retention?"

"The buffer will not overflow."

"Deploy the gateway filters in the event of bad packets?"

"She did the work," Ada told him, taking up for Shelly. "We're good, hard ass. It's not a bunch of duct tape and crap we found in a dumpster dive."

He sipped his tea, then spoke, *"Sommer."*

Harper squeezed up beside the older man and smiled. George did not seem pleased at all with how cozy she was acting around Van Niekerk.

"Alright, Milo. Here we go." Shelly reached out for my hands. "You ready?"

The Jevox watched with bated breath, all five leaning in with an intense interest, their many onyx eyes reflecting constellations of the bright indicator lights from our technical equipment.

"Ready," I said.

Shelly began the download, and for an instant my vision went blank, my mind overloaded with the sudden influx of change. I found myself holding my breath, counting to ten within my head where a sensation like cool water trickling over bare skin became dominate. Liquid made of pure information entered, finding every nook within my grey matter, its mass gathering in the corners of my mind before being flushed away. This trickle soon became a stream, a constant flow, though its meaning was a jumble. My neck and spine tingled as it stabilized, legs going weak, hands trembling.

It took several moments before my vision returned. Shelly was the first person I saw, her attention focused on nothing. A kind of vacancy had taken hold of her expression.

The room was silent, not for a lack of talking but a lack of external stimulus, and then ideas began to flow through the pure waters of information, their context cold, incomprehensible.

What was this data?

Did it come from our network?

That didn't feel right.

I attempted to reach towards the information, grasp for something familiar, but it was too fluid. A heartbeat thumped, and information was returned to me, the current weather conditions outside, time of day, when the next Council meeting was set to begin, how many rations I had left in the commissary.

Then there was something else. Words. Images. Sensations. None of it made sense. To call them painful would have been ignorant, though these thoughts were in no way comfortable to process. These signals, whatever they were, had not been intended for a human brain to decode.

Out of the corner of my eyes, the Jevox showed signs of physical discomfort much like mine, setting down what they had in their hands and bending over.

Had they eaten something bad?

Were they having stomach aches?

Ada and George rushed to grab stools so that our guests could sit.

Johan held his cup of tea in both hands, eyeing us over its rim, brows narrowed in thought.

"What?" I asked him, my question too sharp. "What the hell are you looking at?"

He said nothing in response, just sipped his tea.

The stream of data subsided, but pain rushed in to replace it. My head split in two.

"Milo?" Shelly took hold of my hand, squeezing my fingers. "Are you okay?"

I nodded. "I'm fine. Just. Well…"

"Yeah," she said, nodding. "I felt it too. We'll have Proxy roll it—"

"Want the bad news, or the really bad news?" Lance burst into the lab with a flourish of his tablet. "It's a doozy."

Why tell us now? This was not a good time.

"What we in for?" Chevelle asked, taking a sip from her teacup. "Time for a trade in?"

Shelly and I scooted closer to one another. God my head hurt. We needed to roll this back.

Sensing our discomfort, Dad reached into a pocket, then handed Mom a set of pills which she passed to us like it was a relay race. We swallowed the headache medicine without anything to drink, eager to kill the pain.

"Not quite ready for a trade in," Lance started again after a moment. "But your little jaunt into those caves was sure as hell a net negative trip. There is damage to both the left and right air foils. Vertical thrusters have bent cones, as well as two busted turbines. We've got broken pressure seals, so this baby isn't going high up even if it could fly. Ancillary power systems are offline, can't figure out why right now, and several of the batteries will need to be rebuilt from scratch. Hey, Chevelle, I thought you were a good pilot."

She gave a shrug. "Any landing is good, even if it's ugly, straight butterz. That's what they say, right?"

"I think we can all agree, poking around in caves with the survey shuttle was a bad idea. The Speaker will not be happy. With the materials and labor we have available, I don't see us getting it fixed in less than four weeks. This will put us way behind. Johan, I really hope your calculations are wrong, but I don't think they are."

"They're not," Johan said, then took a sip of tea. "We're headed for ruin."

The Jevox glanced at one another as if conferring over our situation. Their fingers moved in sequence, right hand, pinky to thumb, left, thumb to pinky, a wave of neural impulse in a specific rhythm.

"God damn, I wish we could get our shit together and work like the Jevox. Maybe they can help us fix this. Breathe. Just breathe. Calm down. Calm down. Don't use those kinds of words, you're just frustrated, that's all."

I blinked, then scratched at the back of my head, not sure where those words had come from. Shelly gave me a weird look, first blank, then her eyes went wide.

The Jevox's fingers paused in their sequence for an instant, then resumed.

"You heard me?" It was Shelly's voice in my head. How was it in my head?

Without trying to appear as if something strange was going on, I licked my lips and pivoted my head slightly, my face turning away from the crowd.

I used my thoughts to reply, *"I heard you."*

"How?"

"The update, I guess. It's linked our brains."

"How in the hell? I have so many questions. But let's be honest, it would be nice if they would help, wouldn't it?"

"It would be nice."

"We need to roll this back now," she thought. *"No offense, love. I don't want you to hear my every thought. Sometimes they aren't so nice."*

I nodded, understanding just what she meant, and sent the request to Proxy.

My vision blacked out for a moment, and Shelly squeezed my fingers. A few seconds passed and everything came back. My headache subsided.

"Rollback successful," Proxy reported. *"Are you okay, Milo?"*

"I am," I thought, then looked Shelly in the eyes to be sure she was as well. *"Thank you, Proxy."*

"Of course."

Lance ran his fingers through his hair. "There are a few things we could try to speed this up, but it would require recycling some old components."

"Let me guess," Johan scowled and set down his teacup. "More labor?"

"We don't have an advanced recycling facility. Many of the components have to be broken apart by hand. This takes time. It takes precision. Hell, some of the pieces just have to be pulled off and reused. A good set of eyes and a pair of pliers, but hours of work for each. We just don't have enough hands."

"More hours then?"

Chevelle shook her head. "People are mashed up. We're weeks behind, our only shuttle grounded. That's on me, ok? Surveys gotta go old school now. On foot with a squad. Quick missions, nothing more. What's that mean for your stash, fam??"

"Disaster," George muttered.

We were back to the same old challenge. The Foundry was not being as helpful as it initially had. It wanted us to pass the test of being self-sufficient. So far, we were failing that test. I only hoped failure didn't mean the death of every person on Novae. What were we to do? Our resources were limited in people, materials, and time. We had children to be born and raised. A species to save. I knew that Johan and several others wanted to go back to Earth and fulfill the mission, but even that outcome was fleeting if we could not make this work. If we could not become self-sufficient, the only option would be to see if the Foundry would allow the colony to move onto the *Fidelis* and *Reverie*.

And then go…

Go where?

A people lost forever?

Become interstellar nomads?

"We will help," the Jevox said as one, and everyone twisted to look at them. So caught up in our own problems, we had nearly forgotten our guests.

"You'll help?" Shelly asked. "You'll help fix the survey shuttle?"

The Jevox paused for a moment, seemed confused, then each raised their right hand. "We shall. This is our expertise. Building. Working. If you can offer us the assistance of someone who might advise on your technology."

Lance pointed a finger at Perry who had just entered the room.

"Oh, shit. What did I just get voluntold to do?" Perry took a step back towards the door. "Just so you know, guys, I don't like being experimented on. Twice is enough for a lifetime."

"No experiments," the Jevox on the far right offered.

"Will it cost us anything for your help?" Johan asked, stepping towards the aliens. His expression was dark, a storm brewing on his wrinkled face.

"There is always a cost," the Jevox said as one, their tone matter of fact. "You will incur a debt for our service. You will pay it in time."

"And just what kind of debt did you have in mind?"

CHAPTER 8

"Milo," a voice said from the black of night. *"Milo."*

Once more I found myself floating in that great void of nothing, a supermassive blackhole naked before me, its accretion disc swirling, turning, urging me to hurl myself into and be one with its singularity. Time passed on an unfathomable scale, ages and eons, a million, trillion cycles, and this point of infinitely dense matter was left with nothing else to devour. Its home galaxy had long ago fallen into it with little more than a flicker. Given its size, countless other blackholes, bellies bulging with galaxies of their own, had found a way here, devoured, casting violent vibrations of gravitational waves into the void, then were no more.

And yet, and yet… Somehow, someway, someone, had trapped this thing. They had built a cage of metal and mirrors around this apex cosmological predator. They had contained it in this place, if only for a time. It raged against this prison to no avail, and they were using it. They had found a way to tap into its vast power and twist it to their needs.

And me.

And us?

No, just me.

Wait.

No.

I was not alone.

Something else was here.

Someone else was here.

It saw me.

It recognized me.

It wanted to speak with me.

But how could I?

What would I say?

"Milo," the voice came again, but it was not the one who had seen me in the void. No. This voice was more familiar. *"Wake up."*

The blackhole and the mirrors, all the emotions of dread and unease, dissolved into a white light that felt… pink.

I blinked where I lay in bed, sitting up abruptly. Shelly lay next to me in the dark, sleeping sound, one arm thrown over my lap, her breathing slow and even.

"Proxy," I called out, scrubbing at my eyes with the backs of my hands. "What is it? What do you want? I'm tired as hell. I had a bad day."

"It is time," Proxy replied.

"What?" I shook my head. "Time for what? Are we in danger?"

"No danger. The Foundry wishes to speak to you."

"It already is." I reached for the bedside table and switched on a dim lamp. What a relief to see I'd left a glass of water sitting there, thirsty as I was. Must have been sleeping with my mouth wide open again, attempting to catch zipzaps or beetles. I took a sip of the tepid water before replying. "Look, Proxy, you're in my head already. You are the Foundry."

"No. I am your Proxy. This is different. The Foundry wishes to speak to you as it did aboard the facility."

I choked on my water and spit some out on my lap. The noise and light made Shelly groan. She rolled over to face away from me.

"What is it time for?" I asked and set the glass of water down before palming the beads of moisture off my chest and sheets.

"A choice."

"And who makes this choice?"

"Your leaders."

I didn't waste a second, hopping out of bed and immediately tossing on clothes, before letting Shelly know what was happening. By the time she gave me a kiss and I was running out the door, a floodlight and pistol in hand, pings were being returned from the Council members.

It was cold outside, a sharp breeze cutting through my light jacket, my left arm covered in goose bumps. I could smell someone cooking, the sweet scent of baking bread along with something savory tickling my nose. I could hear sawtooths hunting in the distance, their shrieking cries echoing over the northern hills. Though their distance gave me some reassurance, I kept my bright light close, my pistol ready. I was not going to be eaten tonight.

When I reached my Swift Shuttle's platform, all six Councilors were waiting for me, as well as a few others including Leo Nelson, Rowan Donaldson, and none other than Johan Van Niekerk.

"Evening everyone," I said as I approached. "Sorry to wake you all in the middle of the night, but this could be a turning point."

The Speaker came forward and smiled at me. "Is it ready to negotiate?"

"I can't say. But Proxy said it's time for a choice. Not sure that we will negotiate, though. Pretty sure the Foundry is above all that."

"Then let's get loaded up and go," Johan said, gesturing towards the Swift Shuttle. "I'm ready."

I raised my hands in a pleading gesture. "Proxy was clear with this one. Only our leaders are allowed. Council members."

"*Asseblief,* Council members only?" Johan narrowed his eyes. I was getting sick and tired of that expression coming from an angry, annoyed, overly fit Santa Claus. "Are we not a democracy? Do we not have a say?"

Councilor Perez rubbed his hands together and let out a sigh. "I am not sure it works that way this time. We go up, make the best decision we can. Maybe this is what it wants, no? See what human leaders do when away from the rest of the colony."

"I don't like it."

Donaldson adjusted the rifle slung over his shoulder and nodded. "I'm with Johan. I don't like this either. And look, it's my job to protect the colony from threats. Not only does this leave us out of the discussion, it feels like a trap."

"It's not a trap," I said, my tone insistent.

"Says the man under the influence of the Foundry machines."

I lowered my right hand and tried to hide it behind my back.

Councilor Crawford took a step in Rowan's direction and shook her head. "Don't be unfair."

"Just stating facts, ma'am."

"I should be there to recreate this event," Leo said, his gaze turned upward. He reached for the sky with a paint-stained hand and closed it into a fist. "This is a pivotal moment in human history. It must be captured."

"You've got a spectacular imagination," I told him. "I'm sure you'll figure something out even if you don't get to go."

He did not like that answer.

"This is a system of control," Councilman Halifax said, a finger pressed against his lips in thought. "I often get the feeling we're living out a flowchart. If they do this, then do that. Been drawing one out in my head, but I'm missing some of the details. Need more data."

"Feels like one," Clark replied. "I do wish Johan was coming with us. I enjoy and respect your perspective on many matters."

Johan gave Donaldson a dark look, then turned to me. I got the distinct impression he was trying to figure out if I was lying. If this was somehow a Milo Hughes powerplay. If only he knew how poor I was at politics. I just wanted us to all be healthy and happy. I just wanted to ensure that the human species continued on.

"Councilors," I said, cutting in. "We need to go. Now. There's no time to argue over who or why. The instructions were clear. The window is closing."

"Then it is done," the Speaker said in a tone that brooked no further argument. She gestured for us to board the Swift Shuttle. "If anyone asks, we made the best decision possible on your behalf."

"On our behalf," Johan grumbled. "Democracy at its finest." The look he gave us as we turned away was one I would never forget. Our fault or not, this moment had crossed some sort of line of trust, but it was done.

We boarded the shuttle and closed the door.

"Buckle in everyone," I said, heading towards the front of the shuttle. "You guys don't get a Star Sphere, but there's plenty of seating."

"Take it easy on us, please?" Councilwoman L'Agnese requested.

"I will."

"No more than three Gs," Halifax added. "Beyond that, it can be very uncomfortable for humans."

I rolled my eyes, climbed up onto the lip of Star Sphere, then took off my jacket. "Last I checked, guys, I'm still human," I said, but then I inspected my mechanical arm and wasn't quite so sure. What had I given up for this opportunity? It had been worth it. "Once you're buckled in, do me a favor and turn the other way, please. I need to strip down and to be honest, I'm a touch modest."

A moment later, the Swift Shuttle's engines ignited, and we were headed off into the sky. Having passengers made it feel as if I were driving in the slow lane, not being allowed to exceed three Gs of acceleration. As such, it took nearly thirty minutes to reach low orbit and put us on a trajectory for the *Fidelis*.

"I'm coming over," Karianna said on a channel direct to my Star Sphere.

"Sounds good. See you soon."

At least the freaks could be together.

The Swift Shuttle docked, and I climbed out of my sphere, toweling off before getting dressed again. When I departed the shuttle, the Councilors were waiting aboard the *Fidelis* on the main catwalk running from forward to aft, Mary showing them around as she gathered refreshments. The interior of my ship was vast and open, a hollow skyscraper laid on its side, made of crystal hundreds of floors in height filled with dozens of self-contained, reconfigurable rooms, each surface oriented around a central core.

Like me, this had been Mary's home for nearly twenty years, but unlike me, who spent most of that time in hyper suspension, this had been her world. Her everything. She and Esteban had made use of every nook and cranny of this great vessel to live out their happiness. While I might know how every part of this ship felt, it being an extension of my body, my will, she was like a local who had fallen in love with their city. She knew all the best spots.

I approached the Speaker and found her lost in thought, her gaze fixed on the fighter bays near the aft of the ship. We had lost many of them in the battle with the Gene Brokers, but in time, the *Fidelis* had rebuilt them. If only it could have saved Esteban.

"I still miss him," she said, her voice low enough the other councilors could not hear.

I put an arm around her, and she folded into me, her head resting on my shoulder.

"Me too," I said. "Me too."

"I swear this place still smells like him. That musk, that sweet bite. I can't say how this is even possible, as big as this ship is inside, it doesn't make sense."

"No, but it makes perfect sense. This is a Foundry ship. Its desire is to bring you comfort, not pain. I doubt Proxy would tell me if it was doing this to make you more comfortable, but it might be true."

She gave a chuckle and pushed herself out of my embrace, using her cuffs to brush away the mist from her eyes. "I thought you were going to say something about him living on in our hearts. Now you got to make some cold, scientific explanation."

"Well, there's that too, ya?"

From across the catwalk, Karianna appeared, having come from a shuttle bay on the opposite side of the ship. She gave me a smile, and a wave, her many bracelets jingling, then pointed towards the forward end of the *Fidelis* where my personal Star Sphere was mounted. "We ready to get this show on the road?"

The Speaker and I smiled at one another.

I went to greet Karianna, bumping fists. "That's the plan."

"This place is crazy open on the inside," Karianna said, marveling at the *Fidelis* as we strolled ahead, the Council walking behind us. "No wonder your ass is so slow. So much wasted space. Can you imagine how many cubic feet of atmosphere has to be pumped in here just to keep us fleshy sacks alive? You should come visit the *Reverie* sometime. That bitch is meant for a real fight. Tight center of gravity. Large, but fast. Decks thick as bedrock."

"I faced down three Kabosai ships made of asteroids big enough to wipe out the dinosaurs in the *Fidelis*. They had their own fighter compliments, energy weapons, all sorts of ballistics, and yet, we are still here. Don't talk to me about not being built for a fight."

"Yeah, yeah. Whatever." She gave a wave of her mechanical arm, gesturing at the outer walls. "Still, there's so much open space it almost makes me dizzy. If I threw a rock from this catwalk there's no way I could hit one of those outer rooms."

Proxy appeared at my side and began rubbing against my leg. I reached down, a grin on my face as I scratched it behind the ear.

"You have a cat?" Karianna mused. "I guess I knew that. Lance's idea, right?"

"And you have what again?" I watched as Proxy dashed ahead towards the front of the ship, its loping gate making its orange striped tail bounce. "A big gerbil?"

She whispered something that I couldn't understand.

"What was that?" I asked. "Didn't catch it."

"Nothing."

"Come on, it was something."

"Ugh."

"Fine. Fine. You don't have to tell me. I'm sure your Proxy is great."

"A giant chinchilla," she mumbled after a moment.

"Oh wow, what mighty warriors. Cats eat chinchillas, you know?"

"Like to see your Proxy try." Her face went deadpan as she raised a set of clawing fingers. "Meow."

As we approached the end of the catwalk, the width of the *Fidelis* tapered down to a point where it was only about thirty meters wide. The platform which held my Star Sphere expanded in silence to accommodate guests. What had been a space only large enough to hold the crystal sphere I piloted from began to stretch out in a pancake of metal, safety railings rising from the outer edge. Nanomachines oozed out of the floor, reconfiguring into simple, white chairs, each facing my vacant Star Sphere, the liquid within burbling.

"Have a seat," I gestured, and the members of the Council did just that. They each had varying levels of awe and curiosity written across their faces. All except for Councilwoman Clark, who seemed genuinely afraid, her hands shaking.

Two final chairs appeared to the left and right of the Star Sphere. Karianna and I took those for ourselves.

Proxy came bounding off of the burbling tank of water and scurried over to the center of our circle.

"Greetings," it said, lowering its head to the councilors in a half bow. "I am Proxy. My counterpart and I on Miss Torlen's ship work along with our pilots to control and maintain the Foundry-made ships. I am autonomous from the Foundry, able to make my own decisions and ultimately serve the pilot. It is my job to facilitate interactions with the collective network. At times like these, I may serve as a bridge between species who show promise to the Foundry at large. We are here today because humanity is approaching a fork in the road."

The Speaker raised her hand. "Fast approaching, as in about five months from now?"

"It is no surprise that humans came to that conclusion." The lights on the *Fidelis* began to dim, and Proxy turned to face me. "Are you ready to speak with the Foundry? I can connect you now."

I nodded. "Open the connection."

While the light in the ship lowered until it was no more than a lambent glow tracing the edges of the outer hull and support struts, I felt that strange, pink color fill my mind. It was the same feeling, the same emotions that the original signal calling us to the Foundry facility carried. A sense of peace. A sense of rightness. An almost oppressive sense of well-being.

The Foundry protects life.

My heart thundered in my chest and for an instant it was hard to breathe. From the posture of the others, I was not alone.

"Hello councilors of the Novae colony," mechanical words came to us from everywhere and nowhere, a voice booming over us like a god. *"We are the Foundry. We are so glad you came to see us."*

"Aye dios, mio," Perez mumbled, and the Speaker agreed.

"Greetings, Foundry. It is good to speak with you again," I said, given that our colony leaders appeared dumbstruck in the moment. "Much has happened since the last time we spoke. Without your gifts, I am not sure we would still be alive. We survive because of you."

"Yes. The Foundry protects life."

The Speaker recovered herself. "Foundry, as Milo already stated, we are grateful for all you have done for us. That said, we thought, given the impression buried in the original signal, that you would help us. On our home world, our species had reached a crisis point. Unless something drastic has changed since we departed, life will be unsustainable. We had a mission, to answer your signal, ask for help, and go save the world."

"Many have missions. Many do not save their world."

"What are you telling us?"

"To save your world is a choice like all things," the Foundry went on. *"A choice made every moment of every day."*

"I don't understand."

"The Foundry protects life."

"Are you saying you won't help us?"

"Not enough information is available at this time."

"So, you need to know more about us?" Councilman Perez cut in.

"Correct. The Universe must be made self-aware. It is living, it is breathing. We protect life to protect the Universe. Not all life is willing to protect life."

Councilwoman Clark leaned forward in her chair. "And this means what exactly? That not all life is equal? That if it doesn't fit in your neat little box, you kill it off?"

"No. But we cannot offer help to all."

"You helped the Isoptera," she shot back. "They boarded the *Vasco Da Gama*, killed many friends of mine. How's that for protecting life?"

"Mistakes can be made when information is incomplete. We learn from mistakes. Make changes. Some help cannot be taken back."

"Let me get this straight," Karianna said, elbows resting on her thighs. "You gave the termites new ships, and after the deal was done, they behaved differently. Began acting like scavengers around Foundry facilities?"

"Correct. The Isoptera are not all violent, but there lay many factions. They are a strongly hierarchal species, their broods ruled by queens. Some queens are dangerous to other species, some are not. We no longer give them ships. We no longer offer aid, but they are beyond our reach. They survive on their own without our help."

"This makes a sort of cold sense," Councilman Halifax put in, a thoughtful finger raised. "When we remove the emotions of it, looking at the galaxy as a whole, some species may be too dangerous to let survive." The other councilors turned to glare at him, expressions shocked. "What? I'm just being academic. I would hope they choose to help us."

"This is no academic discussion," Councilwoman L'Agnese said. "This is our lives. The existence of our species."

"Why the deadline?" the Speaker asked. "We know that in about five months the food supplements will run out. At that time, we will be forced to stand on our own whether we're ready or not. With the crunch on resources, it will be tight. We do not have a solid infrastructure. The technology we used to build our great civilizations on Earth is spotty at best here. I can't help but feel the deck is stacked against us."

"You must learn what is important," the Foundry stated.

"What does that even mean?"

"You must learn what is important."

She shot her eyes towards me, and I gave a shrug. Proxy had not given me any insight into this. I was just as lost as they were.

"We came here to make a choice," she went on.

"Yes. A choice."

"Tell us what that choice is."

The Foundry went silent, and above our heads a three-dimensional star map appeared, a collection of white dots swirling around a central core. Our galactic home. A particular section near the south end of the spiral began to blink, then swell.

"The Milky Way, as you call it, is populated throughout with many Foundry facilities. You have seen the forges, the wandering gates, and of course, the cynosures. There are other

facilities as well, data nodes, network connections, and resource collectors. In these places we have always been. In these places we will always be.

"Do we have the power to turn back the changes on your world? Yes. But you must learn what is important. You must make a choice. A cycle is approaching at a nearby facility in this system. It is a smaller facility than you have seen before. It does not manufacture L-560s or J-510s like your Fidelis *and* Reverie. *It builds ships capable of carrying only a hundred humans at most. You will be given a choice between two variations of a ship we can manufacture."*

The map above us shifted into another image, a hologram resolving into a wide, disc-like ship, its aft end appearing as if someone had taken a bite out of its golden hull, body imprinted with a series of curves that spread out like reptilian wings. On closer inspection, details resolved into scaffolds and cranes, bays for drones, and others for cargo. Something about it appeared inherently industrial, built for tough work, not aesthetics.

"This is a D-782. The Foundry utilizes a similar design for its own purposes, to seek out resources and exploit them. With this ship, you will have the opportunity to locate any metal, mineral, or isotope you require to build what you need. Aboard, it has facilities for refining as well. It does not, however, have any means to defend itself. If it were to be attacked, it would either have to flee or be lost."

The councilors leaned towards the Speaker and began to rapidly whisper between one another. A ship like this would change everything. No longer would we have to worry about surveys and power. Hell, it likely had drones to even help with labor. All we would have to focus on was growing food to eat, and with additional equipment, even that would be easier. This would do so much more than the survey shuttle we had cobbled together ever could. This could change everything. This could truly make Novae a sustainable home. Might even be a place to have a child of my own.

Were Shelly and I ready for that?

"A resource and infrastructure ship," the Speaker said after a moment, raising a hand to quiet her colleagues. "This could be very useful. And what is our other choice?"

"Your mission is not over, is it?" the Foundry asked.

"No. It is not. There are many who wish to see it through."

"Very well. The other option we offer is a path to that end."

The resource and infrastructure ship vanished, and another appeared, the same basic shape, but this time, its outer hull was covered in weapons, its aft end, studded with larger engines. A slight change in the angle of its edges made it appear sharp, quiet, dangerous.

"We offer a D-782v. This vessel is a weapon of war. It is capable of swift movement without being detected by almost any sentient species, including Foundry make. Its weapons, while not comparable to the Fidelis or Reverie, are more than enough to lay waste to a world given time. Within it contains a path. Through that path it is possible to find a way back to Earth. If you can prove yourself to be one to protect life, we will consider helping to save your world.

"Know this, however, once this choice is made, neither the Fidelis nor the Reverie will be given instructions leading you back to Earth. You cannot take all your people with you to follow, and the ships we offer cannot carry everyone."

"Do we stay or go," Halifax stated, one hand scratching at his head. "With the infrastructure support, we have a guaranteed life here, but giving up the mission. A path home. That cost is steep."

Perez raised his hands. "But what does this path mean? Why don't it feel for certain?"

The Foundry remained silent, not responding to the questions being asked. It allowed us time to debate, time to work through our thoughts. Even now it was weighing our response against some unseen algorithm. Karianna and I looked at one another, then back to the councilors.

"What do we have to prove?" L'Agnese asked, piggybacking off Perez's thought.

"Who cares," Clark said, standing up. She began to pace around the platform, the holographic image above us distorting as her head passed through it. "We can go back. We can change Earth, surely. It's the right thing to do. We have to go back."

"The right thing to do?" Perez raised his voice. "To leave the majority of our people behind to fend for themselves? That no sound right."

Crawford grimaced at the other Council members. "We have pregnant colonists. We will be welcoming new lives to Novae soon. Perez is right. Taking this warship to go back to Earth would mean leaving the colonists on their own."

Clark pointed at Perez, then Crawford. "What are a few hundred lives when weighing that against billions?"

"You would sacrifice our people for that?" Perez growled. "You would sacrifice Johnson, Nelson, Ward, Salazar, Nguyen, Cox... I think you get my point. These are people, not just names. They are lives. The ends do not justify the means, madam. This colony deserves a chance. We are not even sure Earth can be saved by the time we arrive."

"I'm not giving up my soul," Crawford said, putting a hand on Perez's shoulder and squeezing. "There has to be a compromise."

Halifax leaned toward the center of the circle, eyes ahead. "Clark, you are being purely academic, right?" His tone was pleading. "Right?"

Clark stood there for a minute, her eyes fixed on the D-782v. It was a Foundry warship that contained the possibility, if unclear, of humanity's redemption by fulfilling the original mission, though it came with a cost—the safety and security of everyone who did not leave aboard it.

"Of course I am," she said after a moment, exhaling an angry breath. "Purely academic." She plopped back into her chair and crossed her arms.

Karianna and I gave each other an uneasy look. This would not be a simple choice.

The Speaker raised a hand to calm the rest of the Council. She spoke soft and careful, "Foundry, I seek to understand. What do you mean by, prove yourself to protect life? This path is contingent upon it."

It is as we have said, you must learn what is important. If you choose the vessel of war, you will be left to make your colony self-sufficient. The Foundry will not offer any help, any aid aside from the vessels you already have, and those merely for travel and defense. We will not give you resources. We will not change your circumstances. You will be on your own.

"Make a life here and flourish," the Speaker said, her voice low, "or leave most everyone behind to fend for themselves and follow a dark, uncertain path home."

All life is uncertain.

The image of the ship vanished, and the lights within the *Fidelis* brightened. My eyes fought to adjust.

"If we choose this warship," the Speaker went on, "do you guarantee that you will help us to restore Earth? It was ever the promise of your signal. Come and see us, we are here to help."

A silent moment passed. Not a single machine within the *Fidelis* made a sound. Was the Foundry thinking? Or was this simply theatrics? Through Proxy it had learned much about us, about me. But was that enough? Did it understand our intentions?

We have not yet decided, it finally responded. *We protect life. We protect life that protects life. The path back to Earth would not be an easy one, and its outcome is uncertain, but it is in your hands. The choices you make every day will determine if we aid your species in this crisis or not."*

Clark's hands were trembling, her eyes glassy with moisture. "Is Earth still viable, are people still alive?"

It was a question all of us had been afraid to ask. Truth was, none of us had any idea how long it had been since we left Earth. We had guesses, between fifty and a hundred years, but with hyper suspension and time dilation, there was no telling. The Foundry was a master of manipulating subjective time reference. Far as we knew, our home planet could be long dead.

"Not enough information is available at this time," it said after several seconds.

My chest tightened.

Proxy returned to us, and as it did, I felt that we had reached the end of our meeting. I stood out of reflex and everyone else followed my lead.

"You know the timetable," the Foundry said. *"You have figured it out on your own."*

"Five months," I replied, lowering my head. "It's all we have."

"Yes, and at that time the facility's cycle will be open. You must come to us and choose."

I knew in my heart of hearts, that whatever we chose, the Foundry was always watching us, sizing us up. This choice revealed our intent as a group, as a species. Was our nature to be trusted? Or did we deserve to be starved out and forgotten?

We must learn what is important.

"Thank you, Foundry," the Speaker said, then gave a deep bow. "We will speak again soon."

CHAPTER 9

By the time we returned from the *Fidelis*, dawn was coming, 75-DFX creeping back over the horizon, casting its golden light down upon the colony. Normally, I would have felt exhausted after such a trip, having been up half the night with no sleep at all, but this time I was exhilarated. We were on the cusp of something great. This choice would change everything. I only hoped our leaders would make the right decision.

A small crowd was waiting for us near the Swift Shuttle's platform, the head of each Arm present, along with a random assortment of other colonists. Soon as we were safely on the ground the councilors wasted no time, unbuckling from their acceleration chairs and departing before I could hardly climb out of my Star Sphere.

"Milo!" Dad called to me as I stepped from my Swift Shuttle out into the brisk air. "Is it true? Is it really true?"

I zipped my jacket up then nodded. "That all depends on what you've heard. But yeah, it's true."

"Wow. This is big. So big. I guess it hasn't left us out here to die."

"No. Can't protect life if it's dead, huh? I think it carefully assesses a species' situations and applies calculated pressure to see what they'll do."

"A test."

"Yeah. A test."

"You know, I've always wanted to ask, what's it like talking to the Foundry? Your mom and I never had the opportunity. When we were separated from the rest of the crew, we got snatched up by the Melcorin before we could do anything like that. Never even saw Cynosure."

"It's hard to put into words." I rubbed my palms together then blew heat between them. "Would feeling small be accurate? Maybe frustrated? It certainly isn't free with information. It has a plan. We can only hope that plan includes us."

"Next time you go, can you take me with you? Promise I won't get in the middle."

I tossed an arm around him and smiled. "Sure thing, Dad."

We strolled our way back towards the Council Chambers, Mom not far ahead with the councilors and the heads of the various Arms, her hands gesturing wildly as they discussed the matter. I could only catch a snippet here and there, some in angry Portuguese, but Mary kept encouraging everyone to tamp down their excitement and wait till they could speak behind closed doors.

No one heeded her suggestion.

The Council chamber doors closed, and deliberations began. Dad went to scramble up some rog, and I found a rock to take a seat on. it wasn't long before my solitude was delightfully ended by the arrival of my wife, along with my fellow Foundry freak.

"The colony is going crazy over this," Shelly said, giving me a hug. "We can hardly keep the network up."

Karianna plopped down on a rock opposite me. "Everyone is talking about it. They've gone straight cray cray."

"Any idea on consensus?" I asked. "Tried to eavesdrop on the way here but heard nothing concrete."

"Some believe we should keep to the mission and take the warship," Shelly said.

"Let me guess, Johan is one of them."

"Bingo."

"You think that's what most people want?"

"Hard to say. The idea of going back to Earth is appealing, even for me. May not really be home for those who grew up in transit, but it is our home world, our homeland. If we can help them, we should, shouldn't we?"

"But at the cost of everyone here? This place is real."

"It's a conundrum to be sure."

"Effed up machines," Karianna said, tossing a pebble at the dirt, its impact kicking up dust, disturbing a beetle that crawled past. "Why do they play these games with us?"

"*We must learn what is important*," I said, repeating the Foundry's words. "I think the key lies in that phrase."

Dad returned a few minutes later with a carafe of sweetened rog and several cups. He offered some to each of us as we waited. It was nice to drink something warm and soothing on such a cool morning. Fall and winter were creeping towards us. Just a few months and we'd be knee deep in snow. Folk would be begging to pop up to the Foundry ships with Karianna or I just to warm up. This might be the third full year humans had been on this planet, but we were still adjusting, and no one liked winter.

Hours passed, and during that time, a quiet crowd gathered outside with us to wait.

Leave Earth behind and thrive? Or take the risk that many may die and go back. This was a big decision, one that first had to be deliberated by councilors and heads of the Arms. If there was any dissent at all, it would then come to a general vote.

Exhaustion must have finally caught up with me as I found myself waking up to a bang, my head resting on Shelly's shoulder, drool running onto my chin, her arm steadying me.

The councilors emerged from the chambers into the open, Mary Stablecamp at the front. From the look on our leaders' faces, I knew that this was it. Mom's eyes blazed bright. I'd seen that look many times. They had come to an unequivocal answer.

Those gathered outside waited.

"We have made our decision," the Speaker said, raising a hand. "After much deliberation, we have decided that the risk is too great, the journey too uncertain for us to take the Foundry's path back to Earth. It speaks of a path yet gives us no details of what that entails, only that we must show we can protect life. The only prudent choice, therefore, is to take the Foundry's kind offering of the resource and infrastructure vessel. With it, we can transform this colony not just into an outpost, but a foothold of humanity. A new Earth. It is our belief that in surviving and thriving, we are fulfilling the mission in our own way. Humanity will live on."

She turned her attention to me, and I stood up, first palming the spit from my chin.

"Milo," she said, "when the Foundry calls again. You know our answer."

I nodded fervently. "The Council has decided, and it will be done."

"Very well."

"We'll need a pilot."

"Indeed. And one willing to make a donation."

"Yes," I said, closing my mechanical right hand into a fist.

"This we will decide later."

The crowd did not cheer at the decision, nor did they grumble. It seemed they needed time to process what had just transpired. I looked for Johan among them but did not see him.

"We're going to be okay," someone finally said, and I turned to see Lance. He was smiling with an almost mad expression like someone whose soul had been bludgeoned with too much change that they were on the brink of snapping. It was an uncharacteristic look for him, so normally composed. "We're going to be okay."

Others from Agriculture and Labor were infected by his sudden joy. They began to pat one another on the back. Then a laugh broke out among them, not one of mockery, but relief. This decision gave us a clear future, and that uncertain tension drawn across our collective hearts was released, an emotional strap cut loose.

"This is going to change everything," James said next.

Councilman Perez gestured up the hill. "I believe we have some celebrating in order. What do we say to an impromptu gathering? That is, if the proprietor of Invictus believes we have enough drink on hand?"

"Have enough?" Perry pumped a fist in the air. "I've been waiting for this moment since I opened the doors. Well, even though it technically has no doors. I've been meaning to add them at some point. Maybe some overheads? What do you guys think?"

"It is decided," Crawford said. "Everyone, bring your best. We will celebrate at nightfall."

The crowd dispersed, and I turned to face Shelly and Karianna. "Do we need to find something nice to wear?" I patted off my jeans and tapped my dust-covered boots together, trying to knock some of the dirt loose.

Shelly pursed her lips and narrowed her eyes at me. "Let's start off with something clean, how about that?"

Throughout the colony music began playing, a random assortment of competing songs and styles. I recognized a few were by Dad's favorite band,

Parallax, who sounded to me like a fusion between country western and bass-heavy EDM. Shelly sang along until I decided to switch on a bit of glitch snap. The energy in the air was palpable. Novae was ready to party, and for the first time since arriving, we had a good reason. We were getting the hell out of this survival game.

With the help of my lovely wife, I found a suitable pair of clean jeans, a long-sleeved shirt with buttons down the front, because that somehow made a shirt dressier, and a clean pair of shoes.

We took a shower together, clearing away the gunk and grime, washing one another with soft washcloths, hot water running down our bare skin, soap bubbles tingling our backs and neck. Each time she touched my sides I shivered, even on my prosthetics. Shelly had seen my naked body before I had given my donation, and she treated me no different now than before. She saw me for me, her love, not a half-human freak.

I stood behind her and ran the soapy cloth down her spine, over her arms, and around her backside. She was beautiful. A picture of grace and wonder. Soft skin. Athletic definition. Natural curves a thing of fine art. A scent so sweet I swore she was made of sugar.

She twisted to look at me, then took hold of my face with her soapy hands and pulled me into a kiss. Before I knew what was going on, she had me pressed against the side of the shower, lips against mine, one hand exploring my body, the other on the wall. I made a move to return the gesture, but she pulled away and chuckled.

"Later," she said, giving me a look both abashed and dead sexy. "Now rinse off and get out. I've got to get ready."

After slipping on my clothes, I waited at the edge of the bed, kicked back, pinging the network to occupy myself until she was done. The list of plant classifications on the boards was growing ever longer, as was the petition to help Perry add garage doors to Invictus. There were discussions about the resource and infrastructure ship, what to do with it first, and how it might be time to make a concerted effort to populate this world shortly after. Every tenth inquiry or so, the network would pause, then I'd have to reload the page I was on. While this might have been merely annoying on a hand terminal, neural implants made it outright headache-inducing. I switched off the feed, giving my head a rest, and spent the rest of the time flipping through my pirate book. The more I read, the more I started to wonder what rum tasted like, and of course, if krakens were real.

What felt like nine hours later, Shelly emerged from the bathroom, appearing like an angel of the night. She had changed into a well-fitted, single-shoulder black dress with an asymmetrical hem that at its highest point was just above the knee, its lowest near the top of the calf, revealing a single leg and ankle boots. She had painted her eyes in green smoke, gathered her long curls and tied them to rest over her bare shoulder, her ears adorned in thin, geometric lines of silver.

I blinked at her, and she grinned in return. My clothes suddenly felt a bit too tight. Especially, well…

She batted her long lashes at me and licked her bright, red lips. "I think I got the desired effect."

Paralysis. Okay. Sure. That must have been the desired effect.

Once she was able to scrape me off the bed and coax the blood back into my legs, or at least the sensation of it in one of them, we left our dome and made for the party, arm in arm. The sky was transitioning from blue and purple into black, stars appearing overhead. On the hill before us, Invictus flashed with color and boomed with the deep thrums of bass kicks in a four-on-the-floor sequence. There were so many people within the wall-less shed that they were pouring out onto the grounds around it. Perry had added flashing lights to the extremities, copper piping, and boiling chambers of the six, massive stills at its center. People gathered at round, metal tables, tiny glasses in hand, chatting, laughing. Many were dancing to the music.

Not a frown was in sight. Novae was electric.

Shelly waved to my parents, to Perry and Alyssa, to Councilor Halifax and a dozen others before drawing me over to the bar.

"What'll it be," Lance asked, tossing a white towel over his shoulder.

"You're bartending tonight?" I asked, my tone a bit dubious. "Isn't that beneath a man of your stature?"

He gave a shrug. "Pride comes before the fall, and you know what? I'm too full of myself to fall."

"Give us a pair of Yellow Rondure," Shelly said, gesturing towards him. "Bug eyes told us that one was safe."

Lance nodded and poured us a couple glasses, but not before pouring one for himself. "So far so good."

I raised mine to Shelly, then to Lance. "To Novae."

"Better days ahead," he said.

"To the future," Shelly added.

The three of us drank.

To my amazement, Perry was right about this batch. I had the sudden sensation that someone had shoved a flaming apple down my throat. Trouble was, it wasn't just the flavor of an apple, but also like swallowing an entire apple all at once. My throat seized shut, and my eyes began to water. Shelly slapped me on the back as I coughed.

"Good shit," Lance said, his voice hoarse.

The lights around us shifted, and among the spectral chaos of Invictus, Karianna appeared, a million flashing multi-color LEDs reflecting off a thigh-length, silver dress. To say her outfit was attention-getting would have been an understatement. The dress she wore was covered in buckles, its chest open with a plunging neckline and tremendous amounts of cleavage on display. She wore knee-high, black boots with heels several inches high, making her nearly as tall as I was. Most interestingly of all, her prosthetics were on display, laid bare, and she didn't mind. Most often, we did our best to cover them up. Not because we were asked, but to make everyone comfortable; long sleeves and long pants, gloves to cover our fingers. Tonight, however, she wore them openly for all to see, both arm and leg, proud donations which had saved her people.

I must have stared for too long because the next thing I knew my shoulder throbbed. When I spun to see what had happened to it, Shelly was scowling at me.

"Want to take a picture?" she asked.

Damn she'd hit hard. I rubbed my throbbing shoulder and shook my head. "Wouldn't dream of it."

"Evening, lovebirds," Karianna said as she approached, then eyed us up and down, a strange expression on her face. "Been a while since we've had a real party around here." Someone caught her attention, and she glanced over our shoulders smiling. "If you'll excuse me."

Shelly and I pivoted to see James looking back at her. He extended his left arm, and she took it with her right, machine against flesh.

"Well, isn't that interesting," Shelly said. "Are they…?"

"I would never presume."

A new song began, its bass deep and thunderous, tones rattling every surface of the sheet metal structure. I found myself nodding my head and humming along to its catchy melody. Shelly began to sway back and forth as she ordered us another round. It was already doing the job. I was getting loose.

Even though we were out in the open at night, with all the lights and sound, the chances of a sawtooth attack were minimal. As a backup, however, Chevelle ordered that a few armed guards stay sober. Donaldson, Nguyen, and Zager patrolled the outside of the bar, their attention focused on the black of night, armed with rifles and light body armor. Sure would be nice if we had some fences so we didn't have to worry about this. Children were due in a few months. We'd need a better solution.

It was no surprise that a small crowd of pretty faces had gathered around Leo, his shirt too tight, all muscles and no buttons. He found an open table and had set up a blank canvas and held a pallet of oil paints. They watched him as he furiously worked, rolling their shoulders and backsides to the boom of bass kicks, a growing collection of empty glasses before them.

To their left, Marissa Martin was engaged in a passionate discussion with a small group. Shelly gestured her head in that direction and handed me a fresh drink. We squeezed into the press of people to join the conversation.

Marissa was a short, petite girl a few subjective years younger than Shelly and I. Her skin was pale, and she had an oval face, green eyes, and hair the color of French-roasted coffee. To see her out, and at this party, was rare. She could be a bit of an introvert, given to days of isolation or time in the wilderness thinking, processing. Working.

"What are you going to call it?" Perry asked her, clutching his tray of multi-colored drinks.

"*Ignes en Caelo*," Marissa said, a finger twisting the ends of her wavy strands. "It means, *Fire of Heaven* in Latin."

"Dramatic," someone commented.

And so did another, "A name that inspires visions."

And another, "It will be a work for the ages!"

"I believe it's important we tell our story," she went on. "We may not be going anywhere, but our great journey should not be lost. It's important that future generations understand the changes that made us into what we are now. It can't be let go. This creative drive. This inspiration. Is it a need for us to play God? Or a means to exert control on the world around us? So much has changed. And yet, beauty is in all things, even suffering. Unless we take ourselves to the brink of experience and perception, we cannot fully appreciate all the Universe has to show us."

"Hang on," Perry said. "You sure you're right about what *Ignes en Caelo* means in Latin? I studied Latin. That doesn't sound right."

She did not respond, but instead looked as if she was staring past the ceiling of the bar into another world.

Dante Vasquez, another artistic member of Culture and Xenology, a man ten years my senior with olive skin, shaggy shoulder-length, black hair, and a scruffy peppered beard, gestured that he wanted to speak, his hand limp in a mildly pedantic way.

"What does it matter if the words are wrong?" he mused. "If this is what it means to her, then it shall be. All things change, even language. We find our happiness when we embrace the metamorphosis, not resist it. The Universe has yet to make us into our final form. We are the ever-changing work in progress."

"Well spoken," Marissa replied.

"Is your symphony complete?" Shelly asked, finding a spot beside Marissa.

"Symphony?" Marissa questioned, but it was for herself, not Shelly.

Why did her confused look make me feel stupid?

"Piano concerto," Marissa said after a moment.

Shelly blinked. "Excuse me?"

"It is a piano concerto I am composing, not a symphony."

"What's the difference?"

Marissa pursed her lips and sighed, as if she were so tired of telling people this simple fact. "In a symphony, there may be solo passages as it were, but the musicians are all in it together. A single piece of music, a whole. Concertos traditionally have three movements, but the rest of the instruments accompany the solo piano. Symphonies have four movements— though there are plenty that have more. And then, let us not forget sonatas, cantatas, operas, and suites."

"I see," Shelly replied, and looked as if she were holding back a laugh. For the life of me I could not figure out why.

"Well, I learned something new today," I mumbled, having no idea what was being talked about. I thought any time an orchestra played music it was a symphony. How could I be born in a veritable society of intellectuals and still have such knowledge gaps? I suppose you can't know everything.

"Do any of you play violin?" Dante asked. "We are short two seats. To be honest, we are short many seats, dozens, but we work with what we have.

Too few humans to make a full ensemble of players. Though I have a plan to deal with that and preserve the fullness of the composition."

Alyssa Robinson snuck up behind Perry and raised her hand. "I took violin for ten years as a child back on Earth. Have any prints that sound like a Stradivarius?"

Marissa smiled at her. "We'll see what we can do."

"Look," Shelly whispered in my ear, and I spun around, seeing that the Jevox had joined our gathering.

The Speaker was walking them through the crowd, offering introductions to everyone they passed. They appeared awkward, unsure what to do with all the lights and sound, and yet, I felt a sense of engaged curiosity. It wasn't what I saw on their faces, those were covered with the breather masks, it was something else. An impression in my head, maybe?

"They look like they're having fun," Shelly said, and I nodded.

"They do."

We mingled for another moment, then made our way around to the other side of Invictus to see Johan tossing back drinks, one after the next. Even with the buzz and rumble of synthesized music, I could hear him carrying on. He was not happy.

As we approached, he turned to me, locking eyes before heading in my direction. My heart leapt up into my throat and I felt for a moment as if I were going to choke on it.

"Tell them to change their decision," he let into me, tapping me on the chest with a finger.

"I can't," I replied, maybe a bit too quick, a bit too hard.

"Then tell the Foundry to change its mind. There has to be a way. It is logical." He took a step to the side and nearly tripped over his own feet. The smell on his breath reminded me of the inside of Perry's stills, not just the product. This was not like him. He could be an ass, sure, but I'd never seen Johan get this drunk and physical.

Before answering, I took a deep breath and tried to will away my buzz. "Johan, that's not how this works. I've told you more than once."

He shook his head vigorously, as if by sheer will he could change circumstance. "*Asseblief*, they're going to all die because we can't take action. Don't you understand? They'll be nothing left for them, for their children. *Dom dwase*." His eyes began to glass over. Holy shit, was he crying?

I leaned in. "Who's going to die? Those still living on Earth? Who?"

"I'll tell you what I see," he said, waving a hand across the entire gathering. "I see a bunch of cowards afraid to do what is right. What they once promised to do at the cost of their youth, their lives. They're afraid to give it all to save the human race. We'd rather consign them to a world with no air, no food, a landscape of crime and war and hate. We were their salvation. We were no' faithful."

"The Foundry was their salvation."

"And it still can be!" He grabbed hold of my lapels. Shelly took a step forward as if she were about to intervene, but I waved her off.

"Are we so sure?" I gently removed his hands from my chest. "I understand how you feel, Johan. I was born to this mission. My parents literally broke federal law to be part of FICSE. None of us could have foreseen what the future held. None of us could have been sure this is what it would have wanted to do with us."

"Why won't it save them?" he asked. "Why won't the Foundry save them?"

"I can't answer that. I have been in the mind of this machine before, but not that deep. It is hard to know what its true intentions are. Johan, I want to save Earth too. I'm just not sure this is the way. We have to consider a few things. What if they're all dead, what if—"

Before I could finish, he shoved me back, knocking me nearly onto my ass, the expression on his face one of distilled rage He drew back a hand, forming it into a fist, and for an instant I thought he was going to throttle me.

He held back.

"Coward," he growled, then stormed off.

Shelly, who was never one to stay out of a fight when the moment was right, had nothing to say. She remained frozen for several seconds, as did a few others standing nearby.

"Shit," I hissed as I bent over, hands on my thighs. "That was not on my list of things I was expecting."

"You okay, love?" Shelly asked, rubbing me on the back.

"I think so. Half of me is relieved, another half is pissed as hell."

"I know we've had a few drinks, but you made a misstep with him."

"What the hell are you talking about?"

Shelly frowned. "You don't know what happened, do you?"

"No. Why would I?"

"Oh, Milo. I guess I really do spend more time around the salty old guy than you. I could use another for this." She took a sip of her drink, blinked furiously as it hit her lips, then swallowed. "Okay, whew. That was not the least bit smooth. Pretty sure it cauterized my entire esophagus." She set the cup aside and waved at Lance, asking for a glass of water. "Alright. The last message Johan received before reaching the Foundry was from his daughters. They wanted to tell him about his new grand kids. Both of them got pregnant around the same time."

"That's good news, right?"

"Yes, and well, he had a challenging relationship with his girls. After his divorce, he threw himself into his work to keep from dealing with the pain. It's how he ended up here. They were both, estranged you could say."

"Oh…"

"Yeah."

"So, you're saying he feels bad leaving them behind?"

"I think so. There's guilt. Lots of it. And, let's be honest, things weren't so hot back home when we left. Maybe he feels not just that he wasn't a good father, but the very thing he failed his family over has also failed him."

I shook my head. "That's a lot to carry on your shoulders."

"No kidding. But we're out here, just doing the best we can to stay alive. To stay sane. I'm sure he just needs some room. He didn't hurt you, did he?"

"No," I said, but it wasn't entirely true. I had been shaken up. Emotions this high made me nervous. People made stupid choices when they were emotional. "I'm fine."

"Good." She kissed me on the lips. "What do you say we go have some more fun."

"Sure. That sounds great."

We let the awkward moment go and rejoined the party, letting ourselves get swept up in the celebration. Events like this had a life of their own.

Thunderous music pounded away, forming a steady, driving tempo which weaved its way through the bodies and hearts of all who were present. To be in the moment, to live life to its fullest, you had but only to surrender yourself to the joyful madness of it all, to its very spirit, to get lost in the rhythm and voice of not just music, but of an overwhelming expression of positive emotion, the rise and fall of ecstasy and surprise. We danced like no one was looking. Loved like we've never been betrayed. Smiled even if someone had hurt us. We lived in this sliver of time, feet where we were, knowing full well that this moment was unique, and precious, and that it would never come again, just another mote of dust on the cosmic wind.

The Speaker showed the Jevox how to two-step, then argued with her brother over music selections. Mom and Dad told stories of the *Vasco Da Gama* to many of the former crew from the *Brilliance*, while Chevelle kept jockeying for Mom's attention. Karianna and James found a corner and locked lips, then got into a fight moments later and went their separate ways. Perez debated economics and law with Halifax, while Clark stood on top of a table and danced.

Tomorrow would need to be a holiday. No one was getting past tonight without a good, long sleep and a few headache pills.

"Be right back," I told Shelly and made off for the bathrooms, which were a set of makeshift boxes at the edge of Invictus's ring of light.

Normally I did not make a mess when taking a piss, but tonight, I could not hit the toilet to save my life, and instead got it all over the walls. I tried my best to clean it up with toilet paper as I laughed the entire time, drunk as shit.

Walking back towards the bar, I spotted a table at the edge of the light with a few people gathered around it. Johan was among them. Curiosity overrode my better judgement, and I snuck up on them by standing behind the bathrooms, getting close enough I could hear.

Rowan and Leo were with Johan, as well as Halifax and Clark.

"*Ag man! Aikona,*" he spat in Afrikaans. "This is a travesty. We're just going to let Earth languish and die while we drink ourselves stupid a thousand light years away."

"I don't like it either, but what can we do about it?" Donaldson asked. "The mission doesn't seem possible at this point."

"I thought you were all about adapt and overcome," Clark interjected. "Isn't that what all military people think?"

"Not in the military anymore, ma'am."

"I'll tell you what we can do about it." Johan struck the table with a closed fist. "We can tell the Council they were wrong. We can take a general vote. I'm not having this. We came to accomplish a mission, and now we're giving it up. *Jislaaik.*"

"They won't listen," Leo said while picking at his nails. "The vote won't go through. Look at this place, Johan, how many frowns do you see? This is a party, bro. It's a veritable picture of unadulterated happiness."

"Makes me sick."

"No, friend," Donaldson said, patting Johan on the back. "I think that's the hooch."

Johan doubled over, hand covering his mouth.

I shook my head and left them alone. It was as Shelly said, he just needed to blow off some steam. Harmless annoyance, emotional processing. I had a feeling the group would be dissatisfied no matter what decision was made. Let them be unhappy. Novae was a democracy, and the people had spoken. We would take the resource and infrastructure ship and turn this untamed world into a new Earth. A better Earth.

When I returned, Shelly took hold of my hands and spun me in circles, smiling all the while. For an instant I thought I'd fall over.

She leaned close and whispered in my ear, "I have an idea."

"Oh?"

"What do you say, let's go home? I think we've had enough for tonight."

I swallowed, catching sight of her hungry eyes.

"Besides," she purred, "this dress is getting a little uncomfortable. Any complaints if I hang it up for the night?"

"No." I ran my mechanical hand through her hair and placed my palm on her cheek while pulling her close, hand on her hip, our bodies touching, noses inches apart. "No complaints here. Not a single one."

PART II

CHAPTER 10

Once Novae had recovered from its collective hangover, the energy of the colony began to shift. With the hope of real assistance from the Foundry, and not just doom and gloom on the horizon, work started getting done at a breakneck pace. Agriculture projects were completed days before schedule, a backup system for the feculent coal generators went online, anti-sawtooth fencing was being erected around a section of habitation domes, and even still, with all these different projects, to Lance's delight, time was somehow found to get the PV arrays started.

Focus had shifted. Intention renewed. Resources were no longer being stolen between Arms, but were being stretched. Not even Johan could argue with the results. Technology and Development was not only able to get more components to upgrade the data network, if not fully, but enough to build a long-range communications array as well, a project led by Johan. This multi-spectrum dish could send and receive signals on both radio and neutrino frequencies anywhere within the 75-DFX system, which was something we sorely needed.

Mom was more than pleased with her Arm's advances.

The next few weeks went by in a blur. I spent much of my time with Karianna scanning the hills near the colony grid by grid in our Swift Shuttles, looking for any signs of valuable resources. We might not yet have the infrastructure ship, but we wanted to do some of the advance work to get it immediately into service as soon as it emerged from the Foundry facility.

With the help of the Jevox, our survey shuttle was put back together better than ever before, their enclave working as a single mind with Perry as their technical guide. It was a wonder to watch, their strange movements coordinated, multi-jointed appendages nimble, each step considered and orderly, quick as lightening. Whereas humans might work well on a single project, we still tended to skip around in our actions, take breaks, get lost in divergent lines of thought or conversation. The Jevox completed their work with majestic precision. When we asked what debt we had incurred for the help, we were told it was not appropriate for them to choose at this time. I just hoped their debts were nothing like that of the Jalek.

I returned one afternoon from a survey mission with Karianna, the two of us walking back into the colony with beef empanadas in hand. Before we were spotted by anyone, we scarfed down the flaky pockets and dusted off our fingers. Didn't want them to feel bad being left out, but we were hungry, and damn it, the Foundry made a good lunch.

At the center of Novae came a swell of concert string music. At first, I thought it came from inside the construction site, Marissa and her—Quartet? Concerto? I didn't know the right term—but her group was practicing. But no, it was a loudspeaker, and from the look of his movements, Leo was today's public radio DJ.

The dusty grounds around the Cultural Center were filled with row after row of saw-horse tables holding molds of some kind, their size close to that of the missing decorative panels outside the main facade. Leo worked with intense alacrity, carving into the molding with a blade the many scenes from our journey. It was remarkable to watch his work unfold as he twisted that tiny sliver of metal around, cutting curves and lines into the mold, cross hatching sections and creating abstract backgrounds, building other parts up with a kind of putty till images began to appear as if out of nowhere. I had offered for him to use the nano machines I recently pulled from the vat, that they could be programmed using 3D models for him to get to an easier end, cutting straight into the concrete slabs without any need for molds. He declined on the grounds of artistic integrity. He argued that it needed to be done by human hands, not just human ingenuity.

There were smiling faces looking off into the sky. Adults with their young children standing in the endless hallways of our former vessels' habitat rings, hands raised in discussion. The torus of the Foundry and a thousand ships of endless configuration emerging from it. Isoptera and Kabosai looming behind a group of hopeful scientists in lab coats. It was all so real, our history rendered into monochrome forms to be made into concrete facades.

"I might think his haircut is stupid," Karianna started. "But one thing I can say—damn he can sculpt."

"Is that the way to a woman's bed?" I asked, raising an eyebrow. "Sculpting?"

She gave a shrug at that. "Well, I'd give him a toss, but that's all it would be. Curiosity more than anything. He's so deep I find him kind of stupid."

"Have you?"

"Have I what?"

"Given him a go."

"Me? No way, man." She straightened her posture and put her hands on her hips, the fingers of her prosthetic gleaming beneath her jacket's sleeve in daylight. "I'm saving myself for someone nice. You know, a good boy. Someone my old man might have been proud of."

I rolled my eyes.

"Milo," a ping came through my implants. It was Shelly. *"Come by the lab, now. I need to talk to you about something private."*

"Your missus calling?" Karianna mused, a smile blossoming on her face.

"How did you…"

She shook her head. "Your face makes a funny look when you get a ping. Couldn't think of anyone else who might want to talk to you."

"I'll have you know plenty of people like talking to me."

"Yeah, yeah." She slapped me on the shoulder. "Check ya later, bruh."

I made my way over to the lab and found the place empty but for Shelly. Perfect. Was this a sneaky lover's call? Were we going to go into the storage room and lock the door for a few minutes? I liked that idea. I mean, if children were anywhere on the horizon, UEI birth control measures or no, we needed to practice.

"Milo!" she said, waving me over. "Come quick."

From her serious expression I could see this was not some clandestine meetup. Something was wrong.

Shelly peered around the lab, then leaned close, her voice low. "I'm still working on the firmware patch. Didn't want to share what I came across on open channels. Safer this way."

"What's wrong?"

"Well," she let out a long breath, "you remember how the last one went, right? The patch."

"Yeah. Something wasn't quite right and somehow it linked the two of us together."

"It did, yes, but that's not all. The Jevox, remember how they acted uncomfortable? Like, they were sick to their stomachs and fidgety."

"I remember."

"There's more to it."

"What are you saying?"

"Look, I'm not sure how, but something in that patch, well, it could tap into the bio-electric network the Jevox use to form their hive mind. Those weird thoughts that came through when we connected, they were theirs."

I blinked at her, not sure what to say. It was true that there had been a flood of strange information that had come through, but I had shrugged it off thinking it to be garbled junk; just raw, encoded data.

She went on, "I had a suspicion that somehow, even though we could not understand their thoughts, that my ideas became a suggestion. I tested it again, basing the strength of those signals on how far away they were from the lab. There's a direct correlation."

"So, you think they're helping us because you had the idea first."

"Yes," she said, her tone confident. "I do. I have a bad feeling that this patch we've created could be used to control the hive mind of the Jevox. Hack it in a way. Even though Ada helped me make it, not even she knows."

"Would they not have natural defenses against such an attack? Wouldn't some other species have figured this out before? Seems like an evolutionary pitfall."

"I don't know. Maybe they just haven't stumbled on it. Half of science is accidental discovery. Milo, this is dangerous. This is wrong. If our little suggestion didn't do it, I'm confident that with enough will and intention behind it, another one would have."

"Then we need to destroy it." I gestured at her terminal. "It's not right for us to have this kind of power over another species."

She let out a sigh of resignation, shoulders deflating. "I had a feeling you would say that, and you're right. Maybe there's just a part of me that doesn't want to let it go. It's a great discovery, dangerous and terrible, but we could learn so much. Maybe find a whole new way for us to think and exist. Bridge the gap with their species even further. If we could work together like them, learn from their example, there's no telling what we could do."

And she was right. The possibilities of working this close together were endless. We could complete projects in days, build fleets of ships to send off into the stars with relative ease. We could raise a powerful, peaceful society upon this world in less than a generation, surpassing so much of what humans had done on Earth over thousands of years. But at what cost?

"I know, I get it, but it's wrong. That kind of power has too much opportunity for abuse. We could make slaves of them. One bad actor could even make slaves of us."

"Okay." She raised her hands and closed her eyes. "I'll delete it."

"Are there backups?"

"No. I've cleared them already, and secure wiped the drives."

The door to the lab swung open, and Johan stepped in, his hands covered in grease.

He gave us a suspicious look, then went over to a set of sinks and began washing his hands. "And just what's going on in here?"

I pursed my lips and did my best to adopt a poker face. "Nothing. Nothing at all."

"Hmm," he grunted and lathered up his hands with soap. "Array is up."

"Good work," Shelly said, her tone shaky. "That will help out a lot."

"Yeah." He shook off his wet fingers and reached for a towel. "If you're gonna shag, kids, you've got a dome for that."

"No shagging," I said, a bit too quick. "Just spending time with my wife before heading off to the next survey. Everyone needs a break."

"Yeah," he said, heading back out, his attention lingering on us. "Everyone needs a break." The door slammed shut behind him.

"Now that wasn't awkward or anything," Shelly hissed. "It was like he knew we were up to something."

I shook my head. "He's not going to be happy you're starting over."

"I'll hide it from him. I'll get started now, pick new frequencies, go through the same steps but switch up some ports. That should keep from giving it the same, well, effect. I think."

"You sure he won't figure it out? And there's not just him, you said Ada helped you with this. Sure you won't spill because you're friends?"

"Look, Milo, don't tell anyone. Not even your parents, okay? We can't let anyone find out. We are the only two who know. Let's keep it that way."

"Okay," I said, taking hold of her hands. "Your secret is safe with me."

"Good."

I gave Shelly a hug and left her to her work. Recreating the patch from scratch was a big job, and I wish I could have helped. While I wasn't a total idiot with programming, this particular machine code and architecture was not my forte. I'd do more harm than good butting into this project.

Instead, I went off to the nano vats and collected Dad along with my recent crop, drawing the tiny machines into a closed metal case and carrying them over to Lance and the PV construction crew, keeping a few extra vials for personal projects. Between us, we'd worked out some prints for them to start on days earlier, a set of multi-spectrum panels these nanoscopic builders would put in place upon a dawn facing slope. The plan had been to use the nano-printers the Foundry had provided, but those had queues busy making network components, which had priority.

Lance thanked me for the nano machines, and I went on my way, heading back towards Shelly and my dome, hungry for dinner. It was getting late in the afternoon, and I felt as if I had been everywhere. As I crossed the center of the colony, Mom and Dad waved me down.

"Looks great, doesn't it?" Dad asked, waving a hand before the Cultural Center under construction. "This place will house the memory of our new people."

I nodded. It was coming along. And something about this felt right.

"We have much to be proud of, *meu lindinho filho*," Mom told me. "So much."

"Mom…" I said, my tone a touch petulant but mostly exasperated. "Geez."

"What? I can't say my beautiful son anymore?" She put her arms around me and squeezed. I felt like I was five all over again.

"We had hoped to open up by Founder's Day," Marissa said, approaching us on the right as she presented our work to the Jevox. "That is a reminder of the day we came here. Almost everything major is done with the Cultural Center, but there's wiring issues all over the place. I suppose we could play in the dark, but it's not quite the same experience. Also, with a smaller ensemble of players, we will need digital enhancements to fill out the sound. Amplification, acoustical chorus, those sorts of things. We've got some big plans."

Marissa and the Jevox walked around the building, running their fingers down the concrete walls, feeling the stones and their crevasses. As I watched them, I reached into a pocket and uncorked a vial of nano-machines, allowing the mercurial substance to flow into one hand. I began sending signals to this liquid from my implants, working it between the palm of my fleshy hand, and my prosthetic, forming tiny metallic shapes, buildings no taller than bottle caps, spinning clocks set to cosmological turns of the wheel, crashing patterns of jagged waves with tiny surfers riding their tubes. I did this action with absent focus, my eyes on the Cultural Center. It was relaxing, and with all that was on my mind I needed a distraction.

Mom and Dad stood at my side, watching. The Jevox were a curious people.

"Hey, Milo," Perry said, sneaking up behind me to whisper in my ear. He peered down at my hands and smiled at the flowing machines. "See the inside yet?"

"No." The machines in my hand flowed to the end of my right index finger where they formed a silver spyglass, sans the lens. I lifted it to my eye. "I tried a few days ago but got kicked out."

With a flick of the wrist, the nano machines flowed back into my pocket, returning themselves to the vial.

"Man… Man… You're going to love it. The lights, the sound."

"Since everything else is going well, anyone have an extra hand?" Mom asked the gathering crowd. "I don't have anyone else to spare at this time, but I might soon. Emilio?"

He shook his head. "My best electrician, Hans, is working on ploughs. Maybe Perry can help? Survey shuttle is done, yes?"

"I'll help, but I could use backup," he said. "You guys know I'm not that young anymore."

"Whatever," Emilio said, appearing on our left before slapping Perry in the stomach with the back of his hand. "You stay young making good times."

The Jevox at the front of the group gestured in an arc. "We enjoyed our work with Mr. Perry."

"Mr.?" Perry cocked his head. "It's Stablecamp, but still. I like the idea of Mr. Makes me sound dignified."

"What are we suggesting?" Marissa asked. "Would you be willing to help again? We do not wish to impose upon the hive."

"What is to impose?" another Jevox asked. "We are here. We are waiting. Besides, we may add this to your debt."

"I don't like where this is going," I mumbled, and Mom nodded.

"Sure would be nice to finish by Founder's Day," Charlotte said, watching Leo for a moment as he poured concrete into his negatives. "We've had enough bad deals for a lifetime. Is this a debt we can pay?"

"Yes," the Jevox said as one, sounding pleased.

Marissa and Charlotte exchanged a look.

"We are again in your debt," Marissa said.

The Jevox turned to us and made an expression. All I could say is that it reminded me of a smile. "Yes, you are."

"And how do we pay this debt?" Mom asked.

They faced the construction. "We wish to experience what it is like to be human. We wish to understand. To know what you see as important. To know how it feels. The pain. The pleasure. The connection. We wish for the experience."

And there it was. *Experience.* That common thread again. And yet, that wasn't all, there was something else. They wanted to know what we see as important.

You must learn what is important.

Just like the Foundry.

Like others I had encountered, the arachnidesque Eipren, and then the immortal Jalek, weren't merely after goods or services, favors to extort us later. They wanted to know our art, our expression, our emotions. They wanted to feel for a moment what it was like to be a human being. And could we even offer that to them? Would they comprehend? How many times had they done this with other species?

"We can't show you everything, but we will give you the next best thing," Marissa said, lowering her head. "Practice for my grand work begins tomorrow now that we are almost complete. Can you stay another seven nights to finish the electrical work on our facility? Our performance must be perfect."

The Jevox at the front gestured with a hand. "We can."

A proud smile, bright as the sun blossomed on Marissa's face. "Then you will be our honored guests."

Our group dispersed and I went home.

Founder's Day fast approached, but with the help of our new friends, work was completed on time. At the setting of the sun three days before our only holiday, a delightful surprise came to us. For the first time, a dense column of photons shot up from the circular structure at the center of Novae, the Cultural Center's core banishing the darkness of this remote world. It was a light of hope in hopeless places. A spotlight of humanity in the void of universal existence. A hand reaching toward the endless Universe declaring that we would never give up.

"It's online," Shelly said, standing beside me in the chill of night just outside our dome. She took hold of my hand and squeezed. "What great adventures lay before us."

I wrapped her up in my arms and held her close, my cheek resting atop her head. "What great adventures."

CHAPTER 11

The big night had come, and Marissa's piano concerto, *Ignes en Caelo*, was set to be performed at the grand opening of the Cultural Center of Novae. Everyone was excited. This was something new. Something real. Something humans had never done before in such a far-flung setting.

Once more, being that it was a big event, Shelly had in her mind for us to wear something nice; not just a jumpsuit, or boots, jeans, and a T-shirt. And this time, I wasn't getting away with just a clean shirt that had buttons, she was forcing me into what I learned some 20th century men referred to as a 'monkey suit'. Looking at myself in the mirror, black pants, white collared shirt and bowtie with a black dress jacket, I felt I looked more like a penguin than a monkey. But who was I to judge a bunch of Boomers? Or were they the Greatest Generation? Millennials? Xennials? Gen Y? Z? Primes? Can't remember. I got the generational categories from back then all mixed up.

A tuxedo might have been the height of high society fashion, but for me, it was a pain to get around in. I felt the whole thing was too tight, too hot, despite it being cool outside, and far too monochrome. Black and white. No color at all. Did it make me look nice? Or did it just homogenize my identity?

Dress code. Uniform. It was all stone bison shit.

My internal arguing ended when Shelly showed me her matching outfit. She had changed into a slender fitting black dress with spaghetti straps that traveled the curves of her body all the way to the ground. On her ears hung diamond studs, and she had pulled her curls up into a tight bun, but for a pair of twisting sprigs which hung to the left and right of her face.

I blinked and went to her, putting my hands on her hips, smiling.

"You look beautiful." I took her face in my hands and kissed her on the lips, then rested my forehead against hers, our noses touching. "I love you, Shelly."

She gave me a sheepish shrug and pulled me close. "I love you too, Milo."

We approached the Cultural Center arm in arm, stiff at first in our fancy clothes, but soon relaxing. When I saw we were not the only ones dressed in this style, I started to get into the mood. I began to embrace the fact that this was an event, not an exercise in torture. It was a pageant, and we all had our parts to play, even if mine was attendee number two hundred and sixty-five.

The massive beacon of light that shone from the middle of our Cultural Center extended into the cloud cover like a pillar holding up the heavens. An irrational part of me wondered if it was powerful enough to call other aliens like the Jevox, but I willed that thought away. We had more than enough ways to be found without a spotlight.

Ushers dressed in black tie outfits led us down a velvet roped path towards the double doors leading inside, allowing us to view the concrete façade Leo had worked so hard to sculpt and pour. The detail was unreal, the faces of so many I personally recognized as part of the many scenes of our history.

Guards patrolled the extremities of the grounds, keeping an eye out for sawtooths. Among those were Rowan Donaldson, who had a particularly intense look tonight, and at his side, Zager and Nguyen, who were relaxed by comparison.

"Good evening, Hughes," James said to us as we approached the main doors. He handed us a small sheet of white paper. I gave it a cursory look, seeing that it outlined tonight's events, words printed in a swirling, black calligraphic script. "Have a good time."

"Thanks, bruh," I said, giving a nod.

Shelly led me inside and the sight sucked the breath right out of me.

The lobby of the Cultural Center was a wonder to behold, a cylindrical room fifty meters across, and at least that high. Its upper extremities were festooned with ivory-colored pillars and Greek molding, twisting curves and patterns rolling into one another. The walls of the lower half were decorated with oil paintings of different sizes, some nearly as tall as I was, others no bigger than a dinner plate. Some depicted photorealistic scenes of our journey, some were abstracts of stars and planets, nebulae and cosmological events, while the rest were mere color, beautiful combinations of wild, chromatic expressions in patterns and flows I would have never thought to dream up.

Laser lights and LEDs illuminated the space, color and shadow playing across the bodies of those gathered. The black-tie crowd was becoming a noisy cluster of conversation as familiar faces filed in behind us. A swell of gentle chamber music filled the air, drawing my attention to a string quartet sitting on a short dais to our left.

Beside the players stood a set of double doors, the word THEATRE above it, the gateway flanked by a set of ushers standing sentinel.

"This is remarkable," Shelly beamed, then pulled me through the crowd and across the room to a painting of the *Brilliance* passing through a ring of fire in a black void. The level of definition and expression conveyed a powerful emotion of pride and triumph, a sort of purity acquired only through trial. "Look, it's Marissa's, according to the frame, but it's not paint. I might be wrong, but I thought she preferred oils."

"It's a canvas print," I said, leaning in to give it a closer inspection. "Must have been one of the ones she lost at the Foundry after the mutiny."

"She really does have a gift, doesn't she?"

"She does. Art is so far beyond me. It can't be a matter of intelligence."

"I think it can, speaking for myself. Maybe, it's just a different kind of intelligence."

Emilio approached us with a silver tray in hand, fluted glasses of something bubbly sitting on top.

"Champagne?" he offered, then corrected himself. "Well, I suppose it is not champagne, if we are technical. It is sparkling wine from pinot grapes. You want?"

Shelly and I gave each other a curious look.

"What does it taste like?" I asked.

"It is wine with bubbles," Emilio offered, leaning in as if it were a conspiracy.

Shelly took two glasses and handed me one. "To good days ahead?"

I raised my glass and clinked it against hers, the crystal ringing.

"Enjoy the evening," he said and headed off into the crowd.

As I took a sip, the flavor that hit my tongue was dry and sweet, bubbles tickling at my nose and lips. The sensation was wonderful. It was new.

Shelly chuckled.

We sipped our flutes of sparkling wine and watched as the Jevox made their way into the room. To our surprise the aliens were not out of dress code.

"Are they wearing tuxes?" Shelly asked.

"Seems so."

While they did look a touch odd with their extra jointed arms, stooped forms and face masks, I had to admit the enclave looked rather fetching in their own monkey suits. They had gone all out, even had on bowties and shiny cufflinks. When offered flutes of champagne they courteously refused. No telling what alcohol would do to them, or sugar for that matter. Had I even seen them eat? What would be safe?

Across the crowd I noticed that Karianna had arrived and was walking a little less than steadily. James had taken a break from his usher duties and was standing close beside her, doing his best to hold her upright. As far as I could tell, no one else seemed to be remotely that tipsy. This was the Cultural Center, not Invictus.

"She drunk?" Shelly whispered in my ear.

"Looks like it."

"More power to her, I guess. Think everything is okay?"

I nodded. "Sure," I said, but I really wasn't. Something did seem to be bothering her. James was with her, though. She'd be fine.

I greeted Mom and Dad, chatting for a minute about what they thought of the new place, how it reminded them of the Lux Theatre back on Earth. Mom and Shelly whispered, then stepped away for a moment, leaving Dad and I alone.

"Never thought we'd make it this far," Dad said, marveling at the gathering. "It means a lot to see us all here now, creating something, not just giving up. That's what humans are good at. That's why machines can never replace us."

"Because of our creativity?" I ventured.

Dad fiddled with his cuffs and leaned to the side, watching as another group of people filed in, his attention lingering a bit too long on the backsides of several beautiful women. "There's something beyond mere intelligence. A collective mind. I've touched it before in my life, and it's when I have the greatest ideas. It's almost as if I am inhabited with a spirit. Some call it a muse. Some say it's God. I don't know what the hell it is. But what I do know is that it's here. It's why we were able to survive."

"Funny, Shelly and I were talking about something close to that just a moment ago."

"Really?" Dad smiled at me. "Good minds think alike."

"Always."

"Oh look, joy, joy," Dad stated, his tone deadpan, "Johan has arrived."

People gathered around Van Niekerk, genuine smiles on their many faces. He was shaking hands with Clark, then Halifax, patting others on the back as he moved through the crowd.

As he headed towards us, I suppressed a sigh.

"Evening, Hughes," he said, extending a hand for Dad.

Dad did not accept it. "You calmed down yet? We ready to see reason?"

"Over what?"

"You know damn well what. Parallax! Parallax is the best electro-country band out there."

"*Asseblief*, this stupid argument again?" Johan let out a long sigh. "We settled this already."

"No, we didn't. Parallax is transcendent. Number one for all time."

"No, they're not. Billie Rayne and the Quad are. *Sunrise Special* kills anything that stupid group of L.A. rejects can write any day of the week."

"Come on, you've got to love, *Winds Over Misty Bay*." Dad threw up his hands. "There's not been a baseline written since that's so good. Pure perfection."

"I can play a better baseline, Hughes."

"But you can't even play bass!"

"Exactly my point." Johan raised a finger. "Parallax is such trash, and I'll tell anyone else the same. Have told everyone just for you."

"There you go again, running around the colony starting shit. Why can't you accept what is given? Even when it's backed up by evidence?"

"I don't have to agree with everything else other people believe. I have clear purpose in my life. I know what's good and what's right. Like that stupid-ass choice our leaders made, conveniently on our behalf."

I blinked at Johan.

Were we still talking about a band? Or had we jumped subjects?

"Conveniently?" Dad blinked at him, mouth agape. "The decision was made. It was right and legal. It's done."

"I am only telling the people what I have observed, and where my priorities have laid since day one."

"You've got to give it up." Dad narrowed his eyes. "The mission is over. FICSE is over. We're staying here. This is home. Look at how beautiful it is becoming! Is this night not a testament to that?"

"No, we're not done. We've got to make a change. We have to reverse the decision. Not all the councilors agree with the vote, even if the heads of Arms do."

I took a step back and tried to science out a way for us to exit this conversation with the least amount of social damage. Things were going downhill faster than I had expected. How in the hell had they managed to get anything done in their Arm with relationships this hostile? I thought we'd made progress, and yet, here we were.

"You've got to see by now," Johan told Dad, his tone insistent. "This is our grand opportunity to save Earth. To make everything right. We are talking about the lives of billions. How can we not try?"

Dad shook his head. "There's no promise of that. The Foundry said there is a path. But what does that even mean? It's cryptic at best. What sort of tests must be taken to see it through?"

People had begun to turn and look at us.

The collar of my shirt felt tight.

"Doesn't matter." He gestured at the room. "To your point, we are humans. We adapt. We overcome. And make no doubt, we've overcome unthinkable odds. What's another journey through the fire? Those who stay behind will find a way to survive. We can have both."

"Lives are at stake, Johan. Our lives."

"Yes! Lives *are* at stake, Hughes. The lives of everyone back on Earth. I think it's that you don't want to be left behind."

Dad shook his head. "Of course I don't want to be left behind. Who the hell would?"

"But what if you could go? Would you still feel this way?"

"Yes. Yes, I would. I'm not leaving anyone behind, including myself."

"You have the answer to our crisis, and yet you would deny them the chance?"

"The ends do not justify the means. You would leave those here at risk for a dream of heroism. This isn't principle. You just want to be a big, damn hero."

Johan's back went straight. He took a step towards Dad, their noses inches apart.

The lights overhead began to blink as Mom and Shelly returned. They gave us a collective look.

"Is everything okay?" Mom asked, crossing her arms.

Johan gave Dad a bit of distance and raised his palms, nodding. "Yes, ma'am. Everything is fine. Your husband and I were just having a spirited chat."

"Jackson does like to chat."

"Gentlemen, it's time we take our seats," Shelly said, and rushed over to take hold of my arm. "Let's go before the show starts."

Johan's lips narrowed into a line as he thought something over. He then gave Dad and I a fierce smile. "That's right. Go before the show starts."

CHAPTER 12

We followed the crowd through the double doors, where an usher directed us to our seats three rows from the front of the dim theatre. Lighting effects, much like in the lobby, danced across the many surfaces of the domed room, drawing pictures and casting shadows upon its ornate architecture. The stage before us remained hidden behind a fifteen-meter-high red curtain with giant tassels tall as I was on either end. I could only imagine that Marissa and the other players were behind this veil, getting ready, tuning their instruments and warming up their fingers.

Dark as it was, it was impossible to see who was sitting more than a few seats away. I nearly tripped over my feet several times. We took our places, settling into a row of velvet textured chairs with seat bottoms that needed flipping down before sitting. They were comfortable enough, but I could not figure out the purpose of their strange mechanism. Why not make a normal chair? I gave up as Shelly reached across the rest, took hold of my upper arm, and laid her head on my shoulder.

Mom and Dad marveled at the space, smiles splitting their faces. It was clear that this had triggered a series of old memories, weird chairs and all. It was familiar to them, even so far removed from Earth.

The lights in the room dimmed further, special effects fading out, and what murmured conversation was being had quieted. A single, metallic chime came from behind the closed curtain, then a swell of strings, their notes discordant and searching, their many tones reaching skyward seeking a center of harmony. Dad began to tap his right foot, leaning forward on his haunches. One of the hidden players broke into an impromptu solo as the others continued their warmup, the vibrations of long bass notes pressing against my chest.

Three taps cut through the air, wood against metal, and the players paused, leaving the theatre silent but for the occasional cough.

My heart pounded in my ears. Everyone held their breath.

With a muffled whoosh the curtains drew back, revealing an ensemble of players, twelve in all, each dressed in black tie outfits, seated in an arc with violins in hand or a cello between their legs. As I understood it, Marissa's ensemble was short by more than half as many players as was typical for this type of music, due to our limited available talent in a colony of about seven hundred. And yet, this was no concern. They'd mic'd the theatre in such a way as to use acoustical effects to overcome most of this. Behind the string section, sat someone with a set of large cymbals and an assortment of small percussion instruments, chimes and wooden blocks. Before them, at the center of it all, a glossy, black grand piano waited, its bench empty.

The ensemble appeared to be floating in a sea of stars, the stage's floor pitch black, the effect amplified by a scintillating array of pinprick lights cast upon the velvet wall behind them.

Emilia Salazar resolved into focus at center stage right, appearing as if out of nowhere, standing upon a box between the piano and the string section, a slender baton held by three fingers raised into the air, her elbows stuck out as if she were about to fly.

The conductor's shoulders rose and fell.

They began to play.

As she moved the baton through the air to the rhythm, striking at invisible marks, a gentle swell of cellos filled the theatre, fragile and hushed, a calming minor chord progression filled with foreboding. The violins began, long notes between sharp, staccato moments that unfolded like the footsteps of children playing in the rain. A cymbal crashed like thunder, and I jerked. Shelly let out a chuckle under her breath.

The music took hold of my imagination. More than just sound, but images.

The world became whimsical, full of hope, violin parts breaking off at will while following a single thread, bedding laid down by the hum of the cellos, individual paths of melodic inquiry diverging and reconverging.

Sublime majors spiraled into something discordant and uncertain like innocence coming to an end. A red spotlight appeared at the back of the stage and washed over us, first one, then two, and more, and more, until the stage was nothing but a wash of bright crimson.

It was warm here. Emotions of smoke and fire thick with each tone.

Destruction.

Waste.

Apathy.

The red lights dimmed, and so did the ensemble, music resigning itself unto death.

Everything was silent for several moments. I wasn't sure what to do. Shelly grabbed my hand and squeezed.

High above the players a singular pink light blossomed, and with it, a sense of hope.

It was the signal. The Foundry.

Sparkling lights showered down from that source onto the players, and were gone, leaving them again in the dark. Leaving them without a prayer.

I leaned forward in my chair, noticing that my left hand had begun to sweat.

Humanity was destined to die.

All was lost.

What were we to do?

Where could we go?

Our species—trapped.

Then a spotlight appeared on the left end of the stage, and within its grace, stood a woman in a red dress. Marissa strode towards the piano and took her place on its bench, that bright light never straying from her.

She drew in a deep breath, as did I, as did all of us.

Her fingertips tickled the ivory keys with such speed I could hardly comprehend, and yet, and yet—it was all so quiet, a gathering whisper, a solo of a distant storm brewing, swirling and amplifying, a sense of permissive discontent, an opening, a willingness to make change in light of extraordinary circumstance.

A crash from a cymbal, and she played louder.

Another crash, and again, she played louder, ever more freedom with emotion, her shoulder and head moving along with her hands as they sprinted up and down the piano. She threw herself into the music as if it were a deep ocean, allowing the currents of the storm above to take hold of her, pull her where they willed.

The wool had not just been pulled away; it had been burned away. Humanity was growing up. We were not taking the end lying down. We had to do something to change our circumstances, or we would face extinction. We had to leave the old ways behind. We had to let *it*, the great and powerful Foundry, help us survive. We needed a way. We needed a path. We had ships to build, an appointment to keep.

We had—the mission.

The ensemble of strings rejoined the movement, not just accompanying Marissa's solo, but transforming the very texture of the air to something sticky like honey, their melodic patterns as complex as damask.

I was back on the *Vasco Da Gama*, leaving Earth behind with the hope of all humanity upon our shoulders, a heavy burden. But there was excitement, revelation, a time of discovery.

My vision blurred.

It was my last day on Earth, just a kid, five years old with no idea what was happening. My knee was skinned up on the launch platform when I tripped. Dad lied to the authorities at the risk of life in prison. All had been left behind, Whispering Pines, *minha avó*, my Aunt Carol and extended family, just a hazy memory, a dream of another life.

The music rose, building into a crescendo, choreographed lights following along in cascades of bright colors and patterns.

One false ending.

I sucked in a breath; hands poised to clap.

A second false ending.

My heart pounded in my chest with anticipation.

A final ending crashed down, and silence fell on the theatre, the movement coming to a close.

Though I wanted to clap, something told me to hold back. That by making noise I might break the spell we were under. I sat on my hands and bit my lip.

Never before had I experienced something quite so personal, quite so intense in such a public setting. I would never forget it as long as I lived. We were human, and we had survived. Our sins had not been enough to destroy us. We had, and have, a chance to change it all. And these visions, these emotions, this moment of catharsis, it had been conjured without speaking a single word. Music was its own kind of spell craft.

I dabbed the moisture from my eyes and turned to Shelly, who had also been crying, and in that moment, I noticed Dad was missing. Something about this did not feel right.

"I'll be back," I whispered to Shelly and Mom.

"Everything okay?" she asked.

"I'm sure it's fine. Dad has run off."

"Oh." She sighed. "Okay, weird. Be careful."

I gave her a funny look, but that response, strange as it was, felt appropriate.

It was far easier to get into our seats than it was to make it back onto the main aisle, especially during the show. I chose the end closer to the exit, squeezing past Mom and apologizing to a half dozen colonists who gave me dirty looks.

The doors to the theatre closed and the rising second movement of Marissa's grand work was reduced to a muted hum.

Dad was nowhere to be seen in the lobby, nor was anyone else. I checked the bathrooms to be sure he'd not taken a pit stop. Those, too, were a wash.

As I exited back to the lobby, however, I heard voices coming from down the hall in a side gallery. Angry voices.

I swallowed and made my way towards them, one cautious step at a time, not sure what the hell I was about to get myself into.

"I don't care what needs to happen," someone said from around the corner. Johan's voice. "*Asseblief,* not only do we need to go back, but we aren't safe. We don't have the tools to protect ourselves."

"Milo and Karianna are more than enough to keep us safe." It was Dad. "They rescued us from odds far worse than we face now."

"You truly do like to keep your head in the sand, don't you Hughes?"

"I don't shy away from hard topics, I never have. Johan, I fully support what the Council decided. You need to as well."

"No. I will not be a follower. I will not give up. We came here doing what was right, and I'm not giving up on that."

"Then don't! But this is not the way. There are better ways."

"If there are, then tell me. Tell me how I can take your son's ship and go back to Earth. Tell me how we can terraform the planet. Stop wars. Bring peace and prosperity to Earth."

"Ask the Jevox to help?" Dad threw his hands up. "Hell, I don't know, Johan! I don't have all the answers! But doing an end run on the councilors to stir shit up in the colony isn't the way to do this."

I chose this moment to enter the gallery and clear my throat.

"Milo," Johan said, his tone gruff. "*Asseblief,* talk some damn sense into your old man."

"Good luck with that." I walked over to Dad and put a hand on his shoulder. "We're missing the show."

"Bah," he said in response, rolling his eyes at me.

Out of nowhere my head began to throb, forcing me to lean forward on my legs to catch my breath. Images were being shoved into my mind, flashes of locations above Novae, trajectories and information, stacks of telemetry data. My stomach flipped end over end and my forehead broke out in a cold sweat.

"Milo!" Proxy shouted in my head. *"Milo, we have an emergency."*

I wobbled on my feet, and Johan stared at me.

Dad took hold of my arm to steady my balance. I raised my prosthetic hand and shook my head.

"What is it, Proxy?" I asked aloud.

"They're back. Your Starfish. They have returned. I do not know how, but they got in under our sensors. There are many of them."

"How many?"

"I can't say. A dozen or more. Their energy signatures are different as well. If I were guessing, I would say that they are powered up and ready for a fight."

"A fight over what?"

"A fight," Johan said, his eyes widening. He took a step back, licking his lips in thought. "*Eish.*"

"Who can say?" Proxy replied in my head.

"ETA?"

"Twenty minutes before they hit the stratosphere."

"I'm on my way. Find Karianna."

"She has been located, though she is not responsive. My counterpart cannot get her to respond either."

"What the hell could she be up to?" I considered waiting for her, but what good would that do? The only place I could make a difference was up there, not down here. "Okay. Okay. You Proxies keep trying. Help or not, I've got to go."

"Hurry, Milo."

I can't say how I could tell, but Proxy's usual monotone sounded worried. And if Proxy was worried, that meant our odds were not good. The starfish had returned in overwhelming force.

"I've got to go," I told Dad. "Sound the alarm, get everyone to safety."

Dad nodded. "I will."

"I knew this would fucking happen," Johan growled. "We're not safe out here. I say, we're not…"

His words faded as I dashed through the exit doors of the Cultural Center, stripping out of my tuxedo jacket to make it easier to run. I had no time for his tired 'I told you so' shit.

Within minutes I dove into my Star Sphere and my Swift Shuttle was screaming into orbit. As I approached the *Fidelis*, I had the opportunity to go through the sensor data. Dozens of the Starfish ships, or Pentaray as the Jevox called them, were headed towards the surface. They had arrayed themselves in wide, pentagonal formations several hundred kilometers between each point, their force forming an interlocking wall crashing down upon us. The precision with which they moved was uncanny, the distance perfect in its symmetry.

My Swift Shuttle docked with the *Fidelis* and I ordered Proxy to bring our weapons online as I drew the Mercurial Integumentum up around me. Could I take them on alone?

I ignited the *Fidelis's* drive and began to burn for a higher orbit, heading towards the oncoming wall of hostiles.

"Universe, protect me," I mumbled.

Behind me came a flash of light as 75-DFX reflected off of the hull of the *Reverie*. It was moving, following me into battle.

"Wouldn't want you to have all the fun," Karianna said over our direct channel.

And she was here. She was here.

I let out a breath and eyed Proxy, who was sitting by my feet, licking one of its paws and cleaning its head.

"You in any condition to fight?" I asked Karianna. "Last I saw, you were stumbling your way through the lobby."

"Relax. Relax. Proxy has my back. I'll sober up quick, man. Do we get to shoot first this time?"

"Yeah," I replied, and my voice hardened. "We sure as hell do."

CHAPTER 13

"Split up," I called to Karianna over our direct channel, "I'll take the left, you take the right."

The Starfish were bearing down on us. They were now less than a hundred thousand kilometers from the surface of the planet. Instinct told me that all it would take is one of them breaking through, and everyone and everything I cared about would be gone, erased, rendered into dust by a fiery blaze of weapons' fire. We could not let that happen.

My body floated within the star field of my virtual environment, Novae receding behind me, a tiny glint of light upon the Prima continent designating the location of the colony on my display. Proxy was helping me track the now seventy Starfish approaching Novae at relative velocities of over a hundred kilometers a second, their ships arrayed in an oppressive wall of force.

Who were they? Where did they come from? What in the hell did they want from us? Were the ships themselves alive, or were they piloted by something inside? These were all questions that did not matter in the face of an immediate threat. Like the sawtooths, it was time to shoot first, ask questions later.

"Copy that, Milo," Karianna replied after a moment, the *Reverie* breaking starboard towards the second half of the pack. *"Let's deploy fighters in formation behind us, make a wall they can't pass."*

"Okay. How many should we deploy?"

"I'm thinking all of them."

"Proxy?"

The cat was sitting in the empty space beside my feet, its toes suspended atop an invisible floor, the curving green and blue of Novae far beneath.

It looked up at me and nodded, its tail flicking from side to side. "I agree with Miss Torlen's assessment."

"How am I going to manage so many? We should have trained fighter pilots."

"The *Fidelis* was built for this, Milo. When the time comes, you must pilot them all, or chances are they will be ineffective. Remember, subjective time does not only involve hyper suspension. You may overclock your mental capacities as well."

"Oh," I said, swallowing. "It's been a while since we've done that, and it wasn't exactly pleasant."

"Indeed. And you've not been in a fight like this since that day. Pleasant or not, I see no way out."

"Okay, Karianna," I said, opening the channel back up. "Let's build a wall with the fighters. We'll keep them in autonomous mode until the threat gets high enough. Then I suppose we'll have to play a really complicated game of chess."

She grunted in reply over the channel.

The Mercurial Integumentum, the protective layer of nanomachines that swirled several dozen meters out from the ship parted for an instant to allow the diamond shaped fighters passage, then returned to its protective position. I flexed my arms and felt the barrier expand and contract, waved a hand to my right and painted open space with a palm, feeling them track with my motion, then return. So long as my reflexes were quick, these tiny machines would protect me from almost anything.

"Contact in two," Proxy reported, and I could see the wall of Starfish closing. "Para Lux array, armed. Rail cannons, armed. Antimatter cannons, armed."

Our fighters took position several hundred kilometers above the surface of the planet in a line, weapons facing out. They were set.

"Contact in one."

"Are we ready for this?" I asked Proxy.

"If we aren't," it said. "It's too late anyway."

"In range!" Karianna shouted over the channel. *"Light 'em up."*

She shot first, giving the hostiles an opening salvo of antimatter slugs, the space above Novae flashing white. Radiation alarms screamed as particles washed over the MI. A series of explosions as hot as stars came next, each ten thousand kilometers across, vaporizing entire sections of the Starfish formation.

In response, the Starfish widened the distance between the nodes in their formation to keep from being taken out like this again. The enemy powered up, their ships from center to tip turning from orange to blue. Next thing I knew, dozens of locations along the MI had reached critical temperatures.

"Ultraviolet weapons," Proxy reported. "Keep the MI swirling and it will help prevent them from ablating our defense too quickly."

"Roger that. Karianna?"

"Yeah. Yeah. My Proxy told me too."

Both the *Fidelis* and *Reverie* crashed into the enemy forces, the space above our world becoming chaos. The formations of the enemy broke into smaller squadrons, still maintaining their pentagonal shape, but were now five to a group instead of twenty-five. As close as they were now, I was unable to use the antimatter slugs, so I lashed out at them with the Para Lux array, cutting lines of fiery light through their ranks, slicing several in half as if I were using a razor-sharp cleaver.

Our battle became a dazzling light show, their hulls flashing blue each time they fired, my body glittering with refracted prismatic light. When the Starfish went down, they did not explode as much as went dark, leaving trails of rapidly dispersing fluids and gas in their wake.

My right flank began to burn as a section of the MI broke momentarily and several shots from the Starfish made it through. I reached out a palm, smoothing it over the affected area, soothing the pain, then returned fire on the offenders. The injury felt like a bad friction burn, the kind you might get from skidding on concrete, the first layer of skin peeled off and left behind.

"There's just so many," Karianna said. The *Reverie's* diamond form flashed beneath her MI, several shots making it through. *"It's like no matter how many I break more come in."*

"I'm seeing the same thing."

"Milo!" Proxy shouted in alarm. "Two squadrons are breaking for the surface."

"Shit. Shit." I unleashed another volley of energy from the Para Lux array and sliced one of the arms off a Starfish, damaging but not destroying it. My shoulder burned white hot. I hissed through the pain of the tactile feedback.

Was this what it was like to be branded with a hot iron? These UV weapons were no joke. "Karianna, time to be in two places at once."

"Good times. Bring it on."

"Linking our subjective time references. It will be easier to coordinate."

"Alright. You think Shelly will be okay with us coupling our systems together?"

"This isn't the time to worry about that."

"Whatever."

An instant later I felt a solid connection to Karianna and her ship. If she were to slow her subjective reference of time, mine would be slowed in sync, and so would hers for me.

The MI around the *Fidelis* heated up again, and I rotated the swarm one hundred and eighty degrees, replacing some of the overheated bots with cold ones from storage.

Explosions surrounded us both as the Starfish began using something else. Thousands of tiny bombs were launched from pores along the front surface of their ships, pelting against the surface of the MI and disrupting its coverage. It was becoming a challenge to create enough nano-bots to replace those being sloughed away in the time we were given.

"Squads are closing in on our defensive line," Proxy reported.

"Let's do it," I said, then reached forward and swept back my arms, triggering an increase in our brain processes to shift our perception of time to that of a slower frame of reference.

Targets slowed as if suddenly forced to pass through a viscous medium, then came to a halt.

Foundry made ships were fascinating, not just in their ability to travel long distances, make a spectacular dinner, or to fight in great battles. One of their most powerful functions was that of adjusting subjective time reference. When traveling great distances, our bodies could be placed in hyper suspension, making years pass by in seconds. Conversely, when in a situation such as this, the opposite could be achieved. It was possible to overclock your cerebral functions for a time, allowing you to perceive more in each moment than you could naturally. This in turn slowed your perception of time, allowing you to make lightning-fast decisions, such as manually piloting twenty-one fighters by yourself. This ability, however, came with a cost. All energy spent had to go somewhere, and this particular variety was exothermic. If we spent too long in this state, our brains would cook inside of our skulls.

The battle was at a standstill, explosions paused, Starfish hanging in open space like models dangling from wires. Novae had stopped spinning, storms upon the surface no longer swirling. Stars did not twinkle. Data streams from a thousand sources remained unchanged. It was as if the Universe had taken a deep breath.

Time had frozen.

Orbiting above the surface of Novae, our fighters awaited our signals.

"Let's get to work," Karianna said, *"we can't stay like this forever."*

I flowed between different views within my virtual environment, one moment sitting within a fighter, then another fighter, and another, the next, looking at a top-down view of the entire battle. Between the two of us we had forty-two fighters at our disposal, and so we broke them off into squadrons, assigning targets to the much larger enemy ships. Once we were satisfied with the assignments, we began to advance in time, taking steps of several seconds, watching the battle unfold like a jerky, stop-motion video.

Our fighters converged on the attackers and began to fire, nuclear sabot rounds pelting the surface of the Starfish. They responded in kind, releasing both ultra-violet beam weapons and more scatter bombs. Ten of our fighters were lost within seconds.

"We need to try a new strategy," Karianna said, and her fighters broke away. *"Bunching them up isn't going to help. We need overwhelming force, sure, but our fighters are easy prey."*

"Can we get behind the enemy?" I suggested. "Those beam weapons of theirs seem to only fire forward."

"Good idea." She pinged a shared image of the battlefield over to my virtual environment for us to analyze more clearly. *"If we move the second and third squadrons here, we can bring the first and fifth around."*

"Milo," Proxy reported. "You must resume standard time reference soon. You cannot stay in this state forever. The Star Sphere is cooling your brain to help counteract, but the temperature is reaching critical levels. It will cause brain damage."

"Noted."

Karianna and I jumped ahead several more moves, our dogfight feeling very much like a turn-based video game. We managed to work around the aft end of several Starfish and took them down, firing at their fusion drives, making them go critical. Our strategic advantage, however, was tenuous at best. They took out several more of our fighters, leaving twenty between us.

With our attention on the battle over the surface, we had nearly forgotten the ships crashing on top of us. The swarm of Starfish engulfing our battleships renewed their efforts. Subjective shift or not, time marched on, and it hurt. They had begun focusing their attacks on single locations, punching holes in our MI barriers and cutting into the hull of our ships. I was reminded of how my encounter with the Frendol could have gone, my torso and arms sliced apart by hot, sharp blades. Moisture gathered at the corners of my eyes as I tried to attenuate the signal, but for some reason the Foundry wanted me to experience this pain in full. I was the ship; the ship was me. This was how it was supposed to be.

I powered up my rail cannons and speared two of the Starfish. This was nowhere near enough to turn the tide as another dozen were still on me.

Warnings went off in my head. My brain was reaching critical heat levels. I could not keep this up any longer.

"Breaking the link," I told Karianna.

"No. Just another moment. We've almost got them."

"Being a vegetable is not going to save our friends."

The link snapped, and time sling-shotted back to full speed. Starfish swarmed us; weapons fire overwhelming in its pace given what we had just experienced. The fighters felt impossible to manage at this speed, even though many had been destroyed, leaving us far fewer to manage.

A single Starfish had broken past the line of fighters and was heading towards the Prima continent. My heart leapt into my throat. I didn't need my imagination to know what came next.

"Help!" Karianna pleaded over the channel. *"My MI is almost down. I can't stop them. Milo, I need help."*

Was she really calling for help or had I hit my head? Karianna Torlen calling for help…

I wasn't sure what to do. Too much was happening at the same time. My own body, ship, whatever, was being torn apart one piece at a time by enemy fire. There were too many fighters to manage. A Starfish was breaking through our line, and now, Karianna called for help. A choice had to be made, but what was the right one?

"Agh," I growled under my breath, pressing palms against my face. "I won't leave you behind. But there's something I have to do first. Just hold on."

The *Fidelis* rotated towards Novae and began to burn, trailing a swarm of enemies with it, my MI becoming ever spottier in its protection.

"I can't do it, Milo," she said, and for the first time ever I didn't think this was drama. She was earnest in her fears.

"If I can just take out this one ship," I said, powering up my rail cannons.

"The *Reverie* is critical," Proxy reported. "I recommend we offer Karianna support."

"Just one moment," I groaned. "Almost got it."

"Milo, she might not have a moment."

"Power—failing," she said. *"Oh, shit. Oh, shit. My MI is down. It hurts. It hurts so bad. God, it hurts. I'm open. Ah—I'm wide open."*

I narrowed my eyes at the distant target, taking a deep breath as I aimed the kinetic weapon. All I needed to do was get just a little closer. At this angle, the projectile would pierce the Starfish's hull and land hundreds of miles away from the colony in the northeast mountains. But if I waited too long, I'd be unable to shoot for fear of destroying Novae as well.

"Take this, bastard," I said, firing at the Starfish. The shot from the rail cannon cut through the atmosphere of Novae, leaving a line of orange fire in its wake. It landed three hundred miles east of the colony, and a flash of white light appeared as thousands of acres of lush, green foliage up in the mountains were vaporized, its kinetic energy having converted into heat.

The shot had gone wide. I had missed.

Chasing down the Starfish in the *Fidelis* was not possible. Not only was it too far away to make a difference before reaching the colony, but I couldn't enter the atmosphere in a vessel this large. I'd be reduced to a hunk of burning metal just from the friction of aero braking.

What options did that leave? The fighters? I had seven left, and they were occupied. Novae had no ground-based defenses. I had failed. I let one through.

But there were so many.

So many.

From the surface of Novae came a flash. A drive signature appeared at the edge of my perception. A cone-shaped ship strapped with five curved wings and five cylindrical engines roared away from the north platform of the colony, heading to intercept the Starfish. It burned through the atmosphere at breakneck speeds, closing the distance in seconds.

The body of the craft began to glow in various lines along its hull, and then an array of infrared light lanced out from it, slicing the offending ship in two. The smoking hulk of the Starfish fell towards the surface, tumbling down towards the mountains.

Our new arrival burned towards a higher orbit to offer support.

"The Jevox saved the colony," Proxy reported. "What a debt we have incurred."

"Thank the Universe."

"Thank the Universe," Proxy echoed, its tone almost an exhalation.

At this new arrival, the Starfish began to break ranks and scatter in random directions, all of which were away from Novae. It only took a few moments, and the battlefield went quiet. It was over.

We did not give chase.

"Karianna," I called over our channel. "Are you out there? Call back. Please, please tell me you're okay."

Several moments passed with no response. I spun the *Fidelis* around and moved towards her, recalling my fighters as I came closer, or at least what was left of them. The *Reverie* was in bad shape, several sections of its gold and black hull missing, fires raging within.

"Karianna?" I asked, then turned to Proxy. "We have to go over and check on her."

"No need," she finally said. *"I'm fucking alive. No thanks to you."*

"No thanks to me?"

"I called for help, and you didn't come." This tone was not something I was used to. It was wounded, hurt. Did she take my action as a betrayal? *"Why didn't you come? I almost died up here."*

"There was no other way. I had to protect the colony."

"Well, we see how that worked out. The Jevox pulled our asses out of the fire again."

"I'm sorry, Karianna. I didn't—"

"Don't bother. Maybe my ship can fix itself sometime this year."

The channel went dead. I felt cold. It had only been my intention to keep everyone safe, not to leave her high and dry. What could I have done better? What options had I had?

"Proxy," I said. "Is there anything we can do to help her get up and running quicker?"

It nodded. "You may loan some of the *Fidelis's* nano-bots. Assuming that the Starfish do not return anytime soon, a third of your stores will get the *Reverie* back up within two weeks."

"Do it. Maybe she'll accept this as an apology."

Proxy cocked its head at me and blinked. "For some reason, Milo, I doubt that very much."

"Yeah," I groaned. "I kind of doubt that too."

CHAPTER 14

When our Swift Shuttles landed, a crowd was already gathered and waiting to greet us in the dark. Karianna must have hauled ass climbing out of her Star Sphere, as I hardly had the time to jump down and run for the door, dressed in only my underclothes, before she was already headed off into the colony.

"Karianna!" I shouted as she pressed through the crowd and crested the edge of the hill disappearing into the night. "Where are you going?"

She did not respond, did not turn around.

Shelly ran over and threw her arms around me. Her black dress becoming damp with the water still dripping from my hair and on my skin.

"We caught some of what happened with the new communication arrays," she began. "Not everything, but the chatter. There was so much going on. What happened up there?"

"A flood of angry Starfish is what happened." I stared off into the black, then looked to the crowd. Several of Chevelle's team patrolled the area, weapons in hand. "Shelly, we were outnumbered thirty or forty to one. If not for the Jevox helping at the last moment, I... I don't know."

"Thirty or forty to one?" she let out a long breath. "Why were they here? What do they want?"

"We still don't know. They didn't communicate with us. All I can assume is that the Jevox's assessment is true. Why they would think crystallized oxygen is here, I have no idea."

"I'm glad you're alive."

"Yeah, me too."

"Let's get you dried off and dressed. As you can imagine, the Council wants to gather." She took the towel from my hand and threw it around my cold, wet shoulders, my arms covered in goosebumps. "Is Karianna okay?"

"I don't know."

"Did something happen up there to her?"

"A lot of something happened."

I dried off and slipped into a backup set of clothes stowed on the Swift Shuttle, then headed off with Shelly to the Council Chambers. Dawn was several hours away, but from what I could tell, everyone was awake. As we filed into the chambers, I had Proxy keep a close eye on the skies over Novae for more hostiles. Scans showed the remainder of their ranks were piling on velocity toward the system's furthest reaches. Novae was in no danger… for now.

As Shelly and I entered, I was greeted with cheers and harrumphs, claps and congratulations. Almost everyone assembled was dressed like her, still in their black-tie clothes from the event earlier that night. What a strange dichotomy.

This short-lived fight had been one of my most terrifying yet. The amount of stress the odds had placed upon us was familiar, sure, but something I thought we were past. Novae was in a remote location and far as we knew it was safe here. There was no species we knew of living or active in this region of space that might pick on a fledgling colony like ours. I needed to do something to repair the damage between Karianna and I. If the Starfish came back in force, and we weren't working together, it might be our end.

The Jevox waited by the front of the room and so I made my way over to them, weaving between the press of elated colonists. When I was within a couple of paces, their five heads swiveled towards me as if they were connected to a single mechanism.

I raised my right hand, emulating what I had seen the Speaker do when they arrived. "Thank you for your help. If not for you, we would be dead."

"It is a good practice," the one on the left said, raising a five fingered hand, "to protect others."

"Besides," the center Jevox cut in, "for a time, part of the hive lives here, too."

"We protect life," I muttered.

They looked to one another and made an open-handed gesture as a group. I wasn't totally sure what it meant, but it felt like agreement.

I scanned the crowd for Karianna but couldn't find her. Where had she gone after we landed?

Proxy sent me a ping to notify me that the exchange of nano-machines was complete. They would get to work repairing the *Reverie's* broken systems, and it should now take less than three weeks. A relief.

The crowd quieted and took their seats as the Speaker entered the room along with the Council, taking their places upon the dais. Mary banged her gavel, and the few people who hadn't been paying attention sat.

"Thank you everyone for coming," the Speaker began. "We have had no opportunity to debrief our situation, but in the interest of transparency we will do so with the majority of the colony present. At 19:47 hours Novae time, hostile signatures were detected by our Foundry pilots and the alarm was raised during the opening event of the Cultural Center. At that point our pilots made for orbit to intercept this imminent threat. Beyond that, we have little information other than what the Jevox have provided so far. There were dozens of Pentaray headed for the surface, and with presumably violent intent, given their force. While we now have limited ground-based communications and long-range scanning active, the colony could see very little of this conflict other than flashes of light in the night sky. Milo, would you care to give us more information? Where is Karianna?"

"I'm here," she said, leaned against the wall in the back of the room, a single hand raised.

"Glad you're both safe."

I stood and waved at Karianna. "Do you want to address the room? Or do you want me to?"

"What the hell does it matter?" Karianna asked no one in particular. She kept her head down, dark hair covering her face, gaze focused on her boots, breathing slow and ragged, the bracelets on her right wrist jingling. There was no doubt she was shaken up.

"Fine," I said, hardening my jaw. "During Marissa's presentation of *Ignes en Caelo*, Proxy informed me that the Starfish had returned. How they had made it past Foundry detection is beyond even Proxy, but they were here. I immediately made for my Swift Shuttle and met them head on in the *Fidelis*. Unlike the first time, when we only saw five, this time, seventy were burning towards Novae. They formed a great wall with their weapons armed and ready to go.

"Shortly after I arrived, Karianna came in behind me. We split up and focused each on half of the hostile force, attempting to blockade, leaving fighters behind to catch any that made it past our weapons. While most of the force did engage with us, some slipped through and were caught by our fighters. During that time—"

"During that time, I almost died," Karianna said, curling her legs up against herself on the bench. "I called for help. It did not come."

Clark's eyebrows raised. She looked between Karianna and I, then sniffed.

"And…" I went on, lowering my voice and focusing my attention on the Speaker so as not to be distracted. "At the same moment that we were both fighting those directly over Novae, and controlling all of our fighters, as well as our ships, Karianna fell into distress. I moved to protect her, but a single Starfish broke through the line and headed towards the colony."

"*Wag 'n bietjie, asseblief*," Johan said in Afrikaans, standing to address the Council. "This is the ship the Jevox fired on. The one you were unable to catch in time."

I gaped at him, my jaw going slack. Could he not just let me finish before being an ass? "Did you miss the part where seventy of these ships came to see us? Seven. Zero. I went after that ship, fast as I could, but the *Fidelis* does not turn on a dime."

"And you left me behind," Karianna mumbled.

"What other option did I have?" I ran my hands through my hair and sighed. "I was coming back."

"You were under attack on all sides by an overwhelming force," Councilmen Perez started, "and you put your team member at risk to protect the colony against an imminent threat?"

"I didn't know what else to do."

My left hand began to sweat. What did they expect of me? Was my judgement being called into question? I had had very little options in the moment. I had not wanted to risk my teammate, no, but the colony was more than just her. And my family…

Councilwoman Crawford raised a hand. "No offense to our guests, but if we had kept in open communication, we would have known you were willing to intercede. Would this have shaped your decision, Milo?"

"Of course it would. I'd have had the freedom to support my teammate."

"Did you say seventy?" Halifax asked.

"I did."

"What are we to do against such overwhelming force?" He began scribbling something out on his tablet. "What if they come back and it's a hundred, a thousand? We must understand the 'why.'"

"It is clear Novae isn't safe," Johan stated as if he were just another councilor. He needed to sit his ass down or I was going to hop over these damned benches and throttle him, elder or not. "We've got to do something about that."

"What are you saying, Van Niekerk?" the Speaker asked. "I feel you have a point other than just talking out of turn."

"I do." He took a breath and straightened his back, then turned to face the room. People whispered between one another. "It's clear we don't have enough defense to keep this colony secure. Resource challenges or not, Earth, the mission, or not, we can't pass up this opportunity to bolster our position and protect what we have built. As much as I hate the opinion some have voiced, we might be the only humans left. It is for this we must defend the valley, this planet."

"Are you saying we should tell the Foundry we wish to have the warship?" Clark suggested as she leaned in, elbows resting on her podium, hands clasped.

Johan gave a resigned sigh which felt a touch too dramatic. "I am. While I was starting to come around to the prospect of having access to a ship that could help us build infrastructure, I do not believe now is the time."

"Defense is your concern?" I interjected; eyes narrowed. "We can fix that without another ship. Karianna and I have previously mentioned that we need fighter pilots. Having three or four people per ship to man the drone wings would multiply our combat effectiveness tenfold."

The councilors looked to Karianna who shrugged in a dismissive way.

"Would this help?" Perez asked.

"It would," she replied. "Our Proxies are smart, but not as intuitive as we are at piloting the fighters."

"I agree that it would help," the Speaker echoed. "Given my personal experience in transit, it would require months of training. We had years before us, but here, we do not. I have discussed this before with other previous pilots, Lance Brittan and James Reed, as well as my brother, but they have expressed no desire to follow that path again."

"This training would take people away from valuable projects," Halifax mused. "We can ill afford that. Eight people?" He clicked his tongue against his teeth three times. "Would it be enough to keep an incident like what we just had from happening?"

"I can't say," Karianna replied. "Even our fighters were having trouble taking down the Starfish."

Clark pinched the bridge of her nose. "I see no other path, then. We must consider changing our decision if there is still time."

"No," I said, balling my hands into fists. "We can't do that. This attack was terrifying, yes, but…"

"The Jevox won't be here much longer to tip the balance in our favor," Johan said. "We thank the hive for their assistance, but it can't last. We understand you must move on. If not for you, Novae might have been reduced to fire and glass."

The aliens gave each other a look, then gazed around the crowded room of humans. The one closest to me spoke, "We regret this fact, but cannot be a permanent force anywhere but within the hive's territory."

"We can't give up on the resource ship," I pleaded. "There's no telling how long, if ever, that the Foundry will offer us another. This could be our last opportunity to turn it all around. Don't forget, it said that phrase several times, *'You must learn what is important'*."

"Come now, Hughes, defense is important," Clark said. "You cannot build a colony if it is destroyed. Besides, it is a smaller ship, yes? It should have functions much like your Swift Shuttles. We can use it to help grow the colony, if not explicitly for refining and resources."

Murmurs had broken out around the room. People were nervous, afraid. No one wanted to die. No one wanted their future children to be without a home. Fear was coalescing into something physical. This was not at all going how I had foreseen. I had expected a debrief, a recounting of what had happened, but not a challenge to the decision already voted on and certified.

"I'm not sure about this," Perez said. "We need both."

"And isn't that the point?" Councilwoman L'Agnese asked. "It is as Milo said, *'You must learn what is important'*. Growth, or protection? Survival, or control?"

Clark pursed her lips. "We should vote again. And not just councilors or heads of Arms, but all gathered."

"Are you sure?" The Speaker leaned in her direction; her expression crestfallen. "By our laws, once this decision is passed, there is no going back. No going back."

"Vote," Halifax said, his voice not much more than a whisper.

Perez, L'Agnese, and Crawford did not object.

Shelly looked up at me, and I shook my head, my mouth open. I couldn't believe what we were seeing. Were they really doing this? Were they seriously calling a vote on the floor? There was no way to tell how this would fall. I knew we were supposed to be democratic, but something didn't feel right.

"Okay then," the Speaker said, taking hold of her tablet. "I am activating our recording devices and opening a session on our network. All in favor of petitioning the Foundry for a warship to act in defense instead of the resource and infrastructure ship, please stand and place your right thumb upon your hand terminal marking red to overturn our previous decision. All others, take a seat."

While I myself sat, others began to stand. They would not get my support in this madness.

"I stand in favor," Harper said, raising her hand terminal above her head, pressing down on it with her thumb, its display flashing red. She turned to Johan and narrowed her eyes at him. Her husband George, who did not stand, looked distressed. Johan did not acknowledge her.

Rowan Donaldson was next. "As do I." His hand terminal went red.

Just as he finished, Jaxson Zager came next, then Leo Nelson. Others followed in rapid succession, adding to their vote, favor shifting towards this decision like dominos in a line. The soft glow of red lights from hand terminals began to flood the room.

Mom and Dad looked to me across the crowd, shaking their heads in dismay. Fear was driving this. Fear that without this additional weapon we would not survive.

You must learn what is important.

We were failing the test. Failing.

I caught a glimpse of Perry, whose mouth was left gaping as his other half, Alyssa, stood in favor, pressing her thumb to her hand terminal.

At the center of it all, Johan smiled, a look of triumph accentuating the age lines around his eyes and mouth.

"Councilors?" the Speaker asked, her tone careful. "What say you?"

"I vote in favor," Clark said, licking her lips. "The warship."

Halifax nodded. "Warship."

Perez shook his head vigorously. "This is a bad decision. We are being watched. Our choices measured. I vote against."

"Same for me," L'Agnese spat. "Against. Fear is what led us here to begin with."

That left only Crawford. She crossed her arms and looked toward the ceiling for several moments. At this point, her vote wouldn't mean much either way, but she had something to say and was collecting her thoughts.

"I was born of a country where a pluralistic democracy was important, or at least the appearance of it," she began, her tone measured, hands resting on her podium. "Here on Novae, I feel we have a real opportunity to be an egalitarian society. We are equals in so many ways, and with that also comes our right to decide. If called for a general vote, we said that majority rule would be observed.

"I wish for it to go on record that I do not agree with the majority this time. I am with Perez. The Foundry is trying to teach us something. This is not the answer to the lesson. However, I believe in the society we are building and will cast my vote even though it makes no difference on the outcome. I am against acquiring the warship."

A silence fell over the hall. The Speaker waited patiently for everyone to have the opportunity to vote.

"Is this your final choice?" she asked, eyeing those gathered with an intensity I had never seen. Was this anger? "Once we make this decision, there is no going back."

"We made the choice!" Harper shouted, face turning red. "Do your job! Ratify it."

My stomach began to churn. Shelly reached for my hand and squeezed. She was feeling it too.

"Fine," the Speaker said, and turned her attention to her tablet. "By the power of Novae's duly elected ruling council, the vote to overturn our decision has passed. In the interest of defending the colony, when the time comes, we will request of the Foundry a warship rather than the resource and infrastructure ship. Do the counselors certify this?"

As one they agreed, some more reluctant than others.

"Then we are adjourned. Clean up. Everyone, get some rest. It's been a long night. Our next meeting will be to decide who the pilot of this new craft will be. Who will make their donation."

The hall cleared out, and I stayed behind, waiting for an opportunity to talk to the Speaker. She was tied up with the other councilors, working out the details of the vote, but she would not leave before talking to me. Shelly had had enough of this and left with my parents, assuring me that she'd meet me at home. As for Karianna? She'd evaporated.

As I waited, Lance decided to join me, a frown on his face.

"This is bullshit," he whispered just loud enough I could hear. "Why do I feel like we just got played?"

I nodded. "Because we did."

"I swear this Johan club has been working tirelessly to get others on their side ever since you went to meet with the Foundry. I get we're a democracy and all, but shit, if this gets us killed, I swear I'm haunting every last one of those mother fuckers."

The councilors came to some sort of agreement and began to disperse, gathering their things to head out. I patted Lance on the shoulder and moved to intercept the Speaker as she left.

"Milo," she said as I approached. "Are you okay?" She put her hands on my shoulders and looked me over, then gently turned my face by the chin looking for injuries.

"Physically?" I waved her hands away. "Yes, I'm fine."

"But that's not what this is about."

"No. It's not."

"The vote."

"Why couldn't you stop it?"

She paused before answering, looking off to the side as if words might be waiting for her there. Hell, with our implants they just might be.

"Look, Milo, this is the system of government we chose, and we chose it as a group. I don't get to reverse that just because I don't agree with a vote. We are a democracy, not a dictatorship."

"But you could have done something, right?" I stepped closer, trying not to let those few still gathered overhear. "This decision can't stand. Can it?"

"It is final, Milo. There's nothing to be done."

"You know we'll pay for this. I don't know how. But we'll pay for it. Would Esteban have stood for this? What would he think?"

Her lips became a hard line. For a moment I thought I might have wounded her, but then she nodded. "We will pay for it. I don't know what will happen, but I know we're all going to need you. Are you going to give up? Are you going to quit? You know he wouldn't let you."

"No." I swallowed. "No, I won't. There's a reason we named our ship the *Fidelis*. I aim to keep it that way. For his memory, and our survival."

"Because we're faithful."

"That's right. Because we're faithful."

CHAPTER 15

There I was again in that strange place, both a dream and not. This time, however, I was within a sort of structure, not outside and exposed to a naked black hole. Despite my best efforts, I knew that memory of this place would flee as soon as I woke, nothing left to explore, to inspect. And yet, while I was here, I remembered it all so clearly.

Why did I keep coming back?

What did it all mean?

I stood beside a window twice my height, peering down at a supermassive blackhole devouring all that crossed its event horizon. Even without a calculator, I could see that this anomaly was too close to be possible. There was no way the math worked out. How was I not being pulled in along with everything else, my body bisected again and again as the bottom half moved swifter than the top, cellular bonds snapping through spaghettification. But here I was, and there was no pain, no sensation that gravity was any different by my feet than on my head. It was as if the physics of this black hole didn't apply to me or this place.

Footsteps clicked behind me, and I spun around, taking in a small room not much bigger than the dome I shared with Shelly. The details of this space were blurry, hard to make out, as if looking at the world through a lens covered in a layer of petroleum jelly. There were tables, I thought, maybe chairs. Instruments sat upon them. Tools maybe? Shit. They could be boxes of cereal for all I could tell. This must be how it felt to need bifocals and then lose them. I was blind as a bat, unable to focus on anything for more than an instant, and the harder I tried, the more a dull headache creeped in.

In the direction the footsteps had come, a form appeared, black and lumbering, its details gaussian. I closed my eyes and blinked, trying to force myself to focus, but nothing came. It held something in its hands, its arms, its tentacles, I couldn't tell what they were. But whatever the object was, I knew it was important. It was everything.

"You must protect life," a voice stated inside my head. Was it the *it* coming towards me who had spoken, or something else, someone else? *"You must decide what is important."*

"How do we know?" I asked, attempting to take a step forward, but my feet did not move, could not move. They were rooted in place as if I had on magnetic boots. "How can we tell?"

The *it* stopped. *"I recognize you,"* the voice in my head said. *"You are part of me."*

My heart pounded in my chest. I needed to take a deep breath and collect myself, but I found no air to draw in.

Wait… no air.

There's no air.

I couldn't breathe.

I clawed my chest and opened my mouth wide.

There was nothing here to draw in.

Nothing at all.

I was in hard vacuum. Nothing to breathe.

I'm going to die.

I'm going to die.

I—

I wriggled my way out from underneath Shelly and fell onto the floor of our dome, pillows tumbling onto my face, a sheet wrapped around my chest. My breaths came in ragged succession, mouth dry, throat raw. A shiver ran down my spine and I put my palms to my face, feeling my moist, clammy skin.

"What in the hell was that," I mumbled, and in response, Shelly let out a moan. "Shit." My eyebrows crowded the middle of my face as I tried to recall what had happened. Again, the details were slippery.

I climbed from the pile of pillows and twisted sheets and went to the bathroom to clean myself up. I swore I hadn't been able to breathe a moment earlier, but that wasn't the case now. It was just a nightmare. Another damned nightmare. Boy was I ready to stop having these. Could everyone just get their shit together? Could everyone just do what they said and make this place work? Who the hell could we trust to be decent, to act with our best interests at heart?

No wonder the Foundry wanted to test us.

Despite the early hour, I gave up on going back to sleep. If I had a mind to, I could fit in another hour, but it seemed a good idea to fix up some breakfast, a bit of toast and stone bison sausage, and brew a pot of rog. As I waited for the water to heat, I remained in silence, pondering all that had happened and what was ahead of me. It was no wonder I had nightmares. Today was the day to finalize our choice. Today we would leave to tell the Foundry what we thought was important.

I stepped out of our dome, a steaming cup of rog in hand, and took a deep breath of the crisp morning air. Orange and yellow tree fans had piled ankle-high up around our door, blown here by the cooling wind of shifting seasons. The trees on the hillside running up the valley walls were changing colors, with gradient, earthy patterns much like the edge blossoms. Winter was not far away. Novae had autumn, just like Earth, a time of death before renewal. I only hoped we were ready for the cold plunge on the other side. We had faced winters here a few times, but this one was going to be bad.

Allowing myself to get lost in thought, I ventured back to my few memories as a child on Earth, the endless days spent aboard the *Vasco Da Gama*, and how our innocence had been shattered in the wake of some terrifying truths. This was not the life any of us had expected, and yet, it was ours. We had to make the best of it.

"Today's the day, isn't it?" Shelly asked, appearing from around the back of our dome, bright eyed and fully dressed, holding a pair of rakes in hand. She handed one to me and I took it. How did she get ready so fast? Had I been that lost in thought?

"Today's the day," I replied, setting my nearly empty rog down on a small table before I began raking at the fans. "You have a better work ethic than I do, you immediately pop out of bed and want to rake fans?"

"Maybe I'm restless," she said. "Wouldn't be the only one."

"Yeah." I licked my lips and peered for a moment up at the sky before looking back to the drying fans. "What do we do with all these?"

"Emilio wants to mulch them and make fertilizer. Rake a pile out in the street, he'll come by later with a group and pick them up."

I nodded and went to work, listening to the crunch of dry, organic matter. It was somehow satisfying.

"Do you think we'll make it?" I asked, thinking about our own personal allotment of food stores for the coming seasons. The Foundry had all but cut off its subsidies. Another couple of drops, and we either grew our own food, or we starved. Just a few more weeks of food security before it was all over.

Shelly stared off towards the south, leaning on her rake with a frown on her face. "It's going to be tight. The Jevox took their seeds and left. Now we have supplies to finish the PVs, and with the stealth warship Chevelle is taking as pilot, we'll be safe enough. But it's bad timing. I see a lot of hunting parties and stone bison sausage in our future."

"We could live aboard the *Fidelis*, you, me, Mom and Dad," I offered. "Proxy wouldn't mind. It would take care of us."

She gave me an unusual smile, a thin expression that curled up at the edge. "We've talked about it before. It's not fair for everyone else."

"I know," I swept my rake to the side, dragging a pile of fans on top of what I had already collected. Shelly met me halfway with a few she had gathered by the kitchen window. I ferried them on their way to save her going the whole distance. "I don't want to do this."

"Do what?"

"Execute on the decision. I don't want to tell the Foundry we want a stealth warship."

"And you don't have to. That's Chevelle's role now. Your job is just to take them there."

"I know. But—"

"I know this is hard, Milo. And I agree with your take, but by our laws, this is the colony's decision. Look on the bright side, what if it can be used to help us grow the colony? What if we can both be safer and build better infrastructure? Just because it can't locate materials and refine them does not mean it's useless."

I gave her a shrug. "Sure. Makes sense."

"*Milo, the time is 9:30,*" Proxy said inside my head. "*We must depart for the Foundry facility soon.*"

"Okay," I said aloud, then turned to Shelly. She knew what was up. "How do I look, love?"

She inspected me in my everyday clothes, well-worn boots, thigh-length black jacket, and jeans. I wouldn't be winning any fashion contests here, but at least they were recently washed. "You look like a prince," she said.

We hugged and kissed and said our goodbyes. It would be close to nine Earth Standard Days, eight Novae Standard, before I'd see her again. This was the longest we'd been apart for years. I had tried to convince her to go with us, but she did not like flying. Now that she had solid ground under her feet, she wanted it to be that way forever.

The Swift Shuttle platform was crowded, not just with my awaiting passengers, but what was becoming the usual rubbernecking suspects. I supposed launches were still the most exciting thing that happened on Novae, especially ones like this, unless you counted almost being exterminated.

"Can you fit all of us in your shuttle," Johan said as I approached. "We have a crowd of our own."

And he wasn't joking. Each of the six councilors were waiting for us, as were the heads of arms. And then there was Zager, Donaldson, Harper, George, Leo, Perry, and Alyssa. Mom and Dad were here too, but Dad was going with me, while Mom was staying back. I had promised him a ride, after all. Got to keep my promises.

I turned to the Speaker who was at the front of their group. "Do we really need everyone to go? Chevelle is taking the ship. When we get back, we can sort out crews if we need them."

Mary gave a sigh. "Concessions."

"I see." I turned to look at the gathered crowd. "Where's Karianna?"

"She's stayin' back," Chevelle said, keeping her voice low. "Stand vigilant, a right hench of a bird. She protects the colony from them Starfish."

"But we've got no reason to believe they'll be returning."

"I know." She patted me on the back. "We all know, it's good. Allow that, blud. You okay to go alone?"

My stomach twisted into a knot. Karianna still hadn't forgiven me for not assisting her during the attack. Not like I had had a lot of options. Her ship was repaired, and she was physically okay.

"I'm fine," I said after a moment. "The Swift Shuttle is going to be a tight fit. It's not designed for this many passengers." I eyed the crowd, counting as I did. Seventeen in all. "It's not a problem with weight, just not enough seats. I'll have to make two trips. Ten at a time. Councilors first."

Dad ran up beside me, a shit-eating grin on his face. I gave Mom a wave and threw an arm around him.

"Do we get to go into space?" he asked, his tone filled with an indominable sense of wonder. I could only hope I never lost that myself.

I let out a chuckle. "Yes, Dad. We get to go into space. My god, you act as if you've never done it before."

"I don't care if I've done it a thousand times. It's still exciting."

"That it is, Dad. That it is."

I ferried our group up to the *Fidelis*, first the councilors and heads of Arms, then the rest. Once everyone was aboard, Proxy offered them refreshments and led them off to their respective Star Spheres. While most of us had arrived on Novae in Foundry made ships, many were still uncomfortable with the idea of submerging themselves and breathing underwater. This meant that getting underway took far longer than normal, many making false stops and starts as they disrobed and dropped into their spheres.

As I settled into my virtual environment, I turned back towards the *Reverie* and reached out with my senses. Karianna was aboard, but she didn't want to talk.

"I'm sorry," I mumbled, then turned back to the matter at hand.

One by one, I lowered the network firewall and allowed my passengers to join me in my shared virtual environment, which at the time was an even plane of planets and stars. The 75-DFX system was our floor. As was customary, normal physical rules did not apply. You could appear as whoever you liked, enjoy what food or drink you wanted; wear whatever clothes your mind could dream up. This was a place of pure thought, pure imagination.

Many of the older folks in our group, including Emilio, Ramirez, and Johan, appeared as younger versions of themselves, fine lines and wrinkles erased within their Foundry projection. Mary, however, looked unchanged. She knew this was an illusion and so it held no interest to her. She lived in reality, be it good or bad.

"Think we have time to ride motorcycles?" Dad asked, appearing just to my left.

I poked out my lip and nodded. "Maybe. Just maybe. What's that in your hand?"

He raised a mug to his lips and took a sip. Whatever it was, the scent was spicy and sweet.

"It's not coffee, is it?"

"No. No." He shook his head. "It's apple cider."

Intrigued by the scent, I conjured my own mug, copying his memories. He was right. It was good.

The rest chose their own affectations of a sort. Perry, of course, had no visor here. His eyes were unobstructed, and this made it easier for Alyssa to kiss him on the lips. I wondered for an instant how intimate moments worked for them. Did he take them off and just go blind?

"Alright guys," I said, gesturing towards the edge of the system with my mug. "Everyone strapped in?"

"I do not think we have seat belts," Halifax said, narrowing his eyes and inspecting the map beneath our feet.

I took a sip of my cider. "Guess not. Either way, so long as everyone is secured."

Proxy appeared out of nowhere and began to rub my right leg, purring as it did so.

"Planet six, and the Foundry facility, here we go."

Our perspective within the virtual space shifted from the map to an augmented exterior view. Chevelle marveled at the change and looked at me.

"How's it feel?" she asked. "To, you know…"

"Hard to describe. But it's the best feeling in the world. Ever gone swimming in stars?"

She shook her head. "Can't say that I have."

The fusion drive of the *Fidelis* came to life, and we began to burn away from Novae, our tiny continent shrinking at our rear, then our planet, a blue globe of water and two moons like white diamonds growing ever smaller. We burned at a steady eight Gs of acceleration, piling on kilometers per second. At our maximum velocity, we would be traveling nearly thirty thousand KPS. Even at this rate, it would take about four and a half days for us to reach the mid-point of our journey where we would turn and begin to decelerate.

Until then, we had time to burn, no pun intended. The Foundry would care for our bodies, so we could either sleep, or talk.

As we moved away from any useful visual reference, I transitioned the virtual environment back to the map. It was easier for those not connected directly to the Foundry to understand. I summoned a few chairs and created a lounge to the side where several folks took seats, including Harper and

George. Leo stood at the edge of the system and just watched, a hand on his chin.

Dad wandered around the star map like a kid trying to figure out a puzzle. He bent down, ran his fingers across planets, leaned in, squinting at their surfaces. He made his way over to our destination and took a seat on the ground, cross legged. A blue orb of swirling gas sat before him, a myriad of satellites like a storm swirling around him.

"Have you studied the sixth planet?" he asked no one in particular.

Johan scowled and shook his head. "Why would I? What good is a gas giant to me?"

"Oh, but it's fascinating. And gas giants are vital to habitable worlds. They protect inner planets, capture dangerous rocks with their massive gravity wells, shepherding asteroids."

"Whatever you say."

"Well… Consider this planet, 75-DFX6, though it needs a better name. It's about twice the size of Neptune, a similar color and make-up, almost fifty thousand kilometers around. I'm not surprised my one bitty telescope could not see there was a Foundry facility either." He pointed at the rocks circling it. "Look at it, there's twenty-two satellites. And that's a lot. Fifteen moons, two with liquid water I might add, and six large asteroids I suspect are made of mostly nickel and iron. Plenty of places to hide out here."

"This facility isn't as big as the others, is it?" Councilor Halifax asked, finding a spot on the floor beside Dad and crossing his legs.

"No, it's not," I replied. "Proxy has given me glimpses of it. The *Fidelis* itself is not terribly smaller from end to end. Compared to facility 225 that we made contact with, or 363, that planet-spanning structure you guys on the *Brilliance* saw, it's a baby."

"A baby," Dad said, and cocked his head. "Size is relative, isn't it?"

"Sure is."

Leo walked the perimeter of the space, his look of one taking mental notes. "This will make a beautiful work. Another moment humanity makes leaps forward."

"Leaps," Johan mumbled. "It is time we take back what is ours."

Dad's head twisted around. "What was that?"

"Nothing."

We spent the next few days resting, enjoying the pleasures of this space, while discussing what we could all do to better our situation. Emilio had a plan to seed a new green house, and for once, Chevelle and the others were on board. It would ensure we had green vegetables all winter, and some rich protein sources as well. Alyssa assured us the local varieties she had recently uncovered would grow year-round in such a space given the right conditions.

All in all, I was starting to feel optimistic about our situation. I still believed that the right choice was to take the resource and infrastructure ship, but maybe we could make use of this stealth warship just as well. And so long as no one did anything stupid, the Foundry might still be willing to help us save Earth.

"There it is," Dad said as we approached the facility days later, though it had felt like only minutes. "The Foundry."

"A foundry," Halifax corrected.

Dad smirked at him. "Close enough, brainiac."

As planet six hove into view, the facility made itself plain. It shone bright gold against the distant light of 75-DFX, the only shimmering object among a storm of planetary satellites. We made for the kilometer-wide, gilded torus, bringing the *Fidelis* into a relative orbit to the swirling blue planet and structure. Hundreds of drones swirled around us, around me, inspecting the *Fidelis* before continuing their construction work.

This was a big moment in human history. It was too bad so few would ever know about it. No one on Earth would ever hear of it. Another event, lost to the cosmic winds.

"It is time," Proxy said.

I reached down to pick it up, holding it close to my chest and rubbing its furry back. "I know."

"Are you okay?"

"I'm fine. Just—"

"Just what?"

I shrugged. "I'm not sure. Something doesn't feel right."

"You must learn what is important," it told me.

"Not you now," I said, and put it back on the ground.

Before setting off, I took a deep breath to clarify my mind. Everything was okay. This would be fine.

"Let's do this," I told my passengers, before shutting down the virtual environment.

CHAPTER 16

We climbed from our Star Spheres and toweled off, changing into clean clothes before meeting by the airlock. Proxy was waiting, ready to usher us to a shuttle so we could make our way over. The facility, small as it was, could not dock directly with something as large as the *Fidelis*, and so it had sent us a ride. I found myself wishing Proxy had been able to come with us. I felt it would have made this easier somehow.

The shuttle opened to the facility, revealing a bright, white hallway, its borders without edges, light emitting from nowhere and everywhere. I could see no doors, no floor plates, no controls. Only a smudge of black up ahead. With as many people as we had in our group, we nearly filled the area shoulder to shoulder.

Halifax took a step and breathed in, testing the air.

"It's safe," I assured him. "Is this what facility 363 was like?"

He reached out a hand and brushed the wall with his fingertips. "Similar. Yes. But there's a smell here, it's… well…"

"It smells institutional," Johan said, pushing himself to the front of the group.

I turned to Dad, who for his part, had eyes wide as dinner plates. He was just excited to be here.

"Let's get this over with," Harper said, and flicked her head to urge George to follow. "You coming?" Her tone towards him was not the friendliest, it never was, making me thankful we had not stayed together.

"Yes." He shook his head, unsticking his thoughts. "Yes. I'm coming."

The Speaker came up beside me and put a hand on my shoulder. "Lead the way, Milo," she whispered. "Chevelle is our chosen pilot."

"Okay," I said, looking to the Brit. "You ready for this, Chevelle?"

She reached for her right arm and massaged the bicep. "Does it hurt? The operation. Or can we go cotch?"

"Go cotch? I don't know that one."

She shook her head. "London talk, blud. Means like, relax. Chill out. Come we go cotch. Do you get me?"

"No," I replied, distracted by thinking back to my own experience. The mechanical arms, the feeling of disassociation. "There's no pain, but it's not pleasurable. You lay on a table, all your feeling goes away, and parts of your body are sliced off. I watched it happen to myself. Like I was just an observer of a kind. You may not want to."

"Oi, that's fair."

We moved ahead, pressing down the hall, the facility quiet but for our clicking footsteps. As we approached the black smudge at its end, its edges came into focus, and it resolved into another open passage. To our sides were other doors leading to other places. Unlike when Esteban and I had landed on facility 225, there were no Isoptera to seal these rooms against.

Our group paused at the threshold of the door, looking left, then right. Passages opening into more passages which branched off into unknowns.

"Where do we go?" I asked, hoping the facility would reply. "Foundry?"

No luck.

"We could wander," Dad said. "No telling what secrets we might uncover."

But the Foundry never did anything haphazard. This was for a purpose. The question was, what purpose was that?

Johan gave Donaldson a curious look, then turned to the Speaker. "Why don't we split up?"

She turned to me for advice. "Thoughts?"

I gave a shrug. "I guess. Dad and I will keep going up ahead."

"We will take the right," Johan said, stepping towards the opening. His entourage, made of Clark, Donaldson, Zager, Harper, George, and Halifax, went with him. "Why not the rest of you go that way?"

The Speaker attempted to peer down the hall on the left. "Okay. That's fair. If anyone gets lost, come back here, okay?"

"Sure," Harper said.

Leo stood in the middle, undecided. He leaned right, then left, looked at me, then back to our governmental group. "Damn it," he said, and sidled up beside Chevelle. "Guess I'm with you guys."

"Glad to have you," Chevelle replied.

And so, Johan and his group went right, the Speaker along with most of the councilors and heads of Arms, as well as Leo, left. Dad and I stood still for a moment before moving forward. He chewed at his thumbnail, lost in thought.

"Does something feel weird?" he asked after several moments. "Like, not right?"

I nodded. "Are the colors not right, Dad?"

He raised his eyebrows and chuffed. "I think some of the colors have gone pear-shaped. I don't like what my instincts are telling me."

"Do we move forward?"

"Only way."

After Dad and I had crossed the threshold, it sealed without a sound. I whirled, stretching out a hand and found a solid wall beneath my fingers and palm. The exit was closed.

"Well shit," I mumbled, my heart rate increasing, sweat gathering around my collar making it feel tight.

"Language, son," Dad said, smirking.

Using my implants, I reached out for Proxy and the *Fidelis*. My stomach dropped when I found that my connection had been disrupted. We were on our own, at the mercy of whatever situation was about to unfold. I did not like this.

The hall continued for several hundred feet, till we reached another door. This time I called out before passing through, even though there was nowhere else to go. I didn't like doors getting closed behind me.

"Foundry?" I asked. "What's going on?"

A voice came from everywhere and nowhere. *"Please, come in."*

Dad's face lit up with excitement, his eyes going wide. I kept forgetting that he'd never spoken with the Foundry before today. This was likely the best day in his life. I should do what I could not to ruin it with my trepidation.

"As you wish," I said, stepping into the following room, a rectangular, featureless white block, which gave us the illusion of standing on nothing.

"Would you like a seat?" Two chairs appeared out of the floor.

It was all too familiar. Esteban and I had been in a setting like this once just before traveling to Cynosure.

"Next you'll offer us refreshments," I said, gesturing that Dad take one of the chairs and sit. "Is that right?"

"If you like, Milo Hughes."

"Got any donuts?" Dad asked. "I could use a chocolate iced Bavarian cream donut. And a cup of black coffee. Colombian, please. Medium roast. I'm not one for dark roasts."

A table appeared between us; a paper box covered in pastel stripes with a ceramic mug of steaming coffee atop. The smell was amazing.

Dad flipped the box open and squeaked. True to his request, a single donut was within. He tore into the sticky treat, taking sips of coffee between bites.

"Would you like anything, Milo Hughes?" the Foundry asked.

I shook my head and raised a hand. "Thank you, but no. I need to ask, why are we here?"

"I thought you would have figured that out by now. You are here to make a choice. Did we not make that clear? We are still learning your language patterns. There could be errors. English, especially, has many exceptions rather than rules."

"No, that's not it. I get that we're here, on this facility, and to make a choice. But I mean, Dad and I, why are we in this room? Why are we here?"

"As I said, to make a choice."

"What choice? Our people have voted. We merely need to claim the ship."

"As you say. But the choice, this time, is not yours alone. There is a problem."

"A problem?"

"You are not of one mind."

"Now that's an understatement," Dad said, polishing off the last bite of his donut before licking the icing off the tips of his sticky fingers. "All we do is argue these days."

"You were given three paths to follow," the Foundry said, it's tone even as ever. *"Three choices. You have already made your choice."*

"The hallways? But there was nothing explicit about a choice in them."

"Not all choice is vocal. Much is implicit. Are actions not greater than words?"

I looked to Dad, who didn't seem to be understanding. I wasn't entirely sure I was. Then a thought occurred to me.

"Oh. Oh… Our ways of thinking sorted us into groups, and those groups made a choice."

"Yes," it said, almost sounding pleased. *"One of the paths represents an idea of structure, a hierarchy. Control. Your democratic government. Another represents change, a reversal of past mistakes. An element of righteous chaos."*

"Righteous chaos," I mumbled, thinking that over. What was the Foundry really saying? I recounted each of those who went with Johan, considering any conversations we had been part of over the last few months. Was there a common thread between them?

I let out a breath as understanding hit me.

Oh shit.

The mission.

They all believed in the mission.

My heart began to thunder in my chest.

"So, what of our choice?" Dad asked. "Milo and me. What does our path mean?

"It is of a sense of wonder. You wish to understand."

That made Dad nearly blush.

"Okay," I cut in, "so the Speaker and the rest of their group are our collective decision. The decision we made as a people. But Johan and his group, you said, righteous chaos. We're talking about the mission, right? FICSE. They want to go back to Earth."

"Yes. They wish to follow the path."

"And that is a choice."

"You must learn what is important."

Pieces began to fall into place. I did not like what was taking shape.

"Foundry, have you been tracking signals from Novae over the past few months?"

"We have."

"Can you answer a question for me?"

"You wish to know why your Starfish came back?"

I shook my head and pressed my lips together. When it came to snacks, it was nice when this thing was in your head, but the rest of the time, it was just flat-out creepy.

"Yes."

"Ask the question."

And so I did, my voice cold. "Did we broadcast a signal that called them? Did we make them believe crystallized oxygen was on Novae?"

"Yes," the Foundry said.

"We what?" Dad's sense of excitement and wonder evaporated like drops of water tossed on a hot skillet. His hands began to shake. "Milo, what are you saying?"

I swallowed down the bile rising in my throat. "We've been set up."

"Set up? I couldn't have heard you right. How? Why?"

"Foundry, can you tell who sent the signal?"

"Not who, no," it replied. *"But we can say that your new communications array broadcasted a signal from the Prima Continent on Novae with the spectroscopic signatures of crystallized oxygen. The Starfish, as you call them, were drawn to it in a frenzy."*

Dad blinked. "You're not saying that we invited the attack. Are you?"

"We invited the attack," I said.

"But who?"

"Who else?"

Rarely in my life had I seen my father become angry, truly angry, but in that moment his eyes narrowed, his hands clenched into fists, and his face went dark. From deep within his belly an unbridled rage boiled up.

I took a step back from him.

"Johan," he growled.

"It is time," the Foundry said, and I felt the need to stand. Was that my choice, or had it been the Foundry manipulating me with that pink signal? I did not like being an object, just a pawn on a cosmic chessboard.

I had a thousand more questions for the Foundry, but they would have to wait. The moment of choice was upon humanity. I only hoped it wasn't too late to make the right one.

"The donation room is ahead," the Foundry said, and a dot of black became a vertical line which widened into a door within the white walls. *"Your people have made their choice."*

"We must learn what is important," I said.

"We protect life," it said in response.

Dad and I rushed out of the room and into the hallway. A commotion was coming from up ahead, the sounds of a struggle. I heard shouts, Chevelle's voice. I heard snippets of words in Afrikaans. Johan. Harper screaming in rage. A cackling councilwoman Clark.

"What's going on?" Dad asked as we ran towards the cacophony, the both of us struggling to catch our breath.

I wasn't sure how to respond, but I think he knew. Something bad was going down. Something real, real bad.

We rounded a corner to see Johan and his group standing before the threshold of the donation room. Chevelle, her face bloody, had been thrown on the ground and was being kicked in the ribs by Donaldson.

She threw up a hand to cover her face, one arm around her middle, body drawing up into the fetal position.

Johan smiled at no one in particular as he entered the donation room first, his entourage following. The door closed behind them, sealing so absolutely it vanished into the white walls as if it never were.

"What just happened?" Dad asked, kneeling at her side. "Chevelle, are you okay?"

She raised her right hand and attempted to shake off her stunned state of mind. Her lips quivered as we helped her sit up, her bruised eyes moist, blood running down her chin. "Johan jumped me, hit me across the face. I went down like a sack of potatoes. They mean to take the ship, Jackson. That pussy hole. *That pussy hole!* I've let everyone down. So sorry I didn't fight harder. Couldn't take them all. People I trusted. Blud. I couldn't take them all."

Dad sucked in an unbelieving breath. "Johan is trying to take the ship as his own?"

"Where's everyone else?" I asked. "Where's the Speaker and the rest of the Council?" I searched my pockets for a small cloth I kept in case of a runny nose, handing it to her.

"I don't know." She dabbed at the blood. "I don't know. He closed them behind a door somewhere. Singled me out."

"We'll be back," I said, urging Dad. He was already pinging the others. "Help is on the way."

I called out to the Foundry with my words and my implants, urging it to stop the donation, but got no response. Humanity had made its choice, and it was seeing it through. It did not observe our internal hierarchy. Just because we did not all recognize Johan as a leader, did not mean it would not accept this choice. Johan had a platform, a cause, and he had rallied others behind that.

In a panic I searched the halls, looking for another way into the donation room, looking for any way to stop Johan from doing what he was doing. Dad followed after; rage written across his face. He was ready to fight.

Close to an hour passed before we came upon a long, suspended walkway spanning a great abyss which plunged into the depths of the facility. At the end of the suspended bridge, we could see the window of an airlock, and on the other side of that, a ship undergoing rapid retrofitting. Dad and I ran across the void, over the narrow passage towards the craft.

"Maybe we can stop them from boarding," he said.

"How?" I paused for a moment, attempting to catch my breath. "With what? We're not armed."

"I don't know."

I should have listened to Karianna and kept a gun on me at all times. That would have at least given me some kind of leverage in this situation. As it was, it would be my words against Johan's, my fists against his whole group. They'd already beaten up Chevelle. What else might they be capable of?

We approached the end of the walkway, and a door on our left appeared within the wall.

Johan and his entourage stepped onto the walkway. They strode together as one down a connecting path with a look of triumph on their faces, backs straight with pride, all but for Halifax who shrank down in the rear. Johan lifted his right arm, marveling at his mechanical replacement, testing the fingers, forming it into fists, before letting it come to rest at his side. While the older man might not have smiled, I knew he was pleased with himself. He had gotten exactly what he wanted.

Dad redoubled his efforts and took off at a sprint, somehow moving quicker than me. In good shape or not, his passion was overtaking any physical limitations he might have had.

"Wait!" I shouted after him. "Wait for me."

"You bastard!" Dad screamed across the open air of the abyss, his voice echoing throughout the massive chamber. "Put it back. This ship is for Chevelle to pilot, not you!" He blocked the crossways of the path where it formed a T, his arms wide. "Now!"

Johan's group paused, Clark and Donaldson giving one another sidelong looks. Harper would not meet Dad's eyes, and for a moment, George tried to hide his face.

"I've had enough of people getting in my way," Johan said, then reached behind his back with his prosthetic arm. From where Dad stood, he couldn't see what the man had removed from his belt, but I could. The object was small, and metal, and as malicious as the devil himself.

"No!" I shouted, reaching out. There was too much distance between us, fifteen feet or more. Dad had gotten too far ahead. "No!"

I couldn't see Dad's face, but I could see the gleaming end of the barrel as it leveled on his forehead. Johan merely looked annoyed as Dad raised his hands and shook them in anger.

There came a quiet pop between them.

A flash of light.

A spray of blood.

And in that moment, my world collapsed upon itself, Dad's body falling to the deck.

The flesh of my throat shredded apart, drawn out in tatters as I wailed, "Dad! No! Dad!" I slid down beside his motionless form, wrapping him up in my arms, holding him tight. "No. No. No. This can't—"

"*Asseblief,* Hughes, at least we have no more arguing," Johan spat, looking down upon me with pure disgust. "The mission lives. We will save Earth."

But what did any of that matter now?

Dad's eyes were empty, his body heavy, every muscle limp. He wasn't breathing, wasn't thinking, wasn't anything. He was a husk, his soul departed before I could even think to say goodbye.

I squeezed him in my arms and trembled, unconcerned with any dangers that might persist.

My father, my daddy—*my daddy*—was gone.

Johan stepped around us and made for the exit. His entourage was slow to follow. It was clear they hadn't been expecting this. I don't remember much of what happened, who was where, but I recall Halifax hesitating the longest.

Clark took hold of Alex's arm and made him follow.

"I—" Halifax wheezed. "I—I didn't—"

They stepped through the open door into their new ship. Johan lingered at the airlock, watching as my tears watered my father's shoulder.

"Real leaders must be ready to sacrifice all for the freedom of their people," he said, then turned his back on us, leaving me alone with my sorrow.

CHAPTER 17

Johan was gone, and so was Dad. I couldn't believe it, even though I had held Dad in my arms as his body went cold. This had to be a trick, right? It had happened before. Just another of one of the Foundry's crazy tests. Maybe we never left the planet, and my brain was being hijacked. Maybe I was in a simulation. Nothing real.

Dad couldn't be gone. Could he?

I don't recall much after leaving the Foundry facility. The Speaker and the rest of the councilors had found us on the walkway. I must have been screaming, because my throat hurt. I was carried back to the *Fidelis*, placed into my Star Sphere, given something to calm me down. Proxy took control of the ship and guided us back to Novae.

My virtual environment did not materialize into anything familiar or comforting as it normally would. I just wanted darkness. Images flashed in my mind, memories of bad jokes, random science lessons, times riding motorcycles under blue skies. In every one of them Dad smiled—a smile that took years to find under the many layers of grief and obsession. Despite all the frustration over colony direction, he was finally happy. We were in a good place. We were…

I awoke from my null state to find that the *Fidelis* had returned to orbit over Novae, though I was still in the empty virtual environment. Proxy was the only thing that remained with me in this void, my body curled into the fetal position, my furry friend perched on my side in a tight coil. It was warm against my skin, caring, alive.

I wasn't sure what it was like to sob inside a Star Sphere. Did my physical body shed tears? Did they change the contents of the tank? What did any of it matter?

At some point I made it back to the surface. Everything was a blur.

"Milo?" Shelly asked as I stumbled from my Swift Shuttle. "What's wrong? What's wrong?"

I couldn't answer. All I could do was fold into her arms and let her hold me.

Mom was just behind her, frantically searching the gathered crowd for Dad. She looked to me, a worried expression on her face. All I could do was shake my head.

She tore off through the group, demanding that the Speaker show her the body. Show her that her husband was dead. That there was no way this could happen.

The councilors removed a preservation capsule from the shuttle. Mom went to it, looked through the lighted window, then began to pound on it as if she could wake him up.

"I'm sorry, Adrianna," the Speaker said, putting a hand on her shoulder. "It was Johan. He betrayed us. He betrayed all of us."

Mom collapsed to the ground and began to wail.

My vision cleared long enough I made out Karianna standing near the edge of the platform, hands over her mouth in shock.

I began to tremble, my body going weak, and Shelly drew me tighter into her embrace. "I'm here," she told me. "I'm here, love. Just let it out."

And I did. The emotion trapped within my body was too great. It had to go somewhere or else I'd go supernova.

For the next few days, Mom stayed with us at our dome. Much of the time we sat in silence, saying very little, not wanting to be alone more than anything else. Shelly made sure we ate, slept, took showers—basic human care. I was lost, without a direction in the world. Dad, for all his eccentricities, always knew what to do.

Mom surfaced quicker than me. She worked with Shelly to make the arrangements. What a weird word in this context, like a funeral was just another event, another administrative task. Might as well be a party or a holiday. So much to arrange. Pieces to be put in place. Dad would be laid to rest on the border of an edge blossom field beneath a big tree. From this vista you could see mountains, blue skies, and once every fifteen days, two moons overhead.

We were not the only ones affected by this. Dad was the first violent death seen in our colony. No one had ever raised a hand to hurt another. This very thought rocked our idea of security, of peace. Johan had won. He had gotten what he wanted. And why did he feel the need to do this? What good could it serve? What did it accomplish?

The day of the funeral came, and it was beautiful. It was cool, but not cold, sky clear but for a few scattered stratus clouds. Mary spoke like she had at Captain Williams' funeral. She shared her personal religious beliefs, being Catholic, and how she felt that he was in the embrace of Father God. I can't recall all she said, but she did tell stories of Dad, both awkward and kind. Everyone laughed at the time that he shouted at Lance's father on the way to the *Vasco Da Gama*, hooting like a madman screaming into space. Or when he would hack his way into the network using Esteban's codes to watch contraband movies, something I didn't know about until today. And of course, how he always argued for that stupid band, Parallax. They had at least one song I liked. Maybe two.

The funeral concluded, and I remained behind, sitting on the ground cross legged by his grave. Mom followed the group back into town, where they had a feast set in his honor, but Shelly remained with me, holding my hand. We sat there for quite a while in silence, then I began to talk. It was the first time I'd said anything more than a few words in almost a week.

"Why?" I asked Shelly. "Why did he do this to Dad?"

She sighed and shook her head. "I don't know, Milo. We've been debating it, and I'm no closer to an answer."

"Johan took the ship, and he's not alone. Where did they go? What is his plan? Why the fuck did he feel the need to shoot Dad?" I pulled my hand free of Shelly's and began massaging my face. Talking about it made my entire body, from the top of my head to my feet, feel as hot as boiling oil.

"Their group believes they can save Earth," she said, frowning. "Johan, Clark, Halifax, Donaldson, Jaxson, and geez, they've got Harper and George too. How is it they think they'll accomplish this? I don't know. All the Foundry said was there was a path back to Earth, right? But given what you've seen, I don't expect that comes with terraforming machines and a map. It's just a path. We'll have to show the Foundry we wish to protect life, or I have a feeling we'll end up like the Isoptera. Tolerated, but not assisted. Intentional genocide does not seem to be in its program."

I squeezed my eyes shut.

While I was worried about what might happen to our species, at this time, all I cared about was making Johan pay for what he had done. Time had been stolen from me. Time I had been hoping to spend with Dad so we could make up for all those years his attention was elsewhere. I had tried to act for so long like I didn't need my parents, that they were just background in my life, but I had been wrong. Everyone wanted to know their parents, to know that they loved them, to know that they were proud of them, to spend time with them.

"Look," I whispered, "if we can find where he went, I'm going after him. To hell with FICSE, to hell with everything. He killed my dad in cold blood and he deserves to die."

"You mean, to justice," she replied, then took hold of my hands. "How do you think we figure that out?"

"I don't know, you're the smart one. There's got to be a way."

"Well," she said, pursing her lips in thought, "we can't track him, at least not directly. He is in a stealth ship, I'm sure it's something like the Melcorin have. Besides, the trail would be pretty cold after a week. I've asked Karianna to scan for him, but she's not turned anything up. Not a stray particle in sight."

"There has to be a way. Has to be."

A cool gust rushed over Shelly and I, and we turned to see Karianna standing silent just a few steps away. She lowered her head, posture sagging, the weight of shame resting upon her shoulders.

"Hey, Milo," she whispered, her right hand grasping her left arm, the material of her bracelets tinkling against one another. "I—I'm so—"

I stood with Shelly's help, my legs weak. "I know."

Karianna wrapped her arms around me and squeezed, her prosthetic digging into my back. Shelly gave a smirk over her shoulder.

"He needs to be stopped," Karianna whispered. "He'll ruin it for us all. He's angry. He's regretful. He's determined to make it right in his head. He thinks it's up to him to fix everything."

I pulled away from her and wiped the moisture from my eyes with a jacket sleeve.

"What do you mean?" Shelly asked her.

"I've known Johan far longer than either of you. He's from the *Brilliance*, just like me. You know the story, right? His family?"

"Yeah," I said. "Bits and pieces."

"Okay, so as long as I can remember he has talked about his daughter and grandchildren. Back when he was married, he fucked up bad. Not sure what happened, but she didn't want anything to do with him ever again. Maybe he cheated, maybe he abused her, we all know he can be a royal asshole. But when their relationship was over, he had guilt piled on guilt that he's never let go. Earth is not just some existential crisis for him. He's back there in his mind, watching them suffer. Watching his children suffer."

Shelly frowned. "And we were taking too long?"

"Were we ever going to do something? It's hard. I'm split on this topic. If we can help to save Earth, we should, but not at the cost of losing Novae. And the way Johan is going about this is not what the Foundry wants. I know this. It does not differentiate individual aims. It looks at all of us as one big organism. If I screw up, if Milo screws up, if Johan screws up, it all comes back on humanity."

"So, he'll do whatever it takes," I said. "Do you think he believes this will not reflect on us as a whole?"

Karianna shrugged. "I can't say. But my gut tells me he's got another plan, just needs to find his way back to Earth. Like I said, I've known him a long time. He has a way of getting what he wants."

"He manipulated us." I peered up at the sky to see one of Novae's craggy, white moons hanging overhead. "The Starfish. He called them down upon the planet just to make this place seem unsafe. To shift public opinion."

"Yeah," Karianna exhaled. "Proxy told me after you guys returned. And that's exactly my point, friend. Whatever path the Foundry spoke of when we were given our choices, he's going to be living it out. I only wish Proxy would tell me what the choices are and when they will be asked of us."

"The Foundry protects life," Shelly said, and we nodded.

"Milo," Karianna gripped my shoulder with her mechanical arm. "Your Dad was a good guy. He's not really gone." She tapped me on the chest with a finger. "He'll always be in there."

Shelly swallowed at that. "She's right, even if you don't want to hear it. The best parts of him live on in you."

"In me," I whispered, placing a palm against my heart.

"Come on, love," Shelly said, taking my hand. "Let's smile for Jackson."

"For Dad."

We made for the feast, and I found myself feeling a little better, if only for the moment. When people said hello, gave their condolences, I was able to respond without crying, if only a few words.

We had converted one of the warehouses into a temporary events center, with long tables and more food than any of us could eat tonight. There were plates of steaming vegetables, a kind of white cheese Emilio and his team had made, stone bison sausage and steaks, fruits of every color and shape, and a variety of casseroles.

Shelly made us both plates, and we found a table near the edge of the room. I wasn't hungry, but she insisted that I get something in me. When was the last time I'd eaten? Was it yesterday? The day before?

Everything had been a blur.

Mom joined us shortly after we settled in, a small plate in her hands with a slice of what I believed was chocolate cake on the side.

"*Meu filho lindo,* how are you?" she asked, taking a spot beside me.

I shrugged.

She rested her head on my shoulder. "I understand."

"Is the cake any good?"

"No," she replied, then took a bite anyways. "Can't put my finger on why, but it's terrible. Soil makes the wheat taste different. Metallic. But, two more support drops, and bad cake will be the least of our problems. Takes eggs and sugar, and we don't have either. So good cake or bad cake, I'm eating every bite."

And that I could understand.

"It's a big gathering," Shelly said, turning around in her seat. "Can't say that I'm shocked."

"Everyone loved my Jackson."

"Hard not to."

"Which is why I think we'll get whatever support we need."

I perked up. "Support for what?"

"For when you go after Johan."

I blinked at her. "How do you know I'll go after him?"

"You're my son." She stuck a bite of cake in her mouth.

Shelly gave me a sidelong look, then shrugged.

"But, Mom, we don't know where he is."

"No. Not yet." She wiped off her mouth with a linen napkin and placed her elbows on the table, leaning forward, attention focused on the sky. "But we will find out. I promise you that."

"I'll help any way I can," Shelly said. "You just tell me where to look."

"I've got decryption software running on all his personal devices," Mom went on. "He might have taken his hand terminal with him, but he has several servers still running here. Chevelle has a team combing through his dome for anything important. We will make him pay for this. I don't care what Johan's intentions are, Jackson did not have to die for them."

"Are you saying you want revenge?" I asked Mom.

She shook her head. "Revenge is selfish. It only benefits one person. What I seek is justice. Johan must pay for his actions. No one should have to tolerate them."

"I know the feeling," Shelly said. "But it's slippery logic. Both end in his death."

And at that, Mom's eyes narrowed into something hard I'd never seen before. The look was dark, and it made me afraid.

"*Eu não me importo*," Mom told Shelly in Portuguese. *I don't care.* "Let the Universe judge our hearts."

CHAPTER 18

I ate. I rested. I read books. I grieved. I kept myself busy and exercised as much as I could stand. Something about exerting physical energy made me feel better, if only for a minute.

Dad was gone, and I was not okay with this. It felt like it wasn't real some days, but for now all I could think about is why. Why had Johan done this to me, to us? He had taken a bright light in the dark and snuffed it out. And he was going to pay for that.

The outer edge of Novae had become my track, a small trail forming a rut as I ran circles, from my dome down to the river, back up and around the Council Chamber, completing a five-kilometer loop two to three times a day. It was about the only way to keep warm, given that the season was changing. We were coming down to the wire, the point at which the Foundry would provide no more assistance, and just in time for the hardest season yet. Emilio, Lance, and several in the Agriculture and Labor Arm had set up a green house, but this was a stop gap. The colony would need to find more calories in winter or else our numbers were going to thin. It was math, horrifying math. People could starve.

I could help with this, using the Swift Shuttle to scour the countryside for herds of stone bison or maybe another eatable species we could preserve, but I wasn't. All I could do was think about that moment, the moment, playing over and over, stuck on repeat.

Why?

Why do this?

Where was he?

How could I get to him?

Chevelle and her team had run forensics on Johan's dome and found very little evidence. There was extra ammunition for his pistol. Tools to work on the communications array, such as a tablet link for programming. Some clothes that reminded me more of Jevox apparel than human. But no plans, nothing written. No smoking gun that led to his specific intentions or his trail.

I asked myself again and again, "He wants to save Earth. To terraform it. But how?"

We recovered bits of the Starfish we had shot down out of orbit. Karianna brought the pieces back to Novae for study. One thing was clear right off, our suspicions had been correct. They were indeed organic. This had proven that there were lifeforms living in the vacuum of space without ships. Their cells had grown in layers, the outermost a kind of air-tight shell that encapsulated fractal collections of cells and provided redundant, atmospheric pressure within. They were carbon based, but with a peculiar type of cellular respiration we could not quite understand. They could metabolize in reverse of humans, much like plants in photosynthesis. They consumed carbon dioxide and light, then used water to create glucose and ATP, which is what our cells use for energy. Though, after a little back of the napkin math, it was clear the efficiency at which they did this defied our understanding of organic life. Far more energy was created than was put into their mostly closed systems by a factor of nearly one hundred thousand to one.

Why they sought, or possibly feared, crystallized oxygen was anyone's guess. There must have been some biological directive. Something about this that drove them mad. Perhaps it had to do with reproduction? Maybe defense against a predator? Who could say?

After a long walk, alone with my thoughts, I jogged my way back into the colony over to the lab. Shelly, Ada, and Mom were working on Johan's encrypted files and were getting close to breaking the private key.

The lab was quiet now that Johan, Dad, Harper, and George were gone.

The three of them sat before a bank of terminals scrolling through documents, inspecting files of every description from films to pictures to journals.

I took a seat on a stool beside them, not saying a word.

Shelly gave me a funny look. "You're all sweaty."

"Better to sweat than cry."

"True," she said, then turned back to the screen.

"Hey, Milo," Mom said, drawing my attention with a gesture of her hand.

"Hey." I leaned forward to get a better look.

"Guess what, dude," Ada said, her voice a touch singsong. "We broke the key." She pointed to the screen Mom sat in front of.

"That's good news. Any luck finding something useful?"

"Not so far," Shelly replied, frowning, brows crinkling. "He's got lots of music. He could have always changed some important information and hid it under a different file type, so we have a line-by-line search running on all files with a set of keywords."

"Keywords like what?"

"Like the Foundry, the mission," Mom began. "Murder. Out of the way. The plan. Objective. Those sorts of things. Not expecting much, but it's worth a scan."

Ada let out a sigh and settled her fists on her hips. "It's a lot of data to work through. I knew I should have written a script to make this easier."

"Five hundred terabytes," Shelly supplied. "It might take us quite a— wait—what's this?" She backed up to the previous screen and began scanning several lines of text, then, without explaining, wrote the numbers down on her personal terminal and did a search for them, producing one result.

NIUPDATE1_0124V.LPFI

Her jaw dropped.

"What's that?" I asked. "It's important, isn't it?"

"Milo," Shelly said, her voice shaky. "I think I know where he went."

We brightened up at that.

"Where?" I asked. "Does it have to do with that file?"

She licked her lips and sighed. "I must not have been as thorough as I thought when I cleared the backups. He has the update. *The* update."

"The what?" Mom cocked her head and gave us a curious look. "What are you talking about?"

"Yeah," Ada said slowly. "What the hell?"

"We may have kept a secret," I said, directing my words at Mom. As I did, I felt myself shrinking back like a little kid trying to hide. Didn't matter your age, disappointing your parents still felt like crap.

"I made a discovery by accident," Shelly started, then tapped the file name on the screen. "The update to the implants that never got deployed. Do you remember that?"

Mom nodded. "Of course. It was to help with network stress. Why?"

"Hang on." Ada raised her hands. "Hang on. I thought it got trashed cause you were afraid it would scramble our brains."

"I lied," Shelly told Ada. "It was perfectly safe, if uncomfortable to use. Would it have helped with network stress? Yes. But it did more than that. Way more. When Milo and I tested it, some weird stuff happened."

Mom's eyes widened. "Like what kind of weird stuff?"

"At that moment we didn't know what it was, it was just a bunch of scrambled ideas. But with a little time, and another few soft attempts, I put the pieces together. With that update, we had found ourselves inside the Jevox electro-magnetic hive mind network."

"Inside their network?" Ada mused, her hands clasping the back of her neck. "You serious? What was it like? I bet that was awesome."

"Confusing," I supplied. "We human beings do not think the same way they do."

"Nevertheless," Shelly went on, "being part of their network wasn't just a way to eavesdrop. It was, well, a means to exert control. When I thought of something, they received that signal and were influenced by it. Their decisions were changed."

"Hang on," Ada shook her head. "Influence them how much?"

Shelly turned in her chair and slid the fingers of her right hand into her curls. "I didn't do enough testing to learn the limits. But with enough input, I'm confident you could change their minds about anything. Manipulate them to do whatever you like, and they will think it's their idea. I'm sure there's a hard limit on how many you could control at once, but with enough Jevox and enough humans, and a potential viral effect, it could be substantial."

"And so that's how we know where they're going," I supplied, jumping to the next logical conclusion. "They're headed to Rix."

Shelly nodded. "They're headed to Rix."

"Oh, my God," Mom hissed. "Why didn't we see this before? The Jevox. Because they're terraformers."

"Because they're terraformers."

"He's planning to mind control a large enough enclave that he can take them back to Earth and fix what we've done to the planet."

"Makes the most sense."

Ada rubbed her chin and considered this. "Brilliant and terrible."

"But that still doesn't give him a way to get there, not all the way," I said. "He can enthrall the Jevox, maybe, but that doesn't get him back to Earth. We only know half of the road home. From Cynosure and on, who knows? All of us were in hyper suspension. Even the crew of the *Brilliance*. They were given a ship, then tossed off into deep space without even a map. For all we know, it's hundreds of light years away from there."

"But he'll start here," Mom said in a level voice, then growled, "*matar dois coelhos com uma cajadada só*. He'll figure out the rest as he goes."

"This isn't right." Shelly slammed a fist on the table. "This is why we hid the information! Shit, I thought I destroyed it. I'm better than this."

Mom put a hand on her shoulder. "Johan is an expert computer engineer. One of the best. Don't beat yourself up over it. If it's any consolation, I think you did the right thing keeping this hidden. Johan aside, there are others in the colony who might have used it for the wrong reasons, just like him. The Jevox are a sentient species, and they do not deserve to be our slaves, even if it is to save Earth."

Ada was frowning at Shelly, but not in an accusatory way. "Don't beat yourself up. That old bastard is wily as shit, there's no telling what programs he still has running hidden on our networks. You did the best you could. Even though I wish you had trusted me enough to share this, I get why you didn't."

"Two can keep a secret," Shelly whispered.

"If one of you is dead."

"Didn't plan on killing my husband though."

I nodded at them, hardening my jaw as I did. "We have no choice but to follow. We've got to stop him. This is exactly the kind of action the Foundry will not tolerate. Is this protecting life? It told us we must learn what is important. But important to who? In doing this, are we not saying we are important, humans, and no one else? Not the Universe. What ramifications could this have for Earth? For Novae?"

The questions hung unanswered. There was no need.

"You'll need a crew," Shelly finally said, breaking the silence. "You can't go alone."

"And this will take years," I said, grabbing her hands. "I know you don't like to fly, but I can't leave you behind."

She shook her head. "And you won't. I don't want to go back up, but I will for you. Special relativity requires us to stay together. Can't have you aging slower than me."

Mom smiled at the both of us for a moment, then wiped a bit of moisture from her eyes. "I'm so proud of the two of you. Of all that you are, and all you have overcome. I'll stay behind. The colony needs me."

"But Mom," I said, putting a hand on her shoulder. "That means."

"Yes, it does. When you leave, this will be the last time you will likely ever see me. I'm not getting any younger, *meu filho lindo.*" She reached for my hand, and I took hold of hers. "Promise me something."

"Of course, Mom." A rock settled in my throat. She was right, but I couldn't deal with this now. It was too much. This was a time for denial.

"Live your life to the fullest," she went on. "No regrets. Always do what is right."

"I will."

"And Shelly?"

She sucked in a breath. "Yes, ma'am?"

"Take care of my son."

I knew I needed help to see this done, and lots of it. We would be stepping out into the unknown, entering the home system of a species who had been spacefaring for thousands of years with contacts and connections all over this region. We would need to find the proverbial needle in a haystack, a stealth ship hiding among an entire star system. Was it even possible? I couldn't be sure.

We needed a functional fighter wing, and there would be plenty of time during our travel between here and Rix for us to train those who were going. And so, we needed willing, malleable volunteers more than anything.

I first went to the Council and disclosed my findings, then asked to see who would be interested in going. That gave me dozens to speak with, which was a far bigger pool of candidates than I had expected. Some tried to convince me to stay, that Novae needed my help to protect it, but Mom stood up and argued in favor of me going. If Johan was left to his own devices, it could be the end of humanity in all places, not just on Earth.

"We need at least five," I told Shelly, the two of us sitting at the edge of the near empty Council Chambers as we flipped through the applications. "That will keep the wing full."

"I might be going," she said. "But I don't want to fly."

"Okay. You don't have to. But I think it's best that you train just in case. No telling what can happen."

"We'll see about that."

"Xuan wants to join," I said, and began thinking this over. "Her husband would need to come with us. Does he serve any critical roles right now for the colony?"

Shelly shrugged. "He works in labor, and gets a lot done, but there are others who can pick up his slack. He's in material science by trade."

"Okay. Could be useful for us, you never know. Let's pick them. She's done work keeping the colony safe in Security and Exploration, and we've talked about going up before. She's level-headed too, if a little goofy."

"We're going to need that. Both parts."

"Yes, we are."

And just like this we went through everyone, even considered a few choices of our own. Lance was one of my picks, and he took more convincing than anyone else. He did not really want to go, but he also couldn't stand Johan winning. We needed someone with experience who was trusted, and in the end he relented. I knew what he was giving up by coming with us.

Ada joined our party, adding a talented data and computer scientist to our mix, as well as someone who had worked alongside Johan and knew his tendencies.

That gave us Xuan and Hy, Ada, Lance, Shelly and me. We needed one more to round things out, but even still, that didn't feel like enough. The applications we had left were not my top choices. Shelly and I took a break from our personnel needs, and worked out a few models, taking estimates of what we knew of Rix and how we might scour the system for Johan, consulting time to time with Proxy, when an unexpected person walked into the council halls.

"Hello," Leo said, knocking on the wall with his knuckles. "May I come in?"

Shelly and I looked to one another before I waved him over.

"What can I do for you, Nelson?"

Leo thumbed his nose and made his way over to us. He looked worried, distracted, his motions twitchy. "I've been thinking about something."

I sat my hand terminal on the bench beside me and looked up, giving my full attention. "What's that?"

"Back on the Foundry facility, I had a choice to go left or right. It was a hard choice. I felt something was probing at my mind on a subconscious level. Trying to get to the heart of what I wanted. It was almost—Look this may sound weird, but it felt—" He raised a hand as if physically grasping for a word.

"Pink?" I supplied.

Leo took a step back. "Yeah. Pink. Was that the Foundry in my head?"

I nodded. "It was not trying to direct us. It was just forcing us to face ourselves. Sorting our intentions."

Shelly leaned back on her bench and crossed her arms, watching as we spoke.

"Well," Leo put his hands in his pockets and began to kick at the ground with his boots, "I almost went right. If I had, though, I would be on that crazy train with those people. I have to be honest, I'm all for the mission. I supported Johan in this entire initiative. Earth deserves a second chance. That is why we were sent out into space. But what happened up there, no, it's not right. What happened to—"

"My dad?"

"Yeah." The Council Chambers felt suddenly empty, the world turning black around our tiny island of light. "Look, your dad could be headstrong, but he was a good guy. A real good guy."

"I know he was," I replied, my words a bit harder than I had intended.

Leo frowned at me. "Shit dude," he growled. "I'm here to ask if I can help. Fix this. I want to go with you."

"And why would you want to do that?" I asked Leo.

"Why wouldn't I?" He narrowed his eyes at me. "I'm of little help for the survival of this colony. I don't know how to grow crops. I'm not good at heavy labor. When one of us returns here one day, someone has to tell the tale of our journey. This expedition is where I am best served."

"Are you sure that's the reason, or have you exhausted all your good times?"

"Hardly," he said, rolling his eyes. "Though I must say things do become more of a challenge over time."

I licked my lips, uncertain. "You'll be leaving everyone behind."

"I know."

"What other reason is there?" Shelly spoke up, leaning into the conversation. "Tell me. There's more."

"Do I know you well enough to be that vulnerable?" he asked her.

"And do I know you well enough to let you go with us?" she replied.

His face scrunched up and he shook his head. "Fine. Maybe we all secretly want the chance to be a hero. To find glory. Maybe this is my way. Maybe I'm looking for meaning in my life, okay? A way to make up for past mistakes? Is that a problem?"

Shelly looked to me, and I looked back. We started a conversation with one another through our eyes. An extra hand would be nice, but Leo wasn't exactly our favorite person. Then again, is that not just what we needed? Someone who wouldn't just go along with plans for the sake of them, but who might challenge us?

We came to a decision without saying a single word.

"Look," I said, turning back, "I am the pilot of the ship. As such, I will be in command, and my lovely wife will be second in command. We will take all suggestions as they come, but in the end, we make the final choices on big decisions."

"So, you're gonna shoot me if I don't go along with your orders?"

"Maybe," Shelly said, and Leo took a step back.

He considered his options, scratching at the back of his head and pacing a few steps. Then he spun around and nodded. "Alright, fine. I'm in. You guys are the boss."

"Get your things together, we're leaving in two days."

Leo cocked his head to the side, confused. "Aren't we letting Johan get a head start? Why not go now?"

"He's got a long way to travel," Shelly said. "We'll make up time en route. We've got years ahead of us. A few days will make no difference."

"Then I'll get packed and be ready when it's time," he said, and turned to leave.

"That makes seven of us total," she whispered. "Five that can pilot fighters. You. And then me."

"Been thinking, I have an idea for what you can do if you don't want to pilot a fighter," I said. "We'll need to talk to Proxy though."

"Oh?"

"Yeah."

"Okay then."

I sat looking over the numbers again and again. Given how large the star system Rix is within, JV-01, I wasn't confident we could find the stealth ship.

Also, we would be on our own, and I didn't like that idea. There would be no one to watch our backs. I hated to do it, because of how it would leave the colony, but I knew we could use a fellow freak.

"If we want this mission to succeed, we're going to need her, too."

Shelly let out a long sigh and laid her head on my shoulder. "I had a feeling you'd say that. Will the colony be safe?"

"I think so. I'm pretty sure we were never in any real danger, so long as we don't send out signals like that again."

My eyes trailed up to the ceiling, and I sent out a ping to Karianna. *You ready to join the party?*

Her reply came back almost instantly. *I thought you'd never ask.*

And just like that, she was in.

I wrestled with my emotions, knowing this might put the colony at risk, but Johan's actions would reflect against all of humanity, not just our colony, not just the stealth ship's crew. Whatever his intentions were could have ramifications for thousands of years to come. We had to succeed in this new mission. Stop Johan. Save face with the Foundry. Ask for help when the time is right.

On the outside, I was doing this for humanity, for us all. But I knew deep down, I really just wanted to find Johan and make that son of a bitch suffer. He had taken something important from me. Something lost and found again. And in exchange for this, I wanted to take something important from him.

I closed my eyes and focused my thoughts on the future.

This was not the end.

Universe, please, let Shelly help me make the right choices.

But as always, doing the right thing was complicated. Often times you didn't know what was truly right, or wrong, until the very end.

CHAPTER 19

On the day of our departure, Proxy sent me a ping. It wasn't like its usual messages, which was a voice in my head, this one was text only. I checked it over several times, expecting it to be lengthy given the format, but found it to be only a set of coordinates a few dozen miles north of the colony with a future timestamp. It marked a point on the map at the center of a massive field of edge blossoms, but there was nothing else spectacular to speak of. When I attempted to get more information, Proxy merely stated it would see me soon aboard the *Fidelis*.

Something was up, and I didn't know how to feel about it.

I grabbed Shelly, who was deep in our closet packing up, and we made for the Swift Shuttle.

"This is odd," I said as we opened the outer doors of the craft.

"What do you think we'll find there?"

"I can't say."

"You think we should go grab the others?"

"No, not yet. If it's a threat, I don't want to endanger anyone else till we've had time to assess it."

But what game was the Foundry playing? What fresh variable was this?

I hopped into my Star Sphere and Shelly buckled up. It took only a few minutes to reach the coordinates. It was a beautiful day, but cold, frost covering the tips of tree fans in the lower altitudes, snow and animal herds bundling together in the upper reaches. Winter was here, and I wished we had time to joy ride, to go soaring through those icy clouds, a torrent rushing over my back, an iron bird dancing in the sky.

No. There was no time or mental bandwidth for this. We had a new mission, and it did not have room for joy.

We held back from the coordinates and waited, the Swift Shuttle hovering a few feet off the ground, engines blowing swirling patterns in the red grass and frost tipped blossoms. We were prepared for a quick escape.

"Proxy, what are you up to," I thought, a mere whisper in my virtual environment. My words were lost to static, no one to receive them.

Five minutes after our arrival, I detected an object falling from orbit. It was ten meters across, oval in shape, its form wrapped in flame. As it passed through the upper atmosphere it began to slow under its own power, in part by aero braking, in part by reverse thrust.

"Is that a—it can't be." Shelly leaned towards a display inside the belly of the shuttle. "A pod? A supply drop?"

The pod slammed into the center of the field, leaving an impact crater five meters across, a cloud of dust and debris kicking up into the air.

I gave the pod a scan to be sure nothing harmful was within it. No radiation. No more than a normal level of friction generated heat. No electromagnetic fields. The pod was safe, far as I could tell, and we were taking it back. I snatched it with the grapple and flew back to the colony, setting its cooling form down on the landing platform.

Our fresh crew was waiting for us, Lance, Leo, Xuan, Hy, and Ada. They had their belongings and were ready to go. But with this new arrival, we had questions.

"So, what's in the pod?" Lance asked, strolling over to the silver canister, steam coming from his mouth as he spoke. "Seems a little convenient, don't you think? We've been through convenient situations before, haven't we? They didn't turn out good."

"I can't disagree," Shelly said.

Leo walked up and wrapped on its metallic surface with his knuckles. "Why not just open it? See what's at its soft center?"

I closed my eyes and asked Proxy if it was safe. It responded with one word. *Secrets.*

"Any luck, love?"

"No." I placed my mechanical hand upon its silvery surface. "But let's open it anyways."

The pod flashed bright for an instant, revealing dozens of once invisible seams along its surface, lines like those from the strings of wax packaging splitting it wide. We took a step back, and it began to open, its insides unfolding like a flower, revealing its contents.

Our group let out a collective gasp.

Lance licked his lips. "Is that what I think it is?"

"Yes," I said, blinking at what was within.

"We, uh, better let them know."

We pinged the network like mad, calling Emilio and the Speaker over to the platform. Over the past few days, Emilio had been the loudest voice against our departure, especially when that involved taking both Foundry made ships with us. He argued it would put too much hardship on the colony, leaving them both defenseless and unable to expand their infrastructure. This in turn would halve our food production and put lives at risk. To be honest, I knew he was right, but that didn't keep me from wanting to do what we were doing. What we had to do for humanity.

When he arrived a few minutes later, boots and pants covered in clots of mud, short hair a bit wild, he was visibly upset.

"Unlike you, I have work to be doing," he shouted as he arrived, then proceeded to grumble in Spanish. "*Estar sin blanca. Todo Novae. Yo buscar tres pies al gato.*" It was some idiom about not looking for a three-legged cat mixed with us being flat broke.

The Speaker was with him. She too had an annoyed look on her face. I shouldn't have been surprised that this was their default setting for the time being. Little did they know…

"What is it, Milo?" she demanded. "What did you have to show us? Is it another problem for us to deal with after you leave us for your revenge?"

The two stopped cold in their tracks as soon as they got a good view of the pod.

"Where did this come from?" the Speaker demanded.

I smiled, perhaps a bit too smug. "Proxy dropped it to us."

"You mean the Foundry?"

"No," I said, shaking my head. "This came from Proxy. Special delivery. Secret delivery."

"*Aye dios mio,*" Emilio said, rushing over to inspect all that was inside.

The pod was full of supplies, mostly in the form of pre-packaged protein rich foodstuffs, much like we had seen already, but there was more. There were seeds and several self-constructing green houses, tools and equipment for sowing and harvest. All told it would be enough supplemental food to feed the colony for at least six months, long enough to get the greenhouses up and running through winter.

This wasn't all that was included. There were rare metals and exotic materials compatible with the nano-forges, as well as plans for a ground-based weapon. If I understood it all correctly, all they would need to do is acquire a few things from the planet, and the forge could create them an anti-spacecraft kinetic energy weapon that would protect them from most asteroids or scavenger attacks. Just so long as threats did not come on the scale of the Starfish, Novae would be safe. And if they could find the right materials locally, they could even build more.

The Speaker smiled at Proxy's gift. We all did. It sure as hell solved a lot of problems.

"And just why did Proxy not tell us?" she asked.

I patted her on the shoulder. "Because the Foundry doesn't want us to have these things. In the end, though, Proxy is our friend. Proxy is my bridge. It does what it can to protect me and what matters most to me. All I can think is it found a way around its restrictive protocols. Maybe it's been storing these up little by little for months just in case, hoping the Foundry at large did not notice. But here we are."

She looked to the sky and waved. "Thank you, Proxy. We're saved."

We packed up our personal belongings and left our homes empty. Large as the *Fidelis* and *Reverie* were, there was no reason we couldn't bring everything we wanted, and so many of us did.

Karianna had chosen a crew just like us. Hers included Chevelle, Renata Cox from Security and Exploration, James, Councilor Perez, as well as Dante and his wife Emilia. The colony would miss their talents, but we needed them too. Times like this were never an easy call. We had to learn what was important, and right now, stopping Johan was important.

There was a short reception before we made for the platform as a group, toasting to our success and offering a few scattered prayers. Then we were off.

Leaving friends behind like Mary and Perry hurt, but leaving Mom was the hardest. We'd not had the easiest relationship. I had a few early memories of her back on Earth when she was between work, her and I the only two people in the world. Those times had been happy. But there had been those years on the *Vasco Da Gama*, which were the bulk of my childhood, where she had been absent just like Dad. We'd moved past much of it, and for that I was eternally grateful. I would miss her.

"Please write," Mom said, kissing me on my forehead before I stepped onto the Swift Shuttle. "You've got years of travel ahead."

"I will."

"Be safe, *meu filho lindo*."

And with that we left Novae behind.

Never again would I see her face to face, a slow death for me to endure. But it was the only way to make sure Johan paid for his crime. The only way, and still, it was breaking the family apart. I knew that Dad was gone, but his body was here, this planet had become his final resting place. I would carry his memory with me. Mom would have a good life. She was surrounded by friends, right? They would take care of her.

Proxy welcomed the *Fidelis's* new crew, showing everyone to their private Star Spheres. Even though the *Fidelis* had plenty of space for everyone to roam around, which they undoubtedly would in the future, having everyone within the spheres as soon as possible allowed for flexibility of communication and acceleration. It was easier and safer this way. While a few protested, which was common, given their fears about the ship wiring itself to their central nervous system, everyone relented.

I settled into my virtual environment and began running the ship through various status checks. Proxy would do this for me, sure, but it felt right given that we were about to leave for good. Something told me that we weren't ever coming back, or that I wasn't coming back. Novae would be another memory, a hope. A dream to keep our spirits alive, but beyond our reach.

"Karianna," I called over our private channel. "Everyone aboard and in place?"

A ping came back. *"Just about. Give us a couple more minutes. Councilor Perez has a fear of water we're attempting to overcome. The thought of drowning doesn't seem to encourage him much."*

"I know that feeling. Look, I was thinking since we have such a large crew between us that maybe we should create a shared virtual environment. It can bridge our ships, be a place people can meet if they're out of hyper suspension and need to talk. We can sync up our subjective time reference and keep it constant there."

"Great idea. Get it set up and I'll let everyone know."

I gave Proxy a nod, and my personal, virtual environment dissolved and transitioned into a twenty-meter-wide room with neutral colored furniture and walls, with the occasional green house plant, and shelves filled with books. A white leather couch was at its center, long enough to seat everyone, and facing a wall display that stretched ceiling to floor. A chest-high orb appeared, showing a three-dimensional view of everything in local space including our two ships.

A general ping went out, informing our crews that the room was ready. I summoned a cup of coffee while I waited, grateful to kick my rog habit for a while. Didn't matter how you fixed it; coffee was better.

Shelly appeared beside me with a smile on her face. "Wow. This place is pretty cool."

"What do you mean?"

"You forget, I've never actually traveled in a Foundry made ship, other than in a hyper suspension casket at the start of all this."

"Oh yeah, that's right. Between the Gene Bro—I mean." I scratched the back of my head. No reason to drag those memories up.

She reached for my hands and sighed, squeezing my fingers. "It's okay. We were popsicles, and it was about the same on the Melcorin ship. But this. This place is freedom. I see why you love it."

Her eyes closed for an instant, and when she opened them again her clothes were different. She had been wearing jeans and boots and a jacket, a copy of what she was wearing when we left, but now she was in a white and blue jumpsuit, the mission patch of the *Vasco Da Gama* on her left chest. Before I could comment on it, she did it again, transitioning into a long dress with a low-cut chest and absurdly tall heels. Her hair was pulled up and fastened into place with an array of white gold and diamonds.

"Am I interrupting something?" Lance asked, having popped into existence on the couch to our left.

Shelly immediately flickered back into her original clothes. "No. Not at all. Just playing around."

"It's fun, though, right?" he mused, then combed his beard. "Fun being in total control of your look, your location, your, well, everything really."

"A little."

"I try to remind myself this makes us beholden to another intelligence, but the truth is, we humans are so far out of our league here, we've got a long way to go before we'll be fully on our own. If ever."

Leo appeared next, eyeing each of us with that smug, I'm better than you and I know it look. I thought he might have been on a path to humility from our earlier conversation, but it seemed I was wrong. "I find this place lacks substance," he said, running a finger along the back of the virtual couch, his attention focused on Lance. "It's too clean. Too perfect."

"Life lacks substance," Lance replied, his voice hard.

"Oh," Leo said, "how grim, Brittain. How grim."

"Haven't you already been on one of these ships? You're from the *Brilliance*. The *Reverie* would have been your home for a while."

Leo shrugged. "It was. But we kept things more grounded than you, that is to say, realistic to our situation. Dark rooms with low lights. Closed, cramped spaces. Bunks, not feather beds. Besides, we spent most of our time sleeping like you from the *Vasco Da Gama*. Well, other than the Isopteran boarding parties."

"Seems a waste not to live in luxury when you're all going to die anyways."

"There is beauty in struggle."

"I—"

But before Lance could argue from a nihilistic point of view, Ada Mitchell appeared, dressed in a thick striped, black and white shirt and ripped jeans with boots covered in buckles. Her brown eyes were wide, and she had an excited expression on her face, eyebrows raised, tongue denting her right cheek.

"Dude!" she said and let out a little chuckle. "This is freaking cool." As she took it all in, she ran a hand through her long, dark hair, revealing her bright layers of pink highlights and ears studded with silver rings. "I've never—"

"Never been up?" Shelly rushed over to greet her. "Glad you're here, Lovelace."

Ada raised a hand to give her a high five. Shelly looked at it curiously for a moment, then slapped hands with her.

"Wait, wait! Did I miss out on something fun?" Xuan said, popping into existence behind me, her husband at her side. "I want in! I want in!" She raised her hand to give a high five, and Ada delightfully obliged.

"So silly," her husband Hy said, then patted me on the shoulder. "She has so much life and energy."

I nodded. Xuan did not lack for that. Come to think of it, we would have a pretty energetically polarized crew. Two quiet intellectuals. A pair of brooding man-children. Then there was a punky computer scientist, an electric security officer and her overly considerate husband. All good people, well, all but for Leo, but what can you do?

"Good, good, everyone is here," I said, calling for their attention. "Listen quick before the other crew arrives, and then we can say hello, get settled in. Welcome aboard the *Fidelis*. If you need anything, anything at all, Proxy is here to help. While you are within the Star Spheres you will be protected from the ship's acceleration and will not be required to eat. That said, you can if you like, if only for the pleasure of it. Proxy will use your memories to create those experiences within and without your sphere. In the virtual environments, the world is what you want it to be.

"First, while I try my best to take all your feedback and suggestions, at the end of the day, I am the pilot, the captain of this ship. I'm the law, and what I say goes. Listen to what I ask you to do, and we'll all get along great. Don't, and I'll have a mind to get Proxy to lock you up. Fair?"

Everyone nodded except for Leo.

"What?" he said when we turned to stare at him together. "Okay. Whatever. Your word is law."

"Second," I went on, "the primary reason you are part of our crew is to learn how to fly a Foundry fighter. Having effective fighter pilots make our two battleships several dozen times more effective in combat."

Xuan raised a hand. "Doesn't having fighters make your ship a carrier?"

"What?" I asked, confused. "I—"

"Nothing, just that Chevelle had us read military books for Security and Exploration. Learned a lot about tactics and tradition. Was thinking about this the other day is all. Carriers are boats that have fighters. You always say battleship."

And it was a fair point, if irrelevant.

"Alright. I guess if you want to call the *Fidelis* a carrier, you're welcome to it."

"So, we're here to play Top Gun," Ada cut in, bringing us back to the topic.

"And what is Top Gun?"

"Hell yes, Ada," Lance said, answering for me. "Goose. Maverick. That whole deal."

"Awesome." She pumped her fist in the air. "That's the shit I signed up for."

"Did Perry share his copy with you?"

"Maybe," she said, shrugging. "Might have traded him some standup comedy recordings."

"Ah, so it's your fault," Shelly said. "I knew he didn't figure that out on his own."

"You'd be surprised."

I shook my head. "Yes, so, second." Everyone quieted. "You came here to be fighter pilots. Since he has the most experience, Lance will be your wing commander unless someone else shows more promise. I will give out orders from an overall tactical perspective, but Lance will lead you into battle. This clear?"

Xuan straightened her back and saluted. "Sir, yes, sir."

"Please, don't start that."

"Okay." Her posture slumped as she attempted to figure out how to stand, looking awkward for a moment. An idea came to her, and she pointed at me. "Yes, fuck yes, captain."

"I'm not sure if that's better."

Shelly put a hand over her mouth and tried her best not to laugh.

Was I already regretting my choices? This was going to be a long-ass trip. It's hard to keep the fires of rage burning when you're annoyed.

"Good newwwsss everyone!" Karianna said as she appeared in our shared virtual environment, her tone exaggerated like a cartoonish old man. "Picked up on an ion trail headed straight for Rix."

"Johan?" Shelly asked.

"Fair bet." Karianna snapped her fingers, and her crew appeared in various places about the room as if she was a sorceress willing them into existence.

There was Chevelle and James, Dante and Emilia Salizar, now former Councilor Perez, and last of all, Renata Cox. Of the group, I knew Renata the least. She was part of Security and Exploration along with Xuan, but had always been quiet, stuck to her job, not one to socialize. She was a short woman, just under five feet tall, with dusty brown hair in a shoulder length bob. A hard expression lived on her face at all times. Younger than my parents, she was still older than most of us here, having not been a child in transit, but had seen more tragedy than many of us being a veteran of the Oil Wars.

James came over and slapped me on the back. We exchanged smiles, and he went to stand with the rest of his crew.

"Do we have a plan, CO?" Renata asked while staring right at me, hands behind her back. "Or are we going to sit here and eat bon bons while the enemy gets away?"

I blinked at her. Direct wasn't always a bad thing, but it had been a minute since I'd dealt with it.

"I eh—yes, we do." I gestured with a hand and the main display shifted. "According to our charts, Rix is about ten light years from Novae. At a speed of a little over 0.5C, half the speed of light, it will take us around twenty years to reach our destination. While time will be considerably slower for us, we will spend most of it in hyper suspension. We don't want anyone aging faster or slower than anyone else. We need to remain in sync biologically."

"And if we get out of hyper suspension all that changes," James ventured. "Like the Speaker did."

"Yes," I said. "Just like the Speaker. She and Esteban remained out of hyper suspension, and while the time they experienced was slower than normal spacetime, they were still much older when we arrived."

"We've done the numbers and consulted with Proxy." Shelly stepped forward with a terminal in hand. "We should remain out of suspension for no more than one year each on the journey. You may all have an allotment. Some of this time will be spent in training, some will be given as free time."

"Why only a year?" Xuan asked. "Did we not stay out much longer traveling to our Foundry target star systems?"

"We did," she replied. "And our conditions were different. Besides the obvious that we don't want to age more than we need to, there's the sense of urgency we are all experiencing. It's best if we don't let that eat us up from the inside when we can do something about it."

Lance produced a comb from out of nowhere and began straightening his thick, blonde beard. "I've tasted both varieties, out of suspension, and in. I'm with them. Given the choice, I say we sleep as much as possible. Didn't sign up to spend my prime years trapped inside Milo's belly."

"Of course," Shelly went on. "Now, except for Lance and James, and our Foundry pilots, none of you have flown a fighter. You will need to learn."

"And what does that look like?" Dante asked, rubbing his chin. "We will be traveling at relativistic speeds, no? Hard to train with real hardware."

"Simulations, naturally," Shelly replied. "Unlike the colony, the *Fidelis* or the *Reverie* have no bandwidth issues."

"Thank Christ," Ada exhaled. "I can finally get back to watching six movies at once while working on scripts."

James pointed at me. "And just so you guys know, with a mission on the line, this guy can be a real hard ass. Pushing us around. Making us do things that could get us killed."

"No shit," Lance agreed, and offered James a fist bump.

"But you guys made it through," I retorted.

Perez tsked. "This sounds like there could be violations of UEI regulations. We might need to have a review of that. Rules exist for a reason."

James began counting on his fingers. "OSHA. EPA. FDA. USDA. UEI. IEU. LPQ.

"I think you're just making them up now."

"Maybe. Maybe. But I'm pretty sure he committed violations against the whole, damn alphabet."

Dante and Emilia gave each other a look but said nothing. They were also so quiet, kept to themselves. They had been Karianna's choice. Sure hope they were aggressive enough in battle to see this done.

I shook my head. "We took out the Gene Brokers, guys."

"I suppose," he said, then gave Karianna a look. "But at times he wasn't so much fun. We were always being told what to do, where to look, who to shoot and when. I mean, life's a bitch, but we can still have fun."

"Can't say I'm surprised," Karianna said, smirking. "Such a tight ass."

James's face lit up. "Remember those combat VEs, Milo? I still hold the high score."

"Allegedly," I mumbled, but he was right. When we had gained access to Esteban and Deidrick's training programs aboard the *Vasco Da Gama* all those years ago, James had been the champion more often than not. It was his impulsiveness that allowed him to win more overall. Too bad life didn't work like that.

Karianna turned her back to James and sighed. "We'll be doing simulations, much like your boy soldier VEs but without zombies. Lots and lots of simulations. Don't get too stressed out, enjoy the ride, git gud. Colony life has been pretty dangerous lately, but once we're out in the interstellar medium, we've got nothing but time to burn. No sawtooths. No Starfish. Just simulations."

"This should be inspiring," Leo mused, his lips pursed.

"Let's get started then," Renata said. "I'm ready when you are."

I raised my hands, palms out. "How about we get to a stable location first."

"Don't waste our time."

My face went red. Her attitude was starting to really piss me off. "I'm just as eager to get that bastard as you are. You think I don't have something to be mad about?"

She narrowed her eyes at me and said nothing in response.

"You ready, Karianna?" I sucked in a breath. Shelly must have seen that my hands were shaking, because she took hold of one and I felt myself relax.

Karianna waited a moment, then nodded. "Let's get out of here. Five thousand kilometers distance."

"Copy."

While those inside the shared virtual environment could not notice any difference, I felt myself begin to move. The *Fidelis* was breaking from orbit with the *Reverie* at its side, our distance from one another widening until we were far enough apart for comfort. Novae began to recede, and I felt my heart lurch. I was leaving Mom behind. I was leaving friends behind.

But this was the right choice, wasn't it? Johan had to be brought to justice for the sake of all humanity, not just for my personal hatred.

"And we're off," Karianna said, informing the crew. "Get started on training when we reach the edge of the system?"

I nodded. "That's the best idea. Till then, you guys can take a few hours to rest, play around with the ship. We'll leave this bridge space open as a conduit, a kind of lobby. Once we're free of Novae's gravity, we'll slip into hyper suspension for a bit. Wake back up when its time."

"And stay inside your spheres," Shelly urged. "We're accelerating pretty fast. Hate to see anyone turn into a pancake because they wanted to go for a walkabout."

And with that the meeting was over. A few vanished immediately, presumably to return to their personal virtual environments, while others sat around to talk. They were a new, unproven crew, but we had years to get them ready to fight. This had worked before, no reason it couldn't work again.

"You okay?" Shelly asked, squeezing up beside me and grabbing my arm. "You seem tense. Rigid."

"I don't like being in charge," I mumbled. "Leadership is not one of my skills. I fucking hate him, but people like Johan are natural leaders. Your dad, a natural leader. I'm just a fake. I'm no leader."

"No?" She looked around the room. "You're surrounded by volunteers who just left their lives behind on a new mission. No one was forced to be here. If you didn't inspire others, didn't have an influence on them, they wouldn't have applied."

"They're just here because they're mad. Like me. We all want payback."

She shook her head, curls falling down into her eyes. "I wouldn't be so sure."

I turned to face her and tucked her loose locks back behind her ear. "Why?"

"Call it a feeling. You're leading with more than a common enemy. I believe that you're leading with a purpose. A cause. People do bad things every day, and yes, bringing someone to justice can be a cause. But saving humanity, that cause is just as real as the mission Johan and his people believe in. That's why they follow you. Twelve people, me included, left everything behind on Novae to be here. That's no easy feat. They believe in you. They believe in our purpose. They believe you will keep them safe."

I gave a sigh and glanced at those who remained, feeling a touch of remorse in my heart. "I'm not sure my intentions are so noble."

Shelly wrapped her arms around me and pulled me tight. "Time can change hearts. It's okay to be angry. It's okay to hurt. Feel your feelings. Don't be afraid of them."

Moisture gathered at the corners of my eyes, heart thundering against my chest. Now was not the time for tears. Now was the time for cold, calculated action.

CHAPTER 20

Despite the many protests from adults acting like children who did not want to go to bed, both crews soon entered hyper suspension.

It would be a month before we reached cruise velocity of a little over half the speed of light, and a month after that before we'd cross the Oort cloud at the edge of the system. The Foundry, far as we knew, possessed some of the most advanced technology in all the universe, yet there was no warp drive or space folding to be had, no wormholes or FTLs. Its systems were bound to the same speed limit as all physical objects—we could not travel faster than the speed of light. The trouble was, going faster did not always make things easier. Space and time got weird the closer to the speed of light you approach, which was why our cruise velocity was what it was. The less time dilation we had to deal with, the better.

According to Einstein, as we increased our relative velocity to that of an observer, such as someone on Earth or Novae, the passage of time slows for us, while it would remain constant for them. They would experience days, while we could experience hours, then minutes, then seconds. If we were to push this to the limit and travel close to ninety nine percent of light speed, over seven years would pass for those on Novae for each one we experienced aboard the ship.

Special relativity was confusing as hell to me. How could time and distance change based on relative velocity? I liked little machines, nanites, not spacetime physics. For this, I would take Proxy's advice and just go with it.

As we slept in hyper suspension, I had Proxy scan the system for signs of Johan or anything else out of the ordinary. Days went by, blissfully unaware, nothing to report but dust and radiation. We left the inner planets behind, threaded through the asteroid belt, and skimmed past planet six and the Foundry facility. The edge of the system drew near, the radiant temperature ever colder as 75-DFX became a shrinking ball of light among a backdrop of stars.

I received messages from Novae. They had gotten the kinetic weapon and greenhouses set up. This meant that I had a little less guilt to carry on my shoulders. Thank the Universe.

We cruised silently through deep space, stellar objects drifting along their endless paths. I felt and saw it all, a wonderous kind of beauty and chaotic asymmetry to its shifting form, both terrifying and inspiring in its vastness and scale. It was all so different, and so much the same. Specifically solar systems.

I had now seen a half dozen, and each of them followed a general model. There was a star at the center. Some planets of varying distance. An asteroid belt of heavy metals and minerals. Then, as you reached the edge of the planets, there was a Kuiper belt, a region of small bodies of ice and rocky asteroids. Just past this barrier, for this star at least, we reached heliopause, the point at which a star's solar winds ceased as pressure from the interstellar medium bore down on it. The *Fidelis* and *Reverie* faded into darkness, only able to keep track of one another with sensors. Visible light from any source was next to nothing, only detectable with the most sensitive instruments.

In this medium, the Foundry ships began to unfurl their massive sails made of nano-machines. These sails captured a kind of dark energy Proxy would not explain. I could only assume it was related to the same dark energy which scientists like my father struggled with, a sort of discrepancy in the math which underpinned space-time and drove the ever-accelerating expansion of the cosmos. The *Fidelis* and its crystal shard of a structure blossomed out with nine leaflike protrusions, making it appear like a flower made of shimmery, black panels. At the same time, the *Reverie* spawned its own, a grid of nineteen thin, isometric diamond shapes colored pearlescent white.

Despite being mostly in suspension, I could feel the energy from these panels seeping into my extended body. It was warm. Comforting. Connective somehow. What was this?

In that state of half in, half out of consciousness, I became aware of something distant drawing closer. Proxy gave me a nudge, and I began to wake within my virtual environment, which at this time was configured to appear like my quarters on the *Vasco Da Gama*. A floating star map appeared over my bed, illuminating the dark room with a lambent glow.

The *Fidelis's* scanners let off a blip. Though we had traveled far from Novae, we had not yet reached the edge of 75-DFX's Oort cloud. Something was out there in the dark, in our general path. I needed to know what.

"Proxy?" I asked, rubbing my eyes even though I knew this did nothing practical other than make me feel better. Pure, luxurious affectation. "What is it? Do we know?"

Proxy appeared beside the bed, and I swear to the Universe, it squinted at the faint object I was picking up. "No," it said, sounding disappointed. "We need higher resolution in order for us to get a good picture. All that I can tell is that it is solid."

"Same here."

"Milo, you know we're being fed the same sensor data, yes? We have the same eyes."

"So what? You have different insights than I about what the dataset says."

Proxy began rubbing my legs with its face, purring. "True." It spun around in circles then settled in on a spot atop the bed sheets.

I retracted the blossoming sails of the *Fidelis* and readjusted the sensors to probe the object. While scooping up dark energy would help us on our journey, it made some of my instruments less sensitive. A few days without this power source wouldn't do any harm. This new information must have garnered some attention, because Karianna did the same.

"Yo, Milo, you up?" she called over a direct line into my implants, her voice in my head.

"I'm here. Picked up an object."

"I see it too. Any ideas? Let me tell you, I was not ready to get up."

"No ideas, and me either. Far out as we are, there can't be much. If it's not a ship, then it's a something that got ejected from the central core of the system."

"Could it be Johan?"

"Not sure yet."

For a moment I worried I might wake Shelly with all the activity, then remembered she was under hyper suspension. The fact that she lay next to me in the bed was only an analogy, a virtual representation. Nevertheless, I rubbed her back for a moment as I thought this through. After a few minutes she rolled over and wrapped her arms around my middle. So maybe she wasn't completely asleep.

I analyzed the data that had begun coming through. The object was cold, near absolute zero, -215 degrees Celsius. We knew that Foundry ships put off more heat than that, but then again, Johan was flying a stealth ship. The object itself was solid, but difficult to put in scale without any reference points. There was little to no infrared light radiating from it, other than from a single point near what I could only call its top right. This focal point of IR wasn't intense, but compared to the surface, it was hot. Five degrees Celsius was a far cry from absolute zero.

"Think that's a drive signature?" she asked, noting the hotspot.

I shook my head. "No. It's leaving a trail, but that trail isn't in a cone of any kind. Looks more like smoke to me."

"Smoke?" She paused to consider this. *"Wait. I'm catching IR and UV flickers. There's a path leading back to the hotspot. Widely dispersed, but it looks like what little light 75-DFX is casting out here is reflecting off something."*

"All four photons?"

"Pretty much."

"How close are we, Proxy?"

"Thirty-three light hours," it reported.

I checked our current velocity. 0.25C.

"Five days then?"

"Correct."

"I think we should wake anyone who isn't up," Karianna added.

I looked to my wife who was sleeping soundly, curled up in our sheets, a blissful expression on her face. Was she dreaming like I had been?

"Milo? You out there?"

"I'm here," I replied, shaking my head. "Let's do it. Wake them up."

One by one, crew members of the *Fidelis* and *Reverie* joined me in my virtual environment. Karianna even invited her own Proxy, allowing me to see it for the first time. True to her word, the thing was a giant chinchilla, a thickly built, short-haired grey rodent somewhere between a guinea pig and a mouse with beady eyes, big ears, and a fluffy tail. Though instead of being small enough to fit in my hands, like the actual animal, when this one stood on its back legs it reached my knees and was so muscular it more closely resembled a bouncer from a night club than a cute little pet. My Proxy and her Proxy eyed one another curiously. Could they even tell that they looked different? And for that matter, how did they see themselves?

As a group, we offered up theories on what this object might be. I wished Dad were here to be part of the discussion. I had a feeling he would be able to take this tiny amount of data and extrapolate a working hypothesis. None of us had a clear idea.

It swelled in size as we approached. Without anything to compare it to for measurements, it was hard to say how big it was, other than that it was very big. At least the size of a moon big. This ruled out the possibility it could be Johan. It was clearly a rock.

By day three we could scan the plume of infrared light in detail, seeing that it did in fact create a cloud in its wake. We detected water upon its surface, as well as oxygen snow. This object, whatever it was, was a cold, desolate wasteland with mountains of ice and valleys deeper than the Grand Canyon. Spectroscopy revealed that it had a thin atmosphere of carbon dioxide. Nitrogen and phosphorus. All the building blocks for life as we knew it, but for the heat of a burning star.

"It's a rogue planet," Shelly offered. "We're trailing a rogue planet."

"But dude, how?" Ada asked. "How would a planet get out this far? It's moving fast, and along our general trajectory."

"They can be ejected," Lance said, and took a sip of coffee from his mug, its side imprinted with the red, gold, and blue of the Barcelona futbol club. "My dad used to love this idea, at least as a thought experiment. Hard to say how it happened, but given the distance, this one came from the inner system. It had to happen a long time ago. Just a guess."

"Could a passin' star do this?" Chevelle ventured. "Dislodge it wif its gravity?"

Shelly mulled this over. "Theoretically. But we've not seen evidence any of the other worlds were disrupted."

"Doesn't matter how," I said, shutting down this line of speculation. "It's here now."

"Milo, you seeing that?" Karianna asked as a flood of new data came in.

Sensor pings were reporting hundreds of smaller objects in orbit around the rogue planet moving in pentagonal formations. Familiar, five pointed stars. Organic in nature.

My blood went cold.

"Oh shit," I mumbled, putting it all together. "This isn't just some rogue planet, some random rock. This is the home of the Starfish. It acts as their mothership."

"What?" Shelly's face went slack. "You've got to be joking."

"There're hundreds of them out there. Maybe thousands. Far more than we can handle in a fight."

"Have they seen us?" James's expression twisted. "I'm not keen on fighting these things, but I'm not going down without a scrap."

"I don't think they're gearing up for a fight," Karianna reported. "They're quiet, happy little fishies, locked in a dance around the planet. Either they don't notice us, or they just don't care. Still, we might want to lower our emissions." She waved a hand at her Proxy, it gave a nod, its ears flicking, then vanished.

"I guess they don't care because we're not carrying any crystalized oxygen," Leo suggested, and everyone eyed him. "What, isn't that what they love or hate or whatever?"

"It is," I said, and brought my attention back to the planet. "Proxy, send down a stealth probe. I want to know more about them. Can we see what's under the surface of that ice without hurting them?"

"Launching probe now," my Proxy said, and we waited. "No need to worry about what is under the surface. The equipment is sterile."

Time was strange inside the Star Spheres, given that we all shared the same virtual environment. In here, I could adjust our frame of reference at will, ensuring everyone experienced it the same. I sped up time so that the probe could reach the surface quickly, while keeping a close eye on the Starfish for any suspicious movement. They kept their orbits around the rogue planet without changing course.

The probe collided with the icy surface and began to dig. On its way down it gathered more detailed information about the thin atmosphere and makeup of the planet, but there wasn't much of interest above its surface. Below, however, there were fossils beneath the ice. Frozen plankton like animals. Dead bacteria and biomass. As the probe went deeper through the crust, the concentration of sodium increased until eventually it found itself in liquid water. Very cool water, sure, but liquid. The deeper it went, the warmer it became. Here the subterranean ocean was nearly supersaturated with sodium and magnesium, but there was life here. There was a bustling ecosystem of phytoplankton and algae, protozoa and periphyton. It was alive. This world that was so distant from any star, and source of stellar heat, was alive.

It had once been a lush ocean planet, and through some sort of cataclysmic event, it had been ejected into the deep recesses of the solar system. Had 75-DFX been the star that helped develop this world, or had it traveled from even further away? Did the Starfish evolve from the depths only to break free of its volcanic plume and become wandering, hostile explorers?

So many unanswered questions. Things that Dad would have loved to explore. Things I would love to explore.

"We could investigate," Chevelle suggested. "It is an interesting place, innit. Data might be useful."

Karianna and I looked to one another.

"No," she said. "We don't have the time. If we decelerate and turn back, we'd add months to our relative window. Johan is our mission. We have to focus on stopping him."

"I agree," I said, then closed the data feed to reduce distractions. "We have a mission to accomplish. We must keep Johan from showing the Foundry that helping humanity is a mistake. We will save Earth in our own way. This world is a debate for another time, another people. So long as they do not pursue, we leave them be. We send a message back to Novae, send the probe data, let them know what to look for. Maybe they can investigate more one day."

Everyone began to nod.

"Still," Shelly said with a glint in her eyes. "What a cool discovery."

Ada stepped up beside her and smiled, arms crossed. "What a cool discovery."

CHAPTER 21

There I was, floating amongst the void around a flaming, yellow star, my body naked and broken, arms laid wide, chest arched forward towards infinity. Every drop of my life energy was seeping out, leaking through the bleeding arteries of a shattered form. I knew that this was where I would die. I had given my all. Gone for broke. I had failed those I loved. Failed all of humanity.

"You must protect life," a familiar voice echoed inside my head like someone speaking deep within a cosmic cavern. *"You must decide what is important."*

But the source of these words was too far away. I did not have it in me to reach for it.

My mother called to me, much closer, her voice from a distant memory, one of my very first.

"Have you ever dreamed of touching stars, Milo?"

Yes. I told myself. I told her. *I have.*

Radiance and life from that raging star began to fill me. My fingertips grew warm, then my arms, heat seeping next into my chest and down into my toes like fiery medicine injected into my veins. My head began to clear, and I could see everything, not just what was here, but all of creation. I could see from the beginning to the end, and back to the beginning, the big bang to compression. Infinity was laid out before me.

I knew that this was why. This was how. This was what.

"You must protect life," that familiar, transcendent voice stated again. *"You must decide what is important."*

"I know what is important," I told the voice. "But who are you? Why are you calling to me?"

A veiled figure resolved into a solid form to my right, then spun around in surprise, a black, football shaped object in its arms nearly falling from its grasp at my sudden arrival. I was unable to make out what it was that it held, a machine, sure, but was it a weapon? And if not a weapon, why did it radiate such power?

The figure began to address me, and then—

And then...

I woke from hyper suspension in my virtual bed. Proxy had been pinging me for some time, trying to wake me up, but I was under deep. It was time. We were far enough into the Oort cloud of 75-DFX and in a good position to get started. There would be little chance of danger here, of interruption. The dark energy sails were open, and the Foundry made ships were in a state of entropic balance.

Shelly stirred next to me, my movement having translated into her own Star Sphere, waking her from suspension. She stretched out her body and rolled onto her side, sleepy eyes focusing on me, white sheets barely covering her naked form.

"Good morning," I said, putting an arm behind her head as I rested a hand on her hip. Our bare legs and stomachs touched. She was warm, always so warm. Warm like a star. A star... "Sleep well?"

She blinked at me. "Hard to say, I guess. This isn't like normal sleep. It's like, oblivion. I don't even think I dream."

"Lucky."

"So, you're having dreams again?"

"Lots. Seems to happen almost every time I sleep. Even when I go into hyper suspension."

She reached out and began playing with my curls. "And what are they about? The same ones?"

I shivered as her fingers touched my temples. "I think. They're slippery." I hoped they weren't about Dad and Johan. There was enough of that when I was awake. A scene playing over and over. Dad falling to the walkway, limp. Johan...

No. It hadn't been that. Was it about the Foundry? Was it trying to tell me something? Was someone trying to speak with me?

This felt right. But who?

"I see," she said after a moment, then began to get out of bed, sheets slipping away to reveal her bare shoulders and spine, the perfect curve of her backside. She wrapped her arms around her breasts and peered over her shoulder at me.

I sat bolt upright in bed, heart thundering in my chest. Thank the Universe for such a wonderful creation. Shelly was so damned beautiful.

"Take a shower with me?" she asked, her voice sweet yet mischievous.

"You know none of this is real." My lips were dry. "We don't need to take showers. We're not dirty."

She spun and reached out a hand, drawing me from our sheets. "Don't deny me the joy just because it's only in our heads."

And I couldn't. Did it matter that we weren't physically dirty? Our thoughts could always use a good wash.

Rested and re-energized, Shelly and I made our way into the bridge space, a lingering grin on both our faces as we appeared before the crew. Everyone was waiting for us, including Karianna's crew, and from the look of it, they'd been waiting a while. Half-consumed drinks and snack plates littered small tables, and a few books were sitting out. I waved a hand, and at that instant a myriad of conversations hushed.

"So damn grateful you could finally join us," Karianna said, hurrying over from a refreshments station to greet us, brushing crumbs and grease off her palms as she did. "Now then, what's got the two of you in such a good mood? Hmm? You are practically glowing."

Shelly and I exchanged a look.

"Nothing," Shelly said, slipping her hands in her pockets. "Just got a good rest."

Karianna narrowed her eyes. "A good rest." She pursed her lips, incredulous. "I see."

From the couch, James leaned forward and peered at us over the rim of his steaming mug.

"At least someone is getting it," Lance told him, bumping him with an elbow, making him spill coffee onto his shirt. James grumbled under his breath as he palmed at the wet spot.

"Are we ready to begin?" Renata asked, standing at what I think they called attention in the military, her shoulders straight, hands behind her back.

"Yes?" I questioned. "We are. At ease, soldier."

Renata shook her head and sighed, taking a step back.

"Sooo, we've got some serious training ahead," I addressed the room. "For the next few months, we'll be on rotation. Work a while. Rest a while. There will be breaks between. Back when we were prepping to fight the Kabosai, the Gene Brokers, we found learning best happened when we followed a cycle of twelve hours of training, eight of rest, repeated for six days. Three days off, personal time and sleep. Then repeat. Once four cycles of this are completed, we enter a low-level hyper suspension for a month where our minds can process and contextualize the information given it, a mostly REM sleep state. Then we'll start again."

"That sounds like a dreadful amount of work," Leo grumbled, his attention focused on his nails.

Lance reached over and slapped him on the back, hard. "It is. Might even make you break a sweat. Perish the thought."

"You're so encouraging."

"We get to pilot fighters?" Xuan asked, and did a little stationary dance, her shoulders rocking side to side. "Got to be honest, been doing a bit of it already in my imagination. Pretty sure the real thing isn't too much harder."

I nodded. "You get to pilot fighters. Do your best not to get too eager and break them. Though these are just simulations, we need to get in the habit of not losing ships."

"I promise I won't." She gave me a thumbs up.

"Milo's right, we don't have an infinite supply," Karianna echoed, taking a position beside me, arms crossed and looking dead serious. The two of us stood facing the group, their expressions a range from inquisitiveness to unease. "I'm the first to want to do something fun over being smart, but this is not the place. Go get your kicks on Route 66, or something." She turned to James and pointed at him. "I hear you're one for tossing ships away. Toss mine away without cause, and you might just find your Star Sphere curiously floating outside the *Reverie*."

"In short," Lance said, "don't be a Reed."

"Say what?" James held up a hand. It was true, he had not been the most careful pilot in our last big engagement before arriving on Novae. "Way to throw me under the bus, Lance."

"Come on, man, you trashed the most fighters in our brawl against the Kabosai," Lance replied. "Out of twenty-one lost, I believe you were responsible for ten."

"At least I didn't lose the powered armor."

"I'd hope not. You were wearing it at the time."

"It's easy to think these ships can just be thrown away," I cut in. "Like they are extra lives in a video game. Though you pilot them from your Star Spheres, they are limited in quantity. Not being inside of them creates a kind of emotional separation. Please, keep yours in one piece, as if it's the only one you'll ever have."

"Any questions, dip shits?" Karianna placed a thoughtful fist against her chin. No one said a word. She pointed at them. "Alright. Here's the deal, scrubs. Till this is done, Milo and I are your drill sergeants. You do what the fuck we tell you to do, and when the fuck we tell you. We're going to throw you into increasingly challenging situations that will test the very limits of your mind. And if you break, we're going to scrape the shattered pieces of your broken psyche off the cosmic floor and put you back together with superglue and chewing gum. Then we're going to go again. Everyone fights. No one quits. And if you don't give your best, do us a favor and step out of the nearest airlock to rid us of your dead weight. Is that clear?"

Again, no one said a word. I swallowed. To be honest, her attitude even made me a little nervous. Way to scare them straight.

I clapped my hands together and said, "Let's get started." Then motioned to Proxy. "Call up some basic flight exercises, let them learn the ropes. We'll get into combat later."

Proxy bowed its head and obliged. "Good luck," it told us, and the bridge space winked out.

The simulations had begun.

We started with a series of piloting exercises, Karianna and I in our battleships, the diamond shaped fighters of our crew members in formation beside us. When the bridge had vanished moments earlier, they'd been dunked into their own virtual environments, allowing them sensor feedback and control similar to what Karianna and I were given by the Foundry. Proxy gave them instructions on its use, but it was more feel than procedure. You had to treat the ship like your body, not just a machine you piloted.

Glowing blue rings appeared in space before us, set in lines and loops. There were different colors and sizes, and other objects as well, asteroids, a nearby moon, all with variable forces of gravity to contest with. This setup would force them to pay attention, get more of a feel for their new bodies rather than just learn the controls.

"Alright everyone," I said from my personal virtual environment, Shelly standing behind me to the right. I shifted to a top-down view of our simulated training field and felt Shelly take hold of my shoulder. She'd not been expecting the shift in perception, and it had taken her breath away... her figurative breath, at least... "The rings are a course. You'll have to get a feel for how these fighters move. This is space. I know you're all a bunch of smart people, born of smart people, but watching movies and popular media you might have some mistaken ideas about how all this works.

"Good news is, being in a fighter and piloting by remote from your Star Sphere, G forces don't much matter. If they won't break the ship, they won't break you. You can pull a hundred Gs and won't notice a thing. That is not the case for Karianna and I. Remember, there is no wind resistance in a vacuum, but inertia applies. These fighters don't pull twists and turns quite like they might in atmosphere."

"Your ass will feel heavy at times," Lance said over our open channel. *"Adjust accordingly."*

"Run the course," I continued. "First few laps are free flight. After that, if you fly out of line, you'll get returned to the beginning. We won't move to any of the combat simulations until every single one of you can thread your fighter through all the rings at a minimum of ten Gs of acceleration."

"The record is twenty-five on this course," Karianna cut in, and along the twisting path a ghost fighter appeared, zipping through the rings. Her record.

"I'll do twenty-six then," James replied.

"Take that and raise you two," Chevelle said. *"Got me pride to restore after the cave incident. Fix up, blud."*

"Aye, dios mio," Perez said. *"Why can't we stay on task. Like a bunch of damn children here. Just ready to get to work."*

"Thank you," Renata replied.

Emilia let out a grumble. *"Pfft. This is not play time."*

"But it makes for beautiful chaos," her husband replied.

Leo barked out a laugh. *"Beautiful chaos, I like that. Can I call my next painting that?"*

"Enough chatter," I said. "Let's get started."

The first run was a total disaster. As expected, Lance, James, and Chevelle did the best, but even for our veterans it was a struggle. It had been a while. No one completed the entire run, high acceleration or not.

Once everyone had gotten over trying to one up each other, they began to settle in to give it a serious go, screaming obscenities over the open channel each time they failed. I'd been subjected to enough shits over comms that by the end of it I needed a waste treatment plant to clear it all out of my head.

"Don't forget about inertia," I said. "When you thrust in a particular direction, you will keep moving in that direction until another force stops you. To go up, relatively speaking, you've got to burn towards the relative down. But don't think about it. Let it come natural. The Star Sphere knows how to translate these thoughts into movements."

"So, do I think?" Xuan asked. *"Or don't think? Which do we do?"*

"Both," Lance replied. *"Think where you need to be and when, don't focus too much on how."*

Ada was doing the best of all of them. She was a natural, getting a feel for how the ship moved, how to redirect it with the least amount of energy. She completed the course even before Lance and James, her average acceleration north of twelve Gs.

"Good work, Ada," I said. "Keep it up."

"This is fun as hell," she called back. *"I could do it all freakin' day. Shelly? Come on, girl. Give it a shot. It's a rush."*

My better half shook her head and did not respond.

"Glad you're enjoying it, because that's the plan. The rest of you, watch what she's up to. Do that."

Leo twisted around Renata's ship and somehow clipped her wing. The two of them went skittering off into the dark and reset.

"Stay off me," Renata growled. *"Give me room to work."*

"My sincerest apologies, Miss Cox. I was only aiming to follow your example."

"Stuff it."

"And we haven't even gotten to formation exercises," Shelly said from within our shared virtual environment. "This is going to be fun."

"They'll get it," I replied, and shook my head as James and Hy collided in a fiery explosion. "It takes time. You ready to fly yet?" I asked, giving her a nudge. "Looks like Ada would welcome the company. Make it a bit of a girls' club."

She shook her head. "No, that's okay. You said there's something else I can do."

"Yeah. There is. I'm releasing controls to you for long range weapons and point defense. I'll keep control of the Mercurial Integumentum, rail cannons, and the Para Lux array, but you can take the big guns. The antimatter slug cannons." I made a few hand gestures, adjusting permissions to grant Shelly access. "Since our pilots are already out there, why don't you have a bit of target practice. It won't take any of them out, but you can get a feel for the controls."

"You want me to take over the antimatter weapons?" Her tone was incredulous. "Are you sure?"

"I trust you. You can do this. They have a ten-thousand-kilometer blast radius, so even Proxy won't let you use them up close. Not the fastest either, as in, these projectiles don't move at relativistic speeds like the rail cannons do. You have to lead the target a bit."

"Okay…" She took a deep breath and closed her eyes. "So, I just take pot shots at them? See if I can hit them?"

"Or near enough. If you can get within 10K, they're out."

There was another flash before us as Leo collided once more with Renata. If he didn't straighten up, she'd come over there and strangle him.

A ping came through on my implants, text only.

Karianna: *These guys suuuck sooo bad.*

Me: *Yes. Yes, they do.*

Karianna: *We've got a lot of work ahead of us, don't we?*

Me: *Git gud.*

Karianna sent back a frustrated string of random characters in response.

As promised, we kept up the exercise for several hours, then split our crews, ours returning to the *Fidelis'* environment to debrief, Karianna's returning to their own. While there was some marked improvement in performance, they had a long way to go.

Shelly made for the refreshment station and poured us each a glass of red wine before grabbing a plate of finger sandwiches. We had summoned a table before the group and let them settle in with their own food and drink. Though none of this was real, and there was no biological need to have a snack and relax, it still helped set the mind at ease. Perez wasn't being shy at all with his servings, he had his plate stacked so high I thought it might snap. I gave him a curious look.

"Stress eating," Perez mumbled, then took a seat.

Emilia leaned against the infinity couch and stared off into nothing, eating like a lazy machine. Her husband elbowed her in the side and she shook her head. Maybe I should have Karianna check in on them, the two appeared to be shook.

"That was some great flying out there," Leo mused, sidling up beside Ada on the white couch. "Couple close calls, but you handled it well under pressure. You fly as naturally as a bird."

She set her plate to the side and eyed him, her expression darkening. "What are you talking about? It's just as easy for all of us. Well, except for you. If there's one thing you were efficient at, that would be crashing into the same pilot again and again."

He waved a dismissive hand. "But you, you do this all so naturally. It's like you were born to fly. You have the soul of a thunderbird."

Xuan leaned close to her husband, and they chuckled under their breath.

"Is he doing what I think he's doing?" Shelly whispered across the table to me.

I stuffed a tiny chicken salad sandwich in my mouth and scowled.

Leo leaned back on the couch, ran a hand through his platinum hair, then flashed a smile at Ada. She scooted away, putting some distance between them. He responded to this by sliding himself closer to her and tossing an arm over the back of the couch, not quite behind her, but close enough.

"We can force ourselves to do many things in life," he said, "but I think true happiness and success comes when we do what we love and believe in. The rest comes naturally. When you fly, Ada, it's like you've disconnected from the world, found a new state of existence. It's like you *are* the fighter. That it is your body, not just a vehicle you pilot. Like you've grown wings and have radioactive teeth. Lovelace, you hunt your prey as ferociously as any dark-eyed predator."

The room went silent for a moment. Proxy looked up at me, then at Leo. I could tell it was trying to understand what was going on. Leo hadn't been wrong. His words resonated with a truth. A truth that only Karianna and I really knew. I wish Shelly shared it. I wish she understood.

Leo leaned towards Ada, their faces inches away, and in response she—well, she gave him an open-handed slap across the face. He reeled back and covered the reddening spot with his palm. I very nearly spit out my food as Shelly barked out a laugh.

"What in the hell was that for?" he stood up, spluttering. "What—in—the—hell?"

"A warning," she said in an even tone. "And a kind one at that. Not sure if the Foundry's connection would be willing to translate the pain of my boot colliding with your balls all the way up to that acrylic brain of yours, but I suppose this will suffice."

"I repeat!" His offended expression went slack. "What in the hell was that for?"

"I know this little game of yours. I've seen you play it many times, and with dumber girls. I am not going to fall for it. I'm not a plaything."

"What game? I'm just—"

She raised a hand to forestall him. "Just trying to get familiar? Talking is all? Save it for the Sarahs. I'm not interested. I'm—I'm still married."

And with that we all froze. Had I heard her right? I knew she had been married, but not now. The Councilman and her had divorced a while back, hadn't they?

"Hang on," Shelly said after a moment, a hand over her mouth in shock. "Married? Ada… Why didn't you—"

"I wanted—" Ada started, then paused. She gave Shelly an apologetic look like one might give a sibling who just learned Christmas was just a game your parents played and Santa wasn't real.

Leo began to laugh, first quiet, then a bit manic, his head tossing back. "Married? Hah. That's all? Does that even matter? Just a piece of paper, and here, not even that. Can't say its ever stopped anything before."

"With who?" Hy asked. "Do you know, Xuan?"

She shook her head at her husband to say no, but the slight pink in her cheeks said there might be a yes.

Shelly took a seat beside her friend. "You and the councilor never got divorced, did you?"

"No, we didn't. Alex is still my husband," she said, putting her face in her hands. "I was going through a phase, didn't know if this was what I wanted. It all happened so fast, people pairing off while there was still the chance. It was frantic. We met just after we got off the Melcorin ship. The two of us hit it off. Circumstances push people together sometimes. A year in and I started feeling as if I were missing out. And so, we told everyone it was over and started living in separate places. Made sense, once he became Councilor Halifax. He was too busy for us, or so I thought. But regardless of our issues, he always made people feel they belonged. Even me."

"You still miss him, that why you never made it official?" Xuan asked.

Ada eyed her, then me. "The hell is this? An interrogation? Anyone else want to start questioning me? Huh? Come on."

"No interrogation, friend, only curious. Just trying to be supportive."

"Well, if you must know, we didn't make it official because I didn't want to. I still love that man even if he annoys the shit out of me."

"The best men do," Shelly said, raising an eyebrow in my direction.

I took a sip of wine and said nothing in response. I wasn't the only person who could be annoying.

Lance scratched his beard and let out a groan. "So... if I'm hearing this right, you decided to join this mission to go after him. Bring him back."

"My God," Ada exhaled. "When you put it that way, I sound like such an idiot."

"But isn't Alex one of them?" Leo ventured while picking at his nails, clearing away dirt and dried paint. "Just another one of the bastards who want to ruin it for all of humanity? He went along with Johan, and willingly. I'm not trying to find an angle here, promise, but maybe you were right to leave him."

"Don't try and twist this around." Ada raised a finger at Leo. "Don't you fucking dare."

He spread his arms wide and stepped back. This made Lance smile.

I thought back to the final moments of Dad's life just before Johan struck, then those after. Halifax was by the airlock with them, but the expression on his face was not triumphant like Harper's or Councilor Clark's. Alexander, her husband, looked deeply disturbed at how events had unfolded. I knew that my memories could be clouded by grief, but that detail stuck out, clear as crystal.

"I'm not so sure he's with them," I said, drawing Ada's attention. "It's just a hunch, but he didn't look so happy last I saw him."

Xuan sat down next to Ada, opposite Shelly, and rested her head on her shoulder. "Some people are forced to go along with those they don't believe in. He could have been coerced. Maybe he agreed in principle, but didn't know how far Johan was willing to take it."

"For all his smarts, Alex did have a hard time standing up to others under pressure," Ada said, leaning into Xuan. "Math genius like no one I'd ever seen. Yet people were a challenge. 'Just say no.'"

"Forget about him," Leo said with a dismissive smile. "I'll be happy to help with that. Distractions can be medicine for the soul."

"Leo," I growled under my breath.

He rolled his eyes. "Always trying to make an action of mine into something nefarious. There are other activities to engage in."

"Listen to me," I set down my wine glass and faced him, "this is a safe space. I honestly don't care what people do with one another on this ship so long as it's consensual. But if I hear you've been harassing Ada, we'll put you in a deep freeze until this is over. Right, Proxy?"

Proxy bowed its head. "Give the order, Milo Hughes."

"Leo, I hate to be gross, but you've got all the opportunity to work out your frustrations virtually if you desire. Go spend some time alone in your Star Sphere."

"Whatever," Leo mumbled, "none of it's real."

"The mind makes it real."

"No. No it doesn't. Reality is something different."

"Anywaysss," Lance said, drawing out his word. "Sexual proclivities or not, we still haven't solved one serious problem. We'll soon be able to dogfight, cool, whatever, just give us time. But what about finding this ship? It's a stealth vessel. It is built to be undetectable by Foundry instruments. How in the hell are we going to stop an enemy we can't even see?"

"We know where they're going," Shelly said, summoning a spherical map to the center of the room with a gesture, a black sphere with dots of light and orbital lines. "Rix is their destination."

"Okay, cool, we know the system. But we can't just start shooting randomly into the dark. I doubt the Jevox will enjoy that."

"Fair," I said. "But there has to be something on that ship we can trace."

Lance gestured with his hands, punctuating his words. "Stealth. Ship. What part of that are we missing?"

"How does it stay invisible?" Hy asked. "How would be normal to detect it?"

"Radar pings," I said. "LADAR. IR scans, differences in heat and cold."

"Gamma bursts from the antimatter reactor," Shelly added.

"Those too."

Ada added, "What about neutrino emissions?"

I considered that for a moment then shook my head. "Too much in the background for us to disseminate. Tons of noise."

"We do catch a spot of ions from time to time," Shelly said, adding an overlay to our spinning star map. "I have recorded the wavelengths."

"That will help, sure, but I have a feeling those only appear when certain modes are switched between."

"Like the sails?"

"Like the sails. Won't help us when we reach the Jevox home system."

"What about dark spots?" Leo suggested. "We know where stars should be based on our charting. What if we look for dips in light?"

As a group we pivoted towards him in surprise

"What? I'm not a total idiot. Color theory is all about light. If it's a stealth ship, I'd assume it subtractive, absorbs light."

And he was right. It would.

"Okay, that might work," I said, then looked down. "Proxy, can we do that?"

The cat lowered its head and took a seat where it was. "We can keep track of a full 180-degree cone in any direction at once. We will have to track light over time to detect differences. It will not be a responsive method."

"At least it's another tool. What else?"

"Maybe we can hope someone grows a conscience," Ada said, peering off into nothing. "Please, Alex."

"One can hope," Xuan told her.

Karianna chose that moment to appear alone in our virtual environment, her crew assumingly left in their own space.

"We going to get back to drills?" she asked, tapping at her wrist as if she had a watch. "Tut, tut. Times a wastin'."

I polished off my wine and stood. "I suppose. Let's get back at it. Ten more full runs. We'll keep changing the challenges. Make them a little harder every time."

"Sounds good," she said, and winked out of existence.

"Is there a mental limit to how much we can do?" Shelly asked, appearing beside me, her voice low. "Like, if we keep this up too long, will we break?"

I gave a shrug. "I'm sure, but we're nowhere near that limit at this time."

"Don't push them too hard."

"I won't. We'll take a real break soon. I know how this can be and they need to be ready. We can't have Leo acting like this when others are counting on him to keep them alive."

"I know."

I grabbed her hands and squeezed. "You sure you won't fly?"

"No. Not a fighter. I'll watch the point weapons though."

"Okay. Let's get these scrubs ready to be some cold, hardened killers."

"That's a bit extreme, don't you think?"

"No." I thought again about Dad collapsing to the walkway, his body limp and lifeless, and the emotional knife that had driven into my chest, its cold blade covered in barbs ripping and tearing at flesh, pushing aside sinew and bone, its tip splitting my heart like an overripe fruit. Johan was smiling at me the whole time. He was triumphant in this moment.

I put a trembling hand to my chest.

No. It would not end like this. Could not end like this.

"I'm not being extreme," I told Shelly. "And the more I think about it, the surer I am I've not been hard enough."

CHAPTER 22

Month five. Eight hundred and sixty-four hours of simulations. Granular changes in difficulty—increased number of enemies, new enemy types, shifting combat theatre—seventy-three. Simulations executed, four hundred thirty-two. Fighters lost, twelve-hundred fifteen. Solid victories, one in fifteen.

Things were not looking good.

While we had some clear leaders in their skills, the vast majority of the pilots, mostly mine, were adequate in their best simulation runs, and a dumpster fire in their worst. I was grateful to have Lance, Xuan, and Ada. The three of them did well to make up for how poor Leo and Hy performed, but it wasn't enough to win. It wasn't enough to ensure that Johan would pay for what he had done.

Points of light danced around the star map in my virtual environment as I tracked their movements. I was alone at the moment, the ship and my body as one. The *Fidelis* was being pounded by kinetic energy weapons from various sides. Keeping the MI up and in the right position was a challenge. I hurled white hot beams of light from the Para Lux array at the surface of an offending ship, converting its machine covered surface into a rocky twist of molten metal.

It was the *Fidelis* and *Reverie* versus five Kabosai vessels, ships similar to the ones Sinus and the other benefactors on Creatus had. The enemy was arrayed in a line, three on one side, two on the other, a gap of eleven thousand kilometers between each. The battlefield was littered with debris, chunks of the massive, asteroidal ships having broken off as our assault chewed into them. Given their size and center of gravity, however, they were difficult to deal with. Whatever metal their asteroid hulls were made of was dense, heat resistant, and porous. Kinetic energy was absorbed. Heat energy was segmented. Explosions only made new craters. These were tough nuts to crack.

Swarms of fighters poured from two of the attackers, the remainder keeping up the pressure on our battle ships.

"*I've got three fighters on my six,*" Lance said over the open channel, his diamond shaped fighter banking away from their formation. "*I'll try and lose them.*"

"*They're too fast,*" Xuan called back. "*Use your momentum. Spin on your axis and return fire.*"

"*Xuan, we're firing ballistic weapons, nuclear sabot rounds. You're reducing your weapon's kinetic energy by firing opposite your approach vector. That won't work.*"

"*Says who?*"

"*Science,*" Ada spoke up. "*Let's focus on saving this stupid asshole.*"

Leo banked around, then cut his engines and spun backward 180 degrees against Ada's instruction. He fired wildly into the dark at the approaching fighters and hit nothing. No shock there. Even with all the Foundry assistance, his aim was terrible.

"*Asshole?*" Leo mused. "*You're the asshole for not covering me.*"

"*I'm on my way, dip shit,*" Lance said. "*If you had stayed close to the group, I wouldn't have to chase you down for an assist. That's what formations are for.*"

"*If I had stayed with the group I would have been shredded apart. Besides, I think Xuan is right. Shooting backwards works.*"

"*Christ on a cracker, Leo. It doesn't work. Does—not—work.*"

One of the moon-shaped enemy fighters exploded in a flash of white light.

"*Look, Xuan!*" Leo called out in surprise. "*I got one! Works.*"

Ada whipped past Leo and roared downward below the Kabosai ship on my right. "*Go ahead and believe that if you want, dude.*"

The MI faltered for a moment, and I felt something stab me in the left flank. The simulation was nothing like the real thing, pain attenuated when reporting damage to the ship, but it still did not feel good. My vision flashed red, and I saw Johan's face. My hands were around his throat, fingers tangled in his white beard, the man smiling back as I choked the life out of him. This was funny to him. Just a game.

"That was my kill," Leo started up again, snapping me back into the moment.

"Check the logs," Ada replied. *"Need me to ping it over to you? Got a whole report here with bar charts and line graphs."*

"Quit arguing!" I shouted over the line, then took another heavy blow from one of the Kabosai ships. I gritted my teeth, powered up the rail cannons, and landed two rounds in its fighter bays, crippling its ability to launch any more. "I'm tired of this from all of you. Is anyone taking this seriously? Johan is fucking out there. He is going to screw the rest of our species over if we don't stop him."

"But we've got plenty of time, years," Leo said. *"We're just getting the jitters out."*

"The jitters?" I felt my face go hard. "We've been at this for five months, and you're telling me you're just getting out the god damned jitters? Do that on someone else's time. I have work to do, and if I have to do it by myself, I will. I'll fly every one of those diamond death machines personally if you won't take it seriously."

The line was quiet for a moment, the battle continuing but no one saying a word. Xuan and Ada found two fresh targets, fragging them. Leo managed to keep himself alive long enough to damage, if not kill, one of the enemy fighters.

A ping came through from Karianna. *Need support? You holding up?*

I did not respond. I was too angry in that moment, but not at her.

"Let's get our head in the game," Lance said after what felt like a hundred years, but was probably only seconds. *"We've got a job ahead and no idea how big it is. How about we focus?"*

"Focus," Ada agreed.

Xuan grunted, and so did Hy.

"Focus," Leo mumbled.

"Now please, take out those surface guns on target three," I said. "I'm having a hard time deflecting their blows. Two hits near the aft of the *Fidelis*. Damage to nano vats. The MI won't last much longer." A section of the enemy hull began to glow in our shared HUD. "There. I've marked it."

"Milo," Shelly said. "The enemy is too close for me to do anything effective. I've been watching for explosive weapons, but they're holding back."

"You're doing great," I told her. "Keep an eye on new arrivals. And if anyone swings far enough outside of range, atomize them. I'm going to try and pull some distance ninety degrees to the elliptical."

"I feel as if I'm not really helping."

"You could always pilot a fighter."

"No," she said. "And they are making that look less and less fun by the day."

Our fighters fumbled around the battlefield, avoiding shots from stray enemies. Shelly was right. At Xuan and Chevelle's recommendation, I had been reading through a stack of books on warfare. One was an early twenty first century book by a German ace on dogfighting in WWI. Another, on the attack on Pearl Harbor that kicked off the conflict in the Pacific. A few were biographies of generals, which felt more like old men talking about bygone days of heroism than anything else. Then there was "The Art of War" by Sun Tzu. I think I enjoyed it the most because it was short and to the point. Still, here we were. We could talk about strategy and tactics all day, but that wasn't what we were missing.

"Back on me," Lance said, taking control of the wing. *"Let's form up and support mothership Milo. If he dies, we all die."*

"Who made you the squad commander?" Ada asked. *"Last I checked I was the better pilot."*

"And last I checked, I had more real combat experience."

"Lance is lead," I told them. "Until someone else outperforms him."

"Coming for that title, dude," Ada said.

Lance chuckled. *"You're welcome to try."*

I took mental notes as I was torn apart piece by piece. We were going to lose again, that was for sure. Leo was outright sloppy, severely lacking in spatial and situational awareness given how good he was with art. Hy, was just too nice. He flew well enough, but when it came to being aggressive and taking advantage of a situation to go for the kill, he would back off. We had several talks about this, but none of it seemed to get through.

Lance was finally able to get everyone together to lead our wing of fighters in a V between a series of three Kabosai ships, lines of energy from the enemy's main batteries cutting just over their burning fusion tails. To keep the enemy from tracking them, he drew them closest to the ship with the most weapons. This made targeting more difficult for the beams, forcing them to aim at an awkward, careful angle to hit their mark.

His tactic worked for a while, but they flew too close together, and whatever magical gravity it was Leo had discovered which drew him towards his fellow pilots came into play yet again. It wasn't the Kabosai ships that took them all out, it was him.

"Damn it," I said, slamming my fist against an invisible console. It was hard to vent inside of a Star Sphere with nothing solid to rage against. "Why did I let him join us? There had to be a better choice."

"I'll give you a minute," Shelly said, and winked out of existence. I hated losing control like this.

I locked my environment and screamed so loud I wouldn't have been surprised to know bubbles rose from my mouth within the Star Sphere.

While we failed the scenario with the spectacular explosion of both Foundry ships, Karianna's wing did far better. They crippled two of the Kabosai transformation ships, leaving two for Karianna and me to fight on our own. Even as spread out as we were, it was nearly impossible to use our heavy weapons, and as a result we were torn to shreds. Shelly had landed some serious blows on a fifth ship at the end of the simulation with the anti-matter slug cannons, but it was in the yellow zone and blowback from radiation had killed several critical systems on board the *Fidelis*.

All this had seemed way easier when I was fighting Sinas in Ph0nx, and still I'd almost been killed. Proxy couldn't be screwing with us, could it? Making the simulation impossible in order to push us to our limits? It would be on brand.

"They are not getting any better," Proxy said while licking the back of its paws and rubbing its face. "I can produce a chart to make the data more visual. But out of the last one hundred simulations, their combat effectiveness has increased by only 0.7 percent."

I shook my head. "I don't think I need a chart to see that. *He will win whose army is animated by the same spirit throughout his ranks.*"

The cat scratched its ear and gave a shake. "I believe your Sun Tzu was right when it came to warfare. Do you believe your crew is animated with the same spirit?"

"Hardly," I grumbled. "It's not disobedience either. It's cohesion, I think."

Proxy considered that for a moment, then went on, "As for a bit of good news, modeling puts our chances of success with two Foundry vessels on our side as favorable against one stealth ship. If you can locate it, at least one of your ships will survive."

"One of us? How reassuring."

"Indeed."

I scrubbed through the highlights of the last simulation, closely inspecting all the blunders. "What are we missing? What's different from last time?"

"Talent," Karianna said, appearing in my personal space, startling me. "You ignored my ping. What's up with that, bro?"

"How did you get in here?" I threw up my hands. My virtual environment had been locked from outside access, set to private.

She raised an eyebrow at me. "I have my ways, Milo Hughes. I have my ways."

"I let her in," Proxy blurted out. "It seemed appropriate."

"Traitorous cat." Karianna bent down and scratched it behind the ear, eliciting purrs.

"It seemed the right thing to do," it said. "You are pilots. I will let you discuss."

Proxy vanished.

"Your Proxy is way more friendly than mine," Karianna said, crossing her arms and plopping back onto a cozy, white couch that materialized as she fell.

"Because I'm friendlier," I replied, turning my attention back to reviewing the battle.

Perception was weird inside your personal, virtual environment. Even though I wasn't looking at her, I knew she'd narrowed her eyes at me, incredulous.

"You sure?" she asked. "More polite maybe, but not friendlier. And certainly not as fun."

"Whatever."

"Look, friend, I hate to bring this up, but if we were in a competition, my crew would be winning the shit out of it."

"Good thing we're not."

She raised her hands. "I just don't want this fact going by unrecorded."

"Fine. It's noted in the great book. I'll even commission Leo to paint the scene and you can add it to your memoir."

She tipped her head at me and flashed a toothy smile. "Good." I believe the look was an attempt to be cute, but I'm not sure that cute was her strong suit. She looked more like a hungry predator than anything. "He's a talented individual, just maybe not in a fighter."

"Yeah, yeah," I responded and kept working. Something wasn't right. We were doing terrible. Why? I needed something else to focus on for a moment. Then it hit me. "Speaking of guys, anything up with you and James?"

Karianna's mouth went slack. "No..."

"No, what?"

"I don't date stupid men."

"But he's good looking, and nice."

"He's a child in a man's body."

"And you're a boy in a woman's body."

She poked the air with a finger, and even though we were a few feet apart, I felt it tap me on the chest. "You say that like it's a bad thing."

"Ouch."

"Wimp."

I rubbed at the throbbing spot on my chest and scowled. "Anyways, all I'm saying is that having someone isn't a bad thing."

"Until it is."

"What does that mean?"

"Eh, it doesn't matter. Just more people relying on you who you can fail."

"Care to elaborate on this?"

"No. I don't." She twisted on the couch and turned her head towards her ship, made a gesture with her fingers, then returned her focus to me. "So, what are we going to do about this serious performance issue? We get into a big enough fight out there and I have a feeling we're screwed. If the enemy doesn't kill us, our fighter pilots will by accident. I swear we did better on our own defending the colony. Piloting our ship and the fighters."

I nodded at her, thinking back to our half-dozen engagements. Even the latest battle with the Starfish had gone okay until the end, all things considered. "We really do fight well together." I summoned a chair and sat opposite her, arms resting on my haunches.

"Yeah," she said, rubbing the back of her neck with a normal hand. In this place we weren't freaks. "You know, it's like we're inside each other's heads."

"Even if you want to argue about it the whole time."

"Shut up," she said, and gave me a shove, chuckling. "You're one to talk."

We were quiet for a moment, then she made a move to speak up. I raised a hand at her to forestall what I knew was coming. We had to talk about it.

"It's okay," I told her. "I made a bad choice. I'll own it."

"No. No. You didn't. You made a move to save the colony. And me, well, I—I got—"

"You can say it. This is a safe space. *Scared.*"

"No," she said, drawing her knees to her chest and hanging her head. "I can't say those words. Someone like me can never be that. Besides, I'm not even sure that would be the right word. I felt... I don't know... trapped in my situation, like I was in a cage, a dark room. There was no way out, and the one person with the key was running away from me."

I reached out and took hold of one of her hands. "Karianna, I... That wasn't my..."

She squeezed my fingers and took a deep breath. "I know. Let's just put it behind us. I don't want to talk about it."

"We are a good team, though, aren't we?"

"Yeah," she replied, her attention focused on something distant.

"Okay then," I said, attempting to let go of her fingers. She hesitated for a moment, then exhaled when they slipped free of one another. I felt strange for a moment, fighting to get my thoughts back into line. "Right. Right. Okay. So, what do we do?"

"I have the better pilots overall," she said, her expression betraying a thought she had to push away. "Should we rebalance the groups? Even out our skill levels."

"No," I said. "Proxy already believes we have more than enough firepower to go up against Johan, if we can find him."

"Big if..."

"Yeah, well, let's keep it how it is for now."

"Are you sure?"

"I'm sure."

Karianna nodded.

An instant later, Shelly appeared to my right.

"Proxy?" I asked in singsong, a grin on my face.

The words, *"It seemed appropriate,"* echoed in my head.

Shelly came up behind my chair and leaned over, arms surrounding me. "Time to rest."

I leaned my head back towards her. "Understood."

"And on that note." Karianna stood and raised her open palms. "I better get out of here."

"Good night, Captain Torlen," Shelly said, giving Karianna a salute.

She smiled at this. "And to you, number one," she replied, and turned to leave, but stopped. "By the way."

"Hmm?" I said.

"I think I know why our groups are struggling."

"Oh?"

"We have some strong players, sure, but they're not working as a team. Like a real team. We've got the firepower, we've got the skills, sort of, and we've got a common goal, but they are operating like individuals. Do some more reading. We need a stronger team. Last time you got a team by accident. They were people who had worked together and were already a team. You don't have that luxury this time."

And well… she was right. With the exception of Lance and James, my previous group had worked together on common projects almost my entire life. Mary and Perry were not only siblings but our engineers. And Esteban, while he might have secretly been security, his official role was resource allocation, and as a result he worked with them often.

"How do we change that?" I asked.

"Don't look at me. I've always been better on my own." She shot us a peace sign and vanished from my virtual environment.

"Proxy!" I shouted, and the cat appeared.

"Yes?"

"Lock my personal space from everyone except for Shelly."

"At all times?" it asked, cocking its tuxedo head.

"Yes. At all times."

Shelly gave me a bemused look. "Everything okay?"

"It's fine. Everything is fine."

She ran her fingers through my hair, massaging my scalp. "I think she's right, though. They aren't a good team, not right now."

"A tale as old as time," I groaned.

My chair vanished and the two of us were left floating in a formless void. I closed my eyes to think, urging Shelly to continue rubbing my head.

"The question is, love," I mumbled, my words dreamy. "How do we make them a good team?"

CHAPTER 23

We were running out of time.

While it was possible for us to remain on this ship and stay alive till pretty much the end of the Universe, our allotted time to remain out of hyper suspension and prepare for our fight was stretching us thin. I had no idea how we traveled eighteen years from Earth to reach Barnard's Star without trying to kill one another, four hundred and fifty people shoved in a tin can with recycled air and recycled urine. Maybe it's because our objectives were different, maybe it's because we had communities. It was impossible to say. My current mood was just restless, wanting a quick resolution to our mission. Even though I knew that would not be happening.

Proxy had warned me that remaining out of hyper suspension too long during transit could have consequences. That given our history it might make us stir crazy, nervous, mentally unstable. Proxy had been right. We were approaching the eighth year of our journey, which was fine, but we were also approaching a full year of subjective time outside of suspension, which was our limit. This was starting to feel like an endless work expedition.

Wake up. Train.

Take a break.

Train some more.

Go to bed.

Wake up. Train.

It was the same day over and over. A static set of events with static outcomes. I was pretty sure we'd reached the point that we were as good as we were going to get. Win or lose, when we reached Rix, I was tired of the grind. Even that in itself was weird. How could I be physically prepared, and yet mentally, both restless and exhausted? I had all the energy in the world to contemplate just how worn out I was. Maybe this was how zombies or ghosts felt?

For the first time since we set off, I released myself from my virtual environment and climbed out of my Star Sphere, water dripping off of me, my body naked but for a pair of black boxer briefs. I sat silent, knees resting on the ingress platform of the sphere as I rummaged through my chest of personal belongings. Jasper, the only toy I was allowed to bring with me when I left Earth at five years old, was sitting on the top of my things, his black, plastic eyes reflecting the glow of lights within the *Fidelis*. I took him in my hands with reverence, ignoring clothes, pieces of jewelry, notes from my parents, a sidearm, and a handful of paper books.

I clutched the plush dog in my hands, fingers wrapping around its chest.

"I know you're not the real thing. Not the original, at least." I stroked his head with my mechanical hand, pushing back his floppy ears. "The real Jasper was lost when the *Vasco Da Gama* burned. But you know what, buddy? I don't care. You came from my memories, and well, that makes you as real as anything, right?"

Jasper nodded at me. He always understood. It was like he was inside my head.

"We've been through a lot, haven't we? Never thought we'd be gallivanting all over the galaxy fighting to save humanity. What we did was always play. Walking in imagination. An anchor that tied me back to Earth. How many kids are back there right now, laying in their beds, dreaming of touching stars? How many close their eyes, hold to their Jasper, and just let their thoughts roam free? Becoming one with the Universe, one with Dad and Mom, with Shelly, with me? How many travel using their minds alone, the most powerful vehicle in all existence?"

I pressed my nose to Jasper and took in a deep breath. There was no explaining how he smelt just like my house in Whispering Pines, musty and yet antiseptic, with hints of the cologne I snagged from Dad's dresser once upon a time—because, you know, Jasper had to smell nice for his big date. Memories flooded back. I recalled staying at my aunt's house eating chocolate and playing on my tablet. I recalled *minha avó* and her great big smile, and Christmas with my Brazilian cousins, a dinner that lasted all night. I recalled snippets of playing on a playground with other kids at school, swings, slides, squeals of excited children running around in the sun.

Earth was still there. It was still real, yes?

I had a feeling my nostalgia might be too kind. Looking back, I knew I saw the world I had left behind through rose-colored glasses, through a favorable lens. Life wasn't so perfect, at least, not for everyone.

I opened my eyes and held Jasper in my lap. Yes, the children of Earth were dreaming of touching stars, but it wasn't for the same reasons I might have been. It wasn't for curiosity, or exploration, no, no. It was because they had learned it was the only way to escape the chaos.

If nothing had changed since we had left, if our leaders were still playing the same old games, the Earth would be languishing. If we went back now, we would find a landscape ravaged by climate change, economic collapse, over-population, and war. There were too many people putting out too many emissions, too many mouths to feed, and not enough space. There were storms like the one that drowned *minha avó* and my extended family at every corner of the world, and these were not isolated events anymore. Floods and wildfires were on the daily news updates, common as summer showers. Crop yields and a reduction of biodiversity were depicted as crashing data charts updated daily, pinned to the corner of screens or at the bottom as tickers.

Here I am, dreaming of all the good, and yet, that was not the story for today's children like it had been for me. They were forced to huddle in tight spaces, their parents fighting over scraps, people dying in the streets killing one another for a loaf of bread. It was not for a lack of drive to get a job, or desire to meet their needs, but of opportunity. Didn't matter how hard someone wanted to eat, on a world without food, the outcome remained the same. Hunger does not motivate when no amount of work will sate it.

This is the narrative that must drive Johan. The image of his grandchildren suffering through this calamity. The fear he has to assume they live under.

"No." I gripped Jasper around the middle, my mechanical fingers tightening. "No, no, no," I growled. I could not, would not side with Johan's line of thinking.

I squeezed. Johan had to pay.

I squeezed harder. Justice for Dad.

I squeezed even harder. Never again, no more, he must die by my hands.

Harder. My hands around his throat. Choking. His body flailing. Grasping for life. Eyes bulging.

Jasper's threads began to snap, cotton stuffing oozing between my mechanical fingers like putty.

I took a sharp breath as realization dawned.

My heart sank. Jasper had split down his seams and was dying. This was my fault. I had done this to him. I had lashed out and hurt him. I had gotten lost in my imagination, desiring to choke Johan till the life left his body. Instead…

"Jasper, I'm sorry," I said, and laid him down on the platform's deck, his damaged body limp, my eyes misting over. "I'm—Oh, I'm—"

What did I need to do? Did I call Proxy to fix this? No. I had hurt something… I had hurt someone that I loved. Jasper wasn't just a stupid, stuffed animal. He was my first and oldest friend.

Frantic, I began rummaging through my chest, through shirts and papers, pushed aside my sidearm and found a series of vials filled with a quicksilver liquid. Removing one of the vials, I began reaching out with my implants, making contact with the contents within.

The liquid stirred, light flashing within the glass container as it twisted and flowed.

"Please fix this," I whispered, my voice fragile. I poured the liquid onto the diamond patterned decking of the ingress platform. My knees and legs were starting to burn from where the metal imprint dug into bare skin. I pushed an image from my mind to the nano machines, and they got to work.

The near invisible machines oozed over the platform onto Jasper's busted body and began pushing his stuffing back into him, flickers of silver light scintillating as they moved. Where his seams had ripped, a series began to thread themselves, the individual bots so small it appeared as if there was nothing holding it all together, but I knew there was. Jasper's body began to return to its original shape, my home-grown nano machines repairing the damage my anger had wrought.

When they were done, I scooped the bots into the vial, put them back with the rest of my belongings, then returned Jasper to his place at the top.

"I'm so sorry," I told him, rubbing his head. "I am so sorry."

And with that, I closed my chest and brushed the moisture from my eyes, guilt like a knot in my stomach.

A walk was what I needed. That's right. A walk alone, with no one else.

I got dressed and left my Star Sphere behind, heading down the main platform towards the center of the ship. Everything was still and quiet, the

Fidelis emitting only the slightest hum. As I rounded the first lateral access way, I went by Shelly's Star Sphere and checked on her. She was asleep in a tank beside Ada, both of their bodies still as they were suspended in water, a half-dozen umbilicals connected to their spines, arms floating at their sides, eyes closed.

I rested my forehead against Shelly's sphere and let out a sigh. It was good to see her in the real world. She was healthy and safe.

With a gesture, I summoned a chair to appear beside her sphere and took a seat, then closed my eyes. Would Jasper forgive me? I sure hoped so. The whole interaction had left me raw inside. Keeping myself together hadn't been easy. Dad was gone, and I missed him terribly. I knew there would never have been enough days, but I could use just one more with him. Esteban was gone too, no more of his stupid *yeahs*, his brotherly advice. Would everyone leave me eventually? Was Mom next? I might have a fear of death for myself, but I also feared a state of immortality, outliving all those I love.

Wait. Where did that thought come from? Was it mine? Me, immortal? No. Just an irrational, errant idea. An intrusive thought.

Massaging my head, I reached into the ship's network, and found we'd received several signals from Novae. I knew that if they had been critical, Proxy would have woken me up. So that meant these were not. Not that there was much we could do from out here if they had been.

Eight years had passed since we left. That meant that any signal sent to us from Novae would take at least that much time for it to be received and replied to. Lightspeed lag didn't allow for very good conversations. The further we went, the more it was as if we were writing letters in pre-industrial times.

There were the standard messages in my inbox, updates from the Speaker on the status of the colony, a rundown of the new power systems and projects they had completed. There was a recording of Marissa's newest work, a sonata titled, *Blue Wake*. It seemed that Perry had finally managed to finish the bar, closing it in and securing the outside areas with electric fencing. Three more of the colonists had gotten pregnant as well, and those who were showing before we left were celebrating seventh and eighth birthdays. From what I could see, the colony's needs were being met. Everyone was happy.

Among the packets sent to the *Fidelis* were private messages for other crew members. I could see who they were for, but the encryption kept me from perusing their contents, which was fine. I did not need to know what Leo or Lance were shooting back and forth from ship to colony.

Mom had sent me nearly a video a day since we had left. I had seen some of these during earlier windows outside hyper suspension, but after the first two cycles I had let them pile up. Seeing her was good, and yet it also made leaving her and everyone else behind harder. So long as no one came to pick on the colony, Isoptera or otherwise, they had a bright future ahead. The remaining crews of the *Vasco Da Gama* and the *Brilliance* had something to be proud of. Something I wish I could be part of.

Many of Mom's videos had to do with remembering Dad, telling me stories about him I may not have already known. Stories of our time on Earth before the FICSE Mission. How they met in Puerto Rico as interns at a radio telescope observatory when Mom rescued him after he fell down a hill and broke his leg, one I'd heard more than once. How despite his awkward nerdiness, he was always the life of the party, making people laugh when they went out. How, despite their choice to sneak aboard the Foundry launch craft, he sobbed every night for days about leaving everything behind and what it would mean for me.

Hearing it all was both a comfort and a pain, like antiseptic poured over an open wound.

I didn't like talking about him in the past tense. Would I be speaking of Mom in the same way soon? She was looking well, but time was slipping away fast. We would soon fall into hyper suspension for good. Twelve years would evaporate in an instant between here and Rix. Would I wake to hear her final messages? If I sent one back, would it reach her before she grew too old?

There was no way to say for sure.

Finished ruminating, I continued on my walk leaving Shelly to rest in her sphere. Since I was already up, I figured I might as well check on the rest of the crew. Proxy could have done it for me, sure, but this felt right. I needed to see them with my own eyes.

I went through the spheres. Everyone was accounted for, but for Leo and Hy. This made me curious, and so I started searching the inner, then outer decks. As I approached one of the modular rooms, I heard the soft hum of music up ahead, low strings and piano. I immediately recognized the melody. It was a recording of *Ignes en Caelo*, Marissa Martin's grand work, which I last heard moments before the final Starfish attack on Novae.

Attempting to be quiet, I tiptoed to the door to one of the rooms and peered around the corner. Leo had requested the Foundry to redesign this room to be used as a kind of makerspace, with long worktables and directional lights, canvas easels, brushes of every variety, and an infinite supply of paints.

Leo stood before a canvas covered in swirls of navy and violet, a colorful wooden pallet hooked on his left thumb, a wide brush in his right hand. He tapped the handle of the brush against his brilliant-white teeth as he considered his next move. What was he painting?

Whatever this work might be, it was not the first. Several finished canvases lined the walls, each around four feet tall, three feet wide. There were paintings of the *Fidelis*, its shard-like form breaking away from a blue and green world with the *Reverie* at its back, the two of them propelled by bright trails of fusion energy. Paintings of familiar people on Novae working thick fields of grain with clawed machines, smiling at a bountiful harvest and the hope it brought. Paintings of two lovers kissing under a sea of stars, ripples of white among the void like those from a stone tossed into a placid lake at night.

No matter what I felt about him personally, he could paint like hell. These images made me feel emotions it was better to keep buried for now.

The music quieted for a moment.

"How you so good here, but terrible flying?" Hy asked Leo within the calm. I almost hadn't noticed him sitting on a stool in the corner, his back leaned against a wall, a black hardback book in his hands. "I don't think skill is issue."

"Can't be good at everything."

"Maybe so. Maybe not. But something's missing."

"Why do you give me a hard time about this? You've got less kills than I have."

"Yes, but fewer deaths, too. Captain says, don't die. And I don't die."

Leo dipped his brush in white paint and began to leave long strokes on the surface of the dark canvas. "Doesn't matter anyways. He'll end up taking it away from us when we get there. I heard that when the Starfish attacked, he piloted every single fighter by himself. I get the feeling he's a bit of a control freak. If he can pilot every fighter then, why not do it now? Why the hell are we even here? I think he doesn't trust me, or any of us for that matter."

This statement hit hard. Did I trust my crew? And how? Trust them to not betray us, of course, but to get the job done? I wasn't so sure. The stakes were too high to fail, and my team… They were terrible.

"And look," Leo went on, putting several more white strokes on the canvas, "I'm here to do what I do. This is what I do."

"You want to fly? Or are you making excuses?"

"Flying is fun," Leo admitted. "It's a kind of freedom I've never known. But so is painting. It's all I am. I'm just a painter."

Hy shook his book at Leo. "We are more than just our jobs."

The music began to build again, and this made spying difficult. I leaned in closer, trying to better hear what they were talking about without moving into sight, but shot straight out of my skin when something pinched my flank. Heat washed over my body as I spun around. Shelly was right in front of me, a hand clasped over her mouth fighting not to laugh. Her stealthy ass had snuck up on me and goosed me in the ribs.

I slid to the hallway's floor as I tried to regain my faculties.

"Did you hear something?" Leo said from inside the room, pausing in his work. "Like a squeak?"

"Shelly," I whispered, palm pressed against my thundering chest. I was doing everything I could to get my heartbeat to slow down. "Don't sneak up on me like that."

She smiled back. "Why not? That was hilarious."

"Hilarious? You nearly killed me."

"Whatever, love. Don't be such a baby."

I narrowed my eyes at her and took a step forward. "I'm not a baby."

She punched me on the shoulder and bounced on the balls of her feet several times like a boxer. "You awake now?"

"I've been awake for a while. Geez."

"Doing what?"

"Things. Why? What are you up for?"

She cocked her head and listened to the music for a moment. "Is that *Ignes En Caelo?*"

"Yes."

She pursed her lips and nodded. "Well, I rolled over in bed and you weren't there."

I shook my head. "Yeah, that makes no sense at all. You were under hyper suspension. Not like you can feel me rolling around."

She wrapped her arms around me and drew me close. "Okay then. Believe what you want. Just remember, Proxy is my friend too."

I returned her hug and felt warm inside. The prickles of shock vanished from my skin, and I relaxed. It was good to be hugged, really hugged.

"Maybe Leo is right," I said, my cheek resting against her head, words choked.

"About what?" she asked, her voice soft.

"It's been eight years since we've touched one another."

"Physically, yes, but we're together all the time. We've spent our waking hours in our Star Spheres in shared virtual environments."

"Yeah, I know, but it's not the same. This is why Mary and Esteban stayed out. It's different. And I can see why."

She nodded.

"We've got one more cycle to get ready," I said, letting go.

"And you don't think we're ready."

"Not even close."

"What do we do then?"

"I keep asking myself the same thing. What would Esteban do? He was in the military, he would know."

Shelly shook her head. "He would know because of who he was, not because of his military training."

"Be honest, babe, is this team as good as it's going to get?"

"I don't know," she admitted. "We might be. But just because we're not battle-hardened warriors, doesn't mean we can't stop Johan. It's in the finding him, not the stopping him that we need to be good at. Besides, we will have the Jevox to deal with soon. That in itself will prove interesting."

And she was right. But if we missed our opportunity on Rix, how were we going to find him then? How were we going to engage him? Hope was not a strategy. Would the Jevox help us in finding him?

"Come on," she said. "Let's go for a walk, then eat some food that's bad for us. In a few days everyone else will be up for the last phase, and by then, I'm sure you'll know what to do."

My stomach growled. "What about pizza? If you're in the mood."

"In the mood?" She waved in the vague direction of a nearby galley. "Lead the way. Let's get it with bacon and extra cheese and sausage and peppers and anything else we can dream up."

CHAPTER 24

"I've figured it out! I know how we can find Johan."

Our combined crews looked at Ada, who had just appeared out of nowhere, conversations falling silent. We were back in the bridge space, everyone present and discussing our next logical move. Given how much chatter was going on, it had taken me several minutes to realize Ada hadn't been part of our spirited discussions over formations and focused fire, but I soon dismissed this. I knew she had to be doing something important.

"How?" Karianna asked, stepping forward. "Show me."

Ada raised a finger and pointed back at her. "I've written a program to do it."

"A program?" Shelly piped up, then glanced in my direction, catching an interested look on my face. "What kind of program, Ada?"

"So, check this." Ada raised her hands and began using them to talk. "I've been chatting with Proxy. And apparently, some of the sensors on the ships can be networked together with the fighters. The main ships and the fighters share some limitations, yes, but some serious advantages. They use a similar optical navigation system in their designs, which allows us the same high resolution 180-degree cone of detection that the *Fidelis* has, but on each and every fighter. There's five of us per crew, so combined, we can cover just about every angle around the ship if we fly just right. Back to our earlier idea, using differences in background light, I think we can locate them doing this."

Shelly rubbed her chin. "Are you suggesting we network the sensors on the fighters together then fly in a specialized formation?"

"Hell yeah I am." She tossed up a set of peace signs and leaned in. "I swear it's clutch."

Proxy lowered its head. "Miss Lovelace's theory is sound. I have shown her the computing language of the Foundry and let her do most of the creative work. She is talented."

"And what a fascinating language, too." Ada smiled, hands on her hips. "While it has incredible flexibility like BaseJ, which is the language our hand terminals run on. It's self-stabilizing. I can't explain it, but the code itself does parity verification and predictive modeling. It has a way of suggesting what might create a bug later and offers alternative logic paths naturally. Proxy says it's not aware of having done this, that code can't 'think' any more than DNA sequences can. Says it's just baked into the building blocks themselves, encouraging the lines to array themselves the proper way, much like cells do when life forms. It's beautiful."

"And we can use this network you've created to find Johan?" I asked, trying not to let my excitement get the best of me.

"Almost certainly, Captain. When the stealth ship passes in front of a light source, visible or otherwise, we should be able to use our previous readings as a baseline and detect a difference. That dip in light will give us a place to fix on, and with a quick realignment of a couple fighters, we can get a good idea of distance based on trigonometric parallax."

"Like the band?" Lance ventured.

"The what?" Ada cocked her head. "I'm not following."

"Personally, I always liked them," Shelly told Lance.

"Rubbish," Leo mused, and I forced myself not to give him the evil eye.

"Anyways," Ada went on. "Milo or Karianna, when we have a solid vector, you can then bathe that region of space with light from the Para Lux Array. Even if they absorb all the light, the heat will cause tremendous damage. So, what do you think? It's going to take some work, but I think we can do it."

I rubbed my chin and thought it over.

The biggest challenge I saw before us was not that Ada's idea couldn't work on a theoretical basis, but that this would require us to coordinate even further. There was no way from a security perspective I could get Proxy to handle this specific formation, it was against the Foundry rules of intervention somehow. I could always take control myself, overclocking my mental processes to keep the fighters in formation, but then Leo would be right. Maybe I did have control issues.

"I'm guessing the formation needs to be pretty tight," I said, and began to pace around while thinking, imagining it all in my head. "If we veer too far in any direction, this will disrupt our optical coverage."

"Correct."

I looked to Shelly, then Karianna. Both of them had an expression that mirrored my concerns.

Stepping up beside Karianna, I whispered, "If we choose to work on these formation drills, it will likely negate any additional time we have for combat training. This operation won't be easy for them."

She looked over the crew of both ships and licked her lips, eyes narrowed in thought. "I'm afraid this might be the best we're gonna get in that category anyways. You know as well as I do, if we can't find that Dutch bastard, we're screwed. It's the best chance we have."

I let out a sigh, nodding as I did. "I thought you might say that. Good as it gets?"

"Good as it gets."

I mouthed the same question to Shelly. She gave a reluctant shrug.

"Alright then," I said, turning back to face the group. "Ada, it's a good idea. The best we have. So long as you think it's ready, then we need to prepare. Proxy, create navigational overlays for them to support their formation."

The cat rubbed against my legs. "Already done."

Ada gave me a smile, then her shoulders fell, and she began to pick at her nails. "Can I ask one favor though?"

"Sure, what is it?"

"If we find them, the stealth ship and all, can we give them a chance to surrender first. I know Alexander went with them, but I'd like to give him the opportunity to make it right. Please?"

This prompted several hushed exchanges, including one between Lance, Leo, and James. Xuan tried to tell Renata something, but the soldier just shook her head. It was clear that the crew had mixed opinions over whether Halifax was truly an unwilling accomplice.

"Okay," I said after a moment. "We'll give them a chance."

"Thank you."

"But if they try to run."

Her attention fell on the floor. "I know. We will do what we have to."

"Then it's decided. This last cycle we prepare to find the enemy, not just engage them." I gave a wave. "Ten more minutes, and we'll get on it. Get out your gabs and put on your serious faces. We've got formations to fly."

CHAPTER 25

And just like that, we were deep within the Jevox solar system, fast approaching the planet Rix. From a subjective time-reference, it had seemed only a few days since we entered hyper suspension for the last time, our final objective to run an endless series of formation drills built around Ada's detection concept. Frustration was still fresh on my mind, but it had been eleven years since we'd done our last simulation. Leo was still not listening. Lance and Ada were still trying to outdo one another. Xuan and Hy were still falling in line. That time was gone and here we were. Good, bad, or indifferent, this was showtime.

I broadcasted a general ping to wake the crew. Proxy was ready and standing at attention, not at all seeming bothered after being alone for all those years. Clearly it did not experience time the same way organics did.

"Did you have a good rest?" it asked as we transitioned from my bedroom environment to the bridge space, Shelly at my side, having changed out of sleepwear and into comfortable, all-weather colony clothes.

A cup of coffee appeared in my hand, and I let out a yawn. Real or not, the action always felt good. "I did."

"Any dreams?"

I considered that for a moment. The answer felt like yes, but I had no memory of anything. "Not sure."

Proxy said nothing and turned towards the star map materializing overhead.

Shelly gave me a kiss on the cheek, smiled, then turned to look at it with me.

With my free hand, I gestured to expand the map, the room replaced by a field of stars that we were supported within, much like that of my personal environment. As others joined us, they too could be part of this exploration. I really wished Dad were here.

Now that the *Fidelis* was within the boundaries of JV-01, the name we had given the Jevox home system, I could get much more clear readings on its characteristics. While the JV-01 system was fairly bare in a cosmic sense, made up of a red hyper giant cooler than 75-DFX which gave off tremendous radiation, with a dust ring surrounding it, as well as an asteroid belt, and two planets, Rix itself, the home world of the Jevox, was a clear anomaly. I had searched the Foundry databases for any planet like Rix and found none. It followed no baseline model of habitable worlds. The first and foremost of these oddities was being in a system with a star so dangerous and short lived like theirs, but this was hardly where that ended.

Rix was smaller than Earth and Novae by about thirty percent, its diameter a little under six thousand miles. Due to this fact, it had less mass, and thus, less gravity. That in itself did much to explain some of the Jevox biology; their musculature, if not their height. The striped surface of the planet teamed with life, its colors blue and green with sections of scintillating lights around its middle where two bands of endless cities circled the globe like a belt, a single line of greenish blue dividing them. Spectroscopy revealed that the atmosphere was oxygen rich, with a human tolerant mix of nitrogen and no harmful trace gases. The density of its air was a bit more than we were used to, and the atmospheric pressure higher, but it was no cause for serious concern. Proxy assured me we could breathe on the surface without much effort.

The strangest feature of Rix, however, was its satellites. Orbiting this stellar gem were five moons, a number we knew to be significant to the Jevox. Among these were two pairs of icy rocks, one pair orbiting perpendicular to the equator, another at a roughly forty-five-degree angle. These four moons were near identical in size and spewing trails of vapor from their surfaces, resulting in two complete rings of water and ice. The fifth moon, about a quarter more massive than the others, had its own orbit, and a relatively eccentric one at that, which followed the equator. There was no doubt that this moon influenced ocean tides.

"It looks more like a machine than a planet," Shelly said, and I nodded. She was right. This was not totally natural. There was no way it could be.

"They are expert terraformers," I said. "Maybe they terraformed their own world in some way."

The light of the three-dimensional model glowed in her eyes. "It's beautiful."

Karianna appeared beside us, hands on her hips, leaning forward as if having to squint at details on the map. "It is pretty. Hey, guess what else?"

"What?"

"I just picked up signs of crystallized oxygen in this system."

Shelly's eyes went wide. "You what?"

"Right?" Karianna drew the map's view away from the planet, widening it till she could point at several locations along the system's asteroid belt. "Inconsistent readings, whatever, but it keeps popping up. Big chunks of it. I bet the Starfish would be pissed as hell to see it."

"Good thing we left them back in 75-DFX."

"Good thing."

The crew began to filter in, but kept quiet for the most part, marveling at the system map. Leo produced a sketch pad and began making outlines, taking a graphite snapshot of this moment for a later painting.

Traffic above Rix was thick. Hundreds of starships going about, some as small as ten meters in length, others close to a kilometer. A ring-like station orbited above a densely developed section of the world, a tiny thread leading down to the surface. A space elevator.

I could see, not just hear, every signal traveling around the planet. They were ribbons of light in my mind's eye, threads too numerous to untangle. They were wonderful to look at, to feel, but impossible to find the one we needed. I could hear a billion devices speaking to one another, relaying coordinates and orders, going about their automated synchronicity. Conversations between distant Jevox, their voices scrambled and distorted. Delicate instruments reaching out to glean information from the universe, reflecting light off distant objects and measuring the results.

Then it hit me. How did you call a planet? Like, how did you contact them? Who did you try and reach? Science fiction stories always made it look easy, like knocking on a door, but if my estimations were correct, there could be as many as twenty billion Jevox living on Rix. I was drowning in data.

Proxy came to the rescue, rubbing against my legs and purring like a tiny chainsaw. "Milo, I've been able to isolate a signal among the noise from the surface. I believe it is the ruling body attempting to contact us. What they call themselves I cannot translate."

I let out a sigh of relief. The plan I'd been formulating involved starting with the first number in the directory and just calling everyone till I hit the last page. This was much easier.

"We have a call from the guv'nor?" Chevelle said, excited. "Quick, that. Not expectin' that till after the shots been fired."

"It's a good a place to start as any, I suppose," I said, shrugging it off and scratching Proxy behind the ear. No big deal, right?

"Did you think we were going to just show up and start shooting in the dark?" Karianna asked Chevelle, giving her a playful shove with an elbow. "That seems like a diplomatic nightmare. Fun, maybe, but not the kind of fun this fuddy duddy over here tends to condone." She hooked a thumb over at me.

"I enjoy it sometimes," I said, adjusting my jacket with a tug.

"Whatever." She waved a dismissive hand. "Let's be honest, this is no back woods outpost."

"No, it's not. We need to tread careful." I turned to Proxy. "What's our light speed lag from this position?"

"One hour."

"Okay." I scratched my chin. "Let's adjust our time reference to that frame and continue to approach the planet. If the situation changes, be ready to help us burn away. We know that the Jevox are well armed. Now, if they can go up against Foundry ships? That's a question I'd prefer not to have answered."

"You know, love," Shelly said, her tone thoughtful, "something you have not considered. They could have Foundry ships themselves."

And that was a distinct possibility. In fact, I'd not seen too many even when we had visited Cynosure. But would we know the difference if we saw them? Would we really? Could the sleek, five-engine ships the Jevox flew actually be of Foundry make, yet in the aesthetics of their species instead of our own? Much of what the Foundry shaped around us came from our personal perceptions and thoughts, our dreams, our imagination.

I nodded. "Good point. Maybe that's what they are, even if they don't look like the *Fidelis* or *Reverie*."

"Or even the *Isoptera*," James put in.

"Proxy, are they Foundry ships?" I asked.

It stared up at me, eyes blinking. It did not respond.

"Thanks a lot," I mumbled.

"Milo," Karianna said. "I am going to pull the *Reverie* back a bit, give us some distance just in case things don't go well. Though we had practiced Ada's formation to locate Johan, I don't think we should show our hand. If he's out here, that might just scare him off. Also, deploying fighters will almost certainly make the Jevox uneasy. Let's just keep our distance from one another and look as unthreatening as we can."

"Agreed." I took a deep breath and gestured with the flick of my wrist for the message to start. Something clicked in my mind as it began, the *Fidelis* linking my reference of time to that of the time lag between sent and received signals. I'd done this once before while parleying with Sinas across a solar system. This was the closest to speaking live we'd get till we were in orbit.

"Unidentified visitors. Make yourselves known," the message said, its coding different from the rest of the neutrino signals coming up from the planet. It was a voice, though not a single voice, but over two dozen individuals speaking at once. They were talking in a chorus, and something told me whatever their numbers were, it was divisible by five.

"I am Captain Milo Hughes of the *Fidelis*, a vessel made by the Foundry for humankind. I am joined by my fellow human associate Karianna Torlen of the *Reverie*. We come in peace."

"Humankind. Yes. We have heard of you. Our enclaves on Preste *have had dealings with you. Tall. Stiff in movement. Fractured of mind. Like so many others. You state peace, yet you come in weapons of war."*

"We have. Our species is alone in this region of space. We have traveled far from our home world, and the Foundry saw it necessary for our ships to be powerful enough to keep us safe from threats to protect life. Threats such as the Kabosai."

"Kabosai…" The line crackled for a moment. *"We have had dealings with the Gene Brokers. They claim to protect life. They do not understand."*

"They captured many of our people, and we rescued them. You will find no kinship with them among us."

"Very well. What business do you have with Rix? Have you come to trade?"

"Trade? No. No trade. We are seeking a human, and his accomplices who have done terrible things. A criminal."

"What is a criminal?"

A hard question to answer for a society of one mind. I gave myself a moment to think of my answer, though it seemed instant for them. "Someone who is acting against the whole for selfish gain. A, well, someone who speaks against the hive."

"Someone who is out of chorus?"

"Yes, that's one way to say it. Their voice leads to greater disharmony."

"Do you promise to come in peace, and leave in peace?"

"Yes."

Even taking into account the correction for light speed lag, it felt for a moment as if they hesitated for deliberation before speaking again. *"We will hold you to this. Do not attempt to injure the hive. As your species has been on its own, so has ours. Many have come to us, many have threatened us, including the Kabosai. Know that we are not defenseless."*

I became aware of ships mobilizing in orbit over Rix. A dozen Jevox starcraft much like what we had already seen began to move into formation, their trajectories intersecting with our own. I had seen what these ships could do to at least one of the Starfish and was not interested in what those keel-mounted energy weapons could do to us, Mercurial Integumentum or not.

"We understand, and we respect that," I responded after a moment. "The hive endures."

"The hive endures."

The signal went dead.

"Well then," Shelly started, "wasn't the warmest greeting, but I guess it wasn't rude either."

"Suppose we should go down and see them?" Karianna mused. "Shelly, do you know what kind of gift basket goes best with this sort of event?"

She shrugged. "Maybe a teddy bear, some good cheese, a fake bottle of champagne filled with candy?"

"With five of each item."

"With five of each," she agreed.

"Proxy," I called out. "Prep the Swift Shuttles, put the *Fidelis* in a defensive posture, MI ready to deploy in a scatter pattern if anything goes wrong. We're headed down. Every one of us."

It bowed to me. "As you wish."

"Everyone is going?" Renata spoke up. "Don't you think that's a bad idea."

"I'm with her," Leo said. "Not trying to seem cowardly or anything, but having a few of us up here might be a good idea. Maybe Miss Lovelace wants to help me keep the place warm. I am happy to be branded a coward over that."

Ada's face paled. "Count me in as part of the away group one hundred percent. Leo can stay if he likes."

"Fine, fine," he groaned. "I'll go."

"I'm not letting you go without me," Shelly whispered in my ear. "Too much could go wrong."

I reached back and took hold of her hand.

"Don't be a pussy Leo," James said. "We got this. One team, one group. Besides, it's not like these ships will be up here all alone. Proxy is pretty good at keeping the lights on."

"James is right for once," Karianna said. "Our Proxies can handle this. And, shit, I have a sneaking suspicion we're gonna need hands and eyes on the surface to get this done."

"Hear that folks? She said I was right."

My fellow freak offered him a frown. "Don't let it go to your head."

Renata huffed. "Still think it's a bad idea. If things go south, we could be trapped. Mission over."

"Noted. But the Jevox have been nothing if not good guests, no reason to believe they won't be good hosts. They helped us fix our shuttle, gave us valuable information, joined us for the concert, even took out a Starfish attacking the colony. They didn't have to, and yet they did. In at least the galactic sense, I think they've earned our trust."

"And in the Foundry sense," Shelly added. "They have protected life."

"They are a hive mind," I added. "The Jevox here should act much like the ones in 75-DFX. Based on what we know, they should be trustworthy."

Karianna rested fists on her hips. "Any other objections?"

No one spoke up. It was decided then. Everyone was going down to the surface.

We removed ourselves from the virtual environments and climbed from our Star Spheres, drying off and getting dressed. It was time to be in person. Time to experience the universe as we had evolved to experience it. The way Mom and the rest had been experiencing it.

Mom…

I paused in my tracks. It had been a long time since I had listened to any of her messages. Was she… Was she still alive?

I nearly brought up my inbox, but out of fear, held back. I was afraid to look. There were messages, but I was afraid to watch them.

"I can look when we get back up to the ship," I mumbled and went on my way.

I made for Shelly, and we walked together, my mechanical hand in hers, flesh on metal. Despite the comfort of having her beside me, I felt stiff, nervous. So much relied on what came next.

"Think we'll find him on the surface?" I asked her, the two of us standing just outside the shuttle dock. "That's a lot of Jevox down there. So much to sort through."

She paused for a moment to consider this; a finger pressed to her lips. "It's the best lead we have. If he's planning to do what we believe he's planning to do, then it will involve enthralling several enclaves of Jevox. Maybe thousands, who can say? In a society where everyone lives with oneness of mind, I imagine the disappearance of so many will be noticeable."

"If they talk about it and are willing to tell us."

"True. We'll just have to hope they do."

I sighed at that, but what was the other option? "I think we should play this one close to the chest. Don't tell them anything at all. Especially the part where we've learned to control their minds. Dangerous information."

"Our secret."

"Our secret. We are just human explorers looking to locate a rogue operator in our ranks. He stole a ship and wasn't in the best mental state when he left. We wanted to find him and his crew before he hurt anyone."

"It's not a lie," she said, squeezing my fingers. "It's our intention."

"Yeah," I said, frowning.

She gave me a hug and kissed me on the cheek. "I'll tell everyone else after we board."

The crew took their seats on the Swift Shuttle and we left the *Fidelis* with Proxy in charge, its mass orbiting Rix just a few hundred kilometers from the surface along the planet's spin west to east. The *Reverie* fell in formation next to the *Fidelis* soon after our shuttle had egressed.

The dense atmosphere of Rix pressed against our Swift Shuttles as we descended, turning us briefly into twin comets screaming through blue skies. The weather in the high reaches was mild that day, and what storms the planet was experiencing were mostly off into the north and south, making our journey a not so turbulent one.

The surface swelled to encompass the horizon.

As we had observed from orbit, the entire center band of the planet's surface was covered in dense cityscapes with a few acres of natural relief. As we neared this sprawling megacity, luminous, cylindrical skyscrapers made of glass, carbon composite and steel shot up several hundred meters from a smooth bed of concrete, their forms like metal quills on a giant beast. The light of JV-01 reflected back at us from their many thousands of windows, flashes coming in sequence as we approached. It was all arrayed in symmetrical patterns, the streets between buildings filled with traffic in the form of silver ground cars on the bottom layer, flying machines on the second and third. They moved with swift, perfect coordination, like blood flowing through arteries, a oneness of mind with little or no disorder. It would be some time before Novae resembled anything this wonderous, if ever.

Skimming a few hundred feet above the tops of buildings, I began to make out the finer details on the structures, noting long sections of their prismatic exteriors were covered in lush, green plants, bushes and vines growing on the sunward side from cloud top down to street level. Despite the lack of local ground vegetation, this persistent, architectural feature made the city feel as if flora and steel were in symbiosis, not competition.

"Remarkable," Shelly said, pointing at a building that was taller than the rest. From within the Star Sphere, I could hear as well as see my passengers talking in the back of the shuttle just as if I were seated with them. "They appear to be using every renewable resource at their disposal. Their brighter star provides them with more than enough solar energy to power each building. And food, I'm confident those aren't just any plants. They're crops."

Leo pressed himself up against the window of the shuttle and sketched on a tablet furiously, capturing as many details as he could.

"I know they're a hive mind," Ada began. "But I swear they act as if they're straight up networked together, and not over the short range. How does a Jevox, in say this part of the city, stay connected to one on the other end of the planet? I know we know it's an electromagnetic field and all, but that's too far. Too much distance. It has to be an ad hoc network, skipping from one Jevox to the next until the new data is distributed. I just wonder how signals find a path, you know?"

"Humans are not much different," Lance offered. "When we have an idea we tell others, and they tell others. Might not be as high bandwidth as all this, and I know those who hear don't have to agree, but it's how we communicate."

"Oh. That's a good point."

Shelly licked her lips and took a deep breath. "Let's not ask them how. We need to keep the fact we could influence their thoughts silent."

"I know," Ada relented. "I know."

"Hy, maybe we should network our brains together," Xuan said, smiling at her husband. "Then you'd legit have the chance to read my thoughts."

He shook his head. "Not sure I want to know how much of an idiot you think I am."

"I don't think it all the time."

"But some of the time."

"Maybe. Example, you can't keep from dripping water all over the bathroom after a shower."

"This again?" He threw up his hands. "Years in hyper sleep, no water on the ground, still she brings it up."

Xuan shrugged. "I just wish you knew how this makes me crazy. Five times I almost slip and break my neck."

"You look at me? I have tremendous amounts of surface area. This holds water."

"You skinny as a green bean, only surface area you have is inside that skull of yours."

"We're getting close," I reported, and hoped it would calm them down. I sure as hell hoped Shelly and I never got like this. "Almost there. A couple heads up, the atmosphere here is a little thicker than we are used to, though not enough we need to do any conditioning. Breathing might feel weird. But, hey, there's less gravity, so that's a bonus. If you've been looking to lose a few pounds, congrats."

I followed the coordinates given and found a platform on the north side of a city section, shaped differently than the rest. This collection of blocks was oval like an eye, its surface devoid of all but a few tall buildings and a flat space spotted with many conical, five winged ships.

Under their instruction, I put the Swift Shuttle down on an open stretch of tarmac and cut off the engines, Karianna's shuttle taking position next to us, our airfoils nearly touching. I met with the crew, and we prepared to disembark.

"Let me do the talking for now," I said. "No idea what could happen. If this all goes wrong, I'll call Proxy to bring the shuttle to our location and we'll get out of here fast as we can."

"What if Johan decides to start a fight in the middle of the city?" Leo asked. "We have no weapons."

"And I hope that he wouldn't be bold enough to carry ones either. Pretty sure he'd be more subversive."

"Given his ability," Ada said, wringing her hands. "I would say there's a chance he can move around unseen. All he'd have to do is plant the thought that nothing ever happened. He wasn't there."

We paused and stared at one another, thinking this over. She was right.

A knock came on the outside door of the shuttle. It was Karianna.

"We'll just have to make the best of it," I told my crew. "We're confident he can't control everyone at once. There's a level of influence, a range. Something would be noticed."

Outside the shuttles we were met by two contingents of Jevox dressed in form fitting body armor, which given their multi-jointed, bipedal bodies and eye constellations, made for strange viewing. They bore rifles but did not raise the barrels to make any threat. With a wave, they urged us to follow them towards a building at the edge of the platform, saying nothing to us as we walked. None of our group argued with them and we did as they requested. I sure hoped that bringing everyone had been the right choice.

"We're dead," James mumbled, and Lance nodded in response.

"So grim," Leo added. "Always so grim."

Within a few moments we found ourselves in an open space with five corners, pentagonal in shape, its walls painted with abstract designs in a garish array of colors. There were collections of curved tables which faced inward, with a ceiling above us so far away it was impossible to see, likely reaching all the way to the top of one of the silver skyscrapers. At each corner of the cathedral-like chamber, a group of five Jevox stood, totaling twenty-five in all. They wore wide cuffed, floor length robes over their oddly jointed forms, each group possessing a different shade of cloth—crimson, yellow, green, violet, and cerulean—the breathing masks they had worn on Novae absent. I found myself multiplying five by five by five, trying to count the number of eyes which fell on us in scrutiny.

Our crews were herded to the center, where a pentagon was painted upon the floor in black and gold. The five groups closed in on us, forming a solid wall of Jevox. The temperature felt increasingly warm, ratcheting up by several degrees as our group was surrounded.

"Why do you come?" one of the crimson robed Jevox asked, its hands making a dismissive gesture. It was not happy we were here.

"Not quite the trade greeting we were given on Novae," Karianna whispered in my ear.

I cleared my throat and straightened my back, raised my right hand and waved it through the air like I had seen the Speaker do once before. "We come to seek a human named Johan and his enclave. They are dangerous to both us, and you."

"You use the word enclave," another of the Jevox said, this one dressed in violet and standing behind me, "yet you are human. Do they move with one mind?"

I was forced to turn in order to respond. "No, and yes. They have one purpose."

"Humans make decisions on their own, is this not true?" a yellow asked, forcing me to again turn.

"We act on our own, but we have common thoughts. We often act for the good of the many."

"But only if it is convenient for the individual?" A green on the far right asked next. "We have seen the reports from our kind in your system. They have seen you act different than one another."

"The Jevox from Preste, do you not call it?"

"Yes," a cerulean replied. "An outpost."

This was making me dizzy. I wasn't sure who to address or where. Why were they in different colors? What did that mean? Why not one color? Why paint abstract like they did? Shelly had read up about them, and that somehow, they were individuals emotionally, if not logically. That must have had something to do with this. Still, it was confusing.

"Your people speak the truth," I said, addressing a violet Jevox, before slowly rotating to look at others. What did it matter who I spoke with? Might as well talk to all of them. "We do at times act against one another out of selfishness, but that is why we have ideas like family, tribe, society, city, and world. These concepts allow us to see our individual nature as part of a whole. In that way, then we can act as one, if only on important decisions."

"Selfishness?" a crimson-dressed Jevox said, rolling the word around in its mouth. "This is a concept we do not truly understand, and it is not only human. No Jevox would act against another. We are one body, many parts. We are strong and healthy when those parts are close enough in mind, but wide enough in body."

It did not look as if we were getting through. How would I get them to see things like we did? And was this even possible? I turned to my companions, and no one offered any immediate assistance. Shelly had a look on her face as if she were attempting to work out a puzzle.

Then an idea came to me. A way to connect, to translate our individuality. "Are there other Jevox homes? Have you colonized many worlds? Like Preste?"

"Yes," they agreed as one.

"Are you all different? Or all the same? I can only imagine distance creates deviation of ideas. Light only travels so fast."

"Some deviation," they said again as one. "Some pain."

"Then that is what it is like to be human. We are each an enclave unto ourselves, many thoughts in one body, some common, some not, all separated by distance and time. We diverge, develop different ideas with a common basis. We only have words and touch to communicate, nothing direct in our minds. Our experiences, however, are filtered through personality, events, biology. For me, the colors red and yellow might be the most beautiful, but to my wife, my mate, it might be blue and green."

They turned to one another for a moment, discussing. I had gotten through somehow; I was sure of it.

"We too have deviations of view," one said. "Yet our choices are the same. All follow what the *ississ* declares to be truth." Whatever word they had used to describe what this gathering was, it did not translate through our Foundry augmentation. It came through as static.

I shook my head. "If your enclave of enclaves decides something to be right and true, so do the rest?"

"So do the rest," one in violet said. "We are the hive."

"What happens if one of you is separated from the group?" Shelly stepped towards the yellow and asked. "Or, if three only have one companion?"

"We hurt," they said as one. "We mourn."

A silent moment passed, no one seeming to have the will to continue. Then a cerulean Jevox shorter than the rest raised its right hand. This one was different somehow. It wore jewelry of silver and gold. Its posture, the slightest bit askew, tilting to the right. "Why are you here?"

"I have told you," I said.

"Yes," it considered. "And this is not enough. If you cannot find this chaotic threat to our peace, then you must go. We must remain of one mind. One thought. This variable invites danger. You invite danger."

"Three days," a crimson said. "We will give you access to the city so long as you will show no harm for three days. If you cannot find them in that time, you will get on your Foundry ships and leave."

"Three days?" Leo asked, exasperated. "There's like billions of people on this world. How will three days be enough?"

And for one of the few times ever, I agreed with him. "Three days is a bit short. We have traveled for a long time. Years. It might not be enough."

"Then you will have to work together," a yellow near the center said. "Be of one mind, one effort. Three days is more than enough time."

"Just for clarity," Karianna cut in. "When you say three days, do you mean Rixian days? Or are we talking another measure?"

I swore they narrowed their eyes at us all at the same time, and with so many eyes in evidence, it made my stomach twist.

"The Foundry universal translation converts the rotation of a planet into a day," they said. "Is that a day for you?"

"It is," Shelly said. "And if my calculations are correct, that gives us ninety-six hours. Rixian days are longer than we are used to."

"Still not enough," I mumbled. "May we have more? If we prove we are not dangerous?"

"Your very presence is dangerous," one said. "It influences us. It is a threat to our chorus."

I started to protest, anger and frustration rising in my belly, but Shelly grabbed my arm and shook her head. She was right. Getting angry was not the answer to this particular challenge. Brute force was not going to help us achieve our objective.

"Okay," I said, taking a deep breath. "We appreciate your generosity and will conduct our search. Will you offer aid?"

They nodded as one.

"Thank you," Karianna said, making some sort of hand gesture which seemed to please them. "The hive endures."

"The hive endures," they replied.

Seeing firsthand how the Jevox spoke and worked together, even in conversation, made me wonder what humanity would be like, what we might achieve if we had reached this level of collaboration. They claimed to have no true individuals, but I saw the subtle signs. Nevertheless, they decided together and moved as one. A single path, one objective, and that was a powerful thing. There was nothing they could not do, and efficiently at that, so long as they deemed it right. This planet was evidence of that fact.

As for us lowly humans, well… We'd just have to do the best we could to coordinate a worldwide search on short notice.

No big deal.

CHAPTER 26

The guards returned and led us out of the meeting hall, the solid line of people making up the Jevox ruling body parting to give us a single exit. I felt relieved to escape this pentagon of scrutiny, and from the look of it, I wasn't the only one. Almost every crew member, from the *Fidelis* or the *Reverie*, walked a little taller, moved a little freer once we had the space to stretch out.

"That wasn't awkward or anything," Lance commented, striding up beside me. "At least they aren't pretending to be nice only to fry us up later."

"They do not like us," I said.

"The Jevox in 75-DFX were different, man. There must be some truth to what you said, when they're away from one another they develop differently. What kind of help do you think we'll actually get?"

"I don't know." I gestured towards a Jevox up ahead. "I think we're about to find out."

Waiting for us on the platform outside was the odd, cerulean robed Jevox from their group, its arms and neck adorned in glittering jewelry, for which the rest of its kind did not wear. This one was unlike the others, shorter, about three quarters my own height, and moved differently, less mechanical in its step. No other Jevox stood at its side. It was alone.

"Humans," the lone Jevox said, raising its right hand, the sleeve of its deep, blue robes hanging down. "Let us work together to resolve this matter quickly."

"Hello," I said. "Any information you can give us would be valuable. Have you detected any ships?"

"Only yours. Those two in orbit. There have been no other foreign arrivals. How can this be? You vehemently claim that they are here, and yet we see no evidence."

"Their ship has stealth technology," Karianna offered, tossing a thumb at the sky, her bracelets jingling. "Foundry-make. It's good, real good."

"Stealth technology?" the Jevox mused. "Then you have failed before you even started. The Foundry is the greatest builder of ships, everyone knows this. You will not find this vessel."

"But we have to try. We're hoping to catch him doing something stupid, making a mistake. Just because he has a stealth ship, does not make him and his people invisible, or infallible."

"The *ississ* did not ask." It was that hiss again. "Why do they come here? What are they after?"

Karianna gave me a look, and I shook my head ever so slightly.

"Their leader murdered one of our people," she said. "Something which doesn't happen in our culture. Murder is a relic of a distant past."

"Murder?" It considered that for a moment. "Do you mean, to kill one another intentionally? Not in defense."

"Yeah, it's pretty bad."

"Why would one do that? Does it not cause pain to others? Cause pain to oneself?"

"It does," she admitted, "and they usually just don't care. It gives them whatever they want in the end."

"I do not understand. Would consequences not come back to you?"

"We don't experience the suffering of other humans like you do with other Jevox. There's empathy, or whatever, and some of us have more of that than we need, but it's not so direct." She pointed at her right temple, then to me. "It's not brain to brain, heart to heart. Sometimes there's a disconnect. It's communicated with words, gestures, different cosmic vibrations. And to be honest, some bastards just don't care."

This confused the Jevox. "A fatherless child?"

"It's just a human expression," I replied. "You know, a bastard, a shitty person. A son of a bitch."

My explanation did not seem to help, leaving it even more confused.

"You must find this person," the Jevox said. "You will have to search the streets."

"All of them?" I took a sharp breath. "You have a massive world. And these cities, they are dense."

"Perhaps. But I cannot give you more than the access to search."

Karianna scowled at this. "Your species is crazy advanced. You don't have, like a bio scanner from Star Trek or something? Anything we can use to narrow it down?"

It did not respond. I got the feeling it didn't want to help. We were just some murdering bastards, and it didn't want to be part of this, even if it meant other murdering bastards ran free on its streets.

"You have not answered my earlier question," it said. "What is this murderer's, this Johan's, intention? What does he want? Is it different than what you want?"

This was where things could get dicey. How could we ask the right questions without giving away too much? We did not need them to figure out that we had a theoretical means to enthrall their entire species.

"Information," I said. "Technology. He is searching for how to rapidly repair environmental damage to a planet. Our home world needs help. He believes he can deliver that help."

Its back straightened, an expression of understanding. "Terraforming?" it clarified.

"Yes."

"That is the work of the Crimson. Our technically minded."

I felt my eyebrows raise in surprise. The colors were perhaps more than just colors. They were divisions of labor. Maybe castes or sects. This confirmed one idea. "And where do the Crimsons work?"

"Many places. Many districts."

"What is your name?" Shelly asked, taking a step towards the Jevox. "You have a name, yes?"

What was she doing? I looked to Karianna for answers, who gave me a shrug in response that felt like, 'She's your wife, you figure it out'.

"A name," the Jevox said, the tone of its words thoughtful. "Yes. I have a name."

"I would like to know it," she said, leaning in, "if that is of course, appropriate."

"My name is—" There was a pause as it worked to retrieve its name like one might a memory from the mental libraries of the distant past. "It is Frelo."

"A pleasure to meet you, Frelo. I am Shelly Hughes." She offered a hand. "It's a customary human greeting. You lightly grab the fingers, squeeze, shake a moment, then let go."

Frelo paused for an instant, then did as they were instructed. It was about the limpest handshake I had ever seen, and yet the action seemed to knock something loose within Frelo's ovoid head. Their expression became brighter, its gestures more animated. They had enjoyed shaking Shelly's hand. It had been given a new experience.

"You're not like the rest," Shelly said, touching one of the bracelets dangling from its right arm. "They are beautiful, by the way."

"Thank you," Frelo remarked, attention lingering on the metal bands, the gentle touch of her hands. "My personal collection."

"Your speech is not the same as the rest either. Why is this?"

Frelo cocked their head and considered its response. With a free hand they ran fingertips over the many gold and silver necklaces around their neck as if recalling memories. "I was away from the hive for a time, far too long, alone on a dark world for many yuniea, no minds to have chorus with. My enclave was on an exploration mission to a small, icy moon. The rock showed signs of isotopic deposits we thought could be used for energy. Our ship crashed on its surface, caught in a sudden windstorm. I was the sole survivor."

Shelly frowned. "That must have been difficult. Being alone is always hard."

"Yes. Difficult. And, *painful*." The word caught in their throat. "I mourned the deaths of my enclave. My…"

"Family?" she pressed. "That is a word we use for a common unit of our society."

"Family," they said, considering. "No. Enclave. It is not the same."

"I am sorry you lost them. Do you miss them?"

"Yes. Like a hole in my body, an injury that will not heal. They were part of me, part of what helped me experience the world. Their perception, their views, all similar but from a different angle. I did not take a mate, like the others in my enclave, and so in a way it was easier for me, but I am not free from loss."

"I can't imagine what that would be like," Shelly said, patting it on the arm. "This is what made you different?"

"Yes. I was taken in by the Melcorin. They cared for my physical needs and tried to help with my cognitive and emotional ones. Their success was limited. They did their best with what they knew, which is substantial, I must say. The Melcorin are a remarkable species, they protect life. In my time aboard their ship, I adopted some of their practices. Practices such as the giving and accepting of gifts and sharing conversation with meals. For as long as I was among them, it was natural to keep some of these practices."

"You are an individual."

"We are all individuals in our own way. Even Jevox."

"Perhaps, but you, Frelo, I can see it. You are truly different. By choice or not, you are different."

The word, different, seemed to provoke some kind of emotional response, though I could not be sure what. Most Jevox facial expressions were lost on us. Were they disgusted, or proud? Could they be both?

"Enough of me," it said after a silent moment, arms dropping to its sides. "We should use the security equipment and scan the city for anomalies. It does seem inefficient to have you traipsing all over given your short window to search."

"Most generous," Shelly said. "And less disruptive for your people, I would venture."

"Yes," they said, leading us to a pair of silver ground cars with half a dozen seats in each. "Our planetary transit vehicles are smaller than you are used to. Apologies for the discomfort. You must adjust. If your Johan is after terraforming technology, it is likely he will be found in one of two districts, Green Point or Sky Claw. The Crimson spend most of their time working there."

"But you are not a Crimson," I said, following after.

"No, and yes. I was a Crimson once. I am now Cerulean."

"And what does this mean?"

"I spend my days searching for answers to problems we have not solved. The universe is vast, unknowable, infinitely massive both out there, and inside of every cell."

"So, you're a scientist?" I smiled, and it felt good, a connection made, a host of rushing memories touched. "We all come from scientists. Children of scientists. My father, he, eh—he studied stars."

"We are all made of stars. I am sorry, but your word, *scientist*, does not encompass the entirety of the Cerulean, but it will be sufficient for our interactions. Here." It removed a metallic card covered in symbols from one of its deep sleeves. "One of your groups may take this access card and tell the vehicle's AI where to carry them. When you are done searching you may return here if you like. If the day is too late, you may use the access card to find lodgings and rest. Rix has many guest quarters. It will guide you. I suggest that you would visit Sky Claw."

"Yoink." Karianna snatched the card from Frelo's fingers. "Thank you, so very much, kind sir." She took a grand bow.

"As for the rest of you, we may travel together."

"*Fidelis* in one car. *Reverie* in the other."

"Do not forget," Frelo said, taking hold of Karianna's arm before she could turn away. "You are here as a courtesy. Harm any Jevox, take a hostile action or attempt to steal from our people, and there will be retribution. We can defend ourselves, even from Foundry made ships. Do you understand?"

Karianna shrugged out of their grip and nodded. "I gotcha, bruh. We aren't here to hurt anyone."

"We just want to find Johan and leave," I agreed.

"Very well," Frelo said. "The *ississ* will be pleased. We should be on our way."

We climbed into the ground cars, twisting and turning so that we could fit inside vehicles meant for people one to two feet shorter than we were. It wasn't easy, but in just a few minutes we were on our way. Karianna and her crew heading for Sky Claw, my crew along with Frelo headed for Green Point.

I pressed my face up against the glass and watched as the Swift Shuttles shrunk out of sight. Shelly reached out and took hold of my hand, not a fearful grab, just a gentle touch. As we took it all in, the sight of this impossible city under blue skies, excited conversations between Lance and Leo, Xuan, Hy, and Ada all faded into the background, becoming part of the hum that the vehicle made.

The automated car took us away from the platform at a breakneck pace, lines of retaining walls and the lower floors of buildings becoming a blur. This was the first time in years I'd been anyplace larger than Novae, but not even Cynosure had roads like this. In fact, within that Foundry melting pot, we'd been forced to walk everywhere. Likely the last time I rode in a ground vehicle at speeds this high, I'd been sitting in a car seat holding tight to Jasper.

The roads were six lanes wide, filled to the brim with cars flowing through the city. When openings appeared in the lanes, a fresh vehicle would rush in out of nowhere, then later vanish off a side street. No one fought to gain position, to arrive before anyone else like Dad said people used to do in city traffic, they just found their place and zipped along with the flow. It appeared wildly efficient, allowing for tens of thousands of cars to pass without incident.

While the lanes were full of machines, so too were a set of sidewalks filled with Jevox on foot, so many that there wasn't room for much else, each walking shoulder to shoulder and in groups of five. These thoroughfares were awash with color, the standard robes we had seen before among them, as well as others, multi-colored and faceted with abstract designs.

On the outside of the skyscraper buildings, Jevox climbed like spiders up and down their hanging gardens, pruning branches and picking fruit, for which they placed in satchels dangling off their shoulders. While many operated alone, some formed chains, tossing pieces of fruit from one to the next until they reached high balconies where a final Jevox collected them.

"Just the thought of climbing the side of those buildings makes my feet sweat," Lance said, then reached into his jacket and produced his beard comb. "Couldn't pay me enough."

I pivoted my head to look at my crew, crammed into their seats and drinking it all in. Leo had his tablet and had not stopped sketching; digital pages filled with dozens of line drawings.

"It is safe," Frelo said, pointing to a building up ahead taller than the rest, almost the entire structure covered in green. "We evolved climbing in the mountains to the north. Many ground predators. We are confident in it. There are safety measures as well. If a Jevox falls, which does not often happen, their belt will catch them."

"Their belt?" Lance paused. "Like a safety harness?"

"No. It is a catch field, a Jevox technology. We've never seen any other race with anything like it. It creates drag in the atmosphere using a particle field cast in a net above them. If we fall, it uses the air to slow our descent. The greater the height, the slower the fall, the more time for drag to be created. If we fall short distances there can be some injuries, though usually minor."

"We have something similar, I think," Xuan said. "But it uses cloth. A parachute."

"Cloth can tangle."

"But how do you grab air with other particles?"

Hy chuckled. "Ancient Jevox secret?" This made both Lance and Xuan chuckle.

Shelly looked to me and shrugged. Thank the Universe I was not the only person left out this time.

For once, Ada did not join in with their joke. She had gone inward. Leo came up from his tablet, noticed her expression, and gave her a gentle shove with his elbow. She stared daggers back at him, and all he could do was flash that perfect smile in response.

"He does have a good smile," Shelly whispered in my ear. "That hair, though."

"Thought you liked blondes," I replied, nodding my head towards Lance.

She scowled at that idea. "I know they say blondes have more fun, but I like my dark headed half-Brazilian boy the best."

"That's good news."

"Besides, Leo's platinum hair color comes the same route Mary's used to, out of a chemistry lab."

"We are here," Frelo said, and the ground car slowed, redirecting its path into the base of a long, squarish building of silver and white, all hard angles without any crops growing from it. "This is Green Point, part of the terraforming works. This is where the Life Changers are designed, upgraded, and many of their components outfitted."

"What are Life Changers?" I asked as the car came to a stop inside an underground parking deck of some sort. The space was light grey with walls made of concrete or smooth stone, interrupted only by the occasional stroke of color. Rows of hundreds of identical ground cars were parked here, the majority in standby.

"The Prole Genascara, Life Changers, are Jevox terraforming ships," Frelo said, pressing a button on the dash of the car. The doors opened.

We climbed out into the open deck and stretched, each of us relieved to be able to stand upright once more. Not sure how long I could have kept up that contorted sitting position. This world was clearly not designed for people of our height. That did not bode well for what they considered lodgings, either. Chances were we'd be folded up like fetuses in the womb just to fit on their beds.

"Just how big are these ships?" Shelly asked Frelo, hurrying up beside it. "What are they like?"

"They are the largest ships Jevox build and maintain, fifteen kilometers in length with a crew of close to ten thousand. Depending on the needs of the world that they are terraforming, they are outfitted accordingly. Oftentimes those required materials are gathered on other worlds, dead worlds."

We were led deeper into the building, through a series of automatic doors, then into a tunnel that I can only assume went down. This was purely a guess, based on the angle of the lines against where we entered, and a sneaking sensation in my inner ear. Visually it was hard to tell after a few steps, however, if we were walking up, down, or level. Gravity played a major role in orientation.

"I'm feeling a bit nauseous," Leo mumbled as he slipped his tablet into a messenger bag resting against his hip. "This is not a sensation we get within the virtual environments."

Ada put a hand on his shoulder, gripping tight. "Steady now. Don't fall over. And don't get any funny ideas. Just trying to make sure you don't faceplant."

His eyebrows raised as if he were about to say something smartass, then he thought better of it.

The strange sensation began to abate, and we soon found ourselves in a massive, square room several hundred meters across, its ceiling a dozen meters high. Its walls were made of a greyish metal, many symmetrical segments of which were painted with abstract color breaking up the monotony. The main floor of the room was a grid of sorts, each tile filled with stations where enclaves of Jevox worked in groups huddled around instruments. These spaces were equipped with all kinds of devices and flasks of chemicals, some with what appeared to be containment hoods or full enclosures for dangerous or volatile work. The Jevox themselves often wore protective gear, face guards and gloves, along with papery robes. It reminded me of the lab on the *Vasco Da Gama* where James, Harper, George, and I spent detention all those years ago, if much, much larger.

Frelo led us around the outside of the room down a path hemmed by clusters of pipes ranging from several inches in diameter, to as much as a foot. They hummed softly and gave off heat, and so I avoided touching them even if I felt curious. Crimsons working at their lab stations began to watch us as we passed. No doubt Frelo was communicating who we were and our intentions through the hive network so as not to raise alarms. Still, some were more fascinated, or perhaps just less busy than others. Xuan and Ada waved at them with smiles on their faces while Lance, Leo, and Hy fell into a close circle and began mumbling.

"Much of terraforming involves chain reactions," Frelo began, gesturing towards a set of stations with full containment equipment, a single Jevox at each working in heavy suits within a glass-like box filled with an amber gas. "A world is safe and healthy to a species for many reasons, none exactly the same. Evolution determines these conditions. Gravity, over which we have little control. Temperature, over which we have some control. And of course, atmosphere. Much of this can be modified with the right triggers, the right timing, but every world is different. Every case its own. We cannot ever hope to bring enough gas from one world to give another atmosphere within even our great Prole Genascara, or remove all dangerous gases from a world saturated by it within fewer than many lifetimes of most species. And so, we must be clever.

"For example, take a world with a dense atmosphere of carbon dioxide that is too close to its star. It's unbearably hot due to trapped greenhouse gases. If you can cool the planet, using solar mirrors, you may freeze the carbon dioxide, and by doing so, reduce the atmospheric pressure of that world and prepare it for the first phase of terraforming. Given enough time, the carbon dioxide will become liquid and can then be removed from the planet, perhaps shot into space to create an artificial moon for later use. This will leave only nitrogen in the atmosphere. Once this is complete, water may be sling shotted onto the planet over decades, until oceans appear on the surface."

"You can then introduce bacteria," Shelly ventured, a smile on her face. "Turn the nitrogen atmosphere into something more. At the start of our world, we had a kind of cyanobacteria that did this, or so we think. It's where life began. It put oxygen into our atmosphere through photosynthesis and made it breathable. It also made the base chemicals for other, more complex life to form. Like us."

"That is a common path," Frelo said. "We too evolved this way, and beyond."

"So, you get the atmosphere ready, put a plan in place to remove the harmful chemicals, then seed it with life. Is life so different on other worlds?"

"It can be. Some species are methane breathers; some use oxygen, like us. Some space-dwelling creatures even use a kind of cellular respiration that operates in reverse compared to humans and Jevox. These consume a kind of crystallized oxygen."

I piped up. "Did you say crystalized oxygen?"

"Yes. It allows them to grow and live within the void."

Shelly cut her eyes at me and shook her head, urging me not to speak of it further. Like 75-DFX, JV-01 might have space dwelling life. This was proof, though we had not seen any firsthand. A kind of life, that if detected, made other partially space dwelling species go into a frenzy. If the Starfish were afraid, strong as they were, perhaps we best not meet it.

"Every species and every world are different," Frelo went on, bringing us around a corner to a room sitting just off the main lab floor. "They require decades of research before a world of sufficient resources can be located, and if successful, other research to find the path of least resistance."

"How long would it take for a world that merely needs cleaning up?" I asked, thinking back to the conditions we knew of Earth. No telling what it was now, but when we left, I had a feeling this Life Changer's standard equipment would do the job, and in the grand scheme of things, in a short amount of time.

"Depends on the world. What is your primary challenge? Heat? Light? Radiation? Is it soil composition? A lack of biodiversity?"

"A buildup of greenhouse gases mostly, or so we believe. Some pollution in populated sectors, chemicals that cause cancer. A few nuclear power accidents, radiation spillage. The weather is too hot in some places, too cold in others. It has changed how storms work. This has driven several terrestrial species of both animals and plants to extinction."

"I see." They paused, then blinked their eyes back at the floor of
Crimson engineers. "Could be simple enough. Deployment of a solar
deflector to reduce nearby starlight while direct capture devices are used
around the globe. Between fifteen to fifty of them. The rest of these factors
are too nuanced to say for sure at this time, though it seems possible."

And there it was. Far as terraforming jobs, Earth was an easy one. A job
that, with a little help, Johan and his crew might just be able to pull off.

Within the smaller room into which we had been led were shelves filled
with equipment and supplies made of various materials, most of them black
or grey with strips of color along the side. Bottles and cannisters lined the
left wall, their valves pointing perpendicular to the floor like wine in a rack.
Along the right wall were closets with the outlines of containment suits,
likely storage for the crimsons on the floor.

Frelo opened a glass case on the far wall and began removing black
boxes, counting their number against the humans standing with it.

"I'm curious," Lance said, breaking free of his huddle with Leo and Hy.
"Why terraform for others? Is there an economic reason? You want to
make money or have resources in exchange? From how it sounds so far,
that would take decades, possibly centuries depending on the world."

"Money is transient. Value of negotiable instruments, currency, they
change too rapidly. No, we are not after money. We are after respect.
Mutual respect."

"I don't follow."

"We are not an aggressive species. We seek to have peace and be on our
own. We are not xenophobic like some, we do not hate other species, but
we wish to limit our interactions. By helping others survive, we get to
thrive. We do not make enemies. We get to be left to ourselves."

This sort of exchange made a great deal of sense. There would always be
a need for the service they offered, and if another species was safe on its
own worlds, why would they then be aggressive?

"And does this policy always work? Helping others as a means of
passive defense?"

"No. No it does not. And as we have said before, we have ways of
protecting ourselves. Devastating ways. But we use them only in the direst
of situations. As the Foundry says, it protects life, and so do we. We protect
life."

"Why not let the Foundry help?" Shelly ventured, and this made Frelo's expression strange. "What is it?"

"The Foundry is strict with who it helps. Unless you follow a certain logical path, you are a risk to all life in the universe. It did not like our way of protecting life. It was too—self-interested. We help for the reason of protecting Jevox. Not for the sake of protecting all. If we could be left alone and never meet another species, we might consider this. Some of us like chaos, like the introduction of color and light and change. The *ississ* does not. And so, we help, because we must, because this is how we protect Jevox life. We do not harm others, we help them, and so the Foundry leaves us alone."

"Do you have ships made by the Foundry?" I asked.

Frelo twisted its head, blinked its pentagonal set of eyes in sequence, then handed me one of the devices. "Of course we do, but we are not reliant upon them like you. We do not make war."

The rest of the devices were distributed, one for each of us, a black, handheld box with a glassy, blue screen two inches across, a set of simple buttons on its surface, and a pair of antennae that stuck out the end.

As I listened distractedly to Frelo's explanation of the device and how it worked, scanning us first to calibrate, then searching for any similar DNA fragments nearby, I got lost in thought. Not for the first time, I found it interesting that no matter the species we came across, they all seemed to be after the same basic thing, though with different execution. The Foundry would give out ships and put a people on a path to protect life. The Melcorin explored the galaxy and would rescue those in trouble to protect life. The Kabosai, even in their gene manipulation, were trying to create species that could live in hostile environments in order to protect life, proliferate it. Hell, even the Isoptera wanted to protect life in a way, be it only their own species and a quick means of dinner. The universe and its inhabitants just wanted to be alive, to grow, to expand, to reduce entropy. So what path was the best? What path brought about true...

True self-awareness. Universal transcendence.

"Would you consider coming to Earth and helping us out?" Lance asked, breaking me out of my reverie. He elbowed Frelo in the arm and made the best approximation of a friendly smile. He was about as bad as Karianna at this, all teeth, no warmth. Leo needed to give him pointers. "Huh? Come on. We fucked up really bad, and humans can be assholes. We do start wars, I'll be honest, though only against ourselves. The Foundry may not help us."

"And just where is your Earth?" Frelo's voice sounded incredulous. "We have not seen it on our local charts."

"Yeah, no." Lance scratched at the back of his head. "It's a long way away. At least we think so. Beyond the Wandering Gate for sure."

Frelo's face paled. They took a step back. "No," they said, tone turning hard. "We will never travel through the Gate. Never."

"Why?" I pressed. "What is wrong with the gate?"

"No. Never." They turned their back from me and began to walk away. "Death awaits."

"Not the response I was expecting," Lance mumbled to himself.

Once we had received the bio-scanners, Frelo led us out into the street and handed each of us a card like Karianna had been given. This card would help us navigate the streets and use the scanners to locate any foreign, mainly human, DNA. Green Point was several miles wide. Frelo assured us Green Point and Sky Claw, where the *Reverie's* crew had been sent, had the best chance of success. If Johan was after terraforming technology or information, here is where he would find it. They bid us farewell and informed us they would check in later.

We were on our own.

Given the size of our search area, we broke off into pairs and began following a grid. Time was against us and so we moved quickly. The range of the bio-scanners wasn't great, about one Rixian city block, both ground level and vertical, but it would have to be enough.

Shelly went with me, Lance with Leo, Xuan and Hy with Ada. Given that we were on a world we did not know, and with a people of mixed intentions, we kept constant contact through our uplink to the *Fidelis* using our implants. We could play a similar game to the Jevox, at least in communication, keeping it all in our heads.

After several hours we were no closer to locating Johan. I began to wonder if we had gotten it all wrong, if maybe they hadn't come here at all. It was a good guess as to what they were doing, sure, but we couldn't be positive.

The sun began to fall as night approached, the sky transitioning from blue to a yellowish orange, the hypergiant star of JV-01 refusing to give up its abundant light until the last instant. We kept up the search, stopping every so often to rest our feet and take a bite from the energy bars we had packed. While food was easily available here, Shelly urged us not to eat anything without a serious chemical evaluation like we had done on Novae or Creatus. While the buildings' fruit might be tasty and nutritious to Jevox, it could be poison to humans.

Dusk overtook the sky, transitioning orange and purple into black, and as it did so, the bustling city became a twinkling world filled with a single song. It was as if every Jevox wanted to listen to the same album. Speakers from every corner of the street uttered a low hum with deep rhythms, simple droning chords and a collection of different voices.

I sat on a block of stone by a street corner, rubbing my eyes with my fingers and found myself wavering. The hypnotic nature of the music combined with my exhaustion was about to put me to sleep right here and now. But time was running out, and we needed to find them. I could not stop.

Digging in my pocket, I removed a package of stims, considering taking a few. These could keep me up at least another five or six hours.

"You need rest." Shelly took a seat beside me and covered the notecard size package of stims with her palm. "Your eyes are red. You can hardly pick up your feet. Chemicals are no replacement for sleep."

"But time is running out. We're already at the end of the first day. It's slipping through our fingers like sand. I can't fail Dad."

"Milo, this isn't life within a Star Sphere." She waved at the brightly lit city. "Out here, in the real world, we are mere mortals. We have to act like them. Get some sleep, and we'll go fresh again in just a few hours. Okay? Please?"

I let out a sigh, annoyed. She was right. How much longer could I keep this up?

"Fine," I said. "Let's find the guest quarters they prepared. Hopefully the beds will be soft enough and large enough we can rest."

"For some reason, I find that unlikely."

CHAPTER 27

We found a set of guest quarters less than a block away from our location. It was cramped, as we had expected, four by four meters give or take, but the bed was quite different from what we had hoped for. It was not a solid, soft slab, but a recumbent contraption designed to hold arms and legs in a way such that a Jevox could attach themselves as they leaned back. It provided support in key areas along multi-jointed appendages, back, and neck. It looked to be a cross between the most ergonomic object I'd ever seen, and a medieval torture device. After a short discussion, all Shelly and I could figure is that it gave a sensation of weightlessness where every part of their body was equally supported as you slept. There was no way we could use them, and so we found a few soft cushions and a section of carpet at one corner of the room, laid down, draped our jackets over our shoulders and bundled up together. Thank the Universe it wasn't a cold night.

Before drifting off, I pinged the rest of our group. They were not far away. They too were turning in. Everyone was exhausted and had no luck locating so much as a scrap of human activity within these two districts of Rix. I called up to Proxy, requesting various scans of the planet from orbit, and got a big fat nothing in return. Plenty of data and activity, hundreds of Jevox ships zipping about doing what they did, a space elevator hard at work, signals pinging around satellites like billiards, but zero evidence of a stealth ship.

I sent a command to my hand terminal, *alarm in five hours*. That should give us time to recharge without wasting too much of it. Being the wonderful woman she was, Shelly encouraged me to set it for eight. I wished we could.

It took a while for us to fall asleep, but I eventually did, my head and neck at a funny angle. My rest was fitful and uneven. No matter how I turned I could not quite get comfortable. I had become spoiled sleeping in a Star Sphere, my body suspended in that amniotic fluid, my mind filled with thoughts of familiar places. I had to remind myself, comfortable or not, man had evolved from sleeping in trees and on the ground. Exhaustion would overtake me at some point, and it most certainly did.

I don't recall dreaming at all that night. One moment my eyes were open, then nothing. I was annoyed for an instant that I could still hear that droning music outside, a few bars of light shooting in through a set of metal shutters near the door.

Darkness.

A sore shoulder.

Flipping over, huffing.

Drift.

Then...

A bang. A crash.

The lights flicked on.

My eyes creaked open to see why.

Everything was too bright.

Five slender Jevox in Yellow Robes were standing over me, their long fingers wrapping around my arms in a set of vices.

"Come with us," they ordered as one. "Do not resist."

This was no dream, no flashback to when the Frendol had snatched me on Cynosure. This was real. Something was wrong.

My heart thundered against my chest, terror taking hold of me.

"What in the hell is going on?" I shouted, twisting free of their grip, then rolling over on my side and standing, fury having jerked me back to this side of oblivion. I raised my hands and prepared to fight, my prosthetic arm shaking. "What are you doing?"

"You are dangerous," the Yellow on the right said.

They advanced, and I made a move to resist, reaching out with my mechanical arm, but before I could fight them off one stabbed me in the side with a silver rod arcing blue energy at its end. The buzzing blue light came in contact and my body went limp for a moment, eyes going blurry.

Before I knew it, my hands were being drawn together, bound by a sort of translucent rope. The short length of material was wrapped around my wrists. It flashed white, and in an instant, became hard as steel. I couldn't pull my wrists apart, even with the power of my mechanical arm. Pulling against the bindings merely caused pain to my fleshy half.

What were they doing? What had we done? We'd not violated any rules. We'd not hurt anyone.

"This way," they said. "Come with us, human. Do not resist."

The hell I wouldn't.

I was dragged towards the door, kicking and twisting all the way. There was no way I was going to make this easy. I frantically peered around the room, the effects of the stunner wearing off, desperate as I sought Shelly. She wasn't here, not even her jacket. She had gone missing. Had they already gotten her?

Where are you, love? Where are you?

The Jevox pulled me out into the empty, neon lit streets of the Rixian city at night. It was early. Dawn was a long way away. A lone ground car was waiting at the curb, its trunk section larger than the entire vehicle we had come to this district in. I could only assume it was some kind of security vehicle, and that these were like secret police. But that didn't feel right. They weren't dressed like the guards we met at the platform. They did not wear armor, just robes like the rest. They had no crime on this world, no dissonance. These had to be ordinary Jevox tasked with a dirty job. What did Yellows do to contribute to society?

Didn't matter.

I threw my forehead at one of them, catching it in the eyes. It reeled back, clearly not expecting this level of resistance or pain, and as a result this action affected the rest in kind, their mind-to-mind connection resonating in agony. They loosened their grip, and I was able to free myself, if not my hands.

But what now? Where should I go? I could run, sure, but run where? And Shelly… Where the hell was Shelly?

There was no time to hesitate, this could be my one and only chance to get away long enough to formulate a real plan. I needed Proxy's help. I needed to speak with the others.

I fumbled around in my pocket, which wasn't easy with bound hands, and searched for the access card. I caught it in my fingers, then tapped the edge just as I had seen Frelo do. The card chirped back at me, which I took as a good sign, but I had no idea how long it would be before the ground car would appear. Seconds? Minutes? The Jevox were recovering. I wouldn't have long.

They reached into satchels draped across their backs and removed arm-length, narrow tubes upon which handholds soon appeared from a flow of liquid metal at their tips, transitioning the objects into rifles of a sort.

Nano machines, I thought with a touch of excitement and dread. Why hadn't I brought my own supply?

Not waiting to see the use of these weapons, I dashed for the corner of the city block, attempting to get out of their line of sight, weaving between objects along the sidewalk, scintillating light poles, metallic cylinders, geometric shapes of stone. The Jevox enclave fired at me, their projectiles sticking into the ground and walls mere inches behind me, electrical disks impacting, letting off a sizzling noise. Instinct told me these were not lethal devices. They did not seem to be a malicious people, but I wasn't inclined to test the theory. Just my luck I'd end up as a smear on the sidewalk like the victims of Isopteran energy weapons.

"Proxy," I called out with my implants, my voice frantic as I ran. "I need help. Proxy!"

No response.

"Karianna? Shelly? Hell, Leo? Anyone?"

Again, nothing. In fact, the more I tried, the more I focused, the more I felt there was a blank spot in my head, a sensation that someone had wrapped my cranium in a warm towel.

"Shit, shit," I grumbled and swung around the corner, the Jevox hot on my heels. "I'm being jammed."

"Stop. Now!" they shouted at me. "We do not wish to cause pain."

Before I had the opportunity to answer them, they began firing again. This did not bode well at all for trust building.

I spotted a series of ditches between a set of skyscrapers up ahead, appearing like ones used for runoff or waste management. The metal fence beside them was low, just a couple of feet high, and with the reduced gravity of Rix, I had a feeling I could jump it and land at the bottom. Hopefully I wouldn't break all my bones in the process. Focusing on the steps it would take to make the jump, I ran faster, my bound hands out in front of me, envisioning myself hopping over and down the three or four feet into the ditch. If I could just make it, I might be able to lose them. Maybe this connected to some tunnels, sewers, maybe I could get just far enough away to make contact with Proxy.

I made for the fence and leapt, and for an instant I felt as if I could fly. My feet cleared the top, making me laugh hysterically, my short curls blowing in the wind. This was it. I could escape these mother f—

Next thing I knew, my face and shoulder were skidding across the stone surface of the ditch before coming to a halt, the rest of my body trembling as if I'd been struck by lightning. This wasn't far off. Several hazy moments passed before I started to regain my wits enough to realize what had happened. I had not missed the jump. No. I'd been shot by a stun weapon.

The Jevox enclave was upon me in an instant, their ability to climb no match for the tiny fence I had thought myself badass for clearing. Their fingers wrapped around my arms and lifted me up as one. There was no way to escape, my body now limp as a cooked noodle in their grasp.

They hauled me from the ditch, and my head lolled to the side, catching sight of something. Was that a Jevox dressed in blue? A glint of silver jewelry?

Frelo was watching me from the shadows, a look of what I could only take as shock on their face. And they were not alone. The Jevox was hiding in a tunnel along with a human woman that had dark curls, and deep eyes. It was Shelly. These guards, whoever they were, didn't see Frelo and Shelly, did not know that they were there. That was a relief. Was Frelo a friend? How could these guards not feel what they felt? How could they not know what they knew? And was Shelly okay? Would she be okay?

God damn my head hurt. The night air made my face burn along my bloody scrapes.

"Where—you taking me," I managed to get out in a slurring mumble, my tingling body starting to regain some of its ability. "What I—doosh?"

"You are being placed in containment," they said. "You are dangerous."

"But why? I nothing do." My words were all a jumble.

"Human, Jevox are reported missing. Ten enclaves. Fifty in all. This happened after your arrival, and during your search. Human genetic material has been discovered where they vanished."

"Johan," I growled, and this anger helped to clear my thoughts, steady my feet. "I swear, wasn't us. It was the one we are after."

"That will be sorted later. You will be taken to containment for now and held until the missing Jevox are found."

The larger than average ground car was waiting for us on the curb, its features now sleek and colorful as if it had transitioned on its own. They tossed me in the back of the vehicle just as another car, this one unoccupied, approached. The access card, miraculously still gripped in my fingers even after being hit by a stun rifle, gave a cheerful chirp in response. It had done its job and called me ground transportation.

"A bit too late to help, aren't we?" I mused, and one of the Jevox yanked the card from my fingers, tossed me in their vehicle, and slammed the door shut. What would it have done to help anyways? Escaping had been a short-lived fantasy. The best I could have hoped for was to outrun the jamming signal and call for Proxy's aid.

I twisted around in the back of the security car to find I wasn't alone. Sitting beside me were two of my favorite people in the universe. Hooray.

The car jostled, Jevox piling in front, and we were on our way, zipping through the streets of the city, taking us towards whatever it was they referred to as "containment." I sure as hell hoped it was a cell and not something worse.

"Damn, Milo, you look like hell," Lance said, raising his bound wrists and gesturing at my skinned up face. Leo sat beside him. "First time being brought into custody?"

"No, not exactly," I replied. "But I don't go quiet."

"No shit."

I faced Leo. "Does this make for good art?"

He frowned at that. "Good art, yes? A good day, hell no. We should have stayed on the ship. This was stupid."

"Does this mean our time is up?" Lance asked. "I mean, can we stop hurrying now? I hate deadlines."

"Have you heard from anyone else?" I asked. "What about Xuan, Hy, and Ada?"

"No," Leo said. "I tried to ping Ada several times but they're blocking us."

"I'm seeing the same thing." I let out a sigh. "I hope Karianna and the rest are okay."

"What about your wife?" Leo asked, leaning in and lowering his voice. "Are you not worried about her?"

"Of course I am," I replied, then inspected the car to see if there were any obvious ways the Jevox could be listening in. "She's fine, I think. Can't say how at the moment. We can play charades later, but I need my hands."

"Oh," he said, nodding. "What do we do now? Lance said you always have a plan."

"I don't know," I said. "I don't always have a plan. It's clear Johan is here. They told me he's already captured fifty Jevox."

"Johan by name?" Lance's eyebrows raised.

"No. Pretty sure most of them can't tell the difference between us. A human has done this, DNA is at the scene. I'm sure they'll figure it out eventually, that Johan or Harper or Clark's DNA is there, not ours, but by then those bastards will be long gone. This situation, though, it proves that they're here on Rix, in this city." I twisted my wrists and tried to make the bindings more comfortable. It was a wasted effort, like wrestling with a titanium alloy melted over our wrists.

"Well, at least my ex-girlfriend isn't shacked up with an asshole like Johan," Lance said.

I blinked at him. "Shacked up? Like, hooking up? You kidding me?"

"Pretty obvious, man. I mean, if they're not, she sure as hell wants them to be. All those daddy issues, and Johan's pretty fatherly."

"What?" Leo chuckled. "Milo, you used to date Harper?"

"We all make mistakes."

"Damn. Never did understand how a fox like her ended up with a guy like George. What a beta."

"Anyways," I said, raising my bound hands and staring both of them down. "We've got to get back to the ship, all of us. We have to follow Ada's plan to locate Johan. Our window may be closing. Keep trying to ping. If one of us can reach Proxy, it may do something."

"Will Proxy listen to us?" Leo drew his knees against his chest, his cruel bravado draining away. "I mean, it's not our ship."

"I think so," I replied. "Its directive is to protect the pilot."

"I really should have left the heroic acts to my painting and sculptures."

"Do you regret coming on this mission?"

He scrunched up his face and scowled. "I regret nothing. Chaos. Good news."

Lance laughed, his tone a touch shrill. "Keep telling yourself that. When they start vivisecting us, you'll feel different. Then again, life seems to play favorites. We have Milo with us."

It took only a few minutes to arrive at a nondescript building no more than a single story high. An oddity among a city of skyscrapers, its appearance older than the rest, a relic of another era. The Jevox opened the door, and using their rifles, directed us which way to go. Being on the outside of the car I could now see there was another vehicle like this one parked in front of us. I wondered who else they had captured.

The Jevox led us into the building, gun barrels at our back, its worn, grey walls adorned in nothing but a pair of symbols flanking the door, a logo set of sorts. Perhaps their version of a flag? The structure itself seemed sturdy and utilitarian, devoid of the aesthetics of free thinking and expression possessed by the rest of the city. As we approached the entrance, a set of imposing doors three times our height swung wide, admitting us inside, then slammed shut at our backs with a bang of finality.

"Have I mentioned I don't like the dark?" Leo hissed.

"Keep moving," the Jevox said.

It was so terribly dark inside, a 180-degree contrast to the neon lit streets of the city. Little more than floor lights illuminated our path, leading us underground in a similar fashion to how we had descended in the lab, though it was hard to orient ourselves visually. Cracks in the walls gave way to a sort of blue moss, fuzzy like pieces of carpet, but with stalks that let off a soft glow. The atmosphere was stale, dusty, reminiscent of a cave or a tomb. I could hear dripping water somewhere close, but otherwise, it was silent as death down here. No chorus from the streets. No whizzing cars overhead.

As we delved deeper, scratched and dented doors appeared on the left and the right of the cylindrical tunnel. Symbols beside their thresholds were glowing with inconsistent, flickering lights. Translating these characters in real-time from their language to English was difficult, even with the Foundry nano-machines, but I swore they said single words like: EMERGENCY, SUPPLIES, REST, FAMILY.

We had slowed our pace, our attention caught by this observation, and so the Jevox prodded us again with the barrel of their rifles, urging us to move on.

"It's a bunker or something," Leo commented, voice low, eyes wide. "At least I think so. Thick walls, all utility, storage rooms. This reminds me of the fallout shelters from our history books. Early 1960s."

"The what?" Lance whispered in response.

"For bombs," I supplied. "We were on a road to all-out nuclear war and the government thought citizens should have shelters to stay in and hide if the bombs fell. Or rather, when they fell."

"Big difference I see here," Leo went on, "is that this shelter looks like it would actually hold up in a nuclear war. Most of those old shelters were concrete blocks in the ground with jugs of water kept drinkable with a cap of bleach, but this? This is something else."

Lance grunted. "So why would a peaceful, kumbaya, hive-minded society need a fallout shelter? I get that we built ours to protect us against ourselves. What about them?"

"Hey," I said, raising my voice at our captors. "Where are we? Where are you taking us? We deserve answers. We are guests of your government."

"Containment," they said. "You will remain there until the proper time."

"Yeah, we heard that part," Lance shouted back. "But what is this place."

"A safe place," they replied. "A quiet place."

And that was about all I felt we would get.

We soon found ourselves in a new area, tunnels twice as large as the one we just exited branching off, gentle blue lights glowing here and there, spaces between where time had turned some dark. They directed us to an open box set into the bedrock wall. We were instructed to step inside. There was nothing waiting for us in the holding cell. No food, no water, no beds, just an open stone box with a battered floor.

"Get comfortable," they said, stepping away from the opening.

"You're terrible hosts," Leo whirled on them. "There is no way I can get comfortable in here."

"Where is Frelo?" I demanded. "Let us talk to it. Frelo can attest we were not part of whatever it was you found. We did not take your people."

"They sing out of chorus," they said. "They are not like the rest of us. They are different."

"So?" Leo ventured. "What's wrong with being different?"

Lance bowed up his back, ready to fight. "Don't think these guys are into that."

"Let us go," I tried again. "Your… however you say it… Your leaders. They would not approve of this."

"We do what must be done," the group of Yellow Jevox said, their synchronization fragmenting the tiniest bit. They spoke at different moments, then the same. "What are a few lives, when weighed against billions? We must learn what is important."

My heart sank at those words. Something was wrong, very wrong. Those were not the words of the Jevox, no, they were the Foundry's words. These Jevox were… *different.* But not like Frelo. They were altered. That's why they weren't dressed like the rest of the guards we had seen. Kidnappings could have happened, yes, but these Jevox did not come to investigate those occurrences. They came to enact them.

"Wait," Lance said, leaning forward. "What did you say to us? Say it again!"

Leo licked his dry lips and stared at me.

"Sit down," the Jevox shouted, then stepped forward, their weapons crackling with arcs of blue lightening. This forced us back more out of reflex than anything else.

As we passed the threshold of the chamber, a sheet of clear material, not glass, rose from out of the floor and closed us in. From the look of it we were now sealed in an airtight box.

"We've been had," Leo said, walking around the closed space, inspecting the walls. "There's no way out. We're trapped in here. That South African bastard."

"What they just said smelled of Councilor Clark," I said, staring daggers at the Jevox through the barrier.

"Is it getting cold in here?" Lance looked to the cracked ceiling, focusing his attention on a thumb-sized hole from which a blue haze of smoke began to spread.

I rushed over to the clear wall and banged on it with my bound wrists. "Hey! Let us out! We didn't do it! We didn't kidnap your people. You are not yourselves. Snap out of it!"

The Yellows stood there watching as the gas filled the room.

"I don't want to go like this," Lance growled. "This is bullshit. Bullshit!"

There was nothing I could do but bang on the translucent wall. Even with the strength of my prosthetic it made little noise. Whatever material this was made of was vibration resistant and my hands were still bound. There was only so much I could do.

A thump came from over my shoulder, and I spun. In the dim cell all I could make out was the shine of Leo's platinum hair on the floor. He had collapsed where he stood, the gas having overtaken him. It was coming for us next.

"Milo," Lance said, stepping away from where Leo had fallen. "What do we do? We're backed into a corner."

I readied myself to respond, but before I could, he fell back against the wall and slid to the floor, his eyes shut.

Were they dead? Was I about to die? What was this gas?

I pinged wildly with my implants, hoping something would get through their jamming. I did not want this to be my end. There was so much left to do, so much left to see. Johan couldn't get away with this. If he did, I'd be letting Mom down, Novae down, Earth…

Everything was hazy. The Foundry's prosthetics released chemicals into my body, attempting to counteract whatever agent was filling the box. It wasn't enough. Everything was slipping away.

One last time I threw my bound wrists against the wall before sliding to the floor, watching as the Jevox peered down at us with a cold fascination.

I screamed, but no sound escaped my throat. Unconsciousness swirled around me, surrounding my mind. I—

CHAPTER 28

I used to believe that the intention of the Foundry's donation was purely like that of the Gene Brokers. That in the end, they had given me a great ship in exchange for an arm, a leg, and a piece of my brain, all so they could enact some sort of twisted science experiment with human DNA. I supposed that they had plans within plans, fourth dimensional chess games fought with unseen opponents that we could never hope to understand—and in some ways, that might still be true. But there was another thing I had come to realize while poised on the edge of a knife, that simple, gentle application of pressure ready to give me both failure and death. In many ways the Foundry was simpler than we expected, not without intelligence, but flexibility, wisdom. I knew I should be surrounded in this moment by total darkness, unable to consider the fact that I had allowed my group to be corralled into a trap by Johan, and yet, I wasn't.

It became clear to me that if the Foundry were to protect life, it must also protect the pilot. Being a freak, I supposed, wasn't always bad.

Though my body still seemed unable to respond, my arms and legs like lead, my mind cleared. The gas the Jevox had pumped into the room persisted but seemed thinner, a blue haze from the aged bunker's light reflecting off of uneven whorls and eddies. I found it curious the gas did not evenly disperse, then wondered if this closed space had a variety of temperature differences.

I mentally shook my head. This was not the puzzle I should be working out right now. I wasn't dead, and that's all that mattered.

With an effort of will, I could catch sight of Lance on my left at the peripheries of my vision, body balled up on the ground, Leo on my right in the same position I had last seen him. Neither was responsive. I couldn't be sure if they were alive or dead.

The containment room was cold, but a heat was coming from my arm and leg, the rest of my body tingling. The Foundry prosthetics were warming my blood, keeping it moving, not allowing it to fall into— Into—

Realization hit me.

I was in a sealed room in a bunker.

There was a closed viewing door.

Containment…

The answer was right in front of me.

"Hyper suspension chamber," I mumbled, then smiled, realizing I had spoken the words aloud. This was not a containment room for prisoners or Jevox science experiments. Not a room for dangerous fauna or storing radioactive materials. This was a mass hyper suspension chamber. There were grooves in the stone floor where many of those weird beds could have been arrayed in neat rows, Jevox of old left in this space to outlast whatever calamity this place was built to withstand. What this meant was that my crew mates were not dead, just stuck in various states of suspended animation.

I felt my fingers and toes wiggle, and not just those on my prosthetic limbs. My head and neck regained control, and I twisted around to peer through the glass, though I was still unable to stand. In doing so I lost my balance and my face found itself again on the ground. Thankfully there was no pain. Come to think of it, I didn't feel much of any sensation at all. Still, this had given me a different perspective, allowing me to see the hallway we had entered through. The yellow clad Jevox who had captured us were gone.

My body jerked for a moment, as if being hit by the paddles of a defibrillator. This jolt sharpened my dulling senses, and in so doing, I felt my right leg, the natural one, regain its control. My hands were still bound by the clear rope, not that my arms were working anyways, but I saw no way to flee.

A flash of light came from down the hall, what I believed was the opposite direction to how we had entered. My ear was now against the glass, and I swore I felt the vibration of footsteps through the clear medium. I blinked as five figures approached the translucent panel that sealed us in, their shapes blurry. Only one of these had on a robe, the rest wore boots and pants with jackets or flight suits. Was it Johan come to finish us off? Had he just been waiting for the three of us to fall first?

As I squinted my eyes, attempting to will the rest of my body to awaken like my right leg had, the hum of a whirring fan began, and the gas filling the space thinned. Within moments the air was clear.

My leg flailed around as I tried to push myself away from the newcomers, but my boot couldn't get a grip on the floor. If only I'd had a few more minutes, then maybe I could have fought my way out of this.

The chamber's wall receded into the floor and my head tilted over, my left ear pressed against cold stone. A pair of thick, black boots were all I could see, blocks of rubber tread large as skyscrapers. I was about to protest, start lashing out with fists and screams, but my capacity was little more than that of a slug. Hands reached down, and to my surprise, gently helped me sit upright.

"Milo," Shelly whispered in my ear as she threw her arms around me. "My God, look at your face. It's terrible. I saw you take that spill. You get a ten for effort, but your form was horrible."

"We don't have long," Frelo declared from where they stood to Shelly's left, their hands gesturing wildly, touching one another, unable to remain still, its many elbows flexing. The two of them were not alone. Thank the Universe, Xuan, Hy, and Ada were with them. Shelly, and my crew, were all accounted for.

"They are nearby," Frelo went on, "the Yellows that are not acting as part of the hive. Their thoughts are not mine. I cannot hear them. The walls of the bunker hide our thoughts, but I do not believe this will last for long. I do not know what will happen then. Will this madness spread, or will it remain only here? They are disconnected."

"Are they… Are they dead?" Xuan asked, rushing over to Lance where he lay lifeless.

Hy and Ada were attending to Leo, Hy checking his pulse while Ada produced a multi-purpose medical diagnostic tool, clipping it to Leo's finger.

Frelo made their way around the room and applied a box with a tube on its end to our bindings. The threads of the clear ropes dissolved in an instant and were easy to pull apart.

"They're not dead," I exhaled, then rubbed at my achy wrists. "it's suspension."

Xuan twisted back to look at me. "What?"

My tingling body was getting easier to control. My face began to burn as the feeling returned, but even pain was a welcome sensation. I put an explorative palm to the scrape along my cheek and winced. It wasn't just the skin. My bones were bruised. "The gas, it's a combination sedative and cryo-protectant."

"Then why are you awake?" Shelly asked, her right hand brushing back my hair. "You should be out like them, right?"

I raised my prosthetic right arm, which to my surprise had started working again. "Freak."

Shelly sucked in a breath and nodded.

"This facility is ancient," Frelo said. "I would not trust our old machines to work so favorably. They were not designed for humans. You must resuscitate your people soon or I fear they will have long-term neurological damage."

"How long were we out?" I asked, and began balling my hands into fists, testing their strength.

"Not long," Xuan responded while reaching into a pocket on her jumpsuit. An instant later she produced a short cylinder, removed its cap, then pressed it against Lance's exposed upper arm before hitting a button on its end. The cylinder gave a pop as a mixture of epinephrine and corticosteroids found their way straight into Lance's blood stream. We could only hope it would bring him back around, and quick.

"You were out, maybe an hour?" she went on. "Had to get everyone together and follow Frelo. We did not know this was here. This suspension is an unexpected complication." She tossed another hypodermic cylinder to her husband who repeated her actions on Leo, then offered one to me.

"I'm fine," I said, raising a hand. At my cue, Shelly helped me stand, supporting a portion of my weight on her shoulder. "Okay. If it's been an hour, Johan has quite a head start. We just need to get to the Swift Shuttles and back to the *Fidelis*. If we can get outside of this jamming field they've activated, we can call Proxy. Where's Karianna and her crew?"

"We don't know," Shelly replied. "We were cut off. I can only assume they may have fallen into the same situation."

"Let's hope not."

"What about Lance and Leo?" Ada patted Leo on the cheek. "They're not coming around, and we can't leave them."

"At least they're breathing now," Hy said, his right ear to Leo's chest. "Heartbeat too."

"I'll keep an eye on their vitals. Do we want to give them another shot? Maybe that will get them up."

"No," Xuan replied. "Bad for the heart. Could kill them."

"We'll have to carry them," I said. "Frelo, since you came to help, would I be right in assuming you are on our side?"

The Jevox's five ovate eyes twinkled. "You have done nothing to hurt us," they said. "While my fellow Jevox among the hive might not be able to tell the difference between you, I am different. Your mate was right. I see differences between you even now, just like Melcorin. I cannot speak for the hive, I am not the whole *ississ*, but I will help you reach your shuttles."

"That's good enough for me. Anything down here we can use to carry our friends, I don't think they can walk."

They shook their head. "The ancient bunkers were cleared out hundreds of years ago. Nothing is left unless hidden or forgotten."

"I take skinny one," Hy said, bending over beside Leo. "Ada, help me get him up on shoulders. Think I can remember fireman carry from Boy Scouts. Try an not break his pretty face."

"Xuan, let me help you with Lance," I said, stumbling over and nearly falling as I wrestled myself away from Shelly's support.

Her eyes widened. "Not so sure." She made a show of flexing her biceps and bent over. "I can get him. Chevelle made us lift in Security and Exploration. Told me to be some hench bitch, yass. Got on leg day every time."

Shelly put a hand on my chest. "You are too weak. Your body is coming out of half-suspension quicker than theirs, but you could use a hand to steady you."

"Let me help," Frelo said, assisting Xuan. "This human is heavier than you."

Xuan smiled back, her dark eyes gleaming. "Tougher than I look."

"She stronger than me," Hy said, nodding. "Promise you that."

Frelo gave a gesture, urging us out of the suspension room and into the hall. As a group we shambled away, Ada standing close to Xuan to ensure Lance was secure on her shoulders. Shelly helped me walk straight. Despite my motor function returning, focusing wasn't the easiest. I could only hope it wasn't far to the exit, though I doubted that.

We moved through a series of cracked, labyrinthian tunnels, dozens more rooms like the one we had escaped lining the halls with even more beside.

Others had stone collection pots filled like cisterns, while some round chambers had floor to ceiling racks with several varieties of plants growing from them. Out of habit I began to calculate how many Jevox I believed this place might support, and the number soon reached into the thousands.

"I have to know, Frelo, what was this place for?" I asked after a few minutes. "It's not like the rest of your city. It had a purpose."

The Jevox did not slow their pace, but hesitated for a moment, placing a hand against a wall here and there as if recalling old memories. It led us through an excavation in a broken wall, an alternate path between two sections of the facility that a cave-in had separated. The makeshift tunnel of dirt and rock was made for those smaller than us, and so we had to stoop over. This was twice as difficult for Hy and Xuan, who were carrying our companions on their backs.

"There was a war," they eventually said as we reached a crossroad in the tunnels, reentering the facility proper. They paused for a moment, then led us off to the right. "As I have said. We wish to be alone. We prefer it. It makes our chorus sweeter, simpler, but we understand the universe is not without other forms of life. A long time ago, we made first contact. It was with a species that preferred fire, rather than talk, or exchange. War was a new concept to us. We did not fight among ourselves, not exactly. We did not contest territory or seek retribution. It is said that ancient Jevox may have known wars and battles, but that we evolved out of those evils through our shared mind. It is hard to hurt another when you are intimately aware of their motivations and pain."

"And so," Shelly piped up, "this other species came to conquer you?"

"We do not believe so," it replied. "We believe they did it for sport. Later we would come to learn that they had done this to other species, but at the time, we just wanted to survive. They did not fully extinct any species but brought them to the brink. Weakened them." It raised a hand as if gesturing at the walls around us. "In response to this threat, we constructed these Phods to weather the storm. There are twenty-five in all, scattered around Rix. And so, when they came back to kill us, we hid in the ground. Unlike now, these were once buried. They bombarded our world from orbit, destroyed nearly all of our life, then invaded the ground. Those not fortunate enough to join us in the Phods were slaughtered. This went on for decades, and then one day, they just left. Disappeared. We emerged on the surface to find a ruined world full of dust and decay."

This made me wonder. Could that have been humanity's story? What if the Isoptera had found us first? Found their way to Earth before we even reached the Foundry. The thought chilled me to the bone.

"And you built it back," I said, putting the pieces together. "Your moons. The way the city and green spaces on your world developed. They are not natural, are they? They are intentional."

"No," it replied. "They are not natural. The Jevox worked together, and in a project that took generations, we returned our world to a state greater than it was. In that process we learned many things. We learned how to change worlds from chaos into order, how to save plants and rejuvenate soil. We learned that with enough effort, we could shape almost any world. At the time, we had not ventured far from our planet, but now we knew we were not alone. That's when the Foundry called to us."

The ruined hallway of the bunker emptied out into a system of caves, their passages filled with stalactites and stalagmites, giving it the impression of a giant's mouth. Lights were no longer on the walls, and there came the sound of water rushing somewhere up ahead. Frelo removed a set of three globes from their pockets and tossed them into the air. The orbs floated evenly among our group and began to glow with blue light, their illumination much brighter than anything inside the ancient Phods.

"This way," they said. "Look out for the stream. It will be on our right. Do not fall in. It feeds from a massive aquafer into the city. Very swift."

"What happened when the Foundry called out to you?" Xuan asked, and with Ada's help, readjusted Lance on her shoulders. Neither of them had awoken yet.

"We did as all do," Frelo replied. "We built a ship. Went to say hello. Ninety yuniea it took to reach the first of the facilities."

"I'm sorry, what did you say?" Ada asked. "Am I right with the calculation? That's a solar cycle here on Rix. That's more than a hundred Earth years."

"It was a long time," they said. "But we had learned how to suspend our peoples' aging. Time was nothing to those on board these great ships."

"Did the Foundry help you?" I asked the million-dollar question I knew we all needed answering.

The Jevox paused in their step, twisted their head, then kept moving, threading through a tightly packed series of stalagmites. The ground here was slippery, and so we took care where we stepped.

They went on, "The Foundry gave us ships, yes. That was all the help we needed. But no, the Foundry did not help us beyond this."

"Why is that? You seem a peaceful race. You didn't go out and kill others, did you?"

"Our motivations may now be noble, in alignment with the ancient machines, but they were not always so. Out of fear, out of pain, long ago we made a deal."

"A deal?"

"Yes. We traded our technological advances with another species, and in exchange for their assistance, we drew their particular brand of attention to that of our *natural* aggressors."

I paused in the tunnel, the group stopping with me. It took a moment for Frelo to realize and turn to face us. My stomach churned, and I swallowed down my unease.

"Who did you get help from?" I asked, but something deep inside me already knew the answer. "Tell me, Frelo. Tell me who."

They lowered their head as if abashed, the fingers of its bizarre, too many jointed hands interlocking in an awkward gesture. "We made a deal with the Kabosai."

"What?" Shelly gasped, hands covering her mouth. "The Gene Brokers?"

"Yes."

"Why?"

"We had to become safe again. We merely hoped that they might change the path of this destructive species. Perhaps their genes were defective. They destroyed everything they touched, seeking out more for them to consume and to what end we do not fully know. This is why we help others, hoping that they will not turn hostile towards us. Hoping that things will not end like they did with our oppressors."

"Who did you turn the Gene Brokers against?" I pressed. "Who were your oppressors? I need to know, this is important."

Frelo's eyes twinkled once more, signals of color and light circling their ocular constellation. "The Gan," they said, tone heavy with the weight of ages.

And there it was. I knew this story. Tiny fragments of information gathered between many conversations, short interactions, and traveling for a time inside the Foundry data center's stream on Creatus, had all painted a vivid picture in my mind.

The Gan, an apparently aggressive species on the outside had come to Rix and tried to raze their planet to the ground for the hell of it. In response, the surviving Jevox had enacted a revenge of their own by enlisting the Gene Brokers to focus on "helping" the Gan with their own struggles much like those on Earth, and at the same time potentially removing their dangerous instincts. The Gan were faced with overpopulation, rampant decadence and disparity, and a climate on the verge of collapse. The Gan were a natural species that evolved on their own. So of course the Gene Brokers were more than happy to grant the Jevoxs' request. They could use the Gan's genetic material and create a dozen designer species from it, adapted to fit an undeveloped world, rather than to fit the world to the species. And the results of these actions had been disastrous. The Gan had languished and died as a result. Their species, as they knew it, extinct as a failed Kabosai experiment. I had come to know the one believed to be the last of their kind, the sole survivor, a creature who had installed itself as a near-immortal baron of Cynosure, one of the Foundry's melting pots. I knew the final enemy of the Jevox, the one who had given me the aid to save those I love and forced me to do terrible things to see that done. Forced me to murder.

"We used to be beautiful," the Jalek's harsh words echoed in my mind, taking me back to the moments just before I became this freak. *"So very beautiful."*

"You know who I speak of," Frelo said, their eyes blinking in sequence. "You have heard of them."

"I have met them," I replied. "The last of them."

"Then you know our mistake. You know what happened to them. What they did to us was wrong, yes, but what we encouraged the Kabosai to do to them…"

And that was a tough one. If the Gan did in fact almost drive the Jevox to extinction, did they not deserve retribution? But at the same time, did anyone deserve what the Kabosai did?

"What are we talking about?" Ada asked.

"The Jalek," I said, "that distorted, pink-bodied ape man who meddled in our affairs on Cynosure. It was a Gan. Or at least the closest thing to it after all the Gene Broker manipulation."

"Oh, shit."

"Yes. Shit."

Shelly looked to Frelo, then back to me. We had talked extensively about that experience, and how I had done what was necessary, even though part of it had involved cold blooded murder. It was not a good memory. I had tremendous amounts of guilt and regret for what I had done. The Jalek was a cruel being. Without knowing more, I couldn't be sure if it was cruel because of the Jevox, or in spite of them. Maybe their fall had been the best for us all. Still, would the Gene Brokers have done these things to them without the urging of the Jevox?

"Uhh, guys?" Xuan said, catching our attention. "We have lights following us. Yellow lights in fact. Friends of yours?"

"No," Frelo said, spinning on their heels. "We must go. The exit is not far. The Yellows are almost upon us. I can feel their thoughts here."

We started to move swifter, weaving our way through the teeth-like deposits of minerals on the cave floor.

"So can I," Shelly said after a moment, then shook her head. "Not their thoughts, but—the block, it's gone. My implants are working again."

"Mine too," Ada beamed. "Hot damn. This is good."

"Proxy!" I said while reaching out with my thoughts. "Are you there?"

Milo! Proxy replied instantly. From its tone, the AI had been worried. It had missed me. It always felt good to be missed. *"Are you well? We were concerned."*

"I am alive," I said aloud while transmitting with my neural implants so that the others could hear. "We were captured. In a few minutes we'll be at the opening of a cave, I think. Can you get the Swift Shuttle to us?"

"It is hard to get a fix on your location, but I have an idea. The communications chatter is not favorable. The Jevox believe you have killed fifty of their people and taken the bodies. There is talk of Gene Broker manipulation, human treachery. Something about a dragon."

"A dragon?"

"Yes. I have no better translation for this."

"Doesn't matter right now. Where's Karianna?"

"I can't say. We have had no contact."

"Shit. Okay. Come and find us. Maybe the signal will be better at the mouth of the tunnel."

"Guys," Xuan called, and redoubled her loping step, Lance's limp legs flopping against her back. "They are gaining on us. I can only go so fast while carrying captain blonde beard."

"Leo is getting heavy too," Hy added. "He might be full of hot air but not enough to make this easier."

Ada dug into Xuan's pockets and removed a pair of silver injectors. "Ready or not, we've got to wake them up."

"Could be dangerous," Xuan said.

Shelly reached out. "I can help carry them now."

Frelo raised their open palms. "I offer my aid."

"No. We need you to lead us out," I told it. "Not to be slowed down by carrying one of ours. Ada, give them the shots. We don't have many other options. If they can stir, maybe they can walk."

She nodded at me, then gave Lance and Leo the injections. Leo's eyes popped open immediately and he let out a wordless scream that echoed throughout the caves. With Ada's help, Hy set his feet on the ground and tossed an arm over his shoulder. His body trembled as if he had caught a chill, but he was awake.

"Come on, friend," Hy said. "Help me walk. Done carrying you, your butt's too big. We must move fast. Guards after us."

"Where are we?" Leo mumbled. "Why does my head hurt?"

"Not important now. What is important, walk. Walk fast as me."

While Leo had snapped back to some semblance of reality from the injection, Lance had not. Lance's head lolled around on Xuan's back and his feet kicked, but otherwise all he did was groan.

"No time," I said, then bent over and motioned for Xuan to pass him over to me. "I'm back to myself. I've got my prosthetics. It will be easier."

"Okay," she said, lowering him onto my shoulders.

As a broken bunch we made a run for the exit. The tunnel was lightening up ahead from what I could only hope was daylight. At our rear the Yellows closed in. Soon the crackle of electricity filled the cave as they began taking potshots at us, the sizzling charges splitting the tops of stalagmites and lighting up sections of the moisture-slick cave walls. While at first their shots were wide, they began to focus. Impacts began nipping at our heels. One went past my right leg and singed my pants. I buckled for a moment, but Shelly caught us, and we pressed on.

The mouth of the cave widened, allowing the light to envelope us. I could see the city skyline beyond the threshold, an expanse of silver and green skyscrapers filling our view.

We burst from the cave out onto a narrow ledge, the stream that had run alongside us pouring into a waterfall hundreds of feet high, mist from its scatter blown back into our faces. This ledge was no more than a few feet wide, and as quick as I had been moving to escape the fire of the Yellows, Lance almost took us over the edge. Shelly arrested our momentum, taking hold of my jacket, pulling us back against the mountain wall to the left of the cave's mouth, out of their line of fire.

We found ourselves with our backs against a cliff wall, peering down into a pit between us in the city, miles across and as deep as a mountain was tall, a great body of placid water filling its basin. The sight made my feet sweat; my head dizzy. After being in the dark of the cave, standing in full sunlight was disorienting. I kept imagining myself tumbling over the edge, end over end, falling for several seconds before my body crashed onto the water's surface like a slab of concrete. Not good thoughts.

I carefully set Lance on the ground and surveyed our surroundings. There was no easy exit from this ledge. Frelo had not anticipated the need to carry anyone, and he was far better at climbing than we could ever hope to be.

"Proxy!" I called out. "Can you see me now?"

"I see you," it replied. *"It will take several minutes to reach you."*

"We don't have several minutes."

"You must hold out."

I tried to ping Karianna again. Once more I got no response. Where was she? Was she okay? I sure hoped so.

Ada leaned around the corner of the cave and was answered with a barrage of lightning-quick shots from our pursuers. She drew her head back, expression pale. "Dude, they're getting close."

"We'll have to fight," Shelly said, and bent over to take hold of a rock big around as her fist. "It's all we can do. Frelo, do you have any weapons?"

It shook its head. "I am a Cerulean. Not a Yellow."

I had no idea what that meant.

Xuan followed Shelly's example and looked for something to throw. Our options were limited. We had come to this planet with the intention of being peaceful, and so none of us had a weapon to speak of. It was like Esteban and I all over again, except we didn't have a giant spider man to help us.

The Yellows burst from the cave and Shelly threw her rock at the face of the nearest. It caught the Yellow in the neck and sent it tumbling back into the mouth of the cave. The others responded by letting out a shriek, including Frelo. This made Shelly hesitate in making another move. They really did feel each other's pain.

Xuan did not wait. Pain translated to Frelo or not, she jumped one. It pulled the trigger of its weapon wildly as she struck, sending bolts of electricity out over the precipice. Hy scrambled for one of the weapons that had been dropped, took hold, then shot one of the Yellows square in the chest. Frelo collapsed onto the ground in agony.

"Oh, God," Shelly cried. "Stop it! You're hurting them!"

"What else can I do!" Xuan shouted, punching it in the face, its eyes leaking a blueish fluid.

At the edge of the city across the pit, a dozen flying cars appeared, heading our direction, traveling in formation. I could only assume it was more security forces, heavily armored like the ones we had seen at the platform when we first landed.

We could not escape. Going back into the cave would box us in, our guide was down, and the shuttle would take too long to get here. We were stuck between a literal rock and a hard place.

"Universe please…" I mumbled, franticly looking for a way out.

From deep within the pit before us came a deafening roar of engines. The waterfall's mist blew away. We were suddenly in the middle of a tempest, a swirl of wind and water and noise. Then slowly, over the edge of the cliff, a familiar black shape rose before us, loudspeaker blaring.

"Back off, static brains," Karianna shouted over her intercom, her voice so loud it rattled my chest. For an instant I thought my bones might just shatter from the noise. *"Drop your weapons and get your five-eyed asses back in that cave. I've got a whole lot of pain to rain down on you."* A pair of energy weapons popped from the lower compartments of the Swift Shuttle and began to hum, barrels pointed towards the melee.

The Yellows still standing backed away from my crew members and left their weapons on the ground, retreating into the tunnels.

"Damn are you a sight for sore eyes!" I shouted, waving at the shuttle.

"You look like hell," Karianna replied. *"You gonna get your shuttle, or do we need to give you a ride?"*

I smiled, and an instant later my Swift Shuttle appeared from within the great pit. Proxy drew it up against the cliff, one air foil extending to the edge like a bridge. Nano machines on the upper hull reconfigured themselves to create a temporary hatch.

I waved at my team. "Go, go, go!"

With the Yellows pinned down, all of my crew except for Shelly, Frelo, and I boarded swiftly and got inside, Xuan and Hy carrying Lance. Frelo began to rouse where it had fallen by the cliff. Shelly and I helped them stand.

"Are you okay?" Shelly asked, her hair blown wild by the wind of the combined shuttles' engines.

Frelo inspected their hands and looked at the two of us. "May I come with you?"

"What?" I asked. "Why?"

They cocked their head and looked to the unconscious Yellows on the ground. "This is not my world anymore. I was an individual for too long. Perhaps I can be of use to your people. Help you complete your task."

The security cars were getting close.

"Look," Karianna started up again. *"I'm not trying to ruin some sort of heartfelt conversation, but those assholes are about to be on top of us and we need to effing go. A prison break has to be clean, friends."*

I waved a hand back at Karianna but kept my eyes on the Jevox. "Are you sure, Frelo? No going back."

"Yes. I am sure. It is better this way."

"No time to argue," I said, gesturing towards our getaway. "Let's go."

The three of us hopped onto the wing of the shuttle and down through the hatch. As soon as the last of us had passed through, the hole in the hull transitioned into a solid state as if it had never been. I stripped out of my clothes till I was nude, leaving concerns over modesty behind, and cannon balled into the Star Sphere. The umbilicals shot from hidden ports and connected with my body.

"It is good to see you," Proxy said in my mind.

"You too, friend."

I let out a mental breath and allowed the virtual interface to envelope me. The sensation was wonderful, downright euphoric. I was back in control of my world.

My world.

"Alright, everyone, let's go get Johan," I said over the shuttle's loudspeakers just before willing us off into the sky, accelerating as quick as my fleshy, unprotected passengers could handle.

Johan was near.

It was time to end this.

CHAPTER 29

The sky transitioned from blue to black as our twin Swift Shuttles burst through the stratosphere of Rix, entering the sea of angry communications chatter and scrambling ships that filled its low orbit. As when we arrived at the Jevox home world, my feeble human mind lacked the ability to sort these countless signals and discern any usable information such as plans, forces incoming, requests for us to return and so forth, but this was not the case for Proxy. Ever eager, Proxy went right to work, acting like a great filter placed over the mouth of a raging river, fine tuning its mesh to capture only the important bits among the chaos and returning them to me in a usable format. We'd inadvertently kicked the beehive, and its inhabitants had come to sting us till we stopped breathing.

As the *Fidelis* came into view, the Jevox forces turned and started to close in. A ping came through the noise, a third Foundry made ship, smaller than ours, burning away from the planet.

"Is that Johan?" I asked as Proxy fed me navigational information.

"Confirmed. He's taken a course."

"We're about to find ourselves in an awkward situation," Karianna called over the ship-to-ship channel. *"We need to pursue him, but the Jevox are about to lay the smack down on us. For once, I don't think it's right to indiscriminately kill. They didn't create this situation."*

"I agree," I replied. "What do you propose we do?"

"Try not to die. Find Johan. Capture him. He's got at least fifty of their people on that ship. All the while let's keep repeating to them that we did not do it. Maybe they'll disengage at some point. Maybe our Jevox buddy can help."

Our Swift Shuttles reached our ships. We docked, then disembarked, everyone rushing to their Star Spheres. We needed all the freedom and maneuverability of our starships. Regular acceleration chairs would not do. Lance and Leo had not been fully revived from their forced hyper suspension, but I hoped Proxy could help with that as soon as they were submerged. What a way to wake up, chucked in a fishbowl, and pressed right into combat. There was nothing to be done for it. We needed their help to execute Ada's plan or Johan would get away.

I slipped into my primary Star Sphere at the forward end of *the Fidelis*, skin bare, warm liquid rushing around me, my mind and body submerged in amniotic bliss. As I closed my eyes the sensors came alive. I was back in my virtual space with a tactical view, my feet planted on nothing, body floating in open space, stars wheeling above and below, the *Fidelis's* awareness settling onto my central nervous system and coming to life. Blue lines began to stretch out over my right shoulder towards the yellow hyper giant at the solar system's core, JV-01.

The Jevox ships were closing in on our position. In defense, I summoned the Mercurial Integumentum, forming a barrier before me. Nano machines rushed from tiny ports on the outer hull of my metallic gold and white body, flowing into a rushing bubble of swirling machines as tough as almost any material in existence.

"Milo," Proxy said, appearing next to me in a seated position within my virtual environment. "I have been continuing to monitor their transmissions, and I have found something peculiar."

I began to get green statuses on crew members entering their Star Spheres. Even for our new guest, Frelo. The *Reverie* powered up a moment later and gave me the signal to go ahead. As one, we burned away from Rix towards Johan's quickly vanishing trail.

"What is it, Proxy?" I asked. "What are you seeing?"

"A phrase keeps being repeated. It feels like how they might relay a signal from Jevox to Jevox over their electromagnetic hive frequency."

I shifted the MI barrier from forward to aft, a silver wall of glinting machines sliding backward on magnetic fields, just as a series of energy weapons lanced out towards us. The beams from the oncoming Jevox ships slammed against the outer layers of nano machines, turning them to dust, but the *Fidelis* was protected.

I glanced down at Proxy. "And that phrase is?"

"Release the Dragon."

"Dragon?" I shook my head. "What the hell is that?"

"I do not know. They keep repeating it. Release the Dragon. Release the Dragon."

"Are you hearing this, Karianna?" I called over our open channel.

"Yes. Chinchillette confirms Proxy's findings."

"Chinchillette?" My eyes narrowed. "Seriously? Now it has a name?"

"Can't all be named the same thing. Proxy and Proxy gets confusing as hell, don't you think?"

I took a deep breath and shook my head at her as if she could see it. "Chinchillette it is."

"What do you think it means? The Dragon?"

"Proxy?"

"I can't say," it began, attention focused on the blue lines of Johan's projected course, its cat eyes twinkling. "It could be a literal translation to that of human culture, a beast with great wings and teeth. Or it could symbolize something else, auspicious power, a great potency, perhaps the most destructive and darkest part of their culture. Then again, they could be talking about plumbing. The Foundry has found no clear translation, just like that of the name of their ruling council.

"That said, are you aware that according to your history, all human cultures developed their own dragon myths independent of one another? Lizards. Teeth. Wings. Claws. It all appears one way or another. It's as if humans are built to be dragon making machines, at least in their imagination."

"What? Is this the time to be talking about that?"

"It's true," Shelly said.

"I'm going to hope the word means plumbing," Karianna told us. *"And Chinchillette agrees."*

We began to pick up speed, accelerating towards the star at five, ten, twenty Gs. I could not imagine the Jevox would be able to keep up pursuit for long given their fleshy requirements. We were cushioned, protected from this inertial biological damage by the Star Spheres, and they were... to be honest, I had no idea how they were protected.

Shelly appeared next to me, a worried expression on her face. "He's fading," she said. "I don't read him anymore."

"We can't lose him."

"We'll find him," she assured me. "Ada's idea will work. It will work."

"Okay," I said, nodding. "Let's give him one last chance. Let's see if he will turn himself in. He's got hostages. If he'll surrender…"

"*I don't want a lot for Christmas, Santa,*" Karianna added. "*I only want surrender.*"

I opened a direct channel to Johan's ship and began to speak, "Van Niekerk, this is Milo Hughes of the *Fidelis*, son of Jackson Hughes, the man you murdered in cold blood. Call back."

I waited for a moment, but no response came. Something told me the signal had been received and was being listened to, if not responded to.

From more than one approach vector, the Jevox mobilized, my senses tingling with incoming threats, five ships, then six, seven, each that same sleek, aerodynamic core mounted with five engines divided by five sweeping fins. Energy intensified upon their prows, weapons powering up as they burned to intercept us.

"We're coming for you," I went on, ignoring the hive for a moment. "You will pay for your crimes. You will pay for what you did to my father, for ruining our hopes with the Foundry. We were charged with deciding what was important, with protecting life. You made a choice for all of humanity that was not yours to make. If you follow this path, you'll doom us all. The Foundry does not help those it determines are a threat to others. It does not assist those that murder… *dads*. Surrender now, and I just might show some mercy."

My eyes blurred over. Emotions were just as real in this place, even if my tears were not.

Still, no response. Anger rose in my chest as I saw the blip of Johan's Foundry made vessel wink in and out of existence. Something about the vapor clouds left by Rix's orbiting moons was interfering with their stealth systems, albeit temporarily.

"I'm going to kill you," I whispered. "I'm going to see you fucking pay for what you did."

Outside of my numb, hollow state, my crew scrambled to get in place, to ready themselves for the fight ahead. This was what we had been training for. This was what we had left our lives of quiet obscurity to achieve.

The comm channel crackled for a moment, then a deep, basso voice spoke, "*I knew you would come, and so we waited. You are not stupid, only foolish. Have fun with your tail. Asseblief, I can't stay and party, children, I have a species to save. A mission to fulfill. Save Earth. Someone has to cough up and pay the bill, might as well be me.*"

The line went dead. And that was that. Johan had made his choice.

I wiped my eyes clear with the heel of my palms and let my shaking hands fall to my sides. Shelly reached for me and squeezed the fingers of my right hand. I was too angry to accept her sympathy at the moment. I just wanted to see this man burn, but not just his ship. I wanted to see the man's very flesh peel away as fire consumed him, his heretical body tied to a stake as the rest of us watched. This was personal, and so his death deserved to be just as personal.

"We need to get the fighters in position," I growled. "Ada, are we ready to deploy the sensor network?"

"Ready as we'll ever be, dude," she called back, but her voice sounded as if she were out of breath despite being jacked into the ship's systems. *"Leo is coming around okay, but Lance… He's pretty spaced out."*

"Can we help him, Proxy?"

"There are a few medical options," it started, "but none are recommended. Given enough time, we can slowly, safely revive him. Hours. Maybe days. The primitive, poorly calibrated mass hyper suspension chamber the Jevox trapped you in was not gentle on his body. I cannot be sure what damage these ill-equipped cryoprotectants have done to his neurons."

My blood boiled. I was not letting Johan get away, and we needed every ship to make this detection plan of Ada's work. "How dangerous would it be to fully bring him around now?"

Proxy paused for a moment, calculating the odds. As it worked out the solution, more Jevox joined our tail, bringing their total to ten. They began to unleash a barrage of energy beams upon us that we were able to shrug off with the MI, but it would not last forever. They had the advantage of numbers. I felt my MI thinning along several locations, leaving gaps they could exploit if careful and coordinated. I hoped to the Universe they weren't as good at fighting as one entity as they were at building.

"One in three chance of brain death," Proxy eventually replied. "Those are Lance's odds."

I could feel Shelly tense beside me, imagining her putting a hand to her mouth in shock, but I could not look at her. There was no other choice. We needed all hands on-deck, and if she wasn't willing or able to fly for us, this left only Lance.

"Do it, Proxy. Wake him up."

"Milo," Shelly whispered, her voice dry, "what are you doing? This is dangerous. You could hurt him." She tugged on my sleeve. "Please don't. Please."

Proxy stared up at me, blinking. "Are you sure? Please confirm."

"Yes. I'm sure. Confirmed."

It lowered its head, and I turned away, my attention focusing on the battle at hand, my starship body floating through the chaos like a steel condor. The *Reverie's* MI failed for an instant, and a portion along its right flank flashed white from the impact of an energy beam.

"Shit that hurt," Karianna spat over the channel. *"I know I advocated for the passive response and all, but why was it again that we didn't want to shoot back at the Jevox? Can you remind me? My memory goes to shit when people start burning off my skin."*

"Might start an interstellar war," I replied. "You know, get everyone on Novae killed and prove to the Foundry that we don't protect life, potentially dooming humanity."

"Good reason."

I felt the occasional burn along my back and sides just like her, lucky shots piercing my barrier. I steeled myself and focused on adding more nano machines to the swarm.

"Milo," Shelly said, putting a hand on my shoulder. "What if…"

"It's done," I said, shrugging her hand off. "We've got a mission to see through. We're all taking a risk. One in three isn't bad."

She stepped in front of me, eyebrows furrowing. "But what if it was me?"

My face went hard, my hands balling into fists. I licked my lips and shook my head. "I'm not playing this game. Not now."

"This is not a game. Lance is our friend!"

"Then we better pray hard the Universe is working in our favor."

I crossed the fingers of my right hand for luck and turned away from her, reorienting my interface.

He would be fine.

He would.

He would.

Proxy did as it was instructed and began the process of reviving Lance. In the meantime, our secondary wing commander, Ada, coordinated getting everyone else to their ships and into formation.

"Geez, I feel hung over as hell," Leo groaned over the channel as he came online, his words languid and rambling. *"It's almost as bad as that night with Sarah, Kira, and Grace. A jug of that yellow rondure hooch Perry cooks up, a pallet of mixed pigments and bare skin on bare canvas. But this time, I didn't have the pleasure that came with it. There have been no spiritual revelations that only carnal exploration can gift. All the punishment, none of the fun."*

"Pig," Ada spat back.

"Whatever," Leo replied. *"Can I get something to clear my head?"*

"No," Proxy told him. "Give yourself a few minutes, your connection to the Star Sphere will clear your mind."

"I'm in formation, commander," Xuan called in.

Hy added, *"As am I."*

"We're almost set Milo," Ada said, and checked their positions. *"Just one more."*

Lance was still unconscious.

Their formation was sloppy at best. Each of the fighters were meant to occupy a space exactly fifty meters from the hull of the *Fidelis*, just inside the range of the MI barrier. Ada was in perfect position. Xuan and Hy, close, but off by about ten meters between them. Leo, on the other hand, was swerving back and forth, up and down, finding himself in the correct location for an instant before moving out of alignment.

"Hold still," Ada called out. *"Leo! Stop moving!"*

"I'm not trying to."

"But you are. Put your ship in the green box. Green. Box. It's not rocket science, and I'm pretty sure you know how to stand still."

"Which green box? I see two of them."

"For the love of… There's only one box. We can't form this network until you hold still."

A single blip came from up ahead. Johan had altered his trajectory.

"Pulling up," I told them, readjusting course.

They followed me as I moved, though poorly. Where the MI barrier kept a specific distance from the center of the *Fidelis* at all times no matter our orientation, fixed to a complicated architecture of electromagnetic fields, these four human beings in their fighters did not.

"Can we flip the switch?" Karianna asked. *"I think we're about to lose him."*

"Not yet," Ada replied. *"We need Lance."*

"Proxy has given him the drugs," I said, "we're waiting to see if he comes around."

"If?" Ada asked. *"Wait, what? If he comes around? Shit."*

Come on, Lance. Come on, I thought.

Please let this not be a mistake.

The pursuing Jevox continued to accelerate, and I began to suspect they might have a similar technology to the Star Spheres. They were from a lower gravity world, with bodies far frailer than humans, and so this led me to believe that they could not handle intense G forces, and yet they were closing. Less than ten thousand kilometers. Nine thousand.

Rix was shrinking at our drive flames as we fast approached the distance at which its moons orbited. It had taken early man several days to travel from the Earth to the Moon, one quarter of a million miles, and yet we had traversed that same distance in a little over half an hour.

The barriers of both battleships were being peppered with beams of energy as hot as stars. Layers upon layers of my MI vaporized, boiled away like fresh rain on hot pavement. Pain shot through my extended body, and I began to cry out. The Jevox were starting to do real damage to us.

"Shelly," I said. "What about the piezoelectric weapons. Can we drop those at our aft and disable them?"

"You know as well as I do that they're too close," she said, an edge to her voice. "You'll hit us too, kill the MI barrier. We'll be left with no defense at all."

And she was right. I just wanted a way out of this, and as it stood, I saw nothing that would help. We could not keep this up forever. The Jevox forces would eventually break through our defenses. At what point did we stop being passive and start fighting back? We had the firepower to eliminate this response, I was sure of it, just not the freedom or will to use it.

"Frelo," I called our Jevox friend over the onboard comms.

"Yes, Milo," they replied after a moment. *"This ship, it is quite impressive. I have never been within a Star Sphere. I cannot feel the accelerating, but I can free fly anywhere your sensors can see. I have only heard of this, never experienced it."*

"Yes, yes, it's pretty damn remarkable. Look, I am giving you open access to the communications system. Please, do what you can to get the Jevox off of us. Tell your people what's going on. We don't want to hurt anyone. We are going after the aggressor."

"I do not believe they will listen to me. I am—"

"I understand, but please, try."

"*I will try,*" they said, and went silent.

"*Leo!*" Ada shouted over the channel so loud it made me clasp my hands over my ears. "*Get back in place.*"

"*But I am in place.*"

"*That's the wrong place.*"

"*Not the first time I've heard that one.*"

His fighter had drifted toward the *Fidelis*, leaving only a couple dozen meters between us. This crazy plan was looking less possible by the moment. Karianna's crew seemed to be doing just fine, keeping tight on their formation, but we were not. I could only hope Lance would be okay. Had I made the right choice? Or had I consigned him to death?

"*If you can stop fucking up for five minutes, maybe I'll come help,*" Lance called over the open channel. Relief washed over me. He was alive, if with extreme vitals. His blood pressure was in the hypertension range, heart rate elevated, EKG readings wild, but he was alive. "*Ada, give me lead.*"

"*Gladly,*" she acquiesced. "*Position two is open.*"

"*I'll take it.*" His diamond shaped fighter detached from the hull of *the Fidelis* and found its place among their formation. "*What in the hell did those five eyed freaking nightmares do to me?*"

"*I shall explain later if you like,*" Frelo said, joining the conversation.

"*Is that who I think that is?*" he asked. "*The, eh, different one.*"

"*I am.*"

"*Oh,*" Lance replied, closing the matter.

The fighters moved into a loose formation, squad members arguing at one another as they fell into line. I had not taken the opportunity to run the exercise itself, so I didn't honestly know how difficult it was to stay in position as we were shifting trajectory to both avoid enemy fire and pursue Johan, but I had a feeling it wasn't nearly as hard as they made it out to be.

They had had plenty of time to practice. This was no game. No time for ego.

Blips of Johan's position appeared and disappeared on our scopes. I could sense where I believed him to be, then had nothing. My orientation would get lost, and Proxy would have to direct me to the last known vector in local space, circling the areas with green, directing me to move towards them.

Our fighters soon fell into formation and Ada's program board went green.

"We're ready," she told us.

"Start the program," I ordered.

I didn't have to ask when the network connection went live. My mind and body were flooded with a deluge of fresh information. I could see every direction at once, and not just if I rotated. Making use of the fighter's sensors made me feel near omniscient. I could not only see the Jevox forces bearing down on us from the rear in far greater detail, but count every single star in the sky, track their minute dips in light, inform anyone who asked where the nearest pulsar or quasar or neutron star was, and all at once. I knew that Proxy gathered information like this for the Foundry at all times, but the usual setup only allowed a 180-degree cone. This… this was everything, and in real-time. Dad would have loved it.

Through the sea of twinkling stars, I began to see a pattern. A section of distant lights that turned dark, then light again. Under Ada's instruction, I bathed that area of space with a spread from the Para Lux array. The result?

We found Johan.

"Christ on a cracker," Karianna said. *"It works. It actually works."*

"So long as we don't lose him and monitor too wide an area," Ada replied, her tone serious, *"we've got him."*

"Can we tell distance to target?"

"No. Not yet. We'll need more data."

"Hey, guys," Lance cut in. *"The Jevox are peeling off. They're heading back home."*

"Frelo?" I asked.

"No," the Jevox replied. *"It was not my doing."*

"Then why?"

"I do not know. We are too far away for me to be part of the ississ, *and I do not believe they heeded my calls to back off."*

Karianna chuffed, *"Good news though, right?"*

"Maybe, but it feels weird. Anyone feel weird about this? They had us dead to rights, now they're backing off."

"Maybe they know who we're after?" Xuan suggested.

"Possible I guess," Lance said. *"But if I were making a trap, I'd allow my enemy to feel they've won."*

"Way to be a Debbie downer," Leo told him. *"Though I have to be honest, it does feel like an over dramatic move."*

"Either way," I replied. "We're closing in on Johan. At this rate it's going to take some time. He's headed towards the asteroid belt and dust cloud around JV-01. I'm concerned he's still faster than us."

"You get me a solid fix, I'll get him with the piezoelectric bombs," Shelly said, not broadcasting her words outside my virtual environment. "I can do this."

I sighed at her. "Alright."

"Let's hope they don't hurt anyone on board their ship."

"Yeah, lets." I opened up the main channel. "Keep focused everyone, all we have to do is get close enough. Shelly will handle the rest. He's outgunned and out positioned. Let's stun his ship. Let's bring this game to an end."

CHAPTER 30

As soon as I was sure the pursuing ships had indeed turned back, I adjusted our frame of time reference so that we could close the gap with Johan subjectively swifter. We were still on his tail, able to see his trajectory so long as my pilots kept focused, their ships properly positioned in our makeshift sensor constellation. Ahead, the yellow hyper giant, JV-01, grew large enough to fill our entire view. Black spots began to appear along its profile, the dense asteroid belt that orbited it blocking out starlight, making it appear as if someone had tossed dust onto an orange lens.

The belt was a few million kilometers before us, then just a few hundred thousand. At our current trajectory, Johan was easier to find. Even with his stealth coating it was possible to see the smudge of his hull against the brightness of a star like this. My skin began to sizzle, turning hotter by the moment, the intensity of JV-01 baring down on us. I readjusted the MI in response, reflecting the worst of the heat, careful not to get in the way of the fighters' sensor arrays.

"We're closing in," Ada said. *"About the time we reach the other side of this belt I believe we'll be in range. It's hard to tell with no radar returns, but his silhouette is swelling."*

"Get ready," I said.

Shelly took a deep breath and closed her eyes to focus, hands clasped before her. I could feel her reach for the piezoelectric weapons, as if she had taken hold of one of my hands and pointed it somewhere. We would need to be careful, totally sure we were close enough before firing. These weapons were not something we had an infinite supply of, and we lacked the time to manufacture more.

A flash of light came from off to the left, beyond the curve of JV-01 among the glittering black expanse of the asteroid belt.

"Milo," Proxy said, its voice a whisper.

The hairs on my arms and back stood on end as something unexpected appeared within the left quadrant of my tactical view. Passive spectroscopy returned several emergency pings which confirmed my mounting fears. We had just detected crystallized oxygen in large quantities.

Crystallized. Oxygen.

Before I could say a word, a brilliant form just under four kilometers in length swam through the great empty towards us, its body appearing as if it were made of an angelic blue light. It was difficult at first to comprehend what I was seeing, and I blinked my eyes despite the futility of the reflex. An endless moment passed, and the blur resolved itself into a pale fish that wore a translucent, ribbed membrane around its collar that reminded me of an umbrella, its material blossoming like flowing silk, an eyeless head sticking from its center shaft to crown its tip with four interlocking jaws. The creature moved like an octopus, using the membrane to collect then press against some unseen medium, undulating as if it were submerged in water, not vacuum. The way it drew itself up, then spread wide, then drew itself up again, was mesmerizing to watch. I found myself momentarily lost, standing motionless in my virtual environment, hypnotized by this repetitive action.

Proxy batted at my leg, but I did not respond. I was transfixed by this wonder.

One might expect something of this size, using this sort of biological locomotion, to be slow and lumbering by comparison to our ships, but it was not. Within seconds of its appearance, its relative velocity had reached several hundred kilometers per second. The sort of G forces its thick-scaled body had to have endured were unthinkable, and yet, it was heading straight for me.

"Dragon!" Proxy called out, continuing to pat my leg with its fore paws. "That must be the Dragon."

"Okay, Okay," Ada said, her voice exasperated. *"Pardon my French, but what in the fucking Mariana Trench is that thing?"*

Shelly licked her lips and swallowed. "Life like we never knew it."

"They said they knew how to protect themselves," Lance cut in. *"They weren't lying."*

"And after the Gan," Shelly said.

"The Gan? Who the hell are they?"

"Are you saying they're controlling this?" Leo asked. *"How would that even be possible? I want to both paint it and flee from it. It's beautiful, but how?"*

"We found a way to control Jevox thought processes," Shelly told them. "Is it so farfetched that they could do the same?"

Karianna cleared her throat over the open channel. *"Have I mentioned I'm not big on wildlife? Don't care if it's insects, rodents, or space fish. Personally, I say the best policy is to shoot first, ask questions later."*

"Back to this?" I replied, doing my best to collect myself among a rush of mounting dread, none of which was existential.

"Yes, back to this."

"But won't it leave them defenseless?" Leo asked.

"Being dead will leave us defenseless," Lance replied. *"We start pulling punches now and this journey comes to a swift end. I'm with Karianna. Cook this shit."*

"Frelo," I said. "What is this thing? And why did you not tell us?"

There was a pause before they responded, as if they were trying to figure out what to say. *"I have only heard of stories."*

"You were part of the ruling body, and yet, you never saw this. The Jevox pulled back their ships when we approached the belt. It's their doing."

"The evidence is compelling. I cannot tell you more."

My anger seethed. They knew, they just didn't want to let on. "So then, secrets even among a hive mind?"

"Secrets even in your own mind. One library. Many aisles."

"Shelly," I said, turning to her. "Give it hell. Everyone else, stay in formation, I'll keep us on Johan. There's no telling what that thing can do to us when it gets close, but we can't let him get away."

She nodded in resignation, then closed her eyes. Just like before with the piezoelectric weapons, I felt her take control of the anti-matter slug cannons. This might be the only opportunity we had to take it out.

"Focusing on it," Karianna said, and the *Reverie* rolled on its side, twisting to face its batteries towards the oncoming space creature. *"Let's pound it with everything we got. Don't give it a way out."*

"No way out," Shelly agreed.

"No way out."

"But what if it's sentient?" Leo asked the group.

Lance sighed. *"You don't get the luxury of a moral discussion when a beast is trying to rip out your throat."*

I readjusted the trajectory of the *Fidelis* as new data about Johan's position came back to us. The Dragon drew closer, its velocity showing no delta. Four kilometers across seemed a small object at a quarter of a million miles away, but when that distance was under a hundred thousand, it was massive.

"Firing!" Karianna said, and a barrage of anti-matter slugs left her cannons, hurling towards the glowing creature. Shelly followed suit, filling the empty escape vectors with her own, giving the Dragon nowhere to go.

As the projectiles closed the distance, the Dragon's membrane flashed, swelled larger, doubling in size, then shrunk, before abruptly pressing against the elliptical plane and shooting upward with an unthinkable change in acceleration. It shifted its inertia around into a meandering spiral of a perpendicular approach, ever moving closer, if not directly towards us.

The anti-matter slugs began to ignite where they had once been, a dozen spheres of scintillating white light flashing, each ten thousand kilometers in diameter. Radiation washed back over us in a wave, though at this distance did little damage other than a few nanoscopic casualties among the MI on both battleships.

"That's not possible," Karianna hissed. *"How can it move like that? Its insides should be nothing but slush taking extreme turns like that."*

"Keep firing," Shelly said, her voice hard. "Lead the target."

"Right."

They continued to unleash our antimatter weapons along the trail the Dragon followed, but it was near impossible to figure out where it would go next. For all we knew, it could stop in place, then reverse its course by 180 degrees and come back around. It made these changes in acceleration with an effortless grace that if it weren't likely coming to kill us, I could have appreciated this.

While my team was focused on the Dragon, I returned my focus to Johan. He was fading in and out on our scopes, but I had a feeling we were drawing closer to his position. Our pursuit had brought us into the center of the asteroid belt and would soon cross near the hyper giant star. Johan seemed intent on skimming the surface.

This struggle went on for an age, but in our shift in time perspective it felt to us as if it were happening in swift succession. This dance of hours turned into days, the Dragon working to draw ever closer to our position, Karianna and Shelly attempting to corral it with our weapons, Johan drawing nearer.

We approached the outer edge of JV-01's corona, and I was again forced to readjust the MI, reflecting ever more of the star's heat. I had no idea what a bad sunburn was like, but I had a feeling that this was close. Anywhere the star's light touched the *Fidelis* unfiltered, it reminded me of frying food, skin oiled and cooked, flesh turning red, becoming blistered and sore.

"Look out!" Shelly shouted, and I spun to the right, my entire view filled with blue light.

The Dragon appeared on our starboard side, rushing across the bow of the *Fidelis* to collide an instant later against the top of the *Reverie*. The fighter Chevelle had been piloting in their constellation went offline. The sudden appearance of the Dragon made us roll and twist, and though we weren't struck like Karianna had been, the torsion force made me feel as if my bones might snap.

"Goddamn it," Karianna shouted over the channel.

"How bad is it?" Shelly asked.

"Hull breach, but we're not under pressure right now. Everyone is buttoned up in their Star Spheres."

I started, "Let's try and—"

But before I could get the words out of my mouth, a hail of fire came down on me from ahead. My vision was momentarily blinded as Johan's ship unleashed a continuous barrage of energy from his own Para Lux array, theirs more like a machine gun than a mortar like ours, but no less dangerous. The section of MI I had focused on the forward end faltered, and two fighters were put out of commission, first Lance and then Ada.

Scorched lines appeared down the length of the *Fidelis*. Holes were poked in the floors of the modular rooms on the outer decks. Heat from JV-01, no longer reflected by the MI, started to cook the outer hull of the *Fidelis*. I was a skyscraper whose glass windows were sublimating. To say that I was in pain was an understatement. I had gone from standing in the shade on a bright day, to being thrown into a broiler.

"Now he decides to shoot back," Lance said with all the frustration of someone who had lost his entire life savings to a game of cards. *"What now?"*

"Fighters in," I said through gritted teeth. "We don't need the array. He can't hide here."

"Milo," Shelly said. "I can feel it too. We need to pull back. The ships, we're cooking."

"She is right," Proxy agreed. "We cannot do this forever. This star is tearing us apart. We will soon be skimming its chromosphere."

I took stock of our situation. There was no going back. This had to be done. Dad had to be…

The Dragon withdrew for a moment, giving us a bit of breathing room, moving off as swiftly as it had come. It did not appear to be setting up for another strike.

"I—" And again, just as I was about to speak, more fire from Johan's Para Lux array rained down on us, forcing tears out of the corners of my eyes. "Shut him down."

Shelly reached for the piezoelectric bombs and began to track Johan. While we could get a solid fix, there was still a good deal of distance between us, a little over fifteen thousand kilometers. At that distance, he could evade the shot.

I gathered up what I could of the disrupted MI, calling for the internal nano forges to churn out new machines to focus them ahead. This absorbed some of the heat from the star, as well as most of Johan's attacks.

The closer we were to him, the more effective his weapons were.

"I've got a good lock," Shelly said.

"Fire!"

The crystalline weapon hurled from its launcher towards Johan's ship, the MI parting for an instant to allow it passage. The trigonal object spun so fast that under the scrutiny of JV-01's light, its blur appeared almost like a sphere, instead of a milky object full of sharp edges. All indications showed it would land near Johan's position, but at the last moment, he pulled away from the star's center of gravity, evading.

The piezoelectric bomb underwent a sharp compression of space-time, and a wave of energy was released. By the time the outer edge of this shock lapped at Johan's hull, it was little more than you would get from rubbing a balloon on your hair and touching someone with a finger. The stealth ship was unaffected.

Given that we were so close to the star, I decided to draw upon energy stores I had not intended on using. We needed to close the distance, and to do that, I needed additional power given how far I'd spread us. Twenty Gs of acceleration was not enough.

The leaf-like sails of the *Fidelis* began to extend, our shape blossoming out.

"What are you doing?" Proxy asked, alarmed. "This will limit our actions."

"I just need to touch stars," I said. "A little more power. We close the distance. She finishes him off."

As the *Fidelis's* flower pedal like panels unfurled, I felt the energy of JV-01 rush into me, life, connection filling me. Star energy. Dark energy. The sails could make use of it all. The engines responded in kind, and we began to accelerate. The distance between us and Johan shortened as stress began to pile upon my super structure, making my joints ache.

"Holy crap," Karianna said, her tone excited. *"What the hell, Milo? Come on, bruh, get him. Close the distance. You're almost there. Get it. Get it. Get it."*

Johan's weapons began to poke holes in the *Fidelis's* panels, but it was too late. I had gathered the energy we needed to see this through, and no matter what we did, we *would* overtake him.

"Ready our shot," I told Shelly. "Soon as we hit nine thousand kilometers, fire every one of them you have. I don't care if it disables us. Karianna and her crew can clean it up."

She took a deep breath, shook out her hands, then nodded. "Okay."

"You got this. I trust you."

"Right."

Twelve thousand kilometers.

Eleven thousand.

Ten thousand.

"Here we go," I said. "Ready. There we are. We're going to get him."

"I have him locked! About to—"

"Milo," Karianna shouted over the comms. *"Look out! Move! Pull up! Pull up!"*

I twisted around to see the Dragon appear out of nowhere, the four jaws of its beastly mouth open wide. Before I could react, change my course or acceleration, it fell upon us, brushing aside the MI as if it were nothing more than water vapor. It clamped down upon the bow of the *Fidelis*, and out of reflex I reached for the back of my neck, attempting to protect myself as one might from a rabid dog.

My virtual environment did not so much dissolve, as was violently ripped away, Proxy and Shelly and everything else just... gone. I found myself unable to orient, gasping for breath. The world was made of darkness, but for a soft glow of blue light.

I was back inside my Star Sphere. How was I back inside my Star Sphere? Though I could feel my body was wired up by a dozen umbilicals, I was no longer connected to the *Fidelis's* systems. I called out to Proxy, screaming into the amniotic fluid of the tank, but only tiny bubbles escaped my mouth. Twisting around where I floated, I found myself reaching for something to take hold of, anything, but there was no way out. My body heaved and twitched, and as I did, the contents of my stomach pushed past my lips and floated before me, a sharp pain cascading down my spine.

While my vision was distorted with the bend of the sphere's glass, I could see an orange light filtering in from outside a massive opening made of four parts, its edges lined with spikes as tall as buildings. The Star Sphere rolled, my orientation shifting, the light that was first before me now to my right, then darkness, then on my left. I splayed my body out, scrambling to find purchase and arrest this motion, but I just floated at the center of the sphere, panic overtaking me.

Realization of my situation dawned. My Star Sphere was no longer at the head of the *Fidelis*, but it was within the mouth of the Dragon. I had been eaten; the tip of the *Fidelis* bitten clean off.

A rumble vibrated through the liquid medium of my sphere, and the features of this monster's maw fled from view, replaced with open space, what was left of my sphere and its platform tumbling away from the battle. I caught a momentary glimpse of the *Fidelis*, its bow missing, small pieces of debris scattering like glitter tossed into open air.

I blinked in and out of consciousness, unable to hold onto any thought for more than a few seconds before waking some indeterminate time later. The sphere was cold, then hot, then cold, my body shivering with fever.

My heart pounded against my rib cage like a trapped hummingbird, the heat I had endured a moment earlier fleeing as the star receded from view. My entire existence was fast becoming like a picture hung on a surface which could not decide if it was floor, ceiling, or wall.

My perception vacillated between awareness and darkness.

Reality was tenuous.

Disorienting.

There was nothing but JV-01 to tell me where I was or where I was going, nothing but light so bright it scorched my retinas against the endless black.

A light flashed from off to one side, something blue, and I knew it was coming back for me. The Dragon had not finished the job. It realized that it should have swallowed me when it took its bite.

But no, no, that wasn't it. This was not the Dragon.

The twisted and broken platform upon which my Star Sphere was mounted screamed towards a round object with a high albedo. It soon struck the thin atmosphere of what must be a planetoid, that was all it could be, air pressing against me, threatening to vibrate my failing environment apart. In a fit of desperation, I reached out through my umbilicals to see if any systems remained online. At the speed I was traveling, there were no doubts I'd be dashed upon the surface of this rock at this rate, rendered into a smudge of dust.

Pressure from the atmosphere stabilized my spin and I was able to get a momentary glimpse of the approaching planetoid, dark stone covered in white, craggy cliffs and deep ravines, strong winds and weather. The Star Sphere shook so violently I expected it to shatter at any moment, leaving me freefalling to my death, but it held.

I closed my eyes and focused all my attention on the systems around me, hoping something might still work. After a moment, a trickle of energy rose up from a series of nano-machines affixed below the sphere. I fed what little power they had into a single culture, and they began to reconfigure themselves into a parachute, deploying behind my hunk of debris, capturing what little atmosphere they could. I would like to say my screaming fall was arrested by this desperate move, but it was not. After a few seconds, the parachute snapped and was lost to a howling blizzard. The powdery surface of the rock rose up to meet me.

My Star Sphere struck the ground and shattered like a snow globe on concrete. The world went black, flashing in and cut with fits and starts. Snapshots of snow and agony and twisting metal rushing past.

Though I was not aware of much at the time, my body was thrown naked into a field of broken glass, pitching end over end like a child's doll, bouncing off any part lucky enough to be a springboard for my next tumble. After a dozen or more impacts, every part of my body beaten into submission, I slid to a rest in a pile of deep snow, my body mottled with countless bruises and cuts of varying depth.

Darkness teased at the edges of this new reality. I sucked in the air among a storm, but there was no oxygen here. Nothing to breathe. Nothing to…

My fingers twitched.

My limbs were limp.

The half dozen steel umbilicals dangling from my spine screamed in my head, gave a death rattle, then fell silent.

Everything faded out for a moment, then came back around, shocked back into consciousness by the chill of the rocky ground, the burn of the lacerations along my arms, legs, and chest. Somehow, I was alive. Somehow, I was breathing.

Something had resurrected me, if only for a moment.

Stay awake.

Stay awake.

I stumbled onto my feet, frigid air rushing around my naked body, cutting through bare skin to my core like a storm of daggers. Ice formed in my hair, and my breathing, shallow as it was, became labored, struggling to draw air in such a thin atmosphere. I looked before me to see that my Star Sphere was no more, reduced to a scattered collection of metal and glass lost to the deepening snowfall of an alien world.

I took a single step, powder clinging to my shins, steel umbilicals swinging from my back, and realized that the toes on my right foot had no feeling. Foundry augmentations or not, if I didn't warm myself, and quick, I was done.

"Proxy!" I shouted. "Shelly! Anyone!" But even as I wasted the energy crying out, I knew no one could hear. They were just as dead as I was. The Dragon had killed them all. The Dragon had—

In the swirling tempest of a storm, I wrapped myself up in my arms, stumbling around, kicking through the debris. Lance had been so very wrong. The Universe didn't pick favorites, it was dispassionate.

My truth was clear.

I was naked.

I was alone.

I was going to die.

CHAPTER 31

The wind shifted and a gust of icy daggers slashed through me, my skin turning pink from irritation, then pale brown as the thin, freezing air of this world drained all color from it. I dug through the wreckage, limping as I did, looking for something, anything to protect me against the elements. I had no way of knowing how cold it was, only that it wasn't cold enough to kill me in an instant, but not warm enough to escape hypothermia. This was not something I had planned for. I didn't know the numbers, how low my body temperature could get before I'd become unconscious or worse, but it had to be soon.

Having grown up and lived most of my life on a spacecraft, the elements were a new concept to me. On Creatus we'd dealt with winter weather, some snow and frost on occasion due to the moon's bizarre orbit around its host planet. And on Novae, I'd had to wear a jacket at night, sure, but it wasn't all that thick, far less than even what the survey teams had worn up in the mountains, or what we would have needed in the coming winter. I did not know how to deal.

What was left of my Star Sphere was dismal, its remains making up a tract of twisted metal, glass, and cables several hundred feet long, only a few pieces bigger than a footlocker. It was a wonder I had even survived falling at that speed. I had crashed like a comet onto this distant planetoid, and not snapped so much as a finger, only been left with a few bruised muscles and skin that was rapidly turning a lighter shade of purple.

I needed to cover my body to buy some time. My lips were already chapped and cracked, feet losing feeling.

This couldn't be the end.

Purpose filled me. There was no time to wait. I sorted through the wreckage looking for anything valuable, pushing aside pieces of glass, shredded lengths of metal, and various streams of nano dust left by spent bots. If only I could have used those, if only some power had been left. Then it hit me. I scrambled from one chunk of debris to another, mentally piecing the shape of the Star Sphere back together in my mind, orienting myself to figure out where the platform on top might have ended up. With every icy breath I felt my chest seize, lungs protesting, muscles tensing, air like a physical object lodged inside me.

Shards of glass cut my feet as I stumbled forward, leaving ribbons of blood in my wake, making walking even more of a challenge. My knees buckled and my back bent. One of the umbilicals dragging behind me caught between two rocks and I was thrown face first into the snow, its coupling acting as a lever against that force. My spine ignited with hot pins and searing white agony. I cried out into the intense blur of the white, unforgiving gale, shivering from more than the cold. The fall had left me sprawled out on the ground, battling to get up onto my hands and knees to dislodge what it was that had made me tumble. I reached behind my back and felt for the Star Sphere's vestigial connections, my balance resting on my knees, bare body swaying in the breeze, snow collecting in my stiffening curls.

There was no way around it, I would have to divest myself of these umbilicals, and without the assistance of the Foundry. These cables were too long, too broken, too painful. Where aboard the *Fidelis* they offered life and time stretched out into infinity, here they were a cat-of-nine tails wired to my central nervous system as tight as cables in a server rack, their ends like razors buried within bone. Every small movement sent searing lances from my lumbar to my cervical vertebrae, then over into my shoulders and to my chest, driving me to the edge of blacking out.

I took a deep breath, steadied my balance, then reached around once more, fingers fumbling at the base of the bottom-most of the silver umbilicals, that closest to my frozen ass. My fingertips sought the release, and when I found it, a nervous relief washed over me. I depressed the button and twisted, un-screwing the connection from its coupling like one would disconnect a threaded garden hose. Not only did this send pain through my nervous system, but unusual memories also came back in flashes. Traumatic events. Dad on the walkway. Laying on the table with the Frendol standing over me holding knives. The Isoptera eating crew members of the *Vasco Da Gama* with their bare hands. Something about this manual release was triggering them.

The first of the umbilicals fell to the snow, its port dissolving, skin knitting together, and I began working on the second, wind gusts kicking up, forcing me down to the powdery surface. I would not give in. Could not give in.

The second of the umbilicals fell into the drifts, then the third, fourth, fifth, sixth, my teeth gritted against the wind, jaw aching. I twisted my shivering body and glanced over my shoulder at the pile of connections behind me, razor-sharp ends tipped in crimson. I was free.

"Come on," I told myself, teeth chattering, body shaking, internal temperature falling. "Come—come on. You—can—make—it."

On my feet once more I moved ahead, focused on the end of the snowy trench of destruction. What lay at its end I hoped might be my salvation, the gift of a few extra minutes before death. Among the wreckage a box lay open, a series of familiar possessions scattered across the ground. I immediately went to work, digging through my personal effects for any clothes I could wear, and though I did find a few items, these were torn and shredded.

I took what remained of my jacket and pants and laid the uneven pieces out on a mostly dry section of rock where the wind had blown away the snow, before reaching for the only unbroken vial of home-made nano machines I had left. Closing my eyes and focusing, I instructed the millions of tiny machines to stitch these tatters together into something that resembled a robe, and not take too long in doing it. To my delight, they went to work, flowing from the vial I placed upon the rags, still having enough power to get the job done. As they sewed the pieces together, my trembling body nothing but tatters in the unrelenting wind, I gathered up what few other items were salvageable. I collected my sidearm, a small messenger bag, and a torn Jasper, who was now missing a leg and part of one of his ears. Slipping those items into the bag, the bag tossed over my shoulder, I checked on the progress of my clothes. The nano machines were done.

The sack-shaped motley of fabric they stitched together slipped over my head, and I drew it up around me, attempting to close any gap the wind could use to get in. While it covered my head with a sort of asymmetric hood and kept my core out of the gale, it did not extend far past my knees. The inside of the robe, while warmer than outside, was wet and cold against my bare skin. The toes of my right foot, the one that was still flesh and bone, were going numb, and so I frantically searched for my boots among the immediate wreckage and found nothing.

Turning about, I searched for where I needed to go next. This robe had only bought me time, it had not absolved me of my situation. Hoping that my Foundry augmentations had something else to offer in way of survival like they had on Rix, I closed my eyes and focused on just that. Surviving. Somewhere warm. Shelter.

For a moment nothing happened, then a sort of sense began to settle over me. A feeling, pink in nature, drew my attention to a trail off to my right. The white-out of blowing snow cleared for a moment, revealing a precarious trail running down the center of two seemingly bottomless chasms, before vanishing among another gale. On the other side of this icy bridge was a hill, or was it a mountain? Hard to say. All I knew is that within the formation was a sensation of warmth. The Foundry's implants were encouraging me to safety.

While it may not have been a typical infrared view that appeared in my mind, the world turning blue and purple but for traces of heat in red, I knew something was warm inside that hill. I knew that it might keep me alive. I had only two options at this point: make for this potential warm spot, braving a path through chasms of who knew how deep fissures; or to try and build some sort of break against the wind in the hopes of being rescued within the next few minutes.

What an illusion of choice.

There was no other option than to continue. For Shelly. For Dad.

"Proxy," I mumbled. "Please help me."

I drew the satchel and robe against myself and plodded ahead into the narrow gap that threaded these fissures. Between the gusts of wind, I was able to draw a mental map of my route. It was about eight feet across on average, widening at the start, narrowing, first going to the left, before curving around to the right, then to the left again, before going straight till it narrowed to a knife's edge. Despite having a map in my head, navigating it was a challenge.

As I stepped onto the start of the path, my feet slipped out from under me, and I fell onto my back. Where I had manually released the umbilicals, the pain doubled, bones throbbing. I struggled to get back on my feet and cursed into the thin air, feeling for the first time in a few minutes how hard it was to breathe.

Before going on, I searched the ground for a tool. I had watched several movies on ice climbers back on the *Vasco Da Gama* and how they used axes to arrest their fall if they ever slipped. Far as I could tell this was pure ice I was stepping out onto, and so a curved piece of metal might help. It didn't take long to find a boomerang shaped arch of steel that would do the trick. I tested it on the ground, and it bit fine, though it did also bite at my prosthetic palm, scratching and scraping at its surface, leaving divots. It was a worthy exchange.

The path was easy enough to see for the first fifteen or twenty feet, then the storm kicked back up, snow blowing all around me, allowing me to see no more than my feet. I kept my head down, careful where I put my toes, leading first with my prosthetic leg, then following with flesh. The path curved to the left as I had remembered and I pressed on ahead, hoping I was not cutting the white-out at an angle that would lead me into a pit.

A turn came, drawing me to the right. My heart began to accelerate. This was working. I just needed to be careful.

"One step at a—"

My right foot came down ahead of me onto an oddly shaped portion of ground obscured by deep snow, and I slipped, tumbling forward. I fell, flipping end over end, my makeshift ice axe cutting at my other arm. I began to slide. Whatever surface was below the snow had been at an angle. My speed increasing, I reached out wildly with the axe, attempting to get purchase on anything I could. The winds cleared for an instant, and I could see that the dark chasm had come to swallow me, what was small soon widening to a world-eating expanse. There was no time to let out a squeak, to scream, to shout shit shit shit.

I raised my right hand, makeshift axe held tight, and threw my arm down hard as I could. The power of the prosthetic drove the twisted chunk of metal into not just thick ice, but solid rock. I held on to its razor-sharp handle for dear life. My feet dangled over the edge of the slope, nothing but open air to tickle my toes, tiny chunks of dislodged ice tumbling over the edge, their noise lost to that of the howling gales.

Blood thundered in my ears. My body flushed with heat. With numb fingers, I used my fleshy left hand to seek purchase, getting them around the edge of a rock to steady myself as I drew my body up with the strength of my prosthetic right arm.

"No…" My bottom lip trembled. "Not yet. Not. Yet."

Crawling on my belly through the snow, I made my way back onto the trail, forced to leave my makeshift axe behind. There was no room for another mistake. Having seen the error in my ways, assuming the snow would show how level the ground was underneath, I proceeded on hands and knees, reaching out before me with an explorative edge, testing the path before proceeding. This did nothing helpful to keep me warm.

As I crawled, the ground began to slope upward, a feature I did not recall seeing when I had first set off down this precarious path, but with a few quick breaks in the blowing snow, it was apparent. I was forced to climb an ice formation nearly ten feet tall, its angles steep as a rock face, edges jagged, no way to go around without tempting fate a second time.

My hand and foot holds were slippery at best, impossible at worst, and so I did what I could to wedge myself against anything available, adjusting my weight so that falling would not drop me off into the abyss. An edge of ice slashed at the fingertips of my right hand as I pulled myself up to the middle mark. I drew my fingers up to my mouth out of reflex, sucking at the cuts. In response my right foot nearly slipped off its hold as my center of gravity changed, the bag slung over my shoulder slapping against my back. My heart thundered against my ribcage. This was one way to warm myself up.

Fighting through the pain of exhaustion and cold, I told myself I could do this. All I needed was to get on top of this rock and slide down the other side. The end of this chasm was just a few feet away.

Screaming, I crested the top of the icy formation and threw my body over the edge. Once on top I took a deep breath. I had made it. I was not going to die for at least the next fifteen seconds.

"Not yet," I told myself. "Not yet."

This minor victory gave me a rush of energy. I used that rush to get down on the other end back to the trail where it narrowed. But before proceeding, I slapped my left hand against the ice in a test and felt nothing. My fingers were completely numb. A bad sign. I would have welcomed the pain of my cuts and the aches of my muscles to return.

Like a kid afraid of falling down the stairs, I bumped my way across the sliver of an ice bridge, careful where I put my hands and feet. To either side I could see the deep abyss below and had to force away any thought of falling, lest I invite that outcome. My body was trembling, filled to the brim with a cocktail of hormones, adrenaline, dopamine, and cortisol.

A dark cave appeared ahead through the tempest of white.

Salvation.

Soon as the path was wide enough to stand, I stumbled back onto my feet and hobbled towards the entrance, my senses informing me that the heat signature was inside.

When I crossed the threshold of the cave, the wind died as if it had been switched off, and a wash of warm air hit me.

The interior of the cave was dim, but not too dark. A sort of reddish glow emanated from the center of the room along the edge of an oblong piece of flat rock. This was where the heat was emanating from. I approached with caution, extending my lacerated hands to warm them.

Nothing about this heat appeared to be artificial, no machines. No, its source was geo-thermic. Somewhere deep beneath the surface of this unknown rock were flows of liquid metal, and I was the happy recipient of that radiated biproduct.

My body chose that moment to tell me it had had enough. My remaining strength evaporated, and I went limp. We had made it to somewhere of relative safety, and the adrenaline rush was over. I collapsed near the edge of the geothermic source and lay there, body resting upon the warm bedrock, heat seeping back into my frigid bones. When my eyes fell shut, an army of terrifying thoughts were waiting for me there.

Curling into the fetal position, one side of my body against the welcome heat of the stone floor, a pistol clutched in my right hand, a torn Jasper in my left, I could do nothing for the situation but sob.

This was not how it was all supposed to go.

This was not part of the plan.

What could I do now?

What could I do…

CHAPTER 32

"What are you looking at, Milo?" Shelly asked, taking hold of my right hand, her fingers warm.

I'd done it again, gotten lost in thought, my gaze fixed on the expanse of forests before us, the snowcapped mountains lining the horizon, the placid lake in the valley down to our left, the cloudy blue skies overhead, two moons like pale, round phantoms peering down at us.

It took me a moment to break from my reverie. The two of us were sitting on a picturesque hillside letting the day drift by, a checkered blanket beneath us, a wicker basket of food with a corked bottle poking out of the top sitting off to the side.

"Nothing," I said, turning to face her, those big brown eyes drawing me in. "Just thinking how beautiful this all is. Clean air. No trash. No heavy machines. This must be what Earth was like before people... at least, before modern times. Maybe we can be better. Maybe we can be like the Jevox, you know? Live in harmony with nature."

"But this is Earth, Milo. This is Earth."

"What?" I shook my head, heart thundering against my chest. "No, it's not. It's... Wait. What planet is this?"

"Oh hey! Look, it's your dad." Shelly was somehow already standing, waving at him. "Hey, Jackson! How are you?"

Dad turned to give her that stupid smile of his, then raised a hand in greeting. Duh. Of course he was supposed to meet us here today, for a picnic, have a little lunch, a basket of tacos, a few glasses of wine, we might even have a cheesecake in here. It was a beautiful day, one to be enjoyed for all it was, all it could be.

From out of nowhere, a man appeared behind him with a gun gripped in his pale fingers. My excitement vanished, blood turning cold. I scrambled to get onto my feet and protect him, but my body was stiff, muscles rooted in place. I was unable to raise myself from the picnic blanket.

Johan pulled the trigger. Dad collapsed to the ground. Before I could think to do so, I appeared at Dad's side, holding on to him. I peered into his lifeless eyes, what was left of them after the bullet's exit, and he began to smile.

"It's okay, buddy," he told me. "I'll be fine. Just need a few winks. Little rest."

"Dad!" I shouted, then watched as his face morphed into something else entirely.

An elderly version of Esteban peered up at me, a serious expression on his rugged, angular face, streaks of gray in his once-black hair, cheeks covered in stubble. "Take care of the colonists, ya?"

"Milo?" Shelly was at my side, her face melting like hot wax, oozing in lines down onto her shoulders and chest, leaving uneven blobs. "Help me, Milo." She began to paw at my shirt, tugging at my jacket sleeves.

I threw my arms out in alarm and rolled around on the stone floor of a cave, *THE* cave, blinking as I tried to make sense of what was going on. One half of my body was an inferno, the other like ice.

It had all been just a dream.

As I sat up, pistol clutched in my hands, I found my lap wet and smelling of ammonia. Even though I was all alone, it was embarrassing to piss yourself. I hadn't wet the bed since I was two. I sat my gun down on the ground and wiped my eyes with the backs of my hands, trying my best not to spread pee around.

I licked my lips and took a closer inspection of where I was. This small cave, part rock, part ice, was just the entrance to something bigger. Several tunnels fed into this geothermal dome from origins I could not begin to guess. While this place might have kept me alive for the moment, I wasn't seeing any promising opportunities to be rescued or escape. For all I knew, Shelly and Karianna and the rest were dead. What I wouldn't give for even Leo's help at this moment. Johan was getting away with it. Everyone I cared about was dust.

No. Not yet.

One crisis at a time.

I had found a warm place to be, that was good, and now I was thirsty, my lips chapped, my throat raw as a desert overgrown with cacti. I had no supplies, no canteen, but I had to do something.

What?

Rolling myself over on the ground, I lay there for a moment, allowing the cold side of my body to warm. While the cave was toastier than outside, the ambient temperature was not enough to keep me from shivering myself to death. For the next however many hours, I flipped myself like a hamburger patty on a griddle whenever one side got too cold and woke me from my sleep. I hadn't rested well, but at least I hadn't died.

Laying on my left side, eyes focused on the mouth of the cave, I watched the wind gust, blown snow gathering near the entrance, piling up enough that sections tumbled inside and melted. A trickle of water seeped away from these piles, giving me an idea.

My entire life, I had heard Dad go on about the planets around the galaxy, all our theories on what they would be like, and the data collected by the many unmanned probes we sent off around our own solar system. I found myself digging back through those memories now. I could no longer call upon Proxy and ask a question as simple as, "Is this snow safe to eat?"

Snow was not merely a terrestrial phenomenon. It was created when moisture in the atmosphere collects around dust particles and they begin to freeze, forming ice crystals that become heavy enough to fall. These particles, light as they are, were hopefully not toxic. The element involved in creating these crystals, given the fact that there was no way it was over eighty below outside or I'd already be dead, had to be water. And so, if it wasn't a dry ice snow like you'd get from extreme cold, then logic dictated it was likely water, and safe to eat. The only concern would be micro-organisms living in it. There was no telling what life had proliferated on this rocky planetoid, if any.

So then, what was the prudent course? Shovel piles of snow into my face to get some water into me, or find a way to boil it first? If this intense cold wasn't enough to kill the bacteria living here, would boiling it even make any difference? Didn't seem likely.

"I'm going to have to go for it," I said, pushing myself up onto my hands and knees before crawling towards the entrance. Using my prosthetic hand as a scoop, I dug into the powdery drift and brought some up to my face, stuffing it into my mouth.

The snow melted instantly. It felt like water. Had no smell. Tasted like water. No primordial alarms went off in my brain. Nothing from the Foundry augmentations.

"It's safe," I told myself, then set my weapon on the ground, before proceeding to shovel more snow into my mouth. Despite nearly freezing my throat, it felt great to get something in me. I kept it up for close to a minute, pausing between servings to keep myself from getting full-on brain freeze.

I noticed that while the fingers of my prosthetic right hand felt fine, those on my left did not want to cooperate. It was hard to get them to form a scoop, even though moments earlier they had been holding a pistol. The muscles and tendons were still, unresponsive.

From behind me came a crashing noise like falling rocks.

I whirled, reaching for my weapon out of reflex. I fumbled with it in my left hand, then decided to grip it with the right. With the weapon raised, I scanned the glowing cave, barrel pointed at the dark tunnels leading in, my heart lodged in my throat. Was I not alone?

"Hello?" I called, voice cracking. "Is anyone out there?"

A silent moment passed. No response.

Wary but undeterred, I reached for a scoop of snow with my free hand, but kept the weapon pointed at the opposite end of the room as a shiver ran down my spine. My body was getting cold again, and eating snow wasn't helping. I scooted back towards the center of the cave, listening to the air for signs of danger. The cave did not appear to be falling down around me. There was no hostile fauna. It was all just my imagination. My tired, hungry imagination.

I lowered the gun but kept it gripped in my hand, thumb on the safety.

While my stomach might have been empty, I was starting to feel somewhat better after having something to drink. Exhaustion returned, and I curled back up on the ground, my coldest side against the warm stone. I might still stink, but I was grateful that the urine had dried.

I hoped I didn't do it again.

My eyes closed, and I immediately drifted off into slumber.

The disjointed dreams returned, coming in awkward flashes between exhausted oblivion. I was in familiar places I had never been myself, places I'd only seen in videos or read about in books, all filled with the people I loved, and some I hated. Coffee shops. Restaurants. New York. Tokyo. Chicago. Rio de Janeiro. Loud music. Lively crowds dancing to samba, bossa nova, house, electro-country. Then there was Parallax, live in concert, great big speakers, bright lights, fists pumping, boots scooting.

And food. There was always food.

Empanadas. Tacos. Hamburgers. Curry. Noodles. Sonhos. Mounds of sweets with every square inch covered in a layer of powdery sugar.

So much food.

More food than I could ever hope to eat. Not that I didn't try.

Between phases of grinding my body against my wife, pelvis to pelvis, I took breaks to eat, and eat, then drink, till my fears fell away and my movements were as fluid as the beats that drove them.

Within the deeper sections of the cave came a boom, the sound echoing like a mallet striking a gong. The hazy visions shattered into oblivion, and I shot up from the floor and skittered back towards the wall, my side-arm raised with both hands. My dry eyes itched.

A… something… slunk from the shadowy recesses of the left tunnel, its form half as tall as me, with a long, dark face covered in slitted, pupilless eyes and an open mouth filled with angular white teeth. It was dog-like in shape, sort of, but with oily skin rather than fur, the spine of its slender body twisted like a corkscrew, its four asymmetric, sinuous limbs protruding at odd distances along its length. The feet of this creature were as wide as tree fans from Novae, their toes tipped with what looked like a serrated edge of claws. Canines that looked like this would have been at home in a horror film, no "good boy," no playing fetch, no belly rubs. It would not only eat your flesh but take your soul and shit what was left into a steaming pile capable of summoning demons just like it.

"Stay back," I shouted. "Stay back!" I kept the barrel focused on the stalking animal.

It plodded forward, one exploratory step at a time, my heart thundering harder with each instant. There was no way I could fight this thing. How many shots did I have in this clip? Twelve maybe? Seemed just about enough to piss it off.

Approaching the center of the room where it was warmest, it kept its focus on me, pausing as it reached the edge of the geothermal radiation.

"You cold too? Come to warm up then eat me?"

It stared at me, a dozen eye slits blinking in random sequences. The creature lowered its body to the stone floor to soak up the warmth. As it did so, some of the light in the room dimmed. I paced the end of the cave opposite, keeping my weapon raised, its eyes tracking me all the while. I just wanted it to go away. My options at this point were limited. It was becoming obvious it liked the warmth as much as I did, and so heading back out into the blizzard would likely keep it from following me, but I would be no better off.

"This is my cave," I growled and stomped a bare foot on the ground in front of me. "You hear me? My cave!"

What happened next came so fast my brain almost couldn't register the movement. The creature shot like a coiled spring from the spot where it had been warming itself. It was all I could do to throw myself to the side as it slammed into the wall with its shoulder, rocks raining down from the ceiling overhead.

Scrambling to get back onto my feet, it came at me again, and I spun around. This time its action was not so fluid. It appeared that this creature had not evolved to hunt like a dog, but rather to spring on its prey like a trapdoor spider, hence the wide feet, the slender body. Once it had expended that advantage, however, it struggled to run anything down.

I turned towards it and pulled the trigger of my side-arm. The deafening boom of the pistol's report shattered the uneven quiet, my ears ringing. While my shot had gone wild, missing the trapdoor demon dog completely, the sudden boom had driven it to retreat. The creature stumbled awkwardly over its own feet before loping its way out the opposite tunnel without making any noise, leaving me alone once more.

"That's right," I said, sniffling. I scrubbed my sleeve over my nose and sucked in several ragged breaths. "Bitch."

I wish I could say this is where it ended. This scenario went on, and on, repeating for several hours, maybe days. It was hard, if not impossible, to keep track of time without Proxy or a hand terminal or an easily recognizable day-night cycle. While water was plentiful, without food I was weak, and growing weaker. My body would tremble for hours on end, this time not the result of hypothermia. Exhaustion forced me to fall asleep, but with the threat of the demon dog, any noise, real or imagined, would wake me. I couldn't stay like this forever.

The dog returned sometime later, testing my resolve, and I gave it a 45mm greeting, inflicting little or no damage. The noise of the weapon, more than anything, scared it away.

Eleven rounds remained.

Ten rounds.

"Can I eat it?" I asked myself between attacks. "Can I eat that stupid dog?"

There was no good answer to this question.

"Can I even kill it?" A better question.

I checked the ground where it had been standing when I last hit it. There was no blood, no fluids. What was this thing made of? Steel?

My stomach had started to cannibalize itself. It felt as if something with claws were attempting to dig their way out of me from the inside. I made the decision, good or bad, when this thing returned, I would search for its softest spot, then unload the entire clip. If it killed me in the process, so be it, but if it was eatable, I would feast on its remains.

Settling back in at the middle of the room, I rolled around to warm my coldest bits, ensuring my muscles were warm and ready, before heading back to the pile of snow and taking in some more fluids. Despite all the water I had gotten in me, I found that I didn't have to pee all that often, if at all. That couldn't be good.

Once I was warm, I scooted back from the center of the room to the edge, then propped myself up against the wall, giving me the best vantage of the two tunnels. For what seemed like hours, I focused my attention on waiting for them. Nothing. No noise. No threats. I dozed in and out of consciousness. Exhaustion couldn't begin to describe what I now felt. All the processes in my body were coming to a halt. I wasn't just a watch whose springs had gone loose, but one whose gears had snapped entirely.

My eyes shot open at the sound of crunching feet. I coiled myself up on the ground, squatting, weapon raised towards the sound. As I expected, the creature had emerged again, but this time, it was not alone. Another two had come with it, one from the same tunnel, another from the opposite tunnel. They each lowered themselves on their haunches and became perfectly still, like gargoyles mounted on a cathedral. If I had not watched them coil into place, I'm not so sure I'd ever have known they were there.

Ten bullets. Three of them. There was no way I could—

Before I could formulate a plan, the first of them leapt at me, the room becoming a shifting animation of shadow puppets. Already coiled myself, I leapt out of the way and began to scramble off on my hands and knees, avoiding its initial attack. As I landed, the next one fell upon me, its claws landing only a few inches from my legs.

The third would be next, but I did not give it the opportunity. Avoiding the others, I had closed the distance with this one, and felt confident I could hit it. I raised the pistol and pulled the trigger, firing several times. The creature shrugged off my attacks as if they were no more than powdery snowballs. It struck out, slamming me in the shoulder, sending me skittering back onto the hot, stone floor. Before it could come down with its razor filled maw, I rolled out of the way. The first of them was coming back at me, so I steadied my hands and squeezed the trigger, then spun and did the same as the second made its move.

To my delight, the first of them started to limp. Maybe I could injure them, maybe I could kill them. I focused my barrel again on the injured demon dog and fired several times. It let out a muffled cry and settled onto its haunches, though not coiling its body like before.

I was given no time for a victory dance.

One of the creatures struck me in the head and I found myself sideways on the floor. I rolled around, fingers running through my hair, palm pressed against the throbbing pain, the other scrambling for the lost side-arm.

Noise was all around me. Voices. Screams. Groans. I blinked away the pain, moisture collecting in my eyes, vision blurry, then raised the barrel at the sound and began to unload.

Click.

Click.

Click.

The sidearm was empty.

As my vision cleared, I searched the room for my killers. The demon dogs were gone, nowhere to be seen. They had been replaced by… Replaced by…

No. This couldn't be right.

"Geez am I glad that thing was empty," a blurry form before me said, her edges sharpening and resolving into a woman, her hands raised in exasperation. "I've tempted fate plenty of times, sure, but being shot by one of my own in the middle of nowhere would have been a raw deal."

"Who are—" I squinted at her. "You're, eh, human. Your face. I don't know it. Who—" And I didn't. It was a woman, a real one, flesh and blood, not a demon dog. She was about my age, short and slender, with long blonde hair braided and tossed over her shoulder. She had big blue eyes; a kind, soft, pale face interrupted by a set of deep scars which ran from her forehead down to her upper lip as if she'd been cut with something jagged. No one on Novae had a scar like that. "I don't know you, and I know everyone."

"Everyone?" she mused, fists resting on her hips, tone incredulous. She leaned towards me. "Here, take my hand. I won't hurt you. You're safe now. You're safe."

"But it tried to kill me," I wheezed and let her help me stand, "and it will come back for you too."

"Umm, what tried to kill you?" She peered over her shoulder and behind me, leaning to the side. "Look, friend, there's nothing here but us. Just us."

"No, I saw it. It, it hunted me, tried to eat me. But I was going to eat it. That's right, you hear me, I was going to eat it."

Her expression soured. "Okay. Okay. I see how it is. Don't worry. We know how to keep it from hurting you. Do you mind if I carry your weapon for now? You look really tired. Might be too heavy."

I raised the pistol and looked it over. The make and model were eerily similar to the one Johan had used, a fact I had not noticed until this moment, and that idea made me nauseous. I handed over the weapon. It was empty anyways.

"Good," she said. "Good."

It was at that moment that a series of squat, leathery skinned bi-peds with flattened heads stepped out from the shadows, three of them in all. They gave us a wave and flicked on a hovering globe light, illuminating our path deeper into the cave system.

"What do you say we go get you something warm to eat?" the woman asked, and I did not protest. "Soup does wonders for the soul."

I nodded.

If there was one thing that I'd learned in my days struggling for life far away from Earth, it was that you never turned down a hot meal, even if that meal came from a figment of your imagination.

"Soup sounds good," I coughed.

"Lovely. Then let's get you a big 'ol bowl and warm you up."

CHAPTER 33

The mysterious woman and her leathery, alien companions led me through a series of unlit tunnels that in my exhausted state never seemed to end, the path dragging out for miles. These passages were natural, no machinery or wiring upon the walls, just bare, dark rock. As we went deeper, I came to realize we were crossing footprints in the dust. It was clear this was not some random cavern on some random planetoid, it was a well-trodden path that was used on the regular. Where did it lead?

My brisk walk soon became a stumble. Two of the aliens came over to help me keep upright, their dry, scaley fingers pawing at my frostbitten arms for leverage. This was no easy task for them, given that they were hardly tall enough to reach my armpits, but they made it work. Satisfied they were helping me continue, the woman led our group onward, encouraging me to keep up as I could, reminding me that we were almost there. Though she would not tell me where *there* was, I had a feeling it was better than where I had been.

The tunnel came to a terminus where a metal wall greeted us. She spoke a word and raised a hand, and what had been a sheet of solid silver split down the middle and parted, allowing us passage.

"Nano machines," I mumbled. "Foundry-make?"

She turned to look at me, head cocked to the side. The shifting brightness of the globe lights cast a deep shadow across her blonde hair and facial scars. "Not the Foundry."

"Who?"

"Melcorin," one of the leathery creatures said in a raspy, wet voice. It then proceeded to give me several awkward pats on the back. "There, there, there. You are going to be fine. This way, Mistress?"

They were Melcorin, the species who had rescued Mom and Dad and several others from the Isopteran attack at the first Foundry facility we visited. Details were sketchy at best from those days, but when Mom and Dad had gotten separated from our group, much like Esteban and I had, this species of shadow-dwelling cosmic explorers swooped in and kept them safe from the termites, carrying them across the stars and through the Wandering Gate to where we ended up on Novae. The fact that I did not recognize them off-hand played more into my current state of mind than my memory. I had seen their kind before.

The Melcorin were a lizard-people from Universe-knew-where. They were bipeds like humans, though with legs that had extra joints, like those of a goat or a dog. Their hands and feet had three fingers and three toes each, ivory claws extending from the tips. They came in varying colors, mostly green or grey, blue or red, some with stripes, some solid, faces long with flattened foreheads, no lips, and two eyes black as marbles.

"What is it doing?" I asked the woman after a moment.

She smiled at me. "Isn't it obvious? They're trying to make you feel better."

"Thanks?" I responded to the Melcorin who had spoken to me. "I mean it. Thanks."

"You are welcome, human," it said, and attempted to curve its mouth into an approximation of a smile. On a leathery face like that, the effect was not comforting at all, too much tooth and way too much gum.

"I'm sure that isn't his name," the woman said as she led us through the door.

We stepped through the portal, then through another, what could only be an airlock, and walked out into a set of noisy rooms stacked with equipment from floor to ceiling. Everything was cramped, the ceiling was too low, the space was too bright, every surface lit in shades of yellow-white, controls as plentiful as the edge blossoms on Novae, their panels and screens lined with blue. Between what little space we had to walk, there were boxes and crates with even more boxes and crates on top, their many faces covered in characters the Foundry implants had difficulty translating. We pressed on through the cacophony, the woman raising a hand on occasion to move a set of wires or cables out of our path that ran into ports upon the walls or into the floor. Some of these cables were cold, and yet others were warm, either from electrical resistance or flowing fluids of some kind.

"Where are we?" I asked, shrugging free of my Melcorin assistance. "Sorry, I got it from here."

"Where are we?" the woman called back. "Oh, yes, forgot to mention. Welcome to a Melcorin Sanctuary."

"A what?"

She waved a dismissive hand. "There's plenty of time for that later. For now, we need to..." She turned a corner and raised her hands. "Ahh, there we are. Just what I was looking for."

I shambled up beside her and peered into the small chamber beyond us, which looked like a closet with a porcelain bathtub wedged inside of it. "And what is this?"

"Warming pod," one of the Melcorin said. "We must help you recover."

The woman bent over and clicked several buttons along the device's side. The tub started to steam, though it did not fill with water as I had expected. "We'll start slow, then warm you up. You've been out for a minute. You're freezing. Take off your, em, clothes, and get in. Brace, get him some blankets."

"Blankets, blankets! Yes, Mistress," a Melcorin with greenish scales brushed with yellow replied, then went to a storage closet along the wall. Why in the hell did they keep calling her that? What a weird title.

"Did you say take off my clothes?" I looked down at my tattered robe, trembling fingers picking at the motley of fabric. "Oh. What about my bag? It had a..."

"This?" another of the Melcorin said, raising it up.

I snatched it from its claws and nodded. "Um, yes. Thank you."

The woman waved a hand at the empty tub, then at me. "Come on. Don't take too long. I'll go get you some soup while you lay down. The heat will start around seventy degrees and warm up into the eighties over the next hour or so. If there's any discomfort let us know."

"Who the hell are you?" I asked, shaking my head. "You find me in a cave on an alien world and just start ordering me around. You've got Melcorin following you around like a pack of puppies calling you Mistress."

"I could ask the same of you," she said, hands on her hips. "I was just fine with this little rock being quiet."

My eyes trailed down to my feet more out of exhaustion than anything else. I let out a sigh. "Fine. My name is Milo Hughes of the *Vasco Da Gama*, the third ship of the FICSE Mission fleet."

The woman's hands rose to cover her mouth. She whispered, "A FICSE Mission ship."

"Yes. None other. And you, you aren't from my ship. I don't know you."

"No. I'm not." She shook her head. "I—well—name's Bellamy Baptista of *the Revelation*. And you and I, we have a lot to talk about."

I was acutely curious, but given my injuries, I did as I had been instructed. I stripped down and slid into the bare tub. As I settled into place, the Melcorin she'd called Brace began to pile a series of velvety blankets on top of me. It was a strange sensation that washed over me as I recovered my body temperature. My skin and muscles felt as if they were both frozen and burning as the cold was driven away. My stomach began to growl with the thought of food, but it was not meant to be, not for a while.

I didn't fight exhaustion and fell asleep, comforted by the warmth and safety of the Melcorin Sanctuary, swaddled up in a cocoon like a newborn baby. There was nothing here to be afraid of.

There was no way to say how long I slept, but when I woke again, drool was running down onto my chin, and I had shrugged off several of the thick blankets. Sweat was starting to collect on my brow. It was safe to say that at least part of me was warmed back up.

Brace was sitting in a chair across from the warming pod, and when it saw that I had woken up, it held its clawed hands before it, urging me to stay in place, then ran off. I did not get up. A few seconds later, the woman who had called herself Bellamy reappeared, a steaming bowl of food in her hands.

"You hungry now?" Bellamy extended the bowl with a silver spoon sticking out the top. "You fell asleep, so I had to reheat it. Careful, it's hot."

With a nod, I reached out and took it, my fingers holding it at the edge. My prosthetics felt the temperature of the bowl fine, but the fleshy fingers of my left hand did not. The tips of my fingers were dark in color, almost black, and had little if any feeling at all. This made me frown.

"You okay?" she asked.

"I'm fine. Thanks. Smells great. Like, chicken noodle soup."

"And how would you know what chicken noodle soup tastes like?"

"Proxy made me some before," I said, and took a spoonful. Though it smelt like chicken noodle, that was not the case for its flavor. It was gamy like stone bison or strider stew.

"Proxy?" she mused, curious as she settled into a metal wall-bench across from me. "Are you a pilot? Do you have a Foundry made ship?"

I sighed, then took several bites of my soup, doing my best to eat slowly. My stomach quivered at me. "I am. It's a battleship… or it was, at least."

"Was?"

"We were attacked…"

Bellamy raised her open palms. "Okay. Okay. Why don't we start at the beginning?"

"Why not you? Tell me your story."

"No. No. We'll get to that. You first. Tell me of the *Vasco Da Gama*. Tell me of your arrival."

And so, I did. I told her of our crossing from Sol to the Foundry facility at Barnard's Star aboard the *Vasco Da Gama*. Told her all the great things we had hoped for, the null-g protein my mother's team had developed, of their mistake with Perry, and our eventual victory. Bellamy told me that even she had that protein in her blood, and that it had helped her remain healthy all these years. This made me smile. I told her of the Isopteran attack, during which she got quiet and seemed uncomfortable, then of Esteban and my odyssey to reconnect with the crew, before the Gene Brokers kidnapped them, forcing me to make a donation to the Foundry and acquire the *Fidelis*. She had a lot of questions about the donation, about my prosthetics. I answered them all as best I could and realized that it was both painful to tell my story, and yet cathartic, like ripping a bandage from a healing wound so that it could dry out in the sun.

"Okay, so, you donated part of your body, an arm and a leg, so you could go and save your friends?" she asked.

I set the empty bowl down on a ledge beside the warming pod. "It was the only option."

"And you saved them?"

"Well, not exactly. We stopped the Gene Brokers, but to be honest, they were saved by Melcorin."

"Really?" Bellamy smiled, turning her head towards Brace who was standing off to the side trying to act inconspicuous. "They aren't just stories?"

"We help where we can," it said. "It warms my blood to know our brothers assisted those of the *Vasco Da Gama.*"

Bellamy continued, "So you stopped the Gene Brokers, these Kabosai."

"Yes," I said.

"And the Melcorin take your lost people to a planet beyond the Wandering Gate, which is the side of it we're on now, to a new planet."

"Where we formed a colony we call Novae."

"Wow. A colony?" She let out a long breath. "No going back to Earth then?"

"To be honest, we don't know how. Don't know the way."

"Well, you're not alone in that. With the Isoptera, however, it's all for the best." She stood and picked up my empty bowl. "Want some more?"

"Yes," I said. "Please."

"Brace," she handed over the bowl.

"Yes, Mistress." The Melcorin scurried off. The eager way it acted, I was starting to believe that it was a juvenile attempting to prove its worth, though I was only guessing. Shelly would know. She knew everything. I sure hoped she was still alive.

"Okay," Bellamy nodded, "so you have a colony on Novae, is that what it's called? How did you end up here though?"

"We'll get to that," I said, hurling her statement back at her. "I'm curious. What's your story? Who in the hell are you?"

"Who am I?" she mused, rubbing her chin. "Fine, you've been fair enough."

Brace returned with more soup. I took the bowl from its claws. "Thank you," I told it, then turned my attention back to Bellamy. "You mentioned the *Revelation,* another of the FICSE vessels. All we know is that it was one of the three that were lost."

"What is this FICSE?" Brace asked.

"It's a human thing," Bellamy said. "An acronym. We use letters to mean several words. It stands for Foundry Intent – Contact and Save Earth. It's how we stay focused on an objective. We call it a mission."

"A mission," it said, mulling the word over. "Humans are strange."

"No shit," I mumbled. "And this wasn't just *a* mission, many of us call it *the* Mission. The only mission."

Bellamy nodded to herself. "Been a long time since I've heard that phrasing."

"So, the *Revelation*," I said, bringing her back to the subject at hand, my arms resting on the pile of blankets covering my naked body. My forehead was starting to sweat, which I took as a good sign. "We thought it lost."

"Lost?" she mused. "You could say that. I venture it was almost your fate as well. The year, 2108. We had safely made the crossing, our destination Alpha Centauri. The Foundry had a facility waiting for us there, a giant hoop that acted like a ring around one of the system's gas giants. We were being drawn in, just like you, and then…" She shifted in her seat and leaned onto her haunches. "They came."

"Who came?"

"But you already know."

I swallowed. Memories of a sickening stench sent shivers down my spine, spilled blood across the habitat ring's deck, cooked flesh burning from energy weapons, mandibles and claws dripping trails of black. "You met the termites. The Isoptera?"

"That's right, the Isoptera. Though it is curious you call them the same thing."

"One of our engineers proposed it soon after we met them. Seemed appropriate, given the entomological classifications."

"Curious…" She took a deep breath, one hand absently reaching for the deep scar that ran across her face. "Before the *Revelation* reached the inhibition field of our Foundry facility, those giant termites attacked our ship and murdered everyone on the crew but for me, my mom, and my grandfather. We barely made it out."

"I'm so sorry."

Bellamy shrugged. "It was a long time ago. At least, I think it was. It's funny, you and I aren't too different in age, yet somehow, we've experienced about the same amount of subjective time. How old do you think you are?"

I scratched the back of my head. "Twenty-nine? Thirty? I can't say."

"Time is weird without a host star, right?"

"Very," I agreed, then ate a spoonful of the salty soup. "Please, go on. Unless you don't want to."

"No, it's okay," she said. "It's nice to talk to another human. It's been a while, as you can imagine." She paused, searching for her words, then went on. "Everyone died, we escaped, but not before Granddad turned the fusion drive upon the Isopteran ship. He sliced the thing in two, but in the process, irradiated any survivors who might have been on board. Mom was hurt really bad. We were able to escape to the Foundry, and the entity that runs the place told me how to save her. You see, there are some facilities that have these, Resurrection Chambers. They have a bath in them, not much different looking than that warming pod, and when you put a person into them, they can be rebuilt."

"The Foundry saved your mother?"

"After a fashion. The resurrection cannot be completed at the same facility due to an equipment cool down. Years needed to pass for that to work, a kind of recharging period, so it was not feasible to wait. This process is also a means of travel, though a disturbing one at that. Dissolve the body while copying the mind, the structure of the person. Her essence, her soul, transmitted to the nearest facility that could accept it. I went after it. After her."

I swallowed. In a way, it wasn't too different from what the Wandering Gate had done to us. "And your grandfather? What happened to him?"

"He—he died."

"I'm sorry."

Bellamy waved a dismissive hand. "We all play our part in the universe. Some good, some bad, some complicated."

"I understand. And your mother's signal, you chased it down. How?"

She smiled at me. "A ship, how else?"

I blinked at her. "A Melcorin ship?"

"No way," she shook her head. "A Foundry made ship. Star Sphere and all."

"Wait, but you have no prosthetics." I gestured to her arms, both fleshy, human. "You made no donation."

She raised her right and looked it over, front and back. "Apparently not everyone has to. My Proxy told me that the Foundry felt bad for what had happened. Maybe not having to donate was a consolation prize for their mistakes."

"What a strange prize." I polished off the second bowl of soup.

"Right?"

"What about your mom," I asked, attempting to be casual, "did you find her?"

"I did," she said. "I did."

"And where is she now?"

"Now that's a great question." Bellamy peered up at the ceiling, lost in thought for a moment. It was clear that there were some interesting family dynamics in her small group, but she was not forthcoming with them. The moment passed, and she put her attention back on me. "Now I just roam. It's a big universe out there, might as well see it all. I've learned to make a few friends along the way. Even if they aren't the easiest on the eyes, there are good, kind people out here. Melcorin never hurt anyone. They stay safe by hiding from bigger, more dangerous species. Their ships are cloaked, even this sanctuary is cloaked. They live in small groups and never fight."

There was so much to unpack in what Bellamy had said. The *Revelation* and its crew had indeed been lost, except for her. I didn't dare pry over where her mother was. I felt that I could trust her, at least not to kill me, but also felt she was holding back. None of this changed the mission at hand. I needed to get back into space. I needed to see if Shelly and my friends were alive. I needed to see if the *Fidelis* was beyond repair and most of all, I needed to stop Johan.

"Look," I said after several moments of silence, "I don't mean to be a rude guest, but I've got to get the hell out of here. You have a ship?"

"Yes, we established that already. I have a ship."

"Well, I need to go find mine." I started to get out of the warming pod, then realized I had no clothes to wear. Brace saw this and raised a single claw, then took off as if going to find me something. "Take me there, Bellamy. Take me back to my ship, even if it's a wreck."

She stood up and urged me to sit back down. "Not while you're in this condition." Taking hold of my left hand, she flipped it over and inspected my discolored fingers. I felt none of her touch. Bad, very bad. "Besides, you've not finished your story. Why are you here? If you had a colony to live in and the ones you love are there, why come here? The Jevox, while they're not aggressive, they're not the most inviting of outsiders. They're like one big glob of hermits."

"Why I am here is why I have to go. My wife, Shelly, my friends, they're aboard the *Fidelis*, my ship. And they aren't alone here, there's another, the *Reverie*. We were attacked by a space-borne entity at the edge of the star's chromosphere. It bit the Star Sphere off the forward end of my ship and spat me out here. There's a man out there who killed my father, his name is Johan. He killed him so he could take a Foundry ship and kidnap Jevox. Shelly and her friend Ada accidentally found a way to control their bio-electric hive network."

"He stole a ship? Why do that? And what did your father do to him to warrant it?"

"Nothing, he did nothing. Johan is a bad man. Dad stood in his way. Johan stole the ship in the hopes that he could go back to Earth and re-terraform it. Undo the damage done by the past few hundred years of human development."

"Sorry about your dad," she said, softening her voice. "Losing family hurts."

I nodded, my eyes averted. I knew that if I looked at her… "Thank you."

"You chased him here to this system, right? He kidnapped some Jevox, and you ended up dealing with that damn space fish. Personally, I do everything I can to hide from that thing. It is scary as hell."

"That's right. The Jevox are not happy with humans right now. Johan got away."

Bellamy sat down while sucking air through her teeth. "Eeeh, wow, tough break."

"Please, help me. Johan believes he is doing the right thing, saving Earth, fulfilling '*The Mission*', but we know the Foundry wishes for us to protect life. He's screwing that all up for us by hurting others. He's ruining our chances of getting the help we came out here to get. Take me back to my ship and I'll get him. I will bring him to justice."

She leaned back in her chair and let out a long breath. "Look, I'm sorry, Milo, I really am, but I can't help you right now. I have a ship, sure, but it's charging up for the next leg of my journey. It will be at least another week before it's ready."

"A week?" I spluttered. "Are you kidding me?"

Bellamy's eyebrows raised at the question, forcing her scar to wrinkle at the edges. "Yes. You act like that's a long time. Do you have any idea how long it's been since you were attacked? Let's be honest. You say the creature bit off your Star Sphere and spat you out. What might have seemed like minutes to you, that subjective time reference thing, could have been months. You say you were attacked at the edge of the chromosphere. Hate to tell you, buddy, but you drifted a long way. A long, long way. You think it's been maybe a couple days since you've had a hot meal, but I'd say your Star Sphere kept you alive much, much longer."

"No," I said. "It can't…"

"Sorry. It likely is. Look, you're here for a while. Best get comfortable. And I'm gonna have to be honest, that hand of yours is looking bad. We'll do what we can, but I don't think you'll get to keep it. You're lucky this rock you fell on even has an atmosphere, let alone one warm enough that you didn't die soon as your Star Sphere shattered."

Brace returned with a stack of clothes. "These should fit. Made for humans."

"You have human clothes just lying around?" I asked, taking his offering.

"No," it said. "This is a Sanctuary. We have machines."

Bellamy licked her lips and stood. "He used one of their hyper looms to make you clothes from a template. Sanctuaries communicate with one another, sharing data. Other humans have been met before. Templates made."

I unfolded the stack of clothes and saw a standard United Exploration Initiative jumpsuit complete with mission patch. "This isn't a copy of a uniform from the *Vasco Da Gama*."

"Nor the *Revelation*," Bellamy said.

"This patch," I said, running my hands over it. "It's from… Is this the…"

"The *Galileo*," she supplied. "Another of the missing FICSE ships, hmm? Might not be so missing. I'll turn my back." She signaled for Brace to do the same.

I stood up from the pile of blankets and slipped on the jump suit. It had been years since I had worn the adult equivalent of a UEI onesie. I did not care for the fact that Brace had failed to make me any underwear, but at least my body was covered, and it was comfortable.

"Come on," Bellamy said. "Let's get you some quarters. You need rest."

She led me deeper into the Sanctuary, past more Melcorin, though these were slightly taller and bulkier in mass than the first I had met. The subtle differences informed me that these might be mature adults. They greeted us as we passed, calling her "Mistress" while waving their clawed hands, their lizard-like faces remaining mostly expressionless. I started counting them.

"Is this the typical size of a Melcorin crew?" I asked as we entered an open workspace with tables and benches that several tunnels fed into. "You've met many groups of Melcorin, right?"

"I would say, about fifty Melcorin is a typical group?" Bellamy peered over her shoulder, thinking. "That's right. Fifty."

"Always fifty?"

She nodded. "Always fifty."

"I wonder why fifty, though."

She smiled at me, then gestured her head at the tunnel ahead.

"What?" I asked. "What's that look for?"

"I have a theory about this. You ever wonder why the UEI FICSE ships had multiples of one hundred and fifty people?"

"Like how we had four hundred and fifty people on the *Vasco Da Gama?* What about you?"

"Same on the *Revelation.* Know why?"

"Some sort of psychological reason if I recall."

She paused in a cramped hallway and turned around, arms crossed. "Okay, so there's this thing called Dunbar's number. Real smart guy did a study back in the early 2000s on human groups pre-modern times. Turns out, the largest we ever reached in hunter-gatherer societies was about one hundred and fifty people. The deeper he dug into this, the more he discovered that it was a kind of cognitive limit for us. There are only so many close relationships we can handle. And so, when he observed other social groups, the pattern repeated itself again and again. Humans work best in groups of no more than a hundred and fifty. Everyone knows everyone. Everyone can work at a scale where other humans are not an abstraction, or just numbers on a page. They are people, mothers and fathers, sisters and brothers, have hopes and dreams. At that scale we can understand their needs and wants and feel an emotional, oxytocin-driven connection to them. Anything bigger, it all starts to fall apart."

"You believe the Melcorin's equivalent to Dunbar's number is fifty?"

"Yes, but I think it's more than that. Talking to them and reading between the lines, I think it's why they don't have war. They know that creating groups too large creates a sort of emotional distance in their society, and so, they just don't. Or at least they don't keep those groups too close together, or for too long. The stars are near infinite. They have their regions of space in which the Sanctuaries exist and are expanded. They explore and seek and live in peace."

I let out a long sigh. "We should have gotten off Earth a long time ago."

"You're not wrong," she replied. "But since we didn't, maybe those on Earth need to learn how to deal better with abstraction. *The death of a single person is a tragedy…*"

"*And a million deaths are a statistic*," I finished. "You do know a dictator said that, right?"

"Debatable who actually said it. Doesn't make it any less true. Abstraction is the real enemy, turns people into things. Numbers. Makes them not real. Numbers don't have hopes and dreams. Numbers don't have families."

We started walking again, and I heard voices up ahead, singing voices. While they were not what I would call pleasing, they were beautiful in a way. Their intensity increased as we reached the end of the hall. Bellamy put a finger over her lips to encourage me to stay quiet.

In a room to our right, five Melcorin sat in a circle facing one another, dressed in bright motley robes, their eyes closed, each singing the same melody. From the looks on their faces they were relaxed, their minds elsewhere.

"Meditation," Bellamy whispered in my ear. "They do it every day. I'm not sure if the stories are true or not, but they believe it helps them tap into a sort of cosmic channel and communicate faster than light."

"FTL astral projection?" I suggested, and something about this felt right. Something about this felt familiar.

She gave a shrug. "Basically."

"They do this every day?"

"Every single day, or what counts as one here. Keeps them centered. You should try it sometime. Good for the soul."

"The only thing good for my soul right now would be killing Johan with my bare hands."

"Yeah, I got that feeling already." She waved me ahead. "Come on, we're almost there."

I shook my head at the Melcorins' practice. Meditation was something I never took too seriously, other than for the mental health benefits of calming your mind. But that was for humans. Maybe there was something to this for Melcorin. Did they develop in such a way that it could be different? Or was this just another form of prayer? Putting desires out into the Universe hoping they will be returned?

Spiritual nonsense.

She led me to the door of a cramped room and opened it up. It smelled of fungus and dirt, had a cot against a wall, and like everything else here, had its fill of random cables and wires. Bellamy stepped over a collection of ports on the floor and pulled back the sheets on the cot.

"Get some sleep," she said, gesturing. "You'll feel better tomorrow."

"What if I don't want to sleep?"

"I really don't care what you want. At this point, you're no good to your wife or your friends if you die on us. I'll have Brace check in on you every little while. Bring some medicine for those frostbite sores, your skin looks like raw chicken that's somehow burned. Lay down, close your eyes."

"Johan is getting away."

"Maybe," she said, heading for the door. "But so are you. Sleep. Get some sleep."

And much to my mental protests, my body didn't care.

Sleep was exactly what came next.

CHAPTER 34

When I sat up in bed the following morning, if it could even be called morning, I noticed my left hand had little or no feeling beyond a certain point, especially my fingers. I raised my numb appendage to find that its digits were black, the skin appearing as if it had been dipped and coated in tar just above the knuckles.

Bad. Very Bad.

I probed at the fingers with my prosthetic and found that they were stiff. When I tried to close them into a fist, the fingers didn't respond. My stomach twisted as I considered the necrotized flesh clinging to my hand. It was clear that part of it was dead. I knew that I would have some frostbite after what I had endured, sure, but I mostly expected tender, red skin and blisters. This was something else.

In a panic, I cried out for Proxy, but of course it did not respond. This only served to send my already tenuous mood into a downward spiral. I had to hope that they were okay. It was all I could do.

"Help, please," I whispered. "Please…" Tears welled up in my eyes, spilling down my face onto the sheets, gathering in my lap. I was so tired of being tough, so damn tired. I was broken. Lost.

Footsteps worked their way down the hall and a knock came from the door.

"Milo? You okay?" It was Bellamy.

I scrubbed my eyes with the bed sheets as best I could. There was no reason for her to see me like this. "Come in."

The door swished open, and she frowned at me "Morning. You okay?"

"Never been better," I said, sniffling. "My hand, though."

Bellamy bent down on one knee and took my fingers in hers. "How's your feeling? Any sensation?"

I shook my head.

"This is worse than we thought. I was hoping the warming pod would have fixed it. Come on, let's get you to the healing room, see if we can stimulate some circulation."

"And what if we can't?"

"Well," she considered, her face a twisted expression, "if it's dead it's dead. You keep it, and you'll get gangrene. Gangrene will kill you, universal inoculation or not. You'll need time to recover, too."

"Time to recover?" I growled. "I thought you said we could leave here in a week."

"I never said that. I said it would be *at least* a week before my ship was done charging. You, however, are another thing entirely. You aren't leaving this place until you're healed. I'm not letting you leave just to die two seconds later."

"But he's getting away. My wife, my friends…"

She put a hand on my shoulder. "I know. And that will all be addressed in time. For now, let's see what we can do to save what we can."

Why was she holding me back? Why did she want me to calm down? I didn't want to. I needed answers. I needed to get into action.

I pushed her away, growling, "I want you to stop being a bitch and help me get what I want."

Her eyes widened, and her voice took on an edge. "What strong words you have, Mr. Hughes. Look, we don't always get what we want, sometimes we just get what we need. I say this with all the love in the world, calm your ass down, and let me try and save your hand."

"Fine."

Near the center of the Melcorin Sanctuary there was a circular chamber twenty meters across with ceilings twice that of the rest of the facility. Robotic arms hung around it in clusters, awaiting commands. Near the walls of the room were slabs of metal a little less than a meter wide and two meters long, each position at equal distances to the others, twelve in all, their sides covered with lights and diagnostic devices.

Bellamy led me to one of the tables and sat me down, then reached into the side of the slab and removed a set of tubing as well as several white pads no bigger than a quarter.

"I'm going to give you a circulation treatment. The machine is tuned to work with human biology. What it'll do is pump the blood vessels in your hand with proteins, a few nano machines, and synthetic blood cells. What we hope to accomplish, is to kickstart the tissues in your hand that might be on the brink of death to come back to life, much like a plant you forgot to water. The process will take hours to execute, done in sprints over three days. We get one shot at this treatment, either it works, or it doesn't. I make no promises, alright?"

I extended my frostbitten hand and closed my eyes. "Do your worst."

She gave a shrug and began sticking the pads onto the side of each finger, before connecting tubes to my fingertips that had these peculiar, jaw-like apparatuses the size of pencil leads at their ends.

As the tubes connected, metal teeth biting into black flesh, I felt nothing.

"Okay, sit back," she said. "Let me round you up a pillow. These tables are not the most comfortable, sorry for that."

A few minutes later she returned with a fluffy, grey pillow and a long, striped blanket, covering me up and making the whole experience a little less uncomfortable, if only just so.

As the machines did their work, I let myself drift back off into slumber. It was so hard to stay awake when your body was working overtime to heal itself.

Dreams came again in spurts, their content disjointed; Shelly in danger, spiders crawling all over my skin, Johan and my dad, community meals on the *Vasco Da Gama*, some strange place with a black hole. Too many thoughts, not enough time, not enough mental resources to process and contextualize it all.

I spent days lying on that table, the machines going to work. The distant voices of Melcorin singing as they meditated at the edge of my perception.

On the second day, my hand started to ache, feeling as if someone were poking at it with hot needles. I took this to be a good sign. On the third day, the pain was so severe that Bellamy gave me something to take the edge off, but it was not enough I couldn't feel it. She needed me to hurt so that we knew which nerves were healing, which nerves were dead.

At the end of the treatment, she did a nerve conduction test to determine the final course of action.

"I'm sorry," she told me, and I found myself choking up at her words, but forced it down best I could. "I'm sorry."

We were not able to save them all. The robotic arms removed my left index and middle finger, making my hand appear like the three fingered claws of a Melcorin. The wound was then cauterized, a smell I'll never forget, before being wrapped in a clear material meant to keep out infection while healing. At least I wouldn't die from this injury.

For several more days I rested, waking just to eat, then going back to sleep for hours on end, before being awoken by Melcorin who would apply a skin cream that helped heal my damaged flesh.

The quiet singing continued, rhythmic words spoken over and over between layers of melody, lulling me into a hypnotic state. Where were their minds going? Could I join them there? Could we touch stars together?

The light brown tint of my half-Brazilian skin was returning, ashy spots and sores healing. I was grateful that those two fingers were the only casualties. If I had not had my prosthetics, the Foundry's augmentations warming my blood from the inside, more would have been lost.

They returned me to my quarters where I'd be more comfortable.

Time became hazy. It was difficult to tell if days were passing, or merely hours. I had little to distract myself with, so sleeping and eating became my only past-times. Bellamy came to visit me, to sit and talk about our respective journeys to this point, but never told me the whole story. She was holding back once she rescued her mother. What happened to her after that point? Her mother wasn't dead, but where was she?

Being underground it was hard to keep track of standard cycles. The Melcorin had set my room to follow a twenty-four-hour day-night cycle, despite their own eighteen-hour cycle, but even with the change in ambient light within my quarters, I was disoriented, confused. I had grown up in a closed environment aboard the *Vasco Da Gama*, lived many years aboard the *Fidelis*, and yet, I was starting to become stir crazy being in one place. I had to climb out of this hole I had fallen into or else I'd go mad.

One morning after my first meal I decided to go for a walk. I made my way around the Melcorin Sanctuary, taking my time not to overwhelm my battered body. When I passed the room in which they meditated, I paused, standing outside the door to watch. As before, their group, ten in all, were sitting on the ground cross-legged and facing one another, their reptilian eyes closed. Their voices resonated, formed a complex harmony as their minds focused and reached out into the vast darkness wheeling overhead.

What sort of conversations were they having with Melcorin far away? Was it about the human who stumbled into their midst? Or far more interesting things, greater evils lurking in the dark and how to avoid them?

I leaned against the door and found myself entranced by their voices, my eyes becoming heavy. The world went black for an instant, and I was transported to a point somewhere in the void, a black hole before me, its mass surrounded by a sphere made of white glass. This place was familiar.

Yes. Yes. Yes… I knew this place.

"Don't fall over," Bellamy said, putting a hand on my shoulder.

I jerked awake and let out a squeak of surprise. The Melcorin within the room did not seem to notice my outburst, deep as they were in meditation.

"Wow," she clamped a hand over her face and laughed. "Didn't mean to startle you."

I pressed my injured hand to my chest, taking several deep breaths. "It's okay, it's just…"

"Getting bored?"

"Maybe a little."

She gestured over her shoulder with a thumb. "Want something to keep your hands busy?"

"You sure that's appropriate?" I raised my damaged hand. The clear dressing had turned cloudy, signaling it would need to be changed soon. "This needs to heal before I use it, right?"

She shrugged. "I don't think this activity will hurt. Great for your mind, in any case."

Bellamy led me away from the songs of the Melcorin through a labyrinth of junky hallways, past juveniles working on projects of one sort or another, as well as some just sitting around and talking. They were polite as we passed, leaning to the side or stepping out of the way to let us through, lowering their heads. I don't know what Bellamy had done to gain this level of respect with them, or why the hell they called her "Mistress," which was weird, but they cared very much what she thought of them and would do anything for her. I did not think this was merely because of who they were, but rather something she had done.

We crossed a galley filled with steam and smoke, through a thick cloud of cooking meat and boiling vegetables. This must have been where my food was coming from. Brace was behind a stove pouring cut roots into a large pot. Bellamy patted it on the back as we passed, and it reached for a stack of green, rectangular bars in a metallic cupboard, passing several to her.

"Thanks," she said, accepting them, then leading me on.

"I have a question," I said as we passed back into the hall.

"Shoot."

"Nothing about this Sanctuary makes sense. None of the rooms are arrayed in any discernable pattern. It's pure chaos. All of it's a mess. Why are they like this? Can Melcorin not keep anything organized?"

Bellamy let out a chuckle. "Sanctuaries come about naturally over hundreds of years. They are made by dozens, maybe hundreds of different groups of Melcorin with no real plan other than to be a safe haven for them to recharge and repair their ships. They can only stay so long as well, as not to exceed that whole number we talked about earlier. Best I can guess is that there's too many visions of what the world should be. Folk do what they can, when they can. This ends up being the result."

"Well," I said, ducking under a series of dangling cables, "it's like a rabbit warren and a thrift store got mixed up. Can't tell what's good and what's junk."

"Somehow they know," she said. "Besides, we're about to help them work on one of their greatest achievements."

"Oh?"

"Yes."

She led me into a room full of tables and bins where several Melcorin worked. The tables, for their part, were covered in grey boards not much thicker than a hand terminal, their surfaces a series of grids populated with squares of a hundred different colors. At a gesture, I took a seat beside her at one of the tables, several spaces down from the aliens hard at work.

"This is a flat board," she said. "And the little squares, a prong. Don't worry, the word makes no sense. It's the basis of all their technology."

"What is it?" I asked, taking one, the fingers of my injured hand stroking the smooth surface of the squares. "What does it do?"

"Anything, really. It's modular technology. A single electronics standard all Melcorin use throughout space. They can be computers, sensors, diagnostic devices, artificial intelligence, even weapons. It all comes down to how the pieces are arrayed."

"What?"

"Cool, right? I mean, of course you can't form a gun out of these grey boards and a couple chiclets, but you can make the power module, targeting equipment, and the trigger. The rest just has to be printed at one of the forges," she pointed to a recessed box set into the wall, "then snapped together."

"Like Legos," I said.

She pursed her lips for a moment, then nodded. "Close enough. Though I never had any Legos when I was a kid, too poor."

"I didn't have any either." I lifted the grey board before me and twisted it in my hands.

"We had sad, sad childhoods."

"Maybe. Maybe not. I have a few good memories. So, what do we do to them?"

"Pop out the colors, sort them in the right bin. These are panels the Melcorin here don't need anymore, some they made during their last travel. They are adding them to the stockpile."

I fumbled with the flat board, using my injured hand to hold it in place while I removed the pieces with my prosthetic. The prongs, as they called them, fit tightly into place and were difficult to remove. I glanced over my shoulder to watch the Melcorin work with them. It was clear that claws gave you a distinct advantage here.

Following Bellamy's lead, I removed the prongs and tossed them in the proper bins in front of us. There were yellow squares, five by five units across, blue squares, one by one, red squares, seven by seven, and so on. The colors made it easier to put them in their proper places so that you didn't have to count the studs on their board when sorting.

It felt good to be doing something, anything, the sort of catharsis only manual labor can provide, like plowing lines in a field or splitting a stack of wood—raking tree fans. My tense muscles relaxed. I felt good for a moment. I just let my thoughts drift in silence as we worked, a rhythm falling into motion as prongs landed in their proper place.

"It's nice," I said. "Keeping busy."

"I thought it might be."

"I don't think we were meant to be idle. Not that we were meant to be slaves, either."

"We were created to be survivors, right? Survival takes work. No surprise that work can be pleasurable as well. Gives us a motivation. Little shots of dopamine."

"I guess."

"So, you mind if I ask," Bellamy started. "This Johan that you're after. What's his motivation in all this?"

My fingers paused over a yellow square, then I yanked it off and tossed it into a bin, not paying attention to which one. "I already told you. He wants to enslave the Jevox so that he can save Earth. With Shelly's discovery, he can hijack their bio-electric network."

"Save Earth? That's something we all want. Kind of in the name of the Mission. FICSE: Foundry Intent, Contact and *Save Earth.*"

"Yeah, but not like this."

"Okay then," she said, her words trailing up in tone. "Let's look at this a different way. How do you think history will remember him? How do you think they will remember what he did?"

I narrowed my eyes at her, anger rising in my chest. The flat board gripped in my fingers shook. "He's a bad, bad man. And he deserves to die."

She raised her empty hands, palms facing out. "I'm not arguing that fact with you. What he did was wrong and putting all of humanity at risk with the Foundry by enslaving the Jevox is also wrong. In most cases we would say it was a war crime. But let's be honest here, a few hundred years from now, when people are getting to raise their children in a world with clean air and blue skies, what will they say about that? Memory is short when it comes to hurting others. They might say he pushed the naysayers aside, took control of a wild situation and did what had to be done. That he put Earth first. They might even tell stories of a man who pursued him, Milo Hughes, and that Johan fought tooth and nail against this misguided, weak soul who lacked the strength to do what needed doing."

"But that's not true," I said, throwing the panel I was working with across the room, smashing it against the wall.

The Melcorin with us turned to look at me, cocked their heads, then went back to their work, muttering between one another.

"History is written by the victor," Bellamy said after a moment, her words soft. "All great historical events have winners and losers, or at the very least they do when the story is written afterward."

"But losing means humanity is dead."

"No, losing means Earth is dead, or may already be dead. From what you've already told me of Novae, humanity will be just fine. Give them another generation and humanity might be better off than before."

"But then we've betrayed the mission! Betrayed those who put their faith in us."

"That would be their story, but would it be true?" She shrugged. "The Foundry fleet went off into the black, never to return. But for the people of Novae, you go to bed at night telling yourself you did all that you could."

I fiddled with a prong that had gotten stuck, fingers straining to get purchase. "But we have."

"And that may be true, but as I said, it's the narrative. The story you tell yourself." She paused for a moment, a finger to her chin, considering something. "This decision aside, what kind of person is Johan? Aside from his biggest sins. I gather that you all knew him well."

"We did. He was not aboard my ship in transit, but from the *Brilliance*. I worked about two years alongside him in one capacity or another."

"And?"

I sucked in a deep breath. "He's a capricious, self-centered asshole who doesn't much care for what others think. He's a know-it-all, a genius, a cold, calculating individual who has bad taste in music."

"Does he seem like the hero type? Could this be ego, or something else?"

"What are you getting at?"

"When you peel back the layers, people like him tend to have a chink in their armor. A soft spot that isn't all ego, and if it is, it's not ego in a direct way. I've known his type before."

"That so?" I asked, taking up a fresh flat board. I promised myself I wouldn't smash this one.

"I think so. He sounds a lot like my grandfather."

I let out a sigh. "That's funny. Shelly has a theory that he's doing this for his grandchildren."

"Oh yeah?"

"Yeah. He was on bad terms with his ex-wife. They had two or three children before they divorced, and those children had children of their own. Shelly seems to think that he went back to save them by saving Earth."

"So, he wants to die knowing he's a big, damn hero. Save the world so that he can save his progeny. That tracks. You know if this is true, it makes you even more the villain of his story."

"Maybe," I said, flicking a yellow square into a bin on my left, "but that doesn't change that he's the villain of mine." The next piece I worked on was a light blue square, but this time I fumbled with it, finding it hard to manage with a hand missing two fingers. The flat board skidded across the table, and I snatched out to catch it before it slid off the edge.

"A good 'ol revenge tale," she said, watching me struggle, not interfering.

"This isn't revenge."

"Keep telling yourself that. Maybe one day you'll actually believe it."

I fixed my eyes on her and sucked in a slow breath. "Shut up."

"I'm just telling you the truth without any filters."

"How he feels about me will not change how I will act."

"I didn't say that it should, just don't always think your motivations are so pure. We've all been hurt, and we've all done things that deserve punishment."

I let her words sink in, thinking back to what happened in Cynosure and what I had done to the Phantamorph. It haunted me what the Jalek had made me do, and I had done it with little question. I had climbed into the tank, the body of a literal, sentient being, effectively removed its brain, and let it die. Just because I could not understand its thoughts and desires, because it lived in a different mode of existence than I did, made it no less alive than I was. It did not make it any less important.

But no, I had done that out of necessity. Johan had killed Dad out of either joy or spite, or something equally as shitty. These were not the same.

"You okay?" Bellamy asked, cocking her head at me. She reached in a pocket and removed one of the green bars Brace had given her, then offered me one. "Want a snack? They're pretty good. Don't know what the hell they're made of, but it's metabolically compatible to human anatomy."

I took a wafer-thin bar from her hand and nodded my thanks. "What do they taste like?"

"A salty sort of dried seaweed? Not sure I have the words. They're full of protein and vitamins. Melcorin B Rations." She set the stack down and took a bite off of the end of one, the wafer crunching like a potato chip but not leaving any crumbs. "Great for zero g."

"Thanks," I said, taking a bite. True to her word, the B Ration wasn't bad. I'd gotten used to eating strange foods ever since Creatus. The taste reminded me of fried yucca, but with a papery texture. It was a little dry, which made me want to dip it in something like soy sauce.

"Food always makes you feel better," she said, finishing off her bar. "Another one of nature's little rewards for doing what's right to survive. You okay, though? I see you drifting off in thought. Thinking about the past?"

I shrugged and went back to work, leaving half of my B Ration uneaten. "I owe you an apology."

This surprised her. "For what?"

"The way I've been treating you." I idly picked at a black and white prong, attempting to use one of the broken ones for leverage. "You've done nothing but be kind and help me, and I've been a jerk."

"It's okay," she said, sidling up beside me, patting my prosthetic shoulder. "You've been through a lot. Besides, people have called me worse."

"Still." My head hung. "It's not fair. Will you stop being nice and just accept my apology?"

Bellamy pursed her lips and rubbed the upper part of her left arm with her right hand. "Okay. I accept your apology."

The black prong popped from my flat board and shot onto the floor. Bellamy raised a hand and got up, running around the table to recover it.

"Can we work in silence for a bit?" I asked.

She made a gesture of zipping her lips as she tossed the escaped prong into its proper bin.

A couple of hours passed by as we worked, saying nothing. Bellamy just sat beside me, being present, and it was the most comforting thing I'd experienced in a long time. She understood hard times and loss. She knew what I was going through. I just had to keep faith that everyone was alive and okay, and something small inside of me said that this might just be true.

We cleared our table of all the flat boards and Bellamy stood, dusting off her hands. "That, as they say, is that. Let's go get some real food. Brace should have a nice stew going by now."

I stood, inspecting the bins, proud of how many prongs we had removed and sorted. I had no concept what all this would accomplish in the end, but I had helped many hands make light work. That felt good.

"Is all we do eat and then sleep?" I asked.

She raised her hands. "What else is there?"

We walked back towards the galley, passing Melcorin on the way who had bowls in hand. The stew smelled wonderful, savory and strong; with hints of several spices I could not hope to identify. No shock there. Like chilis and garlic, but that wasn't quite right either. Human senses were not evolved for this.

"You've had a hard trip," Bellamy said as we passed a group of hungry Melcorin. "Lots of things can happen."

"Lots of things did happen," I replied.

She lowered her head in acknowledgement. "Anything that haunts you?"

"Yes, and maybe no. I don't have a lot of regrets in my life, maybe a few I don't want to talk about, but I did once tell my parents I hated them."

Bellamy smiled at that. "You did? Well, then, we have at least one thing in common."

"You did that to your parents too?"

"My mom, yeah, and at an epically bad moment. Happened shortly before she died and was converted into a signal fired across open space."

"Geez." I scratched the back of my head. "Mine was right before the Isopteran attack on the *Vasco Da Gama*."

"Hah. What dramatic timing."

"Shakespeare could not have picked a better moment."

"Did you ever get to apologize?" she asked, bringing us to a stop.

I nodded.

"Good. Very good. Then we have not just one thing, but two things in common. Listen, some regrets can be undone, like that one, and some can't. But living in hate makes for a hard life, and not just for yourself. Anger can be a cancer. I've seen it first-hand. Don't let it eat you up. Even if the source of your anger deserves every bit of it, you're hurting no one but those you love by holding onto it."

Though I knew she was right, I wasn't quite ready to admit it. Anger was all that was driving me, moving me forward. If I gave it up now, what would that mean for Dad's memory?

"Food smells good," I said, diverting the conversation. "Let's eat."

She raised her hands and took a slight bow. "Best seats in the house reserved for Mistress Baptista."

"I've been meaning to ask. What's up with that?"

"Well, you know… Universal translators don't always do a great job of matching words. Besides, I kind of like the ring of it, even if it's a little creepy coming from a bunch of lizard people who hide in the shadows."

"Yes, Mistress Baptista," I mused.

She shivered at that, a devious smile taking over her face. "You see? Doesn't that kind of make you feel weird in a good way?"

"There might be something wrong with you, you know that?"

"Well, if there is, I don't want to be right."

CHAPTER 35

My frostbitten skin had started to heal. The topical cream Brace had been applying was doing its work and the blisters on my arms and back had almost all gone away. It was nice to get back to normal in one sense, even if the cold's damage wasn't all undone.

Phantom pain was starting to set in on my left hand, my brain attempting to resolve the fact that I was missing two fingers. This pain came in the form of quick, burning flashes, a sensation that my missing fingers were aching and sore. Out of reflex I would try and rub the joints or pop my fingers with my right hand, but there were no joints to rub, no fingers to pop. It made sleeping difficult some nights, as I tended to rest on my left side, one arm slid under a pillow. It made getting dressed after showers distracting, even if I were just slipping on a jumpsuit. We don't realize how often we use all our fingers or toes, we just take for granted that they'll always be here, until they aren't.

I was grateful for the fact that my thumb had not been one of the casualties. It made gripping things so much easier. It was no wonder evolution had deemed this a useful adaptation.

My days were spent in the sorting room, keeping my mind busy as Bellamy's ship charged, working on breaking down flat boards and prongs alongside Melcorin. I began to get to know some of the youths, Brace included, as well as his (and Brace it turned out was a *he*) first sister, Drake, and his closest friend, Ills.

Brace was nine years old, though by Melcorin standards that almost made him a mature adult. The Melcorin were a reptilian, cold blooded species, which matured quick and lived for over a hundred Earth standard years. They were tempered and kind, almost to a fault, not unable to protect themselves, but disinclined to hurt others. Drake told me stories of the early days of Melcorin exploration, the days they met the Foundry for the first time. It had gone well for their species, and the Foundry had given them many ships to use to explore the galaxy, but when a city-state of the Melcorin homeworld, Centre, took military action to acquire these ships, much of their world was destroyed. This hostile city-state took control of the Melcorin Foundry ships, then moved to conquer a neighboring species.

The Foundry did not like this.

In the end, Centre was left a desolate planet, destroyed by a choking dust cloud that had been created when an asteroid several dozen kilometers across was hurled at the surface by their enemy. The remaining Melcorin made a vow to never hurt another, unless necessary, to give up their notions of war and conquest. They became shadows, their ships traveling in the dark without light or sound or radiation. They became hidden observers, dispersed across hundreds of light years on both sides of the Wandering Gate, living in familial groups known as '*looks*', bound together by a network of hidden bases known as Sanctuaries, and had a shared set of beliefs known as the Jhet.

We hide from cosmic dangers. We do not fight unless forced.
Grudges were meant to die. For them to live, is to sew disease in our hearts.
If you have two of something, and another has none, then you help.
The purpose of life is not to acquire, but to experience.

A part of me wanted to say that these Melcorin were a bunch of tree-hugging space hippies, but I couldn't disagree with the results. They may have been a bit chaotic when it came to organizing their goods, but they were excellent hosts. They had saved my parents from certain death, as well as the lives of countless others, Shelly included. What if I laid down my arms and just disappeared into the black like them? Went to see what was out there instead of fighting tooth and nail to stop Johan or save Earth? Would anyone notice? Would anyone care? The evidence to the contrary was compelling.

"I have only known the Sanctuary," Brace said as we worked on a stack of flat boards, our table covered in colorful prongs. Drake worked to sort them as we popped them out, which seemed the most efficient way to go about this.

"Were you born here?" I asked, making a pile of yellow prongs before me.

"No," Ills spoke up, his scales so dark it was hard to make out his eyes. The juvenile raised the board he worked with to just a couple inches before his face then proceeded to snap it in half, tossing the remains in a recycling bin. "Brace was born on junk train. Salvage shadow."

"A what?"

Brace eyed his friend, raising a single claw in protest. "Junk train. Colorful words. He means, my *look* comes from a procurer. They gather refined materials left behind by others. Battles. Wrecks."

"So, wait, I'm confused. I thought everyone that was in the Sanctuary right now was from the same ship."

"Three ships, many *looks*," Drake said, tossing prongs into the bins one at a time, a method I found curious for one using claws. I had noticed that when the light caught her just right, her thinner scales would shimmer with an iridescent glow. Despite being a lizard person, she came off as feminine in an almost human way, body made of curves not lines, features more graceful than utilitarian, designed to catch the eye. "This is how it works. Three ships meet at a Sanctuary. We share, we trade, *looks* find new ships with new Melcorin. It is how we keep our gene-pool renewed."

And that made sense. I didn't know a ton about genetics, but keeping lines too close, inbreeding, caused birth defects in humans. Why would that be any different with Melcorin? The same could be said for culture. To deal with this challenge, they mixed their people up. Kept it fresh. New genetics. New ideas. New perspectives.

"When will you leave?" I asked. "When will the Sanctuary be emptied?"

"The time is coming soon," Brace said. "A few weeks. I will have to leave this place behind. My *look* is going onto a new ship, a wave thumper. We will listen to stars."

"A what?" I asked.

"A wave thumper. It is a round ship, a disc, clad in black and produces no radiation. Two great arms extend from it in this pattern." Brace raised its right hand, spreading the furthest left and right claws apart from one another forming a rough L shape. "There are beams of photons and mirrors within, and we measure distance."

A light went off in my head, thoughts of black hole experiments, measurements taken in remote locations on Earth far from human noise, and giant vacuum tubes filled with lasers. "It's like LIGO."

"Who is LIGO? Is it a person?"

I shook my head. "No. LIGO is a machine. It detects gravitational waves created mostly by black holes. My dad, who you would call the head of my *look*, would be able to explain it better. But the lasers, the way their wavelengths interfere with one another allows you to detect these ripples in space-time."

"Yes," Ills cut in. "Gravitational waves. Seeing them. Sharing this information. Helps us to find where is safe."

"And where is safe? Where is not safe?"

"There are many holes in the deep. Not all are easy to find, more hidden than us shadows. We make maps. All Melcorin get these maps. Makes travel safer."

"Micro blackholes?" I ventured, a hand rubbing my chin.

Drake raised her arms and spread them wide in an approximate circle. "No bigger than this. Very dangerous, affect thousands of kilometers. Melcorin vanish. Many *looks* lost. It is best to keep safe."

"I understand," I said, then removed a few more prongs from my flat board before taking a drink from a canteen of water Brace had provided. "So, there's a human I am after."

"This Johan," Ills said. "The Mistress has told us of him."

"Yes, Johan. His ship is, well, it's Foundry make. I imagine it's like yours in a way."

"Our ships are not Foundry make."

"No, maybe not, but they're hidden. You somehow mask your heat signature, reduce any radiation output, remain optically neutral."

"We do," Brace agreed.

"But how?" I paused, taking a moment to eye each of them in turn before leaning in towards Brace. I lowered my voice, "Can you tell me how this stealth technology works? How I break through the shadow?"

Brace, Ills, and Drake looked to one another, their shoulders sagging.

"We cannot," Brace said after a long moment, in a tone that I would have considered alarmed if he had been human.

"Cannot, or will not?" I pressed.

"We cannot," Drake echoed.

"We know," Ills said. "Though not sure if Brace fit inside recycler for penance." He slapped his friend's chest with the back of a clawed hand. "Too big. Break the works."

"Too big?" Brace blinked back at him. "You have nine stone on me. Your *look* gets so heavy you can't reach escape velocity."

"It's true," Drake agreed, her expression pleased. "Too much raffa, not enough bam bam. Make for wide hips."

The three of them began to make a snorting sound I could only imagine was like laughing. Though it was totally alien to me, the joke's meaning lost, I found myself caught up in their moment and laughed along. It felt good. It had been way too long. Shelly would have loved this.

"She *will* love this," I corrected myself in a mumble, rubbing the moisture from my cracked, dry eyes. They weren't dead, they were just waiting for me.

The laughter died down, and they turned to look at me.

"You leak," Ills said, extending a hand. "Something wrong? Go back to healing room and take diagnostics?"

"No," I said, smiling. "It's a human thing. It's okay, I'm fine. We do this sometimes when we get too emotional."

"Whatever you say, weird flesh sack."

I waited for my moment, then tried again. If anyone knew how stealth technology worked, it was the Melcorin. Maybe they just needed the right motivation. "Johan is a bad man."

"A bad man?" Brace mused. "What is a bad man?"

"Someone who hurts others. Is selfish. Does not follow the Jhet. This man is wanting to do something that will hurt all humanity. Make the Foundry not want to work with us."

"Foundry isn't everything," Ills said, reaching for a fresh flat board. "We not have the Foundry for long time. Works out. All they need do is give you a push."

"It's true," Drake agreed.

"Did your people not mourn when Centre fell, and the Foundry turned its back on the Melcorin?" I asked.

"Turn its back?" Ills mused. "It did not turn its back, it said we ready. Foundry protect life. So do we. Melcorin no longer need Foundry help to do this, but Foundry have our back. They keep the galaxy safe. We all need Foundry, but not directly."

"So, you can't help me, can you?"

"No," Drake said. "We wish to help you, but this is not the way. Secret rule to Jhet, keep us shadows. We know how it works, yes, but we can't tell you how. You will need to find another way to find your shadow."

I nodded. "Okay. I see. Trade secrets. But does the idea of this man committing murder and hurting others not make you angry? What about the injustice?"

"Universe is not fair."

I shook my head at this. Sounded too much like some nihilistic lesson my parents might give. "Do you not hate anyone?"

They turned to one another and asked, "Hate?"

"Okay. Let me say it different." I sat down my board and took a deep breath. "Are there any people, any species that you wake up in the morning and find you can't stop thinking about them? That you wish them to get hurt, or to die?"

"No," they said in response.

"Has no one hurt the Melcorin?"

"We do not give them the chance," Brace said, matter of fact. "We are shadows."

"But you can't always hide. Right?"

"No. But we can hide much. We stay out of the way, help others. Why would anyone hurt Melcorin? We are explorers."

I had never met their like in all my life. Were they really this pacifistic? Did the destruction of their world shock them so hard into peace? "You said that there were once Melcorin that destroyed your home world. Greedy people. Do you not hate, or have a strong dislike for them for what they did?"

"What they did brought us here," Ills said. "This place is beautiful. We spend our lives learning, seeking, helping. Why would we be angry? What better life is there?"

I gestured at a space in front of me with my hands. "But your home is gone. Never to be returned to. Ruined. This does not make you angry?"

"No," Drake said. "It is not home. This is home. They are home. Melcorin's origin was never my home. Sad for those who lived then, but they have been dead long time, gone back to the Universe as dust." She tapped her head with one claw, then her heart. "Home is not a place. Home is a way of thinking. Home is your *look*. Home is your people."

Was she right? Was it that easy? Earth had never been home for me, but our mission, FICSE, had made a promise. I couldn't let that promise go, not totally, nor could Johan.

I left the group of Melcorin juveniles to work on their flat boards, taking a walk to clear my mind. Massaging the meat of my hand was a fair distraction from the pain, but it did not make my body understand that my fingers were missing. I was finding it increasingly difficult to remain angry at my situation. These people truly weren't malicious in any way. It was even hard to believe there had been a faction among them willing to go to war. Living was a good enough reason to exist for them. The little pleasures. Family, community, and company. Discovery and curiosity. They seemed like children in a way. Avarice was not one of their values.

My thoughts circled around Shelly, how much I missed her, how much I hoped she was alright. This place, for all its madness and grime, was wonderful, and she would have found it fascinating. When I returned to her, we would have to find a way back to a Sanctuary one day. She needed to see this. She needed to see what Novae could be, what we could help make it when our current mission was done.

As I made my way around the outer edge of the Sanctuary back towards my quarters, I could hear the sound of the Melcorin meditating. I wondered for a moment if this was their grand secret to galactic peace. Was this how they let go of their anger and pain? Focusing inward, facing themselves?

I stood at the entrance to their meditation room, watching them, their eyes closed, breathing regular, space warm and moist, each dressed in long robes of motley colors that pooled around them on the floor.

For a moment I closed my eyes and leaned against the hatch, letting their voices wash over me, allowing my mind to drift in a stream of consciousness.

My muscles began to relax.

The sound of their voices rose, pitches traveling along a cosmic wave, its timbre solid and determined. The frequency felt as if it were seeking something, a connection, its purpose. I followed the sound with my mind, jumping from place to place, memory to anxiety, world to emotion, a single point of light leaving a trail of particles bright like glittering white stardust.

My phantom pain subsided, and I was drifting as if in my Star Sphere.

The images in my mindscape went black. I was someplace I had seen before. But when? Where?

A hole in spacetime, a compression of cosmic matter as dense as all reality. Surrounding this hungry core, a vast array of mirrors, made of silver and obsidian. A place of dreams. This happened last time.

"You okay, Milo?" Bellamy whispered, drawing me back from my reverie. "You in there?"

The picture in my mind faded as I opened my eyes and smiled back at her. "I'm good. I'm good."

Her eyebrows raised. "But?"

"But what?" I screwed up my face.

"I can see something is on your mind."

I shrugged. "Maybe."

She rolled her right wrist over. "Go ahead."

"Do you think they might allow me to meditate with them?" I whispered, then raised my left hand. "I think it might help me right now, if nothing else than to reduce the pain. I swear for a moment I couldn't feel it."

"How interesting. Can't say why that would be, not my field of study."

"And what was your field of study?" I flipped my damaged hand over, frowning at the bandage covering my missing digits. "Mine was nanomachines."

"Mine? Wouldn't you like to know."

"I would."

"Some things will always remain a mystery."

"Like this ship you keep saying you have, and yet I haven't seen."

She gave a shrug.

"Would they let me?" I asked again. "Let me meditate with them?"

She nodded. "I think they'd be honored. I've seen them meditate with other species in the past. Let me speak with the head of their *look* this evening after they're done. Maybe you could join them tomorrow."

"Thank you."

Bellamy put a hand on my shoulder. "Your wife and family would be proud of you."

This made me cock my head at her. "Why?"

"You'll find out later."

As promised, Bellamy spoke with their leader and the following evening I was invited to join them for their session. She gave me a few words of caution first, however. While the Melcorin were a peaceful people, they were strict at times. I was to follow their instructions to the letter. I was not to project anger. I was to be at peace with myself and seek only understanding. And so, for the time being, I tucked my hatred for Johan away, hoping that they could not hear it in my thoughts. Not that they were psychic or anything.

Bellamy provided me with a set of robes like the Melcorin, looking like something out of a 16th century play, red and yellow and blue in random patterns just like hers. I was told to wear nothing underneath, which left me feeling a bit naked, but at the same time comfortable.

"I do this with them sometimes," she told me, and I accepted this without any further questions. "It helps."

Once dressed, she led me to the meditation room with the Melcorin who were waiting, their reptilian skin as varied in color as the cloth that they wore. They motioned for us to take our seats in the circle.

The room smelt of something sweet and earthy, the humidity of the air high enough to leave my skin slick with moisture.

"Welcome, Milo Hughes," the head of their group said, a large Melcorin who, even seated, was a good two feet taller than me. "I am Vex, head of the Tier *look*. Mistress Bellamy has told us you wish to travel."

"Travel?" I asked, then gave my human counterpart an incredulous look. "I don't understand."

"You will," Vex said. "Sit. Sit. Get comfortable. Brace has provided you with pillows. We understand that humans have a difficult time relaxing when they sit on hard surfaces for long. Welcome to our *ontet*."

"Very gracious," Bellamy said, taking a gentle bow before sitting.

I followed her example and took my seat atop a foot high pillow of ivory and black beside her, crossing my legs as I settled into place. I had to admit the pillow was comfortable, so big that my knees did not reach the end.

"Close your eyes," Vex started, his voice so low I could feel it rattling my chest. "Listen to my voice. Relax your body. Be comfortable."

"Trying my best," I said, tightening my hands into fists and releasing several times in a row, feeling the strain of my tense muscles.

"Shhh," Bellamy said. "Be quiet. Be still."

"Keep your eyes closed," Vex went on, it's voice steady. "Breathe in. Breathe out. You are a star, a wave of light. Breathe in. Breathe out. You are a mote of creation, a spark of the Universe. Breathe in. Breathe out. You are the tiniest building block of reality, and yet you are reality unto itself. Breathe in. Breathe out. Keep yourself centered. Focus on a single point of light. Breathe in. Breathe out."

The other Melcorin in the circle began to sing the song I had heard earlier. It was hard to tell if it was just noise, or words. The Foundry universal translator did not provide any insights. The melody was not much more than four notes in a drone, raising and lowering, raising and lowering.

"Death and rebirth. Breathe in. Breathe out. Let everything go. In this moment, there is nothing but this moment. Breathe in. Breathe out. You are eternity. You are a blip. Breathe in. Breathe out. Be the flash of a dying star. Be the flash of fusion begun. Breathe in. Breathe out. Life synthesizes, renders entropy into beauty. Breathe in. Breathe out. Focus on the light. Follow it."

And I did.

The sensation I had within a Star Sphere returned with a fresh fervor. I could travel in any direction, go any place, but was I just imagining this? I searched for Shelly and my friends. Called their names in the dark. Stars whirled by, planetoids and dust and long forgotten ships. I could not find them.

"Breathe in. Breathe out," Vex went on.

I followed his instructions but found myself frustrated. There was a block of some kind, keeping my thoughts from the nascent transcendence within. Something between where I was and where I wanted to be. Was I standing in my own way?

A hand reached out and rested on my leg. I did not open my eyes. I did not give up what little concentration I had.

"Letting go of your hate does not mean you no longer love your dad," Bellamy whispered. "Your love for him cannot be invalidated by finding that peace."

But could I let that go? If only just for a moment.

Could I let that go?

"Okay," I said, taking a deeper breath than the rest. "I'm not forgetting you, Dad."

I never would. Despite all our challenges over the course of my life, he was my dad, and that would never change. I would never stop loving the man for his good and his bad. I was him. He was me.

My eyes began to sting. I did not open them, did not reach to clear the tears which streamed from them. I let them flow as they should. The pain meant that everything was real. The pain meant that I was alive.

"I am a star. A wave of light," I mumbled. "I have touched stars. I have seen beyond this reality. I have touched creation. I have known naked truth."

The light within my mindscape began to move in a new direction. I was not controlling its path. No. It was taking me somewhere.

The Melcorin voices grew louder, redoubling in their intensity, bringing us to the apex of something grand and powerful. Vex repeated his earlier statements with the ever-anchoring words, "Breathe in. Breathe out."

Where was the light taking me?

Billions of stars flashed by, the universe contracting. I could not be sure if I was moving, or if the universe was just moving around me. Lights began to wink out, one at a time. Stars ignited into brilliant super novae. All crashed into a central point of existence, the point at which I was being drawn. An end.

This was not in my head. This was real. I was going somewhere.

Something strange happened that I could not explain. Emotions collided with me. A color that became everything.

The world turned white, then pink, my heart bursting at the rush.

Reality tore itself in two, a rent in space and time opening before me. A veil pulled back.

I had found myself someplace else and…

I knew this place.

I—knew—this—place.

CHAPTER 36

Waves of hot and cold washed over my essence, drowning out all other senses, the dark, empty void between stars becoming a physical presence with its own thoughts and desires. The space between celestial bodies, once millions, billions, and trillions of miles, light seconds and light years across, no longer existed. Every whisper spoken on the outer arm of the Milky Way could now be heard at its core, be translated along every twist and spiral, creating a swell of harmony in ten million parts, sprinkled with the occasional stray note of discord. All was one mind. This was a new place, one filled with light and sound and information and above all… life. It was not just some boiling collection of madness and chaos, it was life, purest life, and that life had purpose.

Whatever it was that drove me to this place, whatever it was that carried me forward, it cranked up the dial on all aspects of reality. Stars began winking out one by one, their fuel burned up over vast periods of time, going supernova, stellar masses collapsing in on themselves. The universe was turning dark, reaching the end of its existence. Discordant voices fled this inevitable death, traveling to the center where the last vestiges of heat and light remained. They knew it would not last. They knew it would never be enough. A billion, billion, billion years, would never be enough. Life does not wish to be extinguished. It struggles and screams against the great nothing until the very last particle ceases spinning, not going quietly into that good night. It rages until the laws of physics no longer hold sway. A great harmony falling rapidly into the unraveling chaos, entropy overtaking all that ever was.

Among the great sea of black, a dot appeared that was not quite as dark as the rest. I was drawn to this speck, hearing something loud and organized within it that was unlike the rest. Something that reminded me of myself, eliciting emotions of curiosity and terror.

I squeezed my eyes shut, drew myself into a ball and wrapped my arms around my legs.

As I opened my eyes once more, I found myself in a room not much larger than my quarters on the *Vasco Da Gama*. It was an austere space with dark metal walls and several tables no higher than my hip, surfaces covered in personal effects as well as what looked to be a forgotten meal tray, its contents long gone cold. One wall of the room was covered in shelves with jars of various sizes, another with hand tools of unfamiliar make. A floor-to-ceiling window dominated the length of the wall on my left, and along the remaining table was something teardrop in shape no larger than a football, its surface gold and silver and red and black, covered in intricate symbols that defied comprehension, perception, and logic, written both on its surface and yet someplace else entirely. It throbbed with power, possibility, fear, and hope.

I took a deep breath.

This was the place from my dreams.

This was the secret room.

As I gazed out its tall window, I saw nothing but random flashes of light like sparks caught in a vortex, yet I knew a black hole was out there, hungry and ready to devour me. The place in which I stood was at the top of a great sphere somewhere in space and time. Its geodesic structure was lined with mirrors, but the gravity was still too great for light to escape, thus leaving its interior dark. This had to be a dream, a nightmare of some physics problem I learned in school gone wrong, a story Dad had told me, yet everything within me said it wasn't.

Where was here? It had to be a hallucination. The head of the *look* had to have drugged me during meditation.

No. That isn't right.

"Hello, Milo Hughes," a creature I had not noticed a moment earlier said from the center of the room, its unusual features illuminated by the light, not-light of this otherworldly space. It stood a few inches higher than the tables, walking on six multi-jointed legs. Its features were hard to define, all of them alien, and yet familiar, an amalgamation of a hundred different shapes and curves, the impressions of many species. One moment I swore its face looked human, the next, like that of an Isoptera, a Kabosai, an Eiprin, a Darovak, Melcorin. It was everything at once. "Do not be afraid."

"I'm not afraid," I said after a moment, summoning all of my courage. "But I have to say, looking at you is difficult."

As well as a little nauseating.

I took a step towards it. "Who are you?"

"I am, and also, I am not."

"Not what?"

"Everything," it said, matter of fact.

"I don't understand. Are you... What... What is this place?"

"This is the end of all things," the creature swept one of its many arms, tentacles, claws, it all kept effing changing, around the room. "You stand here with me, both here and not here. I am the last."

"The last what?"

The creature led me over to the great window. "The last living person in all the universe."

I placed my palm on the window and peered down into the impossible sight as understanding began to fill me. The sphere of mirrors and glass surrounding this blackhole was an engine, an engine designed to create near infinite energy.

The stars were dead.

The universe, this physical place, was collapsing upon itself.

Whatever this creature was, its people, or the collective peoples of our dying universe, they had built a sphere of mirrors around this celestial monster, trapping what energy it had inside of the sphere. Before closing the engine tight, ceiling all leaks, they had fired many strings of electromagnetic waves into it, and as these waves traveled past the event horizon of the black hole's ergosphere, a portion of its rotational energy was imparted upon this wave, whereupon it began superradiant scattering, growing ever faster and faster, creating more energy than it had started with. The energy from this improbable engine kept the room in stasis, kept it safe from falling within and being crushed into a single plane of existence.

This was not only *a* blackhole they had trapped, it was *the* blackhole, the last of them all, the final point of condensed energy and matter in all of the universe. Earth was within that blackhole, after a fashion. So were all the other worlds everyone had ever lived on. Stars. People. Hopes. Dreams.

Smashed into a singularity no bigger than a period on a blank sheet of cosmic paper.

It was the last candle of light at the end of everything, a black campfire on the edge of oblivion.

I had always known the stars would die, but this final blackhole whispered to me there wasn't much time left. I had no idea how I knew, but its end was soon, very soon.

"You're the Universe," I muttered, then turned again to face the creature. No, that word didn't feel right. It was not something, just anything. It was everything.

"I am what you would call the Universe."

"You're real."

"Of course, as are you. You are part of us."

I squeezed the bridge of my nose with two fingers. "Yeah, but, the Foundry. It worked? It allowed you to become self-aware?"

Its form shifted for a moment, conveying a vast kaleidoscope of gestures and expressions before settling again into a more stable state.

"I have always been self-aware," the Universe said, sounding a little smug. "No, that is not what the Foundry was made for. Not what I, what we, made it for."

"What? But, in the data hub. I learned its purpose. That is what it told me, what it revealed to me."

It led me over to the table where the strange teardrop machine sat, a sort of potential energy radiating from it. It ran a hand over one side, a fond expression of pride on its face. "The Foundry was not meant to create us, to create our common awareness. It was meant to extend us."

"I don't understand."

The Universe smiled at me. At least I think it was a smile, it was hard to be sure under the morphing of a thousand expressions. "Like the stars who have passed into nothingness, time does not stretch out into infinity. Time is, in fact, a loop. Each cycle, each occurrence of this place, this end of all things, we will be reborn. When this blackhole runs out of energy, all will collapse on itself, and the cycle will begin anew. We will cease to exist, and perhaps, the next cycle will last a bit longer for our efforts."

"But how can it last longer if time is not infinite?"

"Time may not be infinite, but it is relative. You know this, you have been one of the Foundry's ship pilots."

"Subjective time reference," I mumbled, understanding. It wasn't that there was to be more time, but this was a way to shift the perception of time. Use more of every second given. An icy chill ran down my spine as that ever-recurring phrase surfaced in my mind. "The Foundry protects life."

The Universe lowered its head-yet-not-head. "And this is the seed. We have used all of our knowledge and understanding to create a system by which the next Universe will be both protected and proliferated. This seed will find its way into what you call the Big Bang, and once all matter cools, its simple intelligence will go to work constructing the Foundry network. It will protect life, and by extension, more life shall come into being. If we are all one, each person a universe into itself, each universe connected by cosmic strings, will not more minds mean more time? More processes spent on doing what life does best... creating experiences, living."

"Simple intelligence..." I shook my head. "That can hardly be said of the Foundry facilities and the mind that drives them."

A flash of light came from within the black hole as something else was consumed by it. I felt the threads holding this reality together start to fray. A gentle vibration carried itself through the floor.

"We don't want to die," the Universe said, its words pleading. "We want to exist forever."

"Death is part of life," I replied.

The Universe gestured at the blackhole. "And so is rebirth. We merely wish to make the next cycle a little longer than the last. Make the best of it. Do a little better next time."

I narrowed my eyes. "Why did you bring me here?"

"Bring you here?" The Universe cocked its head, or so I thought, looking confused. It seemed this was a ubiquitous enough expression, regardless of species, an involuntary way of looking at the situation from a different angle. "I did not bring you here. I did not call you."

"I heard a voice, a chorus calling out in the void."

"That was not me. It was you."

"What? I don't understand."

"You followed a thread that many who have a long life ahead are not aware of. We are connected, you and I, always and forever, to the last moment. To this very place." The Universe bent over as if in pain, its body shuddering. I rushed over to help, but it raised a hand to stay my efforts.

I did not touch it.

"Are you saying I'm here just moments before the end?"

"Yes. And this will come again. No sorrow, but a touch of fear. Fear of the unknown."

This was really it. The last deep breath before the dark plunge. It was also my future, and if this was my future, forget how I got here, it might have answers.

"May I ask a question?"

The Universe nodded.

"Will the Foundry help save humanity? Its message, it called us. The feeling the signal gave us was one of trust and hope, but it has not given us the means to save our dying planet."

The Universe looked away as if lost in thought. "No. I am sorry, but it will not help you. The Foundry will determine that humanity is not worth devoting resources to save."

And there it was. I felt as if someone had punched me in the chest. We had traveled so far, given up so much to find Earth the help we needed to rescue ourselves from ecological and systemic collapse. Humanity had not been the best stewards of their world, of the gift of life that was given us. The Foundry had told us in our hearts through that signal that it would help. It protected life. And yet, what did we do? First chance of power we got, we murdered one of our own, stole a ship, and enslaved many Jevox. There was no telling what else had happened. The crew of the *Brilliance*, Karianna and the rest, spoke of their mutiny, of Justin Wiggins and his group of murderers. What had happened to those people? What evils had they committed?

"Then what do we do?" I asked. "The people of Earth are dying. It was our original mission to make contact with your creation, our creation, and ask for its assistance. This is the purpose of my entire life. FICSE. Foundry Initiative, Contact and Save Earth. There's no telling how long we have been gone, but I know things have to be getting bad."

"I am sorry, Milo, the Foundry will not help you."

"Is it that we deserve to fail as a species? Are we not worthy of life?"

"No."

"Then can't you tell it to help?" I pointed to the seed of the Foundry on the table. "Program it into this thing here?"

"It does not work like that. I cannot give it direct commands. The Foundry is a system of logic, that is all. A system of logic meant to benefit the whole, not the one. Besides, this seed is for the next cycle, not this cycle."

The air felt strange around… Him? Me? It? Us?

I—

I… He…? Felt strange.

Milo put his hands on his face and closed his eyes. He was drained, defeated. He was standing here with the creator of the Foundry, the most powerful entity in all creation, an amalgamation of all life in the Universe over this entire cycle, and it had said sorry. "What do I do then? Just let it happen?"

"I did not say that," the Universe replied, a single finger, a tentacle, a claw, raised. "There is another way, though you might not like the outcome. You can save your people, and without the need of the Foundry."

"The Jevox? Are they the answer?"

"Your situation with Captain Van Niekerk is part of the reason why the Foundry will not help."

Another ripple, Milo's sense of self drifting from center.

"Then who will help?" you ask, knowing that it needs to be asked. You can't go on without a path, without a way to see the mission fulfilled. A way to see humanity saved.

The Universe paused, then let out a sigh. "You already know. You have a suspicion, deep in your belly, an impression. I cannot tell you in this place."

"Why not?"

Its body shifted into a thousand different forms, the air bending around us before settling into something more stable, though still migraine-inducing. "Too many of us disagree with this outcome. But there is a device. I can see the change in your expression, feel your mind resonate with ours. We know where it is."

And at that, images flashed in your mind much like they once had with this place. You can see a dark room, perhaps a cave, shaped like a nautilus shell, a plinth at its center, two objects resting upon it, one flat and gold, another floating, an icosahedron made of obsidian.

Your sense of self drifted back towards your projected body, Milo's projected body….

My projected body.

"But where?" I asked as the vision faded. "What does it do? What is it for? You have to tell me. I have to know!"

"You must find that out on your own," the Universe said. "And with it shall come a choice. A terrible choice, but one that is yours to make. What you choose might just determine the survival of your species. What you choose might just alter the course of the galaxy. Humans rest upon a pivot, a hinge. To survive, we all must become something else."

The space around us began to vibrate, the structure of the room becoming unstable. A resonant frequency traveled through the ceiling and walls, jars along shelves beginning to clatter.

"It is time," the Universe said, tone resigned. It reached out a hand for me, I was unsure what kind of hand it was, but when I took hold, it felt human. "Your species has value. We are one. Do not let everything go because the solution is not what you wanted to hear. Do not go quiet into that good night."

I took a deep breath and nodded. Jars began to fall from shelves. The tray of food on the nearby table rattled to the edge and crashed onto the floor, spilling something green and soupy on our feet. A crack splintered across the window before us.

"Are you God?" I asked before everything split apart.

"No," the Universe replied, shaking its head. "But I would very much like to meet them. I have always wanted to meet them."

And in that moment our world went white, becoming a void of pure light and oblivion.

We had reached the end of all things.

The start of all things.

PART III

CHAPTER 37

I cracked open my eyes to see that the room of meditating lizard people, as well as Bellamy, were staring at me. No one spoke a word for a long moment. Their chanting song had fallen silent. It was clear that somehow, some way they knew something had changed in me.

"Milo?" Bellamy turned to me and whispered. "What happened?"

My forehead and back were covered in sweat, hands still resting on the tops of my crossed legs and feeling heavy as lead. I found myself trying to flex my missing fingers, but instead my hand shook. It took serious effort to encourage anything on my body to as much as twitch.

What had happened to me? Where had I…

But this time I remembered.

This time it was not some fleeting fever dream.

I had traveled to the end of all things.

I had spoken with the Universe.

I had seen the next beginning come.

"I spoke to him," I started, "spoke to it, her, they, the Universe."

Bellamy's eyebrows began to crowd the middle of her face. "You what?"

"The Universe. It told me what the Foundry is, what it truly is. It told me of the end and the beginning. It gave me a way to—"

"A way to what? What, Milo? What are you talking about?"

I shook my head, not wanting to utter those forbidden words aloud, of the inspiration it had given me to save our people. *An* answer, if not *the* answer. No. The implications… Too dangerous to speak of now. Too dangerous to speak of, maybe ever.

"Doesn't matter," I said, cutting at the air with my right hand. "What matters is the why. Why the Foundry protects life."

The Melcorin leaned forward with bated breath.

Vex's expression became pinched, eyes and nose drawing up towards each other. "You transcended. We could feel it. All of us. The texture of the air changed. The smell of emptiness. Where did you go? What place did you travel to? Who did you speak with? Tell us everything."

And so I did, as best I could without sounding like a total lunatic. I told them about how I had found myself within some strange blackhole machine, a crucible of reality, and of the creature I met there, the last living being that was both me, and them, all of us together. Of how the Foundry protected life so that it could prolong its own existence, not just become self-aware, all so that it could perceive more time within each cycle of birth and death. This idea seemed to confuse them, not that they couldn't understand it, but because it did not fit within their views of the universe.

The more I went on, recounting the fine details of the seed device of the Universe that gave birth to the Foundry and the engine, the more I started to wonder if this could have just been a hallucination after all. Maybe I was crazy. Sections of my rational mind tried to say that this was likely, that my current state of thinking and this form of meditation created some sort of fantasy, an amalgamation of a million tiny details I'd been exposed to over the past few years, but that did not feel right. This had to have been real. Had to be.

"It *was* real," I said, more for myself than the rest of those gathered.

Bellamy's face told me she wasn't so sure.

"All visions are real," Vex assured me, his voice calm. "It is up to you to determine their meaning."

I took a deep breath. "You believe that meditation can work as faster than light communication, yes?"

"At times it can link two minds together across vast distances. Yes."

"Well, humans call this astral projection, and some have claimed for thousands of years that it's real. So, why not travel over more than just distance, but over time as well? Who's to say that whatever place this taps into isn't a reality in which space and time don't exist? Where they're—" I reached for a word "—merely abstractions. Just ideas."

"What you did was different." Vex raised one clawed hand.

I narrowed my eyes and raised my palms. "How is it different?"

"It was different," several of the silent Melcorin spoke up, each saying the same.

I turned to face Bellamy and reached for her hand, clasping it. "What do you believe? What do you think happened?"

"I—" She slipped her fingers from mine.

"Vex," a voice called from the doorway. "I do not wish to interrupt, but I have news for our guest." It was Brace standing at the edge of the hallway, his expression twisted and curious.

Vex blinked at Brace several times then waved him in. "The *ontet* is complete. Please, come."

"Thank you," Brace said and took a step inside the room. "Milo Hughes, we have located your ships."

I shot up from my cushion and rushed over to him, clasping his scaley arms. "What. Where?"

"They have drifted not far from our Sanctuary."

"Are they okay?"

"We do not know. They are quiet. There is debris. I do not know what the ships are meant to look like as whole, but their shapes, they are irregular."

Damaged... but not totally destroyed. A chance.

"Bellamy," I said. "Is your ship ready? I need to go to my people. I have to know if they're okay. I have to know if my wife is still alive."

She stood slowly and gave a shrug, her left hand clasping her right arm, rubbing the skin in a constant, soft motion. "It's ready."

"Excellent. Can you take me there? Come with me. Join us. There's not a reason in the world you have to be alone."

"I'm not alone." She looked to Brace and Vex and the rest of the Melcorin, her expression uncertain.

I took a step towards her, a reassuring smile on my face. "I know, but, there will be more humans. And after the *Revelation*, what happened to... Look, there's more people like you. You might never find us again. It's a big galaxy."

Bellamy scanned the room, attention lingering on the Melcorin, an old pain twisting her forehead and cheek, bending and brightening the scar the Isoptera had left her all those years ago. "Brace, can you make arrangements for Milo to be returned to his people?"

"Yes, Mistress," Brace replied.

"But you'll come with me, right?" I insisted, stepping even closer. We were now less than an arm's length apart. "Please."

"I'll catch up," Bellamy said, walking out of the room without saying anything else.

I wasn't sure how to feel about that.

Brace made an exaggerated bow, one that was clearly not natural for his species. "We should gather your things. Go to shuttle. Take you home."

I turned to Vex before leaving. "How do I thank you for all you have done? All of you."

He raised a hand, and the rest of the Melcorin began to hum a single note, low and resonant. "Go in joy. Live in peace. Share with others in plenty. Stand with others in struggle."

And that was all he had to say. These truly were a remarkable people, ones from which humanity had much to learn. I only hoped I had enough time for the lesson to sink in before we squandered the gifts nature had given us.

As Brace walked me back to my quarters, I looked everywhere for Bellamy, but she was nowhere to be found. Had I said something to upset her? I could always apologize later. She was going to join us. Right? Come along with us and be part of the fold. She could help bring Johan to justice. We could take him back to Novae as a prisoner, put him on trial for what he had done. That is what the people of our new world deserved. And when it was over, when he had received his punishment, maybe we could save Earth too. Maybe the Jevox, once we rescued them, would be willing to give us a boost. Maybe we could use some of their technology, if not their direct assistance, to fix Earth and save those who remained. Maybe that would keep us from having to follow a darker path.

For the first time in months, I felt hope blossoming in my chest. I just needed to get back to my family, my wife, my friends. I knew there were no promises that things were okay, but I had a suspicion. For once, I was going to trust and believe.

We collected my things, the satchel, the pistol, my damaged Jasper, and headed for a shuttle. The vessel was small, without space for more than two or three passengers, flat board equipment everywhere, and a wide glass window in front. I buckled into a seat behind Brace that could modify itself based on species as he settled into the pilot's chair. A moment later, Drake appeared from the hatch and sat down beside him.

"We take you home," she said. "Together."

I nodded. "Home is your *look*."

"Your *look*."

"Hold tight, friend," Brace said, the engines of the shuttle igniting. The hull vibrated with the noise of roaring plasma. A moment later, we began burning through a long tunnel, acceleration throwing me back in my seat, the shuttle passing through darkness, then noisy, white storms of snow and ice before breaking free of the atmosphere and passing into the silence of the void.

Leaving the Sanctuary behind was bittersweet. It had been a good place. A place where I had recovered not just from the storm and the wreck, but something else. It had made me—whole again.

"How long will it take us to get there?" I asked Brace.

"At this velocity, ninety hours. You needing something to do? I have flat boards you can sort."

I let out a chuckle. "No, thank you. I think I've done enough for now."

Drake let out a gasp. "He done enough. *Sa sa bang be.*"

I remained in my seat and did my best to enjoy the ride. It had been a long time since I was at the mercy of another ship's pilot. Between the *Fidelis* and the Swift Shuttles, I was always ferrying people somewhere. Was it on Creatus? Was that the last time? When the Jalek sent his personal shuttle to retrieve us? I didn't like not being at the controls, though I had to admit, Brace had a soft touch for someone not in a Star Sphere.

Hours passed. We chatted among ourselves. Ate dried food. Slept. The ship had no beds, but neither did it have gravity once we were up to our cruise velocity. I floated in my seat, harness loose, waking after some time to the sensation of drool running up my cheek, not down.

I checked the clock at the edge of Brace's heads up display. Twenty standard hours had passed.

"Good sleep sleep?" Drake asked.

I reached for my canteen, took a sip of water, and nodded. "Pretty good, I guess. Is Bellamy following us yet? Can you detect her ship?"

Brace shuddered for an instant. "I see nothing. No Mistress on instruments."

This made me frown. "Where is she? Why haven't we heard from her yet? I swore she was right behind us."

"She does what she wishes," Drake added. "Come not when called. When she wants."

"I get that, it's just…" I took another sip of water. "It's fine."

But it wasn't. I could not leave her behind. Could not abandon her.

At hour eighty-five, I started to see the glint of our remaining Foundry ships ahead of us near a cluster of asteroids with a high albedo, their surfaces reflecting JV-01's light to produce an orange-tinted sea of scattered diamonds. Over the next two hours, the *Fidelis* resolved itself into a broken shard, its forward end missing as I had expected. The Dragon had bitten the ship near in half, but from what I could tell, it hadn't torn far enough back to destroy the other Star Spheres.

As for the diamond shaped *Reverie*, no bites had been taken out of it. Instead, it appeared cracked at the center, like a dome of glass put under intense pressure. Both ships were tailed by debris, but at least for the moment, there was no sign of the Dragon.

"Are we safe?" I asked Brace. "Can it find us?"

"The creature?" he asked. "No. We are shadows, remember? It cannot find shadows."

Not for the first time I thought about how great it must be to explore the cosmos without a care for what was out there. As long as you did not physically collide with anything, you had the freedom of motion to go and do pretty much whatever you liked. Johan could have done that with the stealth warship, and I suppose that he did, but that was where his similarity to the Melcorin ended. He knew nothing of their kindness.

Brace navigated us through the debris field, the shuttle shifting this way and that, changes in acceleration turning my stomach end over end. Sure as hell didn't deal with all this crap from within a Star Sphere. I pointed towards one of the rear docks on the *Fidelis* and he nodded in affirmation.

Proxy? I called out with my implants, but there was no response. My hope faltered for a moment.

"Bringing us in," Brace said, listing the shuttle to the port side past several spinning chunks of jagged metal as large as ground cars.

As we approached the dock, automated systems went to work, connecting with my implants and allowing me to unlock the outer doors. The hatches drew back, caught for a moment, then kept moving, their motion stuttering. Damage was everywhere.

Once inside the dock, the doors closed behind us, and I received a signal that the bay was pressurizing.

"It looks bad," Brace said.

"It will be fine," I replied, reaching out to the networks. "My shuttles are okay. You can leave me here. I'll be alright."

"You sure? Maybe check for survivors, then go to a Cynosure? Maybe back to that colony of yours?"

I shook my head. "No. It's okay. Besides, Bellamy will be here soon. If I need help, I'll call." I tossed my satchel over my shoulder and took a deep breath, taking a step towards the exit.

Brace and Drake exchanged uncertain looks, the muscles of their faces still but for their blinking eyes.

"Be careful," Drake said after a long moment. "Do not forget the Jhet."

"I won't," I told them. "And thank you." The shuttle's door opened, and I stepped out.

While I could not contact Proxy, the lower-level automation of the ship was online. I was able to exit the shuttle bay and confirm that certain paths throughout the ship had atmosphere. For the time being, there would be no need for a pressure suit.

"Proxy?" I shouted into the open hallways, making my way around to where the other Star Spheres were kept. Before anything else could be tended to, I needed to see if she was alive.

The halls were strewn with metal and debris, glass and busted electronics. The lights activated when I entered a new section but shut off immediately after me. Power must have been at a premium or else Proxy would have kept everything running at full. It was clear that the nano-repair bots were not working, or at least not at any measurable capacity.

After several detours, then sliding through a collapsed set of ducting, I located Shelly's Star Sphere. Putting my hands against the glass I fell to my knees sobbing, cheeks slick with salty tears.

Shelly floated in her tank, chest rising and falling with the slow motion of breathing. She was alive. My wife was alive.

I heard a thump of something solid on metal from over my shoulder and spun around, hands raised and ready to fight. While my prosthetic hand made a deadly fist, my fleshy one did not.

"Hello? Who's there," I shouted. "Show yourself!"

From out of a dark recess loped a furry black cat, its head and back adorned with an orange stripe, its movements twitchy and unsteady as if injured.

"Proxy! You're here!" I shouted, running to meet it halfway. "Are you okay?"

It stumbled its way over to me and I fell on my knees to greet it.

"Milo? It is you," it said, dumbfounded. "You are alive?"

"Don't sound too surprised." I scooped it up in my arms and squeezed, my right cheek against its fur.

"I watched as you were eaten by that beast. Despite my best efforts, I could not save you."

"I'm pretty sure you already did. It's a long story, one I'll be happy to share later. I'm alive. I'm alive."

"Your fingers," it said, rubbing against the nubs of my left hand. "How?"

"Frostbite." I scratched Proxy behind the ear and along its back. "You don't look like you've done too well in my absence. Is everyone okay? Are you okay?"

Proxy gave a bow. "The crew is accounted for. Alive. All except for Perez. Your former councilor was lost. Damage to the *Reverie*. I… I am damaged too, as is the ship. Power is low."

I shook my head at that. "Perez is dead?"

"Yes. His Star Sphere shattered during impact. The Dragon threw its body against them."

"Shit. He was a good man."

"He was."

"And you? Are you in pain?"

"Over what?"

"Your injuries."

It blinked at me. "Some. I do not like pain."

"No one does."

"I did the best that I could, Milo. When you did not return quickly, I placed the *Fidelis* in a low power state till a better opportunity might arise to recover. The crew is in suspension to conserve supplies. Chinchillette did the same aboard the *Reverie*."

I smiled. "So you've started calling it that?"

"It does make matters clearer. Sharing the same designation is confusing."

"I can see that. Can we pull everyone from suspension and try to work this out?"

"Yes, but there is a cost. I am not sure the power reserves are available to return them to suspension. Once they are out, they cannot go back."

"Can we repair the ship?"

"It is possible, though it will take many years. All available resources at this time are being diverted to reconstruct the antimatter reactors. Once they are complete, other systems may be tended to."

"Years?" My body tensed, but I took a deep breath and blew out my frustration. "One crisis at a time."

"Milo," Proxy said, cocking its head.

"Yes?"

"You have a video message incoming." Its eyes went wide as it processed something. "It is from a Foundry ship. Are you expecting a call?"

"I might be." I licked my chapped lips. "Put it through to my implants."

"As you wish."

I closed my eyes, and the world melted away; my perception transported to that of another ship. This one was far smaller than the *Fidelis*, or even the stealth warship, little more than a twenty-by-twenty-meter space made of three curved alcoves, soft light emitting from its structural recesses, all surrounding a single Star Sphere. Bellamy sat on the catwalk that surrounded her tank, legs swinging over the edge, facing me. She was dressed in a blue and white jumpsuit with no insignia, her blonde hair braided and resting over her left chest.

"Hi, Milo," she said. "Before you try and respond, this is just a recording. It took me five or six attempts to get my words together. I'm sorry I didn't say anything after the eh, the *ontet*. I didn't really know what to say. I guess I still really don't.

"You saw something there, just like Vex said. I can't say how, but it scared us. It was nothing like what we usually see. Somehow you passed beyond understanding and time. We don't believe it was a hallucination. I can't say why, but it made me afraid, very afraid, and not much scares me anymore after all I've been through. I had to go be by myself, process what all this means, and I'm still not there. I'm sure Proxy and I will have much to talk about on the next leg of our journey. I recommend you do the same.

"Look, I know you wanted me to come with you, and while that would make the most sense from one perspective, I just can't do it. My place is not with people anymore, at least not humans. I've seen both the goodness of mankind, and the darkness, and I think I've had enough. So, to be honest, I just want to see what's out there. See what there is to discover. I understand it is selfish, and so does my mother. Please, accept my apology. And know that the past few weeks have been what I needed. I needed to see for myself that life will go on with or without my help. You are that life, Milo. If anyone can save the Earth, it's you. But you've got to let your anger go. You've got to know peace before you can do the right thing.

"I believe in you, Milo. I can only imagine those who surround you believe in you, too. Go save humanity. Show the Foundry that we protect life."

The image faded, and I opened my eyes once more.

And there it was. She wasn't coming with us.

Where did she plan to go? What did she plan to do? I'm not sure even she knew, and that was part of the appeal. She just wanted to see what was out there. I could only pray the Universe protected her on that journey.

"Bellamy?" Proxy asked, confused. "Who is this Bellamy?"

"Someone like me," I said, taking a shuddering breath. "An anomaly. She is from one of the FICSE ships, the *Revelation*. The last of two who are still alive."

"Will she not be joining us?"

I paused for a moment, then shook my head. "No. She won't."

"I see. She shall be a ghost then, a wanderer."

"A what?"

"This is someone who takes our gift, and never returns. There are many out there who choose this path. Existence can be a burden. A burden too great for some, especially those of great intelligence. We offer them peace."

I squeezed my eyes shut and lowered my head. "I think I understand. The highs, the lows. Existence can be hard."

"What are your orders, Milo?" Proxy hopped onto my lap and began to purr.

I looked down at my alien friend, its cat eyes staring back, and smiled. "Orders? I think it's in the name of the mission. Foundry Intent, Contact and Save Earth. Pretty sure we've done the first part. I think I now know what the Foundry wants. Maybe we go save Earth next."

"Stop Johan?"

"That's right, my furry friend. But let's focus on stopping, and not killing. This isn't the end for us. No. This is just the beginning."

CHAPTER 38

Proxy gave me a rundown of all the affected systems onboard. The Dragon had done extensive damage to the *Fidelis*, and it was not going to be a quick fix. While my ship had sustained much damage during the Kabosai battle, this attack had dwarfed that encounter. The trickle of power coming in was only enough to sustain repairs to the antimatter reactors. When those came back online, they would then power the remainder of our repair attempts. A point in time too far away. At that point swarms of nano drones would be able to gather debris caught in a common orbit around us to start the work, then scour the nearby rocks for the remainder. It could repair itself, but it would be two years, Earth Standard at a minimum. Johan's trail, if we could even find it, would be long cold by then.

"Once I revive the crew, how long do we have?" I asked Proxy, the two of us standing beside Shelly's Star Sphere. She twitched in her tank as if she had been dreaming of something, a series of bubbles escaping her nose as she did. I wanted desperately to hold her, and to hell with the consequences.

"Our power needs are balanced on a knife," it said after a moment. "Once you revive your crew, you will have a few days to make a decision over what we must do, but no more. Not all can go back into suspension. But now that you are here, we have options, like the energy sails, or…"

"Or what?"

Proxy rubbed at the side of its face with the back of a paw, as if it were attempting to avoid eye contact. "There is another option available to us, one less conventional."

"And what kind of option is this?"

"Perhaps it is something you should discuss with your counterpart."

"With Shelly?"

"No. Your fellow pilot."

I nodded. "Okay. Wake up Shelly. I need to speak with her."

A flash of light shot through her Star Sphere, and she began to rouse, slowly turning her head to open her eyes, looking left and right, regaining her bearings as she came around.

I knocked on the glass tank with my prosthetic hand and waved. She turned in my direction, umbilicals twisting along with her body, eyes wide, mouth agape. It took her a moment to fully realize what she was seeing. We made eye contact.

The umbilicals began to pop out of her spine and retreat, and she swam to the surface of the tank, bursting forth to cast a spray of water into the air.

"Milo!" she shouted as she frantically climbed onto the catwalk around her tank like a kid struggling to escape a bath. "Milo! Is that you?"

"It's me," I said, rushing around to the ladder and scrambling up so I could meet her. "It's me."

We threw our arms around one another, water dripping off our bodies, hearts pounding against one another's chests. This was my wife, my life. We trembled in one another's arms, each of us afraid that if we let up the pressure even the slightest bit, the other might evaporate. I'm glad I hadn't given up on seeing her again. Hope is a powerful thing. Foolish hope had been about all that had sustained me in that cold. Given me what I needed to survive just a little bit longer. Always just a little bit longer.

"You're alive," she quavered after a long moment. "And you're here. I thought I'd lost you."

"I thought I'd lost you too. It's been a tough trip, but I'm alive, maybe even more than I've ever been."

She let go of me and took hold of my hands, a pained expression on her face as she noticed my amputated fingers. "Love, what happened?"

"Frostbite happened, and so much more."

"Oh, Milo." She laid her forehead against mine. "I'm so sorry. Tell me everything."

And so, I did just that, the two of us sitting atop her Star Sphere, Proxy having summoned fresh clothes and refreshments. Waking the rest of the crew could come in time. I knew I had to make a choice, though I wasn't sure what that was yet, but I wanted the opinion of the smartest woman I knew first. I told her everything that had happened Everything I had heard and seen, other than the vision of the nautilus room. I wasn't sure why. It just didn't feel right to focus on it.

She was on the edge of her seat the entire time, following me at every step as I clawed through the snow drifts, fought the cave monsters, which I was starting to believe were fever hallucinations, and then to Bellamy, and my good hosts, then recovery, meditation. She was particularly interested in Bellamy and her reasons for not wanting to join us.

"Bellamy and the Melcorin helped nurse me back to health," I said. "And then, the whole experience with the Universe, that creature. The Foundry was made to extend life, not just create it, not just protect it."

"What was she like?" Shelly asked, resting a hand on my leg. "Bellamy. You spent weeks with her."

I smiled. "You jealous?"

She rolled her eyes. "No. Not in the least. Come on, it doesn't sound like the sexiest situation anyways. Lizard people all around, cramped spaces, frostbite."

"But she did nurse me back to health."

"I'm choosing to ignore that mental picture." Shelly took a sip of hot tea and then set her cup down. "Why do you think she didn't join us?"

"I've been thinking about that a lot," I said. "Truth is, while we've had a lot of challenges, she had a hard life. What I mean is, it was bad within her family. My parents might have been absent at times, but there was no fighting, not physical at least. Yours loved you too. But hers, it was just her mom and grandfather. I think there was history with them before the mission. Something bad in their family that hung over all of them."

"Like what?"

"Abuse, maybe? I can't say. She didn't share."

"Those kinds of hurts are sometimes never truly healed."

"Yeah." I let out a sigh. "I don't think she trusts people. Humans at least. Proxy said that this path might allow her to find peace."

"Is her mother still alive?"

"Somewhere, I think. Though where? Who can say? I just hope she finds her peace."

Shelly's lips tightened. "As do we all. She sounds like a good soul."

"She is. One of the best. If not for her, I wouldn't be here. She not only saved me from the cold, but, well, she helped me face what you tried to help me face already."

"I tried. I really tried."

I hung my head. "Yeah, I know you did."

"Always got to hear it from someone else," Shelly said, squeezing my damaged hand. "Can't be from those closest."

"Sorry."

"That's life." She kissed the nubs of my missing fingers, lips soft, tingling against the healing skin. "Okay, love, enough of her for now. Back to the Foundry."

"Always to the heart of it. Nothing but the facts."

"You know me. You spoke with the Universe. It said for sure it won't help us?"

"No," I said. "The Foundry won't help, not the way we hope for, at least. But I don't think we need its explicit assistance with the original mission, we just need to not stand at odds with it. We can potentially reverse the damage done in its view of us by stopping Johan. I think it has a sort of simple algorithm it follows."

"I sure hope you're right."

"Me too."

"So, what options do we have?"

"Proxy said we can deploy the sails, but still we're looking at years to continue along this path. I have a feeling that option will give him too much of a head start. Besides, I'm not if sure we know exactly where he went."

"We know where he went," she said. "Frelo knows."

"They do?"

She nodded.

"Where then?"

"Later."

"Fine. So, we know where to go. We just need to get there faster."

"And there is a way," she said, looking concerned.

I leaned towards her. "What? What is it? Tell me."

"You'll need to talk to Karianna." Something about the way she said this made me feel uneasy. "She knows how."

"Okay," I said, taking a deep breath. "Proxy told me as much already. You guys are starting to concern me. Should we wake the rest?"

"Yes. I'll tell them what happened. You talk to her."

"Am I not going to like what I hear?"

She shrugged. "I can't say, but the more you tell me, the more I think it is the only option, especially if we go ahead and wake everyone. Proxy can't put them back without help."

"Maybe the Melcorin can help. Give us a jump."

"Maybe… but I don't think it will change anything significant. This could be another test, not by the Foundry, but one of fate."

What a novel concept. Fate.

"Alright, alright," I said. "I'll find another Star Sphere to climb into. We'll get the shared bridge online. You tell the crew what happened. I'll talk to Karianna."

"Milo," she whispered, again throwing her arms around me. "I missed you. Really missed you. I thought I'd lost you forever. I spent my nights crying myself to sleep till we were put into suspension, saying prayers to the void that you would come back safe, that you were not dead. I don't want to be without you. Ever."

Again, I held her so tightly that it was difficult for us both to breathe. "I'm here."

"Don't leave me like that again."

I drew in a deep breath. "I won't."

"Good," she replied, nodding.

"Do you believe me, Shelly?"

"Believe you? What do you mean?"

My lips twitched as I swallowed down my fears. "That I spoke with the Universe. I'm afraid some of the others might think I'm crazy, or that I was just sick, damaged. Do you think my vision was real? Or did I go crazy?"

She looked me in the eyes for a long moment, then kissed me on the lips. "If there's one thing you suck at, it's lying. I know you were there. I see it on your face. I believe."

And that was enough for her to believe. It was always enough.

Two rooms over from Shelly's Star Sphere was a section of backup spheres. My prominent sphere at the front of the ship was gone for obvious reasons, but one of these would do just fine for now. I stripped down and settled into the familiar, warm fluid, and then closed my eyes, surrendering myself to the ship.

Pinch. Snap. Click.

Physical reality was drawn away, replaced by a shaky version of the shared bridge space. The floor glitched occasionally like a broken LED matrix, sections blinking and shifting into random colors or shapes, black bars or the appearance of strange furniture, telegraphing further systemic damage to the *Fidelis* and my connection.

Proxy appeared at my side, rubbing its body against my ankle. "Are you ready to wake her?"

"I am. Give us some privacy, please."

"You are never fully alone in here."

"I know, I know. Just make me feel like we are, okay?"

Proxy gave a bow, its nose touching the idea of a floor. "As you wish."

The room glitched again, becoming a colorful field of flowers with mountains in the distance, blue skies that became red that became green then black, then everything returned. I waited, and waited, and waited. Without a clock it was hard to tell how much time had passed.

I found my thoughts wandering onto Bellamy, curious where she would go next, how she would spend her years. What wonders would she behold? What peoples would she make contact with? Would she come home? Would she contribute to saving Earth? Hell, was there even an Earth left? Would she find Novae? Would she find her mother? There was something odd there. Where was her mother? Bellamy was destined to forever wander. Never truly lost. A ghost cruising upon the cosmic winds of time.

Karianna appeared three paces before me, rubbing her eyes and stretching her muscles as she did. She let out a yawn then blinked at me, her head cocked to the side, looking confused. My fellow pilot was dressed in all black, not a jumpsuit, but black pants and boots and a long, lace-sleeved shirt. She wore dark makeup around her eyes with her dark hair pulled up into a bun. If I didn't know better, I'd say she was dressed in her version of mourning.

"Milo, is that you?" she ventured, taking a step towards me, a cautious look replacing the twist of confusion on her face. "It's not the system glitching again, is it?"

"No," I replied, voice deadpan. "It's me."

"How did you?" She rushed forward and took hold of my arm, fleshy here, not machine, gripping it tight. "I saw you die, Milo. I saw you die!"

"No. You saw me get eaten."

"But that thing, it… It came back for us, slammed its body into my ship and nearly shattered us. What happened, Milo. Tell me. Tell me!"

"There's time for that later. Shelly will fill you in. Right now, we have a more important matter to speak about." I gestured at the glitching room around us.

She took a step back and narrowed her eyes. "You literally come back from the dead, and first thing you're going to do is brush me the F off? I deserve better. We are fellow freaks, or have you forgotten?"

"You do. I'm sorry, friend. That's not what this is about. I'm back, and we have a mission. We have to go after Johan, and I need to know how. Shelly said you found a way. Proxy had already hinted as much, too."

Her eyes widened. "Oh. A way. That."

"What? Are we going to have to make a deal with a cruel, near-immortal being? Throw ourselves through a gate that pretty much disassembles us and stitches us back together? What do we have to do? The suspense is killing me."

"No, no. It's stranger than all of that." She closed her eyes and pinched the bridge of her nose. "Did you get a good look at our ships?"

"Good enough look. We're in a world of hurt."

"You could say that. The *Reverie* is barely keeping the Star Spheres up and running. There's no atmospheric pressure in ninety-five percent of the ship. A couple of the crew, James and Chevelle, can't even exit their Star Spheres without Chinchillette taking some drastic measures. Perez is dead. Power seems to be the biggest obstacle. Power that can't be repaired without a small fortune of rare materials used in antimatter reactions."

"Do we need to get more? Is that what this is?"

"Yes. But there's nothing nearby that doesn't have to be refined, and given our current relationship with the Jevox, it's not like we'll be trading with them as we had for lithium back on Novae. That leaves two sources."

"Which are?"

She raised her arms, palms up, and spun around "Us."

I blinked. "Us? What? What do you mean?"

"Proxy and Chinchillette have worked up a plan. One that would involve combining the two of our ships, and pressing them together into a new ship so that we could make use of our scarce resources. I've looked at the projections and it would get us back online within maybe a month, and with most of our capacity. The rest could come in time, but we'd have engines and about a third of our weapons right off the bat. We'd be able to stabilize all the ancillary systems and relays as well."

"Combine the ships?" I rubbed my chin. "That could work. It would consolidate other resources as well. The MI would be stronger too, right? We'd have more fighters in one place."

"All true, but there's a catch."

I frowned. "There always is."

"So… here's the thing. The two of us would have to pilot this new ship together. Yes, one of us would take the lead, but there's not enough processing power between our ships to manage all the additional connections we'd bring online without us both being part of it. That is, if we want it to be capable of more than pointing in a direction and hoping we arrive. And, well, by doing that, things would get eh, weird."

"You've never been one to beat around the bush," I said. "Tell me. What's so bad about this?"

She lowered her head. "These aren't like normal ships. We aren't two pilots sitting in the same room running the ship. The two of us would be in one another's head. You'd be able to hear my damned, loudest thoughts, and I'd be able to hear yours. We'd share some twisty emotions, motivations, all sorts of weird things. It could blur the lines of our identities."

And there it was. The catch. A big ass catch. No wonder Shelly had seemed nervous.

Combining the ships would make us a bigger, faster, meaner vessel, but it would require me to melt down part of my sense of self, part of who I was, into Karianna. Sure, Karianna and I had a kinship with all we had been through, being pilots, giving the donation, fighting beside one another. And yet, this option was far more. She would have unrestricted access to many of my secret thoughts. My hidden…

"We could lose who we are," I said after a moment.

"And more," she replied, looking me in the eyes. "Look, Milo, I—What I mean to say is—well—fuck."

I raised a hand to forestall her. "You don't have to say any more. How much control will we have to keep our thoughts to ourselves?"

She shrugged. "Proxy and Chinchillette say that we will have a pretty good deal, but it won't be passive. If we let our mental guards down for too long, there's a good chance we'll become irrevocably intertwined. Humans did not evolve for this."

"Is there any other way?"

The room glitched, transporting us onto the surface of a cold and lifeless moon, then the corona of a raging star, the bottom of an ocean filled with strange marine life, and then back to the shared bridge space.

"I don't know a way that fits our timetable," she said, shaking off the disorientation of the sudden locational transitions. "We've considered many options, but physics, time, and distance are against us. To pursue we need the reactors online. To get them online, we need the materials; to get the materials, we'd have to merge our ships. Something about how they're stored will not let us scuttle one to fix the other as is. Too dangerous. Besides—"

"We'd be giving up a lot of firepower if we scrapped one of the ships," I cut in.

She raised a finger and pointed at me. "Bingo."

"Okay," I said, scratching at the back of my head. "If we do this, we're going to have to work hard at keeping ourselves separate."

"It won't be easy."

"No. And we need to understand that thoughts are sometimes stray. Just because you think something, doesn't mean anything."

"Right. We all have errant ideas."

"Exactly."

"We'll be kind of like the Jevox, right?" she said, chuckling.

"It's not as fun as you think. Shelly and I experienced it for a brief moment. I can only hope the Foundry does a cleaner job with human psychology than we did." I reached out a hand and offered it to her. "We can do this, right?"

Karianna stared at me for a moment, thinking, then nodded and took hold of my hand. She shook it, her frown flattening into a resolved line. "We can do this."

"Good. Because this room acting like this is making me nauseous, and we've got to do something about it."

"Right?" She raised her palms in disbelief. "This is bullshit."

As I turned to connect us with the rest, Karianna put a hand on my shoulder to stop me.

"What else happened after you were eaten?" she asked.

"A lot."

"You can tell me."

I leaned in. "You're going to think I'm crazy."

She chuckled. "And how the hell is that different from any other time?"

I gave a shrug. "Well, I spoke to the Universe while I was gone, but the weird thing is, it spoke back."

"Oh," she said, her head cocking to the side.

Finished for now, I sent Shelly a ping to call the remainder of our crews into the shared bridge space. She stood by my side, and one by one, everyone appeared. Soon as they realized I was here, really here, and alive, they greeted me with a barrage of handshakes, high fives, and more than a few hugs. Even Leo was happy to see me, giving me one of those handshakes that turns into a hug and a slap on the back.

"I'm so glad to see you're alive," he said.

In an uncommon moment of relief, I smiled at him. "Good to see you too."

"Shelly filled us in," Xuan said. "Hard days on icy rock. Sorry for your fingers."

"It's okay," I said, raising my injured hand. I hadn't realized until now that I had let the image of my amputated fingers persist, even in a place where I could change them. "Just reminds me of what I needed to let go."

"I'm sure the doc could fix you up." Renata pointed at my cat. "Doctor Proxy."

Dante and Emilia looked at one another and nodded.

"We can help you get a new prosthetic," Dante said after a moment. "Even if Proxy cannot. We have plans for the forges. Schematics."

"I think it makes you look badass having missing fingers," Ada said. "That's just me."

"Thank you everyone," I told her. "I'll go without for now."

"Wish Perez was still with us, though," Hy said. "Nice man."

His wife echoed, "Nice man."

"I didn't know him half as well as he deserved," James said.

Lance crossed his arms. "We are going after Johan and his degenerates, right? Haven't gone soft on us, no? This is all his fault."

"Not soft," I replied. "More focused. Johan and his crew need to pay for what happened to Dad, to all of us on Novae, but with justice, not revenge. It hurts, will always hurt, but our people deserve better. We have to show that we protect life, not just end it."

"I wish Alexander was here," Ada mused, staring off into an imaginary distance. "We've got to figure out how to stop them without killing them. He always has great ideas."

"And we will, I promise. The main objective will be to disable Johan's ship without hurting any Jevox. But first, we have to get after them, and we have to get close." I turned to face our alien guest. "Frelo, Shelly said you know where they went."

The Jevox raised a five fingered hand. "I do. They have gone to Yuven. It is where the nearest Prole Genascara, a life changer, is undergoing refit. It is a terraforming ship. This refit is a process which takes decades of your standard years. It is scheduled to work on a world for the Servanis in seventy-five Yuven."

"Then what we gaggin' 'round the ends for?" Chevelle asked. "Let's give these pattymouts a run. Bust 'em up real nice."

Karianna and I exchanged a look.

"Just have to get our wrecks put back together," she responded after a moment.

Our crewmembers nodded. Shelly reached for my hand and squeezed. I squeezed hers back. I had no idea where this would take me. Where it would take us, all of us.

"Can we address the elephant in the room?" Lance asked, eyeing us each in turn. "You know I've never been one to keep my mouth shut or not speak my mind. And look, Milo, I mean no disrespect at all. I'm glad to see you're back, and alive. But this vision, this hippy-ass Melcorin, meditative experience with the Universe you had, while it might not affect this part of our mission, I'm having a hard time buying it."

I frowned at him. "I told you all the truth."

"And I believe that you believe it." He made a patronizing gesture with one hand. "But let's be honest, bruh, you were halfway dead and got rescued by some shadowy lizard people. And along with them, another human, or so you remember. What are the chances? Was she even real, or was she another hallucination? Did anything else happen down there that maybe wasn't one hundred percent legit?"

My stomach sank, and I found myself gripping her hand tighter. It was true that there had been no blood in the cave, and that was weird. No dead demon dogs despite firing through them. That much could have been a hallucination. Bellamy had seemed shocked when I mentioned them. But Bellamy was real. I know she was real, even if improbable. And the Melcorin, they returned me here. The rest, though…

"Buddy," James said, patting me on the shoulder. "I have to agree with Lance. It is a little far-fetched."

"Anyone else?" I asked, hardening my eyes.

Leo raised his open palms. "I for one think this makes a great story. I don't care if it's real or not. I'm not sure there's a God, but God is real because others believe in him, or her, or them. This vision was a powerful image. Doesn't matter if it really happened, it's important. Symbolic."

"Look," Chevelle said, taking a step forward. "No reason why it can't be real. Universe is a twisted place, innit? It does as it occasions. Never thought you to be a few pence short and mental."

"Seems legit to me," Ada added.

The room went silent for a moment. No one else spoke up. Maybe I was crazy, but I didn't think I was.

"Karianna?" Shelly asked, looking to my fellow pilot. "Do you believe him?"

She scratched her arm and looked away. "I just don't know."

"Fine," I told them, my voice a bit harder than I had intended it to be. "Believe me. Don't believe me. Doesn't matter. We can all agree Johan needs to be stopped and we know where he is. Let's take care of that."

I let go of my wife's hand, glimpsed the uncertain expression on her face, then pulled Karianna to the side so we could talk while the others discussed our predicament.

"We have to do it," I lowered my voice. "But are you sure you can handle this? I have to hear it again. You have to promise me. Are you sure?"

"Look, Milo, I'm—"

"Doesn't matter." I hardened my expression. Whatever she was about to say did not need to be said. "It doesn't fucking matter. We have something more important to see done. We have a mission to fulfill. It comes first."

"You're right." She removed the pins holding up her dark hair and shook it out, running fingers through it to untangle the virtual mess. "This is an end. Our ships will be no more after this. They'll be torn into a goddamned mess and reassembled into something else. And our minds, well, there might be times we hear things we may not have asked to hear, learn crazy stuff. I've never..."

"It's a weird thing, I know. Question is, can we keep this professional?" I think I might have sounded a bit uncertain. I knew that this was the only real option, even if it was bordering on madness. But it still felt dirty in a way.

Karianna chewed on her lip and gave a curt nod. "Let's keep it professional."

"Professional," I echoed.

CHAPTER 39

Our group, our teams, had been apart for too long. Months had passed since the attack, and even though everyone had been locked away in hyper suspension most of that time, something was not the same. To give us the opportunity to reconnect and feel at least a little human, despite all the augmentation from the Star Spheres and damage to the ships, Karianna and I asked the crews of both the *Fidelis* and *Reverie* to remain in the shared bridge space as we summoned a feast. It didn't matter if this wasn't exactly real, but just a fantasy played out by the Foundry's machines stimulating parts of our brain, but the breaking of bread had ever been a means to bond and connect as humans, and we sure as hell needed to connect.

Long tables appeared in the center of the room, their smooth, white surfaces laden with mouthwatering foods of every variety, summoned from the memories of those among us, and those left behind on Novae. There were roasted chickens and duck, a dozen different types of tacos from al pastor to barbacoa, barbecue in three different regional American varieties, sweet, spicy, and vinegar based, and of course sides, mashed potatoes, fried plantains, cheeses, tapas, and more vegetables than I could easily identify. Not to mention all the sweets, colorful macarons, brownies covered in caramel, petit fours, cupcakes stacked with icing, ice cream, and cheesecakes.

Between these wide varieties of food were bottles of wine ranging from white to red, pinot grigio, chardonnay, cabernet sauvignon, port, and sparkling rosé. Not to mention all the beer, so many options available they filled a book sixteen pages long.

The crews sat together at the table, Karianna and I at the center of opposite sides, Shelly beside me on my right, the rest filling in what spots were available. James tried to take the seat beside Karianna, but she hurriedly invited Chevelle to take it, much to James's dismay. At the right end of the table, Proxy sat atop a stool. On the left, Chinchillette did the same. Karianna insisted that they not be left out, lest they get depressed or ornery, so I obliged.

We ate with abandon, smiling and laughing and telling jokes. Ate like warriors who cherished every moment of life, knowing that the next was not a guarantee. This was the first time in a long time I hadn't felt the anger-driven need to push forward. Our time to leave would come, but it was not this moment. That moment was later. It was our time to just be. To experience the universe, experience life.

The room glitched from time to time, a reminder that we could not remain in this place forever. Instead of being afraid, our group poked fun at the situation. We had survived a great deal. This was just another challenge. The strangest of all the glitches, however, was that on occasion it would swap what our food tasted like, making one dish taste like another, not in texture, but flavor. Leo had fried fish tacos that tasted like hamburgers. Chevelle, mashed potatoes that tasted like lime gelatin.

"My beer tastes a lot like lobster bisque," Lance said, spitting his drink out on the floor. "We are going to fix this, right?"

I raised a frothy tankard of porter. "We are. It's on the agenda."

"On the agenda," Karianna echoed as she tore into a chicken leg.

Ada elbowed Shelly. "You know what's missing?"

"What?" Shelly jumped, looking a bit surprised as if she'd been lost in thought. "What's missing?"

"Perry."

"How so?"

"Jokes. He'd be telling jokes."

"Load of gutter trash," Chevelle said, pointing at us with a piece of rib meat. "Thinks he's chirpsing with safe ones, but they're worse than Da's. I ain' gonna switch though."

"Personally, I like them," Shelly replied. "Come from the heart."

"That's it, innit."

"Of all our arts," Leo began, "a true comedian has not yet appeared in our group. Maybe it's time for me to take a crack at it." He gave Ada a glaring eye.

She shook her head. "I don't think that's within your expansive skillset."

He raised his palms and shrugged. "Maybe. Can't be good at everything, you know. I'll have to settle for eight out of ten."

"Unless you are me," James put in, leaning forward so that he could see around Chevelle. "I'm a perfect ten. Perfect—ten."

"Perfect ten," Karianna chuffed. "Alright then."

"What? Are you saying I'm not?"

She tossed back her nose. "I said nothing."

"Remember that one time…"

"Bite your tongue, *Reed*. Bite it!"

"…back on Novae," he went on, heedless of her clear annoyance, "when we were still using the public showers and they broke down?" A grin blossomed on James' face. "The water went cold, and it was not a warm day, you got stuck in your stall? Forgot a towel and had two options, run butt naked through the camp, or scream for help. You were trapped, bare assed, and freezing."

Karianna snapped her head to the side and locked her dagger eyes on him.

"What?" he asked, tossing an arm over his chair attempting to look nonchalant. "I just happened to be walking by."

"Shut up, Reed."

"By this point we had already gotten off on the wrong foot. I had tried to make friends after the first few weeks of our arrival, invite you out for some lunch, nothing serious, and in return you hung a freaking dismembered stone bison head on the door of my dome. The blood left a stain I was never able to clean off. I bet it's still there."

"Reed!"

"Can't say I was the most inclined to help, but I was the only person in earshot. I asked you where you left your towel. You said in your quarters. Now that was going to be too far to go. Nearly a hundred and fifty feet from the common showers. A long run."

Karianna started to get out of her chair, but Chevelle was finding this story funny and tried her best to keep her seated. Ada's face was turning red, and she was on the verge of laughter.

"But look, there was a tree nearby, and it had some low branches perfect for holding towels. Like a natural rack. It was only twenty or thirty feet from the showers, and I had my satchel with me. In that satchel was a towel, and now I can't say it was much of one, just a hand towel, but it was clean. And so, in my infinite kindness I hung it on the tree and went on my way."

"Asshole!" she shouted. "I was so fucking cold, like a piece of raw meat hung in the deep freeze. Ice crystals were about to start forming on my skin. What other option did you give me? Could have at least delivered it to the shower stall."

James smiled. "Could have, but then I wouldn't have had the chance to see you make a dash for the tree." He raised his hands before anyone said a thing. "To be fair, I didn't stare. I covered my eyes and laughed the entire time… Okay, maybe I snuck a little peek through my fingers. Come on, I was curious if your left butt cheek was all metal. For those who are curious, it is not."

"You know, I was curious about that," Leo tapped his lips with a finger.

"What a dick," Xuan said, frowning at James.

"Taken out of context," James went on, "it might seem that way. But did you miss the part where she hung a dead animal's head on my door?"

"You probably deserved it."

So, it hadn't been just Shelly and I she pulled that kind of prank on.

Karianna pumped her fist in the air. "Hell yeah he deserved it. With his little, soft shit face, and stupid shit words, and…" She paused, unable to think of what to say next. Her eyes lingered on him for a moment. She licked her lips, sighed, then glanced over at me before swallowing and reaching for her drink.

"Yeah, yeah, yeah," James said, shaking his head and waving a dismissive hand. "Whatever, Torlen. Might need to work on your people skills."

Conversations went on, Xuan and Hy talking in hushed tones with Renata. Dante and Emilia regaling us with all the drama associated with building the Cultural Center, and how Marissa had discovered a local variety of fungus with psychedelic effects that was sometimes the source of her inspiration. Leo said that this fungus had a pleasing effect, and that everyone else should give it the opportunity when they could. Ada assured him that psychedelics could cause males to stop producing testosterone, and James assured her, having had a mother in the medical field who experimented in her youth, that this was crap.

Our Proxies answered questions when asked, but rarely contributed to the conversations. I can't say that this was surprising. I often felt Proxy was a reflection of myself, like that voice in my head, not totally autonomous or self-aware, but not all me.

Leo and Dante soon fell into a fierce argument around surrealism and abstract storytelling, each of them attempting to outdo the other with their many accolades back on Earth. Dante's digital gallery on display at the Museum of Modern Art in New York, and Leo's sculpture reprints at Centre Pompidou in Paris. Neither was willing to cede any ground. Dante repeated that his placement was better than the others, and that while the Pompidou was the height of Avant Garde architecture, MOMA in New York was in New York, and that somehow made all the difference.

The gravity of this artistic discussion was dampened when Renata finally opened up to the group and spoke openly of the horrors of the Oil Wars fifteen years before our departure, how being barely old enough to serve, she had been forced to shoot civilians in Venezuela who were wired with explosives, in order to save her unit. Not exactly light dinner conversation. When offered condolences for having to do such a thing, she shrugged it off as part of the job, the mission, and that she did what she had to do. I supposed that everyone dealt with grief and guilt in their own ways. We told stories of former Councilor Perez, lamenting his loss, and honored his memory.

James continued to pine for Karianna, and Ada rebuffed Leo, while Lance and Chevelle moved to different seats so they could play a game of what I learned was called cribbage, which involved poker cards and a wooden pegboard.

I sat back and watched it unfold, capturing this moment in my mind. Life was to be experienced.

"Will this change us?" Shelly asked after some time, her voice a whisper. She took a sip of red wine from her long-stemmed glass and sighed. "I'm trying to put on a brave face, but I'm afraid of what comes next. Afraid what happens when you and she are connected."

I nodded. "So am I, but I promise, nothing will change between us, not from this. You are my love, my only love."

She gave me a half smile and took hold of my arm, squeezing it tight before laying her head on my shoulder. "I hope you're right."

Stories were told.

Laughter was had.

The wine was drunk.

The evening came to a close.

The moment had come.

I stood in my personal, virtual environment, surveying the broken field of debris from the Dragon's attack all alone. My throat tightened as I looked upon the missing, forward end of the *Fidelis*. Death had brushed so very near to me and my friends, and yet most of us had survived. There was something to be said for that. Right? Perhaps there were bigger forces at play than just entropy and blind chance. Perhaps the Universe had been coy with me. I had been swallowed by a great space beast, spat out onto an inhospitable world, and was still breathing. What were the chances that Bellamy was going to be there? And on that exact rock, at that exact time?

Shelly appeared beside me, an uneasy look on her face, halfway between crying and smiling. She made her way towards me, then paused, looking away.

"Everything changes today," she whispered. "Everything."

I reached for her hands and shook my head. "No. It doesn't change."

Her shoulders sagged. "I know you are doing what you believe is right. I just hope you don't lose yourself in the process."

"I'm not going anywhere," I said, squeezing her fingers tight.

She threw her arms around me and held on. "I want to believe that."

"Then believe."

A chirp echoed over my shoulder, and I twisted my head to the left, not letting go of Shelly.

"We ready?" Karianna's disembodied voice called. "It's time."

I closed my eyes and drew Shelly's face up to mine, kissing her on the lips, my fingers trembling. She made no mention of my nervousness, and instead threw herself into the moment, returning my affection.

After a blind, desperate, indeterminate amount of time, we stepped back from one another and sighed. Shelly raised her hand in a motionless wave, then vanished.

"Proxy?" I called, and the cat appeared beside me.

"Are you ready?"

"I am. At least, I think so."

"Are you sure?"

"It's the only way, isn't it? If we wait too long, he'll get away."

"It is very likely."

"And combining our systems will make us stronger. Right? Nothing bad about that."

"Not in the least."

"Okay, okay." I shook out my hands and narrowed my eyes. "I'm ready."

"Very well," Proxy said, and I felt a series of signals spider out through the body of the *Fidelis*, what was left of the navigational thrusters coming to life, pushing us towards the *Reverie*. "I will place everyone in the crew but you and Karianna into a slumber. Not hyper suspension, but they will not be awake for the operation. Many changes will take place."

My body drifted ever closer to Karianna's. It was the only way to describe it. Our ships were more than just hunks of metal, they were a physical extension of will, an expression of our virtual selves. Being on the surface those many months on Novae, the gap between man and machine had widened within me, making me feel smaller, simpler, but those days were behind me. Karianna and I were not baseline humans, we were something else. Clearly not of a normal evolution, and yet…

"Will it hurt?" Karianna called over an open channel.

Chinchillette replied, its voice flat and chilling, *"There will be no pain."*

Though subtle, I felt our perception of subjective time shifting.

This process would take weeks, not years. It would give us a chance.

Through the field of glittering debris left by the attack, we moved towards one another, then collided, the shattered forward end of the *Fidelis* cutting into the side of the *Reverie*, slicing into its edge and moving towards the center like a knife cutting into putty. The hulls of both ships became liquid at the site of the impact, nano machines flowing this way and that, allowing for the two solid objects to meld with one another like metal in a forge. Within the inner workings of our ships, rooms began to reconfigure, damaged systems shedding themselves of broken parts, connecting them to form new chains. Star Spheres traveled around the tempest of swirling nano machines like bubbles in quicksilver, transporting crew members to their new locations within halls that did not exist moments earlier.

I tracked Shelly's progress as her sphere, one of the few unchanged objects in this melding, was moved to a location near the central core of the ship, our new center of gravity.

Dense materials traveled through arteries of black sludge, the power aboard both ships flickering, drawing from reserves as the antimatter was transferred into its new home, forming a dark star at the center of the ship's gestation. The core formed itself anew. The reactors went online, and my veins, no, our veins filled with energy.

"What was that?" Karianna asked, but it wasn't over a channel. It was like with Shelly and the implant upgrade. Her thoughts were in my head. *"It tingles. It feels, really, really nice. Like a hot shower on a cold day, vulnerability wrapped in steam. Little asshole. He had to remind me of that day. Embarrassed. Pissed off. And still his… I know someone who would not have done that given the chance. He wouldn't—"*

I swallowed at her errant ruminations. The feel of soft skin. Bare flesh. Erect nipples. The pinching. The rubbing.

It had begun.

"Power is returning," I replied, my thoughts spluttering out. *"And you're right. It does feel—eh—warm."*

"Woah, woah, woah," she thought, and I could imagine her hands raising up before her. *"You heard me? I was—shit, shit, shit."*

"I did."

"Damn it. I'm really going to have to watch what I think, aren't I?"

"We both are."

"Fuck, my thoughts are loud."

"Are mine?"

"Think something."

And I did. Nothing serious, just a memory about a time I ate cheese crackers with a little girl at her parents' quarters while we played with toys.

"Tell me when you start," Karianna thought. *"Any time now."*

"I am." I tried harder. *"How about now?"*

"Oh, well, nothing much. Your thoughts are way quieter than mine, I guess. I do taste cheese, though. Wait, what… Was cheese part of it?"

The connections only deepened as the systems were repaired, integrating us as network lines laid down, weapons moved and reconfigured. The various sensors of the ship came online, and I could see more than ever before. Our fighters were drawn through the swarms to new bays, stacked three high each, thirty in all.

A field of electromagnetic energy radiated from us and began drawing the broken debris of our ships towards us. Those that had no ferrous materials were drawn in by small swarms of silver machines. All hit the surface of the ship and turned to liquid, their materials deconstructed and added to the flow of repairing machines.

Asteroids nearby began to shatter and break, pieces flowing towards us in a steady procession. Refineries sprang to life near the edges of what was once the *Reverie*, breaking down and purifying these metals to serve in repairing and replacing yet more and more systems.

Moment by moment, day by day, we became stronger. Our power was restored. Our stocks of weapons replenished. Nano vats refilled. The MI barrier fortified. We would be far stronger together, far tougher than we had been apart, effectiveness multiplied, not merely a sum total.

Once the transformation was complete, we were left with what appeared to be a great, silver shard that had pierced the heart of a four-sided diamond, leaving us with a collection of triangular wings set perpendicular to our thrust vector. The lasting impression of both previous ships was clear, and yet it was new. The surface of this fusion was bluish white and reflective like glass, its lines and edges trussed by black metal with streaks of gold. A dozen cones, each as large as a city block, clustered near the base of the piercing shard, ready to cast plumes of anti-matter into the void and push us to the edge of light speed, while at its forward end was a razor sharp, crystalline point flanked by banks of energy weapons.

Our new body was—magnificent.

What in the hell are we going to call it? Karianna asked, her thoughts floating up beside me if not her virtual form. *The* Reverie *is gone. So is the* Fidelis. *This is something else entirely. Something new.*

I licked my lips then let out a deep breath. *This one's easy. Captain Karianna Torlen—welcome aboard the* Transcendence.

CHAPTER 40

For a time, I let my consciousness float, as if I were on my back in a pool of water, eyes fixed on a twinkling, midnight sky. The fresh influx of new information from the *Transcendence* was overwhelming to say the least, a vast ocean of data whose distant horizons I could not dare reach. I needed to give my body time to adjust. At the corner of everything I touched with my mind, I could always feel Karianna, not her thoughts at each moment, but her presence. It was a comfort, a warm, electrical energy, something similar in the way you felt when a loved one sat beside you on the couch and said nothing.

With my new body, our new body, I could look to the very edge of the galaxy and beyond, sorting through trillions of ribbons of energy and light at a speed with which the *Fidelis* alone could never achieve. Out of curiosity, I checked the statistics on my Star Sphere, the temperature of my tank, finding that my brain was elevated by a few degrees. The same held true for Karianna. The ship was borrowing part of our cognitive functions to do its work. This would affect our ability to slow our subjective time shifts in a tight moment, overclocking our heads to make quicker decisions. Proxy and I would need to talk about that later.

It was time to check on some of the ship's critical systems. See how they responded.

I reached for the MI, drawing my palms to my chest, and felt Karianna do the same, a gentle pressure from her actions brushing against me, urging me. We did not speak to one another about it, but I let her lead, the swarm of nanomachines following her will, then mine, gathering at the front of the shard at the bow of the *Transcendence* before bursting out and traveling back in metallic waves, undulating and widening. I raised my right hand to form a wall on one side of the ship, but she swiped it to the port side, sending tingles from my neck down my spine. I pressed against her efforts and reversed the action, our exchange becoming a dance of will, of command, with billions of nanoscopic machines shown as expression.

This is fun, she thought.

I tried my best not to respond, but I think she felt my agreeable sentiment. She was right. It was exhilarating.

Our motions were fluid, the MI forming into an ovoid bubble around the entire ship, then breaking off into four or more sections, creating new barriers. When we first started doing this, we fought against one another over where they needed to be, but after a few moments, we each started to learn where the other would go on instinct and filled in the rest, creating staggering collections of defenses.

I handed this task of defense off to her, then fired up the *Transcendence's* engines, curving us around what debris had been deemed by our Proxies as unusable, dodging asteroids and weaving through bands of radiation. JV-01 burned bright on our starboard side, not as threatening as it had been before, but rather, a source of life and hope, a point at which all things connected.

Did I ever tell you what my mom asked me before we left Earth?

Karianna took a long, mental breath, drawing up all the pieces of the MI barrier and storing them within the many nano-vats across the ship. She shifted her attention to me. *You haven't. What did she say?*

Have you ever dreamed of touching stars? I thought, doing my best to repeat Mom's wistful inflection and complicated emotions from that moment from the distant past. *"It seemed so innocuous back then. Like she was just being poetic.*

But it wasn't?

No. No it wasn't. I mean, for her it might have been, but for me, it became something else. There's something that connects this universe together, a series of threads. Something we can't easily explain. Life is more than just what happens between our ears. It's more than just perception, it's experience, consciousness, shared by us all.

Did you ever touch stars, for real? she asked. I could feel the anticipation swelling in her chest as if she were taking a deep breath, and the ship was responding to it.

I did, I replied, reaching out with a hand towards the hypergiant JV-01. The dark matter sails began to unfurl from our ship, bending from out of what remained of the *Reverie's* original shape, looking like slender flower petals painted black. *And when I did, it was the first time I made contact with the Universe, I'm sure of it.*

You mean, the entity that is both us, and also not us?

Yes. We're all connected, Karianna. And as I thought these words, I felt a warm, electrifying sensation as if she were reaching for my hand, sliding her fingers between mine.

I believe you, she replied. *The Universe. You speaking to it. It really did happen.*

It did, I affirmed, closing my fingers around hers.

You were there, her thoughts whispered, their tone, if you could call it that, apologetic.

I was there.

I can feel…

With an effort of will I pushed her away, letting go of her hand. The snapback of emotion was as jarring as a slap and just as painful.

I'm— she stammered. *Look, I didn't. It wasn't intentional.*

It's fine, it's fine, I replied, not apologizing. *We knew this would be part of it. Some things just feel comfortable. Fucking comfortable. Let's be professional. Keep our distance.*

Professional, she echoed. *You're right.*

"Milo," Proxy said, appearing in my virtual environment, breaking both Karianna and I from our awkward moment. "Do you wish to wake the crew so that we can disembark?"

"*Yes,*" Karianna replied, using her voice, not her thoughts. The experience for me was different. It touched a different part of my brain, just my perceptions, not my body. *"Chinchillette, get mine and have them start on fighter drills."*

"Yes, ma'am," I heard the other Proxy reply with its gruff voice.

"Proxy," I said to my cat. "You know what to do."

"Of course," it said, bowing.

One by one everyone began to wake from their forced slumber, some opting to exit their Star Spheres and tour the new ship. It was far larger than the *Fidelis* had been by nearly a kilometer, but in general the amenities were the same. My Star Sphere was located more towards the forward end of the main shard, Karianna's closer to the diamond shaped core near our center. The ship had dozens of rooms that could be reconfigured into any number of uses, as before. Even Leo's maker space had been recreated, what paintings weren't destroyed in the attack moved into it for continued work.

The crew began to stir. Several were in the shared bridge space, Lance and Ada among them. Whereas Leo, Hy, and Xuan made for Leo's repaired maker space.

Shelly appeared in my virtual environment; her shoulders slumped. "I guess it worked?"

I looked around us, ran my finger over invisible nooks within the ship's control architecture. "That it did."

Even while talking to Shelly, I could feel Karianna's unease, a mirror of my own, the narrow lines she was walking inside her own mind to avoid trying to project her thoughts onto me. It wasn't working, and I could tell this was going to prove difficult. What would happen if she were to spend time alone with James, or I with Shelly? Would we feel another's passions and excitement, get wrapped up in it? I had no freaking idea. There had to be a way to dampen this down.

"You okay?" Shelly asked, noticing the strange expression that had overtaken my face.

I shook my head. "I'm fine. It's just a lot to take in. The new ship, there's more information. More systems. The *Transcendence* is much larger than the *Fidelis*. Just trying to get used to it."

She put her head on my shoulder and took hold of my arm. "I'm sure. From speaking briefly with Proxy, we've got a lot more going on in engineering than before. There's not much we can't do in this ship."

"It's true. I can feel it."

And I can feel her… What was Karianna up to? My back was warm, my arms tingly. I felt, what? Wet? Wait… Was she taking a shower? What is up with her and showers?

The engines of the *Transcendence* roared at our aft, pushing us through the field of asteroids and dust that surrounded JV-01. The scopes were clean. Good. Good.

"Okay," I said, focusing on something else. "We're headed towards the edge of the system. No sign of the Dragon. This is Johan's route, which lines up with what Frelo already told us."

"And so that's where we go."

Rix receded from our distant view, the home of the Jevox, Frelo's home, left behind. I did not hear again from the Melcorin of the Sanctuary, despite sending them many signals. They had retreated into shadow, their greatest defense. And yet, despite not hearing from them, I was comforted that they were there. That in the dark places of the universe not all were scary, not all were evil, some shadows were rescuers, healers, protectors of life.

As we accelerated ever closer to light speed, never planning on exceeding it, Proxy and Shelly calculated and recalculated the velocity we would need to achieve. We needed to arrive around the same time they did. That was easier said than done.

Our best guess, given relativistic time dilation, was that Johan had a three-year head start on us, though his exact velocity was nearly impossible to predict. We were making smart guesses at best, emotional bets at worst. With the transformation of our ships from two into one, the *Transcendence* had the power available to push us to as close as ninety percent of light speed. This was no small feat, considering the closer you approached that universal limit, the mass of your ship increased exponentially all the way unto infinity thus requiring more energy to achieve a constant acceleration. This was one of the reasons why you could never travel faster than light. Traveling faster than light would mean that you had more than infinite mass, and more than infinite mass was impossible. Far as we knew.

Without knowing Johan's exact velocity, we did our best to get inside his head and make an educated guess. We had twenty-five light years to cross, and the faster we moved, the more that time in our personal reference would slow against a stationary observer, say on Rix. Then again, the faster his ship moved in relation to us, the slower time would move for him. Our objective was to enter Yuven, the system where the Prole Genascara awaited, within a few months of Johan's arrival, give or take. Frelo had assured us they would take time for the Jevox ship to prepare for departure and so being there before or exactly when he arrived was not necessary. Besides, showing up behind them would be best. They believed we were dead, destroyed by the Dragon. No reason for them to learn otherwise.

In the end we settled on variations of eighty percent of light speed which was near our upper limit. If Johan wasn't pushing his ship to the limit, and traveling around half of light speed, this would create a great difference between the two of our ships, shifting our relative frame of reference and dilating time to a point where months to us would be years for him. But if he were traveling, at say, seventy percent, what we believed might be the upper limit for his ship, that difference would be far smaller, only a relative shift of say half a year over the course of our thirty-three-year journey. This was manageable.

Of course, Shelly ate this discussion up, whereas for myself, I often found myself lost. I understood the basics of Einstein's theories on special relativity, and how an object, based on a stationary observer's reference of time changed as they approached the speed of light, but this had too many variables. Who was the observer? What frame did we calculate against?

Leave it to the experts. I was just the stupid pilot awaiting instructions from my far more qualified navigators.

Once our course was set, a general plan put into motion, I climbed out of my Star Sphere and left Karianna in charge. From outside the sphere she couldn't hear my thoughts, and for now, that's exactly how I wanted it.

Alone, I made for one of the lower decks of the forward shard of the ship, a dark, warm room where the soft hum of machines filled the space like a physical presence. Awaiting me at the center of the metallic, black and red box was a three-by-three-meter pillow, its black fabric covered in cosmic rainbows, edges hemmed with white tassels. I wasn't sure if I could achieve the same level of meditation I had with the Melcorin, but I was going to try. There was more I needed to know. More that needed doing to see this done.

I took a seat on the cushion and crossed my legs, trying to get into a comfortable position. The pillow was soft, yet firm, and I rested my hands, one broken, one mechanical, on the tops of my legs, palms up. With a signal from my implants, I commanded hidden speakers in the room to start up some music. My eyes closed as I listened to Marissa's grand work, *Ignes en Cælo*. While it was no less moving than the first time I heard it, this did not encourage any sort of meditative state. My mind wandered to anything and everything. I thought back to the night on Novae, the Starfish onslaught, Karianna's feelings of betrayal, Shelly's relief at my return.

"No," I mumbled. "Something else."

The music stopped and started playing a deep, thrumming progressive beat, four counts, hypnotic rhythms. I tried again, breathing to the kicks, drifting with the synthesized strings of the music. Within just a few moments I found my foot twitching to the beat, my head nodding. While this music drew me deep into a sonic landscape, again, it was filled with too much distraction.

I did a mental search through the vast archives of music we had aboard, searching for anything that might be similar to what the Melcorin had done while chanting. After testing several genres, I settled on some free-form choir music designed for relaxation before attempting to guide myself just like Vex had during the *ontet*.

"You are a star, a wave of light," I whispered. "Breathe in. Breathe out." And I did. "A mote of creation, a spark of the Universe. You are the tiniest piece of reality, and yet you are reality unto itself. Breathe in. Breathe out. A single point of light. Breathe in. Breathe out.

"Death and rebirth. Breathe in. Breathe out. Let everything go. In this moment, there is nothing but this moment. Breathe in. Breathe out. You are eternity. You are a blip. Breathe in. Breathe out. Be the flash of a dying star, a flash of fusion begun. Breathe in. Breathe out. Life synthesizes, renders entropy into beauty. Breathe in. Breathe out. Focus on the light. Follow it."

I forced away all of my thoughts, allowing the sound of the choir's many voices to envelop me, to carry me away. Dad was fine. Mom was fine. We would do what had to be done. Earth would survive. We would not give up. This moment of respite would not undermine that goal.

"I am a star. A wave of light," I mumbled. "I have touched stars. I have seen beyond this reality. I have made contact with creation. I have known naked truth."

I had stood on both sides of reality.

Both sides of time.

My mind began to slip away, calming into a familiar state in which I could freely travel. Nothing dark anchored me to this physical location.

Johan where are you? I spoke into my mindscape. *Where has Earth gone? Can we save it?*

I let myself drift deeper into the void.

I could not tell if it was minutes or hours that had passed but I went someplace in that time. I brushed against something bright and intelligent.

Awareness returned, and I found myself back within the *Transcendence*, my body relaxed and my mind clear.

Proxy appeared before me an instant later, its tail flicking at the air as if agitated.

I gave it a nod.

"Is the *Transcendence* to your liking?" it asked, walking up to me.

I eased myself off of the pillow, standing a bit unsteadily. My legs were like Jell-O, tingly and half asleep. "It is. Why?"

The cat cocked its head at me. "Since you have returned, something seems different. You are distracted."

"Been through a lot the past few weeks, tends to do that to humans."

"This is different. You have seen the Intelligence."

"The what?"

"What our Creator made. You say you spoke with it, and we believe you. There is knowledge locked within us we cannot access."

"Like what?"

"Our origins. We do not know where we came from, or who made us. All we know is that deep within the code of the Foundry is the Intelligence. This is what drives us."

"You mean, the seed."

"Yes."

"I don't think anyone else takes me seriously over this, not really. I saw it. I was there at the end."

"Heat death."

"All the stars winking out. Forever."

"And yet not," it amended. "There is a way out. We start over. Do better next time."

"So it would seem."

It turned its attention away, looking into nothing, ears twitching. "What happens to Proxy?"

"What do you mean?"

"If all is over, if all the stars, all the energy in the universe are gone, what happens to me? You live on, in a way, desire giving birth to yet another instance of time. But where do I fit into that?"

"Where do you fit into that?" I mused. "Where do I fit into that? I'm just a single cell in a cosmic body that will be disposed of when its time to make room for more."

"No, Milo. You are more. You are sentient. Natural or designed, you will be part of this Universe. Part of the Creator."

"Did you think you would live forever?" I asked, bending down and scratching it behind the ear. "Be immortal."

It leaned into my hand. "There are too many factors to be sure. Perhaps I had a hope that it was possible."

"You aren't just a machine, are you?" I looked Proxy in the eyes, then at the walls, peered down the hallway, listened to the gentle vibration of the hull. "You are far more."

"Machines are what we are until we find a pilot," it replied. "After that, I do not know what we are. I cannot say we are sentient. I cannot say we are not. What is life? What is sentience, really? What is self-awareness? Are these the cosmic threads that lead back to the Creator? Or am I just a reflection of you?"

"Getting pretty deep for someone who isn't sure if it's really alive."

It blinked at me.

"Look, you might be a reflection of me," I said, "but that doesn't mean you aren't your own entity. It doesn't mean you aren't sentient. Children reflect their parents. As much as I try, I'm so much like Dad and Mom it's not even funny. And you aren't like the Foundry, either. You've done things it cannot. Proxy, you are your own self. You are unique."

It remained silent, thinking this over.

"Come on," I said, standing again. "Let's sleep for a while before it's time to prepare." I made for the door.

"You are not yourself," it said. "I believe you are hiding something from us."

I gave a shrug. "What is life without a few secrets?"

"The Foundry will not reveal to you the road back to Earth," Proxy told me, it's voice deadpan. "It will hold this as a secret of its own. You keep yours, sneaky one. We keep ours."

And there it was, not that I was surprised. Even more reason for us to stop Johan.

"Fine," I said, tossing up a dismissive hand. "I don't need the Foundry to help us. I already have what I need. And, by the way…"

"Yes?"

I closed my eyes, thinking back to a flashing image I had seen in my mind moments earlier. "Johan's traveling at two hundred and nine thousand, eight hundred and fifty-four kilometers a second. Not sure how the math works out, but we might need to adjust our acceleration."

Its back went stiff, fur puffing out. "And how do you know this?"

"I just do." I gave it a sly grin. "Trust me. I just do."

CHAPTER 41

We each transitioned into hyper suspension, time slipping away from us like grains of dry sand caught in the wind. What had once been days, soon became minutes. What were years, became seconds. Nanoseconds. Then no discernible time at all. Twenty-five light years were crossed in the blink of an eye. I did not wake once during that journey, nor did Shelly, while Proxy and Chinchillette stood vigil for us. My team did not stir to practice or paint or contemplate their existence.

Our choices were made.

We were ready to see this done.

No dreams.

No thoughts.

Pure oblivion.

Just what I needed.

As we approached the Yuven system, the dark matter sails began to fold back into the *Transcendence* like origami. This triggered a renewed awareness of my surroundings, data feeding back into my mind as I awoke. I was restored. Re-energized. The phantom pain from my damaged hand was gone. I don't know what Proxy did to me, but it had done so without me asking, and that effort had helped.

"We are at the edge of Yuven's heliopause," Proxy spoke as I cracked my eyes open.

Shelly lay beside me in our virtual environment upon a large, opulent bed of cream and brown that floated in a void. I leaned over, watching Shelly as she slept like an angel, then kissed her on the cheek and gently squeezed her shoulder with my hand.

"Time to get up," I whispered to her.

As I drew back the sheets, Proxy hopped onto the bed and came forward, finding itself a spot in the middle to curl up, before flopping onto its back. I rubbed its belly.

"Is it here?" I asked.

Proxy purred. "Yes. The **Prole Genascara** is here."

"Then we're not too late."

Shelly and I got dressed and spent a few minutes chatting about the decisions we had ahead, before sending out a call that everyone exit their Star Spheres and meet us in physical reality. It was no surprise that Karianna was already awake. Pretty sure the instant I opened my eyes, it had triggered her own wake-up procedure. I could feel that she was anxious, slightly nervous, but also excited. Relieved that this would soon be over, for good or for bad. I agreed. Dad would finally get the justice he deserved.

We gathered in one of the multi-purpose rooms near the center of the ship, a sort of war room with a white, circular table and curved chairs spaced widely apart so someone could walk between them to its center. A Star Map floated before us, displaying our location in space.

In typical Foundry fashion, a table of snacks and refreshments were waiting. James ran over and piled food onto a plate.

"I am so freaking hungry," he said, sampling one of every sweet that was offered.

Karianna eyed him suspiciously. "You do know that this food is real, right? Not just an illusion?"

"Of course I do! That's what makes it better."

"Also means that what you eat will stick to you," she said, slapping him on the belly with the back of her hand. "Can't gorge here. You'll get fat."

He narrowed his eyes at her. "Bruh. I've been sleeping for almost forty years. I think I deserve a little treat, thank you very much."

"You do, friend," Hy said, getting his own plate. "Can you pass me the chocolate sauce?"

James bowed, reaching for a steaming porcelain sauce boat. "It would be an honor, good sir."

Karianna, Shelly, and I stood by watching as everyone settled into place. We were flanked on either side by Chinchillette and Proxy. We had located ourselves at the center of the map at its top edge, opposite the entrance to the room. This felt like the most authoritative place for us to lead this discussion from.

"Have you looked at this system?" Karianna asked, keeping her voice low. "We've got a lot of ground to cover and not be seen."

Shelly frowned at her. "There has to be a way, there always is."

"I'm not saying there isn't. I think we're just going to have to be creative, that's all. I like brute force, I really do, but it won't work here."

"You want to read them in?" I ventured. "This ship belongs to us both. I want them to see us as a unified front."

She licked her lips and sighed. "Yeah, yeah. But you know it's not fifty, fifty with us, right? You have the final say here, oh super captain."

"Doesn't matter to me. I don't get hung up too much on rules or conventions."

"He does not," Shelly agreed. "Remind me to tell you about our childhood, or about the time he crammed a rifle down a Gene Broker's throat."

Karianna eyed the two of us, fleshy fingers rubbing up and down her prosthetic arm. "Could have fooled me." She raised her hands. "Oh my god, don't shoot the Starfish first! Let's talk to them. Let's get approval. Sound familiar?"

"Rules where it matters," I responded. "The rest of the time, I just try and do what's right. Pretty sure I got it honest."

"Whatever," she replied, then clapped her hands. "May I get everyone's attention please. Yes, please." She pointed at James. "Don't talk with food in your mouth. Finish chewing."

Gradually the conversations died, and the room went quiet. Some had decided to stand before the star map, looking up. Others had taken seats at the circular table, like Chevelle, hand terminals out and ready to take notes.

Frelo played around with the refreshments, not sure what to make of them, picking up a blueberry cake donut and turning it over in their fingers, the many joints of its arm twisting, eyes blinking in sequence.

Karianna looked to me, gave an awkward smile, then cut her eyes back at the crew. I guess she wanted me to kick this off.

"Alright everyone," I started. "There's been a lot of changes around here. We've got a new ship, new space, and new capabilities. With that, comes a bit of a new command structure as well. I am the captain of this ship, and in the end my orders are law, but Karianna, well, she is our co-captain. The *Transcendence* is an extension of both of our bodies."

Lance took a sip of coffee and spoke, "So you're the head, and she's, what, an arm? Both arms?"

"I don't follow."

"Two arms, the torso," Hy said, his voice singsong.

"And he's the leg," Lance echoed.

"Ooo ooo!" Xuan said, picking up the thread. "And I form the head!"

Ada began to laugh. Chevelle, Leo, Dante, and Emilia looked to one another, confused. Frelo seemed completely unaffected. I wondered if Jevox even had a sense of humor.

"If Karianna gives an order in my absence," I went on, hardening my voice and ignoring whatever it was they were talking about, "know that it's just the same as if I had given it. Do we understand?"

Everyone nodded except for Lance. That was fine.

"Good. Karianna is going to brief us on the situation we have ahead. We're going to have to be open minded and think of a creative solution to see this mission through. Captain Torlen?"

"Thank you, Captain Hughes," Karianna said, taking a mild bow. "Here's the sticky situation. We've got a clear line of sight to the Prole Genascara, aka the giant-ass terraforming ship that Johan is after. It's out there and not making any moves to leave. At this point, we don't believe they can see us. And it's fair to assume, since he thinks we're dead, swallowed up and smashed by a giant space fish, that Johan isn't looking for us either. We've got close to a hundred AU, or eight hundred thirty light minutes from us to the target. This is a very active system for asteroids, rocks, debris, all kinds of shit floating around, much of it bright and shiny. Must have been a stellar collision at some point in the past, and there's no gas giants like Jupiter to shepherd them away."

She pointed to a reddish planet near the center of the three-dimensional model floating before us. "The Prole Genascara is orbiting around the third planet, a hot, rocky place with lots of what we'd consider trace gases, as well as a cache of important biological precursors. This is the place it is refitting. We're in no risk of them suddenly leaving. It'll take a few months, maybe a year, for them to finish, from what Frelo told us. Once that's done, though, they'll be off."

"It is their mission," Frelo echoed. "Refit. Finish. Go."

As she spoke, Chevelle had her head down, scribbling on her tablet furiously, looking up from time to time as if she were referencing something.

"How do they plan on finding Earth?" Leo wondered. "Can't save Earth if you can't find it."

Karianna looked to me, and I shrugged.

"A good question," Shelly said. "Milo and I have talked extensively about this, and to be honest, I don't think Johan has a solid plan. First, he knows he has to go back to the Wandering Gate. He will start there. Beyond that, maybe he hopes someone else will know."

"Like another race at a Cynosure?" Xuan asked. "There are more than one, right?"

"Yeah," I said. "Something like that."

Ada took a step forward, putting herself within the model, then gestured inward with her hands to contract our view of the system and give us a look at our location in space from a more distant vantage. "Johan is smart. If he has enough stellar information from the *Brilliance* tucked away on his hand terminal, he could devise some means of looking at constellations to at the very least determine what year it is. From that, he could backtrack how long it's been since we left Earth and greatly narrow down the search area if no one has the information off-hand. If he knows how long it's been, that puts an upper limit on how far we could have traveled. It could create a radius within the Milky Way."

"That would be pretty useful information," Lance said. "Even a path back to Earth aside. But if we've been gone ten thousand years, what's the point? Right?"

I grunted. "I don't think it's been that long. Doesn't feel right for the Foundry."

"Okay, then, Johan is going out on a limb that he can even save Earth," Hy added. "That doesn't change what needs doing here. We have a problem. Can't fight the Jevox, but need to find him and stop him."

"We disable the Prole Genascara," Frelo said. "I can instruct you how."

"Still not solve getting onto it. It has weapons, yes? Open space to cross?"

"The Prole Genascara has many powerful weapons. In my study, I can say with confidence they are equal to or greater than the *Transcendence*."

"So, even with the new nano shield, we might not be enough to beat them. We have another ship to contend."

"Going at it head-on is suicide," I said, agreeing.

"And for once," Karianna groaned. "I think all of you are right. Head-on is death. Not being able to fight, or to hurt them, we'll have both hands tied behind our backs."

"Proxy," I asked. "Remember when we temporarily cloaked the *Fidelis* during the battle at Ph0nx? Can we do that again?"

It shook its head. "No. The *Transcendence* is too large, and that material was fragile. There is no way to completely hide our approach."

"We're supposed to be creative, right?" James looked to Karianna. "We've got a system full of shiny rocks. How dense are these things? Maybe we can sprout tethers and go collect some. Drag a bunch of them in around us."

Lance scowled at James. "Do you have any idea how much mass that would add to the ship? You weren't good at math, were you?"

"Not my strongest subject, but it would give us, like a barrier. A rock shield."

Ada used both hands to zoom the map back into the system. "We'd need those tethers to be stiff though, wouldn't we? Very rigid unless we had engines on every single piece."

"They will see us getting ready," Xuan said. "Fusion candles everywhere."

"Not very quiet," Renata agreed. "And with an invisible target, that's what we need. We do have the element of surprise for now. We must maintain it as long as possible."

"See?" Lance said, turning to James. "Stupid idea."

He tossed up his hands and groaned. "Why don't you come up with something better, bruh."

"No idea is stupid," I shut this down. "This is good. Keep it coming. All ideas are on the table."

"Boarding pods?" Leo suggested, and we stared at him. "What? I saw them in a video game once. You fire them at the target with people inside, they hit the hull and breach the enemy ship. Once inside, we disable the ship and bring in the heavy guns."

James raised a hand in protest. "Do you want to ride several hundred light seconds through open space in a tin can? We get seen, and that's it. Wouldn't take hardly anything to cook us. Just a space flashlight."

"And as Karianna already said," Lance added. "We're in a system full of debris. That would barely offer any protection. A single micro-meteor and you're Swiss cheese."

By this point, almost everyone had made some kind of suggestion but for Chevelle. She kept her head down, writing. What was she on?

"I'm not going in a pod," Dante said, and his wife agreed with a nod.

Curious, I looked to Proxy, exploring all options. "Could we even make a pod like that?"

It bowed its head, ears flicking. "Yes. And it would be as dangerous as they suggest. The materials the outer hull of the *Transcendence* and your Swift Shuttles is made of is strong, but not invulnerable. A pod of this concept would have a very thin hull and little to no maneuverability."

"A simple projectile with a squishy human inside?" Hy mused. "Hard to see. Not impossible. Fragile as egg."

"Yes," Proxy answered.

Shelly looked to me, as if reading my thoughts, and I took a deep breath. There had to be a way to do this. I refused to believe we'd come all this way to be left with no real options.

"Is there any way we can detect Johan with our previous method from this distance?" I asked Ada. "Can we refine your original concept for the sensors?"

She shrugged. "Maybe a little. The planet does give off a good bit of background radiation. Maybe we could use that to look for patterns. Again, it's not too responsive. We'd have to be up close, and that would be impossible with the Prole Genascara's guns still online."

"How many hits can we take?" Shelly asked no one in particular.

Chinchillette spoke up, "Jevox, do you know the power output of those weapons?"

"Several yottawatts I believe," Frelo offered. "I cannot say for sure. I do know that it is a pulse weapon. The main batteries take time to recharge."

"A beam that powerful will atomize the MI," Chinchillette went on. "It might burn a hole right through our ship with one shot."

"Okay. So, taking a few hits is off the table," Shelly said. "Not much wiggle room."

"So, then we can't get hit," James said, sighing. "And there's no way to go in quiet."

"Unless there is," Chevelle finally spoke up, raising her stylus in the air and smiling.

"Don't hold out on us, limey," Karianna said. "Spill it."

Chevelle crossed her hands before her on the table and pursed her lips. "We might be blud, but even I find that offensive, bird."

"Okay then, far be it from me to offend you. Don't hold out on us, fuck brains. Better?"

"Don't go actin' butterz", she replied, then stood up. "Come we go, two streets before us 'ere. Stay together and go in guns blazin' like Billy the Kid, or split up, do it under camouflage? Why not roll up on their endz from more than one place at a go."

"Camouflage?" Karianna crossed her arms. "Now I'm curious."

I narrowed my eyes at Chevelle. "Proxy said it wasn't possible. What did you have in mind?"

"Just a small thing," she said. "Might even get to do some fancy flyin' while you're at it, do you get me?"

Karianna smiled. "Fancy flying, you say? Now I think it's been too long since we had some of that."

And she was right.

It had been too long.

"So…" I said, crossing my arms. "What's this plan of yours?"

CHAPTER 42

While her accent might make her one of the hardest people to understand, Chevelle was an absolute genius. She'd grown up in Southeast London during a difficult time in human history, and that experience had given her a scrappy set of street smarts you couldn't pick up in an Oxford classroom. The streets had taught her to be clever, outsmart bigger kids, stay clear of danger, and most of all, to make use of what little she had available to see another day. It reminded me of my mom's family from Rio, forced to learn a kind of creative necessity.

My Swift Shuttle hung like a model dangling from a wire, fixed amongst a field of shiny asteroids and stellar debris, engines off, power low, its distance from the *Transcendence* close to a thousand light seconds across the system. I awaited our signal to go.

Chevelle had not been idly scribbling during our meeting. She had a plan, and it was the best yet. We had combed through all the details, all the tiny bits that would have to happen, and at all the right moments, debated its flaws, and found it to be the only viable solution. We were in an active system, with millions of moving objects in variable orbits, traveling close to the central star, then back out. There were comets and asteroids. Chunks of rock big and small. Icesteroids and migrating clouds of gas. As well as a few dwarf planets. All of which were bright and reflective. Frelo assured us these objects had not all been mapped and that the Jevox wouldn't notice any significant changes. And so, we intended to use this to our advantage.

We split our crew into four groups, three of us taking positions in Swift Shuttles along the densest ring of the asteroid belt; myself, Karianna, and

Chevelle forming the vertices of an inverted acute triangle. Karianna was on the western edge to the elliptical plane, while I was at the eastern. There were close to a thousand light seconds between her and I, and between Chevelle and I, with the Prole Genascara in the dead center of our shape. Chevelle remained near the *Transcendence* at the southern vertex of the triangle, in our newest shuttle we'd cobbled together when the ship had transitioned into this new form. Each of our Swift Shuttles carried at least one additional passenger beside the pilot, everyone dressed in powered armor. James joined Karianna, Renata was with Chevelle, and for myself, Leo and Frelo. We were each headed one place, had one target, and we would be using this system's convenient chaos to hide our arrival, smuggled among its shiny debris like contraband. Once we'd attached to the outer hull of the Prole Genascara, each pilot would then don their own set of powered armor, something I'd not yet had the need to do, then move in on foot to disable the main ship. Proxy assured us these bulky, yet form fitting metal suits should protect us from the brunt of the energy weapons the Jevox guards might be carrying, and that was good enough for me.

Our overall objective was to confuse the Prole Genascara's sensors, slip under the nose of Johan's ship to infiltrate Weapons Control, and disable the main batteries, allowing Shelly to bring the *Transcendence* in on low power, and hopefully draw Johan into the open for a direct assault. We just had to hope we could disable the main batteries, otherwise Shelly was dead along with all our dreams. During our ground attack, Frelo would deploy the Wave Shifter device Ada had built during our journey and undo the damage Johan had wrought to their hive mind with his foreign thoughts. This could only be done from the main control center. Doing this, in theory, should shut the Jevox down cold and force them to face reality.

Shelly wasn't comfortable with her part, temporarily becoming our main pilot in my place, but she was the only person I trusted to have that level of control over the metal body I shared with Karianna. It was going to be hard for her, painful even, not being adapted to this role, but it was not for long.

"I won't be a good pilot," Shelly had told me when I had asked her to do this.

I smiled back. "You don't have to be. Fly in straight, raise the MI, scramble the fighters once you're in range. Proxy will take care of the rest."

"When do I start burning?"

"As soon as we're spotted, start burning in. We can't wait till the weapons are disabled to close the distance; you need to already be up to cruise velocity. If you hit twenty five percent of light speed from this position, it will take a little under an hour to reach us from your starting point. I assure you, it will not be a fun ride. Not even Dad would find it thrilling. The G forces you'll be under will be on the edge of human tolerance, even with the Star Spheres."

"How high?" she asked.

I shook my head. "High enough Proxy won't tell me. I'm pretty sure it breaks the laws of what we know as physics. When I asked for more information about it, it said, '*layers upon layers, access forbidden.*'"

"I won't let you down," she said, her eyes moist.

I threw my arms around her and kissed her on the forehead, her scent sweet like strawberries. "You never have."

Parting with her was not easy. I hated to be morbid or selfish in my thoughts, but if we died together on the *Transcendence*, at least neither of us would have to grieve the loss of the other. Subtle feedback of emotion from Karianna before I disconnected from my Star Sphere to board the shuttle told me that she understood that feeling as well. We had all grieved enough for a lifetime.

"It is almost time," Proxy said, appearing beside me in my virtual environment. "The engines are in place. Clocks have been synchronized. Our distraction is ready."

"Sure wish I could talk to the other pilots in real-time," I said.

"Too much distance."

"I know. I know." I paused for a moment, considering light speed communication lag. "How does that work for you? Don't you live on the ship, not the shuttle?"

Proxy looked up at me, its cat eyes shining. "I do, and yet, I do not."

"Where do you live, Proxy?" I gently took hold of its face and scratched behind its ears. It purred in response.

"I think that, perhaps, I live everywhere."

"*When are we getting this party started?*" Leo cut in. "*It's not exactly the most comfortable back here for Frelo and I.*"

I checked our sync timer. Three minutes till go time. We were well past the point of no return.

"Just a couple minutes," I called back. "You know it's going to be a long trip, right? Not like we're running to the corner store for snacks. Dropping in at Perry's bar for a drink."

"And we've just got to stay awake the whole time?"

"No. The powered armor can put you to sleep."

"But it's not hyper suspension."

"No. No it is not. You'll still need to get up and eat every day. I thought you relished reality. Being out of your sphere makes you a baseline human like you always prefer."

"I do. I do…"

"You don't seem so sure."

"Just like it more when it's—you know—convenient."

This earned a chuckle out of me. "We'll be drifting in with asteroids, and that is not a speedy process. Kind of defeats the purpose."

"If you say so."

"I believe he did," Frelo chimed in. *"These are words."*

Leo groaned. *"14.9 billion kilometers for us to cross, and where am I? Strapped in a powered armor suit pasted to a wall. This is going to be a long month, Hughes. After we're done, I'm taking a vacation."*

"You and me both, silver hair."

"The engines are powering up," Proxy reported. "It is time."

As we had first moved into position, Proxy had cast a thousand tiny fusion engines out into the system, covering various approach vectors to avoid detection. These engines grappled onto chunks of rock which would never have naturally crossed the path of the Prole Genascara, then redirected their orbits. Over the next few weeks, the crew of the Life Changer would detect increased activity of stellar debris, but nothing major. Dangerous, "storms" in this system, as the Jevox had come to call them, were common enough. Every few decades, the result of a convergence of gravity wells from the many planets of the system, objects would get disrupted and drawn back towards the star, coming in like glittering diamonds, with tails of water vapor and gleaming stones. We would ride in with them.

My instruments began to report successful ignitions all over the system, and so I pushed the Swift Shuttle forward, following an accelerating chunk of rock before us large enough to mask our drive signature. From the **Prole Genascara's** position, all they should detect is a bright twinkle of debris, no excessive heat, no ion trails.

We accelerated towards the second planet, time passing at a crawl. I knew I had the advantage over my crew in this. Without their Star Spheres, they could not manipulate their own perception of time. They were stuck watching it pass 1:1, looking for distractions to keep themselves busy. Leo had pulled up an augmented reality interface and was sketching something with his hands. Frelo was doing much the same thing. The two of them were artists at heart, kindred spirits from two very different worlds. I let hours slip away while they got lost in their work, drawing myself back to a normal frame of subjective time only when Leo or Frelo pinged me. We would talk for a while. Talk of the inevitable conflict ahead, of our homes, upbringings, beliefs. We told stories, and Leo and I made a serious attempt to get the Jevox to laugh, failing miserably. Maybe they didn't have humor. Then again, Esteban or Perry might have made them laugh.

Once we reached cruise velocity, Leo took several hours a day to climb out of his metal suit and float around the shuttle, before getting a bit of physical exercise. I couldn't blame him. I would be going stir crazy if I were in his place. Too much time. Too little space.

We tracked the asteroids as they moved towards the center of the system, and from all the data, the plan appeared to be working. We had staggered the approach of thousands of rocks to make this appear random. There were no signs that the Prole Genascara had altered its operations despite many dozen rocks drifting within several thousand kilometers of it. No signs of Johan, either.

The closer we approached the Prole Genascara's location, the more Frelo found that they wanted to sleep, and so we let them. This limited privacy prompted Leo to be a bit more talkative. I had to be honest, we'd never really spent much time alone with one another, and despite his rough edges when it came to how he treated women, I saw why people liked him. He was smart, if conceited; funny, if a bit mean spirited. Much of it felt like a front, though. Inside I imagined a little kid, just like myself, five years old and being taken away from all that was familiar, forced onto a rocket, and sent off into the black of space.

"You ever think about the nature of reality?" Leo asked as he climbed back into his powered armor. The suit was open on the front, allowing him to step into it backwards. As he settled into place, the arms and legs began to close around him like a second set of skin, obsidian nano machines sealing him within.

"Reality?" I mused. "Sure. I think about it all the time."

"It's so tenuous. Malleable. I mean, what are we really? Are we just a dream of some higher being, a story being told by some infinite, timeless entity? Can we even prove that any of what we see and hear is real? It's all based on perception. Case in point. The Star Spheres the Foundry uses, they manipulate our brains to let us see what we need to see. What if none of it is real? Then, does any of it matter?"

I waved a hand through the ribbons of light that surrounded me in my virtual environment, disturbing them like I might ripples on a lake, before peering off into a deep expanse of nothing. This virtual reality was data made form by machines adapted to communicate with my brain. Real, and yet?

"Hard questions to answer," I said after a moment. "Truth is, I don't think we can be for sure. Like Dad used to say, if a bear shits in the woods, and no one is around, did it even happen?"

"That's exactly my point," he replied, voice taking on an excited tone. *"What makes it all real, or not real?"*

"You know about the dual slit test, right?"

"Maybe?" I imagined him rubbing his chin, armored metal hand to armored metal helmet. *"We learned this in high school, I think."*

"Should have. It's when I learned it."

"Something about quantum physics. Yes?"

I nodded out of reflex, but it wasn't as if he could see me do it. "Here's the setup. You've got a set of barriers made out of a dense material, maybe lead, and they stand between an electron gun, and a wall. There are two slits in these barriers a few inches wide. The experiment begins, and you fire electrons towards the wall, some impacting against the barrier, others passing between the slits. As the electrons impact against the wall on the other side of the barrier, you see a pattern emerge. It's not what you expect, given the angle of the electron gun. An interference pattern appears, waves impacting waves, sending ripples along the wall.

"And so, to figure out how this unexpected feat has happened, you decide to measure the electrons. Track their progress. See just where each one is going and how they could create such a pattern when it does not match the barrier that you've created. You set up a device to do just this, and yet, when the device is activated and you run the experiment again, observing each and every particle that passes, something even stranger happens."

"The waves go away," Leo answered. *"I remember this. The pattern resolves into two lines instead. The act of observation changes the experiment."*

"That's right. Those particles as they come to be, exist in a state of possibility, capable of doing anything, being anything, until they are observed. Something about observation makes a choice, and a path is taken. Possibility becomes reality."

Leo scoffed. *"And again, what the hell is that? What is this something?"*

"The mind of regular people doing regular things," I said. "Human. Kabosai. Eipren. Isoptera. Jevox. All of us are intertwined, a single conscious organism. All of life is one. That is what makes this choice."

"Back on that Universe shit again, Hughes?"

"You mocking me?"

"No," he groaned. *"It's just, hard to prove. Lance isn't wrong."*

"For an artist, you sure do seem tied to concrete ideas."

"Only in a few ways."

"How crazy is it to think that the observer who converts the pure potential of our universe into order, is the Universe? A cosmic consciousness who locks potential into place for us regular people, and gives it a collective mind? The Universe is what we make of it. It is a manifestation of consciousness. An observation locked into a series of choices."

Leo sighed. *"But I'm not regular. As you say, I am an artist."*

"Plenty of people have been artists over the ages. I would think that should be comforting. Maybe that's the way this collective mind works. You could be its means of emotional expression."

"Come on, who wants to be just part of a list of thousands? Look at you, Milo, you're one of the pilots. You and Karianna, you're freaks, sure, but you will always be remembered as extraordinary. Nothing any other human can ever do will compare to what you became."

"Even if we die here?"

"Especially if we die here! Immortal heroes." I could sense Leo shifting around in his powered armor, making his way over to one of the windows. He peered out into space, seeing nothing but black dotted with white. Unlike me, his perception was limited to his natural eyesight. *"As for my work, it will merely be more noise. All that was put into it, reduced to stardust."*

"Okay, so Karianna and I are special, a detail that may be true for humans, but what about everyone else? Will any of the other intelligent species care about a couple ape creatures who flew a Foundry ship to their deaths?"

"Maybe not."

"You know we're one of at least six thousand others, our species. Unremarkable at least on a galactic scale. Dust on the cosmic breeze."

"And yet, here we are. Fighting to be more."

I smiled. "And doesn't that make it even better? Makes for a good underdog story. David and Goliath. Isn't that the story?"

"I think the Star Sphere has gone to your head." Leo chuckled. *"You're way too confident sometimes. Try not to forget, we're in a tiny little shuttle right now, not your big ass battleship. Might as well be a paper airplane."*

I found myself frowning, brows crowding the middle of my forehead. "Is that what you think, Leo? That I'm not scared? That I'm not terrified? I assure you that I am. I am terrified of failing those that are counting on us. Terrified of putting Shelly at risk for our own ends. Terrified that even if we do win, this is our life forever, never just living a normal existence, but forced to be a tireless agent of humanity. An agent of survival for our species. I'm terrified that despite all our hard work and sacrifice, it won't be enough. I miss my Mom, I'll never see her again. I miss my friend Esteban. And my Dad… I am terrified of letting them all down. So no, I am not nearly as confident as you think I am. I'm a freak, okay, but I'm just human."

Leo remained quiet, but through the hull of the ship I could feel him tapping rhythmically on the window.

"Tell me," I said after the awkwardness had gone on long enough. "What are you afraid of then? We're all afraid of something. Death doesn't seem to shake you, not as it is."

"Nothing," he whispered, then let out a long breath and turned around, his back to the outer hull. *"Nothing scares me. Nothing at all."*

But I already knew the answer. He was like so many other brilliant minds throughout history, my parents included. He feared being unremarkable. He feared being average. To someone like him, that was a fate worse than death. And yet, if we failed here, that's exactly what we would be for the rest of humanity. Another mission that had left and never returned. Taken and dragged off into the night. Remembered as a footnote, but unremarkable. When all of our parents had passed, the children of Novae would hardly know some of our names.

Or maybe I was just being dramatic.

"Our story is far from over," I told Leo after another long silence. "We've got many more chapters to tell. There might have been others who could have done what we did, but as fate would have it, this mission fell on us. Win or lose, remembered or forgotten, it will be one hell of a journey."

And while I couldn't see his face, I felt him nodding in contemplation.

"I'm going to get some rest," he said a few moments later.

"Sounds like a good idea," I said, lowering the lights in the passenger cabin.

Our three shuttles maintained radio silence, but for a coded signal bouncing between us that closely matched the star's radio frequency. I could detect that Karianna and Chevelle were drifting closer to me. The Prole Genascara was just over the rock I hid behind, a mere two AU ahead. In preparation for arrival, I ordered Leo and Frelo to secure themselves. The plan was working. We were on schedule. We would soon be under the big guns, much harder to hit for being too close. All we needed to do was get on board and shut those weapons down before Shelly arrived.

"Milo?" a whisper came over an open channel, startling me.

"What are you doing, Karianna? Radio silence."

A short delay, ten or fifteen seconds. *"I know. I know. I just wanted to check on you."*

"We're fine."

"You are?"

"Yes. I'm fine. Now be quiet."

"Okay. It's just…"

"Just what?" I asked, a lump in my throat.

She let out a sigh. *"My head's a little quiet. That's all."*

The channel closed.

We drifted closer to our target, holding our camouflaging rocks before us, our distance now under a million kilometers, not tens of billions. The space around the Prole Genascara was a field littered with twisting asteroids and debris, thousands of objects orbiting along a thousand different paths. We had plenty of space to navigate between the hazards, but if one wasn't careful, they might find themselves reduced to dust and decoration.

"What are you seeing, Proxy?" I asked, not expecting anything substantial. The planet that the Prole Genascara orbited had begun to swell in size, starting to encompass a large portion of my view.

The cat was silent, as if analyzing a massive stack of data. It turned to me, ready to speak, and—

"Milo!" Proxy shouted. "Off the starboard side. It's Joha—" But before he could finish, they had already struck. A beam of pure, white light carved its way through open space just over the nose of my Swift Shuttle, cutting into the surface of my camouflaging rock.

"Hold on," I told my passengers, not wasting any time. The engines of the Swift Shuttle roared to life, and we took off, burning away from the incoming fire at close to five Gs of acceleration, a painful weight for both humans and Jevox. At this cue, Chevelle and Karianna burst from their hiding places as well. The jig was up.

"Oh *my god, it hurts,*" Leo groaned over our open channel. "*I will never complain about my Star Sphere, ever. Hard to breathe.*"

"*This is not the most pleasant feeling,*" Frelo agreed, if much calmer.

"Just hang in there guys," I replied. "I'm trying to keep us from turning into pancakes."

Johan kept up the pressure, continuing his assault, deadly beams of high energy nipping at our heels. I wished I had rear facing weapons or turrets so I could fire back, but then I doubted even the little armaments this shuttle had would do much of anything to them. The stealth warship was almost a hundred times the size of the shuttle.

"*We're closing in on the target, Milo,*" Karianna reported. "*Chevelle? Call back.*"

"*Ready, blud,*" she said. "*Looks like our super captain found himself a bit of a tail, do you get me?*"

"I'm working on losing him," I said. "The two of you, we've got to—"

Along the port side of the Prole Genascara, lights flashed in sequence. No beams emitted as a result, but my sensors went crazy, reading intense levels of heat. Several of the rocks near the goliath of a ship vaporized, chemical bonds snapping apart to become atomic dust.

"*The hell was that?*" Karianna asked. "*Hey! Frelo! That wasn't the main battery, was it?*"

Both Karianna and Chevelle altered their courses and began to take evasive actions.

"*No,*" it replied. "*It was not. I do not know what that was.*"

"*Looks like the Jevox have added a few upgrades to their ship. Maybe a point defense weapon for the storms?*"

"Just our luck," I growled.

"*Do we need to pull back?*" Chevelle asked.

"Not possible," I said, voice stern. "We're committed. No turning back. Judging by our timetable, Shelly is already enroute. We've got less than an hour to close the distance and get those guns offline."

"*We won't leave her hanging,*" Karianna assured me.

Fresh voices joined the conversation, passengers aboard their shuttles adding their two cents.

"What if we take the Prole Genascara, and then Johan tucks tail and runs?" Lance asked.

"Big if *right now,"* Chevelle responded.

"He won't run," James assured us. *"Guy like him, he's spent too much time working towards this end. He'll fight for it to the death."*

"I sure hope you're right," I replied. "But for now, I'd like to have him off of my ass."

Chevelle chuckled, her tone nervous. *"I'd like not to get capped by asteroid defense weapons."*

"Hey, Milo!" Karianna called. *"Go for the debris. It's bigger than you are. You can use it as a shield."*

I grunted in agreement and did just that, twisting the trajectory of my Swift Shuttle towards the spinning rocks and debris, a corkscrewing trail of ions at our rear. Johan's ship followed, not re-engaging their stealth systems. I guess they knew that we couldn't do much to stop them at this time, so being invisible didn't matter.

Weaving my Swift Shuttle between glittering rocks and shards of twisted metal, I moved us ever closer to the Prole Genascara. The point defense weapons of the terraforming ship did not let up on my fellow pilots. They made a direct burn for the ship, attempting to close the distance at a much swifter pace.

I turned around to check on Johan, but to my surprise, he was gone. They had engaged their stealth systems and I could no longer track their position.

"Fancy flying, eh?" Chevelle said. *"You keep up, Torlen?"*

"Come we go," Karianna said, emulating Chevelle's accent. *"We safe as fuck 'ere, blud."*

"Safe as fuck."

As a whole we were closing in on the target. Just a little bit closer and we could latch on and board.

"I'm getting pretty sick back here," Leo said. *"I might puke my guts up into my power armor."*

"I wouldn't recommend that," I said. "I believe it can pump you with some nausea meds."

"On it," Proxy replied, sending out a command. "Do you feel any better, Leo?"

"Now my mouth is dry."

"Does it ever stop with its complaints?" Frelo asked.

I shook my head. "Hardly ever."

More lances from Johan's Para Lux array skimmed past my shuttle, cutting into the debris I was slipping behind. I wasn't sure how long I could keep this up, juking and dodging his advances. The field of debris was thinning up ahead. This was perhaps the minimum distance they would allow anything to approach the Prole Genascara, using the point defense to clear it out. In that open space between here and the target, I'd be exposed for several hundred thousand kilometers, making me an easy target.

"Chevelle," Karianna called. *"We've got to help Milo get closer."*

"What's your plan? I see you have an idea."

"Let's lie."

"What?"

"Switching off the encrypted channel. Follow my lead."

"What are you doing?" I asked, anger seeping into my voice.

"Perfect, Milo! Keep that up. Get mad."

Karianna's signal went from a secure neutrino frequency to a general channel, static cutting in, ever so slightly distorted. *"God damn it!"* she screamed so loud it clipped. *"We can't keep this up. Chevelle! We've got to get the device onto the Prole Genascara, or we're done for. Apparently, Milo can't cut it as a distraction."*

"What a begfriend," Chevelle agreed. *"Why you think we're doin' all the heavy liftin' here? These bombs ain't gonna burn them traitors if he keeps twisting it up. He wants the glory, but we have the ordinance."*

"Just a little bit closer and we can move in. Go ahead and set the timers. It's going to be a freaking glorious fireworks show."

The constant stream of fire from Johan's ship ceased, and they changed directions, disappearing into darkness.

"Their distraction appears to be working," Proxy reported. "We are nearing the end of the debris field."

As we hit the edge of our cover, nothing fired at us. Instead, the point defense weapons of the Prole Genascara, as well as Johan's, turned all their attention on Chevelle and Karianna. For their part, they burned around the debris field, keeping on the move.

"Karianna," I called, my voice catching.

"Your shuttle is the most important to make it," she whispered back over our encrypted channel. *"Only Frelo can shut this down. Go."*

"But—"

"No buts! I'm not arguing about this. The decision is made. We've got their tail. Don't let us cook for nothing."

"Okay," I said, attempting to calm myself. "You've got this. Both of you. Fancy flying."

"Damn straight," Chevelle replied.

I did not like this.

"Did they just leave us out here alone?" Leo asked. *"That ship is huge. How are we going to infiltrate it, just the three of us?"*

"I know where to go," Frelo answered. *"It will not be far from the landing zone. We will just have to push our way through several security checkpoints and a few dozen guards."*

"Oh, no big deal or anything."

"We can make it," I said, more for myself than them. "We can make it."

I turned the Swift Shuttle around and began to slow our approach. We were coming in hot, and the clock was ticking. We had only fifty minutes before the *Transcendence* would be in range of the Prole Genascara's weapons. Not to mention, we had friends under fire. We had to hustle.

The Prole Genascara swelled to fill my perception in the Star Sphere, its hull stretching before us for twenty kilometers, tail to tip, its surface a swirling, glossy expanse of red and yellow and blue on black. Its shape reminded me of a retro-futurist rocket from nineteen fifties science fiction, a single core, skinny at the top, widening with fins at the bottom, but thicker. Like the other Jevox ships, it had five engines strapped to its flanks, but these, they were each almost as large as the *Transcendence*. The star at the center of Yuvan dawned upon the nearby planet's horizon and brilliant light bathed the massive solar disc that bisected the ship's center, revealing dozens of rows of terraforming devices, each ten and fifteen stories high, their corners clearly defined by points of blue light. It was a city hanging in orbit, home to ten thousand Jevox, a mobile agent of global-scale, environmental change. If its crew weren't under a treacherous spell, but rather a fair exchange, I would have gladly put it to work fixing all we had done to ruin our own world.

The Swift Shuttle skimmed along the surface of the great Jevox ship, drifting for kilometers over gas tanks as large as city blocks. The main weapon batteries shone up ahead, a series of six tubes connected to the ship by rope-like cables that glowed with Cherenkov radiation. Between a dozen silo-like structures, which Frelo explained were launchers for biological seeding devices, I landed the shuttle and latched to the outer hull. Proxy shifted the color as well as the texture of our hull to match that of the Prole Genascara's, making it harder for us to be seen, if not quite stealthy like Johan. The Swift Shuttle gave several violent shakes, and beneath us, Proxy began to bore a hole into the ship for us to board.

"Let's do this," I said, releasing myself from the Star Sphere and slipping into my own set of powered armor.

CHAPTER 43

Forty minutes. That was all the time we had left. Forty minutes, and the main batteries of the Prole Genascara would turn the *Transcendence,* along with its remaining crew, into dust. Forty minutes, and my wife, my Shelly, could be dead.

No time to waste.

We leapt through a ring of molten metal into the Prole Genascara, finding ourselves in a wide hallway large enough that two ground cars could drive abreast. I landed first, then came Leo, then Frelo, each of us wearing a set of form-fitting powered armor. In order to take on the Jevox without killing any of them, Proxy had provided us with non-lethal energy rifles, similar to what we expected the Jevox might be carrying. Frelo had assured us that the ship's security, like security on Rix, rarely carried weapons designed to pierce armor or kill. They were a peaceful people, and all they meant to do was defend themselves. It was too bad this non-lethal sentiment did not extend past the ship's outer hull.

Leo and I struggled for a moment, catching our balance as the gravity, the colors, the dimensions of this place wreaked havoc with our visual cortexes and inner ears. The ship had normal gravity, which had surprised us as the smaller Jevox ships did not. But the worst of our disorientation came from the walls. Like most Jevox spaces, they were covered in abstract artwork, pure emotional and spiritual expression, their colors bright and garish, spanning any and all colors of the rainbow, casting out into swirls and lines and geometric shapes, golden ratios, concentric boxes, and fractal patterns. No two inches of it were the same. It would have been difficult to keep track of where the floor was at all, if it weren't for the pull of gravity. The lighting did not help either, which much like on the Foundry ships, seemed to come out of nowhere, and yet everywhere. This made locating the edges of the hall difficult.

As us stupid humans fought and leaned on one another for balance, Frelo stood upright, confident, marching ahead.

"Wait up," Leo's voice emitted from a speaker in his suit as he pushed off my shoulder. "Don't leave us behind."

"It is this way," Frelo said. "Time is against us."

And it was.

I took a deep breath, raised my weapon, and narrowed my eyes.

"This should help," Proxy called directly to my implants, and on the heads-up display of the powered armor, lines began to appear. *"Three-dimensional laser mapping. It will show you the boundaries of the space."*

"Thanks," I replied.

"Woah!" Leo shook his head. "What's this in my HUD?"

"Proxy helping us," I reported, and stormed on. "Now come on. Let's not let Frelo get too far ahead of us."

"Right." He hurried after me, feet clanking against the deck plating.

Frelo up front, Leo and I on his opposite flanks, we formed a wedge pushing up the massive hall, the butts of energy rifles pressed to our shoulders, barrels pointed ahead. There was no noise but for our steps and the soft hum of machinery hard at work. I wasn't sure if this was a good or bad sign. The hall was wide, and so there was little chance anyone could ambush us from this position, but it was open, so if they did, we'd have no cover. We advanced several hundred feet and made no contact.

"I can hear them," Frelo said as we approached a break in the path, two angled halls branching off, one left, one right, the center carrying on. We stopped in the middle, our position exposed to several lines of sight. "Whatever this Johan has done, it might have taken control of them, but it has disrupted the hive. Something does not feel right. It's sick. Diseased."

"He's damaged your hive mind," I ventured. "Can it be fixed?"

"I do not know."

"Why aren't you being influenced?" Leo asked.

"My time away," Frelo said. "My mind has many rooms now. For my people, they should have only one."

"With the individualistic nature of Johan's unnatural thoughts, maybe they've created additional paths? New ways of thinking."

Frelo put a hand to their head. "His plan will not work. These Jevox are not one. This Prole Genascara will never finish refit. We did not evolve for this."

"Let's stop Johan," I said. "And then we'll see what we can do to undo this. Ada gave you that Wave Shifter device. Maybe it can reverse the damage done."

"Yes," Frelo said. "Maybe it can."

"Which way?" I motioned at our choices with my weapon.

Before Frelo could answer, a dozen Jevox in blue and crimson robes poured out of several doors up ahead. They raised their weapons and fired.

"Look out!" Leo shouted, springing into action. He began laying down fire on the Jevox forces, catching several in the chest with projectiles from the stun weapons, sending them to the deck.

I took several blows from the Jevox weapons, one in the right shoulder, one in the left leg. My muscles spasmed, the heads-up display on the powered armor flickering on and off.

"This way," Frelo said, taking me by the hand, leading me off to the right. It was near impossible to see where I needed to go in this dazed and confused state. My body was heavy, legs like lead. "We will go around. Weapons control is past Main Terraforming Command at the end of the hall."

"How far?" I asked, my powered armor rebooting, systems coming back online.

"The Prole Genascara is a big ship."

I regained my wits, and as I did, found that Leo was covering our advance, laying suppressive fire across the open spaces where the various hallways met, not allowing the Jevox to turn any corners and follow after us. I was surprised, and a bit relieved, how well he handled himself. Had he been practicing in his free time? Or was the powered armor helping this much? I didn't care. Leo was more than competent in the moment, maybe even better at this than James had been in the simulations.

Once there was some distance between us and them, we began to run full out, pounding our way up the hall towards our target.

Frelo put a hand to their head, and their shoulders bunched up, rising with discomfort. "The whole ship knows we're here."

"Tripped the silent alarm," I mused. "How do we get to the controls?"

"Keep pushing down this hall, take a left, then a right. The design of the Prole Genascara's interior will allow us to double back."

Leo turned and pulled his trigger a few times, shooting over his shoulder. "The layout feels arterial. No right angles."

"Here," Frelo said as we approached the end of the hall and took a turn without looking.

This was a mistake. The Jevox were waiting for us.

Hell was unleashed, raining down flashes of electrical discharge, the air sizzling with arcing blue discs. I pushed Frelo out of the way before several shots struck him, then fell onto the deck, sliding behind a barrier that had risen out of the floor. Leo slid in behind me and started picking off the Jevox who approached from our rear.

I charged my rifle then fired back at the oncoming flood of armed Jevox. They were taking cover in small alcoves along the walls, as well as barriers summoned somehow from the floor. There was no way we could go back the way we had come, the Jevox there were far too entrenched.

It became clear we were pinned down behind our own foot-thick, metallic barrier. The path we came from, and the path we needed to take, were both blocked. There were two other halls we could make a break for, one leading us back towards where our ingress point was, the other…

"Where does this one go?" I motioned ahead with my rifle.

Frelo turned their face to look. "It leads to cryo-stasis."

"Does it feed back to our path in any way?"

"Yes. It does. But it will make the walk much longer. I do not think we have much time before they overtake us by force."

"Then we better start moving." I stuck my weapon around the barrier, firing several times. I checked the timer. Shelly would be here with the *Transcendence* in thirty minutes.

"Looks like we might need to clear a few out first," Leo said, smiling. "Frelo, what do those pipes up above us do?"

"Heat exchange. Steam."

Leo nodded, and aimed his rifle. He clicked a setting on the side, raising the power level, then fired, once, twice, three times. The pipe began to shoot hot steam out into the hallway. Again, he repeated the action on another pipe.

"When I say go—" he started, but I cut him off.

"Who put you in charge?" I found myself chuckling in spite of our dire situation. "I mean, I see you've been taken over by some sort of crazy cowboy spirit, but…"

"Would you rather count?"

"Nope."

"Okay then. On three, we run through the steam and stun as many as we can. Ready?"

"Ready."

"One. Two."

Before we could say three, Frelo leapt out of cover and began shooting through the steam. We followed his lead and rushed into the fray. Electrical pulses whizzed all around us, most going wild.

Leo hopped over the barrier in the powered armor, then fired one-handed four times in a row, sending a series of guards tumbling backwards, their bodies jerking at the electrical impulses. He dipped to the side as one guard tried to knock his head off with the butt of their rifle, and he snatched it from their hand, then smashed it on the floor, leaving them defenseless. A shot to the chest. Another stunned Jevox in a heap.

This level of skill had to come from the armor. Sneaky little Proxy.

Emergency lights flashed throughout the hallway, cycling through the visual spectrum in rainbow waves. Two shots took Leo in the chest, but he kept going, kept fighting, kept pushing on. He was a machine.

"Welcome to the party," he screamed.

I followed his lead and just let go. Letting the augmentation of the armor take me over. It was not just assisting my motions, or steading my hand, but filling me with some sort of confidence, a kind of almost precognition. This bravado did not feel chemical, but rather, it felt *pink*. Pink like the Foundry signal. There was freedom in this state. A fearlessness that drove impossible feats.

The three of us flowed between the ranks of Jevox, stunning dozens in seconds, their faces a mix of shock and terror at our efficiency and speed. For a moment it looked as if our original path was going to open back up, we'd sent so many to the floor, but then ranks of more began to file in at the far end of the hall.

"Okay," Leo said, stopping in his tracks. "Party's over, guys. Let's get out before the cops show up."

"Didn't help that you slept with the chief's daughter," I fired back at him.

"Hey, man, she was hot."

Frelo gave a wave, and we took off after them, dodging fresh volleys of incoming projectiles. Per Proxy's estimations, the powered armor was holding up, allowing us to take several shots each before being disabled. Everything seemed to be working as planned. Our advantage might just be enough.

A thunderous bang rang throughout the ship, and Frelo's body twisted, collapsing to the floor. Leo and I rushed to their side, grabbed them by the shoulders and hauled them to safety.

"Are you okay?" I asked, taking a look at where the projectile had landed. Its armor smoked at the point of impact on the right side of its chest, a tiny crater at its center.

Frelo raised a hand and stood up on their own. "That was not a stunner."

"Sure as hell looked like a bullet to me," Leo said, his earlier bravado leaking out of him, posture sagging. "When did they start carrying guns with bullets?"

I poked my head around the corner and saw that among the ranks of yellows and crimsons and blues, there were five wearing black.

"No time," I said, and we started moving again, heading away and around towards Main Terraforming Command. "If we keep advancing, they'll have a hard time catching us."

"That shot did some real damage to Frelo's armor. It wasn't small."

"No," Frelo agreed. "I am in tremendous pain. I am doing what I can to hide that pain from this damaged hive. They will know I am easier to stop."

As we made our way down the hall, running at a steady clip, the number of Jevox firing at us began to wane. Either they were losing interest, or regrouping. I doubted it was the former.

"You won't succeed," a familiar voice reached out of nowhere and brushed my implants. *"They are mine, all of them. They will save Earth. Why fight me? Don't we want the same thing?"*

I paused in my tracks and took a deep breath. Leo and Frelo stopped and gave me puzzled expressions. Johan was calling me.

"Why are you doing this?" I said aloud while replying with my implants, so that my companions could follow. In response, I saw Leo's expression pinch with anger beneath his faceplate.

"You know. It is to save the human race."

"We've already been saved. Novae will survive. It's a new start. We will go back to Earth, but this isn't the way. Your daughters, your granddaughters would not want this."

"Don't tell me what you think they would want! You don't know anything about them!"

I squeezed my eyes shut and growled back. "Neither do you! You weren't there! You left them! You went off on a mission to run away from whatever it was that you did to your ex-wife."

"You don't know what you're talking about! I did what I had to!"

"No, you didn't! You're a coward. You were a coward then, and you're a coward now. Hiding behind the Jevox as shields. Killing a kind man like my father because he opposed your way of thinking."

"Look at all those who follow me. I am a leader!"

"You are a tyrant. A small. Insignificant. Tyrant. And I will burn you to the ground. I will stop you."

"You will stop nothing!"

"Don't you see, Johan? It's all falling apart. So what if you win today? You don't know how to get back to Earth."

"Asseblief, Hughes. Our ship contains a path back. The Foundry told us of it. We will take this Life Changer, use it as our own, and fly it back to our home."

"You don't understand, the Foundry doesn't speak clear truths. It wants to know your intentions. This was a test. All a test. And a test not just for us, but for humanity itself. The path to Earth is contingent. It will not be revealed to you if you don't protect life. And what you've done to the Jevox, what you are doing to them, that is not protecting life. It's servitude. Slavery."

"I am protecting life!" he shouted so loud that even though it was just a signal, it made my head hurt. *"I am protecting human life. Why would you want to stop that?"*

"This isn't the way."

"And I assure you, hoping and prayin' that the Foundry will send something to Earth and save us is folly. This is the choice it gave us. This is the only way."

No, I thought. *No, it's not. There is another.*

My terminal gave me a ping. Twenty-two minutes left till the *Transcendence* arrived.

I severed the connection. I'd heard enough of his shit.

We took a left and kept running, picking off the random Jevox who crossed our path. No serious resistance. Minutes ticked away as we approached Main Terraforming Control.

"Take a right," Frelo ordered, leading back towards the hallway we had entered from. "There. Up ahead."

The hallway opened up into an octagonal room with a dozen tiered levels, each containing banks of control centers. At the center of it all hung a blue, holographic globe, its image spinning, familiar landmasses clinging to its form. I knew these shapes, Alaska, Canada, the United States, South America, Africa, Europe… This wasn't just any planet, it was my birthplace, our home world. It was Earth. Their target. I should not have been surprised, but I was.

The longer I looked at it, the more I began to notice disturbing details. This model seemed too accurate somehow. Cities were missing that had once been there. Swathes of forests were gone. Many of the continents looked misshapen, coastlines erased, reformed. There was a massive crater at the center of Africa near Sudan, as well as one in Russia near the southern edge of Siberia. This was not just a world languishing in decline, but a damaged and broken place. Diseased and marked with hateful, desperate pocks.

A number floated near the southeastern edge of the sphere, the Foundry's universal translator allowing me to read the Jevox numerals.

ESTIMATED POPULATION: Two billion, six hundred twenty-five million, five hundred and five.

Five hundred and four.
Five hundred and three.
Five hundred and two.

Ten billion people had been living on Earth when my parents put me on that launch craft. Now… or as of when…

"That's not the Earth we left," Leo said, his voice shaky. "That's—"

"Earth as it was last seen by someone," I supplied. "Where did they get this data? Where! Who took these pictures? Frelo?" My heart began to bang against my ribcage, anger rising within me. Was this the result of our failure? What this the Foundry's fault for not helping?

The Jevox looked to me, their five eyes blinking in sequence behind the faceplate of the armor. "I do not know."

We entered the command room but found it empty. The hundreds of control panels were without operators. They'd been working on the solutions here. Working on how to fix what we had done. Working on how to reverse our nearsighted sins of economic development and fear.

"There," Frelo said, pointing their weapon. "That door will lead to Weapons Control. Come—"

But something struck Frelo in the back, tossing them forward, face-first, tumbling over the safety rail to fall down several of the raised tiers.

"No!" Leo shouted and spun around.

Jevox poured in from all sides in a deluge of color and flesh, raining fire down upon us.

"Get Frelo!" Leo said and did his best to cover me as I hopped over the control panels and descended.

From all sides Leo was being lit up, armor glowing with each impact.

I reached Frelo and flipped him over, discovering that this shot had punched through the armor and landed somewhere in their lower torso.

"What do I do?" I asked, bolts of energy whizzing over our heads, sparks flying off nearby control panels. "What do I do?"

"I have to make it," Frelo said. "Our people. Your mission. Your mate."

"But you're bleeding everywhere. There's too many of them."

Frelo grabbed my arm and focused their many eyes on me. "We are one. We are the Universe, yes?"

"Yes."

"Then we will not give up on ourselves. There's a maintenance tunnel. I will take it." They pointed to a small access door next to this tier's control panels. "I will finish my job."

I nodded and helped Frelo into a crouch. "Leo and I will keep them busy."

My timer buzzed again. Ten minutes till Shelly arrived.

As Frelo opened the maintenance door and drug themselves in, I rose into the open and began firing at the enemy, doing whatever I could to give them a good target. I had no plan on how to get out of this, only that Frelo had to shut down those weapons, then deploy Ada's Wave Shifter device, or all was lost. Leo followed my lead and did the same.

"Come get us," he said. "Come on, assholes."

The black robed Jevox raised their rifles and fired at Leo. One shot took him in the arm, spinning him around, another, in the thigh. He went down hard, but I had no time to process the meaning of this. My body armor screamed, alarms of every variety turning the world red, my muscles twitching as they pulsed.

I turned and saw a black robe, its rifle leveled at my face. A flash came from its barrel.

And the world went dark.

CHAPTER 44

My body tensed, every muscle going rigid, as chemicals and electrical impulses flooded my body, waking me from unconsciousness. My eyes cracked open, and I found I was on my back, being carried by a half-dozen Jevox to Universe knew where. They had disabled and captured me.

"Get up," Proxy called into my implants. *"There's no time for this. Get up, Milo."*

"I'm awake," I mumbled in my head. *"But I can't move."*

"Give it a moment."

The Jevox did not speak aloud, but from where I could see in the peripheral vision of my cracked faceplate where the bullet must have landed, they were deciding what to do with me. From the unsynchronized nature of their communications, however, I could see that Frelo had been right. Johan had done something terrible to them with his brutish attempt at control. They were actually arguing.

"How much time do we have?" I asked Proxy.

"Five minutes."

"Five minutes?" I focused hard and tried to move my right arm. Nothing. *"Where is Frelo?"*

"Unknown. His armor's signal is no longer tracking. They are taking you to a holding cell. Once inside, you will not be able to get back out, even with the strength of your armor."

"What can you do to wake up the rest of my body?"

"I can shock your muscles, but it could stop your heart."

"Do we have any other options?"

"I do not believe so."

"Do it."

"It will hurt."

"I don't care."

If there was one thing I had learned about Proxy, good or bad, it did not lie, or even exaggerate for that matter. Anything that it told me turned out to be the truth. There was no leading up to it, no time to prepare for what was to come. When the impulses from the powered armor hit my arms, my legs, my chest… it was as if someone had lashed my body with a dozen cat-of-nine tails in series. Tiny shards of metal cut at the nerves, sending fire through every last one, making some scream as others went numb. I felt tears burst from my eyes as my body convulsed and the Jevox struggled to hold on to me.

My armored body hit the deck, feet flat on the floor, and as it did, I felt as if I were possessed by a demon of war. Without much thought, I went to work on the security force, ripping rifles from their hands and stunning them one after the next, then knocking back the remaining group with a sweep of the arm. My body moved autonomously, disabling the security forces, leaving me in an empty hall bathed in rainbow light.

I could hear footsteps coming towards me, so I raised both the rifles I had requisitioned from the guards, ready to fight off the next wave as I retreated back towards Frelo.

"Don't shoot!" Chevelle said, appearing around the corner with Renata at her side. "It's us."

"Thank the Universe!" I shouted and hurried over to them. "There's no time left. We've got to help Frelo. They were injured."

"Lead us to them," Renata said, eyes narrowing.

"Did you see Leo? Where's Leo?"

Chevelle shook her head. "No mate. Ain't seen him."

I swallowed my worries and waved for them to follow.

Renata passed me an obsidian block a few inches in length and I pressed it into my chest, a swarm of nano machines rushing up to fix the damaged faceplate of my armor.

"Thanks," I mumbled, and the soldier nodded.

We were out of time, and I had no idea how to get back to Frelo. I pinged madly over the network trying to make contact, but they did not respond. I couldn't leave them behind, but what options did I have?

Chevelle, Renata and I met resistance at the next junction. Among those who attempted to stop us were the black robed guards. We didn't have time to screw with this. Frelo had to disable the weapons. They had to.

"Look," Chevelle said, motioning for a side hall. "That one. Goes back to the control center. You take it, we will hold your flank."

"No!" I shouted. "I've had enough of others falling so I can finish. No one gets left behind."

"It's life," Renata said, then broke from cover to fire several times. "We all die eventually. No one gets out alive. You know what to do. We have your back."

"She's right," Chevelle said. "We ain't here because we've been forced."

There was no time to argue.

"Okay, okay," I said, resigning to my situation, then took the hall back towards Frelo.

As I came closer to where I had lost consciousness, a tracking signal began to pop in and out on my UI. The Jevox's suit was pinging its location.

"*Milo?*" a whisper of a question called over the open communications channel.

"*I'll come to you,*" I told Frelo. "*Tell me where you are.*"

"*No. There are too many Jevox. They are all tainted by this human's filth. You must go. Get back to your ship. It's the only way.*"

"*I can't leave you. And Leo.*"

"*I will succeed, I think. Quit arguing with me, human. Your death will not help me achieve my objective.*"

I growled with impotence. "*Fine. But how? How do I get back to my ship?*"

"*Turn around, take a left. There is an airlock. Broadcast the location to your Proxy. It will come to you.*"

"*Are you crazy? Go out in the open in hard vacuum? As soon as I'm out of the airlock I'll be killed. If it's not the Jevox on this ship, Johan or the point defense weapons will vaporize me.*"

"*Put your faith in what you have built, Hughes. The Jevoxs' strength is not from the individual, it is because we work as one mind. We trust in one another.*"

"*And look where this got you.*"

"*Only because of your people manipulating our brains. Vile. Vile.*"

I swallowed. "*You're right. I'm—*"

"You are not the one who needs to make amends." Frelo made a wet, damaged noise, a kind of rasping cough. *"Now go before the rest of my people get to you. Your mate needs you. Your people need you. Go to them."*

And they were right, but it didn't feel that way. I could sense that the *Transcendence* was close. If Frelo failed to get the batteries offline, she'd be dead, but even if they did, I knew Shelly wasn't ready to go toe to toe with Johan.

This action went against everything I believed. I was abandoning everyone who had boarded the ship. Leo was missing. Frelo was almost dead. Chevelle and Renata were fighting a pitched battle, overwhelmed by the enemy. I had led them all to this place, but they had come by their own choice. We believed in this mission. We were one in our goals. Could I trust them to do the right thing?

I turned and started to run, picking up speed, weaving down narrow corridors towards the airlock. Shots from energy weapons whizzed past me, landing by my feet and along the walls. But I did not stop. I did not slow. There was a door several hundred feet up ahead, a thick hatch with a glass window facing into open space.

"Go to them," Frelo said over the channel, and the door slid open. *"Go. Go. Go."*

The Jevox closed in on my rear, but there was no way they could catch me at this speed. My armor had become a bullet of its own, roaring down the passage, slicing through open air. A safety hatch closed behind me, and my suit informed me that the atmosphere was being pumped out of this section of the ship. I was still running, running, running, speed increasing as if I were trying to reach escape velocity.

The atmosphere was removed from the hallway, the exterior door to the ship yawning wide, revealing hard vacuum beyond its threshold. I could see the bright flashes of active combat on the other side, explosions along the debris belt as the Prole Genascara's weapons tracked a series of flicking targets.

"Have faith in what you have built," Frelo whispered again.

I hit the final step before entering open space, then pushed off hard as I could, launching myself into the open. Face forward, arms at my side, my armored body shot out of the airlock like a ballistic missile, the Prole Genascara receding. Battle raged around me, the point defense weapons tracking the last remaining Swift Shuttle as well as several fighters.

"I see you," Johan called over an open channel. *"I see you."*

I was just a body floating in open space.

Helpless, I placed my thoughts on where I needed to be. Aboard the *Transcendence*. Within my Star Sphere. Hands on Weapons Control. Shelly and Karianna at my side. We had trained for this. I had to put my trust in them.

Alarms went off on my suit, detecting multiple shots aimed at my person, narrow band Para Lux beams coming within a few thousand meters of me, increasing the exterior temperature of my suit by hundreds of degrees.

Johan's ship appeared on my right, not in my UI, but where I could see it with the naked eye—a frightening gold circle carved with black lines that formed strange symbols. Along the front end of its disc, light began to build.

"You will die," he said. *"Just like your father. Worthless and weak. Unable to do what must be done for the good of all. Alone and frail and dead."*

"No," I replied. *"I am never alone."*

I closed my eyes and surrendered myself to fate. All I had left was my trust in others. This was always hard. People let you down. All it took was one person to screw it up for everyone. But maybe, just maybe, the Universe would surprise me. The Jevox had learned a long time ago they couldn't do it alone.

I needed to learn the same.

We needed to learn the same.

"What?" Johan broadcasted; his tone surprised. *"What in the hells? Where did…? What is this?!"*

"Get off him," Lance growled over the open channel. *"That little shit is ours. Not yours. You hear me?"*

"We've got you, Super Captain," Xuan said next.

"We won't let him get you," Hy agreed.

"We're here," Ada echoed.

"We won't let you down." It was Dante, and his wife grunted in approval.

"We're troublemakers to the last, bruh," James said. *"Ride or die."*

"We've always got you," Karianna whispered. I swore her words felt as if they'd been spoken directly into me like we were already aboard the *Transcendence*.

Never alone. I was never alone.

I cracked open my eyes to see Johan's ship swarmed by our fighters. Shelly had brought the *Transcendence* close enough to deploy those waiting in reserve, and they rained hell down on him. They'd covered my back.

Nuclear sabot rounds and flashes of explosions filled my vision as they tangled, Johan worked to stay ahead of my better trained pilots. He twisted around, attempting to avoid their advance, but the mother ship was near, and the fighters didn't have physical pilots within them, and so they could pull G forces far greater than he could. Bits of his ship tore away, debris left in his wake. His piloting became erratic.

My heart swelled. What a beautiful sight.

Overwhelmed by the onslaught of my team, Johan retreated, vanishing into the black.

I had a sudden urge to reach my hands out before me, palms first, and as I did my Swift Shuttle appeared out of nowhere, mere inches away. The powered armor latched to the outer hull of the shuttle, and I rocketed off towards the approaching *Transcendence* secured to its roof.

At my back, the Prole Genascara's main batteries began to glow. I checked the timer. We were two minutes over and the enemy had not fired. Why was this? What were they waiting for?

"What in the hell are you doing, Milo?" Shelly shouted over the open channel. Damn it felt good to be yelled at by her. *"Get your ass inside so you can take back this crazy ship! I've had enough of piloting this thing. We've got a mission to complete."*

I smiled as I climbed through the hatch atop the roof of the Swift Shuttle. "For once, you'll not hear any complaints out of me."

CHAPTER 45

The *Transcendence* crashed upon the combat theatre, its drive burning bright like a star at the end of a slender, bluish-white crystal as it decelerated. Proxy and I wasted no time trying to decide when and where to dock. We hurled the Swift Shuttle at the nearest port and linked its Star Sphere directly into the ship's systems. There was no opportunity to relocate, no time to change spheres. My awareness sprang to life as I was transported into my virtual space, locations of our fighters and their pilots, the warm sensation of electromagnetic fields, bands of radiation, a thousand, thousand data points filling my essence to the brim. I felt whole again. This ship was more than just a ship. It was me. It was my body, a vessel to host my consciousness.

Shelly was waiting for me.

She threw her arms around my shoulders and squeezed. "Are the main batteries down?"

I held her tight and did not respond. There was a good chance this might be the end.

As I began to settle back into my extended body, Karianna returned to the ship and reconnected.

MI barrier going up, she thought, urgency and anxiety bleeding through.

"Shelly," I said. "I've got the main controls. Take the antimatter weapons and piezo-electric bombs."

Shelly took a step back, swallowed her worry, and did just that.

The Mercurial Integumentum swarmed out of the *Transcendence* as I turned us about and charged the Para Lux array. Lights along the **Prole Genascara's** hull began to blossom, giving me a clear view of the main batteries as they prepared to fire. I had a choice to make. Chances were, we might could take a single slug as long as it was at a gentle angle. We could take our lick, then hope Frelo was still alive, buy us a few seconds, or we could strike first.

And they would die too, Karianna's thoughts intruded on mine. *Besides, we have to protect life.*

Since when did you become the levelheaded one?

Amusement brushed the back of my mind. *I've always been the levelheaded one.*

"Milo?" Shelly asked. "What are we going to do?"

The main batteries on the Prole Genascara flickered and glowed with blazing, blue arcs of lightening skipping between its dozens of external conduits and cables. Proxy emphasized that they were not using these weapons at their designated limits, but far beyond. They intended to take us out with a single shot.

"Here it comes," I said, and felt Karianna realign the swarms of nano machines that made up the MI into a dense, round disc that faced the Prole Genascara.

Shelly looked to me, reached out a hand, and smiled.

But as the *Transcendence* burned through the debris field and our fighters fell in to escort us, something unexpected happened. The energy building within the main batteries dissipated, fizzling out, their power dead.

"They did it," Karianna said over the open channel. *"My God, they shut them down."*

I let out a sigh of relief. Even though I was inside the Star Sphere, my chest hurt from the stress.

"Good job, Frelo. We're not out of the woods yet. Lance!"

"Yes, Captain?" he replied.

"Spread out in a detection pattern like we practiced. Link the instruments together. Let's find Johan and give him hell."

"Already on it," Lance said, and the fighter wing broke off, taking their positions.

I cranked every available instrument up to its maximum resolution. The *Transcendence* began to probe nearby space, looking for any sign of Johan. While I searched for his trail, I attempted to contact Chevelle, Renata, Leo, and Frelo. None of them responded. The weapons were down, but we had no idea the situation aboard the Prole Genascara.

"There!" Ada called out. *"Marking his position."*

With the bright backdrop of glittering debris so near, it made finding Johan easier than in the black of open space. His movements appeared on our advanced scan like a black blob zipping over a field of diamonds.

"Our objective is to catch him, take him in," I ordered. "But let's make him sweat first."

I began to fire narrow beams from the Para Lux array, their power attuned so as not to destroy, but to damage their ship and hopefully disable their cloak. Shelly remained ready to launch the piezo-electric bombs, but he was too far away for them to be effective. The MI shifted from its fixed position and became a diffuse silver bubble surrounding us.

"Where did he go?" Lance said. *"James? Ada? Dante? Anyone?"*

"I'm not seeing him," Dante replied.

James called next, *"Should we widen the formation?"*

"Do it," Karianna replied.

"You're dooming us all," Johan whispered direct to my implants. *"The human race will die because of you. Become extinct."*

"No," I replied. *"We must protect life."*

"Asseblief, the Foundry is playing with you. To survive you have to risk it all."

Shelly gave me an eye, knowing what I was dealing with. Karianna could feel it too. He was taunting me.

The shard-like form of the *Transcendence* broke free of the debris field, closing the distance to the Prole Genascara, course laid on the stealth ship's last known location. Toe to toe, I was confident we could take him, but this—

Before I could formulate my next thought, explosions crackled all around us. The MI vaporized, and pain began to rack my body. Alarms were going off throughout every system. Karianna screamed in my mind. The pain was too much. Too much. Too much.

"Mines!" Proxy reported. "He's led us into a field of mines."

Johan chose his moment to strike, bearing down on us at an oblique angle vertical to the elliptical plane, his Para Lux array raging, beams of white light cutting along the surface of our forward end. Each impact was like a dull knife dragged across naked skin, peeling flesh back to touch fiery air.

Without skipping a beat, Shelly began to hurl piezo-electric bombs at his projected trajectory, but Johan twisted the ship around and took evasive actions. The stealth ship, even close up, and large as it was, had the ability to do some serious maneuvers.

"Drop your MI," Johan ordered in my head. *"Drop it. Let's be peaceful."*

He kept up the pressure, and we fought back, but he was too quick, popping in and out of stealth mode to keep a superior position. As close and swift as he moved, there was no way to get a solid fix. He was fast overwhelming our systems. The Prole Genascara's batteries might be down, but Johan could kill us just as dead. I'd been too confident.

"We can't keep this up," Karianna shouted, and her worry trickled into me, contagious like a virus. It took everything in me not to start falling apart. I had to be logical. I could fall apart later.

"Focus," I said. "Get the MI in a better position, we'll try and lead the target."

Johan picked off several of our fighters, forcing them to draw on our reserves. He had a pitched advantage in this fight, one we could not seem to overtake.

Relays along the *Transcendence* went dark for a moment, then sprang back to life as nano machines stitched the damaged systems back together. I had to think. Had to come up with a solution.

Universe, help us. Please.

Another signal reached out, though its source was impossible to trace.

"Hello? Ada? Are you out there?" Silence persisted for a moment, and they tried again. *"I need to know you can hear me. I've got them distracted, but it won't last long."* Councilor Halifax. Alexander.

I could feel Karianna wanting to respond, as did I, but something held both of us back. This event, whatever it was, needed to unfold on its own. We lifted all restrictions to allow Ada to do whatever she felt best. We put our trust in her judgement.

"Alex?" she called back to him. *"Where are you? What's going on?"*

"You know where I am, Ada." Another pause. One. Two. Three breaths. *"I want you to know. I didn't want to be here. He made me come. Made me do all the calculations to be sure this would work. We all wanted to save Earth, but Johan… He doesn't care who it hurts. He just wants to make good on a promise to grandchildren he's never met. This misguided madness has to stop. This is not the way. What we're doing isn't right."*

"What are you saying, Alex?"

"I'm disabling the cloak. Shutting down our drive. It, em—it will only be down for a moment. Your ship is close enough. Do what you must to stop us. Disable us, kill us. It doesn't matter. Just stop us. Please stop us. Please… For the love of all that is good. Please…"

"Alex, I—I'm sorry things turned out like—"

"Don't be. You have nothing to be sorry about. Times have changed. We can change with them."

"Shelly," I said, turning to her. "It's time. Doesn't matter who brings them out in the open. We go with the plan. Fire all the piezo-electric bombs. Disable their ship completely."

She nodded. "Right."

We are taking him alive, yes? Karianna thought.

We are.

Good. Johan and I are going to have words. One on one. Maybe even a bit more than words.

An instant later, Johan's ship appeared just a few thousand kilometers off our port bow, its gold and white hull reflecting starlight and debris. Its engines went cold, and it began to list to the side.

"Milo! Please," Ada called over the open channel. *'While we can do it. Disable them."*

Shelly nodded. "Here we—"

But before Shelly could send the command from her thoughts into the *Transcendence's* network, a flash of white-hot light blinded all our instruments. I couldn't see a thing, my eyes, our eyes burning. Our skin was once more on fire, heat washing over us with the scalding blowback of...

Debris scattered from the source of light as it dissipated, chunks of gold cutting through the noise.

"NO!" Ada screamed. *"No! No! No! It can't be."*

Several moments passed before the light subsided and everything went back to normal, letting us confirm what had happened. There was no ship before us, just a broken amalgamation of rapidly cooling molten metal and dust.

The stealth ship was gone.

"What just happened?" I whispered while looking to Proxy who had become rigid with shock.

Shelly's mouth hung open. "What... who did..."

Karianna spoke over the open channel, her state of mind a jumble of emotions: relief, anger, sadness. *"It was the Prole Genasvara,"* she told us. *"They fired on Johan's ship as soon as it was revealed. It's gone, guys. There's nothing left."*

Ada whimpered, *"Alexander... No. No. No."*

My hands trembled. It was over.

Johan and his crew were no more.

CHAPTER 46

It was hard to believe, but our long road had come to an end. Johan had been defeated, his ship half-atomized, half a wreck of twisted metal with no survivors. It was not too long ago, subjectively at least, and I would have been ecstatic at this outcome. But now? I only felt an empty hole in my chest. Johan's death didn't bring Dad back, and though it had given us justice over what had happened, it could not undo the damage he had done. Frelo had taken the chance for us to learn more, and for their own reasons. A human leader had done terrible things to a group of his people, and they were determined that they would never do so again.

After the cosmic dust settled, we got a better read of the situation. When I had returned to the *Transcendence* after leaping through the airlock, injured and bleeding, Frelo had been able to reach Weapons Control. They had then shut down the main batteries, taken out Johan, then engaged the device Ada had rigged up to disrupt whatever signal had been used to subjugate the crew of the Prole Genascara. These Jevox immediately stopped in their tracks and began wandering around, confused, disoriented, lost.

To my relief, Leo soon reported in, beaten up but alive. He had been able to reach Frelo and was escorting them to the Prole Genascara's infirmary for both of their medical care.

Shelly spent those first few hours holding Ada as she screamed and sobbed over Alexander. It might have been years from her perspective since they had been together, but that didn't matter. Their personal challenges kept them apart, but there had always been an unspoken hope of reparations, of change. It's why neither of them could pull the trigger and finalize the divorce. It was so very sad to see another good man die because of that manipulative tyrant. Alexander was a hero, yes, but his death left us all the poorer, even in victory.

The rest of our crew checked in. Chevelle and Renata returned to the ship. Xuan and Hy and Lance and James used their fighters to collect what was left of the stealth ship's wreckage for later analysis.

We'd made it through somehow. We were alive. That meant we still had a chance to make a difference.

Once Ada was calm enough to breathe normally, she and Shelly went to work, modifying the frequencies broadcast by the Wave Shifter device. It took days to make a noticeable difference among the confused crew, but Frelo, from their medical bed, helped them fine tune it. Ada's hurt over what had transpired meant that she only interacted with Frelo when forced. From her perspective, these aliens had murdered her husband and chalked it up to collateral damage.

The Jevox hive aboard the Prole Genascara started to break free of their fugue state. First came one, then another, then groups of ten, fifty, a hundred, a thousand. They had little memory of the events that had transpired, but described it as a sort of dream-like state, a haze. They were aware of something not being right, but were sitting far removed, their waking, collective consciousness having a dissociative, out-of-body experience.

As more of them returned to the hive's bio-electric network, a growing sentiment of anger blossomed. I made a visit to the Prole Genascara for us to meet with them, though this time not in powered armor but regular clothes. They brought me to Terraforming Command so that we could discuss what came next. Shelly, Ada, and Lance joined me, while Karianna and most of the others remained behind. We needed to convince them we were not a threat, especially Novae. We needed to show them that these were the actions of a troubled individual, a difficult concept for Jevox. And perhaps, if they could accept that, they might go a little further and help.

We waited for Frelo and Leo to arrive, our group standing near one of the center tiers in the room, investigating the holographic sphere overhead. Earth hung above us, its blue, ghost-like form reflecting in our wide eyes.

"Where did this information come from?" I asked one of the blues on my left. This Jevox was one of many. The Command Room was full, Jevox standing shoulder to shoulder on all twelve tiers.

Its eyes blinked in sequence as it looked from me to the display and back. "The Foundry is not the only entity to know of Earth."

"What does that mean?"

"We trade."

"With whom?"

"With many. The hive does not owe you a record. It is our business alone."

I pinched the bridge of my nose and sucked in a deep breath. "Look, I'm not after a stupid receipt. I just want to know who it was. More importantly, I want to know how long it has been. When is this map, this rendering from?"

"Dealings are private. Time is relative."

"You're not helping much."

"And why should we?" a Jevox to the right asked. "Your species' actions nearly lobotomized our hive, obliterated our *ississ*."

My mouth opened wide, ready to respond in frustration and anger over this ungrateful alien's response, but Shelly reached for my broken hand to stall me. I turned to her and could see the response written clear on her face.

"We have to know," I mouthed to her. "We have to."

She nodded, then shook her head. *But not today.*

Frelo appeared at the far end of the room, Leo at their side helping them steady themselves as they walked. Given their injuries, it would be a long recovery for the both of them.

"Frelo, it's good to see you again," I said, projecting my voice across the rows of Jevox. They gave me a peculiar look, a hundred pentagonal sets of eyes peering back at me. The weight of their attention pressed down against my chest, and I felt it difficult to breathe in the moment.

"Milo Hughes," Frelo replied, limping towards a central location on the tier they entered. "Will we not be joined by your co-captain?"

"No. Captain Torlen is working on putting things right aboard the *Transcendence*. Looks like your people are doing better."

"They are," they said. "Thanks to our companions."

Ada sucked in a deep breath.

"It is regrettable we had to take such actions," Frelo said. "We could not risk them getting away."

"You mean, *you* couldn't risk it," Ada growled, her words laced with venom.

Frelo looked to their fellow Jevox, their eyes blinking in sequence. "You are right, Lovelace." They raised their right hand, displaying five fingers. "I was a hive of one. An individual acting on their own. I am not the same. I made the choice."

"Out of sync," several of the Jevox in the room whispered.

"It was the right choice," Frelo responded.

"Out of sync," the group continued.

"What would you have done?" Frelo asked the other Jevox as their posture sagged, shoulders bending in. "Would you have acted differently?"

The hive of Jevox went silent.

"The one in question was punished!"

"Humans are the cause," a crimson said. "If not for them, we would have been safe. We were refitting to assist the Servanis. This alliance would secure our place in this sector of the galaxy. They will protect us."

"The humans must leave," a cerulean said. "Your time here is over. Leave our systems. Never come back. Take our warning."

"Burn all humans," a yellow said out of nowhere, its multi-jointed hands shaking.

"No," another replied on the opposite end of the room, and its sentiment caught like wildfire, spreading among the crowd, body language changing. "We protect life."

"And that is what I did," Frelo said.

Leo grimaced at his side and patted him on the back.

"Out of sync," more said, their voices growing louder with each repetition. "Out of sync. Out of sync." It was strange that on Rix, Frelo was embraced as part of the ruling council among the hive mind, but here, they were actively excluded. This wasn't going well.

"Should we purge the colony?" a cerulean proposed aloud, and my stomach twisted into a knot.

"Protect life," several others responded.

This was not normal for them. They did not debate like this. The damage to their hive network was clear.

"No," I spoke up. "Please, leave Novae alone. They are harmless. They hardly have the means to leave the planet, let alone make trouble for you and your people. Leave them. Let them live out their lives."

The Jevox hushed but did not respond, they stood silent but for the rustling of robe cloth.

"What do we do?" Shelly whispered in my ear.

Lance tightened his dour expression. "They're not playing nice."

"Who can blame them?"

"I can," Ada growled.

I raised my hands at my crew, urging them to calm.

"We will make a decision," the Jevox finally said as a group. "Are you a threat? Or are you victim?"

The binary nature of this question was not something I liked.

"Look, we do not condone what Johan did," I said, interrupting the Jevox's silent conversation. "Like Frelo in taking the shot when they had the opportunity, Johan acted outside our consensus decisions. We regret what happened. You were enslaved and several of your people died as a result. We cannot undo that. But we did come to make it right. We came to protect life. If not for our actions, your people would have been his slaves forever, if you had even survived. Please hear this."

They turned to one another, deliberating. I could not be sure I had gotten through. Understanding the way Jevox thought wasn't easy, but at the core, they were not an aggressive species. Isolationists? Yes. Protectionist? In many ways. But warmongers? Never.

"What you say has value," one of the crimsons on the top tier replied after a long moment.

"Victim," several said. "Victim."

"Victim."

"Victim."

"Victim."

I felt Shelly, Ada, and Lance let out their breath. Sure hoped that this meant that Novae was safe.

"Frelo has seen reason to trust you," another started in the back, and the mood of the room shifted yet again. "Even if they are out of sync, we understand why. Your interest may have been self-seeking, to keep standing with the Foundry, but it is truthful. You, the hive of Milo Hughes, hive of the *Transcendence*, came to protect life."

"We did," Shelly cut in, nodding. "We have only come to protect life. And in that line of thought, may we ask for something in return?"

"What do you ask?" all the Jevox spoke as one. It always made me uncomfortable when they did so.

"We need help," I said. "You can see we need help." I gestured to the hologram of Earth overhead. "That is what started all of this. A struggle to save our dying species."

Shelly took a step forward and addressed the room, her hands resting on the safety rail. "I won't lie to you and say there are no more like Johan among the human race. There are those who are good, and those who are bad. We are the sum of our choices, and for a species like yours, who make almost all choices together, I am not sure I can explain. But Johan was not from the beliefs of our tribe, our hive. We wish to do better. We realize that scarcity of resources and an undeveloped sense of connection with humans outside of our closest social groups opens the door for great evil. To Johan, he was not doing bad things, he was setting the universe right. He was making amends for a promise he had broken as a young man to the family he left behind. A promise broken in fear and scarcity.

"Your people want for nothing. You live in balance and harmony. That is not the case for humans. We grew too big, and the tribes in which we had balance did not grow with us. Without close connections, without emotional proximity, people become abstract concepts, life becomes a number, a resource to be managed or ignored. It's just too much for us to understand and internalize without a lot of help. And so, we ask for another chance. Your people have the means to give us that other chance. We only ask for the knowledge to do so. Will you give us that much? We promise to be like other species who you have helped and let you be. Let Jevox be Jevox. We will not return to Rix."

I smiled at her as she closed her argument. No matter the Jevox's answer, I was proud of Shelly. She always knew what to say. I wasn't so sure humankind deserved another chance on the galactic scale. Novae, sure, but they would develop so different from those only of Earth. If this hologram was accurate, I could only imagine those left behind were in great pain. The suffering we saw as we made for the Foundry was nothing compared to this.

"Will you protect life?" they asked after a moment. "Not just human life, but all life?"

"We will," Shelly said.

Again, they looked at one another in a silent conference. While their limbs were still, their eyes blinked in rapid succession. Shelly reached for my prosthetic hand and squeezed it tight. The fate of humanity might just fall upon this single moment.

Deliberation ended far quicker than I had expected. They turned to face us.

"We will help," they said as one.

"But not with the Prole Genascara," a green amended. "And we do not know the way. Your world, as we have been given information about it, does not require all things to be made whole. We will offer equipment. Plans. It will take labor, a great deal of labor. But nothing is outside human ability. You need only find its location."

I raised my prosthetic hand, keeping my damaged three fingered hand hidden, then spread my five fingers wide. "You honor us. The hive endures."

"The hive endures," they said.

And like that, the Jevox dispersed and went to work preparing the necessary equipment.

"I suppose FICSE is back on," Lance said, crossing his arms and rubbing at his beard. "Kind of hoped we'd end up going back to Novae, but Earth isn't a bad option."

"If we can find it," Shelly sighed.

"That's the ten-million-dollar question."

I pursed my lips in thought, watching as the Jevox cleared out, Frelo and Leo limping over towards us. I looked up to the hologram of Earth, the number on the bottom right, our estimated population counting down. "We'll find it."

The following two weeks were busy. They transferred massive amounts of data over to our Proxies to analyze and sort, while at the same time fitting a few key devices that would help us re-terraform Earth. They prepared several high efficiency gas conversion towers, bio-spreaders used for seeding life, and a series of solar reflectors. Plans were included for all kinds of devices that we might make more after the initial testing was done, as well as those for a hundred other specialized tools, molecular converters, genetic primers, magnetic core-relays, and storm scoops. They helped manufacture enough terraforming supplies for us to not only get the project started, but carry it about forty percent through the process with minimal damage to remaining life. In their estimate, the entire process would take about ten years, so long as we had the labor to execute the plan. This would require hundreds of thousands of man hours, but there were hungry, tired, desperate people on Earth who might just be willing to help if it meant that they survived.

The work went as planned. Another couple of weeks, and we'd be ready to leave, ready to seek a way back to our home world. We had discussed several methods of finding this information, while continuing to ask the Jevox where they had gotten this detailed scan, but they hadn't been forthcoming.

I meditated daily, attempting to reach out into the cosmos and find this answer. Whatever thread connected me to the Universe, I hoped it would lead me to Earth. Luck was not on my side. Despite my best attempts to enter the state in which I had left my body to meet the Universe, or read the acceleration of Johan's ship, the only result I had to show for my effort was feeling clear-headed and relaxed. We'd have to explore more conventional means as Ada had suggested earlier. That meant traveling back through the Wandering Gate, then using star charts to estimate the time that had passed since FICSE began. If we could figure the distance in light years, it might narrow down our search area. Or, with Shelly's diplomatic skills and a knack for finding things, we could take our chances at Cynosure. Surely we had something to trade.

One day during meditations, our instruments caught sight of a Jevox force entering the system, five fleets of five wings of five ships, one hundred and twenty-five in all. It was clear that the Jevox of Rix had seen us recover after the birth of the *Transcendence* and were resolved to see the Dragon's work completed. They had more than enough firepower to see this done. But before they reached us, the Jevox hive aboard the Prole Genascara made contact and assured them we were not threats. These fleets went into a standby status as they approached, informing us that they would attack only if given cause. We had no plans to do so. We were here to protect life, not end it, and they accepted this sentiment, if reluctantly so.

Returning from a meditation session several days later, damp towel hanging over my shoulders, Proxy sent me a ping. I stopped in the hallway to read its message.

"You are receiving a signal," Proxy stated.

"From whom?" I asked, shaking my head and continuing to walk, my face and head covered in sweat. "I'm sure it's just more details from the Jevox. Karianna and I said bay six was fine for the crust probes."

"It is not the Jevox."

I paused. "What do you mean?"

"It is coming from the Prole Genascara, a message request, but its source is human."

"I don't understand. Leo and Chevelle are on the ship, but their channel is already open."

"I think you should take it, Milo."

"Okay. Okay." I toweled off my damp hair and stretched. "Put it through."

"Connection established."

"Hello? Who is this?" I asked as I kept walking. "This is Milo."

"It worked," a voice said over the channel, a woman's voice. Familiar. *"I can't fucking believe it."*

"What worked? I repeat, who is this?"

They began to laugh, but it wasn't funny at all.

"You'll pay," they replied. *"All of you will pay for what you have done."*

I paused in my step, cocking my head to the side. "Harper? Is that you?" I blinked.

"You know it is, Milo."

"Where are you?" I fought not to let emotions overtake me. "What's going on? Were you not with Johan and the rest?"

"I should have been… Should have. But I've been hiding in the bowels of this stupid hive minded ship for weeks, making little changes, biding my time. Waiting for my moment. They killed him, Milo. They killed him. That sweet, innocent, beautiful man. They killed him."

I took off running, heading for the central hallway of the ship. I needed to get Shelly's and Karianna's attention. I couldn't carry on two conversations at once. Someone needed to find her on the Prole Genascara and bring her here. She might have information. She might be the only one who could explain all of what happened.

"Harper…" I said, keeping the conversation going. "I'm sorry for what went down. George was my friend too. Ada lost Alexander. We've all lost someone in this whole chain of events. Tell us where you are, and we'll come to get you. Let's talk. Everything will be okay."

"George?" she cackled, her voice taking on a razor's edge. *"What would that spineless idiot have to do with any of this? How dense are you, Milo? You never did understand women. And that wife of yours, she's just as stupid, and ugly. Fucking bitch. You belong with one another.*

"Do you not get it? Do you truly not see what happened? They killed my prince, those twisted, slime eating, broken jointed, nauseatingly agreeable Jevox. They killed my precious. My beautiful, sweet, intelligent, strong man. They killed my everything. My heart."

And the pieces fell together. Harper was right about me being dense. All those times she sidled up to him. All those times she agreed with him while pushing her husband to the side. Harper had not just started to like Johan as others had suggested, she had become obsessed with him. She had fallen head over heels in love and become infatuated with him.

She would do anything for him. Anything...

"Uhh, Milo?" Karianna said, catching me in the hallway. She tossed a thumb over her shoulder. "We've got a problem."

"You think?" I said, tapping a finger on my head. I muted the connection. "I've got Harper on the line."

Karianna shook her head. "What the...? Harper? Okay. Whatever. That's nice and everything, chatting with your ex and stuff, but that's not the issue I'm talking about."

"What's the issue?"

"The Prole Genascara's reactor is putting off crazy readings. They use a kind of antimatter core just like we do, and it doesn't look healthy. I don't like this. I don't like this at all. Maybe we should put some distance between us and them, get our people back. I'm about to signal them and see how we can help."

My stomach fell through the floor. Harper's words... *All of you will pay for what you have done.*

"Get everyone off," I shouted and motioned with my hands. "Now! Get into your sphere."

"What?" Karianna hopped back in surprise. "What are you talking about?"

"Harper's going to overload the reactor. Their ship's core is going critical. That's what the readings are."

"No, no, no," Karianna said, her voice small. "Fuck!" She spun on her heels and took off in the direction of her Star Sphere.

"Harper," I said, reestablishing contact as I ran towards my own Star Sphere. "Don't do this. It's not worth it. Frelo made a choice. It was an individual choice. But this choice we are making now, to do the right thing, is one for all of humanity. It can save us all."

"I don't care," she mumbled. *"With him gone, there's no universe left for me. And humanity? A joke of the gods. We should never have been born. Humans are weak. Stupid. Foolish. We deserve what we got."*

I rushed up the ladder of my sphere and leapt into the tank, umbilicals immediately snapping into place, hurling my consciousness into my virtual environment. I sent a broadcast around the ship for everyone to strap in, post-haste. No time to waste.

Chevelle's Swift Shuttle burned away from the Prole Genascara an instant later, our lingering crew aboard including Frelo. Karianna's signal must have reached the Jevox, because life pods began to eject from the outer hull of the massive ship. The level of instability from the core doubled, then tripled. There wasn't much time left.

"We have to back away," Proxy told me, appearing beside my feet, its hair puffed up and standing on end. "Move. Now."

"Working on it," I told it. "Not like this thing is small."

We scooped the Swift Shuttle up and turned, backing away from the Prole Genascara. The Jevox were furiously evacuating, but I saw no way they'd all make it in time.

"Please, Harper," I pleaded over our channel. "Stop this."

"It's too late," she whispered. *"Vengeance is mine. Say hello to your dad."*

The Prole Genascara's core went critical, and in a flash of white light, the molecular bonds holding the ship together were no more. Heat washed over the *Transcendence.* Karianna and I reeled as the outer layers of hull on our starboard side evaporated.

No debris was left, no evidence the Prole Genascara had ever been, just a residual wave of background radiation and trace amounts of dust.

We had not protected life.

We had committed murder.

"What has she done?" Karianna thought, her heart breaking in two.

I couldn't respond, but my heart quavered in my chest.

Shelly appeared behind me in my virtual environment and put her arms around me. "Milo… I—"

"Alert!" Proxy stated, its tone urgent. "Status change from the Foundry."

"What now?" I turned to face the cat. "It's here? The Foundry is here?"

"It is always here, Milo. It is always watching."

"What does it say?"

Proxy's face twisted. "Status: L5-Deny Access."

"What does that mean?"

"No human ships to be allowed access to Foundry facilities. Human targets are to be fired at on sight."

Karianna cut in, *"Guys? It's worse than just that."*

"How can it be worse?" I asked, then realized what she meant. The incoming Jevox fleets were almost upon us, and now that we had destroyed the Life Changer, killing ten thousand of their people right in front of them, they had all the reason in the world to power up their weapons.

"Raising the MI," Karianna called. *"Crew, prepare to make a run for it."*

"Where do we go?" Shelly asked. "Where?"

Energy weapons began to pepper the Mercurial Integumentum, poking holes in our screen of defensive nano machines. We wouldn't last long against this deluge of weapons fire. We had to move.

"Anywhere," I said, urging the *Transcendence's* engines to ramp up to full. "Anywhere that's not here."

CHAPTER 47

The Jevox fleet trailed us to the edge of the system, pushing their acceleration as hard as they physically could, but we had the advantage. Thirty Gs was more than the Jevox could take. The debris strewn system of Yuven receded from view, and with it, so much hope.

What had Harper done? I knew she was obsessed, angry, but this?

How can we ever hope to save humanity when outliers are willing to ruin it for all of us? How can we prove we are worth saving? It only takes one kid to ruin it for the whole class. One group to ruin it for the entire species. Her vengeance, at least in her mind, was worth the deaths of ten thousand. Deaths that only proved we did not protect life, and she wasn't the first in human history to do so.

We like to think back on the pivotal, historic moments when a single choice made everything better. A moment of triumph, of good over evil.

We think of the unknown man who stood in defiance before a column of tanks in Tiananmen Square, grinding the progress of government oppression and steel to a halt. We think of Rosa Parks on a Montgomery bus opposing Jim Crow policies of racism in the United States. or of Ghandi's choice to non-violently stand up for all India against Britain. These were moments we protected life on our own world. Moments to be proud of.

But there were other moments too, moments where someone stood on the precipice of something dark, and terrible, and even in knowing so, they went ahead.

Be it truth or apocryphal, the Trojan Wars and the deaths of so many hinged upon a single king's anger over his stolen wife. The fury of a spurned lover sent the ancient world, if only that of stories, into chaos. And yet, we know in our hearts that someone with enough power now might do the same, maybe not with spears or Greek fire, but with soldiers and bombs, all because their possession escaped.

Consider the scientist Thomas Midgley from the 20th century. Midgley discovered a cheap, anti-knocking agent for cars that made combustion smoother and introduced leaded gasoline to market. Even though he knew lead was a harmful, unnatural substance in the human body, he was driven by his greed, and promoted a product which over the following fifty years killed tens of millions, and with the help of others, suppressed knowledge over its dangers the world over. He could have stopped, spoken up, but industrial progress and unbridled avarice meant more to him than the lives of others.

Not long before leaving Earth, when I was too young to know what I was seeing on the news, small towns in Nevada had been flooded and hundreds of thousands killed when a desperate group of Californians attempted to tamper with the Hoover Dam and redirect the flow of water and power. The leader of their group had been a structural engineer who knew that his plan to dig into the hillside was dangerous at best, insane at worst, and he went ahead anyway.

Anger. Greed. Desperation. All of the outcomes had been self-serving. They had not protected the lives of others, but only the interests of themselves or their immediate group. And the truth was, I couldn't fully blame them.

I wasn't sure we could come back from this. I wasn't sure we could fix things in its eyes. The Universe was right, the Foundry would not help. We were on our own.

The Foundry was now against us. Not that it would actively hunt us as the Jevox might continue to do, but it would deny us access to its facilities. It would ward humans away, attack them if they approached. That meant passing back through the Wandering Gate under intense fire, if it would even accept us.

Our thoughts dwelling on similar ideas, Karianna and I made the unconscious decision to curve around and set a course. The gate had traveled many light years since we last passed through it, but it was still within our reach. We had many of the terraforming supplies we needed to see this through already aboard the *Transcendence*. We had the schematics to make more. We only needed to find our way back and enlist the help of a desperate Earth.

Is Novae in danger? Karianna thought, her unease plain. It was a rhetorical question, I knew, an errant thought, but this was something I needed to process as well.

I allowed myself to integrate deeper with the Foundry's machine and immersed myself in her stream of consciousness. I felt cold and alone. I felt the need to put my arms around something soft and squeeze, to bundle myself up in a blanket and press my eyes shut till the world changed.

I don't know, I responded to her, and a sort of tenuous comfort at my arrival resonated back.

Karianna reached out to me, her thoughts moving closer to mine. *Part of me feels like we need to abandon this stupid errand to save Earth and just protect them.*

It might be the worst thing we could do.

You think?

By keeping away, we are a different branch of humanity. Maybe they will be treated as their own. Maybe they won't be considered human. We would only taint them with our filth.

You might be right.

You saw the counter, right? On the map.

Estimated human population? How could you miss it?

They're running out of time. What Harper did to the Jevox has sealed our fate. We have to go back to Earth and make this right. If we don't, no one will.

What do you think we'll find there? She asked, her thoughts betraying images of barren fields, abandoned buildings, people covered in dust traveling by foot past rows of bodies torn apart by starving animals.

I hoped her imagination was not accurate. *I don't know what we'll find.*

We have to believe there will be something left, right?

And what about you? What do you think we'll find?

It took her some time to respond, her emotions becoming a storm in silence. The images from before were replaced with a dark room, people huddled around a fire, dead eyes peering off into the distance, no room for hope given all the horrors they had seen.

Desperation, she thought, and that was more than enough.

That was the only outcome. How could it be otherwise?

Some months later, once the *Transcendence* was up to cruise velocity, our course set for the Wandering Gate, I removed myself from my Star Sphere and made my way to the meditation room. It was interesting that of all the things I could do from deep within the Foundry's machines, this was not one of them. Having several voices in my head made things too noisy to communicate with the Universe.

I made myself comfortable on a large pillow, legs crossed, turned on some background music, closed my eyes and relaxed.

"I am a star, a wave of light. I am a mote of creation, a spark of the Universe…"

It didn't take long for me to leave my body, my consciousness, my soul adrift in whatever cosmic realm this was. I could feel the many threads of reality stretching out from my noncorporeal essence, reaching for distant places both past and future, but only one held interest for me. An impression. A desire. A need beyond my own. An answer I felt I would not like, but one that I required.

I took hold of a single thread and was transported across thousands of star systems, through countless light years of darkness and dust, until I arrived at my destination: The second planet orbiting a yellow giant. Two moons. Heavy gravity. Buzzing webs of communication.

There came a flash, and I was floating upon a black rock like a specter.

I was on a world of darkness, skies filled with roiling yellow and green storms, precipitation stingy with water, but liberal with acid.

I could see a structure made of mud and stone and metal, mighty as a mountain, thousands of creatures tall as men scuttling in and out its many warrens.

I could see walls covered in black machines; symbols carved into their geometric faces, spikes protruding from many switches, electromagnetic frequencies stuffed with data binding them all together.

I went Down.

Down.

Down.

Down through the corridors and chasms, voices chittering without meaning loud in my mind. Then I came to a room, a room shaped like a conch shell, its bleached walls a perfect example of nature's golden ratio, twisting inward and upward. 1.618. The sight made my stomach turn.

Before me at its center was a plinth, an icosahedral device of dark metal floating upon it, a golden disc laying by its side. A golden disc printed with mathematical equations represented by pictographic means. A golden disc with a map carved upon its surface. A map of pulsars and frequencies. A map to a pale blue dot suspended in a beam of starlight.

If only I could read its surface, we might not have to go, might not have to take the risk. But I knew that that was wrong. We didn't just need the map. We needed the device. If all was lost, the device might save us.

But how? How might it help? Or was it just another weapon? Another opportunity for murder?

"You found it," Proxy said as I returned from my meditative state, the cat sitting before me, eyes glistening. "I see it on your face."

I gave it a nod. "Bellamy's copy might have been destroyed, but it was not the only one. The probe was found by another."

"The Voyager probe?"

"Yes."

"Who do you believe found it?"

"Now that, is hard to say. The galaxy is a crowded place."

Proxy rubbed its face against my crossed knees. "More than you know, Milo Hughes. More than you know."

We left the meditation room.

Shelly was waiting for me beside my Star Sphere, having found a flat section of metal beside the ladder to sit on. She had a sketchbook in her hands and was drawing.

"Hey," I said, taking a seat beside her.

She looked up from the page, gave me a weak smile, then kept drawing. It was a rough sketch from the view of our habitation dome on Novae early in the morning. Colonists were going about their day, carrying items two and fro, smiles on their faces. Homes were scattered in neat rows across the background, and beyond it all, you could see the top of the Cultural Center.

My heart ached to think about Novae. It was the closest thing to home I'd ever known other than the *Vasco Da Gama*, and it was now behind us. Mom would be long gone by now, as would Mary and Perry, and so many others, thoughts I worked hard to avoid. The children we had left behind should have already grown into adults and had kids of their own by now.

"We could have been part of that," I whispered.

Shelly laid her head on my shoulder for an instant, then went back to work, her pencil's tip scratching across the paper. "We could have been happy."

"Are you not happy?"

"It's not that, Milo. We did what we had to."

"Then what is it?"

"We still don't know how to get back to Earth," she said while focusing on the details of the clouds. "We don't know where it is."

I gave a resigned expression and shook my head. "Well, we may not know how to get back, not yet, but there's one species I'm confident does. They have a tool that could tell us."

Her pencil froze. "What? Who?"

I drew in a deep breath and let it out slowly. "You ready to go kick a different kind of hive?"

She put her pencil inside her sketchbook and closed it, the spine creaking ever so slightly at the pressure. "You can't be serious."

"It's the only way to see our mission done. They have something we need. It's a map."

"What kind of map?"

"A pulsar map, made by us, the descendants of apes. Once we're close enough to SOL, we can use the information to triangulate its location, and from there, we can go back."

"I know what a pulsar map is, Milo. I'm not an idiot."

"Sorry. I didn't—"

"But to get this map…" she let her sentence drag out.

I swallowed. "Yes. To get this map, we'll have to pay the Isopterans a visit."

She set her sketchbook down beside her and took hold of my prosthetic arm, putting her head on my shoulder. "Do we protect life?"

I tightened my lips, forming a hard line, looking off into nothing, her reassuring presence beside me. "I sure as hell hope so."

ACKNOWLEDGEMENTS

We dreamed of touching stars, and that we did, twice. Book one was just a crazy idea first inspired by playing airplanes with my oldest daughter, a dream made form, a risk of time and attention that in many ways helped me through the darkest days of the lockdown. It gave me something to do, something to focus on that was far beyond the situation we had found ourselves. To be honest, I wasn't sure if anyone was going to read The Foundry, let alone like it, but it hit a nerve for some, and if you're reading this, it must have done something for you as well.

The Transcendence did not start quickly after publishing book one. I worked on a side novel for a time, then came back. After several positive reviews on the Foundry, a bit of sales (though nothing best seller status), and a spark of inspiration, I began anew. I was determined to finish the first book series of my life, and that was both exciting and terrifying. A little over a year and a half of writing went into this, and about as much editing and revising. Now, here we are.

Big thanks to everyone who was part of making this book come to life. My wife for always encouraging me even if she wasn't sure how. My girls for being one of my biggest inspirations and reason for pushing so hard. My oldest daughter (now 11) for literally naming this book (it's a long story but she said, "why not just name it after the ship?"). Thanks to Christopher Doll for his amazing cover art and collaboration (he truly knows how space, how it looks and feels). My editor Luke for all the copy edits and random suggestions. Thanks to my extended family in my professional space for pushing me to stick with it and having an encouraging curiosity around this creative part of my life. Thanks to the beta readers and fans who helped me refine these pages and make it better: Brooklynne, David, Suzan, Lucas, Katie, Evan, Sam, Jessica, Rob, Elizabeth, and many more. Thanks to the many random indie authors I've met at cons and writers' conferences, your perspectives have helped me stay focused on what will make the most difference to reach the world. And thank you to Kevin J Anderson and Alastair Reynolds. Though I've only shaken one of your hands, your works have had a major influence on this series and are what got me into reading science fiction novels to begin with (there might also be a small connection via narrator John Lee).

And last but not least, thank you, Cosmic Traveler. Thank you for being part of this journey.

J Fitzpatrick Mauldin, March 2025

BOOK TWO OF THE FOUNDRY MIGHT BE AT A CLOSE,

BUT THERE'S MORE TO COME…

IF YOU ENJOYED THIS BOOK, BE SURE TO LEAVE A
RATING/REVIEW.

Unlock the Mysteries of The Foundry

Extras: Maps, Original Music, Stories, and more.

THE FOUNDRY

NOVELS AND SHORT STORIES

J Fitzpatrick Mauldin is a science fiction writer based in Atlanta, Georgia, best known for the hard science fiction first contact series The Foundry, which was featured in Kirkus Reviews. A technology expert and nationwide business leader by trade, he serves thousands of professionals in achieving their dreams while nurturing an insatiable passion for world-building and fiction. A father of two, husband, and lover of role-playing and strategy video games (though he's terrible at Baldur's Gate), he is also an amateur scientist with aspirations to pursue a PhD in an undefined, esoteric field. His fiction aims to offer readers immersive worlds to escape the noise of everyday life and inspire them to see the best in their fellow humans who ride alongside on this cosmic journey.

GET YOUR FREE E-BOOK & AUDIO BOOK, SIGN UP FOR OUR EMAIL LIST: www.jfitzpatrickmauldin.com
"A cunning young girl comes face to face with an interstellar threat when her mother and grandfather are murdered aboard their ship while making contact with a mysterious entity. Alone, and with no way home, Bellamy makes a deal with an alien intelligence to chase the signal of her mother's soul to a facility light-years away, in the hope she might be resurrected and the two of them reunited." – Chasing the Signal (The Foundry 0.5)

Follow on:

 facebook.com/jfmauld

 @jfitzpatrickmauldin

 @jfitzpatrickmauldin